THE FEY: CHANGELING

Kristine Kathryn Rusch

MILLENNIUM
An Orion Book
LONDON

Copyright © Kristine Kathryn Rusch 1996
All rights reserved

The right of Kristine Kathryn Rusch to be identified
as the author of this work has been asserted
by her in accordance with the Copyright, Designs
and Patents Act 1988

This edition first published
in Great Britain in 1996 by
Orion Books Ltd
Orion House, 5 Upper St Martin's Lane
London WC2H 9EA

A CIP catalogue record for this book
is available from the British Library

ISBN : (Csd) 1 85798 484 6
ISBN : (Ppr) 1 85798 487 0

Typeset by Datix International Limited, Bungay, Suffolk
Printed and bound in Great Britain by
Clays Ltd, St Ives plc

To Aaron J. Reynolds,
for all the wonderful summers.
I love you, Kiddo.

ACKNOWLEDGEMENTS

Thanks on this one go to Richard Curtis for allowing me a ten-minute break between books; Tom Dupree for adopting me; Caroline Oakley for her enthusiasm; Renee Dodds for ignoring my moods; Nina Kiriki Hoffman for being honest about my writing; Jerry Oltion for reading fantasy; Kathy Oltion for being my guinea pig; Mike Resnick for keeping me on the straight and narrow, and for covering for me; Kevin J. Anderson for being a friend forever; and to Dean Wesley Smith for all the love, faith, and warmth.

THE THEFT

One

He put words to the memory years later, when he tried to tell people of it. Some doubted he could remember, and others watched him as if stunned by his clarity. But the memory was clear, not as a series of impressions, but as an experience, one he could relive if he closed his eyes and cast his mind backwards. An inverse Vision. None of his other memories were as sharp, but they were not as important. Nor were they the first:

Light filled the room. He opened his eyes, and felt himself emerge like a man stepping out of the fog. One moment he had been absorbing, feeling, learning – the next he was thinking. The lights clustered near the window, a hundred single points revolving in a circle. The tapestry was up, as if someone were holding it.

He turned his head – it was his newest skill, but he saw only the curtained wall of the crib. Voices floated in from the other room – his mother's voice, sweet and familiar, almost a part of himself, and a man's voice – his father's?

His nurse sat near the fireplace, her head tilted back, her bonnet askew. She was snoring softly, a raspy sound that sometimes covered the voices. He could barely see her face over the edge of the crib. It was a friendly face, with gentle wrinkled features, a rounded nose, and generous mouth. Her eyes were closed, her mouth open, her nostrils fluttering with each inhalation. He reached toward her, but his fingers gripped the soft blanket instead.

A cool breeze touched him tentatively, smelling of rain and the river. The lights parted to let a shadow in. The shadow had the shape of a man, but it was dark and flat and crept across the wall. He put his baby finger in his mouth and sucked, eyes wide, watching the shadow. It slid over the tapestries and across the fireplace until it landed on his nurse's face.

He whimpered, but the shadow did not look at him. Instead, it molded itself against his nurse's features. Her hands moved ever so slightly as if to pull it off, then she began twitching as if she were dreaming. Her eyes remained closed, but her snoring stopped.

His mother's voice penetrated the sudden silence. 'You will not give him a common name! He is a Prince in the Black King's line. He needs to be named as such!'

The nurse's breathing became regular. The twitching ceased. If not for the blackness covering her face, she would have appeared normal.

'I thought Fey named their children after the customs of the land they're in.' His father's voice.

'Names have to have meaning, Nicholas. They are the secret to power.'

'I do not see how your name gives you power, Jewel.'

The breeze blew over him again. He peered over his blanket at the window. The lights were no longer revolving. They had formed a straight line from the window to his curtained crib. The lights were beautiful and tiny, the size of his fingertips. They gathered around his crib, twinkling and sparkling. Suddenly he was warm. The air smelled of sunlight.

'I'll agree to the name if you tell me what it means.' The voices moved back and forth, near and away, as if his parents were circling each other in the next room.

'I don't know what it means, Jewel. But it has been in my family for generations.'

'I swear.' His mother sounded angry. 'It was easier to make the child than it is to name him.'

'It was certainly more fun.'

He turned to the curtained wall, wishing he could see through it, wishing they would come to him. The lights hovered above him. They were so beautiful. Blue and red and yellow. He pulled his finger out of his mouth and raised it toward the lights.

By accident, he touched a blue light and pulled his hand away with a startled cry. With the smell of sulfur and a bit of smoke, the blue light became a tiny naked woman, with thin wings shimmering on her back. Her skin was darker than his, her eyebrows swept up like her wings, and her eyes were as alive as the lights.

'Got him,' she said.

His fingers hurt. He snuffled, then looked at his nurse. The shadow still covered her face, and she was breathing softly. He wanted her to see him. But she slept.

The tiny woman landed on his chest, put her hands on his chin, and looked into his eyes. 'Ah,' she said. 'He's ours, all right.'

Her hands tickled his skin. The other lights gathered around her. With a series of pops, they became more winged people, all dark, all graceful and small. The men had thick beards, the women hair that cascaded over their shoulders.

They landed around him, their bare feet making tiny indentations on the thick blanket. He was too startled to cry. They examined his features, poking at his skin, tugging on his ears, tracing the tiny points.

4

'He's one of ours,' the woman said.

'Skin's light,' one of the men said.

'Lighter,' another man corrected. Their voices were tiny too, almost like little bells.

In the other room, his mother giggled. He moved at the sound, knocking some of the little people over. He reached for his mother. She giggled again, deep in her throat.

'Nicholas, it's been just days since the babe.'

His father laughed, too.

The little people got up. One of the men came very close. He squinted, making his small eyes almost invisible. 'Nose is upturned.'

'So?' the woman asked, her wings fluttering.

'Our noses are straight.'

'He has to have some Islander.'

'Rugar said leave him if there is no magic.'

The woman put her hands on her hips. 'Look at those eyes. Look at how bright they are. Then tell me there's no magic.'

'The magic is always stronger when the blood is mixed,' said another woman.

In the other room, his mother's laugh grew closer. 'Nicholas, let's just see the babe. Maybe we can decide what to call him then.'

The little people froze. His hands were still grasping. Outside the protection of the crib, the air was cold. The little people had brought deep warmth with them.

'Stay for a moment,' his father said.

'The healer said —'

'Healers be damned.'

The little people waited another moment, then the woman snapped her fingers. 'Quickly,' she said.

Their wings fluttered, and the group floated above him, as pretty as the lights. He wasn't sure of them. Touching them had hurt, but they were so pretty.

So pretty.

They fanned out around him, holding strands as thin as spider webs. They flew back and forth, weaving the strands. The woman stood near his head, outside of the strands, clutching a tiny stone to her chest.

'Hurry,' she said.

'Nicholas, really.' His mother laughed again. 'Stop. We can't.'

'I know,' his father said. 'But it's so much nicer than fighting. Maybe we shouldn't call him anything.'

'Can you imagine?' she said. 'He's a grandfather and his friends all call him "baby."'

The strands had formed a piece of white gauze between him and the world. The shadow moved on his nurse's face, lifting away a tiny bit, and glancing over its flat shoulder at the flying people.

'Not yet,' the woman said.

The shadow flattened out over the nurse once more.

The gauze enveloped him and his blankets. He felt warm and secure. The little people held the edges of the gauze and lifted him from the crib.

He could see the whole room. It was big. His nurse sat in one corner, the shadow over her face, her eyelids moving back and forth. A bed with filmy red curtains sat on the far side of the room, and chairs lined the walls. All the windows were covered with tapestries, and the tapestries were pictures of babies – being born, being held, being crowned. Only one window was open – the window the people had come through.

Floating was fun. It felt like being held. He snuggled into his blankets, and watched the little woman put the stone on his pillow.

Then the door handle turned. The little woman floated above the crib, shooing the others away with her hands. 'Hurry!' she whispered. 'Hurry!'

'We might wake him up, Jewel,' his father said.

'Babies sleep sound.'

'Wait,' he said. 'Let me find out what the name means. Then we can have a real talk. If it has no meaning, then –'

'Find out who had the name before,' she said. 'That's important.'

They were almost to the window. For a moment, he had forgotten his mother. He remembered her now. He wanted her to float with him. He rolled over, making the little people curse. The net swung precariously. He cried out, a long plaintive wail.

'Shush!' the little man nearest him said.

The shadow lifted off the nurse's face. She snorted, sighed, and sank deeper in sleep. The shadow crawled over the fireplace toward the window.

He cried out again. The nurse stirred and ran a hand over her face. His feet were outside. It was raining, but the drops didn't touch him. They veered away from his feet as if he wore a protective cover.

The nurse's eyes flickered open. 'What a dream I had, baby,' she said. 'What a dream.'

He howled. The little people hurried him outside even faster. She went to the crib and looked down. His gaze followed hers. In his bed, another baby lay. His eyes were open, but empty. The nurse brushed her hand on his cheek.

'You're cold, lambkins,' she said.

The little woman huddled in the curtain around the crib. She moved her fingers and the baby cooed. The nurse smiled.

He was staring at the baby that had replaced him. It looked like him, but it was not him. It had been a stone a moment before.

'Changeling,' he thought, marking not just his first word, but the arrival of his conscious being, born a full adult, thanks to the Fey's magic touch.

He screamed. The little people pulled him outside, over the courtyard and into the street. The nurse looked up, and went to the window, a frown marring her soft features. He cried again, but he was already as high as the clouds, and well down the street. The nurse shook her head, grabbed the tapestry, and pulled it closed.

'Hush, child,' the little man floating above him said. 'You're going home.'

THE
ASSASSINATION
[Three Years Later]

Two

The trees near the Kenniland Marshes grew tall and spindly, but their silvery leaves were thick and provided excellent cover. Rugar, the Black King's son and leader of the Fey on Blue Isle, balanced precariously on the fork between two branches on the tallest tree near the entrance to the marsh. Fortunately the spring air was warm. He had been in the tree since dawn, and his legs were cramping. He straightened them slowly so that he wouldn't shake the branches, or destroy the tiny opening he had made in the leaves. The arrows in the quiver strapped to his back rustled. The bow slipped from its resting place and he dived for it before it clattered down the trunk.

Then he froze, breathing softly, waiting for his heart to slow down to normal.

He double-checked the tiny circle of lights that revolved just above his head. His momentary fear hadn't dissolved them. Good. His escape route remained intact.

So far, no one had appeared on the road, but he didn't want to take any chances. The Islanders had grown careless in the four years of peace, but he had not. If anything, he had become more wary.

Rugar had arrived at the Marshes a week before, keeping off the main roads, and feeding himself from the land. A few times he had had to hide in the brush beside the road. Fey were taller and darker than the Islanders.

He had been surprised to discover that he enjoyed the cross-country trip. He hadn't bushwhacked across Blue Isle before, and he was startled at its varied terrain. The Marshes were at the far south end, and beyond them like the jagged teeth of a Hevish Desert Dog rose the mountain range that encircled the Isle.

Actually there were two ranges, broken in the center by the Cardidas River. The Snow Mountains covered most of the Isle, from the Stone Guardians in the west to the Slides of Death in the east. The imposing, treeless Eyes of the Roca covered the coastline north of the river, from the Cliffs of Blood on the east to the other side of the Guardians on the west. Because of these mountains, Blue Isle was almost impossible to reach by sea. The mountains were tall and sheer on the ocean sides. The only natural harbor was the mouth of the river on the west, blocked by the Stone Guardians.

His invasion force had come through the Guardians five years before, using an old map, an enthralled Nye navigator, and magic. The Guardians were tall rocks partially submerged. Ships rammed the rocks all the time. Without a map, a lot of luck, and a navigator knowledgeable in the ways of the currents, no one could get through the Guardians. From the day the Fey had invaded Blue Isle, the Guardian watchers stopped working the currents. The Islander King, Alexander, had sent the watchers to the settlements in the eastern Snow Mountains. For five years, no one had studied the currents. Blue Isle was completely cut off from the rest of the world.

Rugar would end that soon.

He settled back on the fork, the smooth bark hard against his thighs. He pulled the bow across his lap and stroked the string. Until he had come to the Isle, he had never used a bow. The Fey had abandoned them generations before, preferring swords and their magical talents to fight wars. He started practicing with the bow and arrow shortly after he had stolen his grandson three years before. This plan had not been in Rugar's mind then; only a knowledge that he should learn the weapon the Islanders prefer. During the Fey's first year on Blue Isle, many of them died when the tip of an arrow dipped in poison touched their bodies.

He was going to see how the Islanders would like it.

The marsh smelled of mud and rank, long-standing water. He had been in the tree long enough that thin-legged birds had landed in the water, and were fishing beneath its surface. Grass poked through the wet as did bushes, and more spindly trees. Only the road, purposely built high across the marsh, made the soggy land look any different from the hard ground leading into it.

There were villages around the marsh, but he had avoided them. So far, he had been successful in keeping himself hidden. He was days away from Blue Isle's main city, Jahn, and another day away from the Shadowlands where his loyal Fey remained. To his knowledge, no Fey had ever been this far south, not even the traitorous Burden and the band of deserters who had followed him out of Shadowlands shortly after Jewel's marriage.

The deserters claimed Shadowlands was no longer necessary. Rugar disagreed. He had created two Shadowlands, one to hold the ships, and one to protect his invasion force. Only Visionaries could make Shadowlands. They were boxes so large that a hundred giants could not hold them. The boxes were invisible to the naked eye, but solid to someone inside. The doorways were marked by a circle of lights. Once created, the Shadowlands remained solid until the Visionary destroyed them or until the Visionary died.

The sound of muffled hoofbeats drew his attention. Rugar gripped the bow tightly and leaned forward, peering through the leaves. A single horseman, wearing the black robe of a Danite, rode into view. His head was bald, his feet bare. A tiny silver sword which he wore around his neck glinted in the sunlight. Rugar had done some study about the marshes before he came here. The communities nearby had Danites attached to them to perform the daily religious ceremonies. Danites were the priests of Blue Isle's religious order. This Danite either came from the Tabernacle or from the King.

Most likely, he was an advance man for the King's party. The King had gotten wiser in the years since Rugar's daughter, Jewel, moved into the palace.

The Danite stopped at the edge of the marsh and peered around. The landscape was barren except for the trees, scattered in groups of three and four, across the water. His arrival spooked the birds, and dozens of them took off, the sound of their wings loud in the morning air.

Perfect.

From his quiver Rugar took an arrow, and placed it across his bow. Slowly he raised the bow, and got the Danite in his sights. But Rugar did not pull the arrow back. Instead he watched, aiming, practicing for the crucial moment.

His movements disturbed not a leaf on the tree.

As he had planned.

All of his training as the Black King's son, all of his work as a leading Visionary, all of his years as a military leader had given Rugar a precision that many of his people did not have. Even though he had not had a real Vision in almost five years, he still could invent tiny Shadowlands, and create invisible targets in the air with a startling accuracy. He learned to use that talent when he was practicing his archery. In the last year, it had gotten so that he only missed what he was aiming at when his concentration was destroyed.

Nothing would break his concentration today.

The Danite clucked at his horse and together they rode across the marsh, disturbing birds as they went. Rugar tracked them until he could no longer see them through the small holes he had made in his leaf cover. Then he put the arrow in its quiver, and leaned the bow in its place against the tree trunk.

He was appalled that it had come to this. A lone assassin in a tree. If his daughter had listened to him years before, the Fey would rule Blue Isle now.

Instead, she had taken one of his losses as a failure and negotiated a peace with the Islanders. A peace in which she sacrificed herself in marriage to their prince. She had thought that such a thing would unify the Fey and the Islanders. It had stopped the war, but it had not brought unity. Rugar had heard reports that the Fey who lived outside the Shadowlands, in Burden's encampment, often ran in fear of Islanders with poison.

Poison. The Fey would have owned this Isle within hours of their invasion if not for the Islanders' poison. They used it as holy water in their rituals and had accidentally discovered that it killed Fey in a particularly nasty manner. The Spell Warders, who designed all the spells for the Fey, had stayed with Rugar in the Shadowlands, and were trying to find a way to counteract the poison. They had been close, years ago, when their leader Caseo was murdered. His death had stalled them, and now, for all their work, they were no closer.

Only the Warders could design spells. Warders had the ability to do a bit of all Fey magic. But no Fey had all of the powers of the tribe. Fey were divided into the healing magicks, like the Domestics, Shamans, and Healers, and the warrior magicks, like the Foot Soldiers, Doppelgängers, and Visionaries. Only a few Fey crossed between both camps – Shape-Shifters, Beast Riders, and Enchanters, for example – but even they chose the military or the household when their magickal talents arrived in adolescence.

He wished the Fey had more powers. If they ever found the secret to the poison, the Fey would rule the Isle.

The sound of hoofbeats again drew his attention. This time, there was more than one horse. He pulled the bow onto his lap again, and held his breath. More time had gone by than he expected. It had been decades since he had sat alone in a tree, and never had he done so without a force around him. As a boy, before his magic came, he had served as lookout for his father's army. Today, everything rested on him.

Four riders appeared in the distance, riding two abreast. These riders wore brown pants and tunics – the new uniforms of the King's guards. The King had switched his guards' clothing when it became clear the other uniform was a target. The men had bare heads and close-cropped hair. As they approached, Rugar recognized one of them as Monte, head of the King's guards. Monte was a beefy middle-aged man with ruddy features and a hatred of the Fey. He had insulted Rugar at the banquet following Jewel's wedding, and only Jewel's pleas that the ceremony be peaceful kept Rugar from responding.

Rugar's information had been right. The King was visiting the

Kenniland Marshes on his first trip through the countryside since the Fey had arrived. The marshes were particularly important to the King, since they were, historically, a hotbed of political rebellion. The people in the marshes had led the Peasant Uprising generations before.

Rugar had not known any of the history of Blue Isle when he arrived here. All he had known was that the Isle was rich, and was between the Galinas continent and the Leutian continent. The Fey had just finished conquering Galinas, giving the Fey control of three of the five continents in the world. Leut was next. If his father, the Black King, had not opposed this mission, the Fey might actually be on Leut now.

Or dead. There was no guarantee his father's Spell Warders would have learned the secret to the poison either. But his father's Warders were in Nye, the country on the western edge of the Galinas continent, just as his father was.

The riders did not speak as they rode up. The horses were stallions, proud, dark beasts that pranced with spirit. The men had to use heavy reins to keep them under control. A surprise, and the poorer riders would be thrown.

That was the technique Rugar would have used if he had a force. Alone he had to wait for his target.

The King.

The four guards were scouting the area. They looked into the marsh, and at the trees. Rugar kept very still. If this group got past him, the King would arrive with confidence.

Monte peered into the tree that Rugar was in. Rugar held his breath. It felt as if their eyes met. Then Monte looked away. They rode slowly so that they could scout clearly. It gave Rugar a chance to investigate them. He had not seen the other three guards before. They were all older men who had lived at least three decades, maybe four. They had that same hefty strength that Monte had, and the same weary features. Their blue eyes were pale, their features round. They were shorter and stouter than the Fey, but within that square build lay a lot of strength. Some of the Fey Infantry had learned that the hard way.

They passed within spitting distance beneath the tree. Rugar could smell the horseflesh on the breeze. He watched them pass, then took a deep breath. There should be no more advance teams. The next arrival should contain the King.

Jewel would hate Rugar for this, if she ever figured it out. But he had given her four years to resolve this crisis. Four years to bring the Islanders under Fey control. When she had suggested her plan, she had said that once she was in the palace, she would betray the Islanders. But she had fallen subject to their odd charm. She didn't

15

even realize that the child she raised was a changeling. Her son, Gift, had been in the Shadowlands since he was less than a week old.

If she wasn't going to betray the Islanders by now, she never would. And the King's first visit to the outlying areas provided Rugar with the chance he had been waiting for.

A small dust cloud rose in the distance. Rugar smiled. The King would travel with a party large enough to raise dust even on this meager road. Rugar grabbed his bow, put it across his lap, and rested an arrow on top of it.

He would get only one chance.

As the dust cloud grew closer, the clear air carried the sound of many hooves. The King never traveled alone any more. Before the Fey arrived, he traveled with two guards whom he would often dismiss so that he could talk with his people alone. He stopped that practice immediately, and introduced measures all through the Isle that protected the Islanders from the Fey. Rugar sometimes felt that his biggest mistake was not disobeying his own father's wishes, but underestimating the Islander King.

The cloud was growing bigger. Rugar brought up his bow, placed the end of the arrow against the string, and waited. He could make out tiny figures now – a dozen men, maybe more. Even with all his learning, the King had not yet discovered women as a powerful fighting force. The Islanders' innate dismissal of women probably caused some of the trouble Jewel was having in the palace.

Rugar glanced at the revolving circle of lights. Still there. Still waiting. The Powers were with him. None of this would be worthwhile if he didn't survive. Jewel would not know how to take advantage of the changes, and Gift was too young. Rugar would have to guide them all.

Now he could make out faces, some of whom he recognized from his brief dealings with the Islanders. Lord Stowe rode at the King's right side. Stowe did not wear a hat on his balding head, but his long brown curls were pulled away from his face. He held the reins with a mincing precision that belied his strength as a negotiator.

Lord Enford rode on the King's left. Enford was slender to the point of gauntness, with hollow eyes and sunken cheeks. His blond hair, also pulled back, was thin and scraggly. He was older than the King's other advisors, but had a cunning that Rugar had discovered during his second meeting at the palace after Jewel's wedding.

Four guards rode out front, and four trailed behind, while another four encircled the King and his nobles. Such a large contingent. It made Rugar wonder if this were more than a routine check of the outlying provinces.

Alexander, the King, rode a large black stallion. The animal had a lot of power, yet submitted completely to Alexander's control. Somehow Rugar had not expected the Islander King to be a horseman – another underestimation. This man was the only man in the history of the Fey to defeat a Fey invasion force. Of course he had hidden talents and powers. Even if Jewel had yet to discover them.

Rugar squinted, lining up his shot. The King was still too far away, but it would only be moments now.

Alexander was younger than Rugar by a good decade or more. He had a nonathletic stockiness when Rugar first met him, but that had faded over the years. Alexander was a trim man now who looked only a few years older than his own son, Jewel's husband. The two men resembled each other enough to be brothers. Alexander's hair was shorter, his bearing straighter, his manner less impulsive, all things difficult to determine from a distance.

Rugar had thought of the difficulties in telling the King and Prince apart, then decided that it didn't matter. King or Prince, a death in the royal family would destroy the Islanders' spirit.

Alexander was almost within range. Rugar mentally saluted him. Alexander had proven a worthy adversary. Rugar would mourn his loss.

The approaching force did not talk. The dust cloud traveled with them, surrounding them, but obscuring nothing. The horses' hooves clomped in unison, adding a comforting rhythm to the morning. Rugar leaned forward just enough to make certain his target was within his sights.

One shot.

One chance.

Alexander's perfectly straight torso was within range. Rugar pulled the bow even tighter. He imagined Alexander's heart, beating constantly, rhythmically, pictured it as a target, and then released the bowstring. The snap sounded loud to him, but the arrow flew silently between two guards. It pierced Alexander's breast. He glanced up skyward, a quick moment of startlement, then toppled backwards off his horse.

Rugar didn't move. It would be a matter of moments before they saw him. He wanted to see their reaction before he disappeared into his own private Shadowlands.

The horses stopped. The guards in the rear cried out. The guards up front continued forward another few paces. Lord Stowe yelled his King's name, and Lord Enford was off his mount before the rest. He ran back to the King, and touched him gently, then cradled his head.

Lord Stowe dismounted, as did the remaining guards.

17

'No need,' Lord Enford said in Islander, his voice barely carrying over the marsh. 'He's dead.'

Rugar smiled. Success. It had been so rare these last few years. He reached up and stuck a finger in the circle of lights. The circle grew large enough to accommodate his body. As he stepped inside the swirling gray nothingness, he heard Stowe's voice, high and frightened but struggling for control.

'Where did the arrow come from?'

'I don't know,' Enford said.

'That tree?' asked a new voice.

Then the Circle Door closed behind Rugar and he willed the points of light to become as small as they could. He had made this Shadowlands very tiny, big enough to hold his sitting frame and his weapons and little more. He brushed against the square walls, his head pressed against the smooth sides.

Shadowlands got its air from the outside because the walls were porous. But it got nothing else. He was surrounded by grayness. The Shadowlands was like a great box with nothing inside, but it did have a top, a bottom and walls. They were barriers to the touch and felt solid, but had no visible form.

He could still create Shadowlands – the proper kind – the kind that hid a warrior anywhere on an open plain. He still had some of his Visionary powers. But he didn't need them to know what would happen next.

The Islanders would be in complete disarray. If Jewel stepped into the void left by King Alexander's death, good. But if not, Rugar would. Step one was completed. As soon as night fell, he would leave his tree and head back to Jahn. Then he would implement Step Two.

Unlike his daughter and her friend Burden, Rugar remembered the mission. Blue Isle would become a Fey stronghold. The last five years would become a footnote – the first battle instead of the war.

Three

Jewel stopped at the door of the palace nursery, her hand over her bulging stomach. The baby was kicking – hard – and the sharpness, combined with the constant pain in her chest, made her slightly dizzy. Coming into the nursery always upset her, though. The room was dark and gloomy, no matter what she did to cheer it up. The stone walls were as gray as Shadowlands, and the fireplace did little to heat the place. Whenever she came in, she opened the tapestries and let in the fresh air and sunlight. As soon as she left, the nurse closed the tapestries again.

Not that actions made much difference. Sebastian had not moved from his play rug. He sat, hands on his sturdy thighs, legs outstretched, staring into the fire, just as she had left him hours before. The stuffed warriors the nurse had made him, the tiny carts on their sanded wheels, didn't interest him. Nothing did.

The baby she was carrying kicked again. She had said nothing to Nicholas about her fears for this child. Sebastian had kicked this much when he was in the womb, perhaps more, and now he was a dull, listless child who took not the best traits of his parents, but the worst. If anyone had told her that a mingling of Fey and Islander would result in a child that lacked spark, she would never have made this match.

Or at least not in the same way.

She couldn't imagine life without Nicholas. For all their differences, he was more her complement than any other man she had ever met. She caressed the taut skin hiding their next child. She had tried to prevent another pregnancy, though, using Fey charms and herbs. One month, Nicholas's chamberlain had discovered them and removed them.

One month was all it took.

Still, she couldn't quite bring herself to get rid of the child. She allowed herself the small hope that this baby would be different, that this child would receive all the good traits, Islander and Fey. This child would be what other Fey half-breeds had always been: the most powerful of all.

Fey lore had always said that, in addition to the lands, the Fey needed new blood to keep the magick alive. New blood added freshness, gave the magic room to grow. Fey to Fey matches created magic-filled children, but as the generations progressed, the magick diminished, weakened by too much closeness. Mingling with new races always brought changes to the magick, always strengthened it, and sometimes even created new magickal forms. Lore said that the Fey didn't have Visionaries until they descended from the Eccrasian Mountains.

The dizziness was passing. She took a deep breath and entered the nursery. The nurse was knitting in her chair near the fireplace. Jewel didn't know how the woman sat so close to the heat. The room was already twice as hot as it should be.

The nurse smiled and nodded at her. Jewel nodded back. Carefully, because of her bulk, she moved around the toys, chairs, and tables to her son. Using a chair to brace herself, she sank down beside him and took his tiny hand in her own.

His skin was cold.

And hard. She had always thought a child's skin should be soft. The lack of sunlight in his life – and his mixed parentage – had left his skin a muted gray. Slowly he turned his head toward her. He had the solemnity of a man of eight decades.

'Moth-er,' he said in Islander, drawing the word out, speaking one of the few words he had mastered.

'Hello, baby,' she said, running a hand along his hard, smooth cheek. Just once she wished he would lean into the caress, acknowledge the warmth that a child should feel for his parent. But if she ever had to confess, her warmth for him had faded with his odd behavior. She went through the motions, but the love, once so much a part of her, had disappeared deep inside. 'What have you been doing?'

He shrugged, a movement as slow as all his others. No grace for him, no childlike impulsiveness, no curiosity, no quickness. Nicholas never even came into the nursery any more. He couldn't stand looking at Sebastian, knowing that this child would one day lead the Kingdom.

'How's the heart today, Mistress?' the nurse asked.

Jewel brought her right hand up to the space between her left breast and her rounded stomach. 'It still aches,' she said.

For the last few days, Jewel felt as if her heart were hollow. The Islander healers blamed the constant ache on her pregnancy, but she believed something else caused it. She had felt a sharp piercing pain three mornings ago, so sharp that it had driven her to her knees and sent Nicholas's counselors scurrying for the Islander healers. Then, as suddenly as it arrived, the pain faded, leaving the dull ache.

The Islander healers thought the ache meant she was ill and ordered her to bedrest. But she had never rested in her life. The Islanders had no concept of Fey. Fey women kept moving until the child was born, and often went to war with infants strapped on their backs. Just because she was living in the Islander stronghold did not mean that Jewel would act like a weak Islander woman.

'Perhaps you should rest,' the nurse said gently.

Jewel didn't respond. Instead, she squeezed Sebastian's hand. His return squeeze, when it came, was strong and almost painful. 'Did he show any change at all this morning?'

'None, Mistress.' They had been having this conversation for three years, ever since his naming day. Her father, Rugar, had warned her that giving a child an Islander name might rob him of his power. But she had made a deal with Nicholas. If Nicholas could show that the ancestral bearers of Sebastian's name were great men, then he would win the fight for the name. All the previous Sebastians were great kings. She wanted no less for her own child. She had agreed.

And since that day, Sebastian had shown no interest in the world. He went from a bright-eyed, grasping infant to a listless, lethargic one in the space of a day. In desperation, she had taken him to Burden's colony in Jahn. Burden had formed a Fey Settlement in the city just after her marriage. Many Fey had been disillusioned by her father's rule and hoped that Jewel's marriage to Nicholas would improve their lot. But the Settlement was as much a prison as the Shadowlands had been, just in a different way.

Burden had not taken many Fey with Domestic powers with him when he left Shadowlands, and the ones he had were not great Healers. They had looked at her with pity as if she had failed to understand something, and then they had said that Sebastian was not a natural child, a fact she had already known. They said they could do nothing if she remained outside of Shadowlands.

Her pride kept her from Shadowlands, kept her from asking her father's help. She would go, however, if this new child showed the same lack as Sebastian.

Asking for help would be difficult. Fey did not give help readily, unlike Islanders. The Fey believed that if a person could not figure out something on her own, she lacked insight and intelligence. In seeking help for her children, she would diminish her position with her own people.

She leaned over, kissed Sebastian, and smoothed the thin coarse hair over his forehead. He tilted his head toward her, moving so slowly that the movement was almost imperceptible, and then he smiled.

A true smile.

21

And her heart melted. She lived for these moments, when he actually reached to her, actually saw her. At these times, all the love and hope of his babyhood returned.

She hugged him, and waited until he hugged back, feeling his tentative movements against her back.

'Mistress?' A male voice ruined the moment. She didn't pull out of Sebastian's embrace right away – doing so always startled the boy – but eased her way out, then kissed his hands before replacing them in his lap.

She turned without getting up. She hated feeling ungainly. She was more agile than Nicholas when she wasn't pregnant. Her loss of grace at these times felt like a definite disadvantage.

The man in the door was one of the pages. He had seen no more than seventeen summers, but his voice already had a man's depth. He bobbed in an approximation of a bow when he saw her looking at him.

'Mistress, 'tis yer presence His Highness requests. He says ta make haste.'

Normally she would have smiled and put the boy at ease. She had a way with the Islanders. They expected her to be fierce so she wasn't. She was charming, and that made them forget that she was taller than most of them, her hair black where theirs was fair, and her features up-swept when theirs were square. They still noted her dark skin, and winced when she moved quickly – as if they were afraid she was going to turn them into hogs – but they had become more tolerant over time. She still couldn't train them to use her name, however, in the Fey manner. They insisted on a title, although she could not get used to the word 'Highness.' 'Mistress' was the most she would tolerate.

'Did he say what had happened?'

The boy shook his head. ''Tis something terrible, Mum. He cried out when he heard it.'

Her hand was still over her heart. She pressed, just a little, wondering if her body had foreseen something her mind had not. Visions had been miserly in this place. It bothered her that she had not had one about her son.

'Is he in audience?'

The boy nodded.

'Tell him, then, that I will be there as soon as I can.'

The boy did not wait for her, but bobbed his head again and ran off. Jewel took a deep breath before placing her hands on the chair and levering herself up. Sebastian was still watching her, but it didn't appear that his dark eyes saw her.

'I'll be back, sweetness,' she said to him. Then she glanced at the nurse. 'See if you can get him to do more than stare.'

'Yes, Mistress.'

Jewel took a deep breath and braced her hand at the small of her back. The baby would come any day now. For that, she felt a great relief. She knew this ungainly stage of pregnancy was only temporary, yet on a deep level, it frightened her. She – the most agile of all the Fey, the best swordsman in the Infantry – unable to make quick movements or bend easily. Sometimes she feared that her agility would never come back. She would lose a great part of herself to the child within.

Yet that had not happened with Sebastian. If anything, his birth had made her more agile. She actually practiced swordfighting with her husband. She and Nicholas had met in battle and were evenly matched. When his swordmaster died during the year of the war, he had no one to turn to. Practicing with Nicholas was an exercise in physical strength and mental prowess since they were evenly matched on all sides.

The King, of course, had opposed that from the beginning, at first afraid that Jewel would use the practices as an excuse to kill Nicholas. When it became clear that she would keep her bargain, she was warned by the King's advisors (never the King himself) that such behavior was unladylike. She countered that sewing was unFeylike, although that wasn't true. If she had been raised a Domestic she might think otherwise, but she was the Black King's granddaughter, a Visionary and a Warrior, and she had never held a needle in her life.

The corridor was cool compared to the heat of the nursery. The nursery was on the floor she shared with Nicholas. Theoretically, they were supposed to have separate suites, but they had never managed it. They slept in his. The nursery was off her suite.

What she called a corridor, in parlance she had learned in the Great Houses of Nye, was actually a gallery by Islander standards. It was as wide as many rooms she had lived in and ran the length of the floor. Portraits of Princes and their wives, all looking solemn and square, lined the hall. Her portrait was painted shortly after Sebastian's birth, and even though she still carried weight from the baby, she looked gaunt compared with Princesses of old. Dark and exotic. All of the others had been cut from the same mold – blonde, blonde hair, pale blue eyes, bone-white skin ('alabaster' Nicholas had once called it in a moment of levity), and rosy round cheeks. When her portrait was hung next to Nicholas's, the religious leader, the Rocaan, had remarked under his breath that Jewel looked like a demon in a field of angels.

23

She looked at the chairs lining the corridor longingly. If she hadn't known that they were the most uncomfortable chairs in two continents, she would have stopped for just a moment. But the page had said to make haste, and the quicker she found Nicholas, the quicker she would be off her feet.

She turned before reaching her own portrait, and took the stairs down, using the railing for balance. The stairs were carved of stone, and very sharp. She had nightmares about falling down them, pregnant and unable to get up, bleeding from wounds on her back and sides, the baby dead within her.

Because the nightmares came when she slept, she knew they were not a Vision.

At the landing, she paused. The baby chose that moment to kick again. Jewel placed her hand over the movement, feeling the fluttering –

– and suddenly she was in the west wing. A young girl Jewel had never seen before sat in the window seat, looking down at the garden below. The girl had black hair and skin not quite as dark as Jewel's, but when the girl turned and glanced around the room, her face had a suggestion of Nicholas. Jewel crept closer. The girl wore flowing robes. A maid hovered near the dressing table, exhorting her to get dressed, but the girl leaned out the window, watching something move through the garden.

Jewel stood behind the girl's shoulder. The garden was bright – sun-dappled, the flowers huge and overpowering. There, among them, was a boy only a few years older than the girl. Tall, and thin, and graceful, with black, black hair –

– and then Jewel was back in the stairwell again, leaning against the stone wall, her breath coming in large gasps. The stone was cold against her back, but the ache in her heart had receded.

A Vision. The girl in the Vision had the look of Nicholas with Fey features. And her face was alive, her eyes bright with curiosity, her movements quick, just as Sebastian's were not. A Vision. About her second child, and not her first.

She closed her eyes, and felt relief flood through her. This child would be all right. This child would have all the promise that Sebastian did not have. This child had even provided a Vision. Already. Such powerful magic at work. Visionaries rarely had Visions about babes in the womb.

Jewel continued down the stairs, disoriented from the intensity of her Vision, unable to move swiftly because of her bulk. They probably started the meeting without her. They had done that when she was pregnant with Sebastian. A pregnancy that early had been a mistake. She should have kept her strength in the first few years, not lost it to children and tradition. She was here to unify the Fey and the Islanders, and she was still having trouble. The Islanders did not consider her part of government, merely a wife of the heir to the throne. Only Nicholas felt differently, and he was Prince, not King.

She had other problems as well. Her own people would not work in the palace. A few tried, but left when threatened by Islander poison. She suspected that the Islanders often did not initiate the threat, that they were responding to something, but she fought a losing battle. Her friend Burden had established a colony outside Shadowlands, but it had become merely an isolated Fey community with sunlight instead of grayness. Those Fey were unable to become part of Island society as well.

Fears. She was battling fears and a prejudice she hadn't even known existed when she made this pact. And to have Sebastian be a dullard made matters worse.

She cradled her stomach, glad for the first time for this child. This baby would prove that the match between Fey and Islander was not a mistake, that the two cultures would integrate. And they had to integrate for the rest of her plan – the plan she had once proposed to her father – to work.

When she had married Nicholas, she had believed that the Fey and Islanders would mingle on Blue Isle. They would become a united community. Then when her grandfather, the Black King, finally decided to conquer Blue Isle, he would arrive to discover that the Isle was already part of the Fey Empire. Instead of being conquered by force, it would be conquered by intermingling, by families composed of both Fey and Islanders.

The stairs led directly to the wing with the audience chamber. For once, she was glad for the proximity. It saved her endless walking.

She hurried as best she could through the Great Hall. Her wedding banquet had been held here, one of Nicholas's favorite rooms. The hall was long and wide and had arched ceilings because it connected two towers and had no floor above it. The arched windows matched the ceiling in design, some of the few windows in the palace with rare glass.

The hall was the least Islander place in the palace. Swords hung from the inner wall, and none were ceremonial. The Islanders were not a warlike people – they had never been invaded until the Fey arrived – but they had had their share of uprisings and revolts. The hall had an air of power the rest of the palace lacked.

Still, she didn't linger. A sense of urgency that she hadn't really felt when the page summoned her was growing within. She went through the door that led to the corridor which housed the audience chamber.

Four guards stood in front of the oak door. They were Islander, of course, and did not acknowledge her as a member of the royal family. But two of them did move in unison to pull the door open as she approached.

Nicholas stood inside, his hands clasped behind his back. He wore his long blond hair in a queue. He was as tall as she was – a rarity among Islanders – and, although he was broad, his build had strength. He wore a blouse gathered at the wrists but untied at the neck, and tight breeches that tucked into long black riding boots. His eyes were red-rimmed and he had a tight expression on his face that she had never seen before.

Lord Enford stood beside him. Enford wore breeches as well, something Jewel had never seen. He was covered with dirt, his hair matted against his skull, strands pulling out of his queue. His eyes looked more sunken than usual in his gaunt face.

Instinctively, Jewel put a hand over her stomach, guarding the child within. Then she stepped inside the chamber.

'Nicholas?' she said, even now disdaining the formal forms of address the Islanders insisted upon.

He stared at her as if he didn't see her, as if he were someone else. The thought sent a shiver of fear through her. The Fey had ways of taking over a person – some of them direct, such as a Doppelgänger who absorbed the person, soul and all; and some indirect, such as suggestions made by strong Charmers. Her father couldn't have sent a Doppelgänger to take over Nicholas; all the Doppelgängers had died in the first year on the Isle. No Charmers had come with them either. Still, she went up to Nicholas, took his chin in her hand, and turned his head toward her. His eyes were lined with red, but no gold – the sign of a Doppelgänger – glinted in them. It was Nicholas, but a part of him that she did not recognize.

He moaned at her touch, and wrapped his arms around her, pulling her as close as he could. The babe kicked in protest – did that child never rest? – but he didn't even seem to notice. Jewel held him tightly, glancing over his shoulder at Lord Enford. Nicholas had never been this demonstrative in public. It was something she frowned upon more than he, but he had always honored that. Until now.

Except for Enford, they were alone in the large room. The guards that usually stood beneath the ancient spears lining the walls were gone. On the dais, the throne was empty, which didn't surprise her, since Alexander was on a tour of the countryside –

With Enford.

She returned her gaze to Enford, taking in the brown smears on his traveling clothes. Not all of the stains were dirt. A chill ran through her, so strong that she shivered.

Nicholas apparently felt the shiver and pulled away. He ran a hand through his hair, disturbing its look, a gesture reminiscent of his father. Nicholas walked over to the throne, and stared above it, at the coat of arms that decorated the wall behind. Jewel had always found the fact that the royal family had a coat of arms curious. She found it even odder that the design was of two swords crossed over a heart.

'Do you think that's symbolic of us?' he asked Jewel in Nye.

She knew better than to answer in front of Enford. 'What happened?' she said softly in Islander. She had learned the language well in her years at the palace, although Nye remained her language with Nicholas. It provided them no privacy: Most of the Islanders spoke Nye. It had just become custom between them.

Enford started to speak but Nicholas held up his hand. 'My father's dead,' he said in Nye.

The ache over Jewel's heart dissipated as if it had never been and suddenly, she missed it. She felt hollow. Alexander, dead. In an instant, everything had changed. 'How?' she asked in Islander.

Nicholas turned, faced Enford. 'Wait until the others come.'

'Under the Mysteries,' Jewel said. 'I am your wife. This will affect all of us. I deserve to hear before "the others."'

Enford's gaze held a wariness it had not held before. 'An arrow, Highness. Just one. Through the heart.'

Jewel suddenly wished for a chair. Three days before. She had felt it. She had to have. It took a long time to get to Jahn from the Kenniland Marshes. She had known – but how? 'You caught the assassin, then?'

Enford shook his head. 'Lord Stowe and Captain Monte remain in the area with some of the guards. I came back right away.'

She didn't like this. She wasn't that close to Alexander. She shouldn't have known about his death. It should have been as much of a surprise to her as it was to Nicholas. So far he had said nothing about her sudden heart pain. She only hoped that he would not put it together with his father's death.

She went to Nicholas and took his hand, turning him around. Despite the battles four years before, he was not accustomed to death. She was.

'You're King now,' she said in Nye.

His eyes were empty. She suddenly saw how Sebastian resembled him.

Enford had moved discreetly away, standing closer to the door.

'They will rely on you, expect you to make decisions.'

Finally, Nicholas focused. His blue eyes were wide, red-lined, but dry. 'How? He was my father.'

'And their King. It is time to be strong. Later, when they are gone, you can mourn him.'

He blinked, and straightened his shoulders. Enford was still standing by the door.

'What will happen next?' she asked, her voice soft. She would lead him through this. She owed him that much. Him and the new child. The hope.

'I don't know,' he said.

'You have to know,' she whispered, 'or someone else will fill the gap.'

He nodded once, then pulled his hand from her grasp. He took a deep breath, as if he were steeling himself, then he walked to Enford. 'This is the wrong room for this meeting,' he said in Islander. 'We need to assemble in a place with a table and chairs. I don't want my wife on her feet for the hours it will take to resolve this.'

Jewel mentally applauded him. The decision would also keep him from sitting in his father's chair immediately, so that he would look like a reluctant King.

'Would you please help the servants prepare the Great Chamber? Her Highness and I will follow.'

Enford nodded. 'Certainly, Highness.'

He opened the door, and was about to step out when Jewel said, 'Take a moment for yourself, Lord Enford, and stop in the kitchen for a bite to eat and a bit of mead. I'm sure you're hungry as well as exhausted after your journey.'

Enford turned so that he could stare at her for a moment, his expression unreadable. Then he allowed himself a tight smile and a nod. She understood his acknowledgement. He recognized the courtesy. She had never used his title before, and probably would not again. But they were putting aside small differences at the moment, differences that would cause rather than ease the crisis.

'Thank you, milady,' he said, returning the courtesy as best he could without insulting his new King. 'I will do so after the meeting room is arranged.'

Then he left and closed the oak doors carefully behind him.

'I can't do this,' Nicholas said in Nye.

She had heard this before, in battle, with Fey who had been trained for years to expect such changes. 'You can. You must.'

'Jewel, it may lead to war.'

She didn't nod, even though she agreed. She wanted him to take this one step at a time. 'He was killed with an arrow, Nick, in the Marshes.

28

Arrows are not weapons of choice for my people. We have much more devious ways of killing. Have there been assassination attempts on your monarchs before?'

'None successful.' Nicholas's face was paler than she had ever seen it. A slash of red marred one cheek, as if he had been rubbing it.

'But there have been, right?'

He nodded.

'Against your father?'

'Of course not. Against one of my great-grandfathers. During the Peasant Uprising. A few before that too, I think.'

'So there is precedent.'

Nicholas frowned. 'I suppose there is. But why would anyone want to kill my father?'

She almost started listing reasons: the Islanders blamed Alexander for the Fey's arrival, and for his lack of strength in dealing with the Fey, not realizing that keeping the Fey from overtaking the Isle was a victory. Alexander had made some unpopular rulings in the last few years, from closing trade to outlawing cats. The Islanders had many reasons to hate him. But she said nothing.

'I don't know,' she said. 'But, Nicky, we have to examine that as an option.'

He tilted his head and looked at her sideways. 'So no one will blame the Fey?' The look was almost sly. She had never seen it before.

'Do you?' she asked. Her heart was pounding. The only Islander who had ever supported her, the only Islander who had ever believed that the Fey and the Islanders could work together was Nicholas. Without him, she would have to return to her father with her sparkless child and her newborn girl, to live in Shadowlands and fight a war they had no chance of winning.

'I don't think you had any part in this.'

'So you do blame my people.'

He shrugged, turned. 'I don't understand why my father would die now. As you said, we have to look at all the options.'

She bit her lower lip. Since they were being as honest as they could with each other, she would try one more question. 'There will be objections to me as your Queen.'

His expression softened and he moved beside her, tracing a finger along the fine bone of her cheek. The pull between them was as fine and strong as ever. His people believed their god guided them. Hers believed in Mysteries and Powers. But whatever had brought them together had made it so that the two of them could not resist each other.

'There have always been objections,' he said.

'There will be more now.'

He put his hand on her stomach, and leaned his head against hers. The baby wasn't kicking now, and Jewel realized that she had forgotten to tell him about her Vision.

'You are my Queen, and I am their King,' he said. 'They may not like my choice, but they'll have to live with it.'

'Like you do.'

He kissed her and tucked a strand of hair behind her ear. 'I don't live with my choice, Jewel.' His voice was soft, warm. 'I depend on it.'

Four

He was the King's contact with the people, but Lord Stowe had never encountered people like this. Most of them lived in wood and thatch huts on the outskirts of the Marshes. Only a few lived in the village, and they looked even poorer than the Marsh dwellers.

Stowe had overtaken the kirk at the edge of the village. The building was made of stone, dug up, the villagers told him proudly, from the marsh muck and blessed by the Rocaan himself. The Rocaan, the religious leader of Blue Isle, rarely left the Tabernacle in Jahn, so it was clear the villagers meant the fiftieth Rocaan. He had been dead over four years now, tricked and murdered by the Fey leader Rugar when the Rocaan had tried to make peace. The old Rocaan had spent his training in the Marshes. Stowe doubted the old Rocaan had much to do with the kirk – the building looked too old even for that – but his heritage probably had a lot to do with the building's constant use and cleanliness.

The building was larger than many kirks in outlying areas. It was serviced by a Danite who lived in the village – another rarity since most Danites in an area this small traveled from community to community. This kirk was still made up of a single room, however, about the size of Stowe's entrance hall in his own manor. A dozen pews provided seating for the locals who came to Morning and Midnight Sacraments.

There were no windows. The walls were covered with a white wash that showed through to the brown stone behind it. The altar was a square table, roughly carved, with slots for holy water beneath. An oversized sword, the symbol of the religion, hung from the wall behind the altar, point downward. The silver reflected the light of a dozen candles. This sword was polished and well loved. When he had stepped close to it, he had noted that it was etched with the words from the Roca's Blessing, ostensibly given before he died.

Stowe didn't count himself among the believers, although he attended Midnight Sacrament at least once a week. The Midnight Sacrament re-enacted the Roca's Absorption. The Words Written and Unwritten recorded that the Roca was a man Beloved of God who,

31

when asked to choose between leading his people into a battle they could not win or slaughtering the Soldiers of the Enemy, decided instead to offer himself as a sacrifice. He cleaned his sword with holy water, ran himself through, and was Absorbed into the Hand of God where he spoke on behalf of his people into the Ear of God.

Stowe found the idea of the Roca's Absorption a bit preposterous, and the idea that an entire religion could be based on the good words of one man into the Ear of God absurd. But some part of him found the idea of conducting an investigation into the death of the King here, in the kirk, appalling. Obviously, some part of him had religious sensibilities.

It was not a discovery he really wanted to make.

Except for the Danite who was still lighting candles, Stowe currently had the kirk to himself. He had spent the last few days talking with the people who dwelt near the road where the King was assassinated. They had seen nothing. For his work here, he was relying on the Danite, who knew of several villagers who had made disparaging comments before the King's arrival.

Stowe was glad for the work, and for the help. He had sent Monte back to Jahn with the body and the news that Stowe would stay until he discovered who had assassinated the King. Finding the assassin kept him from focusing on that moment, that thud of arrow against skin, that soft sound of surprise the King made as he toppled over backwards. Stowe had come into his lordship the same year that Alexander had become King. They had been young men together, ruling a country without the vaguest notion of how to do so, learning together, growing together, making mistakes together.

Stowe never believed he would be left to go on. Alexander had always had a golden aura. Even when his first wife died, leaving him Nicholas to raise alone, Alexander had done so, finding time for his son as well as managing a country. His second wife had given him no children, but much comfort. Her death had been a blow to him, one he had barely recovered from when the Fey arrived.

But even the Fey's defeat seemed golden. And the obvious love between Nicholas and Jewel a godsend.

Stowe had never been able to find a wife, let alone find time to father a child. He had spent his years at the King's side, making the King's wishes come true.

Now he was here, sleeping in someone else's mud hut, on the marshy ground of a village that smelled of standing water and sewage, hoping to figure out the secret behind his King's death. Stowe had sent Enford back to Nicholas because Stowe was unable to face the boy. Nicholas was older than Alexander had been when he became

32

King, and wiser in many ways, but the boy and his father had been close.

The news would destroy Nicholas.

The Danite pinched out the candle he had been using to light the others. The kirk was ablaze in light. The white wash seemed cleaner in this kind of brightness.

The room was cold, though. The dampness of marshes penetrated here. At least Stowe's borrowed cabin had a fireplace to dispel the worst of the chill.

'I think we might bring them in,' the Danite said.

'If we're going to interview them, we should do it separately.' Stowe rubbed his hands together. They were turning red with chill, even though it wasn't that cold outside. The dampness in the kirk had to be permanent, and probably quite a relief in the summer.

'They ain't none of them to confess to you,' the Danite said. He was a native of the region, and unlike the old Rocaan, had not yet unlearned the dialect. 'Twon't matter how you approach 'em.'

Stowe suppressed a sigh. He had set up this meeting on the Danite's suggestion. 'Then what is the point?'

'To listen. To hear what they ain't saying. Silences they can tell you all.' The Danite smiled. His teeth were uneven, and one up front was missing. 'And if you listen good, you will learn all you need.'

'I trust you will help me with this listening.'

The Danite nodded. 'Twouldn'ta wasted yer time should I thought it would come to naught. Twould be best if some of the questioning I did.'

'Yes,' Stowe said. 'I think it would.' He waved a hand and headed toward the front where two chairs had been placed in front of the altar. 'Let them in, then.'

The Danite pushed open one of the double doors and gestured the people outside to come in. About a dozen people straggled inside, men covered with mud to their hips, and women whose skirts were patched and mended so many times that the original fabric was unclear. They looked older than Stowe, although he realized as he watched them move that many were younger. One woman had a boy in tow, and he had a large boil on his neck. All of the people were so thin they looked skeletal, and only a few had bathed within the last week.

The stench they brought with them was so great Stowe had to swallow twice to keep from losing his breakfast.

They watched him as they came in, keeping their gaze on him even as they scattered into the pews. Now he understood why the pews had no cushions – the stench would remain.

The Danite closed the door and walked up the aisle toward Stowe. The people sat toward the back in groups of two and three. The Danite stopped beside Stowe.

'His lordship Mr. Stowe,' the Danite said, looking at Stowe.

Stowe nodded his head in greeting. The villagers did not bow or even nod as was the custom in Jahn. They continued to stare at him, eyes bright in their mud-covered faces.

'I trust you all heard about the horrible murder,' the Danite said. 'His lordship Mr. Stowe he wants to talk about it.'

'Ain't none of us done it,' said a man in the back. His hair stuck up on the sides, and his face was so mud-covered his skin looked dark as a Fey's.

'He ain't sayin' none of us did,' the Danite said. 'But we got to find out what happened.'

'Can't see why,' the boy with the boil muttered, and his mother immediately pressed his head against her breast.

'Why?' the Danite said. 'You all know why. Twas our King that died.'

'Not our king,' said the man who had spoken before.

Stowe straightened. He had yet to take the chair that he had set for himself, and now decided he wouldn't. These people were astonishingly forthright. 'Who is your king, then?'

'Don't got one,' said the man. He jutted his chin out as he spoke to Stowe as if that gave him extra strength.

Stowe opened his mouth to argue, but the Danite brushed against him.

'You follow the Roca. The King what died is a son of a son of a son of the Roca. Same family, you know.'

'The Roca does more for us than any king ever done,' a woman said. She was sitting on the opposite side of the kirk. Her face was clean and her hair pulled back in a neat bun. Her skin was unlined, but Stowe could see where age would tug it. Exhaustion had already given her the look of a woman used up.

'Yeah,' said the man who had been speaking for the group. 'We was going to tell the king that when he come. But he didn't.'

'He was assassinated on the way here,' Stowe said.

'And I wager yer here ta blame us,' the woman said. It was as if she and the man had been chosen to speak for the group.

'No,' Stowe said. 'I'm here to see if you have any knowledge that can help me. Have you seen any strangers about? Any Fey in the vicinity?'

'Fey?' The boy turned his head so that he could see his mother. Still, his whisper carried across the room.

'Them creatures as to why we ain't seen no one from Jahn all these years,' the woman said in a whisper just as loud.

'They've never seen Fey,' the Danite said. 'The war is a myth down here.'

It took all of Stowe's diplomatic skills to keep from angrily responding to that. He took a deep breath, then said, 'The Fey are not a myth. They nearly destroyed Jahn and the outlying areas. It is a tribute to your King that you have never seen Fey. In Nye, the Fey rule.'

'How would we know these creatures?' another man asked. He too was scrubbed, but his clothing was worn through on the elbows and knees.

'They look different,' Stowe said, not quite wanting to give away how different.

'Like you?' one of the women asked.

He looked down on himself in startlement. His breeches and shirt were clean. His hair was pulled back and his skin was good. He had never thought how exotic he would look to these people.

'He's just trying to get us to say we done it,' the first man said. 'Then they'll slaughter us like they done when we tried to get our share before.'

'Before?' Stowe asked under his breath.

'The Peasant Uprising,' the Danite said. 'It started here.'

Stowe had forgotten that. To him, the Peasant Uprising was ancient history, the subject of tapestries and wall murals, and nothing more. He hadn't even known anyone who had fought in it – the veterans had all died before he was born. Yet here, it was a living, breathing thing.

'The King was coming here to find out how you were doing,' Stowe said. 'Whether you had had problems with the Fey, what we could do to solve any other problems you might have. That isn't going to change. Whatever grievances you have, you may tell me. But I do need your help in return now. The most important man in the nation has been murdered, and we need to bring his murderer to justice.'

'We don't need ta do nothing,' said the first man.

'He weren't important ta us,' the woman with the child said.

'Our grievances should be obvious,' said the man with the clean face.

Stowe focused on him. The man didn't speak the local dialect. He had a different look, as if the grime had not seeped through his skin. And, although he was of an age with the others, he looked younger.

'Tell me anyway,' Stowe said, speaking to him.

'The Marshes have always been poor,' the man said, 'but at least we could keep fed by selling what we made. Reed rugs, herbs, dyes. It all went and was traded for food. But now you shut off the trade with

35

Nye and with Fillé and no one in Jahn is buying what we make. We got folks who're trying to live off the Marshes, killing the birds, burning the peat, eating the reed grass. It's not any way to live.'

That it wasn't. 'Things should have eased once we made the treaty with the Fey,' Stowe said.

The man shook his head. 'We made most of our money from outside trade, not from the sales in the Isle. Those came back, sort of, for the folks who still had money to spend, but most were trying to recover their own livings. Your precious King never paid attention to what was happening in the Marshes. He figured if Jahn were safe, the whole country was.'

Others were nodding their heads. Stowe had to clench his fists together to keep from showing his shock. The evidence before him was different from all he had heard. The King had been saying throughout the Invasion and beyond that the Isle was self-sufficient, that it could survive without outside trade. Perhaps the Isle as a unit was, but areas were not. Stowe had not thought of that before.

'You were planning to tell the King this?' Stowe asked.

'We was planning to show him,' the first man said. 'Lena, she will lose her boy soon. That goiter'll cut off his air.'

Stowe glanced at the boy. He had thought the bulge a boil, but it was not. It was something more serious.

'And Kel, his children got running sores that he can't do nothing about.' The man was looking at the man beside him. 'And Odeta, she lost her baby when the food run through him like water. None of that was before. We could at least live before.'

Stowe suppressed a shudder. The King would have been appalled. And Stowe didn't know what he could do.

The Danite was watching him.

'How come no one reported this to the Tabernacle or the palace?' Stowe asked.

The Danite shook his head. 'No one talks to the Tabernacle now. The Rocaan is dead. That Elder he left don't believe and has no leadership.'

Stowe had heard this before about Matthias. Matthias was the new Rocaan. He had been chosen by the old Rocaan, according to religious law, and custom. No one could challenge him.

'But the palace –'

'Ain't never helped the Marshes before. Wouldn't do so now.'

Stowe frowned. He didn't like the shifting perspective that this meeting was forcing on him. 'If the King had come here, would you have told him this?'

'This is the group what would have done it,' the first man said.

'And did you believe that he would help you?'

The clean man smiled. The look had no humor in it. 'Talking to him would have at least got us hope. We lack even that now.'

Stowe nodded. He had no more questions. He felt as if he had stumbled into a world he did not know existed, and he would have to understand it before he could determine whether or not the people before him had the capacity for murder.

'If I promise you that I will make changes here in the Marshes, will you help me find the King's killer?' Stowe asked.

'That's a tall order,' the clean man said. 'You expect us to trust that your changes will be for the good.'

'I will do what I can,' Stowe said.

'But you're not king. The king is dead,' a woman said.

'Yes,' Stowe said, 'but his son, the new King, trusts me, and will listen.'

'It's not a guarantee,' the clean man said.

'It's the best I can do.'

'The best I can do is tell you that we didn't kill your king,' the clean man said.

Stowe stared at him. They stared back. 'Someone did,' he said. 'It would help us all if we could find him.'

Five

Matthias flew down the corridors of the palace, his red robes billowing behind him. He had left the Auds with the horses, and none of the Elders had accompanied him. He had never received a message of such urgency from the palace, not at all in his five years as Rocaan. Perhaps something had happened to Jewel's new child, or perhaps something had happened to Jewel herself.

Or perhaps she had finally taken advantage of her position – and the King's absence – to do away with Nicholas.

Matthias had not trusted her from the moment he saw her. She had too much intelligence in her eyes. She was the granddaughter of the man who led the Fey, the daughter of the man who had led the invasion force. She had probably ordered the death of the fiftieth Rocaan. That betrayal and murder that ultimately led to Matthias's becoming Rocaan – a position he never wanted. A position he was not qualified for. A position he regretted holding, even now.

The messenger had said that they all would meet in the Great Chamber, another deviation from standard. Matthias didn't like these changes. They made him even more uneasy.

That and the fact that none of the servants would answer his questions.

His sandals echoed on the marble floor of the Great Hall. He hated the weapons hanging on the wall. The swords made a mockery of the Roca's Sword. They were still stained with blood from past uprisings. Some were rusted, others nicked. The Sword used for warfare, a reminder that death surrounded them all.

Something Matthias wanted to forget.

He touched the tiny flask of holy water in the pocket of his robe. He was the one, in the middle of the Invasion, who had accidentally discovered the powers of holy water. The Fey had invaded the Tabernacle. They had murdered dozens of Danites, dozens of Auds. He had seen more death than he ever wanted to in his life, death he could not prevent.

Then the Fey had come after him. He had run into the servants' chapel, in search of refuge, in search of a weapon, in search of a way to defend himself. He had just reached the altar when the Fey charged him.

He had thought they were going to kill him – rip his skin off while he was still alive, as they had done to an Aud just outside the Tabernacle. He had searched in vain for a weapon, but found nothing.

Then he saw the glittering vials of holy water the Rocaan had blessed the night before for Midnight Sacrament. The vials were made of heavy thick glass. Perhaps they would stop the Fey while Matthias thought of something else.

Matthias grabbed vial after vial and flung them at the Fey, at the group before him, then at the group to his right. The first glass hit the stone and shattered, and the Fey screamed in pain. Then the next glass shattered. Matthias kept throwing until he realized that the Fey were no longer advancing.

The stench in the room had grown. It smelled as if something were burning. It took a moment for him to realize that all of the Fey were clutching their legs and screaming. They had fallen to the ground and were rolling in the blood. He glanced behind him. He had thrown maybe ten bottles, certainly not enough glass to cut that many men.

Then he realized that they weren't bleeding, but their clothes were peeling from them as if trying to get away. He stood for a moment, his hand over his mouth. They were lying in the water, and every time it touched part of their bodies they screamed.

Matthias's hands were shaking – the entire thing had left him terrified – but he had to know. He had to know. The glass couldn't have killed them, so the water must have.

The holy water.

Matthias took a vial and walked down the steps, his heart pounding so fiercely he felt as if he couldn't breathe. He uncorked the bottle and waited until he saw the Fey who had looked at him first. The creature was still alive, his legs and hands a mass of burns, his clothing ripped and tattered.

His gaze met Matthias's, his skin pale and his dark almond-shaped eyes wide with shock. 'What have you done?' the Fey asked in accented Nye.

The words startled Matthias, made him wonder if they were faking, if that was how they had caught all the others. He tossed the water forward, and it landed on the Fey's perfect features. The creature screamed until his lips melted over his mouth. Matthias stood, riveted, tears in his own eyes, watching the creature – the man – flail as the flesh melted over his nostrils and his body could no longer get air.

The other Fey were still moaning, oblivious to their leader's death. But Matthias watched for what seemed like forever as the leader clawed at his featureless face with his misshapen hands. At long last, the body stopped moving.

It was that death he couldn't get out of his mind. He could justify the others: they had attacked him. He had been defending himself. But when he poured water on their leader, Matthias had been experimenting. He had taken a life to satisfy his own curiosity.

Sometimes he thought it made him just like them. Just like the Fey. Demon-spawn.

He shook his head, as if that would rid him of the thoughts. He couldn't keep punishing himself. What was done, was done. In discovering the hidden power of holy water, he had saved hundreds of Islander lives. Perhaps that was what Roca had intended all along.

A guard, no older than fifteen, stood outside the entrance to the Great Chamber. He bowed and said, 'They're waiting for you, Holy Sir.'

Of course they were. The lords lived near the palace and could arrive quickly. A messenger had to leave the stables and disturb Matthias. Then Matthias had to saddle up and hurry over. Of course he would arrive last.

'Then open the door, child,' Matthias said, feeling odd still at using the diminutive. He was old enough to be the boy's father, but the previous Rocaan had been a bent, wizened old man – certainly more the type to call a vigorous boy 'child.'

The guard stood. He came up to Matthias's shoulder, as did most of the Islanders. Matthias was taller and thinner than any other Islander. Until the Fey arrived, he hadn't met anyone taller. Only his entrance into Rocaanism at the age of twelve had kept him from being called demon-spawn. The guard pulled the door open for him, and Matthias entered.

Nicholas stood at the other end of the Great Chamber, his arms crossed over his chest, his eyes dull and sunken in his face. Jewel stood beside him. She placed a hand over her stomach when she saw Matthias. She had no love for him either, and no trust as well.

A table had been placed in the center of the room. At it sat Lords Canter, Egan, and Fesler. Lords Holbrook and Miller leaned against the wall. And Lord Enford sat alone next to the table's head.

Enford. Matthias stared at him for a moment. Enford was covered with dirt. Only his face and hands were clean. His clothing was ripped, and his hair was hastily tied in its queue. Enford was supposed to be with Alexander. A shiver ran down Matthias's back. He glared at Jewel. Now he knew what this meeting was for.

Something had happened to the King.

The door closed behind Matthias and he jumped. No one acknowledged him, an odd thing for this group, since they knew much of the power on the Isle rested with him. But they were silent and somber.

The table, which normally did not belong in the Great Chamber, was made of heavy wood, its legs knobbed and its surface covered with a deep lined pattern. The chairs matched – high, straight backs and arms with knobs at the end, made not for comfort but for beauty.

The lords already seated didn't appear relaxed. Fesler never appeared relaxed though. He was not one of Alexander's trusted advisors, but had become more of a presence since the Fey arrived. Fesler was slender, with hollow cheeks and straight blond hair. His age was difficult to determine, since he never spoke of it, but he had been a lord longer than Matthias had been in Jahn.

Egan sat beside him, his hunched back brushing against the straight chair. Egan crouched to hide his bulk, which never worked. He seemed larger than he had when the Fey arrived, partly because he no longer smiled. Egan was once known as the most jovial of the King's men, but he hadn't laughed since he lost his son in the Invasion.

Canter was studying his well-manicured hands, as if he could find no other way to avoid looking at Jewel and Nicholas. His hair was cut perfectly square, his blouse well tailored, his vest matching his leggings perfectly. He must have been riding when the news came, for Canter usually wore a robe more exquisite than any found in the Tabernacle.

Matthias took the chair closest to Canter and leaned against its sturdy back. Nicholas watched him as if waiting for Matthias to take control of the meeting. Jewel drifted toward Nicholas's side. She looked as if she were going to guide him.

The others didn't seem to care. Miller was tracing the grooves in the paneled wall, his long fingers dancing over the edges as if they were harpsichord keys. Miller was in his twenties, having acquired the lordship from his father a few years before, much to Miller's upset. He had planned on using his musical talents in the Tabernacle, but the Invasion, and then his father's death, had come in the way.

Only Holbrook stared at Matthias. Holbrook was a tinlord, a man who had risen in the ranks and was given his lordship as a reward for good service. If the Invasion hadn't wiped out the ranks of the lordly as well as the ranks of the underclasses, Holbrook would not be in this room at all. Still, Matthias was glad to see him. Holbrook was twice as old as the rest of them. He had lived a long and full life, which he wore on his features like an etching, and his counsel was often based on experience where the counsel of the others wasn't.

Since Nicholas was not taking over the meeting, Matthias leaned forward. He would begin things before the woman did. 'Forgive me,

Highness,' he said. 'I came as quickly as I could. The messenger said this was a matter of some urgency.'

'Some,' Nicholas said. He spoke slowly, something Nicholas had never done in his life. 'My father is dead.'

Matthias heard the words, but didn't feel their import right away. Alexander? But he had grown up with Alexander, had spent his formative years with Alexander, had just the week before taken a cup of late-night mead with Alexander, talking about the fortunes of the Kingdom.

The others hadn't known either. Egan sat up straight and Canter stopped contemplating his nails. Fesler sucked in his breath, and Miller made a small moan. Only Holbrook didn't move. Holbrook, Enford, and that woman.

'Sire,' Enford said. 'If I may.'

Sire. The word focused Matthias more quickly than anything else. Just like that awful day when the Auds came back from the Rocaan's meeting with the Fey, the meeting in which the Rocaan had died. *Holy Sir*, they had said to Matthias. Not Respected Sir, the title for an Elder, but Holy Sir, the title for the Rocaan. They had called him Holy Sir even before telling him that the Rocaan was dead.

Nicholas nodded at Enford, then turned his back. Jewel stood in front of him as if protecting him from the others. Nicholas stared at the wall as if it had a window.

'The King was murdered on the road into the Kenniland Marshes,' Enford said. Miller started to interrupt, but Enford held up his hand for silence. 'He was shot through the heart with a single arrow. No one else was injured. The assassin had to wait through the advance guards and the lone Danite sent to protect the King. The assassin's shot was swift and sure. None of us knew that an arrow had been launched until the King toppled over.'

The phrase was so stark, so casual, as if they were speaking about an animal instead of a man they had all known.

'Who killed him?' Miller asked.

'We don't know,' Enford said. 'Monte and Lord Stowe are still there, hoping to find something.'

'What do you need to find?' Holbrook said. 'You have an arrow, so you have an archer. Archers work within a certain range and distance. There isn't much to conceal a man in those marshes. If you had conducted a search right away, you would have found your killer.'

'There were trees,' Enford said. 'We sent guards there.'

'But these were marshes, right?' Jewel said. 'Couldn't someone be hiding in the water?'

'We searched the surrounding area. They wouldn't have gotten away without us seeing them.'

'But they did.' Fesler's voice was soft, but accusatory. 'Who was in your party, Enford?'

'Besides Lord Stowe and myself, only some guards and a Danite. And Monte, of course.'

'Of course,' Fesler said. 'All trusted. Like Stephen.'

Stephen. Matthias leaned heavily on the chair back, the wood cutting into his forearms. Stephen had been Nicholas's swordmaster. A Fey Doppelgänger had taken Stephen's place, nearly killed Nicholas, and had access to the King.

'We have a treaty,' Jewel said tightly.

'And the Fey are well known for keeping their agreements,' Matthias said.

Jewel glared at him from across the table. 'I was not in that kirk when your Rocaan was killed.'

'No,' Matthias said. 'But you knew about it.'

'I keep my agreements.'

'As well as a Fey can.'

Nicholas turned around. 'Leave her, Matthias. She has kept our agreement from the moment we made peace.'

Everyone in the room turned and looked at Nicholas, all with surprise on their features. But Nicholas didn't even seem to notice his insult. He had never failed to use the proper term of respect for Matthias before. But Matthias would have to let it pass. Nicholas was King now.

'I would rather think that a Fey killed our King than someone in his own traveling party,' said Canter, in an obvious attempt to break the awkward silence. He inclined his head toward Jewel. 'With your pardon, milady. But someone committed the deed.'

She nodded at him. 'It would benefit all of us to find this killer as quickly as possible.'

'As if, milady, you have no knowledge of this,' Matthias said.

She raised her head. The look made her almost as tall as he was, and gave her an imperial quality no one else on the Isle could match. 'Are you suggesting that I would murder my husband's father?'

'I am suggesting that you had knowledge of this, just like you had knowledge of the fiftieth Rocaan's death.'

'And where would I have gained this knowledge?'

'Don't your people confide in you any longer, milady? Aren't you supposed to know all that happens among the Fey?'

'Holy Sir,' Holbrook said softly. 'We have no proof as to who committed the killings.'

43

'It happened in the Marshes,' Egan said. 'There are no Fey in that area.'

'And Fey have other weapons,' Miller said. 'They don't use bow and arrow.'

'But they disappear quickly and without a trace, don't they, milady?'

'Yes they do,' she said. She took a step toward him, but Nicholas grabbed her arm. She shook his hand off, but remained where she was. 'But if we wanted your King dead, we could have done so a dozen different better ways. I could have slit his throat in his sleep many a night. He was only up the stairs from me. Any one of my people could have attacked him during the marriage feast. Or you, for that matter, *Holy* Sir.'

'Jewel —' Nicholas began.

'But we did not. We have kept our side of this agreement. I stay here, in a place that treats women like cattle, because I made a bargain for my people's lives. How do we know that you didn't assign one of your little minions to assassinate the King? You want the war back badly enough. You could then blame it on us.'

'The Holy Sir would never do that,' Miller said, his voice shaking.

'The Holy Sir already has the blood of hundreds of Fey on his hands. What's one more life?'

Matthias could feel himself flush. Always their arguments ended like this, with him accusing her of the murder of the Rocaan and her accusing him of all the deaths caused by holy water.

'Jewel,' Nicholas said softly. 'This will not help us.'

'Neither will his accusations. I am part of your family now, whether he likes it or not. Losing Alexander threatens my people as well. We have a fragile truce here, no thanks to men like your religious leader over there. He would like to shatter it altogether.'

'Is that true, Holy Sir?' Enford asked quietly.

Matthias stood, unwinding himself to his full height. 'The Fey made an agreement to meet the Rocaan in a peaceful situation. They broke that agreement and murdered him.'

'That was five years ago,' Holbrook said.

'I made my pact with Nicholas after that,' Jewel said. 'Because of that awful day.'

'I believe that the Fey have learned that they cannot conquer us by their traditional methods, so they have chosen a more time-consuming, less traditional way.'

'Jewel is my wife,' Nicholas said. 'Be careful what you say.'

'Yes,' said Matthias. 'And the Fey charm and enchant. She has magicked you, Highness.'

'You know nothing of my people,' Jewel said.

'This gets us nowhere.' Holbrook approached the table. 'It doesn't matter who murdered the King. At this moment, we must determine how to control this news, how to prevent the war from starting again, how to stop riots in the streets. There will be a panic, Highness. You are going to have to show them that you can rule, and rule well.'

'He's right,' Fesler said. 'You'll have to take power immediately.'

'He already has,' Enford said.

'Formally, so that the people understand that the wheels of government continue turning,' said Holbrook.

'What about the Fey?' asked Egan.

'We'll ask them for a delegation to the coronation. Jewel will tell us whom to invite,' Nicholas said.

She shot him a curious glance. Matthias saw the reluctance in it. 'Where is the ceremony held?'

'In the Tabernacle,' Matthias said.

'My people can't go in there,' Jewel said.

'They'll have to. It's tradition.' Matthias smiled. 'Or you'll have to step down as Nicholas's queen.'

'I don't think the attendance is important,' Nicholas said. 'It's the invitation that counts.'

Jewel's hand had strayed to her belly again. 'And me? I must attend. And no Fey has come out of that building alive.'

Nicholas put his hand over hers. 'We'll decide location later, Jewel. They're right, though. We need to consolidate power quickly, and you need to be beside me. To prevent any conflict at all.'

Jewel kept her hand in his, but her lips tightened slightly, as if his dismissal bothered her. Matthias leaned on the chair, making certain he looked calm, trying to appear as if he were watching Nicholas instead of Jewel.

Matthias couldn't tell if she was acting. Something about this entire interaction was bothering him. Perhaps the murder of Alexander was deliberate, and perhaps Jewel knew about it. That meant then that she, and her deformed children, would be closer to the throne. What an easy way to gain power. What an effective way.

He would discuss this with Nicholas when the two of them were alone.

'We need to make the announcement about the King's death today,' Enford said. 'Too many people know already. All of the guards who traveled with him, people in the Marshes, and now this room. The secret will out. Better that we control the information.'

'I'll make a formal announcement when we're done,' Nicholas said.

All trace of his earlier anguish was gone. He would handle rule well. If he got a chance to do so.

If the woman let him live.

Matthias licked his lips. They were dry and chapped. 'We'll need the coronation quickly, so that everyone will know you are consolidating power. I would suggest two days hence.'

'Too soon,' Holbrook said. 'If he acts that quickly, he implicates himself in his father's death.'

'We are a nation under siege,' Matthias said. 'If he does not act quickly enough, our enemies will.'

'"Our enemies,"' Jewel muttered and slipped her hand from Nicholas's. He captured it again, and pulled it to his side as if he were holding her back.

'I think Matthias is right,' Nicholas said. Jewel looked at him sharply, as if she couldn't believe what he was saying. He smiled a little at her, a private smile between them only. 'Let me amend. I think he is right that we must consolidate quickly. Two days seems reasonable to me. His reasons are faulty. I doubt the Fey would use this event to overtake our government or to start hostilities again. We have Jewel here, many of them live among us now, and they have yet to learn the secret of our holy water. They won't change the plans from under us now.'

Jewel was watching him closely, her dark eyes glittering. Matthias stiffened. He wasn't certain if he should take Nicholas's comments as support or insult.

'I do believe that our people need to know that the government is functioning normally. They need to know that, even though life has changed these five years, we will still be there for them.' Nicholas paused, and took a breath.

'They need to know,' Egan said into the gap, 'that even when a King is assassinated, the lineage goes on.'

Matthias's gaze met Nicholas's. Nicholas closed his mouth. He flushed and looked away. They agreed on one thing. If Nicholas died, Sebastian could not take over. Nicholas would have to make provisions different from the norm. The norm had always been that the Queen Mother ruled as regent until her son was ready to lead. Such a thing could not happen this time.

'You'll need to improve your own security,' Matthias said.

'I'm fine now,' Nicholas said.

'No,' Fesler said. 'Someone got to your father and we thought he was well protected. You'll need even more protection. Your son –' he bit off what he was going to say. Then he cleared his throat as if the pause were intentional. 'Your son is too young to take over.'

'Even if he were old enough,' Holbrook said, 'losing two rulers in rapid succession would cause a kind of chaos that could destroy the foundation of this government.'

Nicholas ran a hand over his face. He backed away from all of them. 'We'll make sure that doesn't happen.'

Matthias kept his gaze on Jewel. She looked over at him, chin jutted out, as if she expected him to comment on her presence. He would not. He had done enough baiting this day. She was a threat. The others might realize it, but none of them had the ability to say so in front of Nicholas. Matthias had. That would be enough for now.

He would speak to Nicholas later. Matthias would again explain the enchantments. He would point out the disaster of an heir she had given him. He would ask Nicholas to use the precedent set by King Ulysses three centuries before. Set aside his wife. Take a new one. Make a new heir.

And save Blue Isle.

Six

The fire in the cabin had burned low. Adrian put more logs on the flame, then warmed his hands over it. Since his imprisonment to Shadowlands, he had been cold. Five years. Five years without seeing the sun, without feeling the rain on his face, without the wind ruffling his hair. Of course, he had gone out on rare occasions to meet with his son Luke, as agreed, but those occasions only made the return to Shadowlands worse.

Five years before he and Luke had been part of an Islander squad that attacked Shadowlands with holy water. They had thought that the invisible hiding place would disappear when splashed. But it hadn't. Instead, the Fey had been ready for the attack. They had killed most of the troop, captured three members, and taken some holy water to study.

Adrian was now the only prisoner remaining. He had bargained for his son's life. The third prisoner died in Fey experiments a few months later.

The bargain Adrian had made with Jewel forced him to remain with the Fey until he died. He taught them about Islander culture in exchange for Luke's freedom. Once a year, he got to see his son under Fey supervision outside Shadowlands to make certain that Luke still lived.

The last visit had been two months ago, and already he was thinking of the next. But the visits were the only things that sustained him. Life inside Shadowlands was long and fear-filled. The Shadowlands themselves were created by the Fey as a hiding place, a large hole in the sky, like a box. The interior was gray, the walls were invisible, but hard to the touch. Nothing grew here. Colors leached out of clothing, faces, and food. Since Adrian had been captured, he felt as if he had turned gray himself.

He glanced around the cabin one more time. Lately he had been more of a servant than a teacher. Rugar ordered him about like a slave. The cabin was clean and swept as Rugar had commanded, everything in its place, and a fire constantly going. Rugar had been gone a long time now, and he had instructed Adrian to start the fire two weeks after Rugar left. The fire had been burning for a week, and still no Rugar. Such a waste of resources. But Adrian could say nothing.

He sank into the chair closest to the fire and debated whether or not to make some root tea. He wouldn't want to be too comfortable when Rugar got back, but then Rugar couldn't do much to him. Adrian had shown over the years that he could withstand any realistic punishment the Fey dished out. Jewel had requested that no magic be performed on him, and none had been.

At least that he knew of.

One thing he had learned, as the only Islander ever to live in the Fey world, was that Fey magick was subtle and often difficult to recognize. It came in different forms, in strange types, and rarely had the flash he had always associated with magick. If he were spelled, he doubted he would know it.

But his feeling that they had left him alone was another of Jewel's legacies. She had promised, if he cooperated, that they would treat him well within the confines of Shadowlands.

That promise had held.

He was frankly surprised. He had been afraid that when Jewel left, she would take her assurances with her. But Rugar had been too beaten by his own failures to notice Adrian, and after that, Adrian had become too much a fixture in Shadowlands, teaching Fey the Isle language and customs, and helping with manual tasks too menial for the magical to perform.

Rugar had turned his anger on Adrian only once, and then Mend, one of the Domestics, had intervened.

Adrian pushed himself up. The thought of Mend always made him restless. Unlike the other magickal Fey (the nonmagickal were a different matter), Mend treated him with respect. She spoke to him one being to another instead of master to servant. She smiled at him when she saw him, and went out of her way to speak to him.

She was too slender and had deep circles under her eyes – Domestics were overworked and slept little – but her dark hair was glossy, and he found himself at the oddest moments thinking about the upswept angle of her eyebrows and the thin line of her mouth.

Prisoner bonding. Someone had told him about it. Prisoners would eventually identify with and idolize their captors. He had once thought it impossible, but now he wasn't so sure.

At least he wasn't idolizing Rugar.

Voices sounded close outside. Adrian stood guiltily – he didn't want to be caught relaxing in Rugar's home – and wiped his hands on his pants. Then he crouched in front of the fire, straightening the wood-pile, doing makework to look busy. He had heard voices like this in the days previous and nothing had come of it, but he decided then that it was better to act as if Rugar had come home rather than to be surprised.

The voices sounded angry, confused. He couldn't make out the words, but he thought he recognized a few of the Domestics, speaking in urgent tones. The Domestics had been on edge for days because the Shaman was unhappy. She had seen a Vision that had so deeply disturbed her that she came out of her cabin to talk with Rugar who was, of course, gone.

It seemed odd to Adrian that the Fey's Shaman hadn't known that the military leader was gone. But then the more he watched the Fey, the less he understood them.

His back was getting stiff. He switched positions. The fire was hot this close. He would have to leave soon, but he didn't want to while there was a crowd outside. Most of the Fey remaining in Shadowlands knew that Adrian acted now as Rugar's private servant, but not all of them liked the fact that Rugar had a servant. Only Rugar, being the Black King's son and the nominal leader of the group, never heard the complaints.

Adrian did.

He put his hand on the wood floor and braced himself to stand when he heard a voice that made him freeze.

Rugar's voice.

It sounded harsh and biting. Then, before Adrian could stand, the door swung open and banged against the outside wall. The gray mist that swirled inside the Shadowlands drifted in, its chill accompanying it. Rugar stood in the door, his long, thin frame encased in a black cloak that kept the moisture off his body.

A group of Domestics stood outside. From his position on the floor, Adrian could barely see them. They were talking among themselves, like a group about to break up.

'What are you doing here?' Rugar snapped.

Adrian knew better than to provoke Rugar farther. Slow movement, reasonable tones of voice often worked best. 'You had asked me to start tending your fire this week in anticipation of your return.'

'The fire seems fine.' Rugar pulled the door closed. He took off his cloak, shook the water off the outside fibers, and tossed it on one of the wooden chairs. 'Is there any food?'

'No, sir.' Adrian pushed himself up. He had remained in good shape during his stay in Shadowlands, but he was no match for any Fey – especially one like Rugar, trained in all forms of combat. 'I could get some from the Domestics.'

'I could have done that myself,' Rugar said. He pushed another chair back with his foot, then sat. He was drawn and too thin, his normally sharp features almost bony in their prominence. His almond-shaped eyes seemed even more slanted, his high cheekbones more pronounced. Most Fey faces had a whimsical beauty, but Rugar's did not. It had a proud strength, like that of a bird of prey. Not beautiful but striking nonetheless.

And even more so now, on this afternoon, although Adrian would be hard-pressed to say why.

'Your larder is poorly stocked, sir, since we did not know when you would be back –'

Rugar waved a hand for silence. 'I understand the Shaman came out.'

'Yes, sir.' Adrian knew better than to offer more information than was requested.

'The Domestics say her Vision was bleak, so bleak she wanted to find me.'

'I don't know, sir. They never tell me Fey matters.'

Rugar looked up as if seeing him for the first time. 'No,' Rugar said. 'Of course they don't.'

Rugar grabbed the heel of his right boot and pulled it off. His foot was wrapped in thick stockings stained with mud. He tossed the boot at Adrian's feet, then removed the other boot and tossed it as well.

Adrian picked them up without being told. He would take them to Mend – as he had ever since the day she found him trying to clean them himself – and then bring them back in spotless condition.

'Tell me, oh great and wise Islander,' Rugar said, massaging his toes, 'what happens on the Isle when a king dies?'

Adrian's grip tightened on the still warm boots. 'Excuse me?'

'When you lose your king, what happens?'

Custom. Custom and tradition. That was what Adrian was there for, to teach the Fey custom and tradition. Rugar was simply playing with him, taunting him while trying to gain information. And Adrian couldn't lie because the Fey had assured him that if they discovered any untruths, they would murder Luke.

'The kingship is hereditary, is that what you're asking, sir?'

'No.' Rugar put his feet on the floor and stretched. His clothes were wrinkled and stained. Some of the stains were mud, and others looked like grass stains. That too was odd. Rugar was in a position to have Domestic made clothing, clothing resilient to stains and wear and water. 'I'm asking how the country responds when a king dies.'

Adrian let out his breath. He suddenly wanted to sit very badly. He had been in his early twenties when the last king died, and it had affected him not at all.

'They'll send criers from the palace all over the country and announce the death. The new king will be crowned, and life will continue.'

Rugar placed his hands behind his head. 'No one will mourn?'

Adrian shrugged. 'I think that's personal. There is an official period of mourning, but I suspect very few will mourn Good King Alexander.'

Rugar tilted his head toward Adrian, still looking relaxed, but tension filled his body. 'And why is that?'

'Because –' Adrian took a deep breath. It was at moments like these he most resented the order to tell the truth. 'Because he allowed the Fey on Blue Isle. Because so many died under his reign.'

'But I have been told by many Islanders that he was a good king.'

'He was,' Adrian said, 'until he was tested.'

A slow smile crossed Rugar's face. 'Is this common opinion or your opinion?'

'Mine, obviously,' Adrian snapped. 'I haven't exactly had a chance to canvass the countryside.'

Rugar didn't seem to notice the sarcasm. He, like Jewel before him, seemed to believe that it was acceptable, even necessary for Adrian to express himself that way. 'Your opinion is based on what?'

'My situation,' Adrian said. 'If Good King Alexander had defended us as was his duty, I would still be at home with my family.'

'Or dead,' Rugar said.

'Sir?'

Rugar stood so quickly Adrian took a step back. 'I think Alexander did his job. The Fey have always taken countries. Your king prevented us from conquering you. If he hadn't stood in our way, you would probably be dead.'

'He didn't stand in your way. That was the Rocaan and his magic holy water.'

'So the people will think that the religion saved them and their government failed them.'

'Yes, sir.'

'And they will not mourn.'

'No, sir.'

Rugar nodded. He clasped his hands behind his back and paced in front of the door. 'What of his son?'

'What of him?'

'How will the populace accept him?'

'They have no choice, sir. He is the next king.'

'Are you saying they'll be reluctant?'

'Yes, sir.'

'Because he is Alexander's son?'

'Because he married a Fey.' Adrian bit his lower lip. Married Rugar's daughter. 'Sir.'

Rugar stopped pacing and looked over his shoulder at Adrian. 'So the government will be unstable.'

A log popped in the fire. Adrian jumped. He made himself take a deep breath before answering Rugar. 'Not unstable. Unpopular. There is a difference.'

'Unpopular governments lead to overthrows,' Rugar said.

Adrian shook his head. 'Not here. The King is a direct descendent of the Roca. The line has been unbroken for hundreds upon hundreds of years.'

'And what of your Peasant Uprising? It was an attempt at an overthrow, was it not?'

Adrian licked his lips. He never completely understood the Uprising. 'It was, as I understand, a group of peasants from the Marshes who tried to get the government's help, couldn't, and took matters into their own hands.'

'An Uprising, you call it.'

'It was not an overthrow.'

'It didn't succeed.' Rugar leaned on the door, all grace and easy movement. Adrian always felt stiff and awkward compared to the Fey. 'And what if there were a new Uprising? What if it succeeded?'

Adrian felt cold despite the heat of the fire. A heavy ball lodged at the pit of his stomach. 'What did you do?' he whispered.

Rugar smiled slowly. The smile did not soften his face; instead it made him look fierce. 'What do you care? You live in Shadowlands.'

'My son lives outside them. What did you do?'

'Such a rude way for a servant to speak to his master.'

Adrian took a deep breath. That was a warning from Rugar. And warnings were all Adrian could take. He never knew when the Fey would turn on him, when they would renege on the agreement he made with Jewel, when they would slaughter his son. Still, Adrian couldn't bring himself to apologize. All he could do was keep quiet.

Rugar pushed off the door. 'Get me some food. I'll take whatever the Domestics have.'

Adrian swallowed. 'Yes, sir.'

He crossed the room, passing closely to Rugar, able to smell the other man's faintly musky sweat. Adrian kept his eyes downcast, not because he was trying to be a good servant, but because he didn't want Rugar to see the hatred in them.

If Rugar saw hatred, he would know he had won.

Adrian shifted the boots to one hand so that he could open the door and escape the stifling confines of Rugar's cabin.

'You wanted to know what I did,' Rugar said.

Adrian stopped, his hand on the knob, his back to Rugar.

'I opened the door to chaos.'

The chill Adrian felt grew deeper.

'I murdered your good King Alexander.' Rugar sounded pleased with himself. 'In the Marshes.'

The Marshes. Where the Peasant Uprising had begun all those years ago. Adrian pulled open the door and stepped into the grayness, his heart pounding.

He had done that. Somehow, in all his teaching, he had shown Rugar the best way to hurt the Islanders.

The best way to destroy them.

'Don't you have a response?' Rugar called through the door.

Adrian turned, clutching the boots to his chest as if they were a shield. 'I think,' he said, using his slow, measured tone, 'that you did the Isle a favor.'

But for the first time since he had come to Shadowlands, Adrian was lying.

Seven

Nicholas stood by the glass window in the Great Hall, his back to the weapons, his hands clenched at his sides. The glass was old, warped, and bubbled. It let in light and little else. He felt as if its view matched the view from his eyes. His thoughts moved slowly, and each physical movement he made felt as if he were under water. He could stare at something for hours and not see it.

He was King now.

And he couldn't even think.

Yet they expected him to. All of them. They wanted him to make decision after decision as if his world hadn't changed. Jewel had tried to talk with him, reason with him, but she was speaking from a Fey perspective. Fey, it seemed, shut off their hearts and kept walking.

No wonder they could kill with such impunity.

It was amazing she had not slaughtered him in his bed.

He blinked and leaned his head on the cold glass. That thought was not his. Of all the people who had met Jewel, he was the only one who trusted her, and she had returned that trust. He could have as easily killed her in the beginning, but he had never wanted to. She had never wanted to hurt him either.

She was only trying to help now.

But no one could help him. He was alone, more alone than he had ever been. His father had told him after the Fey invasion that Nicholas had learned what he needed, that he was ready to rule. But there was a difference between understanding a kingdom and running it.

Once they had made the agreement with the Fey, the idea of his father's death seemed laughable. His father was only eighteen years older than Nicholas – a man in his prime, a man with years ahead, a man who should not have died.

Nicholas's breath fogged the glass. The hall had a chill, even though the spring had been warm. Nicholas hadn't been outside since his father's death. He didn't know if it was raining or if the sun was out, if it was hot or cold or if frost had visited during the night.

Since he got the news, he hadn't been able to sleep, either. He tried, but as he dropped off, he would hear his father's voice or his father's laugh.

Or see the pain in his father's face as he watched Sebastian stare at the walls and do nothing.

Sebastian was a whole other problem. The boy was mentally deficient. Nicholas's father had suggested – politely – that Fey and Islanders weren't meant to mix, and Sebastian bore that idea out. The next child would prove the statement, and if it proved the statement correct, then Nicholas wasn't sure what he would do.

He needed an heir, but he couldn't set aside Jewel. That would guarantee war with the Fey. The Islanders would win as long as they had holy water, but that would not prevent the constant loss of lives, the gradual erosion of morale. Another battle with the Fey would be bad for the Isle.

It would be bad for Nicholas, and he would have to preside over it.

'Sire.'

The voice made him start. It had a tone of someone who had spoken several times.

Nicholas turned. A page stood behind him, looking small and fragile against the backdrop of the swords.

The boy bowed. 'Forgive me, Sire,' he said, 'but Lord Holbrook said the criers are assembled.'

Sire. That meant Nicholas now. 'Thank you,' he said. 'Tell them I will be in the Great Chamber shortly.'

The boy nodded in his crouch. Then he backed away, running once he felt he had left Nicholas's gaze.

Nicholas was perhaps ten years older, but that decade felt like an eternity.

He followed the boy, moving slowly, the robes he had put on that morning in deference to his new status tangling in his legs. He preferred his breeches. But he was a king now. He had to at least look the part.

The door to the Chamber was open. Someone had removed the table and placed a smaller version of his father's throne inside. Nicholas had told one of the lords in a moment of exasperation that he did not want to use the audience chamber again. The lords could think what they wanted about that decision; the truth was Nicholas felt that the audience chamber belonged to his father. What Nicholas was learning was that his reasons no longer mattered. Only his statements and his actions. The throne itself symbolized that his every wish would come true if it were in the power of his lords to make it happen.

The criers lined up before the throne. There were forty of them, all of them younger than the page. They would cover the countryside, and systematically spread the news of his father's death. Because the coronation was being held so soon after the death, the criers would have to be delicate. Minor lords and land barons from farther climes would be angry at not being invited to the ceremony.

Lord Enford had offered to handle the briefing of the criers himself, but Nicholas was afraid that Enford would impart too much information. This task was delicate, and it was the first he would take for himself as king.

Lord Holbrook stood just inside the door, his solid frame and time-weary face a comfort. When he saw Nicholas, he smiled, and the smile was warm.

Nicholas smiled back.

Lord Holbrook announced him, and the criers knelt on their left knees, their right legs bent. They hid their faces on their right knees. Nicholas stared at them for a moment, a sea of red-covered backs, all of them thin and frail.

This task was too important to trust to small boys.

He almost said something, then changed his mind. Small boys had been criers as long as Nicholas's family had ruled. People found comfort in tradition. Now was not the time for change.

The boys had left a path for him that led to the throne. He swept past them, his robe flowing behind him. The chamber was warm and smelled faintly of little boy sweat. He reached the throne and paused for just a moment in front of it.

This throne was made of wood. It had small swords carved in it – the Roca's Sword by the size and placement with the point tip downward. The arms were carved as well, and at their edges were grooves for his fingers. The seat was depressed slightly as was the back, ostensibly for his comfort. He would have preferred a cushion or two.

He would have preferred to kneel with the boys.

But he turned and took the throne as he would every day for the rest of his life, sinking into place, and understanding for the first time why these things were set on daises. The tiny platform this throne was on was barely high enough to make him tower over the children.

When he was settled, he nodded at Lord Holbrook.

'All rise,' the lord said.

The boys got to their feet. They all studied him, their pale-blue eyes holding identical expressions of fear and curiosity.

'I know it is unusual for you to speak directly to the King,' Nicholas said. The cloud seemed to lift from his brain and he felt clear for the first time since the meeting. 'But I felt this important enough to give you your announcements directly. Lord Holbrook has already told you about the King my father's death. We will be sending you to the far reaches of Blue Isle to make certain all the people hear the news officially.'

The boys watched him, but they were well trained. Their thin chests rose and fell as they took shallow, nervous breaths, but they did not move. No shuffling, giggling or lack of attention which he would have expected. These boys had ceased being children long ago.

'You will announce only what I tell you. You will report any gossip, rumormongering or unrest to Lord Holbrook upon your return. Should there be more serious problems, you will dispatch a person of your choice to the palace to inform us. Is that clear?'

Forty blond heads nodded in unison.

'Good.' Nicholas's throat was dry. He had been dreading this moment. 'You will announce that King Alexander the Sixteenth died on the way to Kenniland Marshes. He is succeeded by his son, King Nicholas the Fifth. Repeat that.'

Forty young, powerful voices recited Nicholas's words verbatim. The sound was deafening. As they spoke, Nicholas looked over their heads at Holbrook, who smiled proudly. He and his men had trained them well. Nicholas would not have been able to repeat so much accurately so quickly.

When they finished, he said, 'Nicely done. Now for the rest of the announcement.'

The boys turned their attentive faces toward him. It seemed odd that they all looked alike: they were all small and fine boned, with a tendency toward squareness. He was getting too used to looking at the faces of Fey.

'Because of the suddenness of the King's death, the advisors have decreed that the coronation of Nicholas the Fifth had to proceed with haste. Nicholas the Fifth received the Roca's blessing on the tenth day of the fifteenth month when the sun reached its zenith. Repeat that.'

They did with equal accuracy. The crush of voices made him shiver, and he hoped it didn't show. That, and his coronation, only two days away. He still hadn't chosen the venue.

'There will be a formal ceremony celebrating the coronation in the second month, after mourning is complete. The ceremony will take place on the sixth day at sundown in Jahn. Repeat that.'

The boys spoke in unison for a third time, a single reedy voice speaking with great power.

'Good,' Nicholas said when they were finished. 'Add the traditional closing, and recite the entire announcement.'

The boys recited all three parts, pausing between them as if inserting a new memory. Holbrook mouthed the words with them, apparently committing them to his own memory as well so that he could help them if they needed it.

They ended with, 'May the Roca guide you in all things.'

The words made Nicholas start. This was where Matthias had always claimed Nicholas had his failings – his lack of understanding of Rocaanism. Nicholas had never turned to the Roca for help. He had never asked the Holy One's help in finding God's Ear. Such things, he had always thought, were for simpler people, and now, at a time he could use comfort, he didn't believe in the one thing that others would have used.

The boys had stopped speaking. The silence in the room was deafening. They all tilted their heads toward him, as if waiting for his comments. Holbrook looked at him too, his grizzled features pressed into a frown.

'That was right,' Nicholas said half a beat too late. 'That was good. Well done.'

He nodded to Holbrook, suddenly tired of talking with these children, these boys who were going to go from village to village announcing the news of his father's death. They would see more of the land than Nicholas ever had. One of them would have to stop at the base of the Cliffs of Blood, another speak to the people who lived near the Slides of Death. Such wonderful adventurous names, such unknown places, places he wouldn't be able to travel to for years, not after what had happened to his father.

'You did well, boys,' Holbrook said. 'Meet me in the courtyard for your assignments. I will be there shortly.'

The boys bowed again to Nicholas, then filed out of the chamber. Finally he saw differences. Some boys were taller than others. Some walked quickly, others hesitated. Still others glanced over their shoulders at Nicholas himself, as if they couldn't believe they had stood before the King.

Had his father been alive, they never would have. Some criers grew into young manhood and were reassigned jobs through the kingdom without ever seeing the King.

Holbrook waited until the last boy had closed the door behind him before coming up front. 'You could have relayed your message, Sire, and I could have told the boys.'

Nicholas shook his head. 'One wrong word and I would worry. No. It's better that it came from me. Even then, there will be trouble.'

'How do you know?' Hidden in Holbrook's question was another: Did *she* tell you?

'It's logical,' Nicholas said. 'Blue Isle is a different place from the one we were born into, milord.'

'The Fey, Sire.'

Nicholas nodded. 'The Fey. The Tabernacle. Here, even the palace. Everything is different. Nothing will ever be the same.'

Holbrook put a hand on the arm of the throne. 'We'll all miss your father, Sire.'

Nicholas made himself smile, although he had never felt less like smiling in his life. 'I suppose we all will.'

''Tis a good decision you made, having the coronation in two days.'

Nicholas shrugged. 'We have much to do before that.'

Holbrook apparently heard the dismissal. He took his hand off the throne, and bowed. 'I have boys to tend, Sire.'

'I know. Thank you. Make sure they have enough supplies.'

'We've done this before, Sire. We know how to send them.'

'I'm sure you do,' Nicholas muttered. Holbrook didn't hear him, and even if he had, he wouldn't have understood. The lords were having trouble realizing that Nicholas was no longer the boy who played at their feet. They had to listen to him now, and they had to treat him with respect. But they also had to stop assuming that he didn't know anything about the Kingdom. He did. A comment like the one he had made about supplies would have sounded like a natural reminder coming from his father. From Nicholas, it sounded like ignorance.

Holbrook let himself out of the chamber. Nicholas stood and rubbed his buttocks. The throne had been hard. He would ask for a cushion. He didn't know how his father had stood it – sitting in a chair like that for hours every day, listening to business and complaints. But Nicholas would have to do the same, whether he did it in the Great Chamber or the Audience Room didn't matter. He was no longer free to roam at will. Everyone depended on him now.

The door to the Great Chamber opened, and Matthias bowed to him. 'Forgive me, Sire, but I would like a moment.'

Nicholas nodded and waved Matthias in.

Matthias entered and closed the door behind him. 'Are we alone?'

'As alone as we can be.' Nicholas would explain no more than that. After his father died, he had ordered guards to listening posts throughout the palace. Four were stationed at posts now, watching all that transpired in the Great Chamber. Nicholas would never be completely alone, but he would probably live through any attack.

He had ordered the guards for himself only. He left Jewel and his son unprotected, an act which he could not bear to contemplate too closely.

The guards had all taken vows of secrecy which, of course, Nicholas had reiterated as he set up this plan with their superiors. Nicholas, however, threatened a harsh and unspecified retaliation should any information escape. So far he believed nothing had leaked, but Nicholas wanted to prevent any discussion, even among the guards themselves.

'We need to talk before your coronation,' Matthias said.

'Yes,' Nicholas said. 'We need to plan the location.'

'More than that.' Matthias came deeper into the chamber. The room seemed empty without the criers in it. 'We need to discuss your future.'

Matthias had said those words to Nicholas many times in a thousand different ways. Matthias had been Nicholas's religious supervisor, and had often approached Nicholas with those same words when Nicholas was not doing his coursework or attending the Sacraments enough.

'Do we?' Nicholas asked. He retreated to the throne and sat in it as his father would have, feet together, hands gripping the arms.

'Yes.' Even though Nicholas was sitting on the platform, Matthias was taller. His unnatural height and thinness made his red robes hang on him. The small swords hanging like tassels from the sash marked his narrow, almost girlish waist. He didn't look like the Rocaan. He looked like a devil of a man dressed as the Rocaan.

Nicholas didn't encourage him to say any more. Matthias was going to be trouble. He had never thought well of Nicholas. Matthias was a scholar and Nicholas had never been. Nicholas preferred swords, horses, and the smell of battle to pens, books, and the clash of minds. Now a former student become King. Matthias would never take him seriously.

'Before we plan the coronation itself, I think we must discuss Jewel.'

Nicholas stiffened. Matthias had opposed the marriage from the beginning. He believed the Fey to be as evil as the Soldiers of the Enemy, the mythical people who had cut down the Roca before he was Absorbed. Matthias only agreed to perform the ceremony because Nicholas's father had talked him into it somehow. And Matthias had done the minimal amount of work on it, giving the ceremony a brevity that wasn't normal.

'Shall I ring for her?' Nicholas asked.

Matthias shook his head. He wasn't wearing his biretta and his blond curls fell in disarray around his face. 'This is between us, Nicholas.'

'Sire,' Nicholas corrected him.

'As long as I am Holy Sir to you,' Matthias said.

Nicholas nodded. 'Point taken. A meeting of equals then, Matthias.'

'Exactly,' Matthias said. 'And as your spiritual advisor, I would like you to hear me through on this one.'

'If you're going to disparage Jewel —'

'I merely want you to think of other possibilities.'

'She is right, you know, about her own behavior. She has been completely trustworthy since she has come here.'

Matthias held up one hand. 'Let me speak my part. Then throw me out if you have to.'

Nicholas sighed. If he didn't give Matthias the chance to speak, Matthias would speak anyway. Or take matters into his own hands, as he had always done. 'Quickly, then. I have other matters to attend to.'

Matthias templed his fingers in front of his lips, bowed his head as if he were thinking how to approach this topic, and then said, 'Five years ago, when the Rocaan died, the Fey lost a major opportunity of a kind we don't completely understand. They tried to learn the secret to holy water, they tried to infiltrate the Tabernacle, and these things did not work.'

'You don't have to rehash history with me,' Nicholas said, allowing irritation into his voice.

'I'm merely setting the situation,' Matthias said. 'What happens if, after that meeting, the Fey decided to take a different approach with us?'

'You've mentioned this before, Matthias. You have no evidence.'

'Your father's death.' Matthias let his hands drop. 'That's my evidence.'

'We don't even know who killed him.'

Matthias took a deep breath, as if he were deciding how candid to be, and then let it out in a great sigh. 'Nicholas, I served as a Danite in the Kenniland Marshes. It was one of the most miserable experiences in my life. I was only there for two years, not enough to make an impression on them, but enough for me to gain an understanding. Your father died on the entrance to the Marshes. You've never been there. I have. There are few trees. The land is flat for miles. A man could not hide there. A Fey could.'

'That's not evidence,' Nicholas said. 'That's speculation.'

Matthias tugged on the silver filigree sword around his neck. 'Perhaps, but you promised to hear me out. Let's assume that after the fiftieth Rocaan died, the Fey decided to change tactics. Let's assume that Jewel's agreement with you was part of that change. Then she would gain your confidence, become important to you, and over time, work her way into this government. The assassination of Alexander would have been part of the plan. When he died, she would become the Queen of Blue Isle. Sebastian —'

'We won't discuss my son.'

'But we have to,' Matthias said. 'If we suppose this was all a Fey trick, then we assume they would have known about Sebastian before he happened. We have never had mixed marriages here. They have all over the world. Perhaps the Fey conquer because they cannot commingle. Sebastian, or the possibility of a child like him, would make Jewel's job even easier. She would become Queen, then you would die, and she would be Regent. Only her regency would be permanent, because Sebastian could never rule. All legal. A takeover without worrying about the threat of holy water.'

Nicholas gripped the arms of the throne even tighter. The smooth wood pressed against his palms. 'It would take an incredibly cold heart to do all of that. You haven't seen Jewel with Sebastian. She sits with him each and every day.'

'The Fey have a history of betraying their own families. The current Black King stole his position from his brother. There are other stories –'

'No,' Nicholas said. His heart was pounding. He didn't want to hear any more. 'They had no guarantee that my father would ever be in a position to allow an assassin access. They had no idea that Sebastian would be – as he is. If they did, Jewel would not have allowed herself to carry another child. She talks to it, Matthias, at night when she thinks I'm asleep. She tells it to be smart and strong and the best of both of us. I can't believe that she would betray me.'

'That's the beauty of this,' Matthias said. 'That you will refuse to believe. We still don't understand all that the Fey can do.'

'We know,' Nicholas said.

'And who did we learn it from? Jewel?' His words echoed in the empty room.

Nicholas sighed. The argument had a curious logic, one that he didn't really want to hear, but one he couldn't ignore. Matthias was twisted, that was all. The death of the Rocaan had put Matthias in an impossible position, and he blamed that on the Fey. He allowed that to fuel hatred instead of creating the best situation he could.

And now he was taking that hatred out on Jewel.

Nicholas wanted him out, but tossing him out would solve nothing. The King and the Rocaan were the most powerful men in all of Blue Isle. If they couldn't work together, then nothing would be accomplished. That much of his lessons Nicholas did remember.

'What do you suggest?' he asked.

Matthias looked up, apparently surprised that Nicholas would even consider his suggestion. 'Set her aside. Now, before the coronation. She can't come into the Tabernacle. The marriage isn't one according the Isle tradition. She was never touched by holy water, never Blessed.

No one would criticize you for setting her aside. Everyone would understand.'

'Except the Fey themselves.'

'Even they might. The settlement in Jahn isn't working. They're being threatened daily, and some Fey are returning to Shadowlands. The Fey are as opposed to this arrangement as the Islanders are. It is a false truce. Everyone knows that but you.'

The words chilled Nicholas. 'Everyone?'

'Yes, Nicholas. You have precedent. Wives have been turned aside before –'

'Not with the Tabernacle's sanction. In fact, the fortieth Rocaan released an edict ordering marriage to be an eternal choice. Your office, Matthias. You, the scholar, are telling me to go against it?'

Matthias pursed his lips. 'The fortieth Rocaan was merely a man. The edict did not come from God or the Roca. No still small voice spoke it. A man simply placed his morality upon the country.'

'The Rocaan is supposed to be the Roca's representative on the Isle, with a direct line to God. You told me that I should always listen for the still small voice,' Nicholas said. 'Has that voice told you to argue against Jewel?'

Matthias studied Nicholas for a moment. Then Matthias licked his lips. 'I'm a scholar, Nicholas. It is what I was before the Rocaan died, all I've ever wanted to be. I look at history, and words, and logic. The still small voice has no place in that kind of world view.'

Nicholas leaned back. The wooden throne made his body ache. 'You taught it to me.'

'Because it is part of tradition.'

'But you're saying no Rocaan has ever heard a still small voice?'

Matthias shrugged. 'We're men, Nicholas. As fallible as kings, just less willing to admit it.'

Nicholas stood and turned his back on Matthias. The loss of his father, the slander against Jewel, the burden of kingship all overwhelmed him, but this was more than he could take. He needed something on the Isle to run well. If it wasn't the palace then it had to be the Tabernacle. And now the fifty-first Rocaan was confessing that he didn't believe in God.

Nicholas clenched and unclenched his fists until his hands were sore. He was shaking. Finally he turned. Standing on the podium, he was almost as tall as Matthias. Nicholas could look at him straight on without looking up.

'You will say nothing of this to anyone ever again, do you understand me?' Nicholas said. He clenched his fists so tightly the nails bit into his palm. 'You will not disparage the Tabernacle's traditions, you will uphold your position as Rocaan and even when speaking to someone as an equal, you will claim to believe all that Rocaanism stands for, including the still small voice. You are the voice of God on this Isle. You defile the name of your predecessor by this kind of blasphemy.'

Matthias went white. 'The Rocaan knew about my feelings.'

'I don't care about what he knew. He's dead. What you feel is between you and the Holy One. As far as the rest of us are concerned, you will be the model Rocaan. An entire nation relies on you. You will *never* speak this way again.' Nicholas was shaking with the force of his words. 'Do you understand me? Never!'

Matthias took a step backwards. He opened his mouth and then closed it. Finally he said, 'Yes, Sire.'

'And one final thing,' Nicholas said. Somewhere along the way he had stopped clenching his fist. He was now using his right index finger as a weapon, waving it in Matthias's face. 'My wife will be beside me at the coronation. Should I die young, she will be Regent, and should it be determined that Sebastian cannot reign, she will choose the person to govern in his stead. You may serve under a Fey Queen. Get used to the idea, Matthias.'

Matthias's eyes were wide. His lower lip trembled. 'Sire, I –'

'No more,' Nicholas said. 'I have heard quite enough from you. More than I ever want to hear. I had to suffer through your lectures when I was a boy, listen to your prattle as a teenager. I am king now. I don't have to listen to you ever again.'

Matthias tilted his head. He no longer looked defeated. He looked angry. 'Are you through?'

'For now.' Nicholas gripped the back of the throne, hoping the solid wood would steady him. Matthias whirled, the skirts of his robe swirling around his sandaled feet. He couldn't seem to get to the door fast enough.

'And Matthias,' Nicholas said.

Matthias stopped but did not turn around.

'The coronation will be held in the palace.'

'It is tradition to hold the coronation in the Tabernacle.'

'But you do not believe in tradition. Make the arrangements with Lord Enford. And do not question me again.'

Matthias grabbed the door handle and let himself out. Nicholas buried his face in his hands. He was shaking so badly that he was afraid to move away from the chair.

He would have to debrief the guards himself. Then find a way to recover from Matthias's announcement. Nicholas had nothing left to believe in, nothing left to hold.

Except himself.

Eight

The fire was warm. Gift sat on a braided rug before the flame, watching the sparks fly up the chimney. The sparks looked like tiny Wisps floating to freedom. His parents were Wisps, but they were only tiny when they needed to be, when they used their magic to make themselves small points of light.

He remembered what it was like touching those lights. His pudgy fingers throbbed with the memory. He knew better than to touch fire.

The rest of the cabin was cool. His mother sang in the other room. She was making lunch. She wasn't as good a cook as the Domestics, but she believed that the family should eat together, without others around them. She believed many unFeylike things. She didn't let him out of the cabin very often, saying he was too young, but he had heard her tell his father that Gift shouldn't play with the other children. They would taunt him and give him bad ideas.

There weren't that many other children in Shadowlands. There was Coulter, who was two years older, and who scared Gift. Then there were a few other children Gift's age, and a handful of babies. That was all. Not enough, according to his mother, to form a good, healthy community for a special young boy.

He didn't mind. His parents kept him busy. They made him do exercises, sing songs and play games with his mind. *Exercising his magic,* they called it, but as far as he could tell, he didn't have magic. No one had magic until they grew tall and thin. Little boys had no magic at all.

He was supposed to be exercising his magic right now. He was supposed to be thinking about the braids on the rug, how they had been woven by Domestics to bring out the power in a room. Then he was supposed to think about his clothing, and maybe concentrate on the fire itself. Domestic magic day, his mother had called it, and his father had laughed.

'That boy will never have a Domestic's magic,' his father had said as he left the cabin. 'Not with his heritage.'

They didn't think Gift understood 'heritage,' but he did. When they used that word, they were talking about the place they had taken him from. The place with the stone walls, and the bright fire, and the strange-looking woman with the shadow on her face, the woman he had known as Nurse. When they flew him over all the bright lights, wrapped in his warm soft blanket, they had taken him from a place of extremes – black and white, red and green, yellow and orange – to this place of grayness, where everyone looked like everyone else.

Something about Gift was different, and it had something to do with that place. The other children had been born into the gray. He had been born into the light.

His mother came into the room with two steaming bowls on a tray. She was slender and tall like the others who lived in Shadowlands, but she had blue wings that folded against her back, and made it uncomfortable for her to sit in chairs. She was light compared to Gift, and she had once told him that was because her bones were hollow.

'Wisps are fragile,' she had told him. 'Most don't survive their childhoods.'

The idea had so frightened him that he had nightmares. Finally, she had to tell him that he would never be a Wisp. His body was too solid, his bones too strong.

'But you and Dad are Wisps,' he had said. 'How come I'm not?'

'Because,' she had said with the same smile she always used when she explained such things to him. 'You're our Gift.'

The answer made no sense to him.

She had that smile now as she stood over him, looking down at him fondly. 'You weren't exercising, were you?'

He shook his head. 'The fire's too pretty,' he said. 'You see the little lights? They look like you and Dad.'

She set the tray on the kneeling table, then sat on the cushion beside the rug. Her wings unfolded just a little, their thin blue edges rustling. She peered into the fire, looking with interest at the sparks rising through the chimney.

'I would hope your father and I are bigger.'

'You are,' Gift said. He moved closer to the table. It was their smallest table, made of wood and spelled to keep food hot. The soup was in black ceramic bowls. The broth was clear, but the meat was white and finely cut. The steam smelled of sage.

'You have no interest in the rug?' his mother asked.

Gift looked at it. He knew it had been given them just recently by a Domestic, but he didn't know why. Now he was beginning to understand. 'The strands are just strands,' he said.

His mother nodded. She had long ago given up asking him where he learned his words. She and his father had decided part of his magic was the ability to know language, and to speak it well. 'Beyond his years,' they would whisper to anyone who asked. 'Gift is beyond his years.'

'You have no interest in Domestic things, then?' his mother asked.

Gift shrugged. He picked up the bowl. The ceramic was cool to his touch, although the soup's steam wet his face.

'I like the way spells work,' he said. 'I like that the table keeps food hot and the bowls don't burn hands. I like my bed and the way it makes dreams come.'

'But you have no interest in creating such spells?'

Gift slurped some soup. It was warm and delicious. The broth had a chicken taste, accented by the spices. He set the bowl down and wiped his mouth with his hand.

'Gift,' she said in her 'mother' tone, although he didn't know if she was referring to his manners or to the fact he had yet to answer her question.

'Anybody can make rugs,' he said, knowing she wouldn't like that answer. So he added to it: 'I want wings.'

Her smile was indulgent. He liked that smile too, although he never told her that. That smile was just for him. She never used it for anyone else, and when she used it for him, he knew that he had done something right or cute or important.

'You know you can't have wings. You would have to be born with them.'

'If Domestics can make rugs, how come they can't make wings?'

'Gift,' she said, picking up her own bowl. 'All the magicks are different. Everyone is born with a special talent. Sometimes it just takes a while for the talent to become obvious. Sometimes the talent is clear from the beginning, like wings.'

'How come you and Dad have wings and I don't?'

'Because each person is different, Gift. We didn't choose to have wings any more than you chose not to.'

'Who chose to bring me here, then?'

His mother set her bowl down. Soup sloshed on the table, but she didn't seem to notice. 'What do you mean?'

'You said I'm different. Is it because I was born somewhere different? Not here in the Shadowlands?'

She licked her lips. He had not seen this glazed expression on her face before. 'I wasn't born in Shadowlands, either,' she said finally.

He had never heard that before. 'Really?'

'Really,' she said. 'Your father wasn't either. Shadowlands is a place, like the place you were born is a place. I was born in Nye, which is far away across a great sea. Where you were born doesn't make you special, Gift. Who you are, and what your talents are, make you special.'

'But you always say stuff about my heritage.'

'Your heritage.' The steam had stopped rising from her bowl. She didn't seem to notice. She leaned back on her hands, her wings closing tightly against her back. 'Your heritage means your talents, Gift.'

He frowned. That wasn't right. She always meant something else when she said heritage. But he wasn't going to argue. Not yet. When his talents came, then he would ask how he got them. Sometimes people treated bigger kids with more seriousness, not because the kids were smarter, but because they were larger.

His mother stared at him for a moment, then she picked up her soup and drank too. He finished first, set down his bowl, and burped. Then he pushed up from the rug. He needed to run, to move a little. He had been sitting all morning.

'Gift.' His mother set her bowl down. 'I want you to sit for a little longer. Your grandfather will be over this afternoon.'

Gift let himself fall back onto the rug. He put one arm over his eyes. 'Does he have to?'

'He hasn't seen you for a long time.'

That was good as far as Gift was concerned. He knew that Grandpa Rugar was the reason they had this cabin and all the wonderful things, but Gift didn't understand why that meant Gift had to be nice to him. 'So?'

'He likes to check on you.'

Gift shrugged. 'He can check when I'm sleeping.'

'Gift!'

Gift glanced at the door as if Grandpa Rugar would come in any moment. The door was closed, as it always was. 'He isn't nice.'

His mother set her bowl down. Then she put her hands on her thighs in her listening mode. 'What do you mean?'

'He talks mean to you.'

This time, her smile was faint, the smile she often had for his father when he said something she didn't like. 'He runs the Shadowlands.'

'That doesn't mean he can talk bad to you.'

She furrowed her eyebrows. 'What do you mean by "bad," Gift?'

'He thinks I can't hear him, and then he says that you should know what I can do by now. He says you don't train me hard enough, that I should have more magic than everyone else combined. He makes it sound like me not doing what he wants is your fault.' Tears filled Gift's eyes. He rubbed them with his fists. He wouldn't cry like a baby.

'He just has high hopes for you, honey.'

'He wants to use me.'

His mother's lips parted slightly, then she closed them and bit the lower one. Finally she asked, 'What makes you say that?'

69

'Because he said so.'

'When?' Her eyes looked unnaturally bright.

'The first time he saw me.' Gift's fists were wet. He wiped them on his legs and watched the moisture bead on his pants.

'Gift, you were just a baby. You can't remember that.'

'Can too,' he said.

She reached over and took his hand, not seeming to care that it was damp. 'You can remember what happened to you when you were very little? Is that how come you can remember words and sentences so well?'

Gift shook his head. 'I always knew words from the time you flew me here. Words are like breathing. I just know them.'

'And how do you know what your grandfather said?'

'I *remember*. Like I remember that we had cake for breakfast. I *remember*.' The fact that she didn't believe him bothered him. His mother had to believe him. She knew everything about him.

'You remember.' She said the phrase as if she were trying to convince herself. 'Do you remember what happened the first time you came here?'

'You had a Domestic give me warm milk and then you held me in my blanket until I fell asleep.'

She nodded, squeezed his hand, and then let it go. 'Why haven't you told me this before?'

'I have,' he said. 'You just explained it away. You would think I was being cute or something.'

'Gift,' she said slowly, 'I've never heard of this.' Suddenly she pulled him close. Her arms were tight around him. His face was pressed against her soft breasts, the faintly sulfur smell of her, familiar and safe.

He struggled to pull free. She had never done this before. Finally, he pulled back far enough to see her face.

'Have I done something wrong?' he asked, his voice small.

She shook her head. She studied him for a moment. 'I just don't think we should tell Rugar. I mean, what could he do? It's not like you have a power. It's not like you could be tested for this.'

He frowned. He shouldn't have told her. Somehow his knowledge of his past made everything different.

Then she nodded, as if something had been confirmed. 'We won't mention this,' she said. 'You won't tell your grandfather.'

'I never tell him anything anyway,' Gift said. He didn't quite understand. If he had planned on telling Grandpa Rugar, he would have done so already.

She grabbed his hand and squeezed. 'I'm sure you don't,' she said.

Then she let go, got up, and picked up the tray. 'Your grandfather will be here real soon now, Gift. Do you need a nap first?'

'No.' Gift picked at the rug even though he wasn't supposed to. She hadn't said anything about Grandpa Rugar's statement that he wanted to use Gift. She hadn't said anything at all. 'Will Daddy be home soon?'

'No, honey. He has river duty today.'

River duty, country duty, sky duty. They were all words that Gift didn't completely understand but that had something to do with his parents' long disappearances. All the grown-ups in Shadowlands had jobs to do. Some of those jobs just kept them away from their homes for a longer period of time.

His mother said he was lucky because at least one of his parents remained with him at all times.

Dishes rattled in the back room. The cabin was small compared to the Domicile and his grandfather's cabin. His parents slept in the back room with the dishes and cookware, while Gift had a tiny room all to himself. The cabin was square. The main room, the fireplace room, was the largest in the place. Gift's was the smallest. His parents couldn't stand up inside it unless they turned to light and reappeared very small.

Maybe he should go to his room. Grandpa Rugar wasn't a Wisp. He didn't have wings. He wouldn't be able to become small.

Gift got up. His eyes felt crusty from the tears. He rubbed at them again. The conversation with his mother had made him sad, and he didn't know why.

'Mommy?' he said. 'I'm going to have a nap anyway.'

'All right,' she called from the back.

But before he could cross the rug, the front door opened. Grandpa Rugar let himself in and hung his long black cape on one of the pegs hanging beside the door. The cape itself scared Gift. The cape always moved. When he was really little, he thought it was alive. But he had never seen it breathe, so it just had to have extra magic.

'Little Gift,' Grandpa Rugar said. He didn't smile or crouch like other adults did. He stood by the door, looking down on Gift.

There was a bang in the back room. Gift's mother came inside the main room.

'Rugar,' she said, sounding breathless. 'You're early.'

'And not unwelcome, I hope,' Grandpa Rugar said.

Gift pushed his lips together. He wouldn't answer that one. He wished he had had the extra moment to go to his room. If he did so now, his mother would yell at him.

'Say hello to your grandfather, Gift.'

'Lo,' Gift said. He hadn't moved off the rug.

'Any progress?' Grandpa Rugar said to Gift's mother, speaking as if Gift weren't even present.

She shook her head just once, a quick uncomfortable movement.

'This is so odd,' Grandpa Rugar said. 'Mixed children usually display sooner than this.'

'We don't use that phrase,' his mother said tightly.

'All of Shadowlands knows. He'll have to get used to it.'

Gift couldn't keep quiet any longer. 'Get used to what?'

'Your heritage, boy,' Grandpa Rugar said. Then he crouched and held out his long slender hands. 'Come here.'

Gift glanced at his mother. He wished he were littler and could run to her, and hide by her legs.

She nodded toward Grandpa Rugar.

Gift had no choice.

He walked across the rug to his grandfather's outstretched hands. But when he got near them, he didn't touch them.

'I don't bite, boy,' Grandpa Rugar said.

Gift still didn't say anything. Up close, Grandpa Rugar smelled of cinnamon and leather. His features were sharp and fierce, his eyes glittery.

'The child should get out more,' Grandpa Rugar said to Gift's mother. 'He's too shy.'

'You had wanted him clear of the other children.'

'But not at the expense of his socialization.'

Gift stood perfectly still, unwilling to move closer, but hating this discussion. Already he had made a mistake, and he wasn't sure what the mistake was.

'He's socialized fine, Rugar,' his mother said. 'If anything he's too precocious.' Her voice strangled on the final word, as if she regretted speaking it.

But Grandpa Rugar didn't seem to notice. 'He seems shy to me.'

'You frighten him, I think.'

Gift clamped his teeth together. The last thing he wanted Grandpa Rugar to know was that Gift was frightened of him. 'I'm not afraid, Grandpa,' he said, although his voice sounded odd, even to him. To prove his words, he reached over and grabbed his grandfather's long hand with his short square one.

The world exploded in color and light. Gift saw a Fey woman wearing a long white dress, lying in the arms of a square man. The man had yellow hair and pale skin. The couple looked familiar, as if he had seen them before. The man was crying out in an unfamiliar language. The words sounded like *Orma Lii. Orma Lii.* His grandpa was beside them.

He pulled a bottle of water from his tunic and poured it on the woman. She cried out as if in great pain.

Gift knew her voice. His mother. And he had never seen her before. Part of her face had melted. Her dress covered her wings. But her hands looked wrong, and her chin.

The yellow-haired man said, '*Ne sneto. Ne sneto,*' over and over to the woman. She reached for him only to have Grandpa Rugar snatch her away. Grandpa carried her out of the room with the yellow-haired man running after him.

Then Gift opened his eyes. He was lying on the floor, his head resting on his grandfather's booted legs. His mouth was open and drool ran down his cheek.

He felt funny. His head felt as hollow as his mother's bones.

His mother knelt over him. She was holding his hands, her eyes small with worry.

'You'll be all right, child,' Grandpa Rugar said. 'Sit slowly.'

Grandpa Rugar supported Gift's back as he sat up. His heart was racing, and he found it hard to breathe. His mouth felt like someone had stuffed it with dried leaves.

'Get him some water,' Grandpa Rugar said to his mother. When she didn't move, he added, 'He'll be fine. But he needs some water.'

She nodded, let go of Gift's hands, and stood. For a moment, it seemed as if she didn't know where the water was. Then she ran for the back room.

'Now,' Grandpa Rugar said. 'Tell me what you Saw.'

'Saw?' Gift asked. How did Grandpa Rugar know?

'You have the Vision, boy. It runs strong in my family, but it will be strongest in you. No Fey has Seen this young. But it is important to share what you Saw.'

It was hard to think. Gift wiped the drool off his face, hoping his mother would return before he had to answer. 'Is this my power?' he asked.

'Yes,' Grandpa Rugar said, 'and it's the one I had hoped for.'

'That was a Vision?' Gift's mother asked as she came back into the room. She was holding a mug, its sides beaded with water.

'A powerful one,' Grandpa Rugar said. 'It knocked him flat.'

'How come it happened when I touched you?' Gift asked, remembering the burn of his fingers as they grabbed at his first Wisp.

'Visions come that way sometimes,' Grandpa Rugar said. 'The first is usually triggered by an event, but only when the Sight is ready.'

'Children this young never come into that kind of power,' Gift's mother said. 'Jewel didn't get her Vision until she was an adult full-grown. He won't understand how to use it.'

'I'll teach him,' Grandpa Rugar said. 'But he needs to tell me what he Saw.'

Gift's mother handed him the mug. Gift drank. The water was cold and clear. It had come from the wooden pitcher, his favorite because it made all water sweet.

The water made him feel a little better. 'Is it all right that I got this Vision?' he asked.

His mother didn't answer, but Grandpa Rugar did. 'It's wonderful,' he said.

Gift looked at his mother for confirmation. Her smile was the tight, disapproving one. 'Should I tell him what happened?' he asked softly, wishing he could speak to her alone.

'I think it best,' she said. 'You'll need help with this.'

Grandpa Rugar's hand never left Gift's back. His palm was warm through the fine weave of Gift's shirt. 'You'll need to leave us. Visions are for Leaders and Shamans only.'

'No!' Gift cried. He grabbed for his mother, almost dropping the mug. 'No!'

She put her arms around him, cradling him as if he were a baby. Then she rocked him back and forth, her warmth like a balm to him. Her wings rustled slightly. He clung to her, unwilling to let her go.

'I think I better stay,' she said to Grandpa Rugar. Gift felt the words rumble through her chest.

'You will not discuss this with anyone.'

'There is much I've kept quiet for you,' Gift's mother said.

'All right. Gift, I need to know what you Saw.'

Gift clung tighter to his mother. She kissed the top of his head, smoothed his hair, and gently worked her hands under his, forcing him to let go.

'Talk to your grandfather, honey. It's important.'

Gift leaned against his mother, his fist against his mouth. He looked over at his grandfather. Grandpa Rugar was still sitting as he had been when Gift woke out of his strange dream. There was a small dent on the side of his boot from Gift's head.

'I was in a place I never been and there were all these yellow people,' Gift said, the words coming out in a rush.

'Yellow people?' his mother asked.

Grandpa Rugar shushed her. 'It's better to let him speak.'

'And one of them was sitting like you.' Gift inclined his head toward his grandfather. 'But he was holding Mommy, and she was hurt.'

His mother's body stiffened. He glanced up at her, but her face hadn't changed. She nodded to him to continue.

'Only she didn't look like Mommy. Her face was funny and I

couldn't see her wings. She was wearing a white dress. It looked like something hurt her head. The man was saying strange things to her. He looked scared. And you were there, Grandpa. You threw water on Mommy. Then she yelled. The other man kept talking to her, but you grabbed her from him and ran with her from the room. He ran after you.'

There was a silence when Gift finished. 'That's all?' his grandfather asked.

Gift nodded.

'Very good. You remember a lot for your first Vision. Now, I'm going to ask you details and see if you can remember them. Were you in Shadowlands?'

Gift shook his head. 'Everything was bright.'

'What else was in the room?'

'Lots of yellow people.'

'Furniture?'

Gift shrugged. 'I just saw people.'

'What did these yellow people look like?'

'They had yellow hair and their skin was really light.'

'Islanders,' his mother whispered.

'Shush, Niche, or I will not allow you here the next time.' Grandpa Rugar spoke sharply to her without looking at her at all.

'See?' Gift whispered. Grandpa Rugar was always mean to her.

She squeezed Gift's arm, but said nothing.

'Was I the only Fey there?'

'Mommy.'

'Besides your mother?'

'Infantry,' Gift said. 'But I don't know who.'

His grandfather leaned close, so close Gift could see the red lines in his eyes. 'Now, this next part is hard. How did you know the Fey woman was your mother.'

'I just knew,' Gift said. He didn't like explaining this. It was like trying to make sense from a dream.

'Did she look like your mother?'

'She was hurt.'

'But –' Grandpa Rugar sighed. 'Let me try this way. Did you know she was your mother before you saw her?'

Gift looked at him, amazed that Grandpa Rugar could understand. 'Yes,' he said.

'Did she speak?'

'She cried when you threw water on her.'

Grandpa Rugar frowned. The look was severe, and frightening. Gift leaned harder on his mother. She put one arm around him.

75

'Were you there, Gift?'

'Yes,' he said. He looked at his mother. She was watching Grandpa Rugar. 'I saw it all. I was just there.'

Grandpa Rugar gave Gift's mother one of those grown-up looks, the kind that proved children were bad. He frowned. 'I know you were there, Gift, but did anyone see you or talk to you?'

Gift shook his head.

'Do you know where you were standing or how you got there?'

'No.'

Grandpa Rugar leaned back as if Gift's answer explained everything. Gift didn't like it that Grandpa Rugar seemed to know more about Gift's Vision than Gift did.

'Is that all?' Gift's mother asked. Her arms had tightened around Gift again.

'For now,' Grandpa Rugar said. 'You did well, Gift.'

Gift smiled at the praise because he knew he was supposed to. But he didn't like it. The whole afternoon had been bad. He didn't want Grandpa Rugar here, and he hated the Vision. If that was going to be his power, he wanted it changed.

To something with wings.

'Will he be all right?' Gift's mother asked.

Grandpa Rugar nodded. 'If it happens again, send for me right away.'

'It'll happen again?' Gift asked. He hated it. He never wanted another.

'All of your life, boy,' Grandpa Rugar said. 'It's not so bad. And when it goes away, you might even miss it.'

'I won't,' Gift said.

'Don't be so sure,' Grandpa Rugar said.

His words made Gift's mother even more tense. 'Are you Blind?' she whispered.

'Of course not,' Grandpa Rugar said. 'But I have watched too many lose their Vision. I know how painful it will be.'

He got to his feet, grabbed his cloak and swung it over his shoulders.

'Rugar?' Gift's mother said. 'About the Vision. What can I do?'

He adjusted the cloak over his shoulders. 'Do about what?'

'The injury that Gift saw. I thought sometimes the point of Visions is to prevent something from happening.'

'It is,' Grandpa Rugar said. 'But you don't have to worry.'

'Gift said –'

'I know what Gift said. I say you have nothing to worry over.'

Gift leaned forward. 'Mommy was hurt.'

76

'No,' Grandpa Rugar said. 'You said that your mother was hurt, but that she didn't look like your mother, isn't that right?'

'Yes,' Gift said.

'Then Niche here has nothing to worry about.'

Gift frowned. Another answer that made no sense. 'Why not?'

Grandpa Rugar looked at him. 'Because she's not your real mother, boy,' he said, and then let himself out of the cabin.

Gift's mother made a soft moaning sound.

'You're my mother, aren't you?' Gift asked.

She didn't answer.

'Aren't you?'

She lifted her head, then kissed his cheek, her lips soft. 'Yes, Gift.'

'So why isn't he worried about you?'

She put her hand behind the back of his head and pulled him close, so close he couldn't see her face. 'Because Visions are odd things. They don't always come true.'

'But you're worried.'

'Only about you, Gift.' She rocked him as she spoke. 'Only about you.'

Nine

Burden was knee-deep in mud, pounding wooden nails into wooden slabs, trying to repair the wall of the Domicile. The spring rain was cool against his head, and his fingers hurt. He would have to get one of the Healers to pull the splinters from his skin when he was through.

The Jahn settlement was a failure. Only his pride prevented him from returning to Shadowlands. Rugar would say that only Visionaries can start new colonies, and Rugar would be right.

In the past three years, the Settlement had gone from a small camp filled with hope to a place full of frightened Fey. The buildings were badly constructed because most of the Domestics had chosen to stay in Shadowlands. Those who had come were younger Domestics, many with textile experience, and no experience on larger homey matters. The Islanders that Jewel had promised had helped early on, but the fights among the Islanders and the Fey had grown so severe that the Fey refused to work with the Islanders. Many Islanders carried poison onto the premises because they were afraid of Fey magic. Many Fey threatened magic because they were afraid of Islander poison.

The truce was great in theory, but in practice it wasn't succeeding at all.

Burden had managed to create a Shadowlands with weather and less protection. So far, no Fey had died out here, but it was only a matter of time.

'Burden?'

He sighed and let the entire piece of wood slide down. The hole still gaped in the side of the Domicile. He turned, his legs squinching in the mud.

The only Weather Sprite to have left Shadowlands, Hanouk, stood behind him. She wore an untreated cloak, hood down. Water poured over her face. Her work with the elements had left her skin so tortured she looked four times older than she was. She had left Shadowlands because she hated the grayness, not because she had believed in Burden's cause. 'Jewel has come to see you.'

'Her Highness wants to see how well the little experiment is working?' Burden wiped his muddy hands on his muddy pants. She would come to see him when he was like this. Not that it mattered. He hadn't ever mattered to her – he saw that now. Their long friendship, their shared experiences in the Infantry, meant nothing in the face of her lust for the Islander.

Still, understanding didn't help Burden's bitterness. If Jewel had to mate with someone who lacked her talents, she should have chosen someone Fey.

She should have chosen him.

Hanouk ignored his sarcasm. 'She is in my cabin. She shouldn't be in the elements.'

'I suppose not, now that the Black King's granddaughter is Queen of Blue Isle.'

He got up, the mud squishing around him.

Hanouk waited until he stood beside her. 'Jewel is with child. We do not want her birthing a mixed baby here.' Then she turned and walked back to the path, her feet staying on top of the mud. Burden envied the Weather Sprites their uncanny control of all the elements.

The pregnancy shook him. He had expected the first child – it was an obligation that she had to fulfill. He had been present when she made the agreement with the Islander. But a second child, so late in the marriage, couldn't be obligation.

He shuddered, the betrayal as fresh as if it had occurred the day before.

He slogged through the mud to the path. There was mud on the stones, but at least they kept him from sinking in the deep. The Islanders were smart. When they had designated this part of Jahn for a Fey settlement, they knew they were giving the Fey river bottom land. It was a flood plain that washed out every spring. Burden had initially said such things didn't matter; the Fey could work with any problem. He was right, of course, but what he hadn't foreseen – what he had lacked the Vision for – was the knowledge that the most magical Fey would remain with Rugar in Shadowlands. The Fey who moved to Jahn were the young, the rebellious, and the underappreciated.

He had so little help, and he was so very, very tired.

The Settlement was fifty buildings big. They were scattered on a series of paths that followed rises in the ground more than any logic. One of the benefits of being outside Shadowlands was the space and materials to build cabins.

The severe flooding had damaged most of them. During this last, long winter, Burden had felt that it was the Fey's fate to live in grayness. The only difference outside Shadowlands was that the grayness contained rain. He had finally asked Hanouk to control the rain and the flooding, and she had given him a withering look. He had not had the power to ask, and she always pretended that he never had.

As he walked, he could see over the walls into the city of Jahn. The walls had gone up shortly after the Fey arrived in the Settlement, another joint project by Fey and Islanders. But unlike the barge on which Jewel and Nicholas held their marriage, this wall was a secret construction. Burden never knew who started it, and he wasn't certain he wanted to know, but one morning he awoke to find one side of the gate built. The building continued during the nights that followed, and he found a few Fey who confessed to adding to the gate. But they never admitted to starting it. He believed that the Islanders had started the gate, hoping the Fey would continue it. And they had.

He wiped his face with the back of his hand, trying not to get too much mud on his features. Hanouk's cabin was straight ahead, its boards the only ones unaffected by the weather which was, Burden had always thought, a supreme irony. Hanouk would help herself, but not her fellow Fey.

The cabin was larger than the others, since Hanouk outranked most of the Fey in the Settlement. She had four rooms where the luckiest of the rest had two. The wood was still its natural light brown, the building still looking sharp and new. The only signs around the cabin of the heavy rains was the standing water on the walk outside.

The door was open. He took a deep breath before mounting the wide stones Hanouk used as steps. It had been a long time since he had seen Jewel alone. He had spoken to her briefly after her marriage, and she had seemed distant, completely unlike the Jewel he had known. The Jewel he had grown up with had been a fierce adventurer, a worthy heir to the Black King's throne. The woman he had seen had been an Islander wife, content to speak about her husband in soft, admiring tones.

He had seen her again when she had brought her strange child to his Healers. He had refused to look at the boy, hearing rumors that the child was not natural. His response had hurt Jewel then, but nothing like the way she had hurt him.

After that, Burden had spoken to Jewel through the Fey channels she had set up within the human palace, and then he had spoken to her only rarely. That she would come to see him was a shock.

He took the steps slowly, his untreated boots sliding on the stone. He knocked as he stepped across the threshold, and someone moved inside the house. Hanouk had not come back. In a moment he would see Jewel.

He wanted the meeting under his control. He stepped inside and blinked at the darkness. Hanouk had left a fire, but it was burning out, and there was no more wood stacked beside the fireplace. A small table stood in front of an oversized chair – clearly Hanouk's favorite place – and decorations of cloth hung from the walls. Burden didn't take the time to examine them, however. Instead he glanced around until he saw Jewel.

She was standing near one of the other chairs, this one filled with stuffing, clearly Domestic made. Her hand rested on its back, and her body was hidden by its frame. Even so, the marks pregnancy had left on her were very visible. Her face was fuller, her hair darker. But unlike most pregnant Fey, she did not seem radiant. Her features were drawn and her skin was ashen.

Then the possibility that had missed him initially came to mind. Perhaps she needed his help. Perhaps the bargain was as bad as he had feared. Perhaps she needed a way to escape the palace.

'Are you all right?' he asked, making certain his voice held the tenderness he felt.

Her smile was small. 'The last month is always hard,' she said.

For a moment, he didn't know what she was referring to. Then he realized she was talking about her pregnancy.

'And there has been a lot of strain.' She brushed a strand of hair off her face, a gesture so familiar that it made his heart ache. 'I need to talk to you, Burden, as an old friend.'

'Certainly,' he said and pulled the door closed. The light from the fire provided the only illumination. For some reason, Hanouk had preferred a Shadowlands tradition – a home with no windows. He took one of the other chairs and pulled it closer to the fire. 'Would you like to sit, Jewel?'

She nodded. She braced herself with one hand on the chair, and emerged from behind its back. He had to work at keeping his expression neutral. Her belly was swollen, and rode low against her hips. She wore a long dress made of a shiny brown cloth he had never seen before. Although she hadn't worn dresses much in the past, this one made sense. Fey women often wore long dresses during pregnancy. She was as thin as ever – the weight gain in her face had probably been his imagination. He had expected to see the pregnancy, but what he had not expected was the slow deliberateness with which she moved. Jewel had always been rapid heat, lightning quick, and full of grace. She had never moved with the care she moved with now.

She grabbed the arms of her chair to pull it closer to the fire, and he shook his head. 'This one, Jewel,' he said.

Her smile was small, tight, and grateful. She brushed past him as she walked, and he recognized her familiar scent of cinnamon and sunshine. A quick flare of desire ran through him. He had forgotten how much he missed her.

She gripped the arms of the chair he was holding and eased herself into it. Then she sighed. Her long black braid brushed his hands. He stared at it for a moment before letting go.

He walked over to the fire and peered into it. The flames were tiny, hesitant, just as he was feeling.

'Aren't you going to sit?' she asked.

He shook his head. 'I don't want to get this mud on Hanouk's furniture.'

'I think,' Jewel said in a tone that told him she was really smiling for the first time since he saw her, 'that Hanouk of all people is prepared for these things.'

Special Domestic-made furniture. Of course, her furniture would be able to handle the effects of weather. He took the chair Jewel had left, pulled it closer to the fire and sank into it. A tingling along the back of his legs told him she had been right.

'You look tired, Jewel.' He leaned back and rested his elbows on the arms of the chair. 'Are you all right?'

'A lot of strain,' she said again. 'And the baby.'

She put a hand protectively over her stomach. For the first time since he had come in, he got a real sense of her. She wanted this child, but she was afraid for it. He wondered what had gone wrong with the other one. Mixed Fey were always more powerful than Fey.

'I need your help,' she said, her voice soft. She paused.

'Is it Nicholas?' Burden asked into the silence. 'What's he done?'

'No. Nicholas has done exactly what he said he would.' She sighed, and brushed her hair away from her face. The gesture was a nervous one. Burden had never realized that before. 'I don't suppose you heard the news. About Alexander.'

'The King?' Burden hadn't been outside the Settlement in days. Not that it would have mattered. He tried not to pay any attention to news any more. Too distracting. He needed instead to concentrate on the Settlement and his own undeveloped – and unknown – magical powers.

'He's been murdered, Burden.' Jewel leaned back and closed her eyes. 'Far from here. In the Kenniland Marshes.'

'The Islanders finally got tired of him, huh?' Burden smiled. He felt no regret about this one, except, perhaps that he should have listened to Jewel in the first place. 'So you're in power now. Good. What do you need me for?'

'It's not that simple.' Only her mouth moved. It looked as if she

82

were talking in her sleep. 'The Rocaan believes that a Fey murdered Alexander. I think he may be right.'

'In the Marshes? Really, Jewel. We have enough trouble getting around Jahn.' A tension built in Burden's shoulders. The relaxed, listening posture he had adopted had suddenly become uncomfortable. He sat up and took his elbows off the chair arms.

'The Marshes are apparently flat and wide with few trees. Alexander was murdered with a single arrow through his heart. Even though his guards searched the area, they found no one. The Rocaan says only Fey can disappear that easily. I think he might be right.'

'Jewel, that man hates us. To agree with him –' Burden sucked in his breath. 'You really do believe him, don't you?'

'It would, as you say, bring me closer to power. But they're trying to blame me for this.' She opened her eyes. She had deep shadows beneath them. 'Not Nicholas, but the Rocaan and the others. They think I did it.'

'So why come to me?'

She rubbed her hand along the top of her belly. Her eyes opened wider and then her gaze pinned him. In it, he saw the fierce Jewel of old. 'Forgive me, Burden, but I need to know. Did you or one of your people assassinate Alexander?'

He felt a slight chill, even though he sat close to the heat of the dying fire. Assassinate the King? It had been the farthest thing from his mind. Mending the houses, staving off the rain, making sure his people had enough to eat. Those things preoccupied him. It should be obvious to her, but it wasn't. She actually thought he might assassinate the Islander King, as if that would make a different to the Fey plight.

'Jewel,' he said, struggling to keep his voice calm. 'If I were going to do something like that, I would slit him with my sword, in the palace, just so that I could get credit for the murder.'

Her lips tightened. 'I'm serious, Burden.'

'I am too.'

She stared at him a moment, her eyes moving back and forth as if she were trying to read hidden messages on his face. Then she sighed. 'Are you sure none of your people did this?'

She was determined. She wanted to pin this death on a Fey. 'Look around you, Jewel,' he said. 'No one in the Settlement has time to travel to the Marshes, plan and commit a murder, and return. We barely get enough to eat.'

'It can't be as bad as all that,' she said.

'Oh, but it is.' The force of his anger pushed him out of the chair. He had to pace to keep from yelling at her. She had to understand. Didn't she know he had done this as a support for her? And then for her to not see what damage this support had done ... The betrayals repeated – or perhaps they never ended. 'Our people are afraid to work with the Islanders. Afraid, Jewel, afraid of that poison. Afraid that they will accidentally touch a surface laced with poison and they will die. Nothing grows here. We get flooded every spring and every fall. We have to find plants that will survive a short growing season. And most of the talented Domestics remain in Shadowlands. We lack resources, Jewel.'

He walked to the fire and back to his chair without looking at her. He could hear nothing from her, not a rustle, not a sound.

'We did this for you. We did this in support of you. We did this because we believed if you could do it, we could too. We could make an agreement with the Islanders work. It hasn't worked, Jewel. And now you accuse us of betraying the very trust we display.'

On the last word, he stopped in front of her, and looked down on her. She had both hands over her stomach now, and she had additional lines around her mouth. 'Their King is dead,' she said. 'Someone killed him.'

'But not me, Jewel, or anyone I know.'

'Burden, the Rocaan has already stated that I should step down. Sebastian will not inherit, and neither will this little one. Worse, the war could start up again. Fey could die as a matter of course. No one has told me of any progress on solving the mystery of the poison. Has there been any?'

He shrugged. 'I don't go to Shadowlands any more than you do.'

All the Spell Warders remained in Shadowlands, theoretically looking for a way to block the Islander poison. They had been unsuccessful last Burden heard.

She shook her head. The lines near her mouth seemed to grow deeper. He could feel the strain on her. It was a live thing, as alive as the child in her belly.

He couldn't stay mad at her long. He had never been able to.

He crouched beside her, and put a hand over her own. She looked up, startled. Her hands were warm, and the skin beneath them stretched taut with the child. He felt a small flutter against his thumb, slid his hand off hers, and onto her belly. The baby was moving inside her.

Burden had never felt anything like that before.

His gaze met Jewel's. She smiled. 'You're lucky,' she said. 'Usually she kicks.'

'A fighter,' he said. 'Like her mama.'

Jewel nodded. 'Let's hope. Her brother kicked too, and he has no fight at all.'

So the boy had not improved. Perhaps the Islanders were trying to get rid of her and pinning an assassination on her was the best way to do so.

'Tell me again why you think a Fey did this,' he said.

'Islanders resolve their differences with words, not murder. There have been assassination attempts in the past, but they were often designed to fail, more warnings than anything else. Except one.' The fluttery feeling in her stomach warmed him. She rubbed her hands over it as if to soothe the child within. 'That attempt took place in the Kenniland Marshes during the Peasant Uprising. It failed because the Marshes were flat, and the assassins could be seen from miles away.'

'So this time the assassin was successful,' he said.

She shook her head. 'Islanders have an odd habit. If something has failed before, they don't try it in the same way again. If they were going to assassinate their king near the Marshes, it wouldn't happen in the same spot as before. It would happen somewhere else, by some other method.'

'That's pretty slim evidence, Jewel.'

'I know,' she said. 'That's why I was hoping you could tell me more, Burden. I hoped you knew.'

He shook his head. 'Jewel, let the Islanders solve this.'

'It's not just their problem any more. It's ours too.'

She was done talking with him. He could hear it in her voice. But he didn't want her to leave. He didn't want to take his hand from her stomach. If the world had been different – if status hadn't been so important among Fey – this would be his child inside her. Instead, it was a mix of Fey and Islander. A mix that had, apparently, failed before.

Strange then, given what she had just said, that she and Nicholas were trying another child.

'You never really answered me,' he said more to keep her beside him than anything. 'How do you know the killer is Fey? Did you See it?'

She tensed. 'No. I didn't See anything.' She emphasized 'see.' He got a sense that she had known something, but didn't want to discuss it. 'The attack just feels wrong. If an Islander were to do it, he would do it differently.'

'You can't go by feeling,' Burden said. 'If a Fey were to kill the king, he would do it publicly, for credit.'

'Unless he was trying something else, trying, perhaps to create dissent among the Islanders.'

'And why would he do that?'

'To start the war again?'

'But it benefits none of us to start the war,' Burden said.

Jewel met his gaze. 'Really?'

He let out a small mouthful of air. 'Unless we have a solution to the poison problem.'

'Or,' Jewel said, 'unless someone were to assassinate Nicholas too. Then I would rule as Regent.'

Burden couldn't tell if that were a suggestion or not. 'Is that what you want, Jewel?'

Her lips parted as if she were stunned by the question. 'No,' she said. 'I do not. I care for him too much.'

Burden looked away. She put her hand on top of his and continued in a soft voice. 'Even if he died, Burden, they would never allow me to lead their government. Sebastian will never be competent enough to take the reins, and none of us know what this child will be like. If Nicholas died, I would have to escape the palace with both children. I'm not sure they'd allow any of us to live.'

'You're Fey, Jewel. How can they stop you?'

'I think you know the answer to that.'

He nodded. He did. 'A Fey killer makes no sense,' he said.

'I know,' she said. 'Yet I can't shake this feeling. Can you find out for me, Burden? Can you find out if one of our people killed Alexander?'

He couldn't refuse her. Not even after all the betrayals. He put his head on her stomach and listened to the baby she made with another man – with an enemy – move inside her.

'I'll find out, Jewel,' he said. And, he promised himself, he would help her set up an escape route.

He had a feeling she would need one.

Ten

Titus stood on the road outside of Jahn. Half a dozen Danites and a dozen Auds stood with him, although he had told Elder Eirman that only a handful of men would do. But Elder Eirman had had an edict from the Rocaan to meet the King's body with the highest contingent possible, and to bring it to the Tabernacle unmolested. Titus had wanted to argue even that order, for the true procedure would be to take the King's body to the ceremonial burial grounds on the hill north of the palace and prepare a casket of proper size. But the Rocaan wanted the King in the Tabernacle, and the Blessing to take place in the Sanctuary, and then have a processional to the grave site for the Burial Service.

Titus thought it all blasphemy.

The church taught that the Services were designed by the first Rocaan with the Roca's wishes in mind. Even though the Roca had been a man, he had been Beloved of God. He sat on God's Hand, and had God's Ear. His wishes were the closest man had to God on the Isle. Titus believed that this made them sacred. The new Rocaan, the former Elder Matthias, believed that this made the Services of mortal design and subject to the whim of the Rocaan. No Rocaan had thought so before, but no Rocaan had claimed the kind of scholarship Matthias had.

Scholarship, Titus was beginning to believe, was the root of all the evil within the church.

But he had no say over this. He was a lowly Danite, appointed to his post after the death of the fiftieth Rocaan, to which he was a witness. That day still haunted his dreams – the Fey creature attacked the Rocaan and then seemed to change *into* the Rocaan. When the Fey/ Rocaan got hit with holy water, he had melted, leaving the small kirk near Daisy Stream filled with blood and bones and water. Later, the Elders had said the Fey were trying to learn the secret to holy water from the Rocaan. According to tradition, only the Rocaan was to know the secret, although at the time, Elder Matthias had known it too.

The Fey had failed in their attempt to take over the Tabernacle and learn the secret of holy water – which they called poison – but they had succeeded in destroying the richness and the unity of Rocaanism. On his most pessimistic days, Titus believed Rocaanism changed forever.

A breeze blew from the south. The road was empty, blocked below by his fellow Danites. No travelers could enter Jahn from the southern roadway today. No one could have the opportunity to tamper with the King's body.

The Auds were milling around Titus. Although some of those Auds had once been his colleagues, and a few of them were older than he was, he felt as if he had years on them. The fiftieth Rocaan had died when Titus was fourteen, and the experience had added ten years on his life. Even though he was only nineteen now, he felt as if he had seen the entire world.

The road was flat and wide here, reflecting all the traffic that came into Jahn from this direction. Before the Invasion, people came up from the south every summer and fall to sell goods, to shop in the city, and to attend at least one Sacramental service in the Tabernacle. Such travel had stopped after the Invasion, and Titus found that he still missed it. He always had a chance to see his family in the summer, and he hadn't seen them since the Rocaan died.

He had lost everything then. Now all he had was the religion itself, and even that was changing. The fifty-first Rocaan seemed to have no understanding of the important things in Rocaanism. He lacked the gentleness that his predecessor had, gentleness that made its way to all the lower echelons of the religion. Instead, the fifty-first Rocaan was concerned with small tricks of language and loopholes in the canon, ways to give himself power, ways to lord himself over the King.

Putting King Alexander's body in the Tabernacle was just one way of doing this. Titus suspected things would get worse now. King Nicholas would probably be no match for the fifty-first Rocaan.

Power. Amazing that it all boiled down to power. To Titus, Rocaanism was about faith, not power. Titus had survived the Invasion. He had survived being in the Fey's lair, and he had survived the ghastly attack on the fiftieth Rocaan. Titus knew the Holy One was watching over him. He knew that he had God's Eye.

The fifty-first Rocaan sometimes acted as if God did not exist.

Simon, one of the other Danites, walked over to Titus. Simon was almost twice Titus's age. He had been a Danite for a decade, and would probably remain one for the rest of his life. He was slender and short, his black robe always impeccably groomed, his feet encased in expensive sandals. Most Danites went barefoot to imitate the Roca's experience in his youth. It was an unspoken idea that only the non believers wore shoes.

Like Titus, Simon was a second son. Only he had never understood the traditions of the church. He had seen it only as a font for his ambitions. He had snapped at Titus when he learned that Titus headed the burial detail for the King. For some reason, Simon had thought it would go to him.

'Are you sure we're on the right road?' Simon asked.

His voice was thin and raspy, a disadvantage when he performed Sacrament at kirks outside of Jahn. One of the Officiates, the men who actually administrated the Tabernacle and the kirks, had told Titus that Simon's voice and ambition were the main reasons he would never go higher in Rocaanism.

'This is where the Elder told us to go,' Titus said. He struggled to keep his voice calm. He too had been wondering if he got the location right. Somehow he had expected the funeral procession to be waiting for them. But traveling across the Isle took time, particularly in the spring when the parties could run into all sorts of unexpected occurrences.

'Perhaps you misheard him,' Simon said.

'Leave the boy alone,' said Gregor. He was an elderly Danite and should, by rights, have been the real leader of the burial detail. But Danites past a certain age served only as assistants and traveling clerics. They were considered to have no ambition and no beliefs, both of which were important in the Tabernacle. 'Your carping will make no difference. You'll need to accept that he is a favorite of Matthias.'

'The Rocaan.' Simon corrected Gregor in a sullen tone.

'Yes,' Gregor said, a small smile playing at the corner of his mouth. 'The Rocaan.'

Titus understood that smile. Gregor had once been one of the Rocaan's instructors, decades ago. Now the Rocaan had risen to the position of God's Beloved, leaving Gregor far behind. 'I am not a favorite,' Titus said. 'Elder Eirman told me to come here.'

'At Matthias's instruction,' Gregor said.

'The boy is a believer.' Simon said the words as if being a believer were a sin.

Gregor looked down at Simon's clad feet. Of all the Danites on burial detail, he was the only one wearing sandals. 'Matthias has a fondness for believers,' Gregor said. 'He always has.'

Titus frowned. He thought back to the changes in the Tabernacle since the death of the fiftieth Rocaan. One of them was that believers often held positions of importance. Titus had always thought that was because the believers struggled to fill positions vacated by the scholars, hoping to protect the Tabernacle. He had never thought that believers held those positions because the Rocaan wanted them to.

'He's doing this wrong,' Titus said. He flushed as he spoke. He knew it wasn't wise to speak against the Rocaan, but he couldn't hold it in any longer. 'We should be taking the body to the palace burial grounds.'

'Believers,' Simon muttered and walked away. He stood by some Auds, far enough away to be out of the conversation, but close enough to hear every word.

'What makes you so certain?' Gregor asked. His voice, unlike Simon's, was deep and resonant. He would have made a great Elder, standing before the congregations every morning and midnight, speaking the words of the Roca.

Titus glanced at Gregor. The older man was watching the road, his time-worn features calm. He seemed more intent on the emptiness before him than on Titus's answer.

'It's ceremony,' Titus said. 'Ceremony developed by the first Rocaan based on the Roca's wishes.'

'Based on what the first Rocaan *thought* the Roca's wishes were. Remember that Matthias is a scholar, one of our best. He may have uncovered information that showed him that the first Rocaan did not follow the Roca's wishes.'

Titus shook his head. 'The first Rocaan knew the Roca. He would have known what the Roca wanted.'

'The way you know what the fifty-first Rocaan wants?'

Titus stiffened. He hated lessons taught in this manner. 'I don't know him.'

'You know him better than you know the Roca,' Gregor said. 'The Roca is a figure of myth to you. You see Matthias daily.'

'But I never speak to him.'

'It's not your job to speak to him, or to guess at his motives. If he wants the body taken to the Tabernacle, he has a good reason.'

'Other than ambition?' Titus's flush grew. He couldn't keep quiet about this. The Rocaan's actions had been bothering him for months now.

'Ambition?' Gregor chuckled. 'Matthias was never ambitious. Only bored. Besides, what kind of ambition could he have? He's Rocaan. One cannot go higher in the Tabernacle.'

'What about King?'

The nearby Auds gasped. Simon glanced in Titus's direction, then quickly looked away. Gregor turned away from the road. Age had blunted his features, made his blue eyes watery, his nose flat. He was the only one who did not seem upset by Titus's comment.

'Young Nicholas is our King now.'

'I know,' Titus said, 'but –'

'No,' Gregor said, his voice firm. 'You don't know. It all seems so simple to someone of your age. A man wants to move on. He wants power. He wants to control the world around him. Once he becomes powerful, he will want more power.'

Simon stopped pretending to ignore them. He came closer. The Auds had turned in their direction as well. The breeze seemed cooler. Titus resisted the urge to wrap his arms around his waist.

'Matthias turned down the position of Rocaan,' Gregor said. 'He turned it down many times, claiming that a scholar had no place in the job. The fiftieth Rocaan said that Matthias was Anointed. Matthias is the one who discovered the powers of holy water. Matthias has discovered secrets behind the beliefs that no one in all the centuries could discover. The fiftieth Rocaan knew this. He appointed Matthias Rocaan twice, first by giving him the secret to holy water early and second by putting him in power before the meeting with the Fey. When you question the fifty-first Rocaan's motives, you question the wisdom of the fiftieth Rocaan for appointing him to the post.'

The breeze grew strong. Dust kicked up on the road, making tiny swirling eddies around Titus's bare feet. The flush in his cheeks felt permanent despite the growing cold. 'I didn't know that,' he said finally.

Gregor put a hand on his arm. 'We all question our leaders, especially after we realize they're as human as the rest of us. The fiftieth Rocaan had been in power so long he seemed the embodiment of the Tabernacle. But when he became Rocaan, two Elders left the church. Were they right to do so? God knows. But we never will.'

Titus swallowed. His mouth was dry. He understood the lecture. Never question, always listen, believe that God knows best. But it seemed to him that the fifty-first Rocaan was walking the wrong path. Wouldn't God be speaking to Titus then?

'So we shouldn't question the Rocaan?' Titus asked.

'Never behind his back,' Gregor said. 'Only to his face, and then only when you are alone. Belief is more than believing in God and the Roca, Titus. It also requires faith in God's Anointed.'

Titus nodded. Even his ears felt hot. He wanted this conversation to end. Quickly. Simon was grinning at him. Simon, who would never make this mistake. Simon was too ambitious.

A thought that Titus shouldn't have. His mother had always said a man should have charity in his thoughts. He had lacked that, even with Simon.

As quickly as it arose, the wind died back. Over the rise, horses

91

appeared. Seven horses with six riders. The center horse, a black stallion, carried a large wooden box on its back. Most of the riders were guards, but Titus recognized one of them as Monte, head of the King's guards. A Danite rode a good distance behind them. He must have been a roving Danite, because Titus did not know him.

A thread of nervousness ran through Titus's stomach. Perhaps Gregor had a point. Titus shouldn't question. To have a body on a horse was considered bad luck as well, but the Words Written and Unwritten stressed that a body must be in the ground within the week of its death. Either the King would have had to be buried in the Marshes, or he would have to come Jahn by horseback. Both traditions could not have been observed in this case.

With a movement of his arm, Titus gathered his Auds. He had chosen them all for their youth and strength. The Danites were Elder Eirman's choice. Simon would sprinkle the casket with sacred herbs, Gregor would make the chant, and Titus would say the Blessing upon arrival in the Tabernacle. The Officiates were supposed to have blocked the road all the way to the Tabernacle so that the King's body would have privacy in its passage. Titus hoped so. He did not believe that the Isle needed any more misfortune.

The riders pulled up a few feet from the Auds. Monte dismounted. His clothes were mud-covered, and he had deep lines in his face. His skin was sallow and sunken against his bones. His hair fell lank and listless over his brow. He nodded to Gregor who turned to Titus in a silent correction. Monte nodded again. Titus returned the nod.

'Thank you, sir,' Titus said. 'We shall take over from here.'

'Any troubles on the ride back?' Simon asked, and Titus bit back a retort. Elder Eirman had stressed that the Danites not ask about the trip.

'None.' Monte sounded tired. 'The news hadn't spread yet. We met a crier on the road yesterday. He was the first.'

'We have no way to express our sorrow,' Simon said.

Gregor put a hand on his arm. 'Forgive him, sir. He took the death even harder than the rest of us.'

Monte's smile was wan. 'I'm sure,' he said, sounding completely unconvinced.

Titus clapped his hands for the Auds. They swarmed the horse, untying the ropes and tugging at the coffin. He approached it too. The horses around them snorted and stirred. They didn't like being so close to the dead.

The coffin was hastily built from inferior wood. A slight odor of decay rose from it. Titus shuddered. This was as close as he would get to King Alexander. The man was the same age as Titus's father, old, but too young to die. The criers hadn't explained the cause of death, but the rumor in the Tabernacle was that the King had been assassinated in the Marsh.

One of the Auds braced the coffin while the rest gripped its sides. As the ropes fell free, the horse backed away, nearly tripping one of the Auds. They grunted as the full weight landed in their arms. Then, in unison, they lifted the coffin to shoulder height. While they took a moment to brace it, Titus searched for Simon.

He had removed the pouch from his pocket, and was preparing himself for the solemn journey through Jahn. Gregor was standing beside Monte, as if providing silent comfort. Titus cleared his own throat. He had been in many processions, but never one as important as this. As a young Aud, he had braced coffins on his shoulders, and as a Danite, he had presided over many limestone funerals – so called because the deceased were so poor, they were unable to have a coffin. They would be wrapped in shrouds, placed in pits, and covered with limestone until the pit was full. Only then would it be covered with protective earth.

Titus hated those funerals. The smell was always ripe, and the Blessing was often lost in the wails of the family.

He wondered if anyone would wail for Alexander. Somehow, he doubted it.

The Auds were looking at him expectantly. Gregor had moved to his place behind the coffin. Simon was beside it, his pouch ready. They were all waiting for Titus.

He took his place in front of the coffin. With another nod to Monte, Titus began the ceremonial walk to the Tabernacle, moving slowly enough for the Auds to keep pace with him.

As they took their first few steps, the breeze carried the sharp scent of the burial herbs Simon was tossing on the coffin. The scent always overpowered the scent of death.

Gregor chanted just loud enough that any bypassers would hear the story of Alexander's life, and the hope for Alexander's future in the Arms of God.

And Titus, who would say the Blessing when the body was placed in the Sanctuary, prayed that God would forgive him for listening to the scholar blasphemer, the newest Rocaan, Matthias.

Eleven

She ran through the streets, her paws coated in springtime mud. Solanda would have loved to stop on nearby steps to clean herself, but she didn't dare. Not in the city. The lovely Islander King had made that impossible years before. Cats were suspect. Orange tabbies even more so. They were to be slaughtered on sight.

Part of that was her fault. She had two forms: feline and Fey. During the Fey's first year in Jahn, she had spied in her cat form, and had been seen. She had even transformed in front of one Islander, an elderly woman whose child Solanda stole. When the news of an evil Fey cat spread through the Isle, the King had ordered all cats killed. If it weren't for the Islanders' love for the animals, Solanda wouldn't be alive to spy for the bastard.

Rugar.

He should have known better than to send his only Shape-Shifter into the city to see if anything were different. But he had *faith* in Solanda; he *knew* she would survive. Hadn't she always in the past?

And just like before, she couldn't say no to him.

She had never been able to say no to him.

That was why she was on the Isle in the first place. Rugar, the handsome young Visionary who had saved her life when she was eighteen, and who asked for no repayment. Until he wanted to conquer an island all by himself.

She was following the river, snacking on fish, and drinking water from puddles. She could no longer rely on the Islanders to feed her when she was in cat form, and when she was in Fey form she was afraid they would attack her with poison. That threat kept her in Shadowlands more than she would have liked. Burden had asked her to become part of the Settlement in Jahn, but fear had kept her away. She had had too many nasty encounters with Islanders to live among them. She wasn't sure how Jewel managed.

Her whiskers smelled of fish. She found a dry spot beside the river to stop and clean them off. At dawn, she had stolen two fresh trout from a fisherman's boat and had hidden with them under the dock before he could see her. Fishermen had started carrying poison with them. The poison had no effect on real cats, but it would melt her. She had seen a number of her cousins, rail-thin, starving, pitiful, thanks to the Islander King's five-year-old decree. Too many times she found dead cats beside the road, their fur in clumps, their ribs poking through their skin.

Perhaps when she was free of Rugar's control, she would ask Jewel to change the decree. Jewel might actually be ruler of the Isle by fall. But Jewel might be able to make the change now. The bad King was dead, and, knowing Rugar, young Nicholas would soon follow him. Then, if Jewel wasn't able to control the Islanders, Rugar would bring out his prize: Jewel's real son, Gift.

Gift. Solanda paused in her washing to contemplate him. Magic crackled from him. When the Wisps had brought him to Shadowlands, she had half expected him to Shape-Shift before them all. But he was of the Black King's line, which meant he had Vision. When that Vision came, it would be powerful. She could feel it already.

Tiny pieces of fish had stuck to her whiskers and she got a second meal by cleaning them off. The sun had risen midway through the sky, but carried no real heat. A breeze blew off the river, adding a chill to the air. The river smelled of mud, fish, and its own particular combination of fetid growths. Much as she disliked getting wet, she loved the river, for it had provided many a meal for her since the decree.

Except for a mangy cat foraging through old bones near one of the warehouses, she was alone on this stretch of bank. She had already had her encounter with the mangy one. He was more concerned with his stomach than with her presence on his territory. She had left part of the second fish for him, and he had eaten it so fast that he had vomited it back up again.

The dead King had been particularly harsh in his decree. He could have limited it to orange cats, but he made it for all cats. He had had no idea the kind of suffering he had caused.

She resumed her bath, using the side of her right paw to clean her eyes and smooth the fur over her face. City cats often followed her, wondering where she got the meals that kept her coat shiny and her body sleek. Sometimes she had had to Shift to her Fey form just to scare them off.

She hated being in Jahn more than she hated the Shadowlands. And so far, she had seen nothing of interest to Rugar.

He had come back to Shadowlands filthy, his eyes glinting like a wild man's. He had found her late that afternoon, catnapping beside a fire in the Domicile, and demanded she Shift to Fey form before he talk to her. She had and he hadn't even noted her nakedness – something that always fascinated him before.

I'm sending you to Jahn, Solanda. I want their reaction. I want to know the mood of the city.

She had told him she wouldn't go, that the city was dangerous for her, and he hadn't even listened. He had told her to protect herself and to return as quickly as she could. Then he had sent her out without even telling her what the Islanders should have been reacting to.

It wasn't until she got to the center of Jahn when she heard the young boy give his formal speech about the King's death that she knew.

Rugar had murdered the King of the Islanders, and he wanted to know how the city was reacting.

He probably wanted to know how Jewel was reacting. But Solanda knew better than to approach the palace in either form. The last time she had gone to the kitchen door – her haven during and after the Battles for Jahn – and had barely escaped the poison with her life. She had only gone once in her Fey form, and she had never been subject to such insults in her life.

Fey were supposed to be stronger than threats. Fey were supposed to crush the peoples who dared taunt them.

For the first time in her life, Solanda understood how a mouse felt when it spent its afternoon in a cat's care. She kept waiting for the teeth in her neck, the sudden sharp shake that would end her life forever.

She hated the feeling. More than that, she hated subjecting herself to it. By asking her to come to Jahn, Rugar was placing her in the enemy's territory. The fact that she had not been spotted had more to do with luck than anything else. And someday her luck would end.

The river water lapped gently against the bank, slowly eroding her dry spot. Another cat was sauntering toward the mangy cat. Soon she would either get another following or find herself challenged to a fight. With a sigh, she got up and, using small shrubs as cover, ran for the road above the bank.

The other cats didn't follow her.

The city spread out before her, dingier than it had been before the First Battle for Jahn. The houses were no longer freshly painted, and some of the wooden ones had lost a board or two. The stone buildings looked the same, except that their front walks were no longer swept. Many of the stores and warehouses along the riverbank had closed.

Blue Isle no longer traded with countries on Galinas or Leut. Ships no longer came into the port. One of the busiest ports in the world now only catered to river boats and small fishing vessels. The Isle wasn't poor, but it no longer had the gleam of the very wealthy.

And Islanders didn't talk any more. She stood at the edge of the road, waiting to see if anyone would approach. In the past, she could find a friendly house, sleep by the fire for a few days, and listen to all the gossip. Now she had to keep to the shadows and hope that she would overhear words on the street.

Two small boys played outside a gray house near one of the abandoned warehouses. A woman hung wash on a line behind one of the stone homes. A man sat on a chair outside a nearby store, waiting, it seemed, for customers, any customer, to enter.

The news of the King's death had been greeted with silence. Solanda wondered what Rugar had expected. Wails of grief? Cheers of happiness? If so, he would be greatly disappointed. If anything happened at all it was that nothing had changed.

No one seemed to care.

Even she, one of the more cynical Fey, could not have predicted that.

'Look, Mommy!' one of the little boys called in Islander. 'A kitty!'

The mother gripped a shirt to her chest as she turned. Her face was filled with fright. She scanned the area until her gaze fell on Solanda. 'Stay away from it!' the mother called. She dropped the shirt and headed for the house.

For the poison.

The little boy was walking toward Solanda, his small companion reminding him that Mother had said to stay away. But Solanda had seen that look before on childish faces. The fascination, the lack of fear.

The determination to catch her tail and pull it.

She bounded off the road and headed back through the shrubs. The other cat, a scrawny black tom, leapt through an opening as she passed, hissing, spitting, and hitting. She hurried past him, hoping he heard the child behind them and knew enough to get out of the way.

When she reached the river bank, she glanced over her shoulder. The little boy was bracing himself on the mud, using one hand as balance as he scrambled down the small decline. His mother had emerged from the house, a vial of the Islanders' poison in her left hand.

'By the Powers!' Solanda snapped, not caring if anyone heard her speak Fey.

The tom who was chasing her stopped in puzzlement, having never heard a cat make such a noise before. She ran along the bank, careful to stay on the driest ground so that she would not leave tracks. She ran as fast as she could, knowing there was nothing faster than she was when she moved like this. Her sleek body was built for hunting and stealth, and she used it. The only problem was that she would not be able to keep this speed for very long.

Then a wall loomed in front of her. It was new, but poorly built, the supports toppling sideways, the wooden boards mismatched, leaving gaps in the sides. She had been here only once before, and then the wall had been partially finished.

The Settlement. They couldn't chase her in here.

She ran on a pile of stones that led out of the muck, glancing behind her once, and cursing when she noticed tiny wet cat prints on the surface. Nothing she could do right now. Nothing at all.

The tom appeared over the rise, the small boy behind him, and the woman yelling as she followed them both. Solanda chirruped at the tom, hoping he would understand and get out of the way, then she dove through the small hole in the wall.

She landed on a pile of slippery, rotted boards. Her paws skidded along the surface and she had to jump sideways. The boards toppled after her, landing on the wet ground with a large thump. Behind her, she could hear the woman yelling. The tom shoved his face in the hole, huffed at her as if disgusted by her choice, then pulled his head out. She wished him luck.

Three Fey were looking at her. She recognized two men as young Domestics. The other was Burden, a tool in his left hand, a board in his right. All three were thinner than Fey should be, their bones appearing prominently through their skin. The buildings were poorly constructed and water-damaged. The great hope of the Fey, Jewel's Vision of peace and harmony among the warring factions, reduced to this.

Solanda was glad for the first time to have Shadowlands.

The woman's voice echoed outside the wall. She was yelling at her child to stay away, then she said something about doing away with threats once and for all.

Solanda sighed, and Shifted.

Her body stretched, losing its comfortable feline form. The pull was almost erotic, the change subtle and great at the same time. Her front paws stretched into hands, her back into feet. Her back and legs lengthened, her ears moved, and her nose shrunk. Her whiskers disappeared, and for a moment – the crucial frightening moment of each Shift – she felt blind. Then her senses Shifted as well, and she found herself positioned awkwardly in the mud – hands and feet on the ground, backside in the air, head facing downward.

She immediately stood, wiped her hands on her bare legs, and faced her male colleagues. The Domestics had seen Shifts before, and sometimes helped the Shaman with the birth of Shape-Shifters, but Burden's magic was marginal. He had probably never seen this before.

His mouth was open, his eyes wide. He brought his chin up as if her change had not disturbed him, and that very movement told her that it had.

Solanda had to suppress a laugh. She knew the effect she made. She was so used to appearing naked in front of others that she was never uncomfortable. Instead, she preferred to see whom it affected, if it affected anyone at all. And young Burden was having trouble. Shifters were the most perfect Fey, physically and magically, and the physical was getting quite a reaction from him.

She tossed her tawny hair over her shoulder, and stood up straighter so that her breasts were prominent. Then she grinned. 'Does anyone have a towel?'

One of the Domestics nodded and disappeared into the nearest building. The other grinned with her. But Burden was still staring, his Adam's apple bobbing as he swallowed.

'Or do you think clothing would be more appropriate?' Solanda asked, unwilling to let this easy victim go. 'That woman did sound as if she were going to charge the gate.'

'You were running from an Islander?' Burden finally understood that Solanda was baiting him. His response had a bit of condescension in it, something Rugar had always hated about him.

'It is a prudent response when they are carrying the poison.' The mud had caked on her hands and legs. The human body had its disadvantages. She would love to crouch on a dry patch of ground and clean herself. But she had to wait for towels and water. She was still enough cat to shudder at the thought of a human bath.

That feeling would pass, of course, but not soon enough. That woman was going to come into the Settlement, and how to explain a naked Fey? Islanders probably never went naked, probably never even saw their mates unclothed.

She would have to ask Jewel the next time she saw her. Odd choices. Solanda had never, not in all her years of warfare, all of her traveling, ever considered mating with an enemy.

Although there had always been embarrassing moments when their toms had looked appealing.

It was a rule among Shifters to avoid change during estrus. Because of her involvement in Rugar's petty wars, she had sometimes been unable to follow that rule.

Burden was still staring at her. Time to take the offensive. 'What is the matter, Burden?' she asked. 'Never seen a naked woman before?'

'Not covered with mud,' he said. His voice was calm, but he glanced away.

'Then you've missed one of the more delightful experiences in life,' she said. The other Domestic came out of the building carrying two towels and a robe. She found herself suddenly grateful. The chill in the air had penetrated her unprotected skin. She never could understand why humans did not have fur.

The Domestic handed her the towels and Solanda wiped mud on them. She almost wiped off her feet, then realized that was a cat trap – she had often stood on three paws in mud, cleaning one paw, and then putting it back into the mud. Another embarrassing feline habit she would rather not think about.

She traded the dirty towels for the robe, and sighed as its warmth enveloped her. Burden watched her, and she thought she caught envy in his expression. She couldn't imagine being marginally magickal – to have the height and appearance of a proper Fey but to have talents so minor as to be unnoticeable. He was one step away from being a Red Cap – the small, squat caretakers of the dead who barely earned the name Fey by their Fey-like facial features. They had no magic, no beauty, and no grace. At least Burden had beauty and grace.

'I'd go to the gate,' she said. 'That woman will probably want in.'

'We usually don't allow Islanders here.'

Solanda snorted. So much for the great experiment. 'Frightened of them, Burden?' she asked.

'I'm not the one who came flying through a hole in the wall a moment ago.'

Solanda resisted the urge to examine her right hand. The cleaning instincts were not yet gone. Instead, she shrugged one shoulder. 'One does what one can to survive.'

'So you are frightened of them.'

The boy really didn't know when to quit. 'No,' she said. 'It is just that royal edict says cats must be slaughtered on sight. Last I heard, Fey could roam the city with impunity.'

'Burden!' someone called. 'We have company.'

Solanda raised her eyebrows. 'You really should listen to your elders.'

'You're not that much older than me,' Burden said.

'Child, I remember when your father was born.' She pulled the robe tighter and walked toward the gate herself. If he wasn't going to deal with this pesky Islander woman, she would.

The path was covered with mud, and she was relieved she hadn't spent the time to clean off her feet. The mud was cool but soothing. Her feet often ached after she made the Shift, partly because they weren't used to carrying all of her weight.

The other buildings that she passed were no better than the first ones. Some actually had holes in the walls stuffed with cloth. Burden may have had an idea, but an idea did not make him a Visionary.

100

Near the gate, the woman stood, surrounded by three Fey. Solanda knew them as Infantry, had often run between their feet on the way to a battle.

The woman was shorter than Solanda, but she had a solidity that Solanda had come to associate with Islander mothers. Childbirth took any slimness they may have had and replaced it with a stoutness that Islanders seemed to find comforting.

'Are you carrying poison?' Solanda asked in Islander.

The woman whirled her head in Solanda's direction. She had not seen Solanda approach. The woman's eyes were the blue of the sky on a sunny day, her nose small and pert, her hair almost yellow. 'It's holy water,' she said.

'Really, Solanda, she's our guest.' Burden said from behind her. He spoke Fey.

'Guest?' Solanda answered in the same language, but Burden had already moved past her. He wiped his hands dry on his pants legs. Then he extended a hand to the woman.

'Welcome,' he said in Islander. 'We don't often get visitors in the Settlement.'

The woman had to shift her vial of poison from one hand to the other. Solanda shuddered as the woman took Burden's hand, half ex-pecting him to start melting. But he didn't. The woman's other hand held the vial tightly.

'My name is Burden,' he said. 'I run the Settlement.'

'Magda,' the woman said.

'We don't have much by way of refreshments,' Burden said, 'but we can at least offer you a chair out of the mud.' He turned, as if to lead her away, but she let go of his hand.

'Actually,' she said, 'I came because I saw a cat run in here.'

'A cat?' Burden faced her again. Solanda pulled her robe even tighter. She felt her nakedness for the first time in years.

The woman nodded. Her eyes had that zealot's gleam that Solanda had seen too often. 'A golden one. The worst kind. It threatened my boy.'

'Oh, for –' Solanda began, but stopped when Burden held up his hand.

'Threatened?' he asked.

'You know they steal children, don't you?' the woman said, her voice low.

'No,' he said. 'I hadn't actually realized.'

Solanda rolled her eyes. She had heard that many times. She should have killed the old woman the day she took Coulter from her. Coulter was an Island child with a powerful magick. If the truth be told,

Solanda had rescued him. These pathetic creatures wouldn't know how to raise a magickal child.

Ever since, though, the rumor persisted that cats stole children.

'They do,' the woman said. 'They come in the middle of the night and steal the child away.'

'It's daylight,' Solanda said dryly. The woman glanced at her as if she had forgotten Solanda was there.

'Actually,' Burden said as if Solanda hadn't spoken at all, 'cats can't steal children. That's a story someone made up to scare people. Cats *spy* on unsuspecting people, and they are often quite cruel, but they never ever go after children.'

'Cruel,' Solanda muttered. He would pay for that remark.

'I heard it,' the woman said, 'from someone who knew.'

'Who, I'm sure, heard it from someone else who knew. But your King reacted badly to rumor, I'm afraid. Cats are God's creatures, like the rest of us.'

God's creatures? Solanda frowned. She had never heard a Fey use that expression. Nor had she ever heard a Fey compare himself to an Islander and get away with it.

The woman was actually listening to Burden.

Solanda crossed her arms over her chest, and leaned back on her heels. This bore some real attention.

'Yes,' the woman said. 'I suppose they are.'

'I'm sure the cat was just interested in seeing if you had any food.'

'It did look thin,' the woman said.

Solanda bit back a retort. Thin, indeed. She was prettier than any other cat roaming Jahn. Fine thick fur, a sleek healthy figure. The woman had no right to call her thin.

'And it probably wanted food. You can't blame it for that,' Burden said.

'No,' the woman said. 'I guess you can't.'

Burden smiled and patted the woman on the shoulder. She didn't flinch, nor did she raise her vial of poison. 'I suggest that maybe in the future, you might want to leave out some milk for the cats, and encourage your neighbors to do the same.'

'Milk gives cats diarrhea,' Solanda said, unable to keep silent any longer.

The woman looked at Solanda and blinked, as if waking. 'It would be breaking the law,' she said.

Burden's mouth formed a thin line, but by the time the woman had turned back to him, he had the same genial expression on his face. 'Some laws aren't right.'

'That's true,' the woman said. Then she smiled at Burden, and

Solanda thought she caught a bit of flirtatiousness in the look. 'I guess I should go back. My boy's outside.'

'Next time,' Burden said, 'maybe you can come in for a bit of warmth.'

'Maybe,' the woman said. She picked up her skirts, turned, and walked out of the gate. She held the vial loosely in her left hand. As she passed through, two of the other Fey closed the gate behind her.

Solanda waited until she could no longer see the woman before speaking. 'You really diffused that,' she said.

Burden shrugged. 'It's fairly easy if you talk to them.'

'I suppose it is,' Solanda said. 'We'll see if she leaves out ... milk.' Solanda shuddered a bit as she said the word. Milk always smelled wonderful and made her very sick.

Burden left the gate and started down the path. Solanda followed him.

'You know, that fire sounds pretty good right now.'

'Right now, I have to work,' he said. 'We don't have much daylight left.'

'Right now,' Solanda said as firmly as she could, 'you have to talk to me.'

He stopped walking and sighed visibly. He couldn't refuse her. Only Visionaries, Shamans, and occasionally Spell Warders had the right to countermand Shape-Shifters. 'I hope this won't take long,' he said.

She ignored his tone. She finally understood the reasons behind it. 'It won't,' she said. 'And you'll be grateful.'

'You're always so sure of yourself, aren't you?'

She grinned. 'Always.'

He shook his head, as if her confidence overwhelmed him. Then he veered off the path onto a mud trail that made her already cold feet even colder. She really shouldn't talk to him. It went against her nature, against Fey custom, against everything she knew. Custom dictated that when a person wasn't smart enough to discover a truth on his own, he didn't deserve to know it. But times were different. Burden was on his own here, without a Shaman or a Warder. Without even subtle guidance.

If he knew, he might be able to help the Fey.

Solanda had to weigh that fact against tradition.

The mud trail went past several cabins until it stopped in front of a small square one. This cabin was at least in good repair, but it was half the size of all the others.

'This is yours?' she asked.

'Did you expect me to be like Rugar?' He climbed the two steps leading to the door, and pushed the door open. The scent of ancient smoke fires rose from within.

She had expected him to be like Rugar. She had expected Burden to take the best cabin, the best site, and the best wood. He had done none of those things. The cabin was near the riverbank and probably got flooded each time the waters rose. The wood looked thin and worn. The floorboards creaked when she stepped on them.

'There's a mat,' he said. He was already kneeling in front of the fireplace, laying out the wood.

She wiped her feet on the mat, and noted that the bottom of the robe was covered with mud. She would track no matter what she did.

He struck the tinderbox, and instantly had a small flame. The wood was dry and lit quickly. Solanda held up the skirts of her robe so that they wouldn't drag on the floor. She stopped as close to the fire as she dared.

The heat felt wonderful against her legs and feet. She longed to have a soft place to curl up and rest. She hadn't slept warm in two days.

'So,' Burden said. 'What was this urgent thing you had to discuss?'

Solanda sighed softly. No nap. Not yet. 'Have you spoken to the Shaman?'

Burden was only standing a few feet from her, but at her question he moved farther away. He was on the other side of the windowless room, in the shadows. Apparently his powers were a touchy topic.

'I know I'm not a Visionary,' he said.

'Very few of us are,' she said. 'I'm not talking to you about the Settlement. I think your lack of Vision is clear. I'm talking about your magic.'

'Solanda, I've heard that feline Shifters were cruel, but I'm not prey. Really.'

That was the second time he had used that word, and she was trying to do him a favor. She drew herself up to her full height and let go of the robe. It fell loosely around her body, but did not open.

'If you're not prey,' she snapped, 'then why are you hiding in the dark?'

He wiped his hands against his pants, apparently a habit he had developed since he had come to live in the mud, and came closer to the fire. Here he looked impossibly young, his features softened by the flame. She hadn't been around for his birth and she didn't pay much attention to him until he became Jewel's closest companion in Infantry. But if he trained with Jewel, he had to be near Jewel's age – about twenty-three or so. Too young for this kind of work. Just as Jewel was. Way too young.

'Good,' Solanda said. 'I can see your face.' She licked her lips and realized she had not had anything to drink since she stopped at a puddle that morning. 'Now, grant me the courtesy of your polite attention.'

He nodded.

'I asked if you had seen the Shaman because I was wondering if she took the time to tell you about your powers.'

'I haven't see the Shaman since Jewel's wedding,' Burden said. 'And I haven't spoken to her since we left Nye.'

'I thought so.' Solanda pushed herself away from the fireplace. 'Have you water?'

Burden smiled. 'Too much.'

'In the house?'

He nodded, bent over, and produced an earthenware pitcher and mug. The water he poured for her was cool and fresh. The minor Domestics he had managed to snag had a few talents.

Solanda drank the entire mug's worth, then set it on the mantel of the fireplace. At least Burden had used stone for that. It appeared to be the only luxury in the place.

'So you have done no work on your magickal abilities?'

'It should be obvious,' he said, his tone sharp. Then he put a hand over his face. 'Sorry. I'm just not pleased with the way my life has gone.'

She almost commiserated with him. Almost. But she understood and he didn't. The key was to make him understand.

'Have you always insulted your betters?'

He brought his hand down. In the flickering light, he looked very young. 'I didn't mean to insult you.'

'I know,' she said. She would have to speak with caution. He was very defensive. 'I was asking the question seriously. Have your betters always heard your words as insults?'

He frowned as he considered. Almost unconsciously, he pulled over a stool and perched on it, his right foot hooked in the rungs, his left on the ground. 'Not before Shadowlands,' he said. 'In Shadowlands, I couldn't say a single thing Rugar wanted to hear. Or Jewel, toward the end.'

'And you didn't think it odd?' Solanda asked.

'I thought perhaps I was overstepping my bounds. But someone had to. Rugar didn't see clearly and Jewel was caught up in something else altogether –'

Solanda waved a hand to silence him. She didn't want to hear his justifications. They didn't matter.

'Yet other people listen to you,' she said. 'Others of lesser importance.'

'I don't think the people who've settled this place are of lesser importance,' he said.

That defensiveness made it difficult to speak to him. The Shaman had failed in her duties. She should have pulled this boy aside when he was in Shadowlands. Solanda would have a talking with her when she returned.

'According to Fey rankings, they are,' Solanda said. 'The highest magic you have here is a Weather Sprite.'

'Hanouk is talented.'

'Hanouk controls the clouds. If we were still in Nye with the Black King, she would never be invited to his home, let alone sup at his table.'

Burden brought his other foot up so that it too hung from a rail. The position made him look like a small child, huddling, awaiting punishment.

'But they all listen to you, don't they?' Solanda asked.

'All but Hanouk sometimes,' he said.

'Like that woman did today.'

He shook his head. 'She was easy. The Islanders are always easy, if you approach them right. Most people don't approach them right.'

'Most people can't Charm,' Solanda said.

He brought his head up so fast he had to put a hand on the stool seat to keep his balance. 'What?' he whispered.

'I can Charm, although I usually choose not to,' she said, ignoring him. 'It's easier in feline form, though, I have to admit. I don't have to say stupid things. But a pure Charmer, those are rare. I haven't seen one since we entered Nye. The skill is so very subtle that it's hard to recognize. But there are some tells.'

'Tells?' He was still whispering.

She nodded. 'The biggest is that Charmers anger those that aren't susceptible. You had no chance with Rugar. A Visionary will not listen to a Charmer. A Visionary has his own version of truth. The fact that Jewel wouldn't listen toward the end only confirms something I suspected – she started having Visions of her own here on the Isle. The Shaman, Enchanters, Spell Warders, and Shifters will never succumb to your talents. But Domestics, particularly inexperienced minor Domestics, Weather Sprites, Wisps, and most of the military will listen to anything you say. If that woman is any indication, Islanders are sheep.'

He licked his lower lip, then bit it. Finally he said, 'You mean I have magic?'

'My friend, you wouldn't look like you do if you didn't. And I would guess you came upon it somewhere in the middle of the Infrin

Sea, before we entered the mouth of the Cardidas. No one noticed in the battle, and once we got to Shadowlands, it became a problem rather than something to be diagnosed.'

'But there are no Charmers on the Isle,' he said. 'They're all in Nye.'

Solanda nodded. She understood the dilemma. She had been born in a war camp and had apparently Shifted the moment she hit air. If the Domestic tending her mother hadn't had experience with Shifters, Solanda would have died then. No one in her family had ever Shifted. No one in the camp had. For the first three years of her life, three very important years, Solanda had learned about Shifting alone.

'I think we'll need to take you back to Shadowlands, and let you talk to the Warders,' Solanda said.

'No,' Burden said. 'I belong here. Everyone depends on me.'

'They depend on you because you Charmed them,' Solanda said. The heat from the fire had gone all the way through her. It was all she could do to keep from asking Burden if he had a rug, and if she could curl up on it. 'If you left, they would realize that they're living in mud and broken-down buildings.'

'It gets better in the summer.'

And worse in the winter, she thought, but said nothing.

'Rugar doesn't want me back,' Burden said.

'Of course not,' Solanda said. 'Your power conflicts with his.'

Burden straightened his legs and got off the stool. He walked over to the fire and peered into it as if it had all the answers to his problems. 'You're not going to tell him, are you?'

'About you?' Solanda asked. 'Of course.'

'You are?' Burden's voice rose. 'You can't, Solanda.'

'I tell him everything. That's part of my job.'

'You're a Shifter. You're the best of the best.'

'I am still Fey,' she said softly. No matter who she was, she still had a debt. No one let a debt go free.

Burden suddenly looked at her, really looked at her, as if trying to peer into her soul. 'Why are you here?' he asked.

'Because a woman was chasing me with poison,' Solanda said.

'No,' Burden said. 'Outside Shadowlands.'

'To see what the reaction is to the King's death.'

He nodded. 'It's been amazingly quiet, hasn't it? If a Black King had been assassinated, there would be riots in the street.'

The thought sent a chill through Solanda. He was right, of course. The Fey never took the death of major leaders well. The Islanders were moving through this as if it were the norm. Rugar's Vision was failing him. If his intent had been to cause civil unrest, he had failed.

Then Burden gave her the appraising look again. 'How did you know about the King's death? The criers hit the streets this morning.'

Solanda didn't answer. It was not his place to know her duties.

Burden put a hand on the mantle as if bracing himself. 'Jewel was here yesterday. She said a Fey killed Alexander. It wasn't you, was it, Solanda?'

'Please,' she said in the most haughty tone she could manage.

'If not you,' Burden said slowly, 'and if it were Fey –'

'We were talking about taking you to Shadowlands,' Solanda said.

'– then it was Rugar, wasn't it?' Burden frowned. 'But Rugar would never hurt Jewel.'

'Who said the Islander King's death would hurt Jewel?' Solanda asked.

'Jewel did.'

Burden's words hung in the air. He rested his head against the mantle. The afternoon had clearly been too much for him. He would have a thousand questions, and by morning, a thousand more. Sleeping on his rug would be a very bad idea.

'Come back with me,' Solanda said. 'Let's talk to the Shaman.'

He shook his head. 'Bring the Shaman to the Settlement. We need a Visionary here.'

'You need to leave this place,' Solanda said. 'It's not healthy here.'

'It's no healthier in Shadowlands,' Burden said. 'No matter what you think of me, Rugar's worse. What was he thinking, killing their King?'

'Perhaps he wanted Jewel closer to the throne.'

'Perhaps,' Burden said. 'But Rugar's motives are rarely that simple.'

Solanda knew that quite well. It had been a fact she had been unwilling to think about. Rugar's complexity had gotten her into trouble more times than she cared remember. 'He does what's best for us,' she said.

'Yeah,' Burden said. 'Like coming to Blue Isle in the first place.'

Twelve

Three layers of Domestic-made clothing had not kept her warm. Jewel put her hands over her distended stomach, willing the baby to move. All this tension, all this turmoil, could not be good for the baby.

She moved closer to the fire. Nicholas was kneeling before it. He had been feeding logs into it, but he had stopped mid-movement. His eyes were glazed, and his lower lip was trembling.

Their bedroom was cold, as cold as the gravesite had been. The household staff had forgotten a fire in the King's room, and placed one in hers instead. Nicholas and Jewel had almost slept there, but Sebastian had whimpered in his sleep in the next room. The sound brought tears to Nicholas's eyes and, without saying a word, he had taken Jewel's hand and led her across the gallery and into his suite.

The King's suite now.

She slowly eased herself down beside her husband, placing a hand on his back. The muscles were stretched tight. He didn't move at her touch, not a flinch, not any kind of response at all.

'Nicky,' she said. 'I have something to tell you.'

He finished placing the log on the fire as if he had never stopped. Then he put the iron grill back in front of it. 'Let it wait, Jewel. I don't need more tonight.'

He was right. He didn't need more. He needed his sleep. The ceremony had been grueling. Jewel had skipped the ceremony in the Tabernacle, pleading fatigue, and had met them at the gravesite. She had come to that out of respect for Alexander and concern for Nicholas. His ability to function had decreased dramatically since the news. Sometimes he appeared to be sleeping with his eyes open. Other times, he seemed too bright, too energetic, as if his movements were all a sham.

'It's good news,' she said. 'Something you'll want to hear.'

He sat back and placed his head on her shoulder, his arm around her, his hand carefully resting on her spine. He rarely touched her belly, and never mentioned the child within her. When she had told him she was pregnant, he had looked at her and said, 'Are you sure that's wise?' Later, one of his men had asked her if the Fey had ways of

109

forgetting pregnancies ever happened. She always pretended that the query had not come from Nicholas.

'It's about the baby,' she said.

A shudder ran through him. 'Not tonight, Jewel,' he said.

'Nicky, she's kicking. She's healthy.'

He sighed. 'Sebastian kicked. He was healthy. All the healers said so.'

'The healers weren't Fey. They didn't know.'

'Please. Let's not talk tonight.'

'Quickly, Nicky. Let me tell you. I had a Vision.'

Nicholas took his hand off her back. He didn't move away from her, but his body tensed. 'Sometimes I don't believe in the magic, Jewel. All that talk about Sebastian being more powerful than any other Fey, it seemed like a special dream. I could never have magic, but my son could.' Nicholas's voice broke. 'He can't even smile at me.'

It had been a long time since Nicholas had visited Sebastian. 'He can smile now,' Jewel said.

Nicholas shrugged and sat up. The loss of his warmth made her chill greater. 'We buried my father today. Let me be a person tonight and not a head of state.'

Jewel took his hand, unwilling to let him get far from her. This closeness she felt with him always amazed her, as if somehow they were fated. Even when they didn't understand each other, the closeness was there, working between them like a subtle magic. 'I thought the good news would help.'

Nicholas shook his head. 'I stood in that glinting sunlight and watched them lower my father's casket into the ground. The Rocaan was saying his Blessing, and I was thinking that I was too young for this. I wasn't even thinking about my father, Jewel. I was thinking about all the burdens of statehood, about all the things we face, and how I'm not ready.'

She squeezed his hand. This she didn't understand. Her father was still alive, and she had never really known her mother. Jewel had broken relations with her father – she had found a separate path – but she still knew how to find him, how to talk with him, and even how to argue with him.

'I'll be beside you,' she said.

'Matthias thinks – God.' Nicholas put a hand over his mouth. His other hand, not the one Jewel was holding.

'Matthias thinks a Fey killed your father so that I could be closer to the throne.'

Nicholas looked at her, astonishment on his familiar features.

'I was there when he made that accusation,' she said gently. She was right. He wasn't paying attention to everything he should.

Nicholas brought his hand down slowly. His fingers were long and slender, Fey fingers on Islander hands. It always seemed odd to her that Sebastian's fingers were short and stubby when neither of his parents' were.

'No,' Nicholas said. 'Matthias came to me later. He said I should disavow you and ... Sebastian ... for the good of the country. He said the next child would be like the first and we would have no heirs. The Roca's line would die. He said you will probably try to kill me now so that you can control the country. He said I should choose an Islander wife.'

Jewel's mouth went dry. She knew that Matthias believed all these things, but she hadn't realized he would plead his case so strongly with Nicholas. She glanced around the room they shared, the big feather bed with its heavy Islander blankets and the single Fey quilt given her by Mend. The tapestries on the window depicted scenes from Kings' lives, and the stone walls were damp in the winter. The chairs weren't comfortable, and the food was often bad. If the servants thought she was going to be alone in a room, they did not light a fire for her in advance. And she never drank water, not even four years after moving to the palace.

She had made a hundred tiny sacrifices.

She had never thought about the ones that Nicholas had made.

The loss of respect. The trouble he would have securing his throne.

Sebastian.

The little boy broke her heart, but she saw him as a child. Nicholas saw him as an heir, as a disaster waiting.

Jewel lifted her hand, the one joined with Nicholas's, and placed it on her stomach. 'I had a clean Vision,' she said. 'As clear as if I had lived it. I saw a girl, a teenage girl, who looked like you if you had Fey coloring. She was here in the palace. She was watching someone move in the garden. She had bright eyes, Nicky, and each gesture, each step, showed a lively active intelligence.'

His fingers tightened on hers, raising his hand just above her stomach. 'A girl,' he said.

'A brilliant girl,' Jewel said.

'And you know it was this child?'

'Yes,' Jewel said. 'The Vision came when I was touching this spot. Always a sign of Seeing the child within.'

'A girl,' Nicholas said again, and Jewel understood finally what he was saying. She lowered his hand, then flattened it and felt its warmth on her skin.

111

'A child,' she said.

'Jewel, a girl can't rule.'

'If she's Fey, she can.' Jewel held his hand in place.

'But this is the Isle.'

'And we're supposed to be unifying two cultures.'

He sighed again and slid his hand off her. 'It won't work, can't you see that? That's what Matthias is talking about. People won't accept us or our children.'

The baby kicked as if she felt the anger Jewel did. The sharp sudden pain gave Jewel a moment to think of a reasoned response. 'You are the Roca's direct heir and Sebastian is your first child. You rule under Isle law. I am the Black King's granddaughter. When my father dies, I lead our people. And when I die, my son does. We have not worked toward acceptance. We have let men like Matthias and my father taint the public response to us. We do not let people see Sebastian, and they probably think he is some kind of freak.'

'He's not healthy, Jewel.'

'But his sister will be.'

'The second born cannot lead. It's written into our laws. And women – it's unthinkable.'

Jewel clenched her right fist, hiding it at her side. 'But you can set me aside?'

'It's been done only when the woman is barren.'

'And the Roca's descendants are notoriously fertile?' Jewel asked.

Nicholas nodded. 'Generation to generation, firstborn sons have led this kingdom.'

'Were daughters ever born first?'

'Not and lived,' Nicholas said softly.

This time the anger forced Jewel to move. She tried to push herself to her feet, but her bulk got in the way. Nicholas grabbed after her, put a hand behind her to brace her, and eased her down.

'I would never kill one of our children,' he said. 'Never.'

'But you would set me aside.' She gritted her teeth, then decided to speak anyway. 'It would start the war again.'

He took her chin between the thumb and forefinger of his free hand and turned her face toward his. His grip was light, his expression tender. 'I have seen you in battle, my demon wife. I don't ever want to cross swords with you again.'

She didn't laugh. She couldn't. The matter was too serious for that. But he pulled her face closer and kissed her so tenderly that the remaining anger eased out of her.

He paused between kisses. 'I would never set you aside. Ever.'

She put a hand on his chest to hold him back. 'But you considered it.'

'No,' Nicholas said softly. 'I never did. In fact, I told Matthias that if I die, he will have to serve under a Fey queen. I told him that he'd better get used to the idea. I'm not going to set you aside or Sebastian. We need to wait to see how he grows. If he can have children, he can be king. You can be his brains.'

'Or his sister can,' Jewel said.

'Or all the other little half-breeds we make.' Nicholas pulled her even closer, then looked down at her belly pressed against his. 'I hope she comes soon. I don't like this distance she puts between us.'

Jewel laughed despite herself. This was what she liked best about Nicholas. He always made her laugh. 'The more children we have, the more advice Sebastian will get.'

'Is that a proposition, dear wife?'

'I thought it was demon wife.'

'Sometimes it is.' Nicholas kissed her again, then caressed her cheek with the back of his hand. 'I will always stay beside you. Always.'

She nodded. She sensed a restlessness within him, though. He still had things to say to her. She leaned into his caress.

'But Matthias has a point. None of the Islanders will accept a Fey queen or Sebastian, not without help.'

Jewel nodded. She covered his hand with her own, then pulled it down again. This time he guided their hands to her stomach. The warmth was comforting. 'I went to the Fey Settlement yesterday,' she said. 'It's a disaster, Nicky. And none of my Fey help have stayed in the palace. Everyone has retreated to Shadowlands. The ones who haven't are living like filth in the Settlement.'

The baby kicked again. Nicholas looked at her in surprise. 'She is active.'

Jewel nodded.

He let go of her hand, and ran his palm over her belly as if he could trace the shape of his child. Then he put his ear against her. Jewel prayed that he would hear the child laughing with delight, as the old stories said active babies did in the womb.

'What were you doing in the Settlement?' he asked as if the question had no consequence.

But she had known him long enough to know these kinds of casually asked questions meant the most to him.

'I went to ask Burden if he had killed your father.'

Nicholas sat up. His face had gone white, but his hand remained on her stomach as if protecting the child inside. 'You believe Matthias, then.'

'I believe Matthias may have a point,' Jewel said.

The shadows under Nicholas's eyes were prominent. He hadn't

slept much since his father died, and when he had, he had pulled Jewel so close that his grip around her shoulders almost hurt.

'I thought it was a lone assassin.'

'A lone assassin who had that kind of success with one shot and who disappeared into nothing,' Jewel said. 'It sounds Fey to me. But Burden said I was imagining this. He may be right. If there is a shot as good as all that, I'm sure Lord Stowe will find him down in the Marshes.'

'You don't sound convinced.'

Jewel shook her head. 'It's too convenient. A King dying in the place where an assassination attempt had been made before. The assailant using one arrow and getting away across flat, marshy ground.'

'Why didn't you tell me before?' Nicholas asked.

'We haven't had much opportunity to talk in the last few days,' Jewel said.

'Did Burden kill him?' Nicholas's voice held fervor. His eyes had narrowed. He looked fierce, like her father rather than his.

'No,' she said. 'If you saw the Settlement, you would understand. They're working too hard to survive. They haven't time for schemes.'

'Then someone from Shadowlands, your father, maybe –'

'Nicholas.' Her tone was purposely stern. She didn't want to lose him on this tangent. 'We don't know.'

He closed his eyes, and tilted his head back. 'You're right.' He let out a long breath of air. 'Jewel, I'm too volatile right now. I'm not thinking clearly. I need to be thinking clearly.'

'You're doing fine,' she said, although she would have preferred cold Fey rationality at this point. She didn't even dare tell him that she would help him. He might hear it wrong, think that Matthias truly was right.

The new Rocaan. Her father had made a lot of mistakes in killing the old Rocaan. The worst was that the death had forced this new man into power, a man with a hatred for the Fey so deep that he discovered and promoted the use of holy water as a poison. She and Nicholas would have made more progress on unifying the Isle if Matthias hadn't been in the way.

When she had approached Nicholas with this plan, almost five years ago now, she had thought that if it didn't work, she would take over the palace with the help of the other Fey. The Black King, if he ever arrived, would accept her children and they would all rule the Isle. It was a slower method to accomplish the same end.

But her desire to take over the Isle had lessened with time and the goal she had verbally expressed to Nicholas – that of unifying Fey and Islander – had become more important to her. The Islanders lacked magic, but they had something, a kind of strength, a resilience, that the Fey had lost. She no longer wanted war with her husband's people. She actually believed that both groups could find a kind of parity.

She also believed that, after all this time, the Black King was never going to come. Her grandfather would die in Nye as he had said he would. He would go down in Fey history as the man who conquered the Galinas continent. When he finally died – and it might be decades from now since some Fey Visionaries lived a long time – one of her brothers would take his place. Then and only then would the Black King venture forth again.

By that time, she would be a grandmother, and her children would be part of the Isle.

Even though Sebastian was flawed, he had forced her to think with that long-term perspective. Sebastian and the child in her belly. When her brother arrived, Jewel wanted to have the Isle a Fey stronghold, but one with powerful magic, one that kept the Islander customs intact according to Fey tradition, and one that required no more bloodshed.

Perhaps she should have been a Shaman. Her Vision was much more Domestic than a Black King's relative's should have been.

'If it was your father, wouldn't you have been able to See it?' Nicholas asked.

No matter how many times she explained, he still didn't understand the concept of Vision. She took a deep breath, using the moment to consider. She didn't want to tell him about the pain she had felt in her heart. She suspected that pain had arrived the moment his father had died – because her father had killed him. The Black King's family was not supposed to murder other members or horrible tragedy would occur. She didn't know if two men related by the marriage of their children counted in that superstition.

'No, Nicholas,' she said quietly. 'I wouldn't necessarily have been able to see it. The Visions are random.'

'Then how do you know about the baby? How do you know that isn't some other woman you're Seeing?'

'Because of what I was doing at the time,' Jewel said. 'I can't explain any better than that. If a Fey killed your father, I will be as surprised as you are. I have no special Vision for that event. I have no Vision for your death either or mine, but we will both die someday.'

Nicholas shook his head. 'Let's pray Lord Stowe finds the assassin. Let's pray it's some crazed, deranged Islander with a vendetta against the Kingship. Let's pray that the killer isn't Fey.'

Jewel didn't know how to pray. But she would ask the Powers for any kind of help they could provide. She had taken a great risk tying her fate to Nicholas's. She didn't want one of her own people destroying that future, not when the child within was finally giving her the opportunity for success.

She put a hand over her heart. The physical pain was long gone, but a new feeling had lodged in its place.

Fear.

Thirteen

The man who led the group looked as if he had risen from the Marsh itself. Lord Stowe followed the group, his personal guards close to him. Half a dozen men from Kenniland surrounded them, their faces weatherworn and purposeful. The Danite had elected to stay behind.

Because the men didn't have horses, the group had had to walk. Lord Stowe realized quickly how used he was to riding. The man who led them – Hector – walked at a fast clip. The fishermen usually used boats, but the hunters walked or slogged, which seemed a better word, through the Marshes proper. Because Stowe was with them, they took the road.

The spring days were fickle. The sun was out, but thin. The air had a chill it hadn't had on the day the King died. The Marsh smelled of mud and decay, a fetid odor that clung to clothes. The village had it as well, but not as strong. Here the odor was a live thing, more powerful than anything around it.

A long-legged bird stood in the Marsh, dipping its bill into the water. It seemed unconcerned by the group of men passing near it. Another bird cawed overhead, but Stowe did not look up. He had long since learned to do as the other men did, for anything else marked him as unusual.

The flat glare of the sun made the Marsh appear as if it extended forever. Since mid-morning, he had been staring at the small group of trees, the one which the guards had searched for the lone assassin. They had found nothing. The group had stopped for its midday meal, and the trees had looked no closer. It was now mid-afternoon, and they were finally approaching the spot where the King had died.

The road looked no different here. Even the blood stain was gone, soaked into the dust. The Marshes were drying from lack of rain while Jahn's winter had been full of water. The differences in climate were one symptom of the problems he had been hearing about. The palace had always governed as if the Isle were one small city with the same problems and the same kinds of people. But not even the weather was the same. And as for the people, Stowe was beginning to think he understood the Fey better than he would ever understand these folks.

117

They stopped at a point directly across from the trees. Even here, the trees seemed both close and far away. Stowe's life in the city had left him ill-prepared to judge distances.

'Time to put them boots to use,' Hector said, pointing at Stowe's feet.

Stowe nodded. He had expected this when the group had insisted on giving him boots that morning. The boots were slightly big, and had rubbed a blister into the bottom of his left foot. But they ran to his thighs and, with luck, would be more than deep enough to keep the mud off his legs.

After the meeting in the kirk, Stowe had investigated a hundred different possibilities. He had examined the homes of the people who had shown up at the meeting and found more poverty than he cared to think about. Only one family had even owned a bow and arrow. The others fished to get food, if they were able to get their own food at all. He also discovered a strong anti-Jahn bias, and an even stronger hatred of the palace. He started taking his own guards everywhere, uncertain what would happen to him in this depressing and hostile place.

Finally, days after the meeting, Hector had come to him. Awakened him, actually, in the Danite's small hut near the kirk. Hector was an imposing presence at any time of day. To someone newly awakened, Hector seemed like a creature from beyond. He was broad and square. His clothing was covered in mud so old that most of it would never come off. His boots appeared to be part of his body. His features were so caked that his skin was invisible. The whites of his large eyes were startling against the black mud, and when he spoke, his remaining teeth were a sickly yellow.

He hadn't introduced himself. Instead, he said, 'If tis answers ye want, tis answers I got.'

Somehow that sentence had led Stowe to this place of death.

One of his guards looked at him. 'I'll go for you, sir.'

Stowe shook his head. He owed Alexander this much. Besides, if he didn't go, he would never be able to explain to Nicholas what had happened.

'Where are we going?' he asked Hector.

'Yonder,' Hector said, nodding in the general direction of the tree.

'The trees?'

Hector tilted his mud-covered face toward Stowe. The man's bizarre eyes appraised him as if he had never seen anything quite that stupid before. 'Anything else ye see?'

'We already checked out the trees,' another guard said. 'There's nothing there.'

'Not ta city men, maybe,' Hector said.

He stepped off the path and instantly sunk to his calves. The marshy water made a large sucking sound. The hair on the back of Stowe's neck rose.

'Ye coming?' Hector asked.

'Of course,' Stowe said. He wished he could close his eyes and pray as he stepped off the firm dirt of the path. Instead, he took a deep breath and stepped down beside Hector.

The Marsh gripped Stowe's boots. He was heavier than Hector and sank to his knees. 'This will be slow going,' Stowe said, hoping for a light tone.

'If'n ye keep acting like a city man,' Hector said.

Stowe bit back a reply. He was a city man, had been all his life. He would like to see Hector try to get a meal in Jahn. But he merely said, as mildly as he could, 'You'll need to tell me what I'm doing wrong.'

'Ye go the way yer supposed,' Hector said.

'I've never been here before.' Stowe's boots had turned cold. The chill in the air almost felt warm compared to the temperature of the water.

'Sure looks like it,' Hector said.

'I mean,' Stowe said, 'I need your help.'

'Ye keep behind me,' Hector said. 'That road ain't the only rise in the Marsh.'

From that cryptic remark, Stowe gathered that there was a less visible path that led to the trees. Hector offered his big, filthy hand, and Stowe took it without hesitation, letting the other man pull him onto the rise behind him. Even though he was still in to his calves, the ground beneath him felt solid.

'Go slow,' Hector said. 'Ye try fast, and ye'll fall. Then there'll be nothing of ye.'

No wonder the villagers had looked at Stowe with a kind of shock when he asked whether one of them had killed Alexander. Given the site, and the impossibility of travel, he should have seen the killer.

'What's so important about the trees?' he asked, not sure if he wanted to plow that distance through calf-deep mud.

'Want to know who killed yer man?'

Your man. Never the King. Or if it was, the name was spoken with hatred. Stowe wasn't quite certain how Alexander had let it get like this. Although he suspected Alexander had little to do with it. Alexander had inherited the problem, just as Nicholas had, just as Nicholas's pathetic little son would.

Hector stomped through the marsh, lifting one foot and placing it heavily before doing so with the second. The manner of walking was stylized and odd. It did, however, keep him from losing his balance or getting stuck. The mucky water made squishy sounds as he hurried across the rise.

Stowe tried to keep pace as he followed, but his legs ached almost instantly. He wished now he had let the guard go in his place. Aside from the dangers of assassination which he and the guards had already discussed, the amount of work crossing this marsh was more than Stowe was used to. He almost hoped for Hector to take some sort of hostile action so that the trip would end.

Although he knew that Hector would leave him alone. Hector could have killed him that morning. The Danite was gone, and the guards were not near the kirk, thinking it protected. If the villagers had wanted Stowe dead, he would have died days ago.

The long-legged bird watched them cross, then plunged its beak back into the marsh. It brought its head up, a small fish wriggling in its beak. It swallowed the fish head first, a bit at a time, until only the tail remained, wriggling as it went.

Stowe had to keep his hands outstretched for balance. The water was black here, the grass a dark green. Things swam around his legs, and more than once something he couldn't identify bumped into him. Hector didn't seem to notice at all. He was almost to the trees. Stowe still had nearly half the distance to cross.

There were four trees. Three were spindly, with thin crooked trunks and stubby branches. Only one tree was big enough to hold a man. It towered over the others, its branches as thick as a man. The leaves were full and cast a shadow on the water.

When he reached the tree, Hector leaned against its trunk. He crossed his arms and waited. He looked like a clump of mud himself. A mud statue, that was it, something made by man but not of man. Stowe shook his head. The whimsy was a result of the events of the last few days. If he didn't laugh, he would cry, and he didn't dare do that. Not until this mystery was solved.

Although he wasn't entirely sure why he needed to solve it immediately. No one from the Marshes would attack Nicholas. Nicholas would remain in Jahn and learn to rule. The villagers only seemed to attack a King when he arrived in the Marshes. If Nicholas stayed away from the southern part of the Isle, he would be safe.

But in the last five years, nothing had been that simple. Stowe knew that if he did not solve this now, he would make up worse scenarios than the one that had already happened. A mud man, like Hector, had shot an arrow into the King, then disappeared into the Marsh. Sure the ground was flat, but Hector seemed to blend in. Stowe doubted that, from the road, the guards could see anything more than a mud blob against the tree.

Stowe wanted to call the case solved, but couldn't. Hector had something to show him, something less subtle than his own body camouflaged against the swamp.

Tiny black bugs rose from the water and swarmed around Stowe's face. He brushed at them with his hands, but it did no good. A few entered as he breathed and he coughed them out, stopping as he did so. More bugs tangled in his hair and bumped against his skin.

'Keep moving. You opened a nest. Leave them.' Hector's tone had that superiority again.

Stowe walked forward, waving his arms like a madman. Hector was right; the bugs started fading away almost instantly. When Stowe looked back, he saw the swarm swirling like a black cloud over that small patch of Marsh.

His home with its seven fireplaces, soft beds, and overstuffed furniture had never seemed more inviting. His back ached from the rough pallet in the Danite's cabin. His legs hurt from the strain of slogging through the marsh. And he still had the bitter taste of black bug on his tongue.

Finally he reached the spot where Hector waited for him. To Stowe's surprise, Hector grinned. 'Ye done that better than most who grew up here.'

'They don't know their way through the Marsh?'

'Not on foot. Takes a special skill.' Hector grabbed the nearest branch and held it. A clump of mud fell off his hand and splashed near their boots.

'What do you want to show me?'

Hector's grin faded. 'I come here after they told me what ye said. Them men of yers, they say they think some of us done this. Yer man, he wasn't well liked here, but we been waiting for him, hoping to get him to change things.'

'I gathered that from the meeting,' Stowe said. The chill in his feet ran through his entire body. He felt rooted in the mud.

'I thought, not many men can shoot so true, and even fewer can hide in the Marsh. Takes a special skill.'

And a willingness to cover oneself in layers of mud. Stowe bit his lip to keep the comment back. He knew better than to alienate Hector this far from the guards.

'So I thought to look around, and I come here.'

'You had no one in mind who could have done this?' Stowe asked.

'Oh, I had someone in mind,' Hector said. 'But I know I didna do it.'

The arrogance again. Stowe almost liked it. 'Is there anyone else who could have done this?'

'Not here.' Hector raised his other arm and swung himself into the tree. Bits of mud flew from his boots and hit Stowe in the face.

Not here. Stowe had already seemed stupid today. Another question wouldn't hurt. 'Do you mean no one else in the Marshes could have done this or –'

'Someone done it.' Hector's voice sounded muffled in the tree top. 'But it weren't any of us. Come see.'

Stowe looked around. There was nothing to step on, no ladder to help him, not even a stone to boost him a little. Hector did not reach a hand down to pull him up. Stowe had never levered himself into a tree, not even as a boy.

'I don't think I can pull myself up like you can,' Stowe said.

'Then climb like a girl.' Hector's tone was reasonable, but his words made no sense. Suddenly his face appeared through the thick green leaves. 'Face tree. Grab trunk. Climb. Swing a leg over like you do on horses.'

It sounded simple. Stowe grabbed the tree branch, his hands sliding in the mud that Hector had left. Stowe laced his fingers together, then pulled one booted foot out of the muck. He braced the foot on the tree. Cold water ran down his boot and onto his pants leg. He brought his other foot up, and climbed, childlike, until his right foot neared the branch.

Hector's hand appeared suddenly, grabbed Stowe's ankle, and yanked his leg over the branch. Stowe cried out despite himself. His hands slipped and pain shot through his right palm. But Hector had given him momentum, and he was able to swing the rest of the way onto the branch itself.

The whole tree shook with his weight. The leaves rustled. No one could have hidden here successfully. Then he realized that Hector had gotten into the tree without making a sound.

Hector sat on a thicker branch to Stowe's left. Hector's boots were braced on Stowe's branch. 'Now look,' Hector said. 'Ye can see how he works.'

Hector pointed to a small hole in the leaves. Stowe leaned forward. The leaves had been pulled away. A few had started to grow back.

He peered through the hole, and got an excellent view of his guards milling on the road. None of them were watching the tree. Not that it mattered, he supposed. They could never have rescued him from this distance across that marsh. But he wanted them to watch all the same. He would talk with them when he got back.

'Shoot through here, nothing moves,' Hector said. 'One arrow, if yer good.'

'He was good,' Stowe said. Too bad, too. If the arrow had gone awry, Alexander might have had a chance.

'He was here long time too.' Hector leaned away from the trunk to show Stowe some scrapes on the bark. 'Maybe hours, maybe days.'

Days, in this precarious place. Stowe felt dizzy just sitting there. The wood dug into his back and buttocks. The air was cooler up here, and the water had made its way inside his boots.

'He was determined, then.'

Hector nodded. They were both thinking the same thing. This was not a crime of passion. No villager woke up one morning and decided to kill the King. This was a planned assassination, done by a patient and deliberate man. Who knew how long it would take for a person to locate the exact spot on the road, pluck the right amount of leaves and then settle to wait on the only nearby tree.

'I still don't know how he escaped,' Stowe said. 'The guards ran out here right away.'

'Not right away,' Hector said. 'They couldn't run in that water. Ye had boots, and it took time. He coulda hid in the water. Hollow a reed, put it in his mouth, breathe through it. City men wouldna see him.'

Stowe was about to deny that, but he didn't. If Hector had crawled under the surface of the water, he would be invisible. It was a good plan, but it didn't feel right. Too risky for a man who would sit days in a tree.

'But I think something else,' Hector said.

Stowe gazed over at him. Hector looked natural here. The mud blended with the tree bark. Even the whites of his eyes reflected the silver lights flickering through the leaves above their heads. Hector, a creature of the Marsh, as alien from Stowe as the Fey.

The lights struck Stowe as odd. He had never seen lights that flickered in a perfect circle before. If he had had time, he would see if the man had tried to pull leaves from the branches higher up.

'This man rooting through the Marsh,' Hector said. 'Nearly killed a crane. I splashed, scared the crane. We don't kill them, ye know.'

Stowe didn't know. He wasn't even certain what a crane was. But he nodded anyway.

'The man, he wasn't from here. Too tall. We got no one that tall.'

'Did you get a good look at him?'

Hector shook his head. 'He was as far from me as the road. But he didn't know customs. And he was thin. Normal thin, not like someone who ain't eaten.'

'Could you see his skin? Was it dark?'

Hector held out his arms, and gazed down at them as if they would provide the answer. 'No darker'n mine.'

Stowe frowned. For a moment, he had thought Hector was describing a Fey. Then he looked at Hector's arms, covered in mud. The deep, dark brown of the Kenniland Marshes. Islander skin wasn't that color. Islander skin would reflect like sunlight off water.

'Like your skin now?'

'Ain't no one with good sense gonna spend time in the Marsh without covering his skin.'

Stowe took that as a yes. Tall, thin, dark. Not knowing the customs. 'Carrying a bow?'

'Had the arrow lined and the crane in his sights. Fine shot, that man.'

'You think he killed the King?'

Hector shrugged. 'Seems right.'

'Do you know where he is now?'

'If I was him, I'd be long gone. Ye gave him time, ye know. If he hid. Ye all come to the village like something's on your tail, and all of ye come. No one stays by the Marsh. No one watches to see if someone comes out of hiding.'

Stowe heard the tone again. City people. City people who were too stupid to know better. But they were panicked and frightened, and Stowe, at least, had been hoping that someone in the village would tell him he was wrong, that Alexander wasn't dead, that Alexander had merely fainted from pain.

No one had told him that.

And he had let the killer get away.

So far.

'You didn't see the man leave or where he was going, did you?'

'He was farther north,' Hector said. 'The palace says the Marshes start here, but they really start north a ways.'

'When was this?'

'Day or so after ye hit the village. I wouldn'ta thought nothing of it if it weren't for that crane.'

North. Toward Jahn. A Fey had come down to the Marshes to murder the king. A perfect murder. It would look like disgruntled peasants. Alexander had been wrong. Even with Jewel in the palace, the Fey would never give up.

But to murder Alexander. Where would it get them?

It would get Jewel closer to power.

Which meant Nicholas was in danger.

A sense of urgency Stowe hadn't felt before filled him. All this time he had wasted. The palace didn't know, and it would take him days to get back there. Days, even if he sent his swiftest messenger ahead.

He was trembling. 'Anything else unusual about the man? Anything at all?'

Hector closed his eyes and frowned. A piece of mud flaked off his forehead and fell on the collar of his shirt. He didn't seem to notice.

Then he opened his eyes, but his stare seemed far away. 'His hair,' Hector said finally. 'I ain't never seen hair like that on a person. It was black as a cat's and it run to his shoulders. First I thought it was mud, but if a man had mud in his hair it wouldn't blow with the breeze.'

That it wouldn't. Stowe didn't need any more. He had all the evidence he needed.

A Fey had murdered Alexander.

Nicholas was next.

The war wasn't over.

The second round of fighting had just begun.

THE CORONATION
[One Day Later]

Fourteen

Charissa's arms ached. She was polishing the silver railings behind the huge dais. The light from the two-story window had faded, and someone had lit torches around the room. One of the butlers had left for candles so that each work area would be illuminated.

Three days to clean the Coronation Hall. Three days to make it spotless. Didn't the gentry know that sometimes what they asked was impossible?

The Master of the House had agreed without conferring with the Master of the Halls. He had been appalled. No one had used the Coronation Hall in centuries. Coronations were held at the Tabernacle – had been for every King except a run of Constantines five hundred years before. Constantine the First had built this section of the palace, and he had tried to wrest control from the Rocaan, even, some said, tried to have the Rocaan killed, although Charissa thought that part a story. One of the chambermaids had told Charissa the entire history of the Hall as they were polishing the brass rails near the door.

That had seemed like months ago, even though it had been a day. The entire palace staff – except for the kitchen staff – had focused on preparing this room, and it would still be a close call to have it done by noon the following day. No one had looked in the hall in years. It had been taken off the cleaning roster when the dead King had been a baby, maybe before.

The Coronation Hall made the Great Hall seem tiny. The chambermaid, whose name was Lis, had told Charissa that the Great Hall had been built first, centuries before this part of the palace, and that you could tell in the way the room was put together. Finally Charissa had asked Lis how she knew so much, and Lis had smiled. Lis didn't work in the palace. She worked for Lord Enford, and his wife taught the servants to read, and actually let them have time in the library. Lis had found a liking for history, especially history of buildings, and had learned everything she could about them.

But Lis had moved to a different part of the Hall that afternoon, and Charissa had lost her companion. The woman who worked beside her now was elderly. She had come from Lord Miller's estate where they frowned on talking at all. Charissa had thought all places were the same, but she soon discovered that she preferred working in the palace to places with rules like Lord Miller's. Lord Enford's estate sounded frightening in its opportunities. What would a woman do who could read and who knew history? It did little for Lis. She had to leave her family and let them continue to farm.

Charissa sighed and sat back on her heels. She hadn't realized until she moved that her knees hurt too. The woman beside her kept stopping and putting pressure on the small of her back. Charissa at least didn't have to worry about that. She was young, and she was sturdy. She had to be. She had worked for days straight with only a few hours sleep a night.

The Master of the Hall let everyone have a bit of sleep. He said it made them fresher, more able to see and attack the dirt. Charissa wasn't certain. She always felt more tired after those naps, as if the time away allowed her body to assess its aches and pains.

She rubbed her neck and glanced around. Men hung from scaffolding, cleaning the arches, and shining the windows. Women huddled on the floor, polishing the gold, silver, and brass that covered everything. Washerwomen had scrubbed the large floor each day, and had finally gotten the grit off of it. They were still scrubbing, and would until the butlers supervised the tables. That, someone had said, would be around dawn. Charissa hoped to be in her room by then.

The Hall did look better than it had. When she had first seen it, she thought the cleaning task impossible. Spiderwebs hung from the arches like gossamer sheets, and the dust was so thick that inches of it covered everything. The great miraculous two-story window was hidden under layers of dirt and grime, and the seats on the second-floor balconies were broken and rotted. When the Master of the Hall had shown the chambermaids the areas to begin polishing, Charissa had thought he was joking. The tarnish was so thick and black it looked as if it had been burned on.

Now the Hall gleamed. Even under the torchlight, the brass rails sparkled. The silver around the base of the window revealed its etchings. The floor was an expensive marble, imported from Nye, and the arches were white stone. When the Master of the House placed the red runner along the center of the floor, and leading up the stairs to the coronation platform, the Hall would be perfect.

Even so, the details weren't done. Whoever had designed this hall had never thought of the people who had to clean it. Tiny bits of silver and gold, small curves under the arches, rotted wood supports beside the stairs. Detail after detail after detail. It seemed that the group got one large thing done only to discover a hundred smaller problems underneath.

'Group Five! Food!'

Charissa looked up. She was in Group Five. The Master of the House stood in the double arched doors, his hands on his hips, surveying the work. He had been the one to issue the food call. He supervised nights, while the Master of the Hall had taken days. The system was supposed to give at least one of them sleep, but it hadn't worked that way. Neither of them had rested since the work began and they looked it. Everyone would have looked that way if one of the butlers hadn't suggested the numbering systems – marking the workers off into ten groups – and having the groups rotate.

She tucked her polishing cloth in the pocket of her large apron, and stood slowly. She had learned on the first long day that rising too fast could hurt. This time she was glad she rose slowly. Her right ankle had gone to sleep.

She braced her weight on her left leg. The elderly woman paused long enough to say sourly, 'It'll be a long time to Group Eight.'

Charissa almost volunteered to let the woman take her place in Five, but the comment seemed designed for that kind of response. Charissa said nothing at all.

The tingling in her ankle had stopped. Group members from all over the hall were getting off scaffolding, setting down cleaning equipment, brushing dust off aprons. Members of Group Four were filing back in. They still looked tired, but the food had refreshed them somehow. Charissa's mother used to say that food was sleep, and Charissa hadn't known the truth of that statement until this project.

She wiped off her skirts, and walked down the steps. Young Prince Nicholas – the King now – would walk up those steps in the afternoon, looking slender and strong and handsome. He had never forgotten her. All those things that had happened to him, all the people he had met, all the servants he had seen, and he still smiled at her when he saw her and greeted her by name. They had only had one conversation years ago, when she had told him about a strange cat that talked Fey and about the changes in an old Master of the House. But the Prince remembered that conversation. Sometimes she would dream that instead of taking her hand on that afternoon so long ago, he had reached over and kissed her. Then she would be queen now instead of that ugly Fey woman.

Dreams, dreams. Charissa's mother used to say that dreaming would only bring her sadness. Chambermaids never became Queen. Queens came from other countries – Nicholas's mother had come from

Nye – or from the peerage, like King Alexander's beloved second wife. Not in all the history of Blue Isle had a chambermaid become Queen.

Charissa knew. Lis had told her.

Charissa was almost to the arched doorway. The walk was a long one. It took her twice as long to cross this Hall as it did the Great Hall. The Master of the House was frowning at her. He waved his hand impatiently, as if by moving the air he could move her. She bowed her head and hurried past him.

She had little to complain about with this Master of the House. He treated her well, unlike the man before him, the man she had talked to the Prince about. That Master of the House had made her do things to keep her job, things the Prince said she would never have to do again. If she ever had the problem with anyone in the House, she was to come to him. She half-wished the new Master had tried something so that she would have had an excuse to see the Prince.

The corridor was warm compared to the Hall. The Hall would never be warm. There were no fireplaces. It wasn't even worth the try.

Voices whispered behind her, and she braced herself. She recognized the tone of the whisper. A person couldn't work in the palace since she was eleven without knowing that sound. Someone important was coming.

She let out a small sigh. This visit would probably delay her dinner. And she hadn't eaten since midday.

She turned, grabbing her skirts in preparation to courtesy and froze in mid-movement. Nicholas. Young Prince Nicholas. Nicholas, the next King.

He was slender with broad shoulders made broader by the jerkin he wore. His clothing had evolved since he married – he had stopped wearing open blouses and started wearing the tight jerkins of the Fey. He wore tight brown breeches that disappeared into his boots, and Charissa had to force herself to keep from looking at the bulge between his legs. His face had narrowed – he appeared to be eating less – and he had deep shadows under his eyes. His long blond hair was loose and curled around his shoulders. Instead of softening his appearance, the hair strengthened it.

The Master of the House hurried to Prince Nicholas's side, and bowed. The others bowed as well, and stood when the Master stood. Charissa had been too stunned to move. The Prince – the King – noted her, and smiled.

She smiled back.

The Master glanced at her, then moved between her and the King. Nicholas.

'Tis welcome ye are, Sire.'

Nicholas nodded. 'I came to see how the preparations are going.'

The double arched doors stood open. The work inside had stopped. 'I will na lie to ye, Sire, tis been a hard few days.'

'That it has,' Nicholas said softly.

'But we'll have it for ye, we will.'

The others had moved on, anxious to be away from the new King. The old King had been volatile when work wasn't getting done. Everyone expected the new King to be the same way. Charissa had tried to tell them otherwise, but no one listened to her. She cleaned the west wing, they said, but had no real interaction with the royal family.

'Good,' Nicholas said, but he sounded as if he didn't really care. His whole being slumped forward as though he were having difficulty standing upright. The Fey woman should have tended to him, but the Fey knew nothing of nurture.

'Been polishing and working since we got the word, Sire,' the Master said. 'Ye'd na a believed this place, what with all the –'

'Tis sure I am his Highness dinna wanna know how much dust grows in the dark,' Charissa said. The Master shot her a horrified look, but Nicholas smiled.

'Charissa,' he said.

Charissa took a few steps forward and curtsied as best she could. 'Tis good ta see ye, Sire.'

'And you,' he said.

She kept her head bent, her gaze on his booted feet. They walked around the Master's foppish shoes and stopped in front of her. The new King's touch on her chin was light. He raised her slowly until she faced him.

It had been years since she had been this close to him. He smelled of leather and the potpourri the housekeeper insisted line the closets. Grief had taken a toll on his face. There were lines near his eyes she had never seen before.

'Ye look tired,' she said.

His thumb traced her jawline and then he let his hand drop. 'Sometimes, Charissa, I think I'll never sleep again.'

That Fey woman. No one could sleep with something that angular and dangerous in their bed. 'I – we – was all sorry bout yer da.'

'My da.' Nicholas's smile softened. Behind him, the Master was shaking his head furiously. Charissa decided to ignore him. 'Yes. I'm sorry about my da, too.'

'But tomorrow, tis important for ye.'

He tucked a strand of hair behind her ear. 'They never tell you that important days often come because of sad ones.'

'Charissa!' the Master said. 'Ye got ta get to the kitchens.'

133

'Let her be,' Nicholas said without turning. 'I'll make sure she comes back when she is supposed to.'

Of course he wouldn't, but it wouldn't matter. He was King now. No one could yell at him.

The Master put his hands on his hips. He looked as if he were about to yell again. Nicholas glanced at him.

'Go back to your work,' Nicholas said. 'I'm sure one small girl won't make the difference between a clean hall and a dirty one tomorrow.'

'Aye, Sire.' The Master shot Charissa one more angry glance and then walked into the hall.

The corridor was empty except for the two of them. Nicholas stayed close to her, so close she could feel the warmth of his body. 'He's not treating you like the last Master did, is he?'

'Tis a good man, he is,' she said.

'You'd tell me if he was treating you badly?'

'Aye,' she said. She felt bold, leaving off his title, but she did so in her mind as well. He didn't seem to notice.

The silence stretched long between them. No one came into the corridor. It was as if the rest of the staff were hiding from him. Finally, he said, 'Where were you off to before I came?'

'Tis supper for Group Five.'

'Group Five?'

'They're feeding us and making us sleep on shifts. Beg pardon, Highness, but twas a lot of work in that hall.'

'I imagine,' he said, but that I-don't-care tone was back in his voice. 'Well, let me join you.'

She ran a hand through her hair. 'Ah, Sire, ye wouldna like the food. Tis just bread and cheese.'

'I've had bread and cheese before,' he said.

'But twould be in the kitchen.'

'I was eating in the kitchen on the day of the Invasion.' His eyes had a faraway look. 'Actually in the pantry, just after dawn.'

'Why?'

'Because,' he said, and then he looked at her, really looked at her. The faraway look left his eyes and she knew he wasn't going to say what he had originally planned. 'Because sometimes I liked to hear kitchen gossip.'

'There'd be none a that tonight. Just whining. The work n all.'

'Yes,' he said. 'The week has been hard for all of us.'

Then she understood all he had been saying. He lost his da. His da. The man who raised him. And everywhere people were congratulating him, and making it easier for him to be King. When she lost her da,

134

she had cried for days. She didn't have to have a ceremony or make decisions.

That Fey woman probably didn't understand. Twas said they had no heart, those Fey.

'Ye poor thing,' she said, taking his hand. 'Here I am prattlin on about silly things and yer havin a gloom night. Come ta the kitchen. Tis sure I am they'll make ye feel like one a us.'

'And put me to work?' His smile seemed real for the first time since she saw him.

'A little good scrubbing never hurt no one.' She dragged him with her, and he let her, catching up to her in two strides. Her fingers were entwined with his, and he didn't let go. His hands were soft except for a few calluses in the middle of his fingers. Certainly not the hands of a man who spent his days polishing silver.

Most days, only the household servants ate in the kitchens. The rest ate in the servants' wing or near their own quarters. For the past few nights, however, the cook had set up extra tables in the main section of the kitchen, near the stairs, and worked almost continuously to keep the staff fed.

The kitchen was Charissa's favorite room in the palace. It was large, with a vented ceiling, and always smelled of food. The hearth fire burned continuously and the stoves were often warm. The last few nights, the kitchen had been an oven itself, especially in comparison with the Coronation Hall.

As they walked through the pantry into the kitchen, Nicholas dropped her hand. They still entered side-by-side, a Queen and her consort, knight and maiden, King and wench.

She didn't like the last. She wished it weren't true. Maybe, on this night, it wouldn't be.

'Lor, tis his Highness,' someone said, and everyone in the room bowed.

The cook on duty was one Charissa had not seen before, but the twenty people spread over the tables were her friends from Group Five. Lis was with them. She had her head bowed, but she was watching Charissa from the corner of her eyes. Lis probably remembered the question Charissa had asked about chambermaids and Kings.

'Please,' Nicholas said. 'Please go back to what you were doing. I don't want to be King tonight.'

Heads came back up, but no one ate. They all seemed to be waiting, to see what Nicholas would do next.

'Tis hungry His Highness is,' Charissa said.

'Let me just have what you're having.' Nicholas slipped into a chair, then pulled one out for Charissa. He sat at a table with Lis, one of the window washers, and one of the scullery maids. Charissa sat beside him.

The cook brought him a plate heaping with cheese, sausages, and freshly baked bread. One of the chamberlains brought a glass of mead.

Nicholas grinned at the cook. 'You've always done this to me,' he said. 'I said I wanted what everyone else was having. That didn't mean all of their food. Just the same portions.'

For a moment, Charissa held her breath before she realized that he was joking. The cook seemed to know it. He smiled.

'I canna treat ye like that, Sire, and ye know it. Ye been tryin this since ye was wee, and it dunna work.'

Nicholas moved the food off his plate onto the plates of those around him. 'Maybe after tomorrow I'll order you to treat me like everyone else when I come into the kitchen to share a meal.'

'Twould be hard ta do, Sire,' the cook said. 'Still and I'd have ta be talking to the chef and all. They'd be thinking I dinna respect ye.'

'Well,' Nicholas said. 'At least someone respects me.'

Charissa frowned. Everyone respected him. At least, everyone she knew. Although they did question his choice of a wife. And they all knew about his son. God's punishment for sleeping with a woman who was evil.

Nicholas's plate was nearly empty. He had left one slice of bread, three slices of cheese, and one piece of sausage. The rest had gone to the others. Charissa hadn't had sausage since she left home. She placed hers on the bread and bit into it eagerly.

'Sides,' the cook said. 'If I dinna feed you right, no one else'd get extra. And the girl, she needs it.'

Nicholas gazed at her fondly. Charissa suddenly wished she hadn't taken such a big bite from her sandwich. 'No,' he said. 'She looks good just as she is.'

She set the sandwich down and resisted the urge to wipe her mouth. Her hands were shaking. She clasped them and held them in her lap. It was her time now. That Fey woman had treated him wrong, had not shown him enough sympathy, had not helped him with the death of his father. He had come looking for Charissa. He needed her.

Lis kicked her under the table, and Charissa started. She glanced at Lis who mouthed, 'Thank him.'

A heat built in Charissa's face. 'Thank ye, Highness,' she said, although she wasn't certain if she felt grateful, honored, or blessed.

The pastry chef came up from the pantry carrying empty trays. He stopped when he saw Nicholas. 'Again, Sire?'

Nicholas shrugged. 'I have had a lot to think about.'

Charissa watched them, not understanding.

136

'When me wife died,' the pastry chef said, 'I dinna sleep for half a year.'

'The same happened to me mum,' the cook said. 'She dinna sleep either and when she did, the dreams made her wake.'

'Tis said Fey can grab a man by the face and make evil dreams,' said one of the washerwomen. Then she went ashen. 'Beg pardon, Sire. I dinna mean harm.'

Charissa felt her shoulders tense. Now he would yell at her. He would yell at them all.

'No harm taken,' Nicholas said. 'My wife says that's true. She says the Fey who can do that are called Dream Riders. Sometimes the dreams they give are good, sometimes bad.'

'Canna she help ye dream?' the cook asked.

'Of course she can,' Nicholas said. His grin had broadened to a leer. 'Just like your wife can.'

The men in the room laughed. Charissa didn't like the warmth in his voice when he spoke of that Fey woman.

'Sire,' the pastry chef said. 'There's women present.'

'Fortunately for us,' Nicholas said. He piled the cheese on his bread, and ate quickly. Then he took his cup of mead and cradled it. 'Someone want the rest? I can't eat any more.'

After a moment, Lis took the sausage. Charissa finished her own sandwich, listening to the banter continue around her. The kitchen staff knew Nicholas, and knew him well. When she had met him all those years ago, he had been in the kitchen with the remains of a meal before him. He must have been coming to the kitchens for comfort and sustenance long before she ever had a conversation with him.

Charissa had just finished her sandwich when the chef glanced at the hourglass. The sand had almost worked to the bottom.

'Ye'd all best be finishing. Group Six is coming.'

He didn't have to speak twice. Chairs slid back, dishes got stacked, and the last of the mead finished. Nicholas was the first to stand.

'I'd best be getting back myself,' he said. He thanked the kitchen staff, then he turned to Charissa and took her hand. He bowed over it. 'Thank you for the dinner invitation. I suspect this night will be the highlight of my week.'

Her cheeks grew warmer. Everyone was staring at her. She almost pulled her hand away, but couldn't. Nor after this public good-bye could she find time alone with him outside the kitchen.

'Yer too kind, Sire. Tis me who should be thanking ye.'

He let go of her hand, stood, and waved. Then he disappeared through the pantry. She couldn't follow him. She didn't dare. Besides, he had made it clear that he wanted to go alone.

'Wouldna wanna be him now,' said the cook.

'Tis thankless. And him always hopin ta be like the resta us.' The pastry chef set his tray down on the counter near the ovens. He wiped the sweat off his forehead with the back of his hand.

Charissa cradled the hand he touched with her other hand. Her skin tingled. 'Why na?' she asked. 'He's King now.'

'Tis na something he wanted.'

'The boy liked fightin,' someone else said.

'We'd be dead if'n na for him,' said one of the women who tended the hearth. 'He helped Cook and the others fight in here.'

'In the kitchen?' Charissa had heard that Nicholas fought. She always imagined it something glamorous, in the streets, perhaps, but not here.

'That woman, his wife, she near ta killed him right where ye are now,' the cook said to Charissa.

'She near ta killed him?'

'Aye,' the cook said. 'They met sword ta sword. Even match, even then.'

Charissa shuddered. 'Tis no great wonder then why he canna be with her.'

'Be with her? Girl, dinna be so sure a yerself. The boy loves her, he does.' The cook said. 'Methinks tis his curse.'

'Loves her? But tis said twas done ta stop a war.' Charissa had always believed him reluctant.

'Her idea. An his. Both das said twas wrong. But they dunnit anyway. And ta see the looks they have for the other. Tis love. Always was something.' The pastry chef opened one of the brick oven doors. The heat in the room rose.

'Group Six,' someone said.

'Aye, and tis trouble we'll be in if'n we're not back soon,' said Lis. 'Let's go, Charissa.'

She nodded. She wasn't sure she wanted to hear more of this conversation, not after feeling his soft touch on her hand. She wanted to dream about him. Maybe, now that he was King, he would come to her more often.

Lis paced her as they left the kitchen. They dropped back from the others and Lis took her arm. 'He doesna see more than a pretty wench when he looks at ye.'

Charissa shook her arm free. 'He talked ta me before. He says he will guard me. Tis a promise years old, and still he mentions it. Na me.'

'A promise to a serving maid. He's King, Charissa.'

Charissa straightened her shoulders. 'He always liked me.'

'And always will. Ye'll never be more than an afternoon's fancy.'

'Ye do na know him. Ye work for Enford.'

'I know enough,' Lis said. 'Ye asked me history. History built that ugly Hall we clean, and history rules him like he rules us. He canna do more than tumble with ye. Ta do more is ta deny history.'

Charissa bit back her first response. Lis was trying to help. 'We ha na tumbled. Tis a friendship, na more.'

'Good,' Lis said. She lowered her voice to a whisper. 'Cause all he'll give ye is a babe. And I dunna wanna be near his wife when she learns ye gave him a bastard. The woman has killed fer less.'

'She'll na kill me,' Charissa said. 'He'll see to that.'

'I hope yer right,' Lis said.

Fifteen

The stables were clean, and smelled of horses and fresh hay. Tel took a deep breath. The stalls were empty, waiting. The King's – the former King's – prized stallions were in the other stable near the servants' quarters. Tel had done most of the work himself. Two of the other grooms had been taken indoors to help with the cleaning of the Coronation Hall. Tapio, who had become head groomsman after everyone learned of Miruts's death, had worked as hard as Tel to make the stables and the yard clean for the Coronation guests.

The day had dawned clear and beautiful. The sunlight sparkled on the raindrops scattered from the night before. The rain had been a light one, leaving the ground damp, but not muddy. Tel and Tapio had been able to move the stallions without worrying about grooming them again.

Tel had volunteered to stay with the stallions, but Tapio wouldn't hear of it. Tel had become Tapio's most valued assistant, a liability on a day like this.

Tel swept the last bit of hay away from the stable doors, then propped them open. Soon the sun would reach its midway mark, and the guests would start arriving for the ceremony. Tel wanted to be gone when they did.

He had thought of disappearing altogether, but he had come back to the stable because he loved it here. Here he could deal with horses and not think about his life. Most of the time, he even forgot he was Fey. He got up at dawn, tended the horses, and went to bed long after sunset. The job didn't leave time for thinking, and he liked that. He looked like an Islander, but he wasn't.

He was a Doppelgänger, a special tool in war. Doppelgängers used the blood of a kill to absorb the life force out of a victim and to, in essence, become that victim. They absorbed the victim's memories, the victim's culture, and the victim's appearance. Tel had been a groom before, but years ago had been ordered to learn the secrets of Rocaanism. He had become an Elder in the Tabernacle, and had been present on that horrible day the old Rocaan died. His fellow Doppelgänger, the one who had overtaken the old Rocaan, had melted in a long-drawn-out way. Only Tel's appearance, and his luck, prevented him from dying that day.

That had been the last straw. He didn't want to return to Shadowlands where he would be ordered to go back to the Tabernacle. So he came back to the stable, where he had been happy, and absorbed another groom. He had lived here, as an Islander, ever since.

If the Fey discovered that he still lived, his punishment would be unspeakable.

Tel didn't want the Fey to catch him, nor did he want to change again. His last change had been particularly horrible. He had snuck onto the palace grounds, still looking like the Elder. Then he had killed a servant, bathed in his blood, and grabbed a young groomsman. The groom screamed as Tel leaped on him like a spider, wrapping his legs around the man's torso to hold his position, his elbows into the man's neck to brace his arms. Tel stuck his fingers in the groom's eyes and his thumbs in the groom's mouth, prying the teeth open and pushing hard against the back of the throat.

Then he pulled and pulled and pulled until the man's essence broke free and fluttered between them for a moment like a frightened child. Tel bit into the mist and sucked it inside, feeling rather than hearing the man's screams. Then he felt his body mold and twist and expand until it became the body of the groom, slender, square, and Islander.

The body between his legs and arms vanished, and he nearly lost his balance before remembering to put his own feet on the ground. The bones clattered to the ground. He sat on a bale of hay as his personality melded with the groom's.

Images mixed in his mind, memories not his own. In those last moments, Ejil – the groom – had thought Tel a demon, come to steal his soul. He had not been far off.

Tel had been weak when he took over Ejil, and he felt a bond with the boy he had never felt with any of his previous victims. Sometimes Tel woke at night, apologizing as if Ejil were there. Tel owed Ejil a lot. He had lived Ejil's life for nearly five years, and they had been the best five years Tel had ever had.

But now he had to be careful on two fronts. Last night, Tapio had told him that the Rocaanists would come early. Then Tapio had told him that Jewel's family would be coming. The Rocaanists could kill Tel by accidentally brushing him with their poison. The Fey could spot Tel – any Doppelgänger – by looking closely at his eyes. Transformed Doppelgängers look like their hosts, except for the gold flecks in the pupils. Those were the only distinctively Fey markings left, and all that was needed.

If the Fey caught him, it would be worse than the instant death he would suffer from the holy water. If the Fey caught him, the Shaman would speak his punishment. Tel had seen a Doppelgänger punished for abandoning his duties just once. The Doppelgänger was forced to go through a dozen Nye prisoners, changing into one after another in rapid succession until his own being broke under the strain. Then he was whisked away by the Spell Warders to be used in their strange and secretive experiments.

No one ever heard from him again.

Tel would rather live out the rest of his life as a short, square, blond Islander groom with no prospects than ever be Fey again. He had had enough. Perhaps if he had stayed on Nye, had been able to pick a body he liked, as some of the older Doppelgängers did, and remain in it for decades, he would have been content. But here, if Rugar knew he was alive, he would be changing bodies every few months, always ahead of the Islanders, always dodging their poison.

As a groom, he had none of those concerns. He rarely saw the religious, and he could choose whether or not to go to the Sacraments. He had found his own way to live the life of a Doppelgänger in peacetime. Denying his Fey heritage wasn't as hard as he thought.

'Ejil.' Tapio emerged from the stable. His short hair had a piece of hay in it, and a black streak marred his light skin. He was younger than most of the grooms by a considerable ways, but he had been Miruts's, the King's, and the Prince's favorite. He was also the best man for the job. 'Twill be soon before they come. We need ta change.'

'Twould be nice if the others was here. Tis the Fey I dinna wanna see.'

Tapio nodded. 'Ye think any of us do? If I let ye go, I let all go. And I canna. Besides, if we can serve the Princess, we can serve her da.'

'The Queen,' Tel said, correcting him. The thought of Jewel being Fey among these people had always intrigued him. When she came to the stables, he watched her from a distance. She always seemed so sure of herself, even though things weren't going exactly as she had planned.

'Right.' Tapio shook his head. 'We get one of them as Queen now.'

Tel almost grinned. Tapio would be surprised that his best friend and best groom was 'one of them.' 'Still, someone has ta be with the stallions.'

'The stallions are alone each night. A day will na hurt em.'

They had had this same argument earlier. No matter how many times Tel tried, Tapio always had an answer for him. 'All right,' Tel said. 'You change. By then the others will be here, and I'll go.'

'Be back on time,' Tapio said. 'I need me best man with strange horses.' Then he walked toward the servants quarters. Orders had come from the House that all grooms were to wear their best clothes, and to polish their leather boots. Tel and Tapio had polished their boots the night before, trading stories and rubbing to get each scratch and nick off the material.

The other grooms had already returned from the palace, but they still had to get their clothing in order. Tel had never seen such fuss. The Fey did not have a ritual for transition of power. The Black King died, and his firstborn took over. It was that simple.

And that complex.

If the firstborn was nowhere near the Black King, the honor went to the secondborn. When the firstborn returned, the secondborn was expected to stand aside. The Black family could not kill each other without causing huge ruptures in the magic. But what was good in theory rarely happened in practice. More than one Black King had *ordered* a member of his family killed. One Black Queen had ignored the edicts and slaughtered her entire family. That action had nearly destroyed the Fey.

Jewel's brother Bridge was probably already preparing himself to take the Black King's place. Fey tradition held that the firstborn took the Black Throne, but Fey history showed that the nearest child always found a way to rule. It would take a miracle for Jewel or Rugar to be at the Black King's side when he died. That left Jewel's brothers, boys who had been little more than babies when the ships sailed all those years ago.

Tel plucked a piece of straw and used it to pick at his teeth. There were disadvantages to these bodies. The teeth actually deteriorated, and aging was not a pleasant prospect. Most Doppelgängers aged by choice, picking a body and staying with it. Tel could find someone younger, but then he would have to learn a new job and find a new place in this strange world.

Guards shouted to each other across the courtyard. Tel glanced at the sun. It was closer to midday. In a few hours, the afternoon would be by, and he would be able to go about his business. All he had to do was be cautious now.

The gate came up on the palace's east wall, and in rode six Danites, followed by five of the ten Elders, and the Rocaan himself. Tel had been an Elder and had been at the meeting when the old Rocaan had announced the name of his replacement. Matthias had not been a popular choice.

But no one could tell it today. Matthias looked regal in his flowing red ceremonial robes. Tiny filigree swords hung from his black sash and another silver sword hung from his neck. His biretta rose from his curls, making his height seem even more unusual. His cheeks were flushed, his blue eyes sparkling. Tel had seen that expression before. Not when the Rocaan had chosen Matthias – Matthias had not wanted the position – but some other time, an older time, in a memory Tel had stolen, a memory not his own.

He would reflect on it later. He was the one who had to deal with the Rocaanists' horses.

His throat was dry.

Behind the Rocaan came several more Danites and two Officiates. Tel had never seen Officiates travel together before. They had probably come to make certain the Rocaan performed the ceremony correctly, that the exact holy pieces were in place.

Two of the other grooms appeared. One was still tying his white blouse. They glanced at Tel, obviously expecting him to approach the Rocaanists.

He had no other choice.

He licked his lips. They were chapped. He hadn't noticed that before. It was as if the dryness from his throat had moved outward. His heart was pounding, his breath coming in small gasps. He had survived days in the Tabernacle, as an Elder, near that poison constantly. He could survive moments near the new Rocaan.

The Rocaan dismounted, followed by the Elders, Officiates, and Danites. Everything was rank and tradition with these people. No room for innovation, no room for spontaneity. Such things normally protected Tel. This time, they trapped him.

His job was to approach the Rocaan first.

The Rocaan, the man who had discovered the evil properties of holy water. The man who would be carrying some now because he was going to Bless a new King.

Tel approached the group, making his way toward the center, toward the most magnificent horse. He bowed his head, hoping his fears didn't show. If the Rocaan were paying attention, the Rocaan would Bless him.

And Tel would melt onto the courtyard, a bubbling mass of flesh, unable to see, to breathe, to survive.

He held out his hand. To his surprise, it wasn't trembling.

The Rocaan slapped his reins in it. Tel let out his breath. Of course. He was too lowly to warrant attention. The fact that both the King and Prince had done so reflected their personalities, not local customs.

He had forgotten that.

'Is there a problem, groom?' Elder Porciluna asked.

Tel had never liked him. Pompous, overbearing, more concerned with the wealth the church could bring him than the status of anyone's soul. Those prejudices had belonged to the Elder Tel had been, but Tel still shared them. The more he knew about the Tabernacle, the more he understood how men like Porciluna defiled it.

'No problem,' Tel said, keeping his gaze averted. It was wrong to call attention to himself. He pulled the stallion forward. He pranced beside Tel, a powerful, delicate piece of horseflesh.

'You'll have a care with that horse,' one of the Danites said. 'It is the sire of the King's.'

Tel knew that. He knew the pedigree of every horse in Jahn. He led it to the stables as the other groomsmen came forward to take the Elders' and Officiates' horses. There was even a ritual order for horses to be stalled.

He focused on his duties; they kept him from concentrating on the religious Islanders behind him, and their danger to him. One quick movement while he had his back turned, a sprinkle of seemingly harmless water, and he would be dead.

Dead.

He reached the stable, and tried not to sigh with relief. Tapio had come from his quarters, his blouse brilliantly white, his fawn breeches creased and tucked into his shiny brown boots. He looked important. He winked at Tel as he passed, then went and gathered the lead Danite horses.

Tel used that moment to take the Rocaan's mount into the stable. He led the horse to the big stall in the back, the one normally used for Ebony, the King's stallion. The Rocaan's stallion went inside without a problem. Tel closed the door before the stallion and leaned on it.

He should have realized that the Rocaan would be first to arrive. He was conducting the ceremony after all. In some ways, he was the most important man there.

Tel had made it through. He would survive the afternoon.

And he would be careful to be gone when the Rocaan left.

Tel passed the groom leading the Elders' horses as he slid out of the stable. Another groom had appeared, and was leading the rest of the horses inside. The Rocaan and his people hadn't left the courtyard. They appeared to be checking their pouches. Several vials of poison glinted in the sun. Tel stopped near the stable door.

Something was odd. They were checking to make certain they had enough poison. That was something they should have dealt with before they left the Tabernacle.

'There it is,' one of the Officiates said. He pulled a small white cloth from his pouch. 'Exactly where you asked me to put it, Holy Sir.'

'Good,' the Rocaan said.

The Officiate put the cloth back into the pouch, and the Danites placed three vials of poison on top of it. Then the Officiate sealed the pouch and tied it to his waist with his sash. All the others replaced their own pouches as well.

Tel was glad that he was staying in the stable with the horses. He had had too many close calls with poison to ever want to get near it again.

Tapio boarded the other horses, then came and stood beside Tel. 'Tis quite the troop, eh?'

'I dinna realize they needed half the church ta make a King.'

''Tis na ta make a King. Tis ta get the Roca's approval.'

And what would they do for the King's son, had anyone thought of that? The day Nicholas died, who would think that the Roca could approve a half-Fey child?

It wasn't Tel's problem. Except for moments like this one, he was no longer Fey. He was Islander and determined to stay that way.

'We dinna have room for many more horses,' Tel said.

''Tis na a concern,' Tapio said. 'The Lords have a processional, and the Fey dinna have em.'

The Fey didn't need them. But Tel didn't say that either. Instead he watched the Rocaanists follow the path that led to the far side of the palace. No going through the kitchen for them.

'Come on,' Tapio said. ''Tis time ta tend horses.'

Tel sighed. The ordeal was over.

For now.

Sixteen

Nicholas's robes were on. His hair was combed and awaiting the crown. The filigree sword around his neck seemed foreign to him. He hadn't worn one since he met Jewel. She had looked at it as if it were anathema, then smiled faintly at him.

'It won't be for long,' he had promised her, and then he had left the room. Her maid was just going in, to put the finishing touches on Jewel's hair.

Finishing touches on most women could take hours. With Jewel, they only took a few moments.

Still, he wanted to be alone. He walked to the top of the stairs, then gazed down the gallery. The chairs leaning against the wall were not comfortable – he had tried to sit in them as a boy, before he learned that they were merely there for decoration – and the portraits themselves were not inviting. The men all had the same face, aged differently and buried in different clothing styles. The women were round and blonde.

Except Jewel.

Matthias hated her portrait, but Nicholas loved it. He walked over to it and stopped beneath it. The artist had captured her spirit, her fire, the fierceness that made her Jewel. If anything happened to Nicholas, she would be able to defend herself, and their children, and survive.

Pity the children weren't worth defending.

The thought made him freeze. If she had known he thought that, she would drag him into Sebastian's rooms even more often. Sebastian. He had seemed so bright-eyed and eager when he was born. Nicholas had never seen a newborn baby with such alert features. He watched everything, and everyone. The nurse said that new borns never tracked as if they could see. It took time for them to learn to control their vision.

Not Sebastian.

Then after the naming, the tracking ceased. He stopped fussing, stopped crying, didn't seem to recognize Jewel or the nurse as he had before. Nicholas hadn't let Matthias Bless the boy with holy water, but sometimes he wondered if Matthias hadn't snuck into the nursery during the night and done something.

The child seemed wholly different after he was named than he had when he was born.

Names have to have meaning, Nicholas. They are the secret to power.

He had insisted on naming the boy Sebastian. There was an order for naming in Nicholas's line, and Nicholas's first born had to be a Sebastian. Nicholas had lied to Jewel, claiming that previous Sebastians had been great warriors. In truth, they had been nothing more than mediocre kings.

For all his knowing talk in the kitchen the night before, he still did not know or understand Fey. When Jewel had tried to explain her Vision to him, she had radiated a kind of joy. She believed that her Vision showed that they would have a daughter, and the daughter would be what she had promised about their children.

She had never had a Vision about Sebastian. After it had become clear that Sebastian would never be like other children, she had confessed she believed that to be the reason she hadn't Seen him. She should have ended the pregnancy there.

The thought of ending a pregnancy had shocked Nicholas then. He understood it now. He didn't want another child like Sebastian. What he hadn't admitted to anyone was that he saw this second baby as a test. If this child were also deformed, he and Jewel would stop having children altogether.

If the Fey had ways of ending a pregnancy, they probably had ways of preventing one.

Then he would deal with the dynastic concerns on his own. His father had had only one child. Nicholas would have two, but those two might not be the right two.

The portrait of Jewel looked fuzzy. He blinked, wiped his eyes, and the edges cleared. Perhaps Lord Stowe had been right that day so long ago, the day that Nicholas had agreed to Jewel's offer of marriage. Perhaps he had been agreed because he lusted after her. But lust didn't feel like this. He felt lust for that serving girl – just touching her aroused him. But he knew that if he slept with her, the lust would fade, and he would be disgusted with himself.

What he felt for Jewel had never faded. It had become richer, despite the troubles. He valued all of his time with her, not just the sexual time. And whenever anyone spoke against Jewel, Nicholas defended her.

She had been well named. He treasured her above all else.

She would be waiting for him. The entire Kingdom would be waiting for him.

He turned and walked back toward her suite. Outside the nursery, he paused. No sounds came from it at all. He had visited many nurseries of the peerage, and they were never quiet unless the child slept. Babies laughed and cried. Children yelled, screamed and talked constantly.

Sebastian rarely talked. He never cried. And he only smiled for Jewel.

Nicholas pushed the door open. Heat billowed out of the room. Jewel always kept it too hot. The nurse was sitting beside the fire, stitching a tapestry. Sebastian sat on his rug, surrounded by blocks. He held one in his hand and stared at it.

Nicholas slipped inside and closed the door behind him. Sebastian didn't turn at the sound, but the nurse did. She smiled at Nicholas, then went back to her stitching. The crackle of the fire and the whisper of thread pulling through canvas were the only sounds in the room.

Nicholas couldn't even hear his son breathing.

The boy looked normal. He had Jewel's dark hair and upswept eyebrows, but his face was all Nicholas's. The stamp of the Roca, his father had called it, passed from generation to generation. The boy's body was square and solid, hard as a rock, even when he was a baby. Nicholas had thought that if the boy's baby fat felt like muscle, he would be stronger than any man when he got older. But the boy would never get a chance to prove his strength. He rarely did anything without someone telling him to.

'How long has he been holding the block?' Nicholas asked.

'Lor,' the nurse said. 'I dinna notice. Sebastian, love, set the block down and rest yer hand.'

Slowly the boy looked to his father, as if he had just heard Nicholas's voice. Nicholas made himself smile at Sebastian, but the boy did not smile back. Instead he gazed at Nicholas with intent gray eyes. Nicholas had no idea where the gray had come from. His eyes were blue and Jewel's were black. She once said that perhaps their combined colors gave Sebastian his unique features.

Sebastian turned his head toward the nurse. Then, carefully, he placed the block on the rug. He let his hand fall on his thigh, and then he didn't move.

'Have you tried playing with him?' Nicholas asked.

'Sire, tis the Mistress's orders. Twice a day, after we break fast, and afore dinner. Tis hard, too. Ye see how the boy moves. He dinna understand play.'

Nicholas had heard that very sentence from Jewel, but didn't understand it himself. How could a child not understand play? It was as if the boy were just a shell with nothing inside. Nicholas had spoken to

149

the healers. They had never seen anything like it, and they blamed Jewel.

They blamed him too, for bringing her to the palace, but they never said so.

They didn't dare.

He should have listened to his father. He should have believed the older council. But his father had botched the war, had caused thousands of deaths by not taking action, and had threatened his own life. Nicholas had not believed in his father's wisdom.

Nicholas had thought that if he brought a Fey into the family, the rest of the nation would follow.

He had thought the wedding would be enough. Jewel had seen that it would take more work, but she became involved in the pregnancy, the pregnancy they needed to cement the relationship and the truce, and she had lost her focus. She had regained it after Sebastian was born, but lost her credibility with the palace staff. They thought that Sebastian was proof the marriage should not have been.

Nicholas's father had ordered that no one except the nursing staff see Sebastian, but it was too late. Those that had seen him spread the news out of the palace. The fact that no one saw the boy at all led people to believe he was some kind of monster, that he looked odd. Finally, Nicholas and Jewel brought him to one of the public speeches so that people would see what a beautiful boy he was.

Beautiful, but empty.

Sebastian hadn't moved since the nurse told him to put the block down. Nicholas knelt beside his son. The boy raised his head. He didn't even have any curiosity. The movement was studied like setting down the block, something he had been taught to do.

Nicholas stared into the boy's gray eyes. They were like flat shiny pebbles. 'Sebastian,' Nicholas whispered, hoping somehow that the sound of his name would bring out the promise of the boy's first week.

The boy continued to stare at him. Nicholas touched the boy's face, felt that smooth hard skin. Jewel's stomach felt like that now as the skin stretched tight over the child inside her.

A girl. Even if the child were normal, a girl would count against them. A girl could not take her brother's place, no matter what Jewel said. The Fey might accept a female ruler, but the Islanders never would. The only thing they could hope for was another son. Or, if they could not have that, then that Nicholas lived until his grandchildren were born.

That seemed very unlikely. He could die the next day. His father's death had shown him how vulnerable they all were. He had thought his father would live to be older than the fiftieth Rocaan. Instead he died at the same age as the current Rocaan, a young man by the standards of Blue Isle. A very young man according to the Fey.

Nicholas let go of his son's cheek. The boy brought up his own hand, and caressed Nicholas's cheek. The boy's hand was cool, but Nicholas leaned into it. His breath caught. Sebastian had never willingly touched him before.

So Jewel was right. There was change. It was just slow.

Sebastian let go of Nicholas's cheek in the same way that Nicholas had done. He did learn. And he could mimic. Maybe there was hope. Sebastian would never be the brains, but he might be the voice for his sister or his mother if the need be.

Nicholas's father was wrong. Hiding Sebastian was the worst thing they could do.

'Nurse,' Nicholas said softly so that he wouldn't startle his son. 'Dress Sebastian for the coronation. Then get yourself ready. We will have him sit near the peers.'

The nurse set down her tapestry. 'The Mistress said –'

'I don't care what the Mistress said. I want my son in that Hall.'

'Yes, sir.' She bobbed her head as she spoke to him, and that made him feel like a child himself.

'Do not let anyone else hold him. Do not let anyone touch him. Do not sit next to anyone. Is that clear?'

'Yes, sir.'

'And bring him right back up here after the ceremony. Do not let his grandfather near him.'

'His grandfather, Sire? His grandfather be dead, beg pardon, Sire.'

'His grandfather,' Nicholas said firmly, not letting himself get sidetracked by a grief he did not have time for. 'Jewel's father.'

The nurse nodded, but not before Nicholas saw the fear in her eyes. 'I willna let ye down, Sire. I'll tend the boy with care, I will.'

'Good.' Nicholas stood. This decision felt right. The boy deserved more than a lonely life in this overheated room. No matter what his problems, he was a direct descendent of the Roca. He would always be the son of a King and a great-grandson of the Black King of the Fey.

Nicholas patted the boy's hand and then stood. 'I'll see you in the Coronation Hall,' he said to his son. The boy didn't understand, but he didn't need to.

Yet.

Seventeen

The Coronation Hall looked like one of the banks in Nye. Rugar had made a room half this size into his bedroom when they had taken over Nye. The Fey had never needed palaces and fine buildings. The Black King was Black King whether he had a fancy hall, a tent in the middle of a bloody field, or a Shadowlands floating silent and invisible above it all. A Black King's power rested within himself, not within a building.

Rugar stood at the double arched doors, his cloak swirling around him. The Hall was full of Island nobles. He had brought twenty of his own people, and had already sent them to the seats near the front. He preferred to stand here, and survey the Hall. Stand here and, with luck, see Jewel before the others did.

He had tried to go upstairs to visit her, but was told that she was dressing. As if Jewel ever spent time on clothing. But rituals were important to these people, and one of the important rituals during a Coronation, apparently, was making sure the Queen was properly dressed.

Rugar had worn his finest clothing too. A black cape woven with good luck wishes. His fighting boots. And a white shirt given him by Jewel's mother when Jewel was smaller than Gift. Unlike Jewel's wedding, this was a celebration. One step closer to Fey rule on the Isle.

One more step and Jewel could be Queen.

Burden, Hanouk, and others from the Settlement sat in the balconies overhanging the Hall. Rugar had noticed them the moment he came in, but did not acknowledge them. When Jewel gained control of the Isle – if Jewel gained control – Rugar would have Burden and his crew shot for traitors. They had no right starting that Settlement. It was in direct defiance to his orders. And, from the things Solanda had said, the Settlement was paying for that defiance. Their blessed sanctuary wasn't a safe harbor after all. They lived in constant fear.

It served them right.

The rest of the Hall was filled with Islanders. Some Rugar recognized from Jewel's wedding. Others he had never seen before. There were also an abundance of Black Robes. One had tried to seat him earlier, but Rugar had kept him back with a hiss and a glare. The Black Robes were as frightened of the Fey as the Fey were of the Black Robes. Only most Fey forgot to use that.

Up front, the Rocaan sat, his red robes marking him like a blood sacrifice. He made Rugar nervous. The Rocaan had touched Jewel once, during the wedding, and Rugar had held a knife then, determined to use it if the Rocaan harmed anyone. Rugar had a knife this time, too, just as the rest of his people did. They all also had bladders of river water, in case things went wrong.

The Spell Warders had learned that the effects of the poison could be slowed, maybe even stopped, if the poison were diluted. Rugar had not had time or the chance to add river water to the vials of poison sitting on the table up front, but if something went wrong – if the Rocaan decided to use the poison as a weapon – then Rugar's people had the river water to spray on each other to slow and, with luck, stop the effects of the poison.

The river water might save lives.

If Rugar had to use it.

He hoped he wouldn't.

Solanda sat near the front, looking radiant in a tunic and pants of soft green. Her boots matched. Most of the Fey wore green at Rugar's request. He wanted Jewel to know they felt joy at the death of the King.

Burden's people did not wear green, however. They wore sedate browns and blacks. Proper everyday colors. Rugar shoved his hands in the pockets of his pants. He had never expected the Settlement to last as long as it had. Even with all the troubles that Solanda had reported, the Settlers hung on. Rugar understood their defiance, but not their determination. Perhaps they knew the punishment they would receive if they ever did return to the Shadowlands.

Two Black Robes passed him, pacing beside the arched doors. He leaned on the door jamb, startled at the cold of the stone. The Hall was warm, but he figured that was the press of bodies. He had not seen so many people sitting in one place before. This many people normally belonged only on a battlefield.

Where he belonged.

Where Jewel belonged.

She should be finding the secret to the Islanders' poison instead of standing beside their next King like a dutiful soldier. Perhaps Rugar hadn't done enough investigating himself. Perhaps the Islanders had some small magicks besides the poison. Perhaps they had the power to Charm.

A rustle in the corridor behind him made him turn. Three people walked toward him: his daughter, her Islander husband, and a woman Rugar did not recognize. The woman was carrying the stone that Jewel called a son.

Jewel had her right hand on top of her husband's left one, and they held their arms outstretched in a ceremonial walk. The new Islander King wore white ceremonial robes with red trim going down the side. A tiny silver sword hung around his neck. His head was noticeably bare, his blond hair combed back in preparation for his crown.

Jewel's hair flowed freely down her shoulders and back, kept off her face by a small cap made of pearls. The pearl trails ran through her hair as well, making her look like a decoration instead of a woman. Her gown matched Nicholas's robe. The high bodice made the gown arch over her stomach. Rugar squinted. It wasn't the bodice that made the arch. Jewel was pregnant again. He let out a small sigh. He didn't really want another grandchild in the Shadowlands, but she was leaving him no choice.

He put his hands on his hips. 'You wear the colors of mourning,' he said.

She wore shoes that added to her height. She was taller than her husband, almost as tall as her father. 'This is not an occasion for celebration.'

'I thought the welcoming of a new king was always a celebration.'

'Not when the old King died before his time.' Nicholas spoke sharply. His Fey was heavily accented, but fluent and clear. He stopped walking a few feet from Rugar.

The woman stopped too. The stone turned so that it could see. Amazing that it had survived this long. It was meant as a golem, and golems normally did not grow or learn. His daughter was powerful, more powerful than she realized.

'You were supposed to be sitting inside,' Jewel said.

'I wanted to see you, to congratulate you on becoming Queen.'

'You could have come at any time during the week. It would have been courtesy to pay your respects.'

Rugar smiled. 'I had none to pay.'

Color flooded Nicholas's face. 'My father bargained with you in good faith.'

'Your father killed Fey.'

'My father did not ask for an invasion of his Isle.'

'Your father should have been prepared for one.'

'Stop!' Jewel moved between them. Her skirts rustled as she moved, the sound Rugar had heard earlier. As she looked back and forth between her father and her husband, the pearls in her hair tapped each other. 'This will get us nowhere.'

154

'Like the marriage,' Rugar said.

'If you had helped, if you had tried, maybe things would have moved quicker,' Jewel said. Her eyes were sparkling. He could feel her rage as if it were a live thing. 'You don't even ask to visit me. Or your grandson.'

Rugar looked at the stone. It had put a finger in its mouth and was staring at him. Its eyes were flat and gray, but not quite empty. Not empty enough. They seemed to reflect something he had seen before.

'I do not consider this thing my grandson,' he said.

'No matter what you consider my son,' she snapped, 'he is your grandson.'

Rugar looked away from the stone. He would not tell her. He could not tell her. If he told her, she would sneak into Shadowlands and steal Gift herself. 'Yes,' he said as levelly as he could. 'I suppose he is.'

'So visit him,' Jewel said. 'Treat us like family. If you act like we're family, the rest of the Fey will follow. The rest of the Isle will follow. We made an agreement. It's time to uphold it.'

Rugar looked her in the eyes. She had lost her understanding of the Fey tradition. Fey did not uphold bargains. Fey subverted them; Fey used them to suit Fey needs. 'You made a bargain, daughter. Not me. I still hold war council in Shadowlands.'

'With half your people,' Nicholas said.

'The best half,' Rugar said.

'If you made war council, you would still be fighting battles.' Jewel pushed herself closer to him. Her skin had a rose scent he had never noticed before. 'You are hiding in Shadowlands. The Black King's son Rugar, Greatest Warrior of them all, hiding from water for five years.'

'I'm not hiding,' he said.

'But you're not fighting, either. You're not negotiating, and you're not cooperating. What are you doing, Father? Waiting for the Spell Warders to find the secret to holy water? Waiting for Grandfather to show up and save you? Is this how you became the Greatest Warrior of all time?'

Rugar grabbed her arm and pulled her close. Her skirts rustled in protest. 'At least, I don't prostitute myself in exchange for safety.'

Nicholas took a step toward them, but Jewel shook her father's hand free before Nicholas could get any closer.

'Safety?' she said. 'Does this look like safety to you? Every day, I face the threat you hide from. Every day, I put my faith in the bargain you deny. *Every day*. And if Grandfather does arrive, I will tell him about your *courage*, Father. I will tell him how you hid while I found a way to save our people.'

'Our people haven't been saved. Look at your friend Burden. His Settlement is as useful as that thing you call a child.'

'Integration takes time,' Jewel said.

'That's what we used to tell the conquered,' Rugar said.

'And who defeated us, Father? It wasn't Good King Alexander. It was you. Mistake after mistake after mistake. The first being your refusal to admit you have gone Blind.'

'I haven't gone Blind.' But he had to look away from her as he said that. He hadn't had a real Vision since the Invasion itself, and Jewel was convinced that the Vision that led them all to the Isle had been one of their defeat. 'Don't go in there, Jewel. Don't ally yourself with them any farther. Take that child you carry and come home.'

'This is my home,' she said. 'I still have Vision. I know I made the right choice.'

Nicholas reached across toward her. 'She is my wife. She belongs beside me.'

'No,' Rugar said. 'She is the Black King's Granddaughter. She should be beside no one. If she didn't marry you, she would rule half the world someday.'

'Wrong, Father,' Jewel said, taking Nicholas's hand. 'If I hadn't followed you on a crazy scheme to save your reputation, I would have been Black Queen. Now the best I can hope for is Queen of Blue Isle.'

'When the Black King arrives, you will regret this,' Rugar said.

'*If* the Black King arrives,' Jewel said. 'And if he does, you had best hope I have this Isle unified because I will give you sanctuary.'

'I won't need sanctuary.'

'You'll need it,' Jewel said. 'If Grandfather is still Black King, he'll have the Soldiers slaughter you and send the pieces of your flesh to the far sides of the globe. No Fey makes the mistakes you made and lives. If Bridge comes as Black King, he will have his faithful kill us both to save his throne. You will have to ally with me, my husband, and the child you refuse to acknowledge. Because if you do not, you will die.'

Her words had a truth he did not want to admit. *Jewel made the only choice for peace*, the Shaman said on the day of Jewel's wedding. *Would that you always do the same, Rugar.*

'Now,' Jewel said, her voice grim and low, 'if you want to support this alliance, you go inside and do not make a fuss. If you want to declare war against the King of Blue Isle, and his Queen, leave. But rest assured that I have the blood of a Black Queen, and I will do everything in my power to win any battle I find myself in. Do I make myself clear?'

Rugar smiled. She made herself very clear. She just hadn't discovered that in war, he held the most important piece. Her son, the most powerful Visionary ever to appear in the Black King's line.

'I'll go inside,' Rugar said. He slipped around his daughter's hand, clasped with that of her husband.

'Promise me,' Jewel said, 'that you won't make trouble today.'

Rugar met her gaze. She had finally asked of him something he could do. 'I promise,' he said.

Eighteen

Jewel put her free hand on her chest. Beneath the brocade, she could feel the warmth of her skin and her pounding heart. Her father turned and, cape flaring, marched through the doorways. From the back he looked like something a Dream Rider would bring, black hair, black cape, black boots, all firmness and power.

And it was a sham, all of it. Rugar had no power. He had never had power off the battlefield, and even then had had to answer to his father. The bid for Blue Isle was a bid for power, and it had failed.

He answered to her now, and he didn't like it.

Nicholas squeezed her hand. His beautiful blue eyes were wide, his face pale. 'Is what you said to him true?' he asked in Nye, apparently not wanting the nurse to understand.

'Which part?' Jewel asked. She allowed herself to be pulled closer to Nicholas's side.

'The part about fighting him if he starts the war again.'

'Yes,' she said.

'But he's your father, Jewel. They're your people.'

'I didn't say I would fight my people, Nicholas. I said I would fight him.' She let her free hand drop. Nicholas didn't know how ruthless the Fey could be. She had tried to warn him, but he couldn't seem to fathom it. 'The only hope for the Fey on Blue Isle is to follow me.'

'Or the Black King will slaughter them when he arrives? Will he arrive, Jewel?'

She nodded. 'Maybe not in your lifetime or in mine, but certainly during Sebastian's. My Grandfather is too old for battle, and I think he's Blind, too. If my brother Bridge becomes Black King, he will consolidate power on Galinas. He is not a warrior and he doesn't need to be. It will be understood that he took the job when the true powers died at sea.'

'At sea?' Nicholas asked.

She nodded. 'Failure is talked about only in the context of living Fey, Nicholas. My father and I can become victims of a storm easier than we can lose a battle. But once Bridge dies, his child, his successor will have to come to Blue Isle because it is the next stop on the way to

Leut. The Fey are warriors. Their leaders are conquerors. We have paused in our travels for a generation or two, but we have never stopped, and we cannot stop until the whole world is ours.'

'Then the Isle should be preparing for this,' Nicholas said.

She squeezed his hand. 'No. I am already preparing. If the Isle is integrated when they come, Nicky, it becomes part of the Empire without bloodshed. The government remains the same, and stays in the hand of your family. But if the Isle isn't integrated, then all the holy water on Blue Isle won't stop the Fey. The Spell Warders my grandfather has make Rugar's team look like infants. They will find the secret to your weapon, and they will turn it on you.'

'What about you?'

'If I am still alive, I'll be executed. My line will be eradicated. We'll all die, Nicky. You, me, Sebastian, and this little one.' Jewel patted her stomach.

He dropped her hand. 'You never said that they would kill us. You said we would become honorary Fey. An important part of the Empire. I remember that. You said it at the meeting when we decided to be married. You made it sound like a promise.'

'It is a promise, Nicholas. It is.'

'But you would betray your own father.'

She didn't know how to explain this to him in the corridor while the entire Isle waited in the Hall for his coronation. Yet she knew it couldn't wait. He had been urged to throw her aside. He would do so if he felt that he had no choice.

'Like you,' she said slowly, 'I have been raised to rule from birth. But unlike you, I was raised in a world of war. Betrayal, coup, assassination. Alliances and counteralliances. My people can make themselves look like the enemy. In the Fey world, no one can be trusted lightly. No one, Nicky. Any betrayal of trust gets tallied, and when the score grows too high, the friend becomes the enemy. There is no other way.'

'So I can trust you as long as I treat you well,' Nicholas said.

She held up her hand. To her surprise, it was trembling. 'Let me finish. The true Black King – or Black Queen – has to be ruthless. It is the only way to survive. No one wants to kill a Black King more than his closest sibling or his child. But the Black King's family cannot kill within its ranks. That causes untold turmoil. So we have to do it subtly, by hiring assassins and not giving direct orders, or by finding other methods. My grandfather sent my father away for a reason. But my father took me as a guarantee that he would not lose his position. His guarantee failed because he had not counted on the strength of the Isle.

'My father was the leader on this Isle and I took that leadership from him, without bloodshed, when I made the alliance with you. He knows it, and I know it. And until the power balance settles, he needs to know I can be as ruthless as he is. Not just for me, but for you. For Sebastian. For this baby. If we don't ally with my father, we will fight a guerrilla war with my own people until the Black King comes. And on that day, we're all dead.'

'But what about me, Jewel? How do I know if you'll turn on me?'

Sebastian was watching them, his little mouth moving as he sucked his forefinger. The nurse was staring into the Coronation Hall. She probably understood some Nye. They should have been speaking Fey.

Jewel swallowed. She had no easy answer for this question. 'Because I haven't turned on you yet,' she said. 'And I won't.'

Nicholas took her hand again and touched each finger with his own before clasping it and pulling her as close as he could. Then he kissed her, his lips so light on hers that they felt like the touch of a breeze. 'We'll do this together,' he said.

She nodded.

Then he took her hand, and held it out as he had all the way to the Hall. As they went through the double arched doors, his grip on her tightened.

Jewel had never been inside the Coronation Hall. She was not prepared for its size. Islanders watched her from the balconies above. Rows of Islanders ten across flanked them on either side. A red carpet had been laid, leading them to the steps and a platform up front. A platform that, in a normal building, would have been a room in and of itself. Matthias sat toward the back of the platform. His red robes matched the carpet. He was too far away for her to see his features.

Jewel and Nicholas processed down the aisle, with Sebastian behind them. A low murmur followed them as people commented on her son. He was a handsome child, his features a perfect combination of hers and Nicholas's. He had her thinness, and Nicholas's squareness. Most of the people in the Hall would see nothing wrong with Sebastian. Only those who caught a glimpse of his eyes would know that he would never be a bright, active child.

She had thought Nicholas's decision to bring Sebastian odd. Now she understood it. Let them know that their king had a family. Let them know the dynasty was secure. Only she, and Nicholas, needed to know that Sebastian could never run a country, especially a country that could, at any moment, be invaded by the Black King of the Fey.

The murmurs were the only sound in the room. She had been prepared for that, but knowing it wasn't enough. The strangeness of a silent march seemed foreign to her, more than almost any other custom. Music was not common here. When she had asked about it, before Sebastian's naming ceremony, Nicholas had looked at her as if she had spoken a hex. Music was considered too powerful for mere mortals. The Tabernacle controlled it, and used it only within its walls.

She had never been to ceremonies without music until she had come here.

Burden and the other members of the Settlement sat in the balconies near the center of the Hall. They looked down on her, their faces solemn. They had tried to make a future on the Isle and she had failed them by being too concerned with her own life. She would not fail them again.

As she and Nicholas walked farther toward the front, Matthias stood. He clasped his hands behind his back, waiting.

They had almost reached the steps. Her father sat in the last seat of the front row, right beside the aisle. Next to him were the important Fey from Shadowlands. They wore green.

Green.

The anger she had felt earlier surged through her again. She almost turned and yelled at her father. Nicholas understood that color. He knew because she had worn green at their wedding to celebrate her joy.

She must have turned, for Nicholas squeezed her hand so tightly that pain shot through her arm. She faced forward, proud Queen once again. She would deal with her father after the ceremony.

In private.

And he would tell her the truth. About everything.

Nicholas guided her up the stairs. Matthias was the only person on the large platform except for them. The nurse had taken a seat on the other side of the aisle, Sebastian cradled in her arms.

On a table behind Matthias stood two vials of holy water, two crowns, and a cloth, like the one he had used at their wedding. Jewel stared at the glittering cut-glass bottles. This was her compromise. This was the risk she had taken for Nicholas. He had agreed to have the ceremony outside of the Tabernacle, and she had agreed to be beside him despite the presence of holy water.

'Blessed be the King and his Chosen,' Matthias said in a voice so loud it echoed through the entire Hall.

'Blessed be,' the congregation answered.

Nicholas took Jewel's elbow and led her to the end of the red runner. They stood together before Matthias. He smiled at Nicholas, but when he turned to her, his gaze was cold.

'When the Roca was Absorbed,' Matthias said, 'his religious mantle fell to his second son. But his power in this world fell to his eldest, and

161

has continued in unbroken line since that day. Nicholas, son of Alexander, son of Dimitri, son of Sebastian, has the blood of the Roca in his veins. He stands before us, heir to the Roca's throne in the world, our leader, our teacher, our healer.'

Matthias held his hands over Nicholas's and Jewel's heads. Nicholas bowed his head and, after a moment, Jewel did the same.

'We honor him. We cherish him. And we will obey him until, in His Wisdom, God chooses another.' Matthias clapped his hands together, then raised them toward the heavens. 'The Words Written and Unwritten say, "And when the Roca Ascended, his two sons stepped forward. The eldest said he would stand in the Roca's place as leader of men." The sun shone upon them, and the warmth of God enfolded them, and they knew it was good. And so it shall be in unbroken generation after generation, the firstborn son shall take the Roca's place in the land, use the Roca's voice to lead, and be the Roca as long as he walks within the world.'

Jewel shuddered. She had not realized how closely tied the King was to the religion. She had known the myth, but not that its power was perpetuated in the coronation ceremony.

'Bow your heads for the Blessing.'

Jewel's head was bowed, but not too low. She could still see Matthias's hands. He backed away from her, and took one vial of holy water. He poured it over the tiny sword around his neck. Then he touched the sword to Nicholas's forehead. Jewel flinched at the nearness of Matthias's saturated hands. But he didn't seem to notice her.

' "Blessed be this man before Us," ' Matthias said. ' "May the Holy One hear his Words. May the Roca guard his Deeds. May God open his Heart." '

Then he let the sword fall to his chest. Nicholas stepped forward, removed the sword from around his neck, and dipped it in the second bottle of holy water. He held the sword up.

'With this,' he said, 'I Bless all before me, and swear upon the Roca's Absorption to serve his purpose within the world.'

Then, out of deference to Jewel, he took the sword off, and set it on the table beside the vial of holy water. He took a pouch of water – water she had given him before the ceremony started – from within his robes, and washed his hands so that the poison wouldn't touch her.

'This King comes to us with a Queen, and a son,' Matthias said. 'This Queen cannot touch the Roca's water. She cannot have the traditional Blessing. But I urge you to accept her nonetheless. She is the choice of our leader, and her son will lead us someday.'

Jewel's heart was pounding. Nicholas had warned her that Matthias

162

would comment on her inability to be touched with holy water. It had to be addressed in the ceremony.

'Still, she will wear the crown of the Roca's consort, and through it, she will fulfill what tradition demands of her.'

Nicholas held out his hand. Jewel stared at it for a moment. She had seen him wash. She had given him the water and had not left his side. She had just told him she would trust him.

Always.

She took his hand.

Nothing changed.

His gaze met hers. Tears swam in his eyes. He had been as frightened as she.

She took two steps so that she was at his side. A kneeling cushion rested just beneath the table, the cushion big enough for both of them. When she was beside him, Nicholas turned, and together they knelt before murderous symbols of his religion.

Matthias stood between them and the table. He took the crown that would belong to Nicholas and held it between his long, slender hands. The crown was large, made of gold, and studded with more gems than Jewel had ever seen. Most were diamonds and rubies, but two were a bright blue, of a kind unfamiliar to her.

'The crown carries the Eyes of God,' Matthias said. 'Its possessor is all seeing, all knowing, all powerful.'

Jewel couldn't help herself. She brought her gaze up so that she could see Matthias's face. He believed what he was saying. *They* believed their king to have the eyes, the ears, the strength of a god. Their king came from the same birthline, and he carried the heritage within himself. Such a firm belief. Such a power to fight against.

Had Nicholas realized this when he chose Jewel? His father certainly had. His father had opposed the joining from the beginning. Only near his death was he coming to accept Jewel. She suspected he was waiting to see what happened to the second child.

'Nicholas, son of Alexander, son of Dimitri, son of Sebastian, heir to the Roca's life, do you accept the wisdom of the Holy One, the Blessing of the Roca, the Sight of God?'

Nicholas's head was bowed, his hair over his face. 'I do.'

'Then accept the symbol of the Roca's power within the world.' Matthias lowered the crown onto Nicholas's head. The crown slipped slightly and Matthias caught it with one hand, then eased the crown into position, messing Nicholas's hair. Jewel kept her hands tightly clasped, resisting the urge to fix it.

'Jewel, daughter of Rugar, son of Rugad.' Matthias was now standing over her. 'You will carry the seed of the Roca within you. You shall stand beside your husband in all he does. Tradition tells us that the Roca's second son, accepting the Charge from God, put aside women. But God, in his wisdom, allowed the Roca's eldest to choose a mate. That mate must also do the Roca's work within the world.'

His phrasing seemed odd to her. If she had carried the seed of Roca within her already, then why hadn't it poisoned her like the holy water had? Perhaps their religion was not poison to her. Perhaps it had no magic at all. Perhaps the word they used to describe the water, poison, was the correct word after all.

'Do you accept your charge as Queen of Blue Isle?' Matthias said.

'I do.' She spoke without hesitation, as loudly as Matthias had. Let them know that their paltry religion couldn't beat her. Let them remember that she was the Black King's granddaughter. And let them understand that she was now a part of their lives, forever.

Nicholas squeezed her hand. She glanced at him. His gaze, through the curtain of his hair, warmed her.

Matthias turned and took the cloth, balancing it gingerly on the tips of his fingers. He placed it on her head. The cloth seemed warm, and it made her scalp tingle. Her mouth went dry.

Then Matthias took the second crown and held it above her. Her crown was smaller, and contained only diamonds and rubies.

'This crown is the symbol of your role as consort. Wear it with the Roca's Blessing.' He snarled the words, almost as if they were a curse.

Jewel's heart leapt. Her limbs trembled with the same energy she felt in the middle of a battle. He put the crown on her head.

Its weight felt unfamiliar. Nicholas tugged at her hand. She was supposed to stand, but the pearls were digging into her skull. Burning her skull. A fire burned beneath her hair.

The cloth slipped forward and brushed her forehead, sending a shooting pain through her. She screamed just once. 'The poison!' she cried to Nicholas in Nye. 'He spilled the poison!'

Her hair was melting from her head. She could feel the burning, the change. The smell rose, familiar and horrible. Nicholas let go of her hand. The crown and cloth slid off her head and clattered onto the marble floor. Nicholas pulled the pouch from his robe and poured the remaining water on her. Matthias bent over her, but Nicholas shoved him away.

'You've killed her!' her father screamed, and voices rose in panic behind them.

Nicholas pulled her close, protecting her with his body.

'Someone help her!' her father cried in Fey. 'Please help her!'

The burning was intense, but it wasn't leaving her head. She had thought her whole body would melt. She had seen others die this way. Their bodies transformed, changed, almost instantly.

Her father stood over her, pouring more water on her. It smelled of mud. River water. More Fey gathered behind him, handing him pouches. Nicholas's robe was wet. His face was wet.

'Jewel. My god, Jewel, are you all right?'

More water splashed on her face. Nicholas raised a hand to stop it.

'Let them!' Her father pulled Nicholas's arms away.

The burning seared her skull. She didn't want to die. Not this way. 'Nicky,' she said, reaching for him. He would never survive this. Not without her.

Her fingers touched his cheek. She couldn't hold consciousness. As the blackness took her, she realized that the Vision she had tried so hard to prevent all those years ago had finally come true. The poison had touched her. Now she had to rely on others to keep her alive.

Nineteen

Jewel's hair was melting into a long black river, the pearls sinking into her scalp. The skin on her forehead had puckered, but the puckering stopped when her father poured the water on it. Nicholas cradled her to his chest. He couldn't lose her. Not now.

Her hand fell away from his face, and her eyes rolled into the back of her head.

'We need help here!' he shouted, but he wasn't sure what kind of help there would be.

Her father was pouring more Fey water on her. The water kept splashing Nicholas in the face. The drops tasted of mud and copper. Behind him, Sebastian was crying. Deep, heart-rending sobs that struck Nicholas as unnatural somehow.

'She's not conscious,' he said to Rugar.

'She'll die. Let me have her.'

If Rugar took her, Nicholas would never see her again. He couldn't lose her too.

'Let me have her. She'll die without our magic.'

'You haven't been able to save any of the others.'

'Let him take her,' someone shouted in Fey from the balcony. 'By the Mysteries. Let him try!'

Rugar bent over and snatched Jewel from Nicholas's arms. The loss of her warmth left him suddenly chilled. Rugar stood and turned, carrying his daughter as if she were as small as Sebastian.

Islanders cringed in their seats, but the Fey were up and running from the Hall. A cat was on the floor, a green tunic pooled around it. It kept pace with Rugar as he ran along the royal red runner. Fey stood in the balcony too. Jewel's friend Burden swung off the wooden sides and leapt to the ground below. He blocked Jewel's body with his own.

Nicholas stood. His robe was sopping wet. It clung to his legs and hampered his movement. He had to follow too. He couldn't leave her with them. After what she had said about her father, Nicholas wasn't certain if the man would help her or kill her for a traitor.

And the baby.

The baby.

The nurse had a stunned look on her face. She was holding Sebastian who had craned his neck around her for a better look at his dying mother.

Nicholas ran down the steps. The crown bounced off his head and fell with a clatter onto the marble floor. No one else followed. The other Fey were ahead of him. Then he heard footsteps behind.

Matthias was coming. His biretta gone, fallen aside, his blond curls flowing behind him. 'Seal the doors!' he cried. 'Don't let them take the Queen!'

The Danites grabbed the doors and were pulling them shut. Damn the long aisle. Rugar would never make it.

'Leave the doors open!' Nicholas said.

The Danites glanced at Matthias. King and Rocaan should never be at odds. No one knew who to follow.

'I am the Roca's representative on *this* world,' Nicholas said. 'Leave the doors open.'

'Close them!' Matthias said. 'She must stay here! The Roca withdrew his Blessing.'

The doors clanged shut. Rugar stopped just in front of them. Jewel's arms swung free, her head back. She looked fragile in her father's arms.

'Are you going to murder all of us?' Rugar asked. 'Or just my daughter?'

'Open those doors,' Nicholas said. He finally reached Rugar's side. Five Danites now stood in front of the doors. They all held holy water. It wouldn't hurt Nicholas, but it would kill any Fey, including Jewel. 'Open them now.'

'The Roca didn't Bless her,' Matthias said.

Nicholas turned on his former teacher. The man wasn't recognizable any more. 'I didn't do what you wanted, did I, Matthias?' he said. 'I didn't set her aside. But she is my wife and carries my child, and by God, the Roca, and the Holy One, if either of them die, I will give you to my friends the Fey here and allow them to slaughter you, inch by painful inch. Now, make your men stand aside.'

Matthias had taken a step backward. 'You can't do this, Nicholas.'

'You are committing murder, holy man,' Nicholas said. 'But it wouldn't be the first time, would it?' Nicholas whirled. The change hadn't spread on Jewel's face, but he had no idea what the holy water had done to the top of her head.

'You –' he said, pointing at the youngest Danite. 'The Words Written and Unwritten say that only God may choose who lives and who dies. Murderers are sent to the Snow Mountains to thrive or fail according to God's wishes. Will you defy me and kill my wife? Because by defying me, you are defying God.'

The Danite glanced at Matthias, then back to Nicholas. The Fey had gathered around Jewel and Rugar, as if to protect both of them.

'I'm sorry, Holy Sir,' the Danite said. He put his vial of holy water in the pocket of his robe, then pushed the door open. The Danite next to him did the same. The remaining three Danites stepped aside.

Rugar ran out the door. Nicholas followed.

'Where are you taking her?' he asked.

'To Shadowlands. It's the only place she'll be safe.' Rugar said.

'Shadowlands is too far,' Burden said.

'We need a Domestic Healer.'

'A Healer can't help her. Not even a Warder can do that.'

'She can't die. She can't!'

Nicholas had never heard panic in Rugar's voice before.

'Then let me take her.' A female voice spoke behind all of them. Nicholas turned. A Fey woman almost twice his height stood behind him. She had white hair that sprung off her head like weeds. Her face was wizened, her mouth a small oval amidst wrinkles. Only her eyes were bright – sparkling black circles of light in a dying face.

The Shaman.

Twenty

'We must take her somewhere safe,' the Shaman said, 'so that the Black Robes do not attack her again.'

Jewel was heavy in Rugar's arms. Her entire body was limp. 'If someone takes her,' he said, 'I can make a Shadowlands.'

'No,' the Shaman said. 'It must be a real place.'

'The Settlement,' Burden said.

'No,' Nicholas said. 'The kitchens.' He pushed past Rugar, his hand brushing against Jewel's face. She did not respond. At least she wasn't changing. At least she wasn't melting.

'Quickly,' the Shaman said.

They ran through the corridor, Nicholas in the lead. The skirts of his robe left trails of wet along the floor. Jewel's arms fell free and were bouncing against Rugar's legs. She felt too heavy.

His daughter.

His fearless daughter.

'Burden,' the Shaman said as she ran beside them. 'Mend is outside the gate with some of the healers. Tell them I want a poultice of red-wort and garlic, and tell them I will need an assistant.'

'I will assist.' Solanda spoke from the floor. She was in her cat form. 'Tell them they do not need to risk their lives to come into this place.'

Nicholas's back was to her, so he didn't see her. His crown was gone and his hair flowed freely. 'The kitchens will be safe. If anyone looks for Jewel in the palace, they will look upstairs. I have help in the kitchens.'

Rugar wondered at that. No man had help in such places. 'It better be close,' he said. 'She isn't moving.'

No one responded. His daughter didn't make a sound. The babe within her pushed against Rugar's chest. He hadn't even known she was with child until today.

Nicholas led them through stone arches into a dark passageway. Suddenly Rugar felt foolish following this man.

'This had better be a safe place,' Rugar said. 'Any attacks and –'

'And what?' the Shaman asked. 'We are here because of you. Allow the boy his grief over his wife.'

'Me?' Rugar's surprise almost made him stop. 'I did not harm Jewel. I didn't even touch her.'

'I warned you,' the Shaman said. 'I told you to allow her to make peace, but you did not. You did not, Rugar. It is your darkness that leads us all here.'

The passageway smelled of roast pheasant and baking breads. Nicholas was leading them to the kitchen. In side rooms, people worked, churning butter, pounding bread dough. Voices rose from a brightly lit front area.

'You knew this was going to happen, didn't you?' Rugar asked. He pulled Jewel closer. He couldn't see her in the darkness. 'Tell me how this is going to end.'

'I cannot do that,' the Shaman said.

'Visionaries can tell each other –'

'Rugar, I had three Visions about this day.'

Despite himself he shuddered. Three Visions. The outcome was in doubt then. Jewel had seen this moment as well. And little Gift.

Only Rugar had been Blind.

As they emerged through another set of arches, Nicholas was already speaking. 'We need a clear area near the hearth fire, and a mattress for my wife. I want all nonessential personnel to leave. Anyone who stays must obey the Fey's Shaman.'

Islanders, men and women, scattered. Rugar got an impression of square, pale faces, blue eyes glancing at Jewel. She smelled of burning flesh. Many Islanders covered their mouths as they turned away.

Nicholas led them to a great stone fireplace where a large fire roared. Kettles hung from iron hooks in the fire, and near the side of the fireplace were more hooks that allowed servants to take the kettles out. A man in a white uniform swept the floor near the fire, and a woman hurried in, carrying a feather mattress that looked none too clean.

Rugar didn't care. He placed his daughter on it. Her skull was almost flat, her hair plastered against her head, and the puckering on her forehead had traveled to her eyebrows. 'The poison is still working,' he said.

'I know.' The Shaman bent over her. 'Someone go to the door and wait for Burden and the poultice. I need her awake.'

Nicholas was standing near the man in white. 'Get my son and bring him here. I want him safe.'

'Sire, I am not supposed to leave the kitchen.'

'Get him,' Nicholas said. 'Now.'

The man nodded and ran from the room. Jewel's stomach was

170

bobbing like the surface of an ocean. Rugar put a hand on it, and the Shaman snatched his hand away.

'You have caused enough trouble for one lifetime. Stand back.'

'She's my daughter,' Rugar said.

'You should have thought of that before you brought her to this place.'

He wasn't certain if the Shaman meant the kitchen, the palace, or the Isle itself. But he backed away. He had no choice. No one had ever lived through this poison. The Warders had said that it could be diluted, but Rugar wasn't certain if the dilution slowed down death or prevented it.

Burden came in from the back door. The poultice he carried overpowered the smell of roast pheasant. He handed it to the Shaman, who slapped it on Jewel's forehead.

'Is she going to be all right?' Burden asked.

'She'll live for the moment,' the Shaman said. 'I can promise nothing more.'

She bent over Jewel, then reached out her hand. 'Rugar, I need your cloak.' When he didn't move, she looked up at him. 'It is a healing cloak, is it not? I need it now.'

He had forgotten the healing properties. It had been given to him by his father before he went into his first battle. His fingers fumbled as he untied the strings around his throat. He pulled the cloak off and handed it to the Shaman, who placed it over Jewel.

'Jewel,' the Shaman said. 'You must wake. You must talk to me.'

Nicholas hovered over her, his wet robe dripping on the dry floor. One of the servants offered to take the robe but he shook his head. His gaze never left Jewel.

The Shaman got on her knees beside Jewel. She put a finger in Jewel's slack mouth. 'Jewel, you must wake.'

Jewel's eyelids fluttered.

'Thank God,' Nicholas murmured and dropped beside her.

'Stay back,' the Shaman said.

Rugar crossed his arms and clenched his fists. He could do nothing. The Shaman at least had access to Domestic medicine as well as her Visions. He had no powers besides his Vision, and it had failed him.

It had failed Jewel.

'Jewel,' the Shaman said. 'Tell me about the child.'

Jewel's eyes opened and for a moment, they were as empty as the stone's. Then she came into them, small and distant. 'The baby. Take her. You have to take her. She's the future. ...'

Jewel's voice faded away. Her eyes closed. The Shaman nodded at Burden.

'I need Mend. I don't care about her fears. I need all the healers outside the gate.'

Nicholas was touching Jewel's face. 'Jewel,' he said. Then in Islander, 'I'm sorry. I'm so sorry.'

'You didn't hurt her, boy,' the Shaman said. 'Now get back and let me help her.'

Jewel's eyes opened. She smiled at Nicholas. She lifted her hand as if it took a great effort, and took his. Then she closed her eyes again.

The man Nicholas had sent for the stone had come into the kitchen, followed by the woman. She had the stone in her arms. It was sobbing hard now, cracks forming on its all-too-human face.

The Shaman looked up, then looked at Rugar. Her mouth was open slightly, her eyes wide with shock. He felt momentarily vindicated. Not even the Shaman Saw everything.

'What did you do?' she asked. 'In the name of the Powers, the Mysteries, and all we hold dear, *what did you do?*'

Nicholas looked up in surprise. Rugar backed away from the Shaman's words. 'I guaranteed our safety,' he said.

'You fool!' The Shaman's voice held panic. He had never heard her panic before. 'I can't save all three.'

'You don't have to. Gift is in Shadowlands. This is a stone –'

'No,' the Shaman said. 'Don't you know what you've done? The boy is part of her.'

'But she's part of me, and I'm fine.'

'She's an adult. He's a child. A half-breed with no support.' The Shaman closed her eyes and keened. The sound stopped all conversation in the kitchen. Nicholas glanced at Rugar, the fear in his face palpable. Only the stone didn't seem to notice. It kept crying as if its heart would break.

Rugar looked at the stone. Of course it was cracking. It only lived because of Jewel. Then he remembered its eyes. He had seen something alive in its eyes. Alive and distant.

Were you there, Gift?

Yes. I saw it all.

'You have to save the boy,' Rugar said.

'He's too far away.' The Shaman opened her eyes, and brushed the damaged skin on Jewel's forehead. 'I doubt I can save anyone now.'

172

Twenty-One

Gift was crying. Niche flew out of the second room to find him on the carpet before the fire, clutching his forehead with one hand and convulsing, his eyes rolled into the back of his head. The other hand was dangerously close to the low-burning flames.

'Gift!' she said. 'Gift!'

She held his shoulders, but she lacked the strength to hold him down. She had seen this before. She had seen it during the First Battle for Jahn when the Black Robes had poured poison on her friends.

But there was no smell. The room smelled of a wood fire, not burning flesh. Beneath his hand, his skin looked fine.

'Wind!' She screamed for her mate. He flew into the room, half changed, mostly wings and small male body. As he landed he grew to his proper size.

'What happened?' he asked as he knelt beside Gift.

'I don't know,' she said. 'I heard him crying and I came in here. Please, go for the Shaman. We need help. We need it now.'

He didn't need to be told twice. With a snap of his fingers, he became no bigger than a spark. But no spark ever flew that fast or with such direction. He disappeared under the crack in the door, gone before Niche could say another sentence.

Gift was moaning. Her beautiful, brilliant boy had drool running down his chin. His hands were opening and closing, his heels pounding the floor.

'Hurry,' Niche whispered. 'Someone please hurry.'

He was supposed to be their salvation, their blessing, their gift. Their reward for serving Rugar so well. The child they could never have. Wisp women were too fragile to have children. Their hollow bones could not handle the weight of a child. Wisps usually accepted this, but Niche wanted a child. She wanted to raise a child with another Wisp. Rugar gave her Gift. He came with a price, but it was a price she had been willing to pay.

Until now.

He had been alone in the room. She had been cooking their lunch and hadn't heard the door. But something had happened. Perhaps he had gotten into some poison, or someone had hurt him somehow. But the room looked no different. No spilled bottles, no water on the floor. The fire crackled and spit as it always did.

Only her son was different.

'Maaaaaaaaaaa!' he cried, and the word broke her heart.

'I'm here, Gift.'

He shook his head and thrashed against her hands, almost rising off the ground. She couldn't hold him. 'Maaaa!'

Beside her the door opened. She looked up, expecting the Shaman. Instead, the horrible little boy that Gift sometimes played with stood at the door.

His name was Coulter, and Solanda had stolen him from the Islanders before Jewel left Shadowlands. She claimed he had magic, but he looked like an Island child, with big blue eyes, brownish-blond hair, and square features. He was small and solid. Even though he was at least five years old, he looked like a child of three.

'Move,' he said with a voice that had no childhood in it.

'What did you do to him?' Niche asked.

'Nothing,' Coulter said. 'Now move.'

Gift's thrashing had gotten worse. Niche pushed down on his shoulders, trying to keep him stable, but she didn't have the strength or the weight. 'Go get the Shaman,' Niche said.

'The Shaman's gone. You only have me.'

'Maaaaaaa!' Gift's face was turning purple.

'Move!' Coulter said. 'Can't you see? He's dying!'

'But you –'

Coulter came all the way into the cabin and, in one sudden movement, shoved her aside. She fell back on her wings, the delicate bones in the tips snapping. The pain brought tears to her eyes. Coulter was leaning over the convulsing body of her son.

He stretched out his arms, then fell on Gift. A bright light wrapped itself around both of them – and for a moment, Niche saw through it. Two grown men, one slender and beautiful and dark, the other short and blonde and pale, standing near the Jahn Bridge on the Cardidas River. Then the image faded.

Wind landed beside her. He grew from a spark into a full grown man. 'The Shaman's gone.'

Niche swallowed, unable to take her gaze off the boy holding her son. 'I know.'

'So are the other healers. We're alone here.'

Niche nodded toward the boys. 'He came.'

The light faded around Coulter, but remained around Gift. He had stopped struggling. Sweat glued his hair to his head, but he had stopped drooling. His hands were at his sides, his feet relaxed, his eyes closed. He looked as if he were sleeping. Bands of light flowed around him like string, binding him together and protecting him from the air.

Young Coulter's hands were shaking as he brushed bangs off his flat forehead. 'Who is the dying woman?' he asked Niche.

She frowned and shook her head. 'There's no woman here.'

'The woman the Shaman is tending. The woman who wears strange clothing, but has the look of a Fey.'

'Jewel,' Wind breathed. He glanced at Niche as if he didn't understand. But she did.

The dying woman. Jewel was too young to die on her own. 'She's his real mother.'

'Ah,' Coulter said. He brought his knees up to his chest and wrapped his arms around them. If it weren't for the ancient wisdom in his eyes, he would have looked like any small, inquisitive boy. 'You realize no one severed the ties between Gift and his mother.'

Niche's wings throbbed. 'Severed the –?'

'She was tended by Islanders during his birth, remember?' Wind said.

'She came to him through their Link,' Coulter said. Niche wondered how he knew this, but he spoke as if it were all natural. 'She tried to save him as she died. But she thought him the wrong child, and by the time she knew he was her son, she was gone.'

Niche looked at Gift. His body shone in the bands of light. 'So he's dead?' she whispered.

Coulter smiled. 'I severed the ties. He's safe now.'

'He was dying because she was dying?' Niche asked.

Coulter nodded. 'But he'll live.' Coulter stood and brushed off the seat of his pants. 'As long as I do.'

Twenty-Two

More Fey hurried into the kitchen. Jewel's grip on Nicholas's hand was loosening. Her hand was turning cold, and he wasn't sure if she was breathing. The Shaman had ceased touching Jewel's face and instead had a hand on her stomach. A small light glowed around the Shaman's fingers.

The kitchen staff kept a respectable distance. Rugar had sunk to his knees beside Jewel, but the Shaman wouldn't let him touch her. Nicholas said nothing, but tried to send his love through his fingers into Jewel's hand.

She had to live.

She had to.

He couldn't survive without her.

The wound on her forehead had spread across her eyebrows. She was still melting, like all Fey did when touched with holy water, but the process was slower than usual.

He wasn't sure how Matthias had done it. He must have touched her with a tainted finger, or splashed her as he placed the crown on her head. But it didn't matter. Nicholas had insisted that she be beside him in a religious ceremony. The responsibility was his.

'Come back to me, Jewel,' he said.

All the Fey surrounding Jewel were huddled over her stomach. A golden cat sat near the fire, licking its front paws and wiping them over its face. The room was too hot, and smelled of pheasant.

Sebastian had stopped crying.

No one spoke. The only sounds in the large room were the crackle of wood in the hearth fire, and the small rustles that people made when they were trying to be quiet.

The silence was eerie. Nicholas wanted to look at his son, but he didn't dare. If he had to choose a life, he would choose Jewel's. He begged the Roca for forgiveness, but his son was a shell, an empty thing instead of a child, and his wife –

His wife was everything.

Her stomach was no longer high and firm. It was rolling like waves on a sea. The small glow from the Shaman's hand extended over the entire womb, showing layers beneath the skin: the blood flowing, the water around the baby, and the baby itself.

Its body was flat. Flat. And its eyes were square, and appeared, even to him, frightened.

'My God,' he said. 'The baby's melting too.'

'No,' the Shaman said. She looked at the Fey around her. Women all, with hair braided and wrapped around their skulls like coronets. Most of them had black hair, but in some braids, silver shone. 'She won't be able to help us. We'll have to do it on our own.'

The cat stood up and walked beside the Shaman. Then it sat, front paws neatly placed before it, and stared at Jewel's womb as if it held a mouse.

'What are you going to do?' Nicholas asked.

'If we don't get the child now, it will die,' the Shaman said.

'What about my grandson?' Rugar asked in Fey.

The Shaman brought her head up. Her dark eyes were fathomless, but there was such fury in her expression that even Nicholas recoiled. 'Your grandson is beyond my help. Now shut up and get out of my way. I will not tell you again.'

'Jewel's face is still melting,' Nicholas said in Nye. His Fey wasn't fluent enough for this kind of emergency. 'Can't you help Jewel?'

'The best way to help the Black King's granddaughter is to remove the child she's carrying,' the Shaman said in the same language.

Nicholas squeezed Jewel's hand. She did not respond. The baby inside her womb had reverted to baby shape, its tiny fists clenched and pushing against the sides.

'We'll have to remove the child ourselves,' the Shaman said in Fey. One of the Fey women got between Jewel's legs, pushed her skirt up, and pulled her knees apart. Another joined her. The third stood and grabbed Jewel's stomach, blocking Nicholas's view.

A spasm rocked Jewel's body, and her hand almost slipped from his. Her eyes were still closed, but her mouth fell partly open. Another spasm jolted through her, and Nicholas understood. They were inducing the spasms in her, trying to make her body act as if it were in labor.

'Will this work?' he asked Rugar in Islander.

Jewel's father looked twice as old as he had that morning. All the power he had carried in his body was gone now. 'I don't know,' he said. 'The midwives do it sometimes when the mother –' his voice broke. He stopped speaking and shook his head.

Nicholas straightened Jewel's head and held it in place for the next spasm. The faint odor of burning flesh wafted around him, but it wasn't as strong as it had been. The Fey woman closest to him was pushing on the womb. A woman below nodded.

'I see the head,' the woman said in Fey.

'Are you sure we have a head?' someone asked. Nicholas didn't see the source of the voice. 'It could be shifting.'

'There's hair, and a skull. Definitely. The form's holding for the moment.'

Sweat was pouring down Nicholas's back. Another spasm shuddered through Jewel. The fire blazed beside them. Even the cat was watching with deep interest.

'Another push,' one of the women said.

'Look,' the second woman said.

One of the cook's assistants screamed. The others, near Jewel's legs, had their hands over their mouths.

Nicholas craned his neck to see around the Shaman, but he couldn't. Something was wrong with this child too.

'Get them out of here,' the Shaman said to him in Nye. 'Please,' Nicholas said to his people. He wasn't feeling commanding any more. Just drained and lost. 'Please leave us.'

The cook gave him a look of alarm. Nicholas shook his head. Jewel's fingers were limp. She no longer seemed to feel the pain as another spasm rocked her. Two of the cook's assistants were sobbing, and so was the woman who tended the hearth fire. They weren't crying because of Jewel. They had been shocked by the baby.

'Leave,' Nicholas said. 'Let them finish here. Please. I'll be all right.'

The cook nodded to the group. Then he spoke to Burden in a low voice, pointing at the ovens as he did.

'I'll take care of it,' Burden said in Islander.

The cook thanked him, then led the others out. Another spasm shivered through Jewel.

'Hurry,' the Shaman said.

Jewel's skin had turned an odd gray. The melting had ceased, the disfigurement stopping near her nose. He hoped the Fey had a way of dealing with that too. He had never seen an ugly Fey. Not even the ones the Fey considered deformed had ugly faces. Those Fey were just short and nonmagical.

'There!' One of the women between Jewel's legs stood. She held a bloody thing with a human head. Its body was long and thin like an eel's. Blood dripped off the ends.

That was his child. This one probably wouldn't live the night.

'Quick,' said the voice that Nicholas couldn't identify. The voice was female, but he couldn't see who was speaking. 'Get it shaped.'

The other woman took the baby, and its form shivered, compacted, and flattened, like it had been in the womb. Suddenly it was square, with eyes and a mouth in the middle.

'Quick!' the voice said.

The Shaman stood and took the baby, cradling it. Nicholas watched, his mouth open, as the flat creature shifted again. In the Shaman's arms, it became a bloody, naked, squalling baby girl.

'You have a daughter,' she said to Nicholas in Fey.

'But what just happened? She looked flat –'

'She's fine,' the Shaman said. 'She Shifted. She'll be a difficult one.'

'Visionaries don't have Shifters,' Rugar said. He hadn't taken any steps toward the Shaman. He huddled by himself, looking small and old. 'Was it the poison?'

The Shaman shook her head. 'There is a wild magic on this Isle. This girl has it. Her Shifting is normal.'

'Actually,' said the voice Nicholas couldn't identify. 'It's too strong. Only one Shift at birth. Not several. That child was Shifting in the womb.'

He looked around for the source of the voice, but couldn't see it. The women were crowded around his daughter, cleaning her off. The nurse sat near the fire, Sebastian still cradled in her arms. He looked as if he had fallen asleep. The nurse was pale, with tiny beads of sweat on her forehead.

'The power this young,' the Shaman said, 'is why we had to act quickly.'

Jewel hadn't moved since they let her go. Nicholas inched closer to her. He didn't like the way her mouth just hung open.

'Now,' he said, 'let's help Jewel. Please.'

The Shaman turned to him. The wrinkles softened on her ancient face. She kissed the baby and handed it to one of the women. Then she came over and crouched beside Nicholas. She smelled faintly of mint.

'I can't help Jewel,' she said. 'I thought you understood that.'

'But someone has to help her. She can't be like this forever.' Nicholas took Jewel's hand and held it to his chest. 'Please. If you don't help her, no one will.'

'Young man,' the Shaman said. 'There are limits, even to our powers.'

'But she's your future.' Nicholas's voice broke. 'She has a child now, a difficult one, you said. And she promised me that she'd be beside me. We need her. You know that. You can't let anything happen to her. We all need her.'

The Shaman gently took Jewel's hand from his grasp, and laid it across Jewel's chest. Then she took Jewel's other hand and placed it across the first. She closed Jewel's mouth, and straightened her hair.

179

Jewel didn't move. She never would move again. With the Shaman's simple ritual, Nicholas finally understood what the others already knew.

Jewel was dead.

Twenty-Three

The kitchen smelled of blood, burning flesh, and woodsmoke. Rugar knelt beside his daughter. Her forehead was puckered, her nose almost gone, her hair a flat mass against her scalp. He should have Seen this. Her Vision carried her to the poultice. Not even Gift Saw beyond that moment. But Rugar was here, now. He should have Seen this.

'Did you know she was going to die?' he asked the Shaman.

She was tidying Jewel's dress. She had pushed Jewel's legs down and pulled the skirts over Jewel's feet. The mattress was soaked in blood.

'No one can survive the poison,' the Shaman said.

'But you said you saw three outcomes. Three Visions of this day.'

The Shaman sighed and pushed her straw-like hair away from her face. She was older than his father, older than any Fey except the Shamans who guided the other divisions. Among them, she was considered young.

'In the first, Jewel did not come. In the second, the Black Robe touched her directly with poison and she died in the Hall. In the third – well. We have lived the third.'

'So she shouldn't have come,' Nicholas said. His voice sounded thick, as though he had a lump in his throat. 'I asked her to come.'

The Shaman put her hand on his. Rugar had never seen the Shaman so tender with anyone. She favored this Islander boy, and Rugar could not tell why. 'If she had not come, her actions would have ended your marriage. You would have set her aside, and there would have been war.'

'You came because of that third Vision,' Rugar said. 'It's no better than the second.'

'It is much better.' Even the tone the Shaman used with Rugar was different than the one she used with Nicholas. She spoke to Rugar with a layer of contempt. 'We have the child. In the second, the child died.'

'So you came here to make certain the baby was born.'

The Shaman tugged Jewel's sleeve to her wrist. 'I thought it best. Until I realized what you had done.'

181

'But you know this will be all right.'

'No,' the Shaman said. 'I know nothing. I only saw the baby in the firelight. I did not know how deeply you disturbed the waters of the future. I hope you did so with Vision.'

Rugar straightened. His heart was pounding. He had Seen nothing, and he should have Seen this. This affected him directly. It affected the family. It affected them all. 'I am the best Visionary in the history of the Fey.'

'Until Jewel,' the Shaman said. 'And you killed her.'

Nicholas was kneeling. His face was whiter than the linen on his robe, his eyes nothing more than sunken blue bruises. 'Matthias killed her,' he said.

'Your holy man would not have acted if Rugar had listened to me.' The Shaman turned to Rugar. Her entire being radiated power. 'I told you that Jewel took the path for peace. I told you to follow her. But your ego brought you to Blue Isle, and your fear forced you to bring the only person whom Rugar would have chosen to take your place on the Black Throne. Fortunately for us, Rugar, your father is still alive. He will not give the Black Throne to Bridge unless nature forces his hand.'

'So I can still become Black King,' Rugar said.

'See the man who bargains for his future over the body of his dead daughter. No, Rugar,' the Shaman said. 'Black Kings may lose their Sight, but they never assume the office Blind.'

'I'm not Blind,' Rugar said.

'You are Blind. If you had Sight, you would have known about this day. It is to my shame that I did not realize how Blind you were. I thought you loved Jewel enough to prevent her death. I did not realize that you didn't even See it.'

'Jewel did.' Nicholas's voice was soft. 'She told me. She first saw me in a Vision. The day we met, she asked me what *Orma Lii* meant. She pronounced it wrong. Later she told me that I had said that to her in a Vision. I said it to her this afternoon. In my own language, I asked her if she were all right, and I didn't remember. I didn't know.'

A tiny light glowed from the Shaman's hand around Nicholas's. He didn't seem to notice, but Rugar did. The Shaman valued the boy. She knew something about him, too. Something she wasn't telling.

'Did Jewel tell you of this Vision, Rugar?'

He didn't answer. The Shaman would block his move to become Black King, and now Jewel was dead. And probably Gift. Rugar's heart twisted. Little Gift who had had a Vision younger than anyone in history. He would have been so strong.

But this baby girl was strong. This Shifter. A child born to Visionary parents had to have Vision. This newborn girl would have Vision and the ability to Shift. That would make her very powerful.

'The new child is a Shape-Shifter,' Rugar said. 'An Islander can't care for a child like that. Let me take her to Shadowlands. She'll be –'

'No,' the Shaman said. 'You will not touch that child.'

'She's my granddaughter. She could be Black Queen someday. I have the right to make certain she will survive her babyhood.'

'And so do I.' The Shaman let go of Nicholas. She reached across Jewel and grabbed Rugar's hands, placing them on Jewel's forehead. The skin was spongy, the bone gone. 'This is what you do, Rugar. This is what you caused. Jewel told you her Vision, didn't she? You ignored it for your ambition, just as you ignored my warnings.'

'I told Jewel not to marry the boy,' Rugar said. He tried to pull away, but the Shaman was too strong. She held him tightly. 'We thought the Vision was about the wedding.'

'You should have heeded the Vision, Rugar,' the Shaman said. 'When did she first have it?'

The spongy mass beneath his hands was caving inward. Jewel's hair brushed against his fingertips. It felt like oily hemp, not like hair at all.

'I don't know,' he said.

'She said it was in Nye.' Nicholas held his hands over theirs, then slid them back. 'Please don't hurt her.'

'It's too late for that, child,' the Shaman said. 'He hurt her when he decided to come here. The Vision in Nye would not have been about a marriage. When did she have it?'

'She said when she was waiting for her father to finish planning the trip with his father.' Nicholas clenched his fists and held them to his chest.

Rugar glared at him, then pulled his hands away. They were covered with blood, bone, and flesh. 'Why didn't I melt?' he asked.

'Because the poison seeps inward,' the Shaman said. 'Even if she had lived, she would not have had a mind left.'

Nicholas made a small cry. Blood ran from Rugar's hands onto his wrists.

'You knew, Rugar,' the Shaman said. 'You knew and you ignored for your own glory.'

'But I Saw her, in this palace, holding a baby. It seemed right.' He wanted to wipe off his hands, but didn't feel right doing so on the legs of his pants.

'It seemed right because you wanted it to seem right. You did not check with me or the other Shamans. And you did not check with your own daughter, the daughter of *two* Visionaries, to see if her Vision had come yet.' The Shaman glared at him. 'You killed her, Rugar, as clearly as if you had placed that poison on her yourself.'

He shook his head, stood, and backed away. He had been a good father. He had given Jewel what she wanted. She had been a brilliant fighter, a strong person, a good daughter. He had helped her move forward. Bringing her to Blue Isle had been for her own good as well as his own.

'Now, you want the child. Do you have a Vision for her, Rugar?'

He held up his hands. The blood had run past the wrists to his elbows.

'Of course not,' the Shaman said. 'If you had Seen her, you would have known Jewel was pregnant, and you did not. You didn't think of the child until we tried to save it.'

'Jewel Saw her.' Nicholas sounded numb. 'Jewel Saw her only a few days ago.'

'When I decided to come here,' the Shaman said.

'She Saw her in the palace.'

The Shaman nodded. 'This baby shall remain with her father.'

'But he can't care for her. Shifters require magick.'

'Yes,' the Shaman said. 'And Vision. And love. Her mother had the Vision. Her father will give her the love.'

'And who will provide the magick?'

'Not a Blind man,' the Shaman said.

Rugar shook his head. Finally he grabbed a towel from one of the tables and wiped off his hands. The blood had dried between his fingers. He couldn't get it off. 'I want the child.'

The Shaman stood. 'You will not have her. As long as I live, the girl lives here. If I discover that you have stolen her, I will bring her back. If you tamper with her, I will come after you, Rugar.'

'And do what?' Rugar said. 'I lead this company.'

'I am the only one who can challenge your power, Rugar. And I will.'

Rugar shook his head, then pointed to the body of his daughter. 'You can do nothing to me that hasn't already been done.'

'Ah, but I can, Rugar, and I will. I will take my place at the Black King's side, pronounce judgment and execute you if I must.'

'You'll lose your powers.'

'It is a price I am willing to pay.'

Rugar glanced over her shoulder. Mend was holding his granddaughter. The little girl had thick black hair and a delicate face. She would look like Jewel. 'The girl is that important?'

'You are that destructive,' the Shaman said. 'Now get out of this place and do not come back.'

Rugar didn't move. 'I can bar you from Shadowlands.'

'You can,' the Shaman said, 'but I do not think it wise.'

'You won't survive among the Islanders.'

'She will,' Nicholas stood too. 'She will have my protection.'

She smiled at him. 'Thank you, boy, but I will return to my home. Rugar knows as well as I do that if he banishes the Shaman, the Fey will not follow him. He may be the Leader, but that is only because he has war powers. We do not need war powers here. We need Healers. And Rugar, no matter how talented you are, you cannot heal.'

The little girl had her eyes open. They were deep like the Shaman's. The Shaman was right. The Fey would not follow him if they thought he banished the Shaman. But she had not Seen him take Gift. She would not know when he took the new baby either.

Neither would Nicholas. The boy didn't realize that the thing he called a son was no more son to him than the ovens were. No Fey would ever tell him. Fey believed Islanders inferior. Not even the Shaman would tell him because his inability to see proved his inferiority. Once Rugar took the baby, no one would come after her.

Rugar took one last look at Jewel's mutilated body. Then he walked around the Domestics, and headed for the door.

'Rugar,' the Shaman said. 'Think on your daughter. Before you take any action, remember her.'

He stopped, and closed his eyes. Jewel, her thin body warm beside his on the deck of the wedding barge. *We beat the Visions, Papa.* She had seemed so sure that day, so sure the Vision she saw had been about her wedding, not about her death. But the Visions always win. She didn't know that.

He hadn't known that.

Until now.

'I will never forget my daughter,' he said, and left.

Twenty-Four

Rugar's head was bowed as he walked, his back stooped. He was not the tall, proud man he had been when he confronted Nicholas and Jewel in the corridor only hours before. Nicholas watched him go, but said nothing. He allowed his own shoulders to sag slightly in relief.

The Fey women had rigged up a bottle with a nipple and were feeding the baby. She was cradled in one of the women's arms, her head tilted back, drinking hungrily. Sebastian slept in the nurse's arms, his face beautiful in repose. Two difficult children. One who could not think for himself and one who could not hold her human form.

And his wife, dead at his feet.

'What are the Islander death customs?' the Shaman asked.

Nicholas blinked. He didn't know how long he had been standing in one position, staring at the door Rugar had left through. It took a moment for the Shaman's words to register. 'I think,' he said slowly. Another decision. This time about Jewel. 'I think she would want to be buried Fey.'

'We do not bury our dead,' the Shaman said. 'We use them.'

'Use?' He had to come out of this stupor. He swallowed, turned, and faced her. Even she was taller than he was, and she was bent with age.

'Forgive me,' she said softly. He realized then that she was speaking flawless Islander. 'Our customs developed during war. We take the skin and use it to create magic. Some of our people use the blood in their spells. And the bones become tools for the weavers and the other Domestics.'

The idea made his stomach churn. But so did the thought of putting Jewel into the ground, where she would, over time, disintegrate into nothing.

'I think she would prefer that.'

The Shaman shook her head. 'We cannot use her that way.'

'Because she is the Black King's granddaughter?' He didn't understand their customs. He would never understand their customs.

'Because the poison robs us of our magic. We can only use magical

186

beings for the death rituals. Parts of the nonmagical go to the Warders for experiments. Those experiments would not be fitting for Jewel.'

Experiments. On skin he had touched, a body he had loved, a woman who had been strong and feisty and brilliant all at one time. 'I don't know how we can bury her,' Nicholas said. 'It was the Rocaan who killed her.'

The Shaman watched him for a moment. 'It would be more appropriate to keep her with you.'

He couldn't think about it. He didn't know what to do. Her own people didn't want her. He would take her. He wanted her, always. 'I'll figure out what to do,' he finally said.

'Good,' the Shaman said. 'Mend, fix another bottle. Then give him the child.'

The Fey women started collecting their things. The woman holding the baby handed her to another woman, and began preparing a new bottle.

'Wait,' Nicholas said. 'You're not just going to leave her with me?'

'Of course,' the Shaman said. 'You're her father.'

'But I've never – What if she changes again?'

'Change her back,' the Shaman said.

'I can't. I'm not Fey.'

'She got her wild magic somewhere,' the Shaman said. 'It had to come from you. She is your daughter. No full Fey child would have such pale skin and such blue eyes.'

'I don't know how to keep her in one piece,' he said. 'Please. Help me.'

The Shaman smiled. 'You will do fine.'

'No,' Nicholas said. But the woman holding his newborn daughter handed the baby to him. She was light, weighing no more than his sword, and warm in her makeshift blankets. Her features were small and wrinkled, and she had a tiny birthmark on her chin.

'I will check with you when I can,' the Shaman said. 'You will send word to Shadowlands if there will be a ritual for Jewel.'

'Wait!' Nicholas said. 'Please, tell me, will the baby be all right? My son, he – isn't – and if this child isn't, then I don't know what I can do.'

'Your son,' the Shaman said slowly, as if she were mulling over the words. 'Your son is lost to you. Jewel called this child the future. She is right. This baby is more precious than anything on the Isle.'

'Then help me care for her.'

'I am,' the Shaman said. She nodded to the women. They took their belongings, and left through the same door Rugar had. The Shaman left last. She did not look back.

Except for the scent of garlic, it was as if they had never been in the palace.

Nicholas turned to Burden.

'What should I do?' he asked.

Burden's too-thin face looked haggard. His eyes were bright with tears. 'Listen to her.'

'Can you help me?'

Burden shook his head. Then he paused next to Jewel, and lightly touched her hands. He murmured something too soft for Nicholas to understand, then stood and left with the others.

The nurse huddled in the corner, watching him, her lower lip trembling. Sebastian slept in her arms. His skin looked old and cracked, as if the grief had broken something inside him. The cat was curled next to the fire, but it was watching Nicholas. The baby gurgled, and reached her tiny hands toward his face.

This morning he had awakened and thought he would end the day in a feast celebrating his coronation, his wife beside him, his child as yet unborn. Instead, he stood alone in the kitchens of the palace, holding the baby that he hadn't even acknowledged until this week, his wife dead at his feet.

'I don't know how to care for you,' he said to the child in Fey. Not that she would understand Fey. She was too young to understand anything. But it was easier to deal with her than the body of her mother.

'I do.' The voice that spoke sounded familiar. It took him a moment to recognize it as one of the Fey voices that had been consulting over Jewel.

He glanced around, but the kitchen was empty except for the nurse and himself. The nurse looked as startled as he did.

'I always said Islanders had no imagination.' The voice sounded exasperated. 'Look here.'

'Where?' he asked.

'The fire, you idiot.'

The cat was sitting up, her front paws pressed together, her black eyes staring at him. He had never seen a black-eyed cat before. The cat sighed.

'You would think a man who took a Fey to wife would be able to see beyond surfaces. But Jewel never was very deceptive that way.'

The cat stood and stretched its long form, tail curling behind it. Then its mass wavered like a heat dream on a hot day, shimmering before him, changing, growing. The fur receded, revealing skin the color of gold. Then the shimmering stopped. A woman crouched on her hands and knees. She stood, completely naked. She had small breasts and narrow hips, but her hair wasn't dark like most Fey. It was tawny. She had a birthmark on her chin, and a feline look to her face. Even so, she was the most beautiful woman Nicholas had ever seen.

The nurse made a small squeak, and placed a hand protectively over Sebastian's head.

'It's all right,' Nicholas said reflexively, although he wasn't sure if it was. This was the creature that he had heard about. The one who had appeared before the odd deaths five years before, the one who stolen the baby from a settlement near Daisy Stream. The one who had provoked his father's decree outlawing cats.

'The Shaman is wrong,' the woman said. Her voice was husky and feral. Her long vowels almost sounded like meows. 'That child will need expert care.'

'How can the Shaman be wrong? She's the expert among you.' Nicholas didn't know that. He had merely assumed that from the way the others had been treating her.

'Shamans are experts, yes,' the woman said. 'But she's young and inexperienced. That's the only reason the Black King let her come. There hasn't been a Shape-Shifter in nearly a century. I'm the last. The Shaman who birthed me assigned me my own Domestic, and I still came close to death seven times before the end of my first year.'

'You steal children,' Nicholas said, mostly because he didn't want to think about what she had said.

'Oh, of course, especially when I think their magic will be ignored. But I can't very well steal this one, can I? The Shaman made that clear. This little girl can't go into Shadowlands or her evil grandfather will – I don't know – force her to turn into the Black King or something.' The woman rolled her eyes. Her face and tone held a layer of contempt that sounded almost familiar. 'It's time to face my heritage, I think.'

'Face your –'

'Didn't Jewel teach you anything?' The woman sighed again, and placed on hand on a slender hip. 'Of course not. Jewel didn't need to. She thought she'd be here.'

Nicholas tightened his grasp on his daughter. She was quiet, her tiny face turned toward the woman's voice.

'It is said that Shape-Shifters steal babies because they can't have any of their own. The Shifts get in the way, they say. It's actually a misunderstanding of the Shifter way. I can hold my form for as long as I want. But we're delicately attuned to the magic within others and cannot bear to see it mishandled – ah, you don't care. You just want to know if I'll take that little girl from you.'

He said nothing.

'I can't. And I won't. I'm here because you need help raising that child. The only help you'll get is me.'

Nicholas put his arms around his new daughter. She was all he had left of Jewel, all he had left – in some ways – of himself. He turned his back on the woman and paced through the kitchen, cradling the tiny, warm form to his chest. When he left this room, he would have to find a way to bury Jewel without the help of the church. He would have to comfort his own people. He would have to face Matthias.

And he would have to protect this little girl from her grandfather, for reasons he didn't entirely understand.

Nicholas stroked the baby's soft black hair. It was long already, but the Shaman was right. The baby's skin was tan – darker than his, but lighter than a Fey's.

She Shifted, this little girl, formed other shapes, and that threatened her somehow. The Fey's Shaman thought he would be able to take care of her, but what if that were another ploy, another way to show the Islanders' ineptness.

A way to kill without committing the crime herself.

What had Rugar said? The Shaman would lose her powers if she killed someone. But did that mean she could leave a child with someone who couldn't care for it? Would that be considered killing?

And if so, why would she do such a thing? Because this little girl was important? Because Rugar wanted her?

Or because she was the last link between the Fey and the Islanders?

He kissed the baby's soft head. Already she had taken a place in his heart. Lord knew he had room. Everyone else he loved had left during the same week.

'How do I know I can trust you?' he asked without turning around.

'You can't,' the woman said. 'But she can.'

Suddenly she was beside him, her hand reaching over his, stroking the baby's hair. The woman moved silently. Everything about her was catlike, and eerie.

'She's not even an hour old. She was born on the day her mother was murdered. Her grandfather sees her as a bit of territory to be squabbled over, and her father has no idea what she is.' He looked in the woman's eyes. The pupils were not round, like human pupils, but oval, like a cat's. 'She can't trust anything.'

'That's where you're wrong.' The woman reached into his arms and tilted the baby's head so that he could see her chin. 'That birthmark on a Fey marks a Shifter. I have one. We are sisters under the skin. No one understands what it is like to be two creatures at the same time except another Shifter.'

190

The woman let go of the baby's head. The little girl gurgled and snuggled closer to Nicholas. The movement warmed him.

'The Black King's family has always used us. They find a way to hook us and then we become theirs, forced to run little errands, to risk our lives for things so petty that no one would remember what we have done when we died. That is what it is like for those born outside the Black King's family. Imagine what would happen to a member of it.'

Nicholas couldn't. The machinations of Fey politics were beyond him. 'What can you do for her?'

'Help her learn to control her Shifts early. Help her choose her second form. Help her to gain the wisdom and independence she'll need to survive in this world you brought her into.'

'What do you get from this?' he asked.

A smile played at her lips. 'I get you to remove the decree against cats. I get my freedom within Jahn.'

'It seems like very little.'

'You've never had small boys chase you with knives.' She pushed her hair away from her face.

He brought up his arm, blocking her access to his daughter. 'If I am to trust you with her, I need the truth from you. Always.'

The woman shrugged. 'The truth as I know it.'

'Then tell me why you do this.'

'For the child,' the woman said. 'That much is true. And for the decree.' Then the smile crossed her lips completely, slitting her eyes, and making her look wholly feline. 'But I do it for revenge.'

The calmness in her remarks made him cold. 'Against whom?'

She looked up. Tiny dark freckles dotted her cheeks like whiskers. 'Rugar.'

She spoke the name slowly and with such hatred that Nicholas backed away.

'Yes,' she murmured. 'Rugar. He wants this little girl. He'll never have her. There are ways he could steal her, you know. It's been done before.'

She looked at Sebastian. A chill ran down Nicholas's back. Was Rugar the reason that Sebastian had no mind? 'He stole my son?' Nicholas asked.

The woman nodded.

'But my son's here now,' Nicholas said.

She made a small huffing sound as if she couldn't believe how stupid he was. 'You believe that is your son?'

'What else could he be?'

She shrugged. 'A bit of stone? A lump of clay?'

He frowned. That child was not stone. Nicholas had touched him, had been touched in return. If the child wasn't theirs, Jewel would have known.

The woman peered at him for a moment, and then when he didn't respond, she made the huffing sound again. 'It doesn't matter,' she said softly. 'I will help your daughter, not you.'

'You'll make sure she doesn't end up like my son?'

The woman smiled. 'I'll guarantee it.'

That was all Nicholas needed. Somehow Rugar had interfered with his son, probably to ruin the marriage, but this woman would make certain he couldn't do it again.

The woman put a hand to the baby's lips. 'I'll protect her, and raise her, and make her strong.'

'She's my daughter,' Nicholas said.

The woman smiled at him. 'Delicious irony, no?' She walked over to Jewel. 'The thing is, Jewel wouldn't have been able to raise this child either. It takes special skills to form a Shape-Shifter.'

'Jewel was talented.'

'Yes.' The woman crouched beside Jewel. The woman was so sleek and well-formed that the muscles in her legs, back and buttocks showed with each movement. 'Jewel was talented. But not in my kind of magick.'

She plucked at Jewel's sleeve, then brought her face close to Jewel's head. Nicholas walked back to his wife's side. The woman's nose twitched. She was actually sniffing the corpse. When she saw Nicholas, she grinned, but there seemed to be a bit of embarrassment in the look. 'Cat tendencies,' she said. Her voice was soft. 'I never liked Jewel much, but she didn't deserve this. I suppose I'm here for that too. The Shaman is right. Jewel would still be alive if it weren't for her father.'

'Or Matthias.'

'I trust you'll take care of that creature.' She put her hands on her knees and leveraged herself up. 'I personally would slit him from throat to gullet. You are probably more refined than that.'

Not the way he was feeling. Not at the moment.

The nurse was watching all of this, and obviously understanding none of it. Only Nicholas, his father and a few of the lords had learned Fey. Her arms were wrapped around Sebastian as tightly as Nicholas's were around his daughter.

The woman followed his gaze. 'I suppose that tends to the baby's needs?'

'The nurse?'

'Whatever it is. Besides frightened. I don't do diapers, bottles, or vomit. Just training, intelligence, and Shifts.'

192

Nicholas smiled in spite of himself. The smile was almost involuntary. The woman's energy pleased his aching and tired soul. 'I will monitor everything you do,' he said.

'Please.' Her tone had an air of condescension. 'If that child were in any danger, you would have no clue. I didn't have to show myself to you, after all. I could have taken her in the night, like I did Coulter.' She shook her head. 'Mistake there. Such power, and all of it goes to Rugar. Still, the boy is young, and the power won't develop until adolescence. You should thank your god for that. If the boy's power existed now, you Islanders wouldn't stand a chance.'

Nicholas didn't know what she was talking about. He didn't care. The baby had wet his hand. 'Will she Shift again soon?'

The woman shrugged. 'Probably not. Babies tend to involuntarily Shift in moments of fear or stress. The danger comes after the first month or so, when they tire of staring at the world, and want to test new muscles. Arms, hands, feet – and Shifting.'

'What next?' Nicholas asked.

The woman plucked the nurse's shoulder. 'Looks like the King's daughter needs diapers,' she said in Islander.

The nurse looked at Nicholas for confirmation.

'It's fine,' he said. 'Let's get Sebastian comfortable and see what we can do for his sister. I'll watch over him.'

The nurse took off her cloak and wrapped it on the floor, then she set Sebastian in it. She shot a wary glance at the woman, then went into the kitchen proper. Something was burning in the ovens, probably whatever the chef had asked Burden to watch.

'You asked what we do first,' the woman said in Fey. 'First we make introductions. My name is Solanda. I shall call you Nicholas. If you insist on Highness or some other slop, the deal is off.'

The smile touched his lips again. It was good he could smile. He needed to know that he would feel lighter emotions again. 'Nicholas is fine.'

'Good,' she said. She paused over Sebastian, then shook her hand. Nicholas had seen cats make that gesture with a front paw when they were near something that disgusted them. 'Jewel allowed you to name this lump, didn't she? Big mistake. Probably part of the reason Rugar won that round. Fey children need Fey names.' She walked over to Nicholas and peered into the baby's face. 'We'll go back to my generation. No "meaning" names. That's a L'Nacin tradition, not a Fey one.' She ran a hand over the baby's head. 'We're going to call her Arianna.'

'She's also Islander,' Nicholas said. Then he stopped. He remembered this discussion with Jewel. *I swear*, she had said. *It was easier to make the child than it is to name him.*

Solanda shook her head and rolled her eyes. 'Arianna was a great Shape-Shifter who disappeared into enemy lines when she was a toddler. She took as her second form that of the general who adopted her, and after he died, used his visage to convince his troop to surrender to the Fey.'

'What an auspicious name,' Nicholas said dryly.

'It is a name worthy of her talents and her future. Go ahead,' Solanda said. 'Name her as you named your son.'

Nicholas sighed. The day had defeated him. 'Right now, one name is as good as another.'

Solanda peered at him. Then she turned as the nurse approached carrying towels torn up as diapers. 'You must decide where this child will sleep. I would suggest boarding her in a crib in your room until Rugar realizes he cannot steal her.'

'I'll take care of everything,' Nicholas said. There was no one else to. And he had hours before he could even think of sleep. First he would care for Arianna. Then he would take care of Jewel. 'I'll need you to stay with Jewel and scare off anyone who tries to touch her.'

'Ah,' Solanda said. 'The evil feline. It could get me killed.'

He looked at her sideways. 'I'll rescind that decree soon. Until then, I think you can take care of yourself.'

She chuckled, then slipped into her feline form. Her body shifted, molded, compacted. Fur grew on her skin. Only her eyes remained the same.

'I promise you, Nicholas the Highness,' she said when the change was complete. 'We will bring this girl up right. She'll be prepared for anything her grandfather throws at her.'

'I hope you're right,' he said, looking over his daughter's head at the body of his wife. 'I really do.'

THE SCHISM
[The Following Day]

Twenty-Five

His whole body hurt. He woke slowly, his eyes glued together by sleep and tears. Gift had the feeling that Coulter was on the bed next to him, but when he opened his eyes, he was sleeping alone. But he wasn't in his room. He was in the front room, the door closed and bolted. He was lying on the rug, but someone had put something soft – a pad? – underneath it. His mother sat on a cushion, her wings bandaged and taped to her sides. Her eyes had deep shadows under them and she appeared thinner than she had before.

She had been hurt.

Dying.

And she had cried when she saw him, and cursed his grandfather, and told Gift that she loved him.

Or had she?

A fire burned in the fireplace, the smell of woodsmoke at once comforting and alarming. He had just been somewhere near a fire. In his dreams. . . .

'Gift?' His mother asked. She half-stood, as if she needed a better view of his face. 'Gift?'

He lifted a hand. White light dripped off it like water. 'Mommy,' he said. 'I had a bad dream.'

'We all did, little sweetness,' she said. 'It's over now.'

But it wasn't. Not the way he felt. He felt as if the dream had been true. For the first time in his life, he wanted to see his grandfather. His grandfather had been there, in that strange room with the Domestics and the yellow people. His grandfather had cried for the woman on the mattress.

Gift's throat was sore and his forehead felt like something bad had happened to it. He brought up his hand, dripping white light, and touched his forehead. The skin was smooth. His hair fell over it, as it should have, and his head felt solid.

Somehow, he had thought it shouldn't.

'What happened?' he asked. His voice was raspy. When he spoke this time, he noticed that his stomach hurt too. And the back of his legs.

197

'We don't know, honey,' his mother said.

'What happened to you? Who hurt your wings?'

She shook her head. 'It's over now,' she said.

'What's this white stuff?' He held out his arm. The white dripped off it and splashed on the floor. The light spread like water before disappearing into the wood.

'It made you better,' she said. Her eyes wouldn't meet his when she spoke. For the first time in his life, he realized that his mother didn't want to tell him what had happened.

Gift closed his eyes. He saw the woman – *Mother?* – on a mattress in a strange room his grandfather called a kitchen. She wasn't moving. Beside her stood a yellow man holding a little baby. He was watching a cat.

The whole thing seemed very real. The crackle of the fire beside Gift echoed the large fire in the kitchen with the woman. But it wasn't real. He had seen these images in his dream: these and others, like the ones he had seen when his grandfather was here. This time the Vision had lasted forever, and it had made him cry.

He opened his eyes. His mother was watching him closely, as if she were afraid something was going to happen to him with his eyes closed. 'I had that Vision thing again, didn't I?' he asked.

Her lips got tight, and she shrugged, a tiny movement he almost didn't see. Then the door opened, and he turned, thinking it would be his father. Instead, Coulter came in.

Coulter looked bigger somehow, older, not like his friend, but like a grown-up. Coulter's blue eyes seemed brighter than they had ever been before. Gift could feel him almost more than he could see him.

The light around Gift grew brighter, almost blinding. Coulter waved his arm over Gift, and the light dimmed. Gift could no longer see it, but he could feel it, encircling him like a warm hug.

'You woke up,' Coulter said.

Gift nodded. 'What happened?'

Coulter looked at Gift's mother. Gift recognized the look as one grown-ups gave each other. It sent some sort of secret signal. Gift's mother stood. She moved gingerly, as if her wings hurt her.

'You be careful,' she said to Coulter. 'I'll just be outside.'

Coulter didn't answer her. Instead he waited until she left before he sat, crosslegged, beside Gift.

Gift had always liked Coulter. He looked funny – kind of like the yellow people in Gift's Vision – but he was big and friendly and had a sparkle that surrounded him. The sparkle had grown stronger all winter, and now it was as bright as the light had been around Gift. In fact, the light made him think of Coulter.

'You did something to me, didn't you?' Gift asked.

Coulter nodded. 'I want you to think in your grown-up way before I talk to you.'

Gift frowned. He hadn't told anyone except his mother about his grown-up think, and she hadn't believed him. He knew she hadn't told Coulter. Gift raised himself on his elbows. 'Something awful happened, didn't it?'

'Do you remember how you came to this place?' Coulter asked.

Gift nodded. 'My mother and her friends brought me here when I was very, very little.'

'Solanda brought me,' Coulter said. 'I was a year old.' He leaned forward, his arms resting on his thighs. 'You and me, we aren't real Fey.'

Gift frowned. He could see that about Coulter. Coulter didn't look like anybody else. His hair was yellow, his eyebrows were straight, and his eyes were round. But Gift had seen himself in a mirror. He had the eyebrows, his hair was dark, his features were swept up in proper Fey fashion. 'I'm Fey,' he said.

'No,' Coulter said. 'Part Fey. Your daddy is what they call Islander, like me.'

The man who held the baby. That was Gift's father. He knew that as clearly as if he had been with the man every day of his life. 'Then why am I here?'

'I don't know,' Coulter said. He bit his lower lip, finally looking like a kid again. Gift wasn't sure he wanted to talk to a kid. Coulter glanced around as if he were making sure they were alone. 'Yesterday, I heard you screaming. No one else seemed to. They all did the same stuff they always do. But I heard you. In my head. And it was like this door opened in my brain, and all this stuff I knew came to my mind.'

'I was screaming?' Gift pushed himself all the way up. No wonder his throat was sore.

'Not really, I don't think,' Coulter said. 'I don't know. I heard you in my brain. Then I came here. You were dying, Gift.'

Gift frowned. He was sore, but other than that he felt all right. 'I'm all right now.'

'I know,' Coulter said. 'I came here and the closer I got to you, the more I could see what was happening to you. You had ties to someone else – your real mom – and she was dying, and you were dying with her. And everybody knew, and they were letting you die.'

'Everybody?' Gift asked. 'Even my mom and dad?'

Coulter shook his head. 'Your dad went to get help. All the Domestics and Healers were gone. Even the Shaman was gone.'

'Because they didn't want to help me?'

199

'Because they were helping your real mom. And when I came in the door, I heard – through you – the Shaman saying she was too far away to help you.'

Gift frowned. He remembered that. He remembered her standing beside him and saying that. 'Was my grandfather there?'

Coulter nodded.

Gift put the heel of his hand on his forehead. This sounded so familiar. He closed his eyes. He could see his grandfather, demanding they save the boy, and when they did not, wanting that baby.

As if they were interchangeable.

'I don't understand.'

'Me, neither,' Coulter said. 'But I knew what to do. It was like I knew it already, like it had been in my brain all along. I cut that link you had with your mom, and I wrapped my light around you. That's why you still have light now.'

Gift looked at his hand. If he concentrated, he could still see the light dripping off it. No wonder he had thought Coulter was with him. Coulter was.

'How long do I need this?' Gift asked.

'I don't know,' Coulter grabbed Gift's hand. Coulter's grip was tight, his skin clammy.

Gift didn't pull away, but he wanted to.

'I'm scared,' Coulter whispered. 'Something happened to me, and what happened to you started it.'

'Maybe,' Gift said slowly, 'when my grandfather gets back, we can talk to him.'

'I thought you never liked your grandfather.'

'I don't really,' Gift said. Then he told Coulter about the Vision. 'Grandpa knew what it was. He said it would happen again, and that's where I was when you came here. In that place, with those people.'

Coulter let go of Gift's hand. 'Your grandfather scares me. He doesn't look at people. He looks through them.'

Gift nodded. He had seen that. 'He wanted to trade me,' Gift said. 'For that baby. When he thought I was dead. He wanted that baby.'

'Baby?' Coulter said.

'She was there, where my real mother was dying. My grandfather wanted her if he couldn't have me.'

Coulter bit his lower lip again. Then he rubbed a fist against his cheek, leaving a smear of dirt. He didn't really have parents. Everyone at the Domicile watched him, and sometimes they let him go without a bath for a long, long time.

'Something's wrong,' he said. 'I don't know what any of this means, Gift.'

200

'Me either,' Gift said. He was more frightened now than he had been when he woke up.

'But I think we should be careful around your grandfather.'

Gift nodded. 'Can I keep the light?'

Coulter grinned. 'Sure.' He got up. 'I'm glad you're all right.'

'Me, too,' Gift said, although he wasn't sure, after this conversation, if he was all right at all.

'Look,' Coulter said. 'You and me, we're different. Neither of us live with our real mom and dad. And when you got in trouble, somehow I knew. I think we should stick together.'

Gift held up his hand, and watched the light drip from it. 'I don't think we got a choice,' he said.

Twenty-Six

Matthias hadn't slept. He sat on the kneeling cushion, which he had moved beneath the slitted windows in the fiftieth Rocaan's worship room. The room smelled musty and damp. Cobwebs hung from the ceiling and dust had gathered on the tiny altar. The Sword, hanging from the wall beside the door, was covered in rust.

The fiftieth Rocaan had used the room to be closer to God. Every morning, he had taken the back stairs to this tiny, unadorned place, and spent an hour listening for God's still small voice. Toward the end, he had said he never heard it. Matthias hadn't even believed it existed. Yet he found himself walking the cramped steps himself during the night, searching for some kind of solace.

The Tabernacle had once been a small saint's cottage filled with an incense burner, an altar, and a kneeling cushion so that the itinerant worshiper could feel closer to his God. The original stone room remained, although three centuries earlier, the thirty-fifth Rocaan added a window, covered by tapestries. The window became an arrow slit, which he used to attack assailants who were trying to eject him from the Tabernacle.

The light coming through the window was just enough to allow Matthias to blow out the candles he had brought. From here he had a view of the river, and when the sky was clear, a view of the palace.

He leaned his head against the damp stone wall. Nicholas had sent a page over in the middle of the night with a message. Two words.

Jewel's dead.

He still remembered Nicholas's face. The Fey held his pregnant daughter close, and Nicholas followed, already looking bereft. *You are committing murder, holy man. But it wouldn't be the first time, would it?*

Nicholas didn't understand. He had never understood. As a boy, he had shirked his duties and tried to avoid his religious studies. As a man, he had fought Matthias each and every step along the way.

He did not understand what they were facing.

No one did.

But the answer lay in holy water.

The Roca had used the holy water to clean his sword before he

202

allowed the Soldiers of the Enemy to run him through. The Words Written and Unwritten said that at that moment, the Roca was Absorbed to the Hand of God. Rocaanist tradition said that Roca's actions provided a sacrifice which saved his people from the Soldiers of the Enemy. Nothing in the Words or in the traditions said that holy water had murderous properties.

The fiftieth Rocaan had decided that they had misused the holy water. He thought perhaps the Fey were the new Soldiers of the Enemy, and he agreed to meet with Rugar, Jewel's father, in the hope that he could drive the Fey back by himself.

It was a vain and arrogant hope. The Rocaan was putting himself in the position of the Roca, thinking that if the Fey ran him through, he would be Absorbed, and the Fey would leave Blue Isle forever.

The Fey had killed him, using their magic, and nothing had changed. Instead Nicholas had married a Fey and an uneasy truce was born.

But the holy water had its effect on the Fey for a reason. No one else suffered so at its touch. All the others on the Isle took part in the Sacraments, and they touched the holy water daily. The worst that had happened to an Islander was a small rash. People born near the Cliffs of Blood wore gloves during Midnight Sacrament to prevent the allergic reaction. But even if the holy water touched them, it did not kill them.

The sun sparkled on the river water below. The Cardidas was wide, the ports empty now except for fishing vessels. Jahn's wealth was slowly disappearing. All because of the Fey. Even Nicholas's marriage hadn't allowed trade to reopen. Both Nicholas and Alexander were afraid to let the Fey off the Isle, afraid they would send holy water back to their Black King, and his magicians would find a way around it.

But what if the Fey couldn't find a way around it? What if the Islanders had holy water for a reason, and that reason was to stop the Fey?

Six years ago, Matthias would never have believed this. But, as the Words said, *The belief of cowards was assured*. As time passed, he believed more and more.

It was almost as if the fact that holy water could be used against the Fey proved God provided for the Islanders. The old Rocaan would have called – and once did call – that idea blasphemy. But it was no more blasphemy than thinking a man fifty generations removed could take the place of the Roca.

Matthias leaned his head against the cold stone wall. The slight breeze blowing in the window off the river was warmer than the stone. But he didn't mind the chill. He needed it to remind him of what had happened.

He had tried to warn Nicholas. When Nicholas had asked that Jewel not feel the touch of holy water during the marriage ceremony, Matthias had agreed. He wanted to wait and see what would happen. His role as Rocaan was still too new. Perhaps he was wrong. Besides, he thought there would be a number of options. If the marriage did not work out, Nicholas could have set Jewel aside.

Then the baby was born, and again Nicholas asked that Jewel and her son not feel the touch of holy water. It soon became clear that God was not with the boy. He had no brain to speak of. He moved slowly, acted slowly, and even slept slowly. Alexander had worried that the child would not be able to rule. Matthias worried that the child was such an abomination that God might not want it to live.

From that point on, he had tried to talk to Nicholas, but Nicholas would hear nothing of it. *Other families have problem children*, he would say. Matthias would point out that those families were often in God-less areas, like the Marshes or the Snow Mountains, but Nicholas would point to the few who had made their way to Jahn.

When the new pregnancy happened, Matthias became desperate. He did not want Jewel to solidify the marriage. Nor did he want another half-formed child that close to the Roca's throne. Nicholas did not believe, and because he did not believe, he did not understand that he was polluting the Roca's blood with that of the Soldiers of the Enemy.

Tiny figures crossed the Jahn bridge. Matthias twisted on the cushion so that he could see better. No horses. No one from the palace.

Yet.

Matthias was accused of not believing – and he had told the fiftieth Rocaan that he hadn't believed – but what he had meant by that was that he didn't believe in the miracles. He still felt that if he studied enough, he would learn the secret behind the Absorption. Perhaps it was a simple trick designed to scare the Soldiers of the Enemy. He felt that the Rocaanists honored a man. A great man to be sure, but a man just the same.

That the Roca had lived and influenced life on Blue Isle, Matthias had no doubt. That the Roca had powers from God, Matthias did doubt. Still, the systems established after the Roca's death had served the Isle for generations. And one of those systems including passing the Roca's blood through the King's line, unbroken, from the days of the Roca's sons.

Nicholas had polluted that blood. The pollution produced an abomination like Sebastian. For the sake of the Isle, for the sake of Rocaanism, for the sake of Nicholas himself, Matthias had to stop that.

He had thought a simple test would have been enough. The cloth had not been dipped in holy water. It had been stored with holy water. That way, if God intended the water to touch Jewel, it would. God prevented the abominations from continuing, not Matthias.

Matthias had simply been God's instrument.

If that is the case, Matthias, why can't you sleep?

He sat up and glanced around the small room. The door was still closed. He was alone.

He had come here to hear the fiftieth Rocaan's voice, but not with words from his conscience, speaking inside his head.

Matthias had not been able to sleep the night of the Invasion either. Whenever he closed his eyes, he had seen Fey melting, grasping at their featureless faces, suffocating before him. It had taken him weeks to get beyond that.

And he still saw the face of their leader, asking, *What have you done?* in accented Nye, as Matthias poured holy water on his face.

Matthias shuddered.

Even when faced with an Enemy seeking to destroy everything a man held dear, that man still had twinges of conscience.

Conscience that spoke with the voice of a former friend and mentor.

Matthias sighed. He had told the Rocaan it was wrong to appoint him to take his place. But the Rocaan hadn't listened.

– You are my choice, Matthias. A Rocaan needs strength and a certain love of knowledge. You have both of those.

– I would want the church to be led by someone who believes.

– Why? You don't believe yourself. What should it matter to you?

– I have always thought that my failure to believe was my failure. Having a Rocaan who believes, being surrounded by those who believe, reinforces that feeling. But if the Rocaan doesn't believe either, that makes Rocaanism a hollow shell. An institution with no heart, a hypocritical place that pretends to provide comfort and answers and in truth can provide nothing.

– There have been disbelieving Rocaans in the past.

– Yes, and one was assassinated, and another nearly brought the church down with him. I don't want to be that kind of man, Holy Sir, I can't be.

– You won't be.

The Rocaan had been so certain that day. Yet that certainty had never made its way to Matthias. The Rocaan had said, just before he died, that he hadn't heard the still small voice in years. He believed it hadn't spoken in generations, leaving the Rocaans to discover truth on their own. He had said he thought such a discovery the only way to continue faith.

Matthias had discovered truth. Nicholas simply hadn't wanted to hear it. He would be grateful, though, one day, when his real son and heir, born of Nicholas and an appropriate Island woman, would be born.

A knock on the door sounded close in the small room. Matthias stood, his knees almost buckling beneath him. He had been sitting a long time.

The knock sounded again, and then the door opened. Elder Reece leaned in. Reece was thin to the point of gauntness. He was also small, and preferred his Danite's robe to his Elder's robe. Matthias had to threaten him with a special decree to get Reece to wear the proper robe during the day.

Reece was wearing his Elder's robe now. The sash was belted loosely, making the robe hang off him like a sack. He still went barefoot within the Tabernacle, and his feet were filthy.

'Forgive me, Holy Sir,' he said, 'but the Elders have been looking for you everywhere.'

'This is a worship room,' Matthias said. He was glad they had sent Reece. Reece was easy to manipulate.

Reece bobbed his head, but did not let go of the door. 'I know, Holy Sir, but we have been looking for you since dawn. I-I-I thought one last try –'

'I will appear when I am ready,' Matthias said. He wasn't ready yet. He was still unsettled by the suddenness of Jewel's reaction to the holy water.

And by Nicholas's anger.

In all of the history of the Tabernacle, there had never been a split with the palace.

'Forgive me, Holy Sir, but Porciluna, he said . . .' Reece paused and bobbed again. The light from the window fell on his sallow features, and they were drawn with fear.

'Yes?' Matthias said. They had sent the timid one because he would deliver the message. Sometimes in his absorption in Tabernacle matters great and small, he forgot that none of the Elders approved of his appointment to Rocaan. And why would they? They had been in the running for the position as well.

'Porciluna said that they would start without you.' Reece ducked his head as if he expected to get hit. 'Forgive me, Holy Sir.'

'Start what?' Matthias said.

'The Elders' evaluation. They – Porciluna – ah – they all wonder – forgive me, Holy Sir, but they wonder if you've gone crazy.'

'Crazy?' Matthias asked. 'And on what do they base this idea?'

'The Queen's death, Holy Sir. One of the Officiates says you planned it.'

'Really?' Matthias felt cold. He should have expected this. A distant part of his mind wondered why he had not. 'You were present, Reece. Do you think I acted like a crazed man?'

'You – ah, please, Holy Sir. I only deliver the message.'

'Do you?'

Reece let go of the door and looked down at his hands. 'Holy Sir, you did not let the Fey leader out with his daughter. You tried to prevent his leaving.'

'And that's a sign of craziness?'

'It – seemed odd, Holy Sir.'

Matthias took a deep breath. He had expected trouble from the palace, but not from the Tabernacle. None from the Tabernacle at all. 'Tell them I'll be at the meeting shortly.'

Reece did not move.

'Tell them,' Matthias said.

'Forgive me, Holy Sir,' Reece said. 'They've been waiting all morning. They said if I were to find you, I was to take you there.'

Like a prisoner. Matthias would not allow himself to be treated like a prisoner. 'I will show up there when I am ready. I assume they're in the audience room?'

'Yes, Holy Sir.' Again, Reece did not move. Matthias was getting irritated.

'Reece, I am capable of finding the room on my own.'

'Yes, Holy Sir.' Reece stepped out of the room, and pulled the door closed.

Matthias leaned back against the wall. Its chill seeped through his robe. Crazy. An excuse. They were making up an excuse to get rid of him. They didn't want him to be Rocaan. No one had, except the fiftieth Rocaan, and even he did not believe he would die anytime soon on the day he appointed Matthias.

The only power Matthias had was in being Rocaan. The Rocaan was the Keeper of the Secrets. Unlike his predecessor, Matthias had not shared even one secret with anyone else. He also had not appointed Elders to fill the vacancies left when he went into the Rocaan's chair, and when Elder Andre disappeared. Under canonical law, Elders could only act against the Rocaan when all Elders agreed. All *ten* Elders.

He took a deep breath. He had planned for this moment in some ways. He had always known they would challenge him. He just hadn't expected it over the Fey. For some reason, he thought they were all agreed on the Fey.

Matthias let himself out of the chamber and took the stairs to the main level. He walked slowly – any appearance of haste might be mistaken for panic – and made his way to the audience chamber.

The double doors were open, waiting for him. All the Elders were inside, including Reece. His slender hands were gesturing as he spoke, apparently telling the others that Matthias would be along soon.

The Audience Room was so large that eight men disappeared in it. The chairs were pushed against the walls. The chandelier was lit, but whoever had done so had failed to pull it back to the ceiling. The carefully crafted glass baubles hung at the height of Matthias's head, and candle wax dripped from one bauble onto the floor.

Porciluna stood in the center. His robe was plush velvet, the small swords hanging off his sash made of polished silver. Even after the Invasion, Porciluna managed to have the best of everything in his rooms – the best food, the most comfortable bed, the finest jewelry. Like Matthias, Porciluna had been a second son forced in the religion. Unlike Matthias, Porciluna had decided to make himself as comfortable, if not more comfortable, than the family that had forced him to this place. Porciluna had never hidden his ambitions, or his lack of faith.

Unlike the man standing next to him. Ilim was squat and older than many of the Elders. He wore a plain robe and kept his hair uncut, preferring to tie it into a ponytail down his back. He supervised the spiritual guidance of the servants and rarely involved himself in Tabernacle business.

The six remaining Elders were scattered around the audience hall, conferring in groups. Only Timothy didn't seem to be paying attention. Timothy, whose hair had touches of gray in it, but who moved with the quickness of youth, had a naïveté about him that the others mistook as a lack of intelligence. Timothy was staring at the wall panels which depicted the reign of the first Rocaan as he converted the countryside, and subdued his brother, the King.

'It has been one hundred and sixty-five years since the Elders last summoned the Rocaan,' Matthias said. 'I trust this matter is important.'

'If you consider murder important,' Porciluna said.

'Murder!' Linus whirled from his place near the wall. He walked beside Porciluna. 'You condemn a man before giving him a chance to speak.'

'Close the door, Vaughn,' Matthias said to the Elder nearest him. Vaughn closed the doors as Matthias walked into the room. He looked at his former companions. 'Elder Reece said you all thought I was crazy.'

'One needs to be crazy to kill the Queen at the King's coronation,' Porciluna said.

'Porciluna!' Linus took his arm. 'This was not how the meeting was planned.'

Planned. Matthias looked at Linus. Linus and Ilim resembled each other enough to be brothers, but Ilim appeared embarrassed by this meeting and Linus did not.

Porciluna shook Linus off. 'Let me explain this to you, *Holy* Sir. We all know that you never believed in the Roca or in God. The Rocaan told us that the day he appointed you. He said your faith was tainted.'

'He also said a man cannot become an Elder without faith.' Timothy spoke from his place near the wall. 'Do you believe that, Porciluna?'

Matthias suppressed a smile. Perhaps the group was not as unified as Porciluna thought it was.

'Just because the fiftieth Rocaan said it doesn't make it true,' Porciluna said.

'Obviously,' Matthias said with a pointed glance to Porciluna.

'Don't change this,' Porciluna said. 'The fact is you committed murder.'

'That's a heady charge,' Matthias said. 'On what do you base it?'

'On the ceremony yesterday. She died, Matthias.'

'She did,' Matthias said. 'And it is regrettable. But it happened.'

'You make it sound as if it were out of your control.' Eirman had been standing in the shadows. He came forward, under the light of one of the torches. 'You knew that holy water would kill her.'

'I didn't use holy water on her,' Matthias said. 'I kept my agreement with the King. I had told him I would place a cloth on her head before touching her or allowing anything to touch her, and that is exactly what I did.'

'Officiate Danesfen says you instructed him to keep the cloth in his pouch with the holy water.'

'I instructed him to keep it in his pouch. I do not know what else he kept there,' Matthias said.

'At the stables, you asked for the cloth. I was there when he pulled out the holy water, then the cloth,' Linus said.

'The vial for the water should have been sealed. The cloth seemed dry. It looked fine to me.' Matthias shrugged. 'The cloth was dry when I spread it on the Sacrificial table. I kept it away from the vials. How do we know that the cloth killed her? How do we know it wasn't her husband's touch? He had been near the holy water. You are quick to assume I did it.'

'She didn't change until you put the crown on her head,' Porciluna said.

'Yes, but the transformation was a slow one. Most Fey melt quickly.' Matthias looked at them all. 'Or am I the only one who remembers that?'

'You didn't want to let her out of the Hall,' Porciluna said.

'We don't know what caused her change. I believe that God and the Roca were signaling their displeasure. I thought she should remain so that we could understand what was happening.'

'The Fey thought they could save her.'

'They were obviously mistaken,' Matthias said. 'It is clear that her death was God's will.'

'Just as the use of holy water as a weapon is God's will?' Timothy asked from the corner.

'If God did not want it used that way, he would not have revealed its properties to us,' Matthias said. He walked farther into the room, until he was standing in front of Porciluna. 'How many of us can say that we have not deliberately used holy water to kill a Fey? Hmmm? Timothy, perhaps. Andre before he disappeared. Any of the rest of you?'

He looked at Eirman. Eirman dropped his gaze. So did the rest of the Elders as Matthias turned to them. Only Porciluna continued staring at him. 'You were the one who discovered how to kill. You were the one who convinced the last Rocaan to use holy water in that way. And you are the one who used it to kill the woman that our King had taken to wife. You cannot pass blame so easily.'

'I am not passing blame,' Matthias said. 'I am merely pointing out that the standard cannot change from case to case. Murder implies a deliberate act. If you want to put this in human terms, what happened to her was an accident. If you prefer it in religious terms, it was an Act of God.'

'God does not commit murder,' Porciluna said.

'Of course not,' Matthias said. 'He acts in the best interest of his people. He gave us holy water. He allowed us to be the only people in the world with the power to defeat the Fey. You cannot believe that he would allow our blood to mingle with Fey blood and call it good. Look at the child Nicholas created with that woman. Look at what happened to the Roca's blood. Jewel carried another child. God ended her life before another abomination could appear.'

'If that were true,' Ilim said, 'then the child wouldn't have been born.'

Matthias felt as if someone had poured cold water down his back. 'What?'

'The palace kitchen staff were present when the child was born. They say it is a demon.'

The Elders gasped. Matthias felt the blood drain from his face. Another child to contend with. 'I thought Jewel died.'

'She did,' Ilim said. 'But the kitchen staff said that Nicholas and the

210

Fey saved the child. Then when they saw what it was, they made the staff leave.'

Still it continued. Matthias clenched his fists, then rubbed his fingers together, allowing none of the emotion he felt to show. Nicholas would have to throw these children over. But Matthias had time on this. He could eventually convince Nicholas to do so. And Nicholas would.

He would have to.

No monstrous child could rule Blue Isle. It would not be allowed.

'The child is a demon because the Fey are demons,' Matthias said. 'They have powers which should be reserved for God. My instinct was right. We should have forced the Fey to remain in the Hall until we were convinced Jewel had died.'

'Why?' Timothy asked, his brow furrowed. 'Doesn't the survival of the child argue against your position?'

'No,' Matthias said. 'The Fey have abilities only God can subvert. We allowed them the freedom to perform those abominations. We should have prevented it.'

'You seem so certain,' Linus said. 'I don't understand how you can be so certain.'

'There is nothing in the Words Written and Unwritten that mentions abomination,' said Ilim.

Matthias was trending on very thin ground here. They would not listen to him if he didn't convince them properly. 'The Words Written and Unwritten talk about the Soldiers of the Enemy and the threats they brought to Blue Isle. The Roca sacrificed himself to them to prevent them from taking over the Isle. In doing so, he was Absorbed to the Hand of God.'

'We know this,' Vaughn said.

'But you do not think about it,' Matthias said. 'The fiftieth Rocaan believed the Fey were the Soldiers of the Enemy. He went to meet with them hoping that God would be present at the ceremony, believing that he would become the Roca in the World, believing he would be Absorbed, believing that he would lead the Fey off the Isle.'

'He died because of that belief,' Reece said softly.

'He did,' Matthias said. 'But did he die because he was mistaken in his belief or because he was too arrogant? Or because he misunderstood an element of the Words.'

'He would never misunderstand the Words,' Vaughn said.

'Really?' Matthias asked. 'Were you listening to the Coronation Ceremony? The Roca's representative in the World is the King. We are not part of the Roca's direct lineage. The King is. What if he made a mistake mating with the Soldiers of the Enemy? Wouldn't God show that by giving him deformed children? What if he were to face the

Soldiers of the Enemy head on, be Absorbed, and the Fey were to leave because of it?'

'Is that why you used a religious ceremony to commit murder?' Porciluna asked. 'Because you heard those words and made a mistaken belief according to your inept scholarship?'

'I have already addressed your murder charge,' Matthias said. 'I have done nothing.'

'Try convincing the palace of that,' Porciluna said.

Matthias crossed his arms over his chest. 'Do we run our religion according to what the palace thinks?'

'No,' Porciluna said. 'But the fiftieth Rocaan was an old, sick man when he died. His delusion about being the Roca proves that he was not thinking clearly. He appointed you believing he would come back. He did not. I think it is time for the Elders to choose a new Rocaan.'

'This has not been done in the history of the Tabernacle,' Timothy said.

'But it has been tried,' Linus said. 'The Rocaan who did not allow it nearly destroyed the church.'

Matthias let a slow grin grow on his face. 'So, Porciluna, you believe you should be the next Rocaan. Upset because the fiftieth Rocaan did not choose you and you could not go on plundering the church?'

'I have Rocaanism at heart. I believe more than you do, Matthias. I would never, ever murder to achieve my ends,' Porciluna said.

Matthias let the lack of respect slide by. For the moment, he had a greater concern. 'Well,' he said. 'I'm sure that Nicholas would approve of all of you choosing a new Rocaan. I suspect he is not pleased with me at the moment.'

'It would help relations with the palace,' Linus said, as if he were trying to convince Matthias.

'It would, wouldn't it?' Matthias smiled at Linus, then shrugged. 'I think it would be fine if you all chose a new Rocaan.'

Porciluna's small lips pursed, making him look as if he were waiting for a kiss. Linus grinned. Ilim frowned, and Timothy peered at the panels as if they had changed in the last few moments. Vaughn and Reece stared at Matthias as if he had lost his mind, and Eirman was shaking his head.

Then Matthias raised himself to his full height, almost a head taller than anyone else in the room. 'But if you do, realize that you break canonical law. It takes ten Elders to choose a new Rocaan, after a ruling made by Officiates and Danites about the health of the current Rocaan. You will have to assemble those needed, and it will take time. Then when it comes to the choosing, you will have to do so with eight Elders, because I do not plan to appoint two more. I believe that right there takes you outside canonical law, although I could bow to my friend Elder Eirman. Am I correct, Eirman?'

Eirman glanced at his colleagues. He was standing far behind them, so that they couldn't see the panic on his face. 'I – ah, would have to check the literature,' he said.

'Even if we determine that eight Elders can choose a new Rocaan, this goes against the Words Written and Unwritten. Before he died, the Roca chose his successor, and the Rocaans have seen that as an order by example to do the same. I am too young to choose my successor. In fact, I believe it would be a detriment to my position as Rocaan to do so.' Matthias gathered the skirts of his robe together. 'Besides, I don't believe any of you are qualified. There are a few Danites that I have my sights set on. It will take a few years before I know if they are Officiate material, let alone Elder material. I hope I have a few years to make those determinations.'

'If we choose the new Rocaan, it is your duty to follow us,' Porciluna said.

'That's where you forget yourself,' Matthias said. 'My duty is to lead the faithful in the best way I can. I am doing so.'

'We don't agree.'

Matthias shrugged. 'Elder Andre did not believe in using holy water as a weapon, yet he did not try a split from the Rocaan.'

'Elder Andre disappeared on the day of the Rocaan's death,' Linus said.

'I think he died,' Reece said softly. Reece had been there. His description of the confusion on that day still made Matthias shudder.

'My point is,' Matthias said, unwilling to get distracted, 'that I am Rocaan, no matter what Porciluna calls me. I am Keeper of the Secrets, and I am the Roca's Spiritual Heir, designated by his previous Spiritual Heir. You can designate one of your own to be Rocaan, but he will never be a real son of the Roca. I will tell my successor the Secrets of the Office, but I will only tell the successor I choose.'

He stared at them all. 'I will not choose someone because you force me to. Throw me out if you like. Kill me if you like. But remember: Until I choose a successor, the Secrets of the Office will leave with me.'

He did not wait for an answer. He whirled and walked out of the Audience room. Let them think on that. They needed him more than ever now. For one of the secrets he held was the secret behind holy water. Without it, the entire population of Blue Isle would be defenseless against the Fey.

213

Twenty-Seven

His entire body ached. Lord Stowe felt as if he were attached to the saddle. He had been upright for three days, stopping only to allow his horse a rest. He felt that getting back to Jahn was more important than anything else he could do.

But the unease he had felt since the King died stayed with him. Jahn was not the same city it had been two weeks before. As he rode in, he noted that homes were shuttered and children did not play on the streets. He hadn't expected so much change. He remembered when Alexander's father had died, and while the death had shaken up the city, it had not changed it.

Nor had Nicholas ordered the change. Stowe had listened to three separate criers on his journey, and the boys had said nothing about national days of mourning. They had instead explained the haste of the coronation in a way that had not alarmed the populace. But Stowe was alarmed. His unsettled feeling increased the farther he got into Jahn.

The sunshine and spring warmth usually invited citizens to spend their afternoons outside. The air smelled of mud and the Cardidas, but the breeze was fresh, carrying with it a bit of summer. But no one seemed to be enjoying it. Not even the old men who ran the shops were sitting outside. The doors were shut, the signs inside. It was as if everyone had gone away.

Even the gates to the Tabernacle were closed. They had not been closed since the night of the Invasion, years before.

That had distressed him, but not much as what he saw now.

He had taken the back route to the palace, unwilling to face his friends and neighbors on the streets of Jahn. He had planned to go to his own home first to clean up and get a fresh horse, although this view changed his mind.

The road to his home took him past the Fey Settlement. He often rode past it and reported on its progress – or lack thereof – to Nicholas. The Settlement took up a large area of river bottom land. Stowe had seen that land flood year after year, and had argued against giving it to the Fey, but Alexander had been adamant. *If they are committed to living*

214

in Jahn, he had said, *they have the abilities to turn poor land into good land. Let them use those abilities.*

It appeared, in that at least, Alexander had overestimated the abilities of the Fey. The land flooded on cue every year, and the Fey had rebuilt their homes just as Islanders would have. Only one house in the middle of the Settlement had seemed unaffected, and Stowe didn't know if that was because of the land it was on, or because the Fey had done something to it.

Still, each time he had ridden by, he had seen Fey. In fact, as the years progressed, and the wall was built as a protection around the Settlement, he had seen more and more Fey.

This afternoon, however, he saw none.

He reined his horse near the gate and peered inside. The gate's door was open, as were the doors to several of the cottages. The mud from the last rain was still thick here, and the stink of the river even stronger.

The place looked abandoned.

His heart pounded hard. He clucked at his horse, and together they went inside the gate. It took a moment for the horse to find the path that the Fey used. It was a raised bit of dirt, mud-covered as well, but the horse's hooves did not sink into it.

The cabins were poorly constructed, as if they were made by boys who had no sense of form. Wood had been pounded on top of wood, mismatched pieces held together by thick wooden nails. Some of the wood near the foundation of the cabins had already rotted away.

Stowe stopped his horse near the first open door, and dismounted. He supposed that this could be a trap, but he doubted it. The Fey were smarter than this. Most Islanders would never come into this place, abandoned or not. If the Fey wanted to get to the Islanders, they would have to do it in subtler ways – ways that they were capable of.

The mud was slick, but the ground was firm beneath his feet. He followed the path to the steps leading into the cabin, calling hello in Fey as he did so. His voice echoed. The horse whinnied behind him, and shook its head as if the silence made it uncomfortable.

It made him uncomfortable too. Not even birds sang here.

He peered inside. The cabin was dark. It had no windows. The light through the door provided the only illumination.

A table sat in the middle of the room, surrounded by makeshift benches. On the table's surface were woodworking tools and the remains of a meal. Whomever had lived here had planned to come back.

Stowe moved away from the door. He walked through the deep mud, not caring that his boots got soaked, and went to the next cabin. This door was closed. He knocked on it, then opened it.

Everything was put away here, except for a robe lying over one of the chairs. Again, it appeared as if the owners were going to come back.

Something had happened. Something that made the Fey leave this place quickly. Had they known about Alexander's murder? Had something else happened in Jahn to cause this quick exodus?

Ice settled in the pit of his stomach. His throat was dry. He hadn't felt this way since Alexander was killed beside him.

Stowe ran out of the cabin, and quickly mounted his horse. He snapped the reins, and let the horse pick his way out of the Settlement. When they reached the road, Stowe turned away from his home. He had to get to the palace first. He had to know what was going on.

The main road leading from the bridge to the palace was empty. No one was outside, and most of the small shops – those that were still in business – were closed. His horse's hooves made small clomping noises on the road. The sound echoed. Had everyone disappeared and left him as the only inhabitant of Jahn, bearer of bad news that everyone already knew?

He reached the palace walls quickly. The gates were closed here as well. Two guards stood in the tower. They had bows up and strung before he reached the gate.

He held up his hands. 'I'm Lord Stowe. I'm here to see the King.'

He hoped.

One of the guards called down to the ground below. A grating sound started almost immediately, then the gate came up. Stowe nodded his head in thanks as he cantered inside.

The courtyard looked more or less normal. The kitchen door to the palace was open, and smoke rose from the fireplaces. The grooms were tending the palace horses, and servants went from their quarters to the main buildings.

The difference, though, chilled Stowe farther.

Guards stood beside each doorway. They were armed with swords, daggers, and bows. Many had their quivers at their feet. They all watched him approach warily.

He led the horse to the stable and dismounted. The groom who came out had a thin, drawn face. He looked as if he hadn't slept for days.

'What happened here?' Stowe asked.

The man ran his hand along the horse's flank. The stallion was filthy. He had been groomed as well as possible, but Stowe had run him to his limits. 'Ye best talk ta nother lord, sir,' the man said. He started to lead the stallion away.

'Wait!' Stowe said.

The man stopped, keeping his back to Stowe. The man was stocky, younger than he expected, and immaculately groomed. 'That horse has been traveling at top speed for three days. Give him your best care.'

'Aye, sir.' The groom took the horse inside.

As he did, one of the guards came over. The man was beefy, his arms solid muscle. His blue eyes were small in his large face, and his lips were thick. Tiny white scars marred the skin on both cheeks, as if he had been in dozens of fights, and wounded in most of them.

'State yer business,' the man said.

'I'm here to see the King,' Stowe said. He had never been quizzed quite like this before. He held out his hand for what had become an obligatory holy water testing.

The guard looked down at it. 'That don't matter,' the guard said. 'I need yer weapons, instead.'

Stowe brought his hand to his side, unwilling to let go of his weapons until he knew what was going on. 'What happened here?'

'Ye came from the Rocaan, did ye not?'

'No,' Stowe said. 'I was one of the lords traveling with King Alexander. I've been investigating his death. I'm here to report to his son. I would have gone home to clean up, but it seems something strange has happened here.'

'Ye dinna know?'

'Know what?' Stowe asked.

'About the Rocaan killin the Queen.'

The breath left Stowe's body. He felt as if he had been hit in the stomach. 'What?' The question came out in a rush of air.

'Twas at the service. Melted her, he did.'

Stowe blinked, trying to grasp the change this implied. Jewel was dead? A Fey had murdered King Alexander and a few days later, Jewel was dead at the hands of the Rocaan?

'He put holy water on her?' Stowe asked.

'I dinna see it. Twas told ta me. But I seen her body n all, n she look like a Fey what met with holy water.'

'My god,' Stowe said. He made himself breathe. He needed to go in now, just to see what kind of shape Nicholas was in. 'When did this happen?'

'Yestadey. Them Fey twas in n outta the kitchen until the wee hours. Taint seen em since.'

So that was why the guard forewent the holy water, and had asked if Stowe was from the Tabernacle. At the moment, Nicholas was not treating the Fey as the enemy; he was treating the Rocaan as one.

Stowe ran a hand over his face. His skin was oily and dirt-covered from his long ride. His news would change things again. He sighed against his palm, then brought his hand down and slowly removed his sword and dagger. He handed them to the guard.

'I need to see the King,' he said.

'Taint no one seen the King since he come out to say the Queen was dead.'

'After the Fey left?' Stowe asked. He didn't want to get inside and learn that Nicholas was dead too.

'Aye, Sir.'

'Well, then. He may not like my intrusion, but he's going to need it. Do you know where he is?'

''Tis sorry I am, Sir, but I got orders. Taint no one ta go in.'

'He'll want to see me.'

The guard glanced over his shoulder. There were no other guards of higher rank.

'I'll go to Monte if I have to,' Stowe said.

'I dinna know where he is, Sir.'

Stowe waited. The guard shifted back and forth. Finally he indicated to another guard to come closer. When the guard approached, the first guard handed him Stowe's weapons.

'He asked ta see the King. I'm takin him,' the first guard said.

''Tis glad I am taint me,' said the second.

Stowe swallowed. His mouth was still dry. He probably looked terrible, all dirt-spattered and sweat-covered. He knew he smelled like his horse, and probably the foul mud of the Kenniland Marshes. Still it was beginning to sound as if things would not wait. More changes had occurred in Jahn in the last week than in any other time since the Invasion.

The guard nodded at Stowe. 'Come with me, Sir,' he said.

He clasped his hands behind his back and led Stowe into the kitchen. The chef was kneading dough on one of the tables. A housekeeper had his head inside one of the brick-lined ovens, scrubbing a black substance off the walls. The kitchen wasn't as warm as usual. The hearth fire was burning, but apparently the ovens weren't in use.

More housekeepers scrubbed at the floor before the hearth fire. Dark stains covered the flagstones. Stowe remembered the last time he had seen this: two days after the Invasion, when it became clear that the Fey had been routed. The Islanders had finally started cleaning up the blood.

Stowe said nothing as he was led through. The guard paused just as they entered the pantry and held up a finger, indicating that Stowe was to wait. He peered back into the kitchen. No one smiled. No one even met his gaze. Seeing these people unnerved him more than the silent city had. They were working hard, but it seemed as if the work were merely a way of keeping busy, not a way to do their jobs.

The Rocaan and Jewel.

Stowe had not expected that at all.

The guard was talking to the Master of the Hall. They were at the far end of the pantry, and Stowe couldn't understand them. The Master was gesturing with his right hand. His face had fatigue lines, and a long smudge of dirt marred his brown shirt. Finally the guard nodded and returned to Stowe, but said nothing.

They continued to walk through the corridor. They went past the audience hall and stepped into the Great Hall. Stowe grabbed the guard's arm, holding him back.

There, in the center of the Great Hall, was Jewel's body. She lay on her back, her hands clasped over her breasts. She wore a bloodstained white gown. Stowe went ahead of the guard, and circled Jewel. The top half of her head had been destroyed. In the remains of her face, her beauty still showed.

Candles burned around her, and someone had placed a single rosebud at her side. It must have been the first flower of the season, beside a woman who would never see it.

'What's she doing here?' Stowe asked.

'They dinna know what ta do with her,' the guard said. 'The Fey left without her, n tis the Rocaan what killed her.'

The Rocaan. And the Tabernacle, who were in charge of the graveyards and the burials. Stowe shook his head. What a mess he had walked into.

Someone had tried to arrange a small cloth around Jewel's forehead, but Stowe could still see the disfigurement caused by the holy water. Poor woman. He had never liked her. He hadn't disliked her either. He had just not trusted her, always wondering what she was about, what she really wanted from Nicholas.

Perhaps she had been honest all along.

Then he realized what was missing. 'What happened to the child?'

'The Fey, sir. They dinna leave until twas born. Tis said twas ugly thing. A monster, not even human.'

Stowe closed his eyes. Another one. Ah, Nicholas. He was half afraid to find the new king. With all these tragedies, the boy might well be mad. If that were the case, then, the lords would have to appoint a regent. They would have to know how Nicholas was.

They might as well know now.

Stowe walked around Jewel's body. It seemed appropriate to lay her out in the Great Hall, where she and Nicholas had their wedding feast, surrounded by real weapons, swords from the Peasant Uprising and before. She looked like a warrior queen which, in fact, she was.

The guard gave her one final look, then moved in front of Stowe and led him up the stairs to the family quarters. They walked through the gallery and turned to the queen's side of the hall. Stowe shot the guard an uneasy glance which the other man missed. Nicholas was hiding in Jewel's apartments? Already the signs were not good ones.

The guard stopped outside the door near Jewel's suite, and knocked. When the nurse pulled the door open, Stowe understood. The nursery. Nicholas was in the nursery.

A wave of heat floated out the door, and on it, the choking sound of a child crying. The nurse peered at both the guard and at Lord Stowe.

Stowe clicked his heels together, and nodded to her. 'Please tell the King that Lord Stowe is here to see him.'

'He's na seeing anyone,' the nurse said.

'I think it important that I see him.'

'Let him in.' Nicholas's voice came from the room, sounding strong and sure of itself.

The guard looked in the door. 'Do ye wan me ta stay, Sire?'

'No, thank you,' Nicholas said. 'You may return to your post.'

Stowe also thanked the guard, then slipped into the nursery. The room was large. A fire burned high in the hearth. A cradle stood in the center of the room. Sebastian sat on the floor beside it, sobbing as if his tiny heart had already broken. The nurse went to him, picked him up, and cradled him to her chest.

'Maaaaaa!' the boy wailed.

Stowe shuddered. He hadn't even known the boy could talk, let alone understand that his mother was dead.

Soft couches and chairs lined the back of the room. A bed with curtains stood in one corner. Rugs covered the area before the fire. Two chairs sat beside the fireplace, and the nurse sat in one, holding Sebastian tightly. He didn't move as he cried. He just clung to her and sobbed.

Nicholas stood beside one of the windows, looking out. He wore his fighting clothes – a dark blouse and black trousers. In one arm, he held the baby.

Stowe closed the door behind him. A cat stood up near the hearth, turned around three times, and lay back down. It was a golden tabby, and before it settled, it looked at him with its large black eyes as if measuring him.

The cat sent a shudder through him. He remembered the woman who had come to his estate years ago, claiming a cat had stolen her child. Alexander had banned all cats after that.

Nicholas followed Stowe's gaze. 'I'll explain in a moment,' he said.

Stowe walked over to Nicholas. The boy looked a hundred years older, his face gaunt. His eyes no longer had a gleam in them. They were dull and dark. A day's growth of beard was on his chin, and his clothes hung around him.

The baby, on the other hand, looked fat and healthy. She had a Fey face – sharp cheekbones, swooping eyebrows, and a thin mouth. Her head was covered with dark hair. She had the look of Nicholas in her face, but Stowe couldn't say where. He just felt there was a resemblance.

He reached out, tentatively, and touched her small fist. She opened her eyes. They were a startling blue. Then her fingers wrapped around his. Her grip was amazingly tight.

'Blue eyes,' he said.

Nicholas nodded.

'I guess I'm used to the Fey,' Stowe said. 'It surprised me.'

A small fond smile crossed Nicholas's face. 'She looks like her mother.'

'She does,' Stowe said. Her skin was darker than his and very soft.

Sebastian's hiccuped sobs eased. Nicholas looked over his shoulder toward his son. The nurse had a hand protectively around the boy's head.

'He's been crying off and on since yesterday,' Nicholas said.

''Tis the most he's done his whole life,' the nurse added, speaking softly. 'Poor baby.'

The cat sat up and yawned, then padded over and wove around Nicholas's legs. It looked up at Stowe and yowled.

'Solanda,' Nicholas said in a chastising voice.

'A Fey-named cat?' Stowe said. 'I thought they'd been banished.'

'I changed the decree this morning.' Nicholas ran a hand over his daughter's hair.

'You know about the cat that stole children?' Stowe said. 'They said it looked like this one.'

The cat bumped Nicholas's leg, then sat beside him and purred loudly.

'Jewel explained it to me,' Nicholas said. 'We're safe from it.'

'How do you know?' Stowe asked.

'I just know,' Nicholas said.

The baby's grip loosened on Stowe's finger. She made smacking sounds with her little toothless mouth. He touched her cheek. It was soft as down.

'She's beautiful,' Stowe said.

'Yes.' There was pride in Nicholas's voice. 'You sound surprised.'

Stowe sighed. The moment had come. 'Nicholas, you've had a lot of shocks this week. If you would like me to come back, I will.'

Nicholas shook his head. 'You have news for me. You wouldn't have come straight here if you hadn't.' The shadows beneath his eyes were so deep the skin looked folded. A few silver hairs mingled with his blond bangs. He was only in his twenties, and yet he had lived through more this week than most experienced in a lifetime.

'The news can wait,' Stowe said.

'I would rather have everything at once,' Nicholas said. 'I would rather know what I'm up against.'

Stowe couldn't tell if Nicholas had the strength for this or if he were merely pretending. 'The guard told me that the Rocaan caused this. Is it true?'

Nicholas nodded and turned his head toward the window. The view from the nursery was of the bridge and the towers of the Tabernacle beyond. 'I haven't decided how to handle that yet. I threatened his life yesterday.'

'Do you know why he did this?'

Nicholas licked his lips before replying. The baby watched Stowe, her eyes alight with an intelligence he had never seen in a baby this young. 'He did it,' Nicholas said, 'because he believed I was wrong. He believed I should set Jewel aside, deny these children, and start again. He thought Arianna would be – like Sebastian.'

Arianna. A Fey name. Stowe said nothing about the name, though. 'I seem to remember Sebastian being alert in his first few days.'

'Something changed him.' Nicholas glanced at the cat. 'Some think his Fey grandfather might have hurt him, but Jewel was convinced it happened at the naming ceremony. We'll have no ceremony for Arianna. She has her name already.'

A Fey name. They blamed the name for Sebastian's condition. Odd and interesting. 'You didn't want to set Jewel aside?'

'She is – was – my wife. Setting her aside never crossed my mind.' Nicholas turned back to Stowe. 'Even if it had, it would have been wrong. The Fey would have turned on us. The war would have continued, and the deaths –' His voice broke. 'I guess that's where we'll be now.'

'But I don't understand,' Stowe said. 'If the Rocaan was that opposed to the marriage, why didn't he stop it before it actually happened?'

'He tried,' Nicholas said. 'He almost refused to perform it. My father convinced him. I think Sebastian's condition, and my father's death made the Rocaan decide that Jewel had no place here. He thought that the Fey killed my father, but he had no proof.'

'He does now,' Stowe said.

Wood snapped in the fire. Sebastian took a deep breath. The cat mewled softly. The nurse was watching them all.

Nicholas sighed, then leaned his head against the window frame. One more burden. But Nicholas was strong. In some ways, he was stronger than his father. The boy had fought in the war, and then fought to marry the enemy, to form a truce.

He had to be strong now. If he wasn't strong, the country would disintegrate, and he knew it. Unlike his father, Nicholas had no one to take his place.

Finally he said, 'Jewel was afraid a Fey had killed my father. She told me that it sounded like something a Fey would do. She actually went to the Settlement to see if they knew something about it.' He bowed his head and placed his lips against his daughter's ear. 'Why isn't she here now?' he murmured.

The cat sighed heavily and fell across his feet.

'It's not the same,' Nicholas said. 'It'll never be the same.'

Then he opened his eyes, kissed his daughter's forehead, and carried her to the cradle. He gently set her inside it, then covered her with a soft white blanket. The cat jumped on the changing table beside the cradle and curled up on a clean cloth diaper.

'What kind of proof do you have?' Nicholas asked.

'A witness. A man who saw a Fey there, a Fey man carrying a bow and arrow.'

Nicholas shook his head. 'What were they thinking?'

'Apparently someone in the Fey camp was as upset about the way things were going as the Rocaan was.'

Nicholas snorted. 'Wouldn't that stun Matthias? Show him that he was just like the dreaded Fey.'

'This is serious, Highness,' Lord Stowe said.

'I know it is,' Nicholas said. 'Someone murdered my father, and then the Rocaan killed Jewel. She thought he was right. She thought someone was trying to get her closer to the throne.'

'Would she have gone along with it?'

Nicholas shook his head. 'She wanted us together. She thought it best for the Isle and for the Fey. And she had such high hopes for this little one.'

Stowe looked down on the baby. 'Below, they're saying she's a monster.'

'Jewel?' Nicholas said.

Stowe shook his head. 'The baby. You'd better let the public see her, and soon. Let them know that she is different from her brother.'

Sebastian was asleep, his hand tucked against his mouth. The nurse was rocking him just a little. She was staring out the window, pretending that she didn't hear the conversation. Stowe hoped she was trustworthy. If she wasn't, Nicholas would be in even more trouble.

'A monster.' Nicholas made a sound that was half a laugh and half a sob. 'That's my fault. I ordered the kitchen staff out at the wrong time. Her birth was difficult. She wouldn't even be here if the Fey hadn't acted fast. Jewel was dying. They got the baby out while they could. They saved her, even though they could do nothing for Jewel. Now what do I do? Get revenge on them? The loss of Jewel was their loss as well.'

'Do you plan revenge against the Rocaan?' Stowe asked.

'He killed my wife.' Nicholas's voice was hard. Suddenly Stowe recognized the look in Nicholas's eyes. They weren't empty. They were full of rage.

And hatred.

The ice in Stowe's stomach grew. 'Nicholas,' he said. 'The Fey were planning to fight us before Jewel died. They killed your father. Her death was an escalation in a war they already started. We need the Rocaan. He's the one who provides holy water.'

'I should remain close to a man who murdered my wife? A man who makes a weapon that can kill my children?' Nicholas shook his head. 'You're being unrealistic, Lord Stowe.'

'Your responsibility is to the Isle, Highness.'

Nicholas whirled. 'Yes, it is. Jewel had a Vision for this Isle. She believed that if the Black King came, he would be able to conquer the holy water. She thought that the only way to maintain Isle traditions was to bind the Fey and the Islanders together.'

'I remember,' Stowe said. 'I was there when she proposed the marriage.'

'We are bound. My children show that. And yes, maybe Sebastian isn't what we had hoped, but Arianna will be more than we can hope for. I think Jewel's Vision was an accurate one, and I will fight for it, no matter how the Rocaan tries to ruin it.'

'And what if the Fey try to kill you?'

Nicholas looked at the cat. It had its head on its front paws. Its eyes were half open. 'They wouldn't dare.'

'They killed your father.'

'Jewel is no longer here to take my place.'

'Do you seriously believe the lords would let Sebastian rule?' Stowe asked. 'The baby is too young, and even if she were old enough, she's female. She can't.'

'I know the problems,' Nicholas said.

'This is something we'll have to resolve, and quickly. If something happens to you –'

'I know the problems,' Nicholas said again. His voice was firm. 'I will have a solution for you tomorrow. Gather the lords after lunch in the audience room. Tell them to come with open minds.'

'What are you going to suggest, Highness?' Stowe asked.

'I don't know yet,' Nicholas said, 'but I can guarantee you that it will be something which will not jeopardize Jewel's Vision. We are going to make Blue Isle safe if I have to fight every lord, Rocaan, Elder, and Fey to do so.'

Twenty-Eight

Shadowlands was as bleak as ever. The Circle Door closed behind Burden, shutting out the greens of the forest, the fresh pine smell of the air, and the chirping of the birds, leaving him shrouded in gray. Gray ground, gray walls, a gray box around him and everything inside. Sometimes he wondered if that gray reflected the gray in Rugar's mind. But he knew better. He had been in different Shadowlands before. They all looked like this. The Fey simply weren't supposed to live in them for so long.

No one sat on the Meeting Block, and the doors to the cabins were closed. Smoke came from the roof of the Domicile and from the Spell Warders' cabin. Some of his own people were standing near a wood-pile in the back, but he did not go to them. He had not given any orders for people to come here. They had, though, expecting trouble after Jewel's death. The Shadowlands was, more than anything, safe.

Hanouk stood by herself, as if she had set a personal vigilance to see if he would come through the door. He nodded at her, but he didn't want to talk with her. If she wanted to return to the Settlement, that was her right. She had always told him she preferred the world outside, that it was her domain. Perhaps she should have dominated it more than she did. Perhaps if she had, Jewel would still be alive.

Burden wiped his hands on his pants. A Charmer, Solanda had said. Someone who got other people to do his bidding with a minimum of effort.

He would need that ability now.

There were no familiar paths in Shadowlands, only buildings rising out of the grayness. He already missed the mud and the rotten wood, the rain and the floods and the smell of cooking from the Islander houses outside the Settlement.

He wouldn't be able to stay in here very long.

He walked through the cabins to the second largest. Jewel and Rugar had built their cabin to be a meetinghouse at first, then took it over once the Domicile was completed. Burden had always thought that unfair, but Rugar was the one who made the Shadowlands. It existed because he did. He was the Black King's son, and subject to special privileges. Those privileges, though, were a fact of Fey life. Something Burden had hoped to change, with Jewel's help. When she married the Islander prince, she had abandoned Burden. She had abandoned them all.

Still, when he last saw her, she sounded like the Jewel of old. She seemed wiser from her experiences, willing to make the changes needed to let a place like Shadowlands thrive.

When he had leaned over her body in that hideous kitchen, the place he had first seen as a young Infantryman, he had made her one last promise: No matter what it took, no matter how many years he worked, he would avenge her death. He would do it alone if he had to.

He hoped he wouldn't have to.

The steps leading to Rugar's cabin were covered with dry mud. It had dried in the form of bootprints down the middle, as if caked boots had climbed them some time in the past. Burden stepped around the footprints, and stopped on the stoop.

Fey peacetime tradition allowed a mourner three days alone before he had to face the rest of the people. It gave the mourner the chance to work through the grief, to let the emotion of the event overwhelm for a short time. It also allowed the great warriors to cry in private, where the tears would not compromise the image of strength they presented the rest of the time.

Peacetime tradition.

Even though there were no battles raging, Burden did not consider this peace. Rugar would not have the luxury of mourning the daughter he helped kill.

Burden pounded the wooden door with the side of his fist. The knocks sounded heavy, furious, and strong. They echoed throughout Shadowlands, a weak echo that damped after the first circle, as if a great hand had clamped down on the noise.

A door in the cabin behind Burden opened, but Burden didn't turn. He knew the others wouldn't approve of his visit to Rugar. He didn't care.

He knocked again, more insistently this time.

Finally the door opened. Rugar stood before him, a changed man.

This Rugar had deep haunted eyes, long lines around his mouth, hair stringy and unkempt. He wore a shirt stained with the morning's meal, and his pants were untied. He blinked at Burden before it became clear that he recognized him.

'What?' he said.

'Let me in,' Burden said.

Rugar shook his head. 'I got three days.'

'Let me in now, or we'll have this discussion in front of everyone.'

'In three days.'

'No,' Burden said. 'Right now.'

He pushed past Rugar and let himself into the cabin. It was cold and dark. A single candle rested in its own wax on the table, the wick flickering in the darkness. The room had the faint odor of urine. A chamberpot stood beside the door. Rugar hadn't even left the cabin to relieve himself in the community baths.

She had been dead less than a day. It was amazing that a man could let himself go so quickly. But, apparently, that was what this period of mourning was for.

Burden had no need of it.

'I have three days,' Rugar said. He still stood in front of the open door.

'You have no time at all. Close the door.' Burden walked over to the fire place, crouched, and started building a fire.

Rugar stared at him for a moment, then pushed the door closed. It shut with a snick.

Burden layered the wood on top of kindling. When he had made a good base, he took the tinderbox and lit the fire. It took a moment for the kindling to catch but when it did, the fire spread through the wood. Burden replaced the grate and stood.

'You have no time at all. The mourning period is for peaceable Fey, not for Visionaries and warriors.'

'My daughter died,' Rugar said.

'And the Shaman says you had a hand in it. Before she died, Jewel came to me wondering if I had killed the Islander king. She said it sounded like a Fey job. I suspect it was. How did the mud get on your stoop, Rugar?'

'Yesterday.' Rugar waved a hand. His movements were vague, unfocused. 'I brought it yesterday.'

Burden shook his head. 'The mud's too old for that. And there's none inside. If you had tracked it in here yesterday, it would still be here, like your piss.'

Rugar looked down. 'I was supposed to have privacy.'

'You're not going to get it,' Burden said. 'You didn't let any of us know that you were escalating the war again. Have you a solution to poison?'

'If I did, do you think I would have let Jewel die?'

'Then you better have had a damn good reason for killing their king.'

Rugar sighed and slumped into one of his chairs. The faint odor of unwashed flesh rose from his clothes. 'I have her son,' he said.

'What?' Burden crossed his arms. 'What good will that thing do us?'

'Not the thing,' Rugar said. 'It's a golem. Her son. The actual boy. The Wisps stole him when he was less than a week old.'

Burden sat heavily in the nearest chair. It had no cushion and the impact stunned his spine. A real child. Not the slow-moving creature that they had all figured to be the product of an Islander and a Fey, but a real flesh-and-blood being. 'What do you expect to gain?' Burden said. 'When Nicholas learns this, he will have even more reason for revenge.'

'The child is a Visionary,' Rugar said.

Burden shook his head. 'Now I know you're making light with me. The boy is three years old. To have powers at that age is impossible.' Then he frowned. 'Didn't the Shaman say the boy was dying?'

Rugar nodded. 'I checked on him as soon as I returned to Shadowlands. He had a strange bout, a reaction, I guess, to Jewel's passing, but he's fine. After my mourning, I was to talk with his stepmother.'

Burden leaned forward, put his elbows on his knees and wiped his eyes with one finger. A Visionary at the age of three. A child with more powers than the Fey had ever seen. A baby girl with Shape-Shifting abilities born to a Visionary. Jewel had been right after all. The union between Islander and Fey made them both more powerful instead of less. Burden pinched the bridge of his nose.

'You ruined Jewel's chances of survival,' he said.

'What?' Rugar looked up and blinked at him.

Burden let his hand fall to his lap. 'You ruined any chance of that alliance succeeding. If the Islanders had been allowed to see the gifted child born to their King instead of the thing you replaced him with, then Jewel's alliance would have worked. You ruined her from the start.'

Rugar shook his head. 'I was helping her. I was helping us.'

'I don't see how,' Burden said. Bile had risen in his throat. He had to swallow to keep it down. Rugar had done more to hurt the Fey than anyone else ever could have.

'A Fey child couldn't be raised in an Islander world,' Rugar said. 'The moment the boy showed any precociousness, someone would have sprinkled him with poison. You saw what that 'holy man' did to Jewel. Imagine that happening to a defenseless child. As soon as I can, I'll get his sister as well.'

'You will not,' Burden said. He stood. 'You will not interfere any more than you have done. I was there when the Shaman said that little girl should not come to Shadowlands. The Shaman still has her Vision. You do not.'

'I have something better,' Rugar said. 'I have my grandson's Vision.'

'Did your precocious grandson see Jewel's death?'

The bluster Rugar had a moment before subsided. He leaned back in his chair and looked at the fire. The flames played across his face, making his features dance. 'Yes,' he said softly. 'He did.'

'And you did nothing? You prepared for nothing?'

'He was a child,' Rugar said. 'It was his first Vision, and it was very confused. I had no idea the mother he saw on the ground was Jewel. I had no idea that what he called yellow people were Islanders. It's only in hindsight –'

'It's not in hindsight,' Burden said. 'You're just unwilling to admit that you had been warned and did not take appropriate action. Of course you've gone Blind. You never deserved Sight in the first place.'

Rugar didn't move. 'Say what you want,' he said. 'I did not know.'

Burden paced in the small cabin. He touched the table where Jewel had once sat, fondled the cup she had preferred. He would never see her again, never talk to her again, never have the chance to apologize to her for all the things he had said. All the things he had thought.

'It was your mistake that brought us to this place,' Burden said. 'Your lack of Vision that allowed us to get slaughtered by these Islanders, and your lack of wisdom that prevented you from listening to the others around you.'

Burden walked to Rugar's chair, put his hands on the arms, effectively trapping the older man. Rugar turned toward him, eyes dull, and hopeless.

'You're going to listen to me now,' Burden said. 'We have a responsibility in all of this. But so do they. We have never survived by hiding. We have never made our way in this world by sneaking around and ignoring our Visions. We are a world power because we have abilities that we use.'

Rugar didn't move. He was watching Burden as if Burden were a child having a tantrum.

'We also have a responsibility to Jewel. The Black King's granddaughter was murdered when she was operating in good faith with the enemy. We must seek revenge.'

'We can't,' Rugar said. 'Their holy man makes the poison.'

'You have always been a weak man,' Burden said. 'It was your weakness, your desire to be something greater than you are, that brought us here in the first place. You never acknowledged your limitations, you never listened to your betters. You just brought us all with you and doomed us to this life. And then, when your daughter tried to improve it, you abandoned her and kidnapped her child. You're not a leader, Rugar. You're certainly not a Visionary. You're a weak and pathetic man who thinks only of himself.'

'You have no right to talk to me that way,' Rugar said. 'I'm in mourning.'

'See? Only of yourself. I have every right,' Burden said. 'There is no time for mourning. We have to make their holy man pay. Once we do that, we will be able to negotiate with Nicholas again.'

'Their holy man could kill more Fey by himself than Nicholas could with his guards in a month,' Rugar said. 'For all we know, the poison is a part of the holy man. Quest died too quickly for us to discover if we can ever get near their holy men.'

'Quest,' Burden said. He clasped his hands together. He hadn't been this angry in years. 'Quest was a Doppelgänger who sacrificed himself for a solution we never got. Then Jewel sacrificed herself. All because of your mistakes. One of your greatest mistakes was a failure to use our resources. Our Warders found a way to slow the effects of the poison. How come they haven't found an antidote?'

'They've been working on it,' Rugar said.

'Working on it? For years? If Caseo were still alive, he would be appalled by that. How long has it been since the Warders left Shadowlands? Have they tried other methods of discovering what creates the poison? Did any of them ask for help from the Settlement or from Jewel? Of course not. The one thing that could save us all, and you let the Warders piss the advantage away, encouraging them to hide in here while your daughter sacrificed her life for us.' Burden paused to take a breath.

Rugar finally sat up. His face was only inches from Burden's. 'We have limited talent among our Warders.'

'Of course we do,' Burden said. 'You cover them with additional excuses. Since Caseo died ... or finding a solution is difficult ... or we have limited talent. You never look at the situation. Is Rotin still among the Warders?'

'Of course she is,' Rugar said, adopting Burden's tone. 'We have only lost one Warder.'

'And I suppose you still allow her to play with her herbs. How can a drugged mind find any creativity, Rugar? Have you even chosen a leader for the Warders now that Caseo is dead?'

'It's their duty to choose a leader,' Rugar said.

'And they always choose the oldest, not necessarily the best. You know better, Rugar. It is our lives you're toying with here. Go in there, discover the best Warder and put that person in charge. Get rid of the drugs, give the Warders a deadline with real consequences, and see if they come up with a solution for you.'

231

'I can't give the Warders consequences,' Rugar said, and closed his eyes.

'Yes, you can,' Burden said. 'If they haven't found a solution by whatever time you set, kick them out of Shadowlands. Make them search for answers on Blue Isle – which is where they should be looking anyway.'

'And lose our Warders?' Rugar said. 'You're the one who is short-sighted, Burden.'

Burden grabbed Rugar by the shoulders and pulled him forward. Rugar opened his eyes, but his expression remained impassive. Burden crouched beside him so that their faces were close. 'What have the Warders done for us since we came to the Isle, Rugar? Any new spells? New ideas? If they had all died in the First Battle of Jahn would we have noticed? Yes, they slowed down the effects of the poison, but Jewel died anyway. *They have made no difference at all.* If you force them to work, they will make a difference.'

'I cannot force answers where there may be none,' Rugar said.

'Your father could, and did,' Burden said. 'So did your daughter. Learn from that.'

'You want me to divide this community,' Rugar said.

'I want you to get revenge for your daughter,' Burden said. 'I want you to save our lives.'

'Killing their holy man will only create more problems.'

'Like killing their king did?'

Rugar stood, forcing Burden to let go of him. But the effort to stand appeared to be all that Rugar had in him.

'If you don't lead, I will,' Burden said.

'You can't,' Rugar said. 'No one will follow you.'

'Like no one followed me to the Settlement?' Burden stood as close as he could to Rugar.

Rugar took a step back. 'I'm the Leader here.'

'And they're all waiting for you to do something,' Burden said. 'Your daughter was murdered. Fey do not let that happen.'

'Jewel had a treaty with those people.'

'A treaty which you broke before her death. Don't hide behind things you never believed in, Rugar. You subverted that treaty the moment you stole Jewel's child.'

'I didn't steal the boy,' Rugar said. 'He belonged here.'

'Without his parents' permission? When he was supposed to represent the unification of both states? The improvement that Jewel sought? I agree with the Shaman, Rugar. You engineered your daughter's death. You did it slowly and over time, probably from the moment you agreed to have her come to Blue Isle. Were you afraid your father would pick her to take the Black Throne, passing you over entirely? That would have been humiliating, wouldn't it?'

'I had nothing to do with Jewel's death,' Rugar said. His voice rose. 'The holy man killed her.'

'Maybe I'm wrong about you,' Burden said. 'Maybe you have Vision. Maybe you saw Jewel's death from the beginning and that's why you brought us all here. Well, Rugar, what does the future hold? More Fey deaths? A union with Blue Isle? Or is your father due at any moment?'

'The situation here is as it has always been,' Rugar said. 'We're in Shadowlands, besieged by the outside, and my father is nowhere in sight.'

'Because,' Burden said, 'your father did not believe us worth rescuing. He wanted you dead, Rugar, just like you wanted Jewel dead. It makes me wonder what you want for her son.'

'The boy has Vision.'

'And so did Jewel.'

They stared at each other, breathing in unison, their chests rising and falling together as if they had just had a pleasurable joust instead of a verbal tussle.

'You should get out of here,' Rugar said.

'I think I will.' Burden walked toward the door. He grabbed the handle and stopped. 'But I want you to realize something. If you do not act, I will. The holy man will die, the Warders will work on the antidote, and the Fey will become powers again.'

'You can't do that without my help.'

'I can and will. No one believes in you any more, Rugar.'

Rugar hadn't moved. He was still breathing hard.

So was Burden. The anger that had brought him here had not abated. 'One more thing,' he said. 'The Shaman thought your grandson died. You care enough to find out that the boy lives, but not how he lives. Or what saved him. The Shaman thought the boy was doomed without her help. I remember. I was there. Have you ever wondered what really saved him? I would wager the Shaman had nothing to do with it.'

'Sometimes,' Rugar said through his teeth, 'even the Shaman is wrong.'

Burden shook his head. 'Not like you,' he said. 'No one has ever been quite as destructive to our people as you have.'

Twenty-Nine

They made him sit in a small room off the Great Hall. Tel rubbed his hands on his knees. The tiny window was actually an old arrow slit. He was in an ancient part of the palace. Lord Enford had promised that the King would be here soon.

Tel hoped so. He couldn't stand being inside Islander dwellings unless he knew that the Islanders had no interest in their awful religion.

He stood and walked the length of the room, from door to arrow slit, then back again. There wasn't much point walking the width. The room was the size of a closet, and the four chairs that lined its walls had the look of old furniture little used. He almost felt like a prisoner, although he knew they had no reason to suspect him of anything.

As far as they were concerned, he was a groom with a story, not a Fey. If they knew what kind of Fey he was, they never would have promised to bring the King into such a small room. They would have to stand near each other. Tel could find a knife, leap across the room, and be transforming into the King before anyone realized what had happened.

He just didn't want to.

He never wanted to leave this post as groom.

He owed a debt to Jewel.

He also wanted to do something about Matthias. If Tel could strike a blow against the Tabernacle – a damaging blow – he would. And after hearing about Jewel's death, he knew he could.

The door opened. Tel froze in place, uncertain what kind of greeting he faced. He had seen a lot of reactions this morning, from anger to disbelief to barely hidden joy, and he wasn't sure which he would get now.

Lord Enford entered. He was shorter than most Fey but tall for an Islander, and slender to the point of gauntness. His complexion was an unhealthy waxy yellow, and his hair was thin in front. It hung down his back in a thin queue. No matter how much wealth and opportunity some people had, they still looked as if they would die tomorrow. Lord Enford was one of them.

'The King will see you,' Lord Enford said.

Tel's throat closed up. Enford had come into the room alone. This meant more travel through the corridors of the palace, more chances of seeing someone who might be religious, more opportunities to touch poison.

'Follow me.'

Tel nodded. Enford went out the door, the skirt of his robe swaying, and entered the corridor. Tel had to hurry to keep up. Enford moved silently, but Tel's boots slapped the polished floor. He made himself swallow. He had come this far. He could go to the King.

Early that morning, Tel had awakened with the knowledge that he had to speak out about Jewel's death. He had gone to the head groom, Tapio, who had urged him not to get involved. When Tel insisted upon being involved, Tapio had pointed him to the Master of the House, who had sent him to the Second Assistant to the Lords, who had sent him to another assistant who had finally led him to Enford. Enford had listened silently, left Tel alone in that tiny room, and now had come back with the news that the King would see him.

Guards stood in front of large double doors. Tel clenched his hands. He had heard that anyone who got close to the King got tested with poison. If they tried that with him, he would run. He would run and then he would lose his comfortable home.

But the guards nodded to Enford and two of them pushed the door handles down, sliding the doors open to reveal one of the largest rooms Tel had ever seen. Ancient spears lined the walls, looking almost decayed. At the room's far end, a throne stood on a dais. Behind it was a coat of arms. Tel had never seen that before.

Two swords crossed over a heart.

Curious. If Rugar had known that somewhere in their past the Islanders had had a military tradition, would he have attacked this place?

Probably.

Rugar had believed that he was invincible. And, until he had arrived on Blue Isle, he had been.

A man moved in the corner, near the curtains hanging on either side of the dais. Tel hadn't seen him at first because the red of his robe matched the red curtains. He recognized the King – indeed, had spoken to him many times – but something was changed about him.

The King looked older. Decades older. His face was lined, his eyes weary. His hair, which he normally wore in a queue like Enford did, was hanging free. His movements had a quick, odd nervousness to them, as though he wasn't concentrating on anything, even walking.

'What now, Enford? We have the lords any moment.'

Enford bowed. Tel did the same.

'Forgive me, Sire,' Enford said. 'But I believe this groom has something you need to hear.'

The King peered at Tel, but remained on the dais. How odd to be in a room alone with the King. There should have been guards inside. Perhaps there were. Perhaps they had secret hiding places, like the guards in the throne rooms at L'Nacin.

'You're Tapio's assistant,' the King said. 'Ejil, is that correct?'

Tel was both astounded and flattered that the King remembered his Islander identity. Especially with all the trauma and turmoil of the last week. 'Aye, Sire,' he said. ''Tis sorry I was ta hear of yer wife.'

The King waved a hand, dismissing Tel's comment. 'I trust you didn't ask for an audience to give me your condolences.'

'No, Sire.' Tel walked down the long runner in the center of the room. He stopped at the stairs below the throne. The King looked down on him. 'I came because I saw something the day yer Queen died that I think ye need ta know.'

Lord Enford stopped beside Tel. 'I agree, Highness. I would not have brought him here at this moment if I didn't believe you needed to hear this before you spoke to the lords.'

The King's shoulders went up and down in a sigh he released quietly. If Tel hadn't been trained to watch the bodies of others, he would never have noticed the movement.

'Very well,' the King said.

Tel bit his lower lip. He had learned all sorts of bad habits in this body. He licked the lip, then swallowed. 'Sire, on that day, twas Rocaanists what arrived first. I was takin their horses. Twas what the Rocaan was doing what stopped me.'

The King was watching him now, eyes hooded, expression guarded. He didn't move at all.

'Afore they went in,' Tel said, 'they took them holy water bottles from their pouches. Twas an Officiate what pulled a white cloth from his pouch and said, "Here it is," flashing it at the Rocaan. The Rocaan nodded.'

'They were supposed to bring the cloth,' the King said. 'It was . . .'

He turned his head away, then brought his right hand to his face. With his thumb and forefinger, he rubbed his eyes.

'It was,' Enford said, keeping his gaze on the King to see if he should speak or not, 'it was to protect the Queen during the ceremony.'

'I know,' Tel said. 'But that's the odd thing. Twas already kept in the pouch with the Officiate's holy water. When he put the cloth back, twas three vials he put on top of it.'

The King brought his head up, but his hand remained in place, fingers open as if expressing the shock he would not allow his face to express. 'What?'

'When he put the cloth in the pouch, he put three bottles on top. All holy water.' Tel's throat had gone dry again. Didn't the King understand? Was Tel going to have to spell it all out for both of them?

'Those vials are stoppered,' the King whispered. His gaze was on Enford's. 'Sometimes water leaks.'

Enford nodded.

Suddenly the King's movements were focused. He came down the stairs and stopped so that he was standing across from Tel. 'You're saying the Rocaan watched this?'

'Aye, Sire,' Tel said. ''Twas he what started it. He got em all lookin for that cloth. He dinna say nothing when he saw the Officiate put it under the bottles a water.'

'I need you to be very clear here,' the King said. 'You are telling me that the Rocaan sanctioned this.'

'I dinna hear him give permission, Sire, but he watched it and he dinna say word one. If he dinna like it, he coulda got a new cloth or something.'

'God's will.' The King spat out the words. 'God's will with the help of Matthias.'

'Highness,' Enford said. 'There's no proof. It could have been a simple mistake.'

The King whirled. His eyes, dead a moment before, had a spark within them. 'If you believed it was a mistake, you would have not brought this man to me.'

Enford said nothing. He continued to meet the King's gaze levelly.

'Sire,' Tel said, 'yer wife was a good woman. She dinna deserve this. But I wouldna a said a thing if I thought twas an accident. But with that check, with the way they was talking, t'all seemed on purpose ta me. Even then. I thought what they done was strange, but I dinna know how twould end up.'

The King nodded. 'Thank you,' he said. Then he took Tel's hand. Tel suppressed a wince. 'I cannot thank you enough.'

Tel dipped his head, trying to be courteous. He had one more thing to say, and he had thought all morning about the way to phrase it. 'Forgive me, Sire, but tis one more thing I gotta say. I know twas the Old Rocaan what picked this one. And I know he done because he thought twas right. But Tapio – the head groom, Sire – he says a man shows himself when he talks ta his horse, and well, that new Rocaan, he dinna talk ta his horse. T'all. Tis as if I could give him a brown mare taday and a black stallion tamorrow, and he wouldna know the difference. Tis not ta say he's cruel ta the animal. He just doesna seem ta know anything outside himself, Sire.'

The King was frowning slightly. A blush was building in Tel's cheeks. So many small incidents he could relate, incidents he had seen in the Tabernacle. Incidents that didn't seem important then, but did now.

But he couldn't say anything about them. He had seen them when he wore a different body, the body of an Elder. A groom would never have seen these things. It was a situation he had not been in before. The Fey had always known what he did, how he changed himself. The Islanders never would.

'Are you saying I should forgive him for what he's done?' the King said.

'Nay, Sire!' Tel actually took a step backwards. 'I think tis a betrayal of the worst kind. Ye and yer lady ye trusted him. Ta attack her in yer celebration, and at a time a peace is a crime that canna be outdone. I guess what I'm saying, Sire, tis that this might be something ta thinka. I dinna believe that he thinks beyond himself. If the time comes agin where he sees a need ta act according ta his lights, he will. Sire.'

The King nodded. 'You're a good man, Ejil. I understand you spent a lot of time getting to me. I appreciate your candor.'

Tel knew a dismissal when he heard one. He bowed. 'Tis glad I am ye took the time fer me, Sire.'

'No,' the King said with a firmness Tel hadn't heard before. 'I'm the one who is pleased. Come to me whenever you need something. I will see to it personally.'

'Sire,' Enford said.

The King waved his hand to silence Enford. 'I mean that, Ejil.'

'Thank ye, Sire.' Tel bowed again, then backed away. The King returned to his throne. Tel turned and walked out of the room, his heart pounding with relief.

He had survived this. He had been able to avenge the Black King's granddaughter, and he had been able to strike a blow against the Tabernacle.

It was time to become Ejil the groom fully and completely.

Tel would never be Fey again.

Thirty

Nicholas sat on the steps and buried his face in his arms. The darkness did not soothe him. Nothing soothed him, except his infant daughter.

Arianna looked so much like Jewel. She had Fey qualities, qualities that would make her more than an Islander, more than a Fey, if Solanda were to be believed.

Arianna was the thing that kept him moving. If he didn't resolve all of these crises, her parents' people would forever be at war.

'Highness,' Enford said in a shocked voice. 'The lords will be here shortly.'

Even Nicholas's stomach was trembling. His eyelid twitched, something it had never done before Jewel's death. He sat up, pressed his right forefinger against the offending lid, and looked at the near-empty audience room.

He had no answers.

The Lords would want him to make decisions.

The simple gut reaction was easy. He would go to the Tabernacle himself and slit Matthias's arrogant throat. Murder his wife, would he?

Murder.

Nicholas stood and walked to the throne. He ran his hands along the carved back.

Two murders.

Some Fey – some male Fey – had killed his father.

Matthias had known.

Jewel had known.

Only Nicholas had not wanted to believe.

But if Matthias had just given it some time, he would have learned that Jewel was on his side. Jewel had wanted to find the killer as much as Matthias had.

Jewel had gone to her old friend Burden.

She had suspected someone.

Her father?

What had she said to him that last afternoon?

She had said that he hid.

He hid.

Like an assassin.

Nicholas pressed the heel of his hand against his forehead.

And Matthias had murdered Jewel with trust. He had taken the scheme they had made to save Jewel's life, to allow her to participate in Islander ceremonies, and he had turned it against her.

He too had hidden behind the rituals of his religion.

Behind his God.

'Sire?' Enford said. 'Are you all right?'

Was the man a fool? How did he expect Nicholas to be all right after this week? The fact that Nicholas was still on his feet made him stronger than most people he had ever met.

'Sire, we need to discuss what we will do with this news.'

'We will discuss it when the others arrive,' Nicholas said.

His voice sounded hollow in the large room. Empty, like he was empty. His dilemma was impossible.

And he had promised Lord Stowe answers today.

Answers.

The only answer Nicholas had was to make the Isle safe for Arianna. He had only one way to do that now. The threat to his daughter did not come from the Fey.

He walked around the throne and sat on its carved wooden seat. He put his hands on the chair's arms, fists gripping the ends. 'Send pages for the lords. If they're not here within the next few moments, we will start without them.'

Enford looked up, the surprise clear on his too-thin face. 'Sire?'

'I gave you an order, Lord Enford. I expect you to carry it out.' Nicholas's tone was imperial. It was a tone he had never used, a tone his father had used only rarely, a tone he had learned from his grandfather – a cold harsh man who had never had time for anything but his Kingdom.

Nicholas would have time for Arianna.

But he had to be cold and harsh to get through this next few days.

Enford frowned, peered at Nicholas as if he didn't recognize him, then scuttled from the room. Nicholas kept his grip tight upon the chair arms. He held himself rigidly, holding his body in place, his emotions at bay. He would get through this afternoon. Then he would get through the next day and the next until Arianna was safe.

Until the Isle was safe.

And he would do it through the strength of his own will.

The doors opened and Lord Stowe entered. He bowed, revealing the bald spot on the top of his head. Since Nicholas's father had died,

Stowe's brown hair had turned grayer – not the light silver of a distinguished man, but the gray of a man who worried too much. He stood, clasped his hands in front of his robe and walked to Nicholas's side.

'Enford says you wish to start early,' he said.

'I have pressing matters,' Nicholas said.

Stowe nodded, as if that were enough. He was cleaned up from his ride the day before, but his features were still haggard. He looked as if he had not slept much, if at all, since he had returned.

The doors opened again. Lord Fesler came through, leaning on a cane. In the last week, his hands had started to shake, and fine webbing lines appeared on his face. The age Nicholas had never been able to determine was becoming clear. Fesler had been a contemporary of Nicholas's grandfather, although most forgot that. His work as a lord had been relatively routine until the Fey arrived. Then the stress had seemed almost too much for him. This week had to be especially hard.

Lord Miller followed him. Miller was still wearing his riding clothes. His boots trailed mud onto the clean floor. Miller was the youngest lord and, until Nicholas's ascension, had not taken his duties very seriously. It still looked as if the perks of lordship interested Miller more than being lord itself.

He bowed to Nicholas, and Fesler did as well, barely bending at the waist, as if his back pained him.

'Forgive me, Sire,' Miller said. 'Enford said you wanted to meet now. I was planning to change.'

'I don't ask formality of my lords,' Nicholas said. At least not now. Protocol was the last thing on his mind.

Miller looked around for a moment, and, seeing no chairs, took his place beside Stowe. Stowe glanced at Fesler.

'Sire,' Stowe said. 'May we get a chair for Lord Fesler? His joints have grown swollen and sore in the last few days.'

'By all means,' Nicholas said. 'There are chairs in the back room. Take one.'

He stressed the word 'one.' He wanted his lords uncomfortable for this meeting. He wanted them to forget young Nicholas whom they had teased and Nicholas the tragic king whose wife was murdered at his coronation. He wanted them to think of him as King. So much King that they would forget that anyone had ever come before him.

Now that he was concentrating on his grandfather, his grandfather's words were coming back to him. *When you become King, boy, everything will rest on you. If you do not remember this, you will lose all you have gained. You will harm Blue Isle more than you will help it.*

Nicholas didn't know if his father had lived by these words. He

241

doubted it. Although he wasn't certain. His father had become a different man after the Fey arrived. His response to the invasion had been confusion, and he had allowed Nicholas's wishes to supersede his at the marriage with Jewel, but Nicholas was no longer certain that was a mistake. If the marriage failed, it could have been blamed on Nicholas's youth, not on the King's bad decision-making.

Stowe disappeared into the back. He spoke to the guards there, and then he and a guard emerged. The guard carried a chair and placed it near the stairs. Fesler sat in it, then sighed softly, as if just standing had been too much for him. He set his cane across his lap, and held it, flush against his stomach, as if he were going to use it as a weapon.

The doors opened again. This time Lord Canter entered wearing a robe finer than the one Nicholas wore. Canter's hair was cut perfectly square, ending below his chin in a fashion that had just begun before the Fey arrived, and had been adopted by some of the fighting men. Canter's cut was always precise, as if he had his man trim it every day. His robe rustled as he moved, the gold embroidery adding sound as well as weight, and his slippers shuffled across the floor. His hands were white and well-manicured, unlike Stowe's, which still bore the stress of his trip, or Fesler's, which were cramped and swollen with pain.

Canter stopped in front of Nicholas but did not bow. Nicholas stared at him, a chill running down his spine. If Canter did not give him obeisance, the others would think they could get away with it too. This meeting was more important than any other. Nicholas knew it and they knew it. This was the meeting that would decide who was in control of the Kingdom.

'Lord Canter,' Nicholas said, 'are we unworthy of your acknowledgment today or are you merely forgetful?'

A dull flush crossed Canter's face. Nicholas had never used the royal we in the presence of the lords before. 'Forgive me, Sire,' he said as he bowed. 'I have been quite forgetful these last few days.'

'Would that we all could be so lucky,' Nicholas murmured.

Canter remained bowed. Nicholas waited an extra moment before bidding Canter to stand.

As he did, Enford entered with Egan and Holbrook. All three men walked down the runner, then bowed in front of Nicholas. They had apparently seen the last part of the interaction with Canter.

Egan nodded his head again, then approached the stairs. His robe was tight around his middle, and he huffed as he climbed toward the throne. Beads of sweat had formed on his forehead. He bowed again when he reached the step below Nicholas then leaned toward him.

'Sire,' Egan said so softly that he almost whispered, 'I wish to give you my deepest condolences and my deepest understandings. I hope you don't think I outstep myself here, but if the nights grow too long for sleep, you may feel free to summon me. We can share hot mead and conversation until dawn.'

Egan's kindness nearly shattered Nicholas's resolve. Of all of the lords, Egan was the only one who had suffered devastating loss. His only child, a son, had died on the day of the Invasion. Egan had searched for the boy for three days before finding the mutilated body beside the river.

Nicholas made himself smile. 'Thank you, milord. I will remember your offer.'

Egan nodded and went back down the stairs. Enford watched the entire exchange closely. Holbrook had been studying Fesler. Fesler's obvious aging had apparently disturbed them all. Suddenly Fesler looked older than Holbrook, who had always appeared twice as old as the other lords. Nicholas had never realized the two men were of an age, an age his grandfather, and his own father, had never seen.

'Now that we are all assembled,' Nicholas said, 'let's begin.'

'Forgive the intrusion, Sire, but the seating seems to be limited,' Canter said.

Nicholas stared at him for a moment. So this was how it would go. The dissenting lords believed they could gain control quickly, now that the King's Fey wife was dead. 'Have you forgotten yourself again, milord?' Nicholas asked. 'This is the second protocol error you've made this afternoon.'

'Highness, I was merely noting that Lord Holbrook also appears uncomfortable and –'

'Fight your battles alone, Canter,' Holbrook said. 'My feet have borne my weight for decades and will continue to do so without complaint.'

'This forgetfulness of yours seems to be quite serious, Lord Canter,' Nicholas said. 'I believe we shall have to keep it under observation. If it interferes with your functions within this House, we shall have to ask you to step aside and allow your son to fill your seat.'

'My son is just a boy, Highness,' Canter said. 'I'm sure that even with diminished capacity I could perform better than he.'

'Your son and I are of an age, milord,' Nicholas said. 'We surpassed "boy" a long time ago. I would be pleased to have him work at my side. It certainly appears easier than dealing with your new affliction.'

Canter stared at Nicholas, jaw working. Nicholas met Canter's stare. Finally Canter looked away, and slowly bowed.

'I shall, Sire, make certain that my affliction does not interfere with my duties.'

'See that it doesn't,' Nicholas said. 'I shall be monitoring you.'

When Canter stood the flush had left his cheeks, but the speculation had not left his eyes. Nicholas purposely turned away from him.

'My friends,' Nicholas said, emphasizing the word 'friends,' 'we face the largest crisis to hit Blue Isle since the Roca faced the Soldiers of the Enemy. I'm sure by now Lord Stowe has told you about the Fey seen in the area where my father was murdered.'

The lords nodded.

'Just a few moments ago, a groom told me that he saw Matthias place the cloth he was using to protect Jewel in a pouch with vials of holy water. My wife's death was no more accidental than my father's.'

Fesler's hands tightened on his cane. Enford looked down. Stowe frowned. Canter and Miller didn't move. Egan closed his eyes and shook his head.

Only Holbrook seemed unmoved. 'That's a very serious charge, Highness.'

'I realize this,' Nicholas said. 'I would not make it if I did not know it to be true.'

'I have heard the groom's testimony as well,' Enford said. 'He is unimpeachable. I tried before I brought him to the King.'

'You cannot base something this serious on the word of a servant,' Fesler said.

'I do not,' Nicholas said. 'I base it on the word of a groom, on my own knowledge, and upon Matthias's actions. He did not want Jewel to leave the coronation hall. If she had stayed any longer, we would have lost her and the child.'

'Forgive me, Highness, but wouldn't that have been a blessing? They're already saying that the babe is more of a monster than her brother.' Canter spoke softly, as if he didn't mean to offend.

Nicholas rose slowly from the throne. He walked down two steps, stopping on the last step and looking down at Canter. 'I will tolerate no more of this from you.'

Canter squinted. 'You will have to, Highness. If you don't hear it from me, it will be whispered behind your back. Already on the streets, they are saying that it is good the Fey woman died. It is good that the royal blood will no longer be polluted with the blood of the damned. They are saying you were bewitched and that Matthias broke the spell.'

Nicholas raised his chin just enough so that he could look down his nose at the man. 'You are speaking of my wife and children.'

'I am speaking of the state of the monarchy.'

'The state of the monarchy.' Nicholas tested the words. 'The state of the monarchy is this: I am taking over my father's place. Cross me and you will commit treason. Speak ill of my wife or my children, and you will also commit treason. Treason is and always has been punishable by death. Do I make myself clear, Canter?'

Canter put his well tended hands behind his back. 'Yes, sir.' He did not sound docile.

'Whether or not you punish the citizens for speaking ill of the royal house,' Holbrook said, 'will not solve the problem, Highness. Your marriage to Jewel was an unpopular gamble that unfortunately resulted in a first born who cannot rule. Her death in a religious ceremony, at the hands of the Rocaan, divides our people. You must deal with these things.'

'I plan to,' Nicholas said. He returned to his throne and made a ceremony of sitting down. The men watched him, their expressions more wary than he had ever seen them. He gripped the arms of the throne so tightly that his hands hurt.

'I understand the problems that Matthias's act of murder has created. I know that he has fanned sparks that were growing already. We face battle on two fronts, gentlemen. On the first, the Fey, who began this by sending one of their own to kill my father.'

'Then Matthias was justified in retaliating,' Canter said.

Nicholas raised one hand for silence, keeping his gaze on Canter. 'On the second, we have the Tabernacle. The actions of the Rocaan split this Isle down the middle. People must choose between their faith and their King. I hope to quash the first and negate the second.'

'Impossible, Sire,' Fesler said. 'You cannot force the people to choose loyalty.'

Nicholas smiled. The smile felt strange on his face. The smile was something he wore, like his robe. It was not connected to his heart. 'I most certainly can,' he said. 'Matthias reminded me of that during the ceremony he used to kill my wife.'

'You're being mysterious, Sire,' Stowe said.

Nicholas shook his head. 'I am being deliberate, Milord. There is nothing in the Words Written or Unwritten that provides for the Tabernacle. The only thing – the only thing, gentlemen – in the Roca's words that allows for the Tabernacle at all is His admonition that the eldest son become King and the second son lead in the spiritual realm. Perhaps, gentlemen, we have failed. Perhaps we did not follow the Roca's second admonition. Perhaps that is why we were so ripe for conquest in the first place.'

Enford's face went white. Holbrook grinned, then quickly suppressed the look. Miller leaned his head back, looking interested in the conversation for the first time.

'The only true representative of the Roca on Blue Isle is me, gentlemen. I carry his blood in my veins. Leaders in Rocaanism must live chaste lives, an odd choice, I think. Or they would have been able to follow in the path of the Roca's second son. The Roca meant for his family to rule Blue Isle, not second sons of average people. The failure of the fiftieth Rocaan, and the destructiveness of Matthias prove that God is not with the Tabernacle. God is here, in the palace. With me.'

'If God were with you,' Canter said, 'your son would be able to think for himself.'

'Watch yourself,' Enford said softly. He hadn't taken his gaze from Nicholas's face. Apparently Nicholas was looking as fierce as he felt.

'If I split with the Tabernacle, will you stand with Matthias, then?' Nicholas asked.

Canter shook his head. 'Fortunately,' he said. 'I am not a practicing Rocaanist.'

'The faith's tenets demand that the King do the Roca's work in the world and the Rocaan do the work within the spiritual realm,' Fesler said.

Nicholas shook his head. 'The faith's tenets, which I learned from Matthias himself, only say that the second son must do the work within the spiritual realm. Our current Rocaan is not related to the Roca. He has no right to lead in the spiritual realm.'

'You would forego the spiritual, then?' Fesler asked, his voice cracking just a bit.

'It seems,' Nicholas said, 'that we already have.'

No one spoke. Only Lord Enford continued to look at Nicholas. Lord Stowe studied his hands. The sweat dripped down Lord Egan's face.

They thought he was crazy. They clearly thought that the events of the last few days had driven him over the edge. He opened his mouth to defend himself –

– and stopped. *No matter what the course, steer steadily and with great control*, his grandfather used to say. *You must show them strength*, Jewel had told him once. *People respect strength, Nicky.*

Just as he had respected hers.

'You leave us with a divided country if you do this thing,' Holbrook said.

'No, I won't,' Nicholas said. He continued to speak with great firmness, pretending a confidence he wasn't sure he had. 'I will take over the Tabernacle. I will run it until we find others to do so, or until one of my children can.'

'The girl?' Miller asked. He swiveled as he did so.

'The girl,' Nicholas said, 'will act as regent for her brother when she gets older.'

'You're planning to have more children, Highness?' Lord Stowe asked.

'I'm not planning not to,' Nicholas said. 'It is much too soon to think of another wife.'

His heart couldn't bear it. Inside, he apologized to Jewel, yet he knew of all people, she would understand the most.

'You cannot allow a woman to run the country,' Canter said.

'You were the one who said that my son would not be capable,' Nicholas said. 'A point which we could debate. My daughter will be capable. She may serve as regent should something happen to me.'

'But, Sire, what if something were to happen to you before she comes of age?' Egan asked.

'We'll have to make certain it won't, won't we, milord?' Nicholas said.

A slight frown creased Holbrook's lined features. 'I still do not understand how you will set Matthias aside.'

Nicholas leaned back. The wooden back of the throne gave his spine the stiffness it needed. 'I will use Matthias to solve our other problem.'

'The Fey?' Stowe said. 'How would you do that?'

'They have the same difficulties we do.'

Miller started to speak and Egan shushed him.

Nicholas nodded his thanks to Egan. 'My wife knew nothing of the plot against my father. She went to see her friend Burden, the Fey who started the Settlement, and asked him if he had sent someone after my father. Burden had known nothing of it either and had, in fact, been surprised that a Fey was even connected to the crime.'

'How did your wife know?' Fesler asked. 'Stowe didn't return until yesterday.'

'She listened to Matthias like the rest of us. Only unlike us, she agreed with him. She knew that the murderer had to be Fey. The crime was committed in a way that was too cunning and calculated – and unmotivated – for an Islander. She went to see Burden, and told me of their conversation the night before she died.'

'Do we know who committed this crime?' Egan asked.

'No,' Nicholas said, 'but I think Jewel did. She wasn't ready to tell me until she knew for certain.'

'We already know that the Fey murdered your father,' Fesler said. 'I don't understand how that compares.'

Nicholas tilted his head, looking down on Fesler. Even his jaw was swollen. His hands, resting on his cane, were shaking. He looked wrung out. Fesler wasn't siding with anyone. He was trying to make sense of events.

As they all were.

'*The* Fey didn't murder my father,' Nicholas said. 'A Fey murdered him. A single Fey, acting alone. I learned that much from Jewel and from the others at the coronation. If the Fey had unilaterally opposed the marriage and the alliance, they wouldn't have worked so hard to save Jewel and Arianna.'

'You believe they had someone acting without authorization from their leaders, creating a situation the way Matthias did,' Stowe said. His thin, exhausted face had a puzzled look to it, as if he were having trouble following Nicholas's argument.

'Exactly,' Nicholas said. 'I believe my father's death caught most of the Fey by surprise.'

He didn't discuss the interlude in the kitchen after Jewel's death, the fight between the Shaman and Jewel's father over the placement of Arianna. Or Solanda's mysterious comments about Rugar.

'So the Rocaan was right in retaliating,' Canter said.

'Matthias was wrong in retaliating, especially against Jewel who, for the first time in her life, actually agreed with him. She was the one who could have resolved all of this. He killed the very person we needed to help us.' A lump grew in Nicholas's throat. He had to swallow – hard – to make it go away. 'Matthias should have spoken to me. Jewel and I would have resolved this. Peaceably.'

'Dreams,' Canter said.

Nicholas shook his head. 'Reality.'

'I believe the King is right,' Enford said. 'The situation we have now is untenable. The Queen's death only made things worse. But I'm not sure I like your proposal so far, Highness.'

'You may like this part even less,' Nicholas said. 'I propose we do not fight the Fey. I –'

'We couldn't fight them anyway,' Miller said. 'You forget, Highness. The Rocaan is the only one who makes holy water. If we anger him, we lose any advantage we have against the Fey.'

'Do we?' Nicholas asked. 'I contend we have no advantage now. The Fey may be planning something even now as a retaliation for Jewel. And they won't come for me. They'll go for Matthias.'

'Or the rest of the Isle,' Fesler said.

'That isn't the Fey way,' Nicholas said. 'They won't destroy the place in order to win it. Jewel taught me that. You have to listen to me. I think I have the only way out of these conflicts. The only way that will leave Blue Isle intact.'

He was begging, but he no longer cared. They had to listen to him. They had to understand.

'Go on, Highness,' Egan said.

Nicholas took a deep breath. His heart was pounding. Hard. His palms were so damp they were sliding on the arms of the throne. 'I will propose to the Fey that they turn over their killer to us, and we'll turn over ours to them.'

'What?'

'Highness!'

'You can't mean that!'

The cries were so uniform that he couldn't tell who had spoken. He kept his grip on the chair. He might be nervous, but he couldn't show it. Not now.

'I do mean it,' he said. 'It's the only way.'

'And what if they don't turn over their killer?' Holbrook asked.

'Then we don't turn over ours.'

'But what if they give us the wrong person?'

Nicholas's mouth was dry. He hadn't thought of that. 'I'll make the exchange with their Shaman. She'll know.'

'How will she know?' Canter asked. 'Magic?'

Nicholas nodded. 'Some Fey have a gift of clearness. The Shaman is perhaps the most gifted of all in that area. She will be honest with us.'

'You're putting a lot of trust in them,' Egan said softly.

'They saved my daughter's life.'

'They had benefit in that too,' Enford said. 'She is their ruler's great-granddaughter.'

'Jewel believed that they had benefit in the alliance,' Nicholas said. 'She believed it was the only way for Fey to survive.'

'Not if you give them our Rocaan, it's not. Then they can attack us with impunity, especially if you take over the church. Who'll make the holy water?' Canter asked.

'I will,' Nicholas said.

'Forgive me, Highness, but you don't know how,' Holbrook said.

'Matthias will teach me,' Nicholas said, although he wasn't sure how he would accomplish that.

'Giving you the secret to holy water would be useless,' Canter said. 'You would never use it against them.'

'Exactly,' Nicholas said. 'That is one of the things that gives them safety in this bargain.'

'But that will never protect us,' Canter said.

'Of course it will protect you,' Nicholas said. 'As long as the agreement remains alive, the Fey will not attack us. They will work with us.' He stood. 'I have said I will do anything to save my daughter and to save this Isle. I mean that.'

'Do you?' Holbrook asked softly. 'Do you really mean that, Highness?'

Nicholas cocked his head and looked at Holbrook. 'Why are you asking me that, milord?'

'Because, Sire, it seems to me that your actions now will destroy this kingdom. To separate the state and the Tabernacle is like severing the Isle down the middle.'

'I find it ironic,' Nicholas said, 'that you men are blaming me for the severing. Matthias murdered my wife. Matthias already severed this Kingdom. If I let him go without punishing him, then we are all at risk. The Fey, and our own people, will believe that we will do nothing if the royalty is attacked. So they will attack. Matthias murdered Jewel. He did so in front of the elite of the Kingdom, and in front of her people. Witnesses saw that he planned this murder. If I do not punish him, I lose what little power I gained upon taking this throne.'

The lords were watching him, open-mouthed. He had been speaking loudly and with a force he rarely used.

'If I do not punish him,' Nicholas said, 'Blue Isle as we know it will disappear. Chaos will reign, and eventually the Fey will win.'

'The Fey will win under your plan. They almost did,' Canter said. 'If your wife had lived, we all would have lost.'

'That's treason,' Stowe whispered to him.

'No, let him say this,' Nicholas said. He walked down the stairs until he faced Canter. 'If he's saying it, so are others. I am only going to explain this to you once more. By your definition, the Fey won when they invaded. They breached our impenetrable walls, and slaughtered people in a nation that had never seen outside war. They changed the face of our land, of our religion, and of ourselves. If we do not acknowledge that, then we are fools.'

Canter's eyes narrowed. He was frowning.

'We had beaten them back, but we couldn't let them leave. They can never leave. All we can do is wait for the Black King to arrive. He may never arrive. He may believe that Blue Isle is lost to him. He may have sent his son here to get rid of a rival. He may have no interest in the Isle. That's what we hope for.'

'Then why do we ally with them?' Canter asked.

'Because we do not know. This Black King may not come. The next may not come. But the next will. And what do we do with all the Fey? They have more magicks than we know. Some will survive. And when the Black King comes, with his superior magicians, we will die. They will find a solution to holy water, and we will all die.'

'We may not live that long,' Canter said.

'And some of us might,' Miller said.

'Some of us,' Holbrook said slowly, 'care about the future we give to our children, and our children's children.'

'If my alliance with Jewel had been allowed to stand, we would have secured that future. Jewel and I would have kept the Isle running as it always ran. She was even willing to support the religious traditions which were deadly to her. Matthias changed all of that. *Matthias*, and people with attitudes like yours, Lord Canter. I will still try to meld both cultures into one. That is my job now. But I will do so my way. And my way does not include Matthias.'

'Would it include another Rocaan?' Egan asked.

Nicholas took a deep breath. This was an option he had considered and discarded. 'I don't know,' he said. 'I only know that a man who has purposely taken a life in the name of religion does not belong in charge of that religion.'

'Are you suggesting a puppet leader of the church?' Holbrook asked.

'If need be,' Egan said.

'There will be no need,' Nicholas said. 'I will make arrangements to give Matthias to the Fey, and get their killer in return.'

'I cannot support this plan,' Canter said.

The fury Nicholas had suppressed all afternoon rose and he almost brought up his fists. But he took a deep breath, as his father had taught him, and waited until the anger surged through him.

'You will support it,' Nicholas said in the most measured tone he could manage. 'You will support it and all I do or so help me God I will take your lands and your title and all you are from you so quickly that you won't see it coming.'

'You wouldn't dare,' Canter said. 'You're a new King on shaky ground, a Fey-lover, and an appeaser.'

'I can and will,' Nicholas said. 'Except for Sebastian, I am the only heir to the throne, with no possibilities for a regent. None of you can lead this country. You are stuck with me and no one else. And you are stuck with my policies. One of my policies is, *Lord* Canter, that you support me in all you say or do or I will confiscate all that you own, all that you are, and all that you will ever be. Is that clear?'

'A man cannot rule by tyranny,' Canter said.

'A man must rule with force and dignity,' Nicholas said. 'My father ruled with kindness and a weak hand. It got him killed. I have to survive until my daughter reaches her majority. I will do so any way I can. Will you support me, Canter?'

Canter stared at Nicholas.

Nicholas nodded, feeling as if he had gotten his answer. He grabbed the skirts of his robe and started up the stairs.

'Wait, Highness,' Canter said. 'I will support you.'

Nicholas smiled to himself before he turned around. He didn't know where this coldness had come from within him, but he was learning to work with it, to survive with it, to allow it to show him the way. The smile had disappeared by the time he faced Canter.

'You will support me in all things, *Lord* Canter,' Nicholas said. 'You will support me in action, in word, and in deed. If I hear so much as a whisper of your misconduct, I will strip you of your lands and titles so fast that you will not have time to steal a prized possession from the house.'

Holbrook frowned. 'Highness, a man says things –'

'Men say things, yes,' Nicholas said. 'But Lord Canter cannot and keep his title. If you talk in your sleep, milord, I suggest that you sleep alone. Am I making myself clear?'

'Very, Highness,' Canter said. The dull red had risen in his cheeks again.

'Can you do this?'

Canter's lower lip jutted out slightly. 'I'll have to, won't I?'

'Only if you want to keep your position,' Nicholas said. He gave Canter's clothing an appraising glance. The gold embroidery sparkled in the candlelight. The rings on Canter's fingers were worth more than Ejil, the young groom, would spend in his entire life. 'And it looks as if you'll be lost without your position.'

The red in Canter's cheeks grew even darker. To his credit, though, he gave no other indication of his great anger.

'Highness,' Enford asked quietly. 'How will you achieve this exchange with the Fey? Do you need our services?'

Nicholas shook his head. 'I know how to speak to them. I will do so my way.'

He climbed the stairs back to the throne and sat. Then he stared at his lords. Impossible to say which would be loyal to him. Even Egan, who had touched him with kindness earlier, had reason to oppose Nicholas's policies. After all, the Fey had slaughtered his son. Stowe had been loyal to Nicholas's father, as had Enford, but who knew how such loyalties transferred.

'I will be acting quickly,' he said. 'But if word of this reaches Matthias before I take action, heads will roll.'

'Literally, Highness?' Canter asked.

'Possibly,' Nicholas said. He waved a hand. 'You're all dismissed.'

This time the lords were careful to bow on their way out. They did not speak as they filed past. Fesler struggled with his chair. He set his cane aside and attempted to pull himself up. Nicholas waited until the last lord had left the room before going down the steps. He put a hand beneath Fesler's elbow and eased the older man to his feet.

Fesler's arm was fragile in Nicholas's grasp. The bones were thin and brittle. Fesler trembled as he rose to his feet.

'Had I realized movement was so difficult for you,' Nicholas said, 'I would have arranged a better place for this meeting.'

Fesler's smile was sad. 'Movement has been difficult for years. I used to hide it better. I think this week destroyed the strength I used for pretense.'

'I had never realized you were in such poor health,' Nicholas said.

'It is not poor,' Fesler said. 'My condition is chronic. Your father knew. We had to discuss it when I first became ill. There was no one to take on my estate.'

'And now?' Nicholas asked. He had not had time to look into any of the records.

'Now I shall wait and see if the plans I made are the plans I should follow,' Fesler said.

Nicholas nodded. He understood that. Fesler looked at him. They were standing closer than they ever had, in all the years Nicholas had known him.

'You reminded me of your grandfather today.' Fesler patted Nicholas's arm. 'This is good. We need strength, particularly now.'

'I don't feel strong,' Nicholas said.

'But you act it. That is enough.' Fesler braced his cane on the floor and shifted his weight from Nicholas to the cane itself. 'It is a shame your strength had to come from events as tragic as these. But we cannot choose how we are forged.'

'I would have preferred an easier way,' Nicholas said.

'As would I, boy. As would I.' Fesler leaned on the cane and slowly made his way up the aisle. 'You know you made an enemy today.'

'I know,' Nicholas said. 'My grandfather used to say that a strong man made an enemy every day.'

Fesler stopped walking. He peered at Nicholas over his shoulder. 'Your grandfather,' Fesler said, 'was not always right.'

Thirty-One

Rugar knocked once on the door to the Wisps' cabin, then let himself in. The cabin smelled of woodsmoke and fresh baked bread. Gift was sitting on the floor, as he often was. When he saw Rugar at the door, he let out a small yelp and backed away. Rugar terrified the boy and he wasn't sure why.

'Mama!' Gift cried, then stood and backed away until he was braced against the wall. Rugar smiled at him, but that did not put him at ease.

Gift was a beautiful child. His hair was so shiny black it reflected the flames from the fireplace as blue. His eyes were round, startling, and full of intelligence. His upswept brows, high cheekbones, and thin features made him appear Fey, but his face belonged to his father. Anyone who saw him and Nicholas together would know Gift's paternity.

Rugar could never forget it.

Niche peered out of the back room. She was holding a towel. Wind was at her shoulder, his delicate features haggard. They had the look of people who had gone days without sleep.

'I thought you'd be in mourning,' Niche said. Her voice was cold. She set the towel on a tiny table to her left and came into the room.

'I heard the boy had some trouble.'

'He's fine now.'

Gift was watching them from the wall. For one who had supposedly come close to death, he looked the healthiest of all of them.

'The Shaman had said he would not survive the night. I would like to know what happened,' Rugar said.

Niche looked at Gift. His eyes were wide. 'Gift, will you leave us, please?'

'No,' he said, his tone surprisingly adult.

'Gift,' Niche said. 'I need to talk with your grandfather alone.' She had turned toward the boy to speak with him and Rugar saw that her wings were bandaged and held close to her side. Something had happened here. Something serious.

'Come, boy,' Wind said. 'Let me take you outside.'

'No,' Gift said again. He hadn't taken his gaze off Rugar. The boy's old eyes had a malevolence to them that they had never had before.

Rugar crossed the room in two strides and crouched in front of Gift. The boy tried to push himself even farther into the wall. 'Do you have something to say to me, son?'

Gift pursed his lips. Niche shook her head at him. He didn't even look at her. His eyes narrowed, and he looked just like his father had when Rugar tried to take the baby.

'You let her die.' The boy's words were stark, flat and cold.

Rugar took a step back.

Niche put a hand over her heart and looked at Rugar, as if asking him to explain. Wind straightened his brows in confusion.

Rugar felt as if the air had been knocked from him. 'What?' he asked.

'I been thinking about it,' Gift said. 'You let her die.'

'No one's dead, Gift,' Niche said.

'Then why should he be mourning, huh? And why do you make me call him Grandfather? You don't call him Father. Neither of you.'

Niche looked at Rugar as if pleading with him. But he couldn't get a footing on this situation. Too much had changed for him too quickly.

Rugar swallowed. 'I didn't let anyone die.'

'You let my real mother die.' Gift spat the words at him. They felt like little arrows entering Rugar's skin.

Niche gasped. Now it was Wind's turn to look at Rugar in shock. They both thought he had told the boy. He hadn't said a word.

'I didn't let anyone die,' Rugar said again. The sentence sounded weak.

'You did,' Gift said. He still leaned on the wall. Rugar still frightened him, but not enough to stop the boy from speaking. 'I been thinking about it. You knew she was going to die. You said I Saw something and I Saw her die. And you knew that would happen and you did nothing.'

'You don't understand, boy,' Rugar said.

'I understand. I understand real good.' Now the boy pushed off from the wall, the depth of anger propelling him forward. He wasn't yelling, but the power behind his words gave him a force that Rugar couldn't ignore. Rugar felt riveted to his spot. Apparently Niche and Wind did as well.

'You don't care about nobody,' the boy said. 'When that old lady told you my real mother was dead, you turned to me. And when the old lady said that I was dying, you said you wanted that baby. Not because you like us or want us, but because we can do something for you.'

255

'I'm sorry, Rugar.' Niche came up behind the boy and put her hands on his shoulders, holding him back. 'But he was very ill.'

'I wasn't ill,' Gift said. 'I was dying. The old lady said I almost died because of him.'

Niche's gaze met Rugar's over the top of Gift's head. 'The old lady?' Niche asked.

'The Shaman,' Rugar said. He was breathless with wonder. 'He Saw the fight I had with the Shaman.'

'But how?' Wind asked. 'He's just a boy. I thought that Vision was an aberration.'

'I thought Vision didn't break the fog of the present,' Niche said.

'Sometimes it does,' Rugar said. He had seen Gift watching, but hadn't realized that the eyes belonged to his grandson. Until now. 'But that's not what happened here.'

'You lied. And you killed her. You killed my real mother.' Gift strained at his mother's grip. Her hollow bones wouldn't be able to restrain him much longer.

'What happened then?' Wind asked.

Rugar looked at Niche. She would understand. 'The golem lives.'

'Still?'

The boy didn't seem to hear. 'I don't want you coming here any more. I don't ever want to talk to you again. I want you to leave us alone!'

'Gift,' Wind said. His tone was mild. The boy ignored him.

Rugar crouched. He couldn't be afraid of this child. The boy was his best hope for the future. 'I am your grandfather, Gift, the only blood relative you have.'

'Lies,' the boy hissed. His composure startled Rugar more than the words. If he had shouted or thrown a tantrum like most children his age, Rugar would have been able to ignore the boy. But he couldn't. 'The yellow man, he's my father. And the baby, that's my sister.'

'Where did you hear all this, Gift?' Wind asked.

'I Saw it. I Saw it all.'

Niche looked over her shoulder at her husband. 'I'll explain later,' she said.

'Gift,' Rugar said. He had to quiet the boy. He wasn't sure how. 'I would never want you dead.'

'I didn't say you wanted me dead. I said you didn't care,' Gift said.

Rugar closed his eyes. He had heard that from too many people this week. Couldn't they see that Jewel's death had torn him apart? He had not planned for this. Blue Isle was supposed to be his triumph, not his torment.

He opened his eyes again. Gift was staring at him, his small face contorted with rage. Rugar had been wrong. If Niche let go of Gift, he would attack Rugar and beat him with his fists. 'I can't leave you alone, Gift,' Rugar said. 'To do so would be to betray everything.'

'You let her die. You knew and you let her die.'

Rugar had to calm the boy. He had to get Gift back on his side. He needed the boy's Sight. 'There are many things you don't understand about Visions, Gift.'

'You're going to lie to me again, aren't you?' he said.

Niche was biting her lower lip. She swallowed hard. Wind was behind her, supporting her so that any sudden change in Gift's position would not send her flying back and break her fragile bones.

'Gift,' Wind said quietly, 'you're not an expert just because you had one Vision.'

'But I told him my mother was going to die and he didn't listen! He said it would be all right.'

'I didn't understand your Vision,' Rugar said. 'It was powerful, but you're very young.'

'That's what you all say!' Gift was shouting now. 'But I Saw her die. I Saw it. You can't change that. I Saw it and you did nothing. You didn't even believe me.'

'I believed you.' Rugar reached out his hands. 'I just didn't understand.'

'Her dying almost killed me.'

'I know,' Rugar said. 'I'm sorry. Your Vision was unusual, Gift. How much more can I explain this?'

Gift's features narrowed, and then his lower lip trembled. 'She loved me,' he whispered.

Rugar held his breath. Niche put a hand over her heart.

'She loved me. She didn't even know I was here, and she loved me.'

'You saw her?' Rugar asked.

Gift nodded. 'She came to break the tie. But she thought I was going to be someone else.' He raised his eyes to Rugar. 'She cursed you.'

Rugar worked to keep his features impassive. Jewel had given her last energy to save her son. She had known that the ties weren't broken, and she had slid along the Links to save him. Only instead of finding the golem, which she had been looking for, she found Gift.

And knew what Rugar had done.

If only he had had a chance to explain. If only he had been able to tell her that he had taken Gift for the good of the Fey.

'Rugar?' Niche asked.

He glared at her, this Wisp. Just because he had deemed her worthy of watching his grandson didn't mean she was worthy of talking to him.

The fierceness he felt must have seeped into his features. Gift backed into his mother, looking for the first time since Rugar arrived, like the child he was. 'I don't get it,' he said, and despite the fear he was displaying, his words held bravado.

'Get what?' Niche asked softly.

'If a person can See the future, how come he can't change it?'

The words were an attack. The boy was leaning on his adopted mother, taking her strength, and using his protected position to bait Rugar.

He wouldn't be baited. He would win the boy any way he could. 'Sometimes a person can change the future,' Rugar said. 'If he understands.'

Gift crossed his arms. 'But you didn't understand?'

The difficult admission. The one that would reveal he was not all-powerful. But if Gift thought him all-powerful, then he would always blame him for Jewel's death.

'No,' Rugar said softly. 'I didn't understand. That's not unusual. Sometimes I don't understand my own Visions. No one does. They become clear when they happen.'

Gift bit his trembling lip. 'So what's the point of having them?'

Rugar wished he knew. He had thought he had known once, but Blue Isle had changed that. 'I was told,' he said, 'that a man has Visions of things he cannot change so that he will believe the Visions he has of the things he can change.'

'That's stupid,' Gift said.

Rugar grinned in spite of himself. 'I thought so too.'

Gift looked at him, expression young and suddenly trusting. 'You did?'

'I did,' Rugar said.

Wind bent over and took Gift's hand. The boy looked at his adopted father, the moment with Rugar broken. Rugar almost admonished Wind. Almost. But to do so might mean alienating the boy again, and the boy was alienated enough.

'Come on, Gift,' Wind said. 'Your mother needs to talk with your grandfather alone.'

Gift sighed. He glanced again at Rugar, that look of trust gone. 'I'm not going to say I'm sorry for yelling,' Gift said.

'Gift!' Niche said.

'It's all right.' Rugar stood. 'He has a right to his anger. He has been through a lot.'

Even though he spoke to Niche, he made certain he looked at Gift. He wanted Gift to forget that moment when Rugar had dismissed Gift's death, when Rugar had tried to reach to a future the Shaman had shut him out of forever.

'I want to talk some more,' Gift said. 'You gotta tell me how to make the Visions go away.'

'They don't go away,' Rugar said. 'But I can teach you how to use them.'

'Come on,' Wind said. He led Gift around Rugar and out of the cabin. As soon as the door closed, Niche crossed her arms.

Such anger around him. It was as if he were suddenly attracting it. Now, when he couldn't handle it any more.

'What happened to your wings?' he asked so that she wouldn't be able to start the conversation.

'I fell on them,' she snapped. 'Tending my dying son.'

'You blame me for that, don't you?'

'Gift is right,' she said. 'You should have listened to him.'

'And done what? He thought you were threatened. You were warned. There was nothing I could do.' Rugar kept his hands loosely at his side. He held his place in the center of the floor like it was a battlefield he had conquered. He would not show her the depth of his own despair. She needn't know that he was already defeated enough.

'None of us were warned. I spoke to the Shaman. She says he had the Vision because he was threatened.'

'If she knew that,' Rugar said, 'then she should have stayed.'

'I spoke to her after she returned.'

Niche's words hung in the air. Behind Rugar, wood snapped in the fire. He jumped, despite himself. She noted the movement and he wished he could take it back, make it go away.

'We had no way of knowing that he was threatened,' Rugar finally said.

'The Shaman said that a Vision which comes young is usually of a child's death.'

'The Shaman would be wise to share such knowledge with other Visionaries.' Rugar couldn't keep his own temper in any longer. 'Is that why you wished to talk with me alone? So that you could tell me my failings? I already know them. I lost a daughter this week and almost lost a grandson. I am very well aware of where I stand.'

'I asked you to talk with me alone because I am concerned about Gift,' Niche said. Her haggard features told him that more eloquently than she ever could. She and Wind must not have slept at all since Gift's illness. 'He is too young for these Visions. He is too young to be saddled with the burdens you're placing on him.'

'I have placed no burdens on him. I can't control his Visions.'

'But you brought on the first,' Niche said.

Rugar raised his eyebrows. 'Did the Shaman tell you that too?'

Niche shook her head. 'I saw it. I was here, remember?'

'If Visions were that easy, Visionaries would be infallible.' Rugar sighed. If only he could have a Vision whenever he wanted one. 'He touched me. That triggered the first Vision. And he was so young he didn't understand half of what he Saw, and he communicated it even more poorly. If I had known, truly known, what he Saw, then I might have been able to help Jewel.'

'But not Gift.'

Rugar shook his head. 'None of us knew of the boy's link to Jewel. Not even the Shaman. Had she known, she might have stayed here to care for the boy. She was doing her best to save Jewel.'

'You should know,' Niche said. 'You're the Leader of this pitiful troop. You should know about Links and you should See what will happen next. You didn't even warn me that Gift might die. I could have used warning.'

'I didn't know,' Rugar said. 'I can't know everything.'

'You should know,' Niche said. 'My son is alive because of luck, nothing more.'

'Your son?' Rugar glared at her. 'Your son? My *grand*son, woman. You care for him because of my good graces. Not because of any blood tie.'

'My son,' Niche said. 'And you're right. I care for him. You do not. You took the Shaman, the Domestics and the Healers with you that day. If Coulter hadn't been here, Gift would have died. Wind and I certainly weren't able to help him.'

'Coulter?' Rugar put out a hand to steady himself. The anger that had held him dissipated with the shock of the name. Burden's words came back to him. *Have you ever wondered what really saved him? The Shaman thought your grandson died.*

Died.

Rugar sank onto a cushion and sat there for a moment, his heart pounding hard. 'Coulter?' he asked again. 'The Islander child? The one Solanda stole?'

Niche nodded.

'What could an Islander do?'

'He wrapped him in strings of light.'

A chill ran through Rugar. 'You were here? You saw it?'

Niche was standing over him. She smelled of a fresh breeze blowing off the ocean. 'I saw it all,' she said.

'Was there a Vision? In the light? Did you see something other than light?'

She frowned, as if she hadn't expected him to ask that question. 'I saw both boys as men standing on the Cardidas River.'

Rugar closed his eyes. The contents of his stomach churned. He wondered if Burden knew of this or if Burden would have known what to make of it if he heard.

The Islanders don't have magick, Rugar had said when Solanda told him of the child.

This one does, she had replied.

This one does.

She had known. She had known from the beginning. Which was why she took him and brought him here.

We can't use the powers of a baby to fight a war, Rugar had said.

Not yet, she had replied.

Rugar swallowed, and opened his eyes. Niche was watching him, her features furrowed in concern.

'Are you sure that Gift didn't do this himself?' Rugar asked.

Niche nodded. 'He was screaming, his eyes rolled in the back of his head, and ...' her voice faltered a bit '... and it smelled like burning, like someone had poured that poison on him. He couldn't have done anything.'

'Are you certain?' Rugar said. 'The boy has powerful magic.'

'Coulter came in,' Niche said. 'When I wouldn't move, he pushed me aside. That's how my wings broke. I was watching. The light came from him, and cradled Gift. He saved Gift. He did. I saw it.'

Rugar shook his head. 'It's not possible.'

'It happened.'

'But the boy is Islander.'

Niche shrugged. 'Gift is part Islander, and you say he's powerful.'

'But that always happens when Fey breed with outsiders. The magic runs truer.' Rugar looked away from her. The fire was burning high and bright, the flames orange with a blue center. The wood glowed.

An Enchanter. Only Enchanters could do that sort of spell. Shamans had all sorts of talents, from healing to Visions, but they could not do light or fire spells.

Enchanters could do everything.

'What does Gift think of this?' Rugar asked.

'He asked for Coulter when he woke, and Coulter came to the door. They seem closer now.'

They would. They were bound. Gift wouldn't be free until Coulter let him go.

An Enchanter.

An Islander Enchanter.

This made everything different.

'Do you know where the boy lives?'

'Coulter?' Niche asked. 'I thought the Domestics cared for him.'

'I need to find him and discover what he's done.' Rugar stood. He started for the door, then felt Niche's light hand on his arm. Her expression was fierce.

'Coulter saved Gift's life. Don't do anything to reverse that.'

Rugar put his hand on hers. She flinched at his touch. 'Believe me, woman,' he said, 'I would never harm my grandson.'

'You have before.'

He gripped her hand just tight enough to threaten her hollow bones. 'Gift belongs to me. I can take him any time I want.'

She nodded. 'He may be your blood, but he loves me.'

'Love is worth a bucket of piss in the end.'

'A bucket of piss is worth a fortune in a drought.'

He had no answer for that. One of the reasons he had chosen her to raise Gift was the fierceness she showed now. He had thought it would protect the boy.

Maybe it had.

'I will not harm Gift,' Rugar repeated.

'Perhaps not intentionally since he is all you have now,' she said. 'But if he needs those cords to survive, and you cut them, you will hear from me – and from all the others. Coulter said that Gift lives because Coulter lives. Remember that. Don't harm my son.'

'Have a little faith,' Rugar said.

She pulled her hand from beneath his. 'Even a little faith is difficult given your record,' she said.

Thirty-Two

The Warders stared at each other across the long table. From Touched's point of view at the foot of the table, their bald heads looked identical, their long robes costumes they put on when they became Warders. Due to his youth and inexperience – in six years as a Warder, he had yet to develop a working spell – he sat nearest the fire. Sweat ran down his forehead and dripped off his chin onto his cowl.

Rotin was supposed to lead the group, but more and more often, she ground her herbs, placed them on her tongue, and lost herself to the ecstasy. Warders were forbidden any sexual contact and the herbs mimicked the experience. When Touched first became a Warder, Rotin had done her herbs in private. Now she did them whenever she felt like it, and she didn't care who watched her round face go red and her eyes glaze.

The remaining Warders, the dregs of the Warding group, would wait until her spasms were done, then continued as if nothing happened.

More often than not, nothing would happen.

Four years before, a Red Cap had murdered Caseo, the most talented Warder who had come to Blue Isle. Red Caps had no magic, and Caseo had believed that the Islanders' poison would not work on someone who lacked magic. He demanded that the Cap take part in the experiments. The Cap had fled. When he returned later, he murdered Caseo.

Red Caps were unimportant Fey. They tended the dead during and after battles, and no one paid attention to them. The Warders knew that the Cap who had killed Caseo was named Scavenger, but they didn't know any more about him. He looked like any other Cap, short, squat and ugly. Magickless. A search of the forest never revealed him. He got away after the murder, and no one really cared.

Except Touched. Touched was startled to discover he missed Caseo. They had been at odds when Caseo was alive, but at least Caseo had led the Warders. Rotin did not.

They still worked in the same cabin, and still had a few vials of poison to experiment with, but they had ceased using the poison in the experiments two years before. They never took the skin and blood from the last battles out any more either. And Rotin only called group meetings once a week. Most of the Warders had gone their own way, trading tiny spells with the Domestics in exchange for extra food or a private cabin.

Touched felt that he alone remained focused on the poison, and he was going nowhere. Rotin didn't teach him the discipline as she should have – a new Warder always apprenticed to the senior Warders – and he had only his talent and his experience to draw on.

His talent was considerable – it was what made him a Warder in the first place.

He had no experience at all.

The Warders cabin was one of the larger cabins in Shadowlands. It had several rooms off the main one, most of them filled with Red Cap pouches from the honored dead. Pouches that should have been used in experiments but were mostly forgotten. There were also beds and equipment Touched didn't understand.

The main room had the long table, enough chairs for all the Warders, and a fireplace. Caseo had kept the fire burning constantly, but Rotin had allowed it to burn out on many occasions. Touched suspected that the loss of the original fire also interfered with the Warders' abilities.

The other Warders made no complaint, and Touched had no one else to turn to. Most of the time the other Warders acted as they did now, staring at the walls, waiting for the meeting to end. They had become faces to Touched, colleagues no longer.

In the early days on the Isle, when Caseo was alive, the Warders met every day and had heated discussions. Spellmaking was a joint art, fraught with jealousies and insecurities, but fascinating all the same. Now the Warders appeared to meditate while waiting for Rotin to excuse them.

She often forgot to excuse them when she was taking her herbs.

Touched stood. The sound of his chair sliding back was the only sound in the room.

'We aren't done, Touched,' Rotin said, her words slurred.

'I am,' he said. He couldn't sit a moment longer. He threaded his way behind the other Warders and went out the door.

The grayness of Shadowlands seemed warm and familiar next to the interior of the cabin. He stepped across the wooden porch, past the spot where Caseo had bled after being stabbed by the crazed Red Cap, and sat on the steps. Touched always avoided the spot where Caseo died. The Domestics had long ago pulled the blood from the wood, but Touched still saw it, like he still saw Caseo's body there when he closed his eyes.

He certainly wouldn't have been locked in this gray windless weatherless place with these passive Warders if Caseo were still alive. Caseo took the fact that he couldn't neutralize the Islander poison as a personal affront. He had stayed up each and every night, striving to find the solution.

Striving to find the solution before Touched did.

Touched still worked on it, but he lacked the experience. Even though he was trying to learn how to do simple spells no one took the time to teach him. Rotin had laughed at him when he asked.

Here's your chance to be the greatest Warder of all time, boy. Teach yourself.

He hadn't realized until Caseo died that Rotin had hated him too.

Through the silence of Shadowlands, a door slammed. The slam echoed off the invisible walls. This place had the hollowness of a crevice, something Touched believed he would never get used to. After a moment, he saw Rugar. And the sight surprised him.

Rugar was supposed to be mourning. Jewel's death affected them all except, of course, the Warders. When Touched had brought up the even greater need to solve the riddle of the poison, Rotin had laughed at him.

Bit late for that now, isn't it, boy? Can't make points with Rugar by saving Jewel. The girl's dead. We don't dabble in revivals.

As usual she had twisted his words and then had done nothing. The other Warders hadn't backed him. They all hated working with the poison, believing that even touching a vial of it might kill them. They would be happy to have the silent meetings about the poison and do nothing for the rest of their days.

Rugar leaned against one of the newer cabins, hand over his face, his body motionless. He wasn't wearing his usual cape, and without it, his shoulders looked small and frail. His boots were scuffed and his pants ripped. It was as if witnessing Jewel's death had robbed him of what little power he had left.

Rugar dropped his hand and his gaze met Touched's. Touched felt his cheeks warm, but he didn't look away. Rugar cocked his head as if he had gotten an idea, then walked toward Touched. Rugar's movements had an intensity that Touched hadn't seen a moment earlier.

Touched didn't move as Rugar came to the Warders' cabin. Rugar stopped in front of him, placing a hand on the railing beside the steps. His eyes, sunken into his face, looked dark and angry.

'Touched,' he said. 'We haven't talked in a long time.'

'No, sir,' Touched said. They had never talked. The only reason

Rugar knew his name was because Touched was a Warder. If Touched had been Infantry, Rugar wouldn't know him at all.

'Is Rotin still running the Warders?' Rugar asked.

'I guess,' Touched said. He couldn't give her credit for something she wasn't really doing.

Rugar peered at him as if he hadn't quite expected that answer. 'And she's inside?'

'Her body is,' Touched said.

Rugar's jaw worked for a moment, but he said nothing. Finally he glanced away, then sighed. 'She's still taking herbs?'

'She never stopped,' Touched said.

'How much progress has there been on the poison?'

'None,' Touched said. 'We don't work on it.'

Rugar swung his head back quickly. 'You don't –?' He couldn't seem to finish the question.

Touched shrugged. 'We meet every so often and discuss it. No one is working on spells.'

Rugar took a step up. 'Why not?'

'No leadership. Everyone is afraid of the stuff.'

'Even you?'

Touched shook his head. 'I'm the youngest. The inexperienced one. The one who doesn't understand.'

He said the last three words with great emphasis, repeating the phrase he had heard from both Rotin and Caseo.

'My daughter just died from that poison.'

'I know,' Touched said. 'We stay in here because of that poison. We lost the war because of that poison. But it's safe here. And Rotin likes to be safe.'

'What of the others?'

Touched studied Rugar. He truly appeared not to know. Ah, well. Touched had nothing to lose. He had never gained anything in the first place.

'The others?' Touched said. 'Your father gave you Caseo for reasons I don't understand, but I understand why he gave you the others.'

'Caseo was my personal Warder,' Rugar said. 'But my father chose the others.'

Touched shook his head. 'If Caseo chose the others, he wouldn't have chosen me. He hated me. Thought I was talented, but hated me nonetheless. Upstart, he said. Inexperienced. And I was. I am.'

Rugar frowned, as if trying to assimilate this news. 'But the others?'

'Are no better than Rotin. Your father had to have had a hand in this. He sent the worst of the Warders with you. Me, the youngest ever; Rotin, so addicted to herbs she doesn't care about anything; Ceel, who has never been able to do more than Domestic spells – I could go on if you want.'

Rugar shook his head. 'I think you're exaggerating.'

'If I were exaggerating, we would not be sitting in Shadowlands,' Touched said.

Rugar walked up the stairs. His weight bent the wood. He rapped on the door, and then opened it.

Touched didn't move. He didn't even turn around. He knew what Rugar would find, and he knew that it would make him angry. The door snicked closed, and inside he heard voices.

The air was chill. Shadowlands always made Touched think of a deep fog bank, so deep that a man inside it couldn't see the house on the next rise. The analogy wasn't quite apt – he could see everything in Shadowlands – but it looked as if it grew out of fog. No trees, no ground, no wildlife. Only houses, and Fey, and grayness.

Rugar's voice sounded loud but his words were impossible to make out. Then Rotin answered him, her voice fainter than his. Rugar responded again and this time Touched heard a word that made a shiver run down his back.

Enchanter.

He had felt an Enchanter years ago, had actually developed a spell for one before Caseo laughed at him and told him the spell was worthless. No Enchanter had come on the ships to Blue Isle. No Enchanter, but the troop did have a second-rate Shaman, and a Visionary who was Blind. Even a Blind Visionary should have been able to see that such a journey was doomed.

Rugar hadn't seen at all.

Touched had been too young to understand the ramifications, the others too uninformed. Caseo had known, but Caseo, like Rugar, had believed that the Fey were strong enough to beat any odds.

The conversation rose to shouts, then the door opened and Rugar came out. He slammed the door behind him and whirled, a movement that would have been dramatic had he worn a cape. As it was, the movement made him look even smaller than he had a moment ago.

'Four years of nothing?' he said to Touched, voice still raised. '*Nothing*?!'

Touched shrugged. 'Some of us tried. But none of us were capable alone.'

'We stayed here because of four years of nothing.' Rugar was speaking softly, almost to himself. 'Nothing.' Then he looked up. 'Do you think you can come up with an antidote to their poison?'

Touched felt the back of his throat go dry. He had once thought he had a solution, only as Caseo reminded him, there was no one to perform it. 'I think so,' he said. 'If you introduce me to that Enchanter you mentioned.'

Rugar put his hands on his hips. 'Were you listening in?'

Touched shook his head. 'It shouldn't matter. I should have been in there in the first place.'

A small smile played at Rugar's lips. 'Yes,' he said. 'You should have.' The smile disappeared. 'I don't know if we have an Enchanter. If we do, it's from an unlikely source.'

Unlikely source, and one that did not come across the Infrin Sea. Gift? There seemed to be no one else. 'I can conduct tests if you like.'

Rugar tilted his head. 'I should have the Shaman do that.'

'The Shaman won't conduct the kind of tests we need. We need to know if we have an Enchanter and if the Enchanter is powerful. The Shaman will simply Look and give us a vague pronouncement based on a future she doesn't want to reveal.' Touched's heart was pounding. He hadn't moved, but he felt as if he were showing too much eagerness. He had grown up with an Enchanter, and had been there when the Shaman came in and tested him, then when the Warders had. Nothing would erase the moment from his mind when Warders looked at his friend with shock mixed with awe.

Enchanters were the most powerful, the most feared of the Fey.

'All right,' Rugar said slowly. 'The quicker we resolve this, the better.' He walked down the steps with the purpose he appeared to have regained.

Touched got up and followed him. Touched was thinner than Rugar and younger, but at the moment, the older man led him. They made their way to the Domicile. Rugar bade Touched wait, and Rugar went in.

Touched hadn't expected the Domicile. He had thought they were going to the Wisps' cabin. The Domicile made him nervous. The size of the building was intimidating, and its multitudinous rooms were full of Fey he didn't know or like. The Healers' section up front always made him feel uncomfortable and inadequate, as if he couldn't quite measure up to the gentle part of his art.

He had never been able to do Domestic spells, although they were supposed to be the easiest of all the spells, the most logical. Perhaps because of how he was raised, and because of his early friendships, 'easy' tasks were never easy for him. But he could weave wonderful labyrinthian spells, perfect for Enchanters or other Warders.

Enchanter Spells are easy for all of us, boy, Caseo had said. They fill in the gaps for us, make spells that are awkward seem elegant.

Perhaps. Or perhaps that was Caseo's jealousy speaking. Perhaps

Enchanter spells were more difficult than the others. Perhaps Touched had had a skill Caseo hadn't.

It would come into play now.

The door opened. Rugar came out. Touched moved to one side so that he could see Gift with a new perspective. But Gift did not follow Rugar.

Coulter did.

The Islander boy.

Touched frowned. The Islander boy. When had he first felt that Enchanter signature? When Solanda brought Coulter into camp? Was it that long ago? If it was, the signature had been so faint that no one else had felt it.

Faint because the sender was a baby?

'It's not possible,' Touched said to Rugar.

Rugar nodded. 'Perhaps we've underestimated them all along.'

Touched crouched in front of the boy. He had never really looked at Coulter before. Coulter did not hide behind Rugar's leg as most children would have done. He stood and stared at Touched as if Touched were the one being judged.

Coulter was shorter than a child should have been at – what? – five? six? His hair was the pale blond that Touched had only seen in the Islanders. His eyes were an ice blue, and they were round. His eyebrows didn't rise like wings, they hugged the bone over the eye and turned downward, toward his fat cheeks. His nose was small and stubby, his lips pink and full, and his ears had rounded, not pointed, tips. If he had any Fey blood at all, it was buried in all his Island ancestry.

Fey blood told. Not a single race had mingled with the Fey without obvious change. Even Gift, whose father was as blond and icy-eyed as Coulter, had dark skin, upraised brows, and ears whose tips pointed slightly.

'It's not possible,' Touched said again.

Coulter frowned at him. Something in the boy's eyes made Touched peer deeper. No gold rims to the pupils. This was not even a Doppelgänger. This was a real Islander child.

Touched cast through his brain, remembered the Enchanter spells he had been taught. Warders, like Enchanters, had a facility for all nature of spells. Unlike Enchanters, however, Warders had a limited range and ability with them. Warders could not actually use the spells to good or long effect. Warders could, though, develop more spells. No other Fey could do that, except accidentally, as new talents emerged.

Coulter was watching him, mouth a thin line. The boy's eyes were different. They had an adult wariness, and a large intelligence behind them. He seemed to know that Touched was there to evaluate him.

Touched found the Enchanter spells. He sent a small lick of fire across the air. The flame was blue, almost invisible in the gray of Shadowlands. If it hit the boy, it would burn him slightly, and they would have to take him inside to have a Domestic heal him.

Coulter's gaze darted toward the flame, then back to Touched. A frown creased the boy's forehead. Suddenly he held up his hand and the flame stopped mid-air as if it had collided with a wall. Then the flame went out, leaving a tiny black puff of smoke.

Rugar had missed the entire exchange. He was still watching Touched, as if Touched were going to say something.

But Touched wasn't. He had deliberately started with flame, something even an Enchanter should not be able to control at Coulter's age. The powerful Enchantments didn't arrive until after puberty. The children had only lines and ties until then. Binders attached to them through which they could send and receive, but never initiate.

Touched blinked, then mentally felt through the grayness for a Binder. One led from Coulter to Gift. Touched glanced at Rugar, wondering if he knew. Probably. This was probably what led him to Coulter in the first place. Another led through the Domicile and to the cabins beyond. Touched did not explore that one. It had the blue of a parental Binder. Whoever had raised the boy here benefited from that.

It was the strong blue strands that disappeared out the Circle Door that Touched traced for a moment. These strands were old, a path laid for someone who had not – or could not – follow them.

'How old were you when you came to Shadowlands?' Touched asked.

Coulter started. He had not expected Touched to speak aloud. Had he felt Touched's presence on his Binders?

'Since I could walk.' The boy's voice was strong and beautiful. With his Binding sight, Touched could see sparkles along the edge of the boy's mouth. He had Charm as well.

These skills were too developed for a child.

'Solanda brought him here,' Rugar said. 'He was little more than a toddler.'

Touched ignored Rugar. He didn't want Rugar's answers, he wanted Coulter's.

'Who taught you spells?' Touched asked.

'No one,' Coulter said. 'You all think I'm not like you.'

'You look different,' Touched said.

'Doesn't mean I am.'

– *Ah, but you are*, Touched sent the message to the boy in a flicker of light. The light left a small trail between them.

Coulter blocked the light as easily as he had blocked the flame.

When the light went out, Touched felt a small tug on his forehead. The boy had tweaked him. Purposely.

'Either you let me in voluntarily,' Touched said, 'or I find a way in on my own.'

Coulter jutted out his lower lip and shook his head. The movement was slight. Touched wasn't even certain that Rugar saw it.

The boy was defended. That's why the flames didn't go past him, why the light broke around him as if he were wearing a shield. He was wearing a shield. All over.

But he was a child. He had probably forgotten to shield one place.

Touched sent a new message – *Who helps you?* – and had the light drill a hole in the ground in front of Coulter's feet, then bend up and touch his toes. Coulter tried to send his shield down, but too late. The message went in.

Coulter frowned.

Then the air shimmered around him, and a bolt of light shot from his forehead. Touched didn't even have time to put up his hands to ward it off. The light beam hit him with the force of ten men and knocked him backwards. The air left his body, and as he gasped for air, he felt rather than heard Coulter's response.

No one helps me. No one ever helped me. No one ever will.

The boy turned and ran up the stairs. He let himself into the Domicile, the door slamming behind him.

Rugar started to go after him but Touched grabbed his leg. Rugar looked down and Touched shook his head.

Touched took several deep breaths. Rugar crouched beside him. 'You all right?'

Touched nodded. He rubbed his head, amazed that it didn't ache. The boy had deliberately hit him with that force. Deliberately and yet gently.

But not all his skills were in place. If they were, he would have known that Touched and Rugar needed to see him. He wouldn't have been caught off guard, and he would never have allowed Touched to get the better of him.

The boy had power, but not all of it was ready for use.

When the boy became a man, he would be astonishingly talented. Perhaps the most talented Enchanter the Fey had ever seen.

Only he wasn't Fey.

Now Touched was getting a headache, but it had nothing to do with the bolt of light Coulter had sent to him.

'He must have developed young,' Touched said. 'There's no way he can be Islander.'

Rugar had a hand behind Touched's back. 'I remember when he

271

arrived here. Solanda brought him. His parents were killed during the First Battle For Jahn. They were Islander. An elderly woman took him from the Foot Soldiers and hid him away in a village. But he had left a trail for the parents to follow. Solanda followed it instead, and brought him here. The Domestics did everything when they saw he had some magic. But he never proved to be Fey. Not ever.'

'Why didn't you know he was this powerful until now?' Touched's head was spinning. An Enchanter. An Islander Enchanter.

'He never called attention to himself. I had forgotten he was here,' Rugar said. 'Then he saved Gift's life.'

Touched knew that Gift nearly lost his life when Jewel died, but he hadn't heard how Gift survived.

The boy. Coulter.

The Enchanter.

'This changes everything,' Touched said.

'I know,' Rugar replied.

Thirty-Three

The air glowed green around him. Bright green like light filtering through an algae-covered pond. Matthias opened his eyes. The room was dark. The green was gone.

A board creaked in the main room of his suite.

His hand went to the tiny sword around his throat. Someone was in the room with him. The guards outside should have kept him out.

Then Matthias remembered.

No guards. The Auds refused to stand near his door, as did the Danites. There were no Officiates in the Tabernacle.

He was alone.

The sound of the blood in his ears was so loud, he was convinced the stranger could hear it too. He tried to breathe evenly so that he sounded as if he were still asleep. Then he pulled his left arm slowly from under the blankets.

Another board creaked.

Matthias scanned the darkness. He could see nothing. He slept with his tapestries pulled down, the fabric so thick it kept out the moonlight. The layout was as familiar to him as the back of his hand: the bed in the center of the second room, a fireplace on the wall at the foot, two tables on either side, and two chairs in the corners.

The other room had sofas, chairs, tables, and another fireplace, as well as windows that opened onto the balcony. He had been in these suites since he had become an Elder. When he became Rocaan, he had the option of taking the old Rocaan's suites, but didn't.

Now he was glad he had chosen to stay here.

He slowly slid his arm to the bedside table. The hair on the back of his neck rose. He had no idea who was out there: Someone Nicholas had sent? Someone from inside the Tabernacle? A Fey?

A Fey.

The prospect made him cold. He hadn't thought until now that they too would want revenge. Even if Jewel wasn't doing what they had wanted, she was, after all, their leader's daughter.

She was important to them.

His hand was shaking. He could no longer hear anything from the front room. His eyes still hadn't adjusted to the darkness. He had been too successful at shutting out the light, and the fact that he hadn't made a fire tonight meant that not even coals illuminated the room.

Could the Fey see in complete darkness? He had no idea.

Slowly he eased his hand onto the bedside table. The cool, polished wood felt reassuring under his fingers. He walked them along the surface, careful to move slowly so that he wouldn't knock anything down.

A soft exhalation of breath, not his. He paused. He wasn't sure if he had actually heard the sound or not. No more creaks, no banging against furniture, nothing.

The person had to be familiar with his room.

His whole body tingled with anticipation. He continued to walk his fingers along the surface of the table until his index finger brushed cut glass.

The vial.

He resisted the urge to grab it. Instead he eased his hand around it and lifted it just high enough to pull it back to the bed.

Another breath. Soft. Almost impossible to hear. But this time he knew he heard it.

The person had to be in the same room.

Matthias rested the vial against his own chest. With his free hand, he pulled out the stopper. If the person in his room wasn't Fey, this would do no good.

Except maybe to startle him.

A slight 'huh' of air beside him, a faint warmth near his left side. Someone was standing beside him.

Matthias tossed the water in that direction. It splashed on the bed, on the table, on Matthias's hand. A voice made an odd, almost panicked cry.

And suddenly the green glow that he had been dreaming about filled the room. A young man stood in the center of that glow, radiating light throughout the room. He was short and stocky, his features Islander, and he was blinking as if the light had blinded him.

The holy water made him glow. Did that mean he was a Doppelgänger? Or another kind of Fey?

Or was he an Islander, like he appeared to be?

Then the man moved his right hand and light flashed off a blade.

He was carrying a knife.

Matthias rolled away from the man and got out of the opposite side of the bed. The light made everything green as if they were underwater. Matthias breathed shallowly, half afraid that water would fill his lungs.

274

The man turned. He was wiping his face with his left hand. As he did, the green glow faded. It was the contact of his skin and the holy water that caused it.

Matthias thought all these things as he ran through the door. He banged a shin on a table and the thunk resounded through the room. The glow came after him, casting that same eerie green light throughout the suite.

The balcony doors were open and a cool breeze rattled the tapestries.

'You stop!' the man shouted. He had no accent. His Islander was perfect.

Matthias didn't stop. He weaved his way around the soft sofas toward the double doors. His nightrobe had gathered around his thighs, making movement difficult. The tiny silver sword banged against his chest with every movement.

He had forgotten to grab more holy water. Perhaps if he threw more at the ghostly vision, it would dissolve.

But he didn't have time for that. The man was gaining on him. A table fell over with a bang, and the green light got closer. Matthias's shadow looked like a bruise on the far wall. The green made the etchings glow.

The man was almost upon him when Matthias grabbed the door handles and pulled them down with all his strength.

The candles were lit in the corridor, but no one stood outside his door. He scurried through the doors and, with a flick of the wrist, yanked them closed.

The green light glowed from underneath them.

The man was close.

Matthias screamed for help, half afraid that help wouldn't come.

But he lived with the other Elders on this floor; They had to help him. Had to.

He ran down the hall, pounding on doors with his fists. The doors finally opened, the Elders peeking out. Danites came up the stairs, and a sleepy Aud pushed off the wall where he had been dozing instead of guarding.

Matthias was taking deep pulling breaths. His hair was matted and falling over his face. The stench of his own sweat was overpowering. He pointed toward his rooms.

'In ... there,' he gasped. '... a ... man ...'

The Danites hurried in that direction. Elder Reece held Matthias's shoulder in a light grip, as if afraid to touch him more. Elder Linus was peering down the hallway as if he wasn't sure whom to believe.

Porciluna came out of his doorway, breathing heavily. Even the slight exertion seemed to tire him.

'What kind of man?' he said, and from the bluntness of his question, Matthias could tell that the man had not come from the Elders. He had come from outside the Tabernacle.

'... I ... don't ... know ...'

He was shaking and ashamed of it. Not once had he thought of God or his faith or the Roca. Not once had he turned to his religion for help. Instead he had used the holy water as a weapon.

Like the old Rocaan feared it would be used.

'Don't know?' Porciluna sounded disbelieving. He slept in a satin robe that hung off his bulk. His hands looked naked without their jewelry, his eyes oddly vulnerable as they squinted from lack of sleep. 'Didn't you see him?'

'I saw ... him,' Matthias said. His breath was coming back. '... later. Much ... later. The room was so dark ... I heard ... him first.'

He wasn't explaining this well. One of the Danites had come back down the corridor from Matthias's room.

'The balcony doors were open. There's a rope still tied to the railing. That's how he got in. He climbed up.' The Danite appeared to be reporting to Porciluna, not Matthias. 'We're looking through the rooms, but we don't expect to find anyone.'

'Get ... someone down ... to the courtyard,' Matthias said. 'See if we ... can catch him.'

The Danite nodded and hurried down the stairs. The sleepy Aud followed him. Reece stared after them.

'Someone should have been guarding your door. Don't the Auds keep care of you any more, Holy Sir?'

Beside Matthias, Porciluna shook his head slightly. Matthias pretended that he didn't notice. 'Apparently,' Matthias said dryly, 'only God watches ... out for me.'

His heart was still pounding, but his breathing was slowly coming under his control. Reece frowned at Porciluna. Not all the Elders were agreed, then, about ostracizing the Rocaan.

Matthias put a hand on his back and made himself take a deep breath. He would say no more about the man in his room. No one needed to know that holy water made the man turn green. He would investigate that himself. The man may not have been Fey, but something about him had triggered a reaction to the holy water. Matthias seemed to remember hearing something about that before. He would see what he could recall.

The Danites trooped out of his room. Another came toward him. 'Did you throw holy water on him, Holy Sir?' the Danite asked.

Matthias nodded. 'Why?'

'Because you had an empty bottle on the bed, and the blankets are wet. We sent for an Aud to replace the blankets, but we weren't certain if the intruder had done something to them. We can't be too careful any more.'

'No,' Matthias said. 'We can't.'

'If you threw holy water on him,' another Danite said, 'then he wasn't Fey. No smell, no body in the room.'

'It startled him, nothing more,' Matthias said. It felt odd to lie to the Danites. They had once had complete truth in the Tabernacle.

Porciluna was watching him. Matthias felt his own skin crawl.

An Aud came up the stairs. He was older, and took the stairs cautiously, hand on his back as he walked. When he reached the Elders and Matthias, he stopped.

'They found nothing in the courtyard,' the Aud said. 'It looks as if the intruder got away.'

'We need someone to stay in the Rocaan's rooms,' Reece said.

Matthias shook his head. 'No. I'll remain alone.'

'At least let us put an Aud on the balcony –'

'No,' Porciluna said. 'He would like to be alone.'

Porciluna was agreeing a bit too easily. Matthias studied him until Porciluna squirmed and looked away. Then Matthias turned to Reece.

'You're right, Reece. An Aud on the balcony would be a good idea and two more at the door.'

Reece smiled and touched Matthias's arm once more as if for reassurance. 'I will see to it, Holy Sir.'

He disappeared down the stairs. Despite everything that happened, Matthias still trusted Reece. Porciluna was the one who looked guilty. Of what, Matthias was not certain. Perhaps he was just guilty of impure thoughts.

Thoughts of overthrowing the Rocaan.

Linus excused himself and peered into Matthias's rooms. The Danites went down the stairs.

Matthias's heart rate had slowed. An exhaustion like one he hadn't felt in years crept over him. 'It has never worked, you know,' he said softly to Porciluna. 'No one has ever overthrown a Rocaan.'

'But more than a few have left voluntarily,' Porciluna said. 'You're the scholar. What are the circumstances behind those?'

'If a Rocaan leaves each time the Elders find his actions unpardonable, no Rocaan would have remained in office.'

'No Rocaan has murdered before.'

'You forget the thirty-fifth Rocaan.'

'Tis said those deaths were an accident.'

Matthias smiled. 'A happy accident then, facilitated by the arrow slits he carved in the old kirk worship room.' With his left hand, Matthias moved the hair off his face. 'Don't be deceived by history, Porciluna. None of the Rocaans were saints. They were all too human.'

'I am aware of that,' Porciluna said.

'Then don't punish me for taking the right action. Elders have been forced to resign under less trying circumstances.'

'The right action doesn't lead to assassination attempts in the middle of the night.'

'Sure it does,' Matthias said. 'That's why the Rocaan usually doesn't live on the same floor as the Elders. Rocaans are always threatened by their assistants.'

'Perhaps I phrased that wrong,' Porciluna said. 'The right action doesn't lead to assassination attempts whose source can't be determined. An Islander attacked you? Was he from the King? Or did he have ties with the Tabernacle? Or was he acting alone? And those examples don't count what would have happened had the Fey been involved. You didn't take the right action, Matthias. Your action may have doomed us all.'

'You have a flair for the dramatic, Porciluna,' Matthias said.

Porciluna squinted at him. 'No, Matthias. I have a penchant for truth.'

'Really?' Matthias said. 'Then you wouldn't pass yourself off as a believer, Porciluna.'

Matthias pushed past him and went back to his own rooms. The Danites had left the door opened, and the furniture moved. The balcony doors were closed and bolted, and someone had pulled the blankets from the bed.

Matthias's heart pounded just upon re-entering the room. No green glow. No man. How odd he had been dreaming about it before the man appeared. Perhaps the man had been glowing green even then.

Islanders didn't glow. Neither did Fey, to Matthias's knowledge. But he knew less about Fey than he wanted to. He always believed he should understand his enemy.

'Holy Sir?'

Matthias whirled, his heart already in his throat.

An Aud stood at the door, blankets piled high. 'Should I remake the bed, Holy Sir?'

'Please,' Matthias said, although he doubted he would be getting any more sleep this night. 'And when you're through, I would appreciate it if you could start a fire as well.'

'As you wish, Holy Sir.' The Aud went into the bedroom. Another Aud knocked on the door.

'You want someone on the balcony, Holy Sir?'

Matthias nodded. He half felt like checking the Auds for weapons, but he knew better. No one would dare attack him with his own guards. Still, he would play it as safe as he could. He would remain on guard until he figured out the best way to protect himself.

The Aud left his bedroom and two more stationed themselves in the hallway. The Aud on the balcony closed the doors behind himself and sat in one of the chairs in the shadows. Matthias pulled the tapestries, and closed the doors to the hallways. He couldn't bear to let the Auds watch him pace in fear.

And he was frightened. Whoever the green man was, he had accomplished his mission.

He had frightened Matthias very badly.

But Matthias wouldn't stay frightened for long.

Thirty-Four

The tapestries were pulled back, letting the early morning sunlight into the nursery. Arianna cooed in her crib. The wet nurse had just left, and Sebastian's nurse had just finished feeding the lump. The fire had gone out in the night, but the coals were still warm.

Another morning in the palace.

Even though Solanda was in her cat form, she ignored the warmth. Instead she had gone to the window and let the cool breeze ruffle her fur. Three stories below her, the garden glistened in the early-morning dew. She licked her whiskers, remembering how, years before, the cooks used to leave out milk for the cats.

Those days were gone now. Long gone. She hadn't even left the nursery since Arianna was born.

She didn't dare.

And still no one trusted her. The nurse never left Solanda alone with the baby. So Solanda had to spend her time in the nursery with the lump of clay Nicholas insisted on calling a son. She had tried to tell him, but he hadn't listened. He insisted on believing that Jewel would have known if the lump was not her son. Jewel hadn't known. Fey couldn't see everything.

If he wanted to remain loyal to his dead wife, fine. Let Rugar keep Nicholas's real son. It didn't matter to Solanda. All that mattered to her was keeping Arianna alive. She would stay as far from the Islander King as she could. She didn't need to get involved in his life. If he couldn't see that what he called a child was nothing more than an animated hunk of stone, then he probably couldn't see other things.

Solanda didn't need to be mixed up in that. She would take care of Arianna and nothing more.

She glanced over her shoulder at the baby. From her perch on the sill, she could see into the crib. Arianna's pudgy baby hands were grasping at air, her laughter making Solanda purr. These quiet moments were rare, and they made Solanda uneasy.

Arianna was proving to be a difficult child, more difficult than Solanda had imagined. Solanda hadn't left her side since she was born. Thankfully, the nurse was afraid of Solanda's Shifting, so any order Solanda gave her the nurse would fulfill.

She fulfilled the orders faster when Solanda gave them as a cat.

But the nurse also threw Solanda out of the baby's crib when she was in cat form. Old superstitions died hard. The nurse believed that cats would suffocate babies. Maybe real cats would. But this child was more Solanda's than anyone else's. She wouldn't harm a spot on Arianna's delicate body.

So far, Arianna had Shifted twice since her Birth Shifts.

Neither time had she done so in response to stress, which frightened Solanda.

No. It seemed Arianna was playing.

The first Shift had been major. One moment the little girl was staring at the ceiling with her tiny eyes open. The next she was a puddle of water in the crib. Shifters did not survive as water outside of the womb. Solanda had had to reform the baby herself, using Shifting techniques she hadn't thought of since she was a little girl.

The nurse had not seen that one.

But she had seen the second.

Arianna had grown a tail, just like Solanda's. It was even calico, like Solanda's tail, with the same markings on the end. Solanda had unswaddled her, and found that tail and fur had ended at the baby's bottom. Arianna had added it so that her tiny fingers had something to hold.

Partial shifts weren't supposed to be possible, but Arianna was clearly testing the limits of the possible.

Arianna had her own realm of possible.

And that scared Solanda. All Fey followed a predictable pattern of maturation. And, as Solanda's mother used to say, such a thing was a blessing. Imagine a Doppelgänger infant, grabbing anything that came its way, slaughtering it, and then taking its form. Or a Foot Soldier stripping the skin off anything it touched. Or even a Domestic creating a blanket out of thin air, and then suffocating in it. The chaos would have been enormous. The Fey would never have survived over the generations.

Only the great magicks leaked into childhood. An occasional Visionary had a single important Vision before puberty. A Shaman sometimes healed a parent. Enchanters had binding powers from the womb.

And Shifters chose their form before the age of three.

Or died.

But the Shifting rarely happened when a newborn was playing.

Shifting happened under stress or in moments of great fear. A child didn't learn to control Shifting until after it learned to speak and walk.

Solanda was already tired. She didn't know how she would feel when Arianna reached her terrible twos.

So far the baby had attempted to Shift each day of her life. She had only been successful twice, if Solanda didn't count the Birth Shifts.

Those scared her the most. One Shift at birth was all she had ever heard of. And then one Shift back. Never four Shifts. Not in all the Fey history. Never four.

The breeze had a bit of humidity and smelled faintly of the river. Solanda's stomach growled. What she wouldn't give for fresh fish, held between two soaking paws, her muzzle buried in its flesh, eating it scales and all.

She was beginning to fear such luxuries were far in her future. This morning, after the nurse had awakened her, she daydreamed about a rat getting loose in the nursery. Even tough, filthy rat would provide some sport, some fresh meat.

But she would have none of that now.

And she didn't dare leave Arianna alone.

Not even to find out how to care for her.

No Fey would come here to help her either. They were so afraid of the Islanders that the Shaman would have let Jewel's daughter, the Black King's great-granddaughter, survive on her own rather than place a guardian with her.

Perhaps the Shaman thought Nicholas up to the task.

But he panicked each time he heard of one of Arianna's Shifts. Solanda couldn't imagine how he ever would have cared for her during one.

More likely, the Shaman had Seen that Solanda would care for Arianna. That probably was part of the Shaman's plan.

'There,' the nurse said in that sickly sweet Islander baby talk. ''Tis a good boy ye are, Sebastian.'

Tis a good boy ye are, Sebastian, Solanda mouthed to the air. How could it be anything but good? The lump made no conscious choices. And here the nurse was praising it for eating its breakfast. Of course it ate its breakfast. It tried to keep up appearances. That was part of its mandate. The Wisps had given it that much. But they hadn't given it the ability to live this long.

Someone else had been giving it that.

Both Rugar and the Shaman believed that Jewel's love had kept the thing alive. But the more Solanda stared at it, the more she wondered. Jewel was dead. Nicholas seemed a bit cool toward it, although he did speak to it. The nurse cradled it like her own, but she had no blood ties to the real child, so her affection shouldn't matter.

Someday Solanda would discover how the lump kept moving. But not this day.

Solanda reached out her front paws and stretched, first pressing her belly toward the ground, then arching her back. The breeze was still a bit chilly to sit in long.

She leapt from the sill to the table, then picked her way across the toys various nobles had brought for the baby until she reached the edge of the crib.

'Now, none a that!' the nurse cried. She left the lump beside the dying fire and hurried toward the crib. 'I will na ha yer filthy fur in with me girl.'

'First of all,' Solanda said, refusing to Shift into her Fey form, 'I am not filthy. I bathe constantly. Secondly, this child is not your girl. She is mine, and I would do nothing to harm her.'

Arianna grasped the nurse's finger. 'Twas not sayin that, mum,' the nurse said, refusing to look at Solanda. ''Tis not right, though, fer a babe ta breathe fur.'

'You don't know what's right and what isn't right for a child like her,' Solanda said.

The nurse wrapped her own fingers around Arianna's tiny hand. ''Tis true, mum, I dinna know. But I figure she's like most babes, weak n helpless n needin love.'

Solanda tilted her head. The phrase intrigued her. *Weak and helpless and needing love.* No one ever spoke of Fey children that way.

'N with her ma gone, she needs even more. Her da will na be able ta see her much as she needs. Someone's gotta care for her.' The nurse stroked Arianna's dark head with one hand.

'I care for her,' Solanda said. 'I'm going to train her how to be a proper child. I will be working with you. You'll be tending her physical needs.'

'Beg pardon, mum, but at her age them needs is most important.'

The woman was insufferable. And she had learned a way of speaking to a cat. She could talk just fine if she didn't look at Solanda.

'Then serve those needs,' Solanda said. 'But when she needs to know how to survive in the world, she'll come to me.'

'Ah, tis only right, mum. Ye got special ways, ye do. And so does she, poor thing.'

'Poor?' Solanda straightened, resting most of her weight on her front paws. Her tail was twitching.

'Oh, mum. I dinna mean no harm. Tis sorry I am. Tis just they been squabblin bout her from the moment she come into the world, and her being loose dinna help, I think.'

'Loose?' Solanda asked. She was half intrigued with the way this woman's mind worked, and half appalled.

'Well, what do ye call it, mum?'

'She Shifts.'

'Aye, but na like ye. Ye become something. She just changes.'

The description was accurate, Solanda supposed, if a person only understood Shifting from the outside. What Arianna was doing was what most children tried after they had chosen their shapes. They tried to Shift to make pieces of the Shape, getting that perfect and then attempting another piece. When they had all the pieces right, they then tried to Shift into the whole.

'Your people won't like this about her, will they?' Solanda asked. Her greatest fear was that Arianna would grow up in Islander culture only to have it repudiate her. Sometimes Solanda was tempted to take her to Shadowlands.

Until she remembered Rugar was there.

The Shaman's warning stuck in her mind. She already regretted bringing Coulter to him. Rugar didn't need more power. The way he had acted around Jewel's death was reprehensible.

He had always been reprehensible.

She had to remember that.

The lump cried out. The nurse turned, and the lump reached up with its hands. It had done that a lot since Jewel's death. If Solanda hadn't known it was a lump, she would have thought it needed reassurance.

The nurse untangled her hands from Arianna's and went to the lump, picking it up with a grunt. It buried its face in her shoulder and sighed, then sobbed once, and sighed again. The nurse patted its back and cooed at it as if it were a real boy.

Solanda sighed. The mysteries of the nursery. She would lose her mind if she didn't find a way to leave here from time to time. The entire spring would go by without the chance to eat a blade of fresh grass or to dig in the newly-turned dirt.

She leapt off the table and walked to her robe, tail high. Then she Shifted, feeling the fur absorb into her body, her limbs stretch, her tail retract. Her Fey form made the room seem even smaller, more confining. And the urges spring gave her in this form were even more uncomfortable. She would have to talk politics with Nicholas soon and discover how he meant to avenge Jewel's death. The sooner the threats to Arianna were gone, the sooner Solanda could go outside.

Whenever she went from cat to Fey she became instantly cold. She grabbed the robe and slipped it on, thankful for its silken warmth. Maybe in a few days, she would get the nurse to bring her Islander clothes. Maybe she would start looking like they did.

Maybe.

The robe would do for now. Nicholas had insisted on it, saying that he couldn't leave a naked woman in the room with his two children.

For a while she had thought it more than that, but then she realized that he didn't see her. He didn't really see anyone except Arianna, and he probably saw her because she was the last tangible part of Jewel he had.

Amazing how he never thought of the lump as a part of Jewel.

Behind her the baby gurgled, then laughed. She didn't think a baby could laugh so young, but Arianna did. She laughed and cooed and appeared to look a person straight in the eye.

The baby laughed again. Solanda tugged on the sleeves of her robe to straighten them, then tied the sash around her waist. Her bare feet were chilled. Maybe after the chamberlain brought up her breakfast, she would insist on a new fire. Then when everyone was gone except the nurse she would stretch out before it and nap.

The baby's giggle stopped mid-sound. Solanda whirled. Arianna was half transformed. Her neck and chest were feline, but her head remained the same.

She was choking.

The kitten-sized air passages couldn't handle the human head. This was Solanda's fault. Already Arianna was watching and mimicking.

She hurried to the crib. The nurse didn't seem to notice. Arianna was thrashing and kicking, her tiny hands pulling at her throat. She wasn't changing back.

'Put that lump down and get over here!' Solanda snapped at the nurse.

''Tis sad he is. The boy knows his ma is gone.'

'I don't care. His sister will be dead if you don't help me.'

'Lor. Not again.'

Solanda grabbed the baby's hands. Her eyes were wide and frightened, her blue pupils almost black. The nurse set the lump down – too slowly for Solanda's taste – and stepped tentatively to Solanda's side.

'I dinna know yer magick,' the nurse said.

'I don't care,' Solanda said. 'You have to hold her still. Completely still. Do you understand?'

'Aye, mum.'

The nurse put her hands into the crib, reaching for Arianna's transformed shoulders.

'And don't touch her fur.'

'Sorry, mum.' The nurse gripped Arianna's waist with one hand, and held the baby's hands with the other. Arianna's feet still kicked. Her face was turning blue.

Solanda stroked Arianna's chin, feeling the ridge that went from fur to skin, and she pushed the skin downward. It did no good. In her panic, Arianna fought.

'Work with me, babe,' Solanda whispered in Fey. 'Work with me.'

But Arianna turned her head from side to side, continuing to thrash.

'I said hold her!' Solanda said in Islander.

'I dinna have enough hands, mum,' the nurse said.

Incompetent help. 'Then hold her head and body still. Keep her hands off me.'

'Aye, mum.'

Solanda bit her lower lip. The previous times she had guided Arianna to change on her own. This time that wasn't working. She would have to instigate the Shift herself.

She only hoped she could do it.

Arianna's tiny tongue protruded from her lips. Solanda grabbed Arianna's shoulders and willed herself to Shift slowly, hands first. Her nails became claws, her hands paws, and fur grew on her skin. Solanda's Shift stirred something inside Arianna and she stopped struggling.

Then Solanda Shifted her hands back to normal.

Arianna's neck and shoulders Shifted with her.

The baby took a deep shuddery breath, then another, and another. The nurse and Solanda leaned against each other for a moment before they realized that they had touched.

'I dinna know, mum, but seemed twas close ta me,' the nurse said, still holding Arianna.

Solanda took her hands off the baby, not wanting to trigger another Shift. She wondered if her own Shifts were causing Arianna to experiment or if something about the Shift triggered the baby. She wouldn't be able to stand remaining in the same form every day. She would have to teach Arianna how to control the Shifts first. Maybe by holding her and doing slow Shifts until Arianna gained control.

'It was close,' Solanda said. 'If we hadn't been here, she would have killed herself.'

'Beg pardon, mum,' the nurse said. 'If ya tweren't here. I dinna know magick.'

'You know enough,' Solanda said. 'You concentrate on what she looks like, remind her of her Fey form, and talk to her until I get here.'

'But twould be na way ta get ya, mum. I'd be with her sweetness.'

Solanda bit back a response. She was trapped here. She had made this bed, and she would have to remain in it. 'I'll stay here,' Solanda said. 'I won't leave until she has this controlled.'

'Aye, mum, even us tenders need ta get away else we do na good.'

'How would you suggest I leave her?' Solanda asked. The question came out harsher than she expected. Arianna looked up at her. The baby's breath was coming normally now and her skin had returned to its natural color.

'I dunno,' the nurse said. 'Perhaps twould be all right ta send Sebastian for ye.'

'That lump?' Solanda looked at it. It had gotten up and come to the nurse's side. It was half-hidden in her skirts and peering into the crib.

'Mum, please. Dinna call him such things. The boy is slow, but na deaf.'

Solanda sighed. These ignorant creatures had no idea what they were thinking was a child. But as long as she was here, she could avoid saying 'lump' in conversation. 'I don't think sending *him* after me would be a good idea. What if he forgot? Or worse, stopped moving?'

'Twouldn't do that,' the nurse said.

'But he knows so little of the palace. He wouldn't be quick enough.'

The nurse nodded. If anyone considered the lump as a true child, the nurse did. The woman had a good heart. She just wasn't much smarter than her charge.

Solanda sighed. 'If I need to leave the room, we'll bring in someone else you trust to watch Arianna. Then we can send that person for me. Or maybe I'll leave when Nicholas comes. We know he has a vested interest in this little girl.'

'Aye, mum. Tis a good idea, that.'

Obviously. Solanda was known for her good ideas. Like this one. Her heart was still pounding from the closeness of that Shift. Perhaps there was a way to get the Shaman here to examine this child again. Or maybe a way to have a Domestic here permanently. Solanda would ask Nicholas the next time she saw him.

He wouldn't object, but finding another Fey willing to live in the palace after what had happened to Jewel would be almost impossible. Solanda did it because she had to – she had to take care of Arianna – but no one else felt that need. Not even the Shaman.

Solanda wondered what the Black King would think of that.

A small movement beside her caught her attention. The lump had pushed closer to her. Its skin was surprisingly warm. Its forefinger was in its mouth and it was staring into the crib.

Slowly it brought its finger from its mouth. A thread of saliva ran from the fingertip to its tongue. The nurse caught its hand before it could touch the baby.

It looked at the nurse. 'Is that my sister?' it asked. The words came out hesitantly. Slowly. As slowly as its movements.

The nurse shot an uncertain glance at Solanda. Solanda wondered what the problem was.

'Of course,' Solanda said. 'Her name is Arianna.'

'Airy,' the lump said. 'Airy Anna.'

Tears had filled the nurse's eyes. 'He's never said more than two words. Except when he cried for his mother.'

'Airy Anna,' the lump said. 'Pretty.'

'What's he saying?' the nurse whispered.

A chill ran down Solanda's back. She hadn't realized. No wonder the nurse hadn't understood.

The lump was speaking Fey.

Thirty-Five

Nicholas was still in his chambers, finishing the last of the pastries the cook had sent up for his breakfast. He was nursing a cup of herbed tea, and ignoring the warmed milk with the tiny skin on top. The cook had included the milk ever since Jewel's death. Nicholas didn't want to know why. It probably had to do with taking proper care of one's self while grieving.

A fire burned in the grate. He had left his bedroom and was sitting in the main suite as close to the fire as he could get. He wasn't sleeping well – some nights not at all – and found that lack of sleep meant he was always chilled. He didn't even open the tapestries, like he used to do in the spring. He didn't want to see the empty chairs around the room, the places where Jewel used to sit with him, the places where they used to talk.

He was dressed for the day, in breeches and a peasant shirt, but he wasn't ready to start working yet. First he had to see his daughter, then he had to determine how to care for Jewel's body. That, of course, would lead him to Matthias, a subject he didn't want to consider at all.

When he saw Solanda, he would ask her how best to contact the Shaman. The quicker he made the trade, the better they all would be.

The knock on his suite door didn't surprise him. He had already been in his chambers longer than he had planned. The urgency of the knock did, however.

'Sire?' the voice belonged to his chamberlain. 'Beg pardon, Sire, but tis a lord here ta see ya. Says tis urgent.'

It was always urgent these days. 'It can wait until I open the audience chamber.'

'No, Sire, we need to talk now.' The voice belonged to Lord Stowe. Nicholas sighed. Now. Everything was now. Someday he might have time for then.

'Stowe, I have other business –'

'Not as important as this,' Stowe said. 'It concerns Matthias.'

So other people weren't calling Matthias the Rocaan any more either. How very interesting. Nicholas took the last bite of his pastry, wiped his mouth with a cloth, and pushed his tray aside. After a second's consideration, he grabbed the mug of herbal tea and cradled it against his chest.

'Come.'

'Sire, I'm bringing your chamberlain with us. I assume you trust him.'

That sentence alerted Nicholas. He sat up. Something was odd here. 'I do,' Nicholas said.

The door opened. The chamberlain came in first. His elderly body was bowed as if the weight of the meeting oppressed him. He normally stood very straight and interfered with nothing. He slipped to the side and stood there, as if prepared to bolt for the door. But beside him was Nicholas's sword.

Nicholas noted that, and nodded to the chamberlain. The man did not nod back.

Lord Stowe entered. He appeared even more fatigued than he had the day before, if that were possible. He wore breeches and a white shirt, untied at the neck. The dagger around his waist was turned toward the front so that the man behind him could not grab it easily.

Nicholas recognized the third man, but it took a moment to place him. He was young, about twenty, and stocky, with thick blond hair. His eyes were an electric green. He wore a crudely-dyed red shirt – the color blotched along the middle – and a pair of brown pants that had been mended several times. His boots were covered with mud, and his clothing looked as if it had dried damp.

His hands were tied.

'Luke, isn't it?' Nicholas said to the third man.

He nodded, but wouldn't meet Nicholas's gaze.

Luke had been part of a military troop that had been captured by the Fey over five years before. His father had bargained for Luke's life, offering to remain in Shadowlands in exchange for Luke's freedom. Luke got his freedom, and the opportunity to see his father once a year, but the Fey had done something to him. Something odd.

When touched with holy water, Luke glowed green.

Nicholas had seen him after the return, and had asked Lord Stowe to remain in contact with the boy. Luke had once visited Jewel to get his father's freedom. She had left the meeting cursing her own people under her breath. When Nicholas asked her about it, she had snapped at him, claiming there was nothing she could do. Then or ever.

Nicholas had not seen Luke since.

'The boy asked that we tie him up before we brought him here,' Lord Stowe said. 'But he wouldn't talk with anyone except you.'

'Then how do you know this story is worth my time this early in the morning?' Nicholas said.

Lord Stowe stared at Nicholas for a moment, as if trying to get used to the new, harsher version. 'Luke arrived at my home a few hours ago, soaking wet and carrying a knife. He said he had just come from the Tabernacle. He smells of holy water.'

Nicholas set his tea mug down. He stood so that he was of an height with Luke. 'You're not glowing.'

'It fades, Sire,' Luke said. He still didn't look up.

'What's so urgent that you disturb me before breakfast?'

Luke lowered his head so that his shaggy blond hair covered his eyes. 'I tried to kill the Rocaan.'

Stowe took a step away from the boy. The chamberlain put his hand on the hilt of the sword.

'Did you know this?' Nicholas asked Stowe.

'Only that he said he had come from the Tabernacle and it had to do with Matthias. And that he had to see you. Now.'

'Do you want me to lock you up?' Nicholas asked. 'Lord Stowe could have done that just as easily.'

Besides, Nicholas wasn't certain he wanted to. The boy had taken the action Nicholas had wanted to take.

'I don't know if that would do any good.' Luke brought his head up, shaking the hair out of his face. Nicholas finally recognized the look in those green eyes. It was fear.

'Tell me then,' he said.

Luke's face had broadened in the years since Nicholas had seen him last, yet he still looked young. The innocence was gone from his eyes, and so was the hope.

Luke had once had hope that his father would get out of Shadow-lands, and that all would change.

Once they had all had hope.

'I was on the farm yesterday when I learned about the Queen. I am so sorry, Sire. I – She – well, she got me free from Shadowlands. She's the one who made the agreement to get me out.'

Nicholas nodded. He had known that much. He had also known that the boy had a crush on Jewel so severe that it scared Nicholas. After Luke's single meeting with Jewel, which Nicholas saw the end of, he didn't ever want the boy near his wife again.

'And I felt real bad. I was doing my chores, though, so I could think through it. Mourn her in my own way. I was wondering if that meant that my dad would go free now or if he would still be there forever, and then I heard a voice. It was soft and I can't remember what it said.'

'Did you see where it came from?' Stowe asked.

Luke shook his head. 'Then it's night and dark and I wake up and I'm glowing green. I'm standing over a man's bed and I'm holding a knife like I'm about to stab him. He's running around the bed, and I follow because I don't know where I am. I can see him in the green light, and he's really tall, and then he opens the door and I recognize the Rocaan.'

Nicholas's hands were cold. He wished he were still holding his tea mug. He clasped his hands behind him as Stowe had done. 'And you don't know how you got there?'

'No,' Luke said. 'I lost a whole day.'

'How did you get out?' Stowe asked.

'I ran to the other doors. They led to a balcony. A rope was tied to the railing and I scaled down it. As I did, the green faded. I ran across the courtyard and jumped the wall, and didn't stop until I got to your house.' Half a sob broke out of Luke. 'I'm so sorry. I don't know what happened.'

Nicholas did. Or thought he did. And he didn't like it. 'I want to get the sequence straight,' he said. 'You heard a voice, and then you remember nothing until Matt – the Rocaan threw holy water on you.'

Luke nodded. 'That's right, Sire. I was already glowing when my mind came back.' He glanced at Lord Stowe. 'I can't go into the churches any more. The Danites are afraid of me. I don't do the Sacraments because I glow.'

Stowe's gaze met Nicholas's. Nicholas no longer cared that he had been interrupted. He called to the chamberlain. 'Get my holy water.'

'Yes, Highness.' The chamberlain tapped the sword hilt as if reluctant to leave it, then went into Nicholas's bedroom. He emerged carrying a vial.

'I want you to pour it on Luke.'

The chamberlain nodded. Luke cringed, bringing his shoulders up and his head down, his hair again hanging over his face.

'Does it hurt you to glow, Luke?' Nicholas asked.

'No,' Luke whispered.

Nicholas moved his head slightly, indicating that the chamberlain should pour the water. The chamberlain uncorked the bottle and poured the contents onto Luke's back. Luke didn't move. The water flowed over him as if he wore a green shell. Slowly it absorbed into the shell and onto his clothing.

A slightly bitter smell mingled with the woodsmoke.

'Do you feel any different?' Nicholas asked.

Luke stood up and wiped his face with the side of his arms. The movement was awkward – sticking his hands into the air – but Stowe moved between Luke and Nicholas just the same.

Nicholas touched Stowe's arm. He appreciated the gesture, but he doubted it was necessary.

Luke frowned. 'I feel just the same.'

'You can untie him,' Nicholas said to Stowe.

'No!' Luke said. 'You don't know what I'll do.'

'Actually,' Nicholas said. 'I do. I'm safe around you. It's Matthias – the Rocaan – who has to worry.'

All three other men looked at Nicholas in surprise. 'How do you know, Sire?' Stowe asked.

Nicholas smiled. 'Do you remember bringing Luke to me in the first place?'

Stowe nodded. 'We didn't know why he glowed.'

'And now we do,' Nicholas said. 'They put a spell of some kind on you, and they haven't used it until now. The Fey tried to get you to kill Matthias for them.'

'Me?' Luke's skin went white. 'I've never killed anybody in my whole life. Why would they try that with me?'

'Because they could. Because someone had the opportunity.' Nicholas looked at Stowe. 'I have to move quicker than I thought. I will need to set up a meeting with the Shaman today. I'm going to need to send someone to Shadowlands for her.'

'I can go,' Luke said. 'Maybe I should go. They can't do anything more to me.'

'They might be able to,' Nicholas said. 'And besides, I can't really trust you. I don't know what will happen there. I will send someone else.'

The chamberlain untied Luke's hands.

'What are we going to do with him?' Stowe asked.

'We're going to have to lock you up somewhere,' Nicholas said, 'Although I wish we didn't have to. I see no reason to put him in a cell. Is there somewhere in your home that he would be safe, milord?'

'I have a section that is both comfortable and safe.' Stowe frowned a little. Nicholas had been to the section. It had once been a small keep hundreds of years before. Stowe's grandfather had turned it into servants' quarters, but the servants hadn't liked it. The lack of windows bothered them. 'I'll put him there.'

'I don't care about comfortable,' Luke said. 'Please make certain it's safe. I don't want to kill anyone. I've never harmed anyone in my life. I couldn't face it if I did.'

'If you did,' Stowe said softly, 'it wouldn't be your doing. It would be the Fey's.'

'No.' Luke's voice held a plaintive note. 'It would be my hands. My doing. If I had stayed with my father, none of this would have happened.'

'We don't know that,' Nicholas said. 'We don't know how things would be right now.'

Maybe things would have gone so different that Jewel would still be alive. A longing rose in Nicholas's chest, a longing so deep it hurt. He turned away from them, went to his table, and picked up his mug. The tea was cold.

'I will see the Fey Shaman,' Nicholas said. 'I see if she can help you.'

'Jewel said no one could. The spells were too deep.'

'Maybe,' Nicholas said. 'I'm beginning to learn that there were some things Jewel didn't know.'

Like Arianna. He had no idea what would have happened to that child if Jewel had birthed her normally, without Fey present. The Islander healers wouldn't have known what to do.

'If we're done, Highness,' Stowe said, 'I'll take Luke to my place.'

Nicholas nodded. He made himself turn, the mug cupped to his chest. 'I will do what I can for you,' he said.

'I was so afraid you'd want me killed,' Luke said. 'I was afraid that I made things worse.'

'I don't know how you could have made things worse,' Nicholas said.

Both Stowe and Luke bowed, then they left the room. The chamberlain followed them, closing the door behind them.

Nicholas stood alone before the crackling fire, his hands wrapped around a cool mug of lukewarm tea. He didn't know how to tell the boy that his action hadn't bothered Nicholas at all. Someone had to avenge Jewel. It would have been so much easier if Luke had been successful.

So much easier.

No Matthias to worry about. The Rocaanists would choose a new Rocaan, and Island life would go on as usual.

But it couldn't be that way.

Unless Nicholas did nothing. Then the Fey would avenge Jewel's death.

And in doing so, would ruin an innocent life.

Nicholas was sworn to protect those lives. And even though Matthias administered the oath, the oath was still valid. Nicholas's father would have been so disappointed if Nicholas had done anything but follow the life he was born into.

Jewel would have been disappointed too. All her life, she had done her best for her people. Even in marrying him.

Especially in marrying him.

Nicholas went to the window and pulled back the tapestry. The irony bit into him. Jewel was the only one who would have understood why he couldn't avenge her himself.

Thirty-Six

Adrian's small cabin had become home. Mend had helped him fix it up. He had a thin cot, two chairs, and a tiny fireplace, barely big enough for three logs. When he arrived, the Fey had tried to give him Fey lamps to hang overhead, but he had refused. Somewhere along the way, he had learned that those lamps were lit with the souls of the enemy dead. He didn't want to see by the remains of his own people.

He used candles instead.

The result was a tiny room that was always smoky. The cabin had no windows, of course, because all they would look on was grayness, but sometimes he wished for a window so that he could open it. The smell of candlewax and woodsmoke was sometimes too much to bear.

But it was better than being in the Shadowlands proper where the Fey could watch him.

He had no real duties any more. He was more of a prisoner than he had ever been. And his teachings had led to the murder of King Alexander and, possibly, the death of Jewel.

Not that he cared about her. She was the one who had made the bargain that sealed him in this gray place forever.

At least Luke was all right. Even now, years after Adrian had made the agreement, the fact that Luke had survived and done well was a comfort. The third prisoner, Ort, had died rather horribly a short time into their captivity.

Adrian stretched out on his cot. He was sleeping more and more, finding less time to do the handful of things they assigned him. There were no books in Shadowlands, and the Fey believed he was unteachable, so they didn't try to work with him. Instead, they gave him menial tasks and didn't care if he completed them. An occasional Fey would ask him for lessons in Islander, but even those had become rare. Most of the Fey who wanted to know the language did.

He heard a thump outside his cabin, then the door swung open. Coulter ran in as if something were on his tail. He launched himself at Adrian, wrapped his arms around him, and held on. Coulter hit with such force that it knocked the wind from Adrian's body.

The door slowly swung closed behind him.

Adrian put his arms around the boy and stroked his hair, as he used to do for Luke, when Luke was young and frightened. Coulter had never allowed Adrian to hold him. They had a tentative relationship, formed more out of defense than anything, the only two Islanders in Shadowlands, both prisoners. Adrian at least knew what he had lost; Coulter hadn't been outside the grayness since he was a year old.

It took a moment for Adrian to catch his breath. The boy was clinging to him so tightly he would have finger-sized bruises later. Coulter was shaking and if Adrian hadn't known better, he would have thought that Coulter was suppressing a sob.

Adrian had learned through all the years of raising Luke alone that the best way to handle a boy this upset was to give him time. And since Adrian had time – and a lot of it – he would wait.

Gradually, the boy's shuddering eased. Then his grip loosened. For a moment, Adrian thought Coulter had fallen asleep, but the boy didn't take his characteristic deep breath and shuddering sigh. Adrian had gotten used to the boy's breathing on the long nights. Coulter could still sleep and sleep hard. Adrian, no matter how much he tried, had trouble sleeping longer than an hour or two.

Which was one reason that he napped as much as he did.

Coulter usually slept on a mattress that they rolled up during the daytime – or what the Fey declared to be daytime, since the inside of Shadowlands never changed. Adrian had taken Coulter in when he found the toddler sleeping on a pile of garbage near the Circle Door. Apparently the Domestics who were supposed to tend him didn't pay much attention to him. He didn't belong to anyone, so no one took care of him.

Until Adrian.

Even then, though, Coulter had refused to let him close. And not once, in all those years of sleeping in the same cabin, and talking about the history of the Isle, had Coulter ever demanded to be held.

'You ready to talk now?' Adrian asked.

His shirt was damp. Coulter *had* been crying.

Coulter's breath hitched the first time he tried to speak. Then he pushed himself up on one elbow, careful to keep his arm on Adrian's cot instead of his chest, and wiped his face with his sleeve.

'They said I can't see Gift no more.' His voice sounded young and pouty. Coulter never sounded young. That was one of the things that Adrian marveled over.

'Who said?'

'Rugar.'

Adrian stiffened. If Rugar were involved, something serious had happened. 'Why did he say that?'

'Because Touched told him that I was too powerful.'

They were speaking in Islander, as they usually did when they were alone. Adrian believed that Coulter should learn the language of his own people. But sometimes Islander didn't cover the nuances of Fey magic.

'Tell me in Fey,' Adrian said. 'What did they mean by powerful?'

'Rugar brought Touched to me,' he said, switching languages, and lying back on Adrian's chest as if he didn't want to look at him, 'and he tried to get me –'

' "Get you?" '

'It was strange. He shot fire at me and light and words and I had to block them.'

Adrian's hands froze on Coulter's soft hair. 'Block them?'

Coulter nodded, his head moving against Adrian's chest.

'Were you able to?' Adrian asked.

'It was hard, and once I couldn't.'

'What they say about your being able to block?'

'Touched kept saying it was impossible.'

That was what Adrian would have thought too. The Fey used the word 'block' very specifically to mean prevent an attack by the use of magic.

Adrian swallowed. He wanted to ask the next question as carefully as he could. 'Did you block using your hands or your mind?'

'My mind,' Coulter said. 'How do you block?'

Adrian stroked Coulter's hair again. He didn't want this conversation too seem any odder than it was. 'With my hands,' he said.

'That doesn't work,' Coulter said.

'I know.'

'What about thinking? Can't you block by thinking?'

'No,' Adrian said. Obviously Coulter could. Coulter. Blond, round-faced, blue-eyed. So clearly Islander that the Fey treated him little better than a dog.

Except Solanda. She had brought him here, spoken of magic, and left, never to care for him again. Mend thought Coulter had magic too, but Adrian had thought that woman-talk for a child's specialness. He had never thought she was serious.

'How do you keep them from hurting you then?' Coulter asked.

Adrian buried his face in Coulter's hair. It smelled of Domestic soap and child-sweat. 'Sometimes I don't,' Adrian said.

Coulter was silent for a long time. The fire was burning low and a chill was building in the cabin. But it didn't matter. The heat of Coulter's body was more than keeping Adrian warm.

'How come they won't let me see Gift?'

'I don't know,' Adrian said. 'Did you block something Gift sent you?'

Coulter shook his head. His grip had tightened on Adrian. Gift and Coulter were the only two children of their age in Shadowlands. A few other children had been born in the last year or so, but they were much too young to interest three-and five-year-old boys. Forbidding Coulter to see Gift was like forbidding him to eat. Coulter only had two friends: Gift and Adrian. And of the two, Gift was the one he relied on the most.

'Member the other day when I left here?' Coulter asked.

Coulter had left the cabin at full-tilt run. Adrian had asked him where he was going, but Coulter hadn't answered. Adrian figured that Coulter was going to do boy things, and never questioned beyond that.

'Yes,' Adrian said.

'Gift got really sick. The Shaman and the Domestics were gone. So I helped him.'

'You –?'

Adrian stopped himself. This conversation had become surreal, but he didn't want to sound disbelieving. Coulter was hard enough to talk to without doubting his every word.

'How?' Adrian asked.

'He was still Bound to his mother. She was dying. I cut the Link.'

So simple. Fey terms. Magick terms that spoke of concepts that Adrian only dimly understood. He thought about what Coulter said for a moment. Cut the Link. With Jewel.

Gift's mother.

No wonder Rugar took credit for the boy.

'How did you cut the Link?' Adrian asked.

'I Linked him to me,' Coulter said as if that were the most simple concept in the world.

'And that saved him?'

'Everybody's Linked,' Coulter said. 'Some Links are better than others. You got a strong one that goes out the Circle Door.'

All Adrian's Links went out the Circle Door. He had none inside. Except for Coulter and Mend. Much as he hated to admit it, he too had two friends in Shadowlands. A five-year-old frightened boy, and a Fey woman.

'And one to you,' Adrian said softly.

'Yeah,' Coulter said.

They were silent again. The silence was comfortable. And Adrian found he liked the feel of the boy's body against his. It had been a long time since he had shared an affectionate touch with anyone. He missed it. He missed his own child. But Luke was not a child any longer. He was a man full-grown.

The flames were burning blue. Soon he would have to add another log or the fire would go out. Adrian didn't move. He couldn't lose the warmth. And he wanted a chance to think.

Coulter was Islander, but raised among the Fey. He had never left the protection of Shadowlands, never seen the green grass or the blue sky. Since he was a baby barely old enough to walk, every person he touched, everything he did, had a Fey focus. The only Islander he knew was Adrian, and Adrian had sought out that Link, not Coulter. Adrian wasn't even certain Coulter knew he was different.

But he was.

And perhaps the difference came from being raised in Shadowlands, breathing the Fey's magick air, thinking in the Fey's guttural language. Perhaps magick wasn't innate as the Fey insisted. Perhaps it was learned, just like mannerisms, language, and food preferences.

'I don't want to stay away from Gift,' Coulter said quietly.

'I don't think you should,' Adrian said.

'They said I have to until Touched was done with me.'

Adrian had to work to keep his body relaxed after that statement. No one cared about this boy, no one except him. No one thought about what it would be like to have his best friend taken away. No one thought about how a boy would react to experiments.

Experiments had killed Ort.

'You have a Link to Gift, don't you?' Adrian said. 'They can't take that away, can they?'

'If they do, he might die,' Coulter said.

Maybe Adrian shouldn't worry about Coulter. In some ways, Coulter was far ahead of him.

'What does Touched plan to do with you?'

'See how far my powers extend.'

The words had to be Touched's. Coulter had never spoken in concepts like 'extend' before.

'Can you just tell him?' Adrian asked.

Coulter didn't move. For a moment, Adrian wondered if the boy had heard. But he had to. He had his ear pressed against Adrian's chest.

'I think he knows,' Coulter said.

Adrian frowned. Sometimes the Fey were as alien to him as fish. 'If he knows, then why the test?'

'Because he's afraid,' Coulter said. 'Really afraid. Once he saw what I could do. He and Rugar said that what I can do, it changes everything.'

Adrian closed his eyes. Of course Rugar would see it that way. He saw his own daughter as a way to achieve his own ends. He had somehow brought his grandchild here. And now he had turned his attention to a child he hadn't thought worthy of such attention. Coulter.

And the truth was, it did change everything. If Islanders had the ability to learn as Coulter did, the Fey weren't as all-powerful as they believed.

'What can you do?' Adrian asked.

Coulter frowned. 'I never thought about it,' he said. 'I just do.'

Adrian nodded. He didn't want to push Coulter, but he needed to know. This could be important to both of them. It could be important for the Isle itself.

'What do you do?' Adrian asked.

Coulter shrugged. 'Like the Link. I didn't think about it. I just did it.'

'Did Gift call to you? Is that how you knew to do it?'

Coulter shook his head. 'I knew I had to see him. And I didn't question it. I just went.'

Adrian took a deep breath. Something fluttered in his stomach – a kind of excitement, a bit of hope. He ignored those feelings. He would have time to sort those out later.

'Was that the first time that's happened to you?'

Coulter shook his head. 'I've always been able to do things. You know that.'

Actually, Adrian hadn't known that. Coulter had been a very private child. Interesting that he assumed Adrian would know what he had been doing. Perhaps their connection was closer than Adrian thought.

'Explain this to me,' Adrian said. 'Rugar called it a power? What kind of power?'

Coulter raised himself on his elbows. He squinted at Adrian. 'Why do you want to know?'

Adrian gazed back at him levelly. He could lie, he supposed, and just say he was interested. Or he could tell a partial truth, that he was concerned for Coulter. Or he could be completely honest. 'Islanders don't usually have powers, Coulter,' Adrian said. 'We are non-magickal beings.'

'You're saying I'm Fey?' He had hope in his voice. Adrian winced.

'No.' Adrian had to quash that idea quickly. 'I'm saying that you may have taught us something about the Fey. Magick might be a learned thing. All Islanders might be able to learn it.'

'So I'm not Fey?'

'No. You're too old and too Islander to be Fey. But you could be as good as the Fey. Maybe even better.'

The hope had left Coulter's eyes. It had shocked Adrian more than anything in this conversation. The boy wanted to be Fey? It made sense, he supposed. Coulter couldn't remember life outside of Shadowlands. All he had ever known was that he was not Fey. He didn't really understand his own heritage.

'How can I be better?' he whispered.

'Rugar didn't know what you were,' Adrian said. 'He brought in Touched, a Warder who should have been able to tell too. They wanted to know how far your powers extend. Boy, if they could tell what kind of magic you had, they would have *known*. They wouldn't have had to check.'

Coulter nodded. He looked thoughtful. The adult expression was back on his face. Adrian studied the boy, finally understanding. The adult attitudes Coulter adopted were a cover, a way to pretend he didn't care. He was more mature than the average five-year-old and smarter, too, but he was still a child.

A child who was trying to make sense of a world that didn't care for him.

Adrian heard the unspoken questions. Will they like me better if I have magick? Will I become one of them if I can act like them? Will they value me?

Adrian suspected the answer to all those questions was no.

But he wasn't about to tell Coulter. Not now.

'How far do your powers extend?' Adrian asked.

'I don't know,' Coulter said.

Perhaps the question was wrong. 'What kinds of things can you do?'

'I don't think about it,' Coulter said. His tone was guarded.

'Then how do you know when you can do something?'

'I just do it.'

Adrian propped himself up so that his eyes were level with Coulter's. 'Coulter, trust me for a moment. I want to help you and I can't without understanding what's happening here. It's new to me too. How do you do these things?'

Coulter bit his lips, then licked them and swallowed so hard his small adam's apple bobbed visibly. 'It's like the Links. I know they're there, but I mostly don't think about them. I feel like there's all kinds of things I can do, but I don't because I don't need to. I don't really want to. Like blocking. I had never done that before, but it was there when I wanted it.'

'If I ask you to do something, can you do it?'

'Some of it,' Coulter said. 'Why?'

'How do you know you can't do all of it?'

302

Coulter shrugged and looked away. For a moment, Adrian thought he had lost him.

'Coulter, please,' Adrian said. 'This is for both of us.'

Coulter turned back toward Adrian. Tears filled Coulter's blue eyes, but didn't spill onto his cheeks. 'I – they – I know parts aren't ready. Like someday I'll be able to do this, but I can't right now. And I'm really scared –'

His voice cracked on the word 'scared' and he broke off.

Adrian put a hand on Coulter's back. 'Scared of what?'

'Scared that I'll need to do something and I won't be ready.' Coulter blinked and the tears ran down his cheeks, silent streams of misery. Adrian brought the boy close, cradled him against his shoulder. The boy didn't sob, but the tears continued, long and hard. Adrian rested his own cheek against the top of Coulter's head.

No wonder the boy was so tense all the time. He carried so much responsibility, even now. The incident with Gift, instead of giving him confidence, had added more responsibility. What if Coulter hadn't been able to save him? What then?

Adrian knew that feeling. He had lived with it for four years. When the time had come to protect his own son, he had been unable to do so. He had to sacrifice his own life to save Luke's. It had been the only way, and even then it had seemed too little too late.

'Coulter,' Adrian said quietly, 'you do more than anyone else could have. You did very well. You saved Gift's life.'

'But they won't let me see him now.'

'They're scared of you. You're not what they expected. People are scared of things they don't understand.'

'How come they don't understand me?' Coulter asked. 'I'm just like them.'

'I know,' Adrian said. 'But they believed no one else could be like them. You've proven that wrong.'

And they would try to see how similar the boy was. Adrian wouldn't let them experiment on Coulter. He wouldn't lose another son to these people. Like he lost Luke.

The Fey had said if Adrian left, Luke would die. But maybe, just maybe, Coulter could prevent that. Especially if it took the Fey a while to learn that Adrian was gone.

That way, Adrian could save both his sons, his real son and his adopted son.

Adrian frowned, remembering something he had heard, years ago, from Jewel. 'Coulter, have you ever opened the Circle Door?'

'No,' Coulter said. 'Why?'

'Because,' Adrian spoke slowly. 'Because the Fey say that only magical beings can open that door. I can't. But maybe you can.'

'Why would I want to?' Coulter asked.

'To go home,' Adrian said. 'To go back to the Isle, to get out of this place.'

'I've never been out of here.'

'Except as a baby.'

'I don't really remember it,' Coulter said.

'If I left, would you go with me?' Adrian asked.

'And leave Gift?'

'For a while. Maybe find your family.'

'My family is dead,' Coulter said. 'They told me that a long time ago. I remember it.'

'What do you remember?'

'Them screaming. The woman taking me.'

'Solanda?'

Coulter shook his head. 'An old woman. She –' he took a deep breath as if this next were hard to say. 'She loved me.'

The words echoed between them, filled with loss and hopelessness. No one had loved Coulter since he had come to Shadowlands. Even Adrian had held himself back, afraid of losing another child.

'Don't you want to see her?' Adrian asked.

Coulter shook his head, brushing his tear-soaked face deeper into Adrian's shirt.

'Why not?'

'Because she didn't come for me. She didn't want me.'

It was as if a window had opened into Coulter's soul. Adrian finally understood the boy. 'She couldn't come for you, son. Islanders can't get in here.'

'You did.'

'I was taken prisoner. I can't leave.'

'She can't get in?' Coulter asked.

Adrian shook his head.

'Really?'

'I'll walk to the Circle Door and show you if you want to see. I can't open it. I have no magick, and I'm sure she didn't either.'

'Oh.' Coulter spoke the word long and soft, almost like a sigh. His entire body relaxed against Adrian's. They remained like that for a long time, so long, in fact, Adrian thought maybe Coulter had fallen asleep. Then Coulter said, 'If I let you out the Circle Door, will you help me find her?'

This time, Adrian heard the subtle question behind the practical one. 'Coulter,' he said, picking his words carefully so that the boy wouldn't feel used yet again. 'I consider you part of my family. You will always be welcome at my side and in my home. I'll help you find her. I promise.'

'All right,' Coulter said. He leaned back and smiled tentatively at Adrian. Then Coulter wiped the tears off his face. 'If they want me to stay away from Gift, I will. I'll leave.'

The loss of Coulter would terrify Rugar. Adrian smiled. For the first time in years, he could taste freedom.

Thirty-Seven

The Shaman stood in the door to his private suite. She was so tall. In the last few days, Nicholas had forgotten that. Her white hair floated around her head like a nimbus, and her nut-brown eyes were deep, deep as any reflecting pool. She wore a white robe that shimmered with each movement; he had never seen such material before.

Nicholas got off his chair and ushered her in, closing the door behind her. The sofas and chairs were empty. He had cleared a place in front of the fire because the tapestries were up, and the cool morning air floated in with the sunlight. The windows overlooked the garden which was empty.

He had arranged the meeting in his suite so that they would have complete privacy. Lord Stowe had complained when he heard that Nicholas had dismissed his guards.

But the Shaman had had her chance to kill him the day Jewel died. He knew she would not.

'Thank you for coming,' Nicholas said. He wasn't used to looking up at a woman. Even Jewel had been of his height. 'Especially coming here. I hope my emissary relayed that we could have gone somewhere neutral.'

'I needed to come here,' the Shaman said. Her voice was deep and calm, not at all the clipped command tones that she had used a few days previous. 'I did not want the others to know I had come.'

Nicholas nodded. He had stressed to the page he had sent that this meeting be completely private. The boy was trustworthy – Nicholas had used him before – and completely terrified to see a Fey. Jewel's presence in the palace had never changed that.

Jewel. They had buried her late the previous day in the palace grounds. No Rocaanists had been present. The servants had dug the grave, and the lords had helped Nicholas preside. None of Jewel's people had been there.

He couldn't get her from his mind. Every morning he woke up and reached for her, half feeling her presence still in the bed. He would discuss her with the Shaman as well.

'I have several problems, Shaman,' he said. 'I think they are joint problems.'

She threaded her hands together. 'I suspect they are,' she said.

'Some of my lords are advocating an attack against the Fey. There has already been an attack against the Rocaan, not from my people.'

'The boy,' she said.

He glanced at her. She hadn't moved from the spot he had led her to. Obviously more was happening than even he knew. He moved a chair closer to the fire. She took it. He sat across from her. The breeze kept the fire low. The air had a smell of rain.

'The boy,' Nicholas said, not yet willing to pursue that topic farther. 'We also know that one of your people killed my father.'

The Shaman sighed softly. 'It would have worked, you know,' she said.

Nicholas tensed. 'My father's murder?'

'No,' the Shaman said. 'Your marriage.'

A sharp pain drove through Nicholas's heart, as if she had wielded a knife with her words. He couldn't sit. He stood, walked to the window, and looked out at the garden below.

The tree branches were no longer bare. The leaves had sprouted, and flowers were budding beside the path. The gardener had tilled the vegetable patch on the far side of walled off area, the dirt looking black and healthy in its patch of sunlight. Clouds were forming to the west, and he could see a haze of rain over the river.

When he had control of his voice, he said, 'It does us no good now.'

'Perhaps,' the Shaman said. 'Perhaps not. A try is always good, Nicholas.'

He shook his head, and placed his hands flat on the window sill. The stone was cold against his palms. It was all too new. He had steeled himself for this meeting, and the Shaman had immediately seized control of his emotions.

'I have been thinking of this since I last saw you,' she said. 'I wonder if I could have done more.'

'You did all you could to save Jewel,' he said. His voice had a roughness to it that it didn't normally have.

'I did,' she said. 'But I wasn't talking of that. I meant on your marriage day.'

That caught his attention. He turned and rubbed his cold hands against his breeches. 'My wedding day?'

She was staring into the fire. In repose, her face had a gaminish quality. 'I said to Rugar that Jewel made the only choice for peace. I asked that he do the same.'

'Rugar?' Suddenly Nicholas's hands weren't the only part of him that was chilled.

'I was too subtle. I should have told him to stay away from Islanders. I should have told him he would bring disaster.'

'Rugar.' Nicholas swallowed. 'Rugar said he had nothing to do with my father's death.'

The Shaman turned her head. Her eyes absorbed the sunlight coming in the windows. 'Did he?'

Nicholas frowned. He didn't remember the words exactly, only the impression. 'I thought he did –'

She smiled. The wrinkles on her face deepened. 'Rugar is good at making people think what he wants them to think. He is a master at it. Did Jewel believe he was uninvolved?'

'She never said.' Nicholas was silent. Their last night together, they had sat in front of that fireplace, his hand on her taut stomach, Arianna kicking from the womb. 'At first she thought Burden did.'

'But?'

'She went and spoke to him. She was convinced he hadn't.'

'And still she thought a Fey had killed your father.'

Nicholas nodded. He returned to his chair, sat, and put his hands on his knees, guarding himself but remaining as open as he could.

Rugar. He had the most to benefit from giving Jewel a step closer to the throne.

'You mentioned the boy when I told you of the attack on Matthias.'

The Shaman nodded. 'Before I tell you more of this, young Nicholas, I must tell you I believe you to be a good man who has an affinity for Fey. We are a warrior people. When in battle we make interesting choices.'

He raised his head. Something in her tone caught him. She was warning him. 'Jewel told me that.'

'Good,' the Shaman said. 'Then you will find it easy to forgive her.'

His hands tightened on his knees. 'Jewel? What has she to do with this?'

'She made the agreement.' The Shaman leaned back in her chair. 'With Adrian and young Luke. The idea was Jewel's.'

'The agreement to exchange Adrian's life for Luke's? She never told me that.'

'There is much she never told you,' the Shaman said. 'The Fey are warriors. We share secrets on a need-to-know basis. If we believe that the information will hurt us or our cause, we will not impart it. Unfortunately, that tendency becomes part of our private relationships as well.'

He knew that. He had learned a lot in the last few days. Even that, however, did not diminish his feelings for her. All he had learned made sense. He had not been living with the Fey. Jewel had been hoping to change her own people. She had been living as an Islander, with an Islander. Some of what she had known would have interfered with his response to her and her people.

'It strikes me that there is more to this agreement than the exchange,' Nicholas said.

The Shaman nodded. 'For the agreement to work, we needed to be able to find Luke at a moment's notice. That way, if Adrian escaped, we would punish his son. Since we were spelling Luke, we added two other spells, one at Rugar's request.'

Rugar again. Nicholas's father-in-law had a lot to answer for.

'He asked that we place a Charm on Luke, a suggestion, that if something were to happen to any of the Fey leaders, he would get revenge. The Charm was powerful. It lasted for years. Someone in Shadowlands triggered the Charm after Jewel died. Someone seeking revenge.'

'Rugar?'

The Shaman shook her head. 'He lacks the skill to enact a Charm without help. Someone else. I have speculations, but no proof.'

'What was the other spell?' Nicholas asked. 'Is Luke carrying another suggestion that will kill us in our beds?'

The Shaman shook her head. 'The Night Riders gave him false memories. Of Jewel. To keep him attached to Fey and Shadowlands.'

Jewel had seen Luke and left cursing her own people, claiming she could do nothing to help him. Luke, who had a strong, eerie crush on Jewel.

False memories.

Nicholas should have asked Jewel more about the Fey when he had the chance. His father had tried to learn everything he could about the Fey. First he had interviewed that odd little man, the spooky Red Cap who had disappeared years ago, and later his father talked with Jewel. Nicholas's father had always worried that Jewel wouldn't tell him everything, that she was keeping things hidden from him. He had feared that she and her father were planning something.

But she had assured Nicholas that she wouldn't do that.

It had been the last thing she had done.

And she had risked – and lost – her life to prove that.

The Shaman was watching him, as if she were waiting for him to stop remembering. He wondered how well she could read him. It seemed that she could read him very well.

When she saw him staring at her, she said, 'I cannot guarantee that Luke will stay away from your Rocaan.'

'Between you and me,' Nicholas said, 'I wish he wouldn't.'

The Shaman didn't move. It was as if she were waiting for him to say more.

'Jewel worked very hard, and lost her life, to make certain that the Fey and Islanders were united,' Nicholas said. 'Yet one of her people killed my father, and one of my people killed Jewel. Both acts are enough to start the fighting again. I do not want to preside over a war. Both sides will lose – the Fey early on, and the Islanders later, as attrition takes the young away. Jewel believed her grandfather would come eventually, and so even if the Islanders won, the Fey would take over the Isle after a few years.'

The Shaman's hands were still folded. She hadn't moved at all as she watched him. He had only seen Sebastian be that motionless. His son had more Fey than he thought as well.

'I have a proposal,' Nicholas said. 'I will give your people the Rocaan, if you give us the person who murdered my father.'

'Give?' the Shaman asked.

'Trade,' Nicholas said.

'To do with as we will?'

He nodded.

She stood, her calm shattered. She hadn't expected this, clearly. If he hadn't seen her agitation the night Jewel died, he wouldn't have believed this now.

She walked over to the fire, crouched before it, and held her hands over the flame as if for warmth. Her hair shimmered red and gold in the fire's light.

'It's an elegant solution,' she said.

He frowned. Something in her tone sounded sad.

'Elegant.' She bowed her head. 'But impossible.'

'Impossible?' He had expected that argument. 'I think you can make it possible. We both face difficulties here, but what are two lives compared with hundreds? I will give you the religious leader of Blue Isle in exchange for your killer. I will shatter centuries of unity with the Church and the Crown for this. I think the Fey can make the same sort of sacrifice.'

'You don't know what you ask,' she said.

'I do,' he said. 'I know. Rugar has not led your people well since he brought them here. No one has supported him. Jewel did tell me that.'

The Shaman put her hand on the stone wall of the fireplace, bracing herself as she stood. 'So you know, but you do not understand.'

'I understand that twice now he has interfered in ways that have nearly destroyed our two peoples. Just as Matthias has done. If we get rid of them both, we can live in peace.'

'Peace cannot be built on death,' the Shaman said. 'Nor can we survive more battles. We have some semblance of peace now. Let's work to keep it.'

She grabbed her skirts and walked away from the fire. She appeared to have aged since he saw her face a moment before. 'What you suggest,' she said, 'is too horrible to contemplate.'

'More horrible than your people dying as we throw holy water on them? More horrible than the kind of war we saw years ago?'

The Shaman raised her dark eyes to him. 'The Fey are trained in war. We expect death. I do not object to the death. Were it anyone but Rugar, I would do what I could to make certain my people comply.'

'You have no reason to protect Rugar,' Nicholas said. Her words were all the confirmation he needed. 'The man single-handedly slaughtered your people. He murdered the fiftieth Rocaan. He murdered my father.'

'He is the Black King's son.'

'Yes,' Nicholas said, 'and the Black King sent him here, to fail, so that he wouldn't pretend to the throne.'

'You don't understand,' the Shaman said. She almost spoke in a whisper. 'The Fey are sworn to protect all who aspire to the Black Throne.'

'Anyone?' Nicholas asked. For anyone could aspire to any throne. Achieving it was another matter.

'Anyone in the Black King's family,' the Shaman said.

'But Rugar lost his chance to become Black King,' Nicholas said. 'You and Jewel both told me that.'

The Shaman shook her head. 'It's not so simple.'

'It doesn't seem that difficult. He will plunge you back into a war you cannot win. Why defend him? Give him to me. I'll be responsible for his life.'

The Shaman closed her eyes. Her eyebrows met in a single line. 'That would be worse.'

'I have no stake in your throne,' Nicholas said. 'Blame me.'

'Your stake is greater than mine,' The Shaman said. She opened her eyes. They were so dark they almost seemed black. 'Your children will inherit. They both have aspirations.'

Nicholas sighed. 'Jewel had brothers whom she was certain would become Black King. Surely my children have no chance at that Throne. Rugar was effectively sent away, sent to fight and win or fight and lose. Apparently his father didn't care. You make it sound so ominous. It can't be. Let me have Rugar.'

'If you have Rugar, the world will erupt in flame.'

311

As if to accent her words, a gust of wind stirred the fire. The flames shot almost to the chimney. Nicholas got up and closed the grate so that no sparks would escape.

'You're very good,' Nicholas said. 'Does Rugar know how well you defend him?'

'Don't make light of what I'm telling you,' she said.

'What I do or what my children do will not affect the entire world,' Nicholas said.

'The Black Throne is held together by Blood Magick. That Blood flowed through Jewel. It flows through your children now. If the Blood turns on itself, insanity reigns. And when insanity reigns, whole cultures die. Your children are part of the Blood now. You are part of the Blood. Do not take responsibility for Rugar's life. If he loses it while you hold responsibility, the Blood will have turned on itself. You will unleash a fury.'

Nicholas shook his head. 'I may not know much about the Fey, Shaman, but I do know the stories. I know that one Black King went Blind and the Shamans and Warders picked another to succeed him, from a different line. I know that an entire family who would have inherited the Black Throne was slaughtered almost a century later. I know that you have provisions for this sort of thing. Jewel said Rugar was Blind. You are here, talking with me. Obviously you think something is wrong.'

'You know the stories?' the Shaman said, her voice thrumming. 'You do not know the stories. You *do* not know the stories. Only one Black family turned on itself. The deaths you mentioned were in that family. Three thousand people died after the Black Queen and her family killed each other. *Three thousand.* It was said to be a raging madness that made fathers turn upon sons, sons upon mothers, mothers upon daughters. And it happened throughout the Fey Empire. Only one in ten survived. The Fey Empire was small in those days. Now it covers over half the world. Do you want to be responsible for such a slaughter?'

'I don't believe old myths,' Nicholas said. 'If I believed in myths, I would not offer our Rocaan to you.'

The Shaman stopped, her eyes glittering. Her hair had stopped shimmering. Now it was a soft, brittle white. 'What fate do you tempt?'

'The Rocaan is Beloved of God,' Nicholas said.

'You tempt your own God?' the Shaman asked.

'I have never met my God,' Nicholas said. 'In the last week, He has taken my father and my wife from me. He leaves me with a child who cannot hold her form and another who has no real mind. He lets me

312

rule a nation that may not survive another day. If I will gamble for the lives of two cultures versus an angry God, I will save the lives.'

The flames in the fireplace had died down. The Shaman's hands had let go of each other and were clenched, her knuckles almost as white as her hair.

Her silence felt like a judgment.

Nicholas's heart was pounding so hard he thought she would be able to hear it. But he didn't move either.

Finally, she stood. 'You have courage that I lack.'

He stood too. 'It's your lack of courage that will kill us all.'

She placed one fist against her stomach. 'I can See your daughter, your almost-grown daughter, standing in that garden, holding the hand of her brother, their dark heads glistening in the sunlight. I hear birds and I know that all is right in our world. But I don't know how we get to that place. I can't See next week or even next year. I know Rugar's father lives, and I know he has not abandoned Blue Isle. And because I know those two things, I am unwilling to risk even the least of the Black King's family. I am unwilling to strike the tinder that will light the wrong flame. And if that means I condemn us to a decade of battle, so be it. Better a hundred lives than a hundred thousand.'

'Better two lives than a hundred,' Nicholas said.

'Your lack of belief gives you such certainty,' the Shaman said. 'It is a certainty I cannot afford.' She bowed her head to him, then walked to the door.

As she put her hand on the handle, he said, 'I will avenge my father.'

She rested her forehead against the door for a brief moment. Then she said, 'But first, you will avenge your wife.'

Thirty-Eight

Burden was sitting at the Meeting Rock, waiting. Shadowlands was nearly full. Since Jewel's death, most of the Fey remained inside. The Fey from the Settlement were trying to see if their families would take them back into the cabins. The other Fey appeared to be waiting for Rugar.

Burden had seen Rugar go into the Warders' cabin, and then leave, taking Touched with him. They were heading toward the Domicile. Burden had been about to give up waiting when the Circle Door opened and a man slipped through. He was wearing an Islander face. It shimmered and became his own for a brief moment as he stepped through the door, then it returned to the illusion: round eyes, round cheeks, blond hair.

'I was expecting you last night,' Burden said.

The illusion shimmered and vanished. Veil stood before Burden, slender, dark, almost a shadow himself. Spies had a wispy quality that placed them in the same category as Dream Riders and other creatures of the night. Almost invisible, barely existing, with little personality of their own, Spies had only the power to create a simple illusion around themselves. They could change their appearance and the unwary wouldn't notice. The watchful would see the dark eyes peering through, the Spy's real height, the lips that didn't quite move with the words. Burden hated the Spies among the Fey, but this time he needed them.

And he might need them again.

'I couldn't get away,' Veil said. His voice was as shadowy as he was.

'Right,' Burden said. Spies never had trouble escaping a situation. They established their illusions and left.

'No,' he said. 'I couldn't. I had to see what the Islanders would do.'

Burden crossed his legs and rested his arms on his thighs. 'I don't care what they would do,' he said. 'I want to know how the murderer died.'

'He didn't,' Veil said, and cringed.

'He didn't?' Burden made his voice cold. The plan was simple and foolproof. Jewel had told him about the Charmed boy years ago.

Burden had gone to the Domestics to get the boy's name. Once he had that, he was able to send a message which the boy received and then the boy left. No one would question an Islander in the Tabernacle.

'The murderer woke up, tossed poison on the boy, and the spell was revealed.'

Burden pushed himself off the Meeting Block. The gray mist of Shadowlands swirled around him. He hated this place. It was like being in a perpetual fog.

'Spells are never revealed,' he said.

'This one was. I saw it.'

'You saw it?' Burden asked. 'Don't tell me you had enough courage to go into the Tabernacle.'

Veil raised his chin and stretched himself to his full height. He looked like a shadow at twilight, long and black and too thin. 'You told me to report. I had to be able to see to do that.'

'You went into the Tabernacle and came out to tell of it.'

Veil nodded. 'I pretended to be one of their lower religious ones, the Auds. I watched the boy climb the wall, then I went in myself. I went to the proper floor, dismissed another man there, and said I would take his place as guard. So I did. When he was gone, I went to the door, but by then, there was a horrible green glow. I heard the murderer run toward the door, and I could barely get to the stairs where I was supposed to be.'

'So you saw nothing,' Burden said. Incompetence again. If he had known when he signed on this mission almost six years before that he would be surrounded by incompetence, he would never have come.

Although, in truth, he would have. He was only seventeen, then, and deeply in love with Jewel. He would have followed her anywhere.

If I am going to choose a non-magical king, Burden, I will choose someone whose blood will enhance my line.

He had discovered his own magic years too late. Too late to even tell her.

'I saw enough,' Veil snapped. 'I saw the murderer run out of the room, and he smelled of that poison. I saw the green glow. I heard him describe what happened when the poison touched the boy. It startled him. The spell became visible and frightened them both.'

'So you escaped, and waited a day to come see me?' Burden asked.

Veil shook his head. 'I knew you wouldn't believe me, so I followed the boy. He went to a lord who took him to the King. After they saw the King, I heard them talking. They think that the poison broke the spell's hold on the boy. He said he came to himself when the water hit him.'

Damn Rugar. Damn them all for failing to find the secret to that poison. It had ruined everything. Burden sighed, folded his hands together, and pressed his thumbs against his lips. This plan had seemed so simple. So perfect. No one would have blamed the Fey. He could have avenged Jewel and kept his own people out of it.

He let his hands drop. 'The man still goes free, then.'

'No one is doing anything to the murderer.'

'They approve?'

Veil shrugged. 'Most Islanders seem to. The leaders appear to be paralyzed.'

Like Rugar was. The shock was too great for all of them. That would give Burden another chance to act.

'I can't use the boy again, can I?'

Veil shook his head. 'They know now.'

'But you got into the Tabernacle with no problems.'

'I looked like one of them. I made myself into a lesser one so that no one would notice at me.'

'And the boy got in as well.'

'They don't appear to be guarding the murderer. It seems, from talk I overheard, that not all of his followers agree with what he did.'

The Tabernacle was easy to get into. That much was clear. 'Not all of them agreed,' Burden said, more as a stall. Rugar would do nothing about Jewel's death. Rugar might even have maneuvered it, just as Rugar attempted to maneuver Rugar's death.

'No,' Veil said. 'They seemed to think it was wrong to kill Jewel.'

'Because of Jewel?'

Veil shook his head. 'Because it happened in a religious ceremony.'

Such a thing was only logical. Jewel hadn't been thinking when she planned to be part of that ceremony. At least the child had survived. Burden would leave the child with Nicholas.

For now.

'So the Tabernacle isn't well guarded, and the murderer's own people disagree with him,' Burden said. 'We can no longer use our boy, but I promised Jewel that she would not remain unavenged.'

'I think that we should talk with Rugar about this,' Veil said.

'If Rugar wanted to get revenge for his daughter's death, he would have done so on the day she died. No, Rugar only thinks of Rugar. I'm the only one who thinks of Jewel.' Burden paced around the rock. The gray mist was so thick that he couldn't see his feet. The Weather Sprites should give up their experiments in Shadowlands. No matter what they tried, they produced fog.

'You could get back into the Tabernacle,' Burden said.

Veil's jaw worked before he spoke. 'I – Spies can't kill.'

'Life would be so much easier if they could, wouldn't it?' Burden asked. He wasn't going to let Veil intimidate him simply because Veil wanted no part of this plan. He needed Veil. He needed others as well. 'If we send in two spies to guard the murderer's door, the rest of us could enter from the balcony, as the boy did.'

'The rest of us?' Veil said.

Burden nodded. 'A Dream Rider and as many Infantry as I can gather, maybe a few Foot Soldiers, don't you think?'

'Riders can't hold through torture. I saw that in Nye. The pain breaks the spell,' Veil said.

'Too bad,' Burden said. 'Because the man should suffer. Jewel did.'

'You could take him from the Tabernacle and bring him here.'

'Too risky,' Burden said. 'He's too well known and too many Islanders like what he did. We'd lose our troops if we did that. Better to attack quickly, kill him the old-fashioned way, and escape.'

'Would you go?' Veil asked.

Burden stopped pacing. The mist swirled around him. 'I sent a boy the last time, a boy who was spelled and who should have done exactly what I told him to. He did not. We only have one more chance.'

'If that,' Veil said. His voice was shaking. None of the Fey liked the Tabernacle. They were all frightened of it.

'Then we shall take only necessary risks. We will not leave until the murderer is dead.'

Veil ran a hand over his slicked back hair. 'We might all die,' he said. 'The poison is everywhere in that place.'

Just the mention of poison brought the smell of burning flesh back to Burden. He had seen so many friends die from one drop of the poison. So many friends.

And Jewel.

Burden clasped his hands behind his back, like Shima, his former Infantry captain, used to do when she wanted the unit's attention. 'We used to face death every day, or have you forgotten that, Veil?'

'I haven't forgotten,' he said. 'I went to the Tabernacle for you.'

'And you'll do so again,' Burden said. 'Only you're not going for me. You're going for the Black King's granddaughter.'

'Jewel doesn't care if we die for her,' Veil said.

'No,' Burden said. 'But I do.'

Thirty-Nine

Arianna slept in her crib, tiny fist pressed against her cheek, her breathing soft and regular. Solanda sat on the windowsill, her long legs extending to the floor, the robe she wore warm. The sill was not comfortable when she was Fey, but she had no choice. Arianna was the most playful baby she had ever seen. The girl Shifted on a moment's notice, and not all of her Shifts were part of the same animal. Mostly she had Shifted into a cat, like Solanda, but once, she had mimicked the tree outside her window, and another time she had tried fire.

Solanda had stopped that one quickly, but not before the baby blanket was scorched. She had sent the nurse in search of another blanket, and the nurse had brought back Domestic weaves which Jewel must have gotten for the lump. The weaves kept Arianna calmer, but didn't stop her from experimenting.

No wonder so many Shifters died in their first weeks of life. Their own mothers strangled them from frustration.

Fortunately the late morning was clear and cool. The air was refreshing. Solanda had let the fire burn out, and she had turned the crib so that Arianna only saw blank wall when she was alone.

Although Solanda didn't know if that was the answer either. She worried that Arianna would turn to stone if given the chance.

But at least Solanda had a momentary reprieve. The nurse and the lump had left the nursery, to visit the garden and enjoy the sunshine. Solanda had let them go. She could only be feline so long and pretend that no one else existed. At times she absolutely had to be alone.

With Arianna asleep, this was as alone as she would get.

Solanda leaned her head against the chill stone of the window frame. The depth of her own loyalty surprised her. Normally, once the frustration of any task started, she left. But although the frustration, the hours, and the confinement wearied her, she had no real desire to leave. Her destiny was tied to this child. She would stay at Arianna's side as long as necessary.

Suddenly the door opened. Solanda was on her feet beside the crib almost before the door swung against the wall.

'You have no right –' she started and then stopped herself.

The Shaman stood at the door.

'No right to be here?' The Shaman asked. She looked twice as old as she had a few days before. Jewel's death had affected them all.

'Forgive me,' Solanda said. 'I didn't know it was you.' The Shaman's presence had Solanda's heart pounding. The Shaman never left Shadowlands without a good reason, never came visiting without notice, never appeared suddenly for fear of her own life.

'I came to see the child,' the Shaman said. She entered the room and closed the door. The Shaman's walk was slow, her skin ashen. Perhaps more was happening here than Jewel's death.

'Are you all right?' Solanda asked.

The Shaman smiled. 'I'm fine, child, and relieved you are here with Arianna.'

Solanda almost asked how the Shaman knew the baby's name, then paused. Of course the Shaman knew. The Shaman knew everything.

The Shaman peered into the crib. Arianna looked like a little innocent, docile and undemanding. Her cheeks were flushed with sleep, her long lashes resting on her dark tan skin. She was one of the most beautiful children Solanda had ever seen – and Solanda had seen a lot of children over the years.

'She's stunning,' the Shaman said.

'When she's asleep,' Solanda said.

'Chafing already?' The Shaman had a bit of judgment in her tone. Didn't any of the Fey believe Solanda could be constant? She could. She could do any task they asked of her. The problem was that they never really asked.

'I can't leave her side,' Solanda said. 'She Shifts at whim.'

The Shaman tucked the blanket under the baby's chin. 'A morning or two to yourself wouldn't matter,' she said.

'It would,' Solanda said, 'if she Shifted while I was gone.'

'You worry too much, child. Shifters have grown without round-the-clock care.'

Shifters had grown. Of course they had. But they weren't like Arianna. Solanda didn't know how she would convince the Shaman of that. The Shaman clearly wasn't listening to what Solanda was saying.

The Shaman's gnarled fingers played with the baby blanket. Arianna was so tiny. It was so hard to believe something that small could totally control another person's life.

'I don't complain too much,' Solanda said. She walked to the corner, picked up the burned blanket and tossed it at the Shaman. The Shaman caught it with her other hand. She gazed at it for a moment, noted the brown-tinged holes through the middle and ran her fingers

319

along them. 'Last night, she was fire. A day before that, she was half cat – the wrong half. A day before that, water. She Shifts whenever she's awake, and she does so based on what she sees. You and I may think she is too young for this, but the fact is that she does it. The Islander nurse and I guard her. I can only sleep when the nurse is in the room.'

The Shaman let the burned blanket fall to the floor. She bent over the crib until her face was as close to Arianna's as she dared. She touched the baby's cheek. Arianna cooed, and brushed at the Shaman's finger with her small hand.

'Don't wake her,' Solanda said softly.

The Shaman stood, wonder on her ancient face. 'She hums with magick. It flows around and through her as if she were the bed for a river.'

'Please don't give her that image,' Solanda said tiredly. 'She might try it.'

The Shaman walked to the window. Her back was bowed. She looked out. 'The garden extends around the palace?' She sounded surprised.

'It's large,' Solanda said, wondering at the Shaman's change of subject.

The Shaman placed her hands flat on the sill and stared out, much as Solanda had been doing the last few days. 'It seems that the wild magic here is stronger than we thought.'

'I know,' Solanda said.

'It will require a deep commitment from you, one that will last until this child can control her Shifts and maybe beyond.'

Solanda said nothing. She didn't have to. She had already made the commitment in her heart.

'You cannot allow this child into Shadowlands,' the Shaman said.

'I may not be able to control that,' Solanda said. 'She already has a mind of her own.'

'Never,' the Shaman said. 'It will ruin us all.'

'If she can't go there,' Solanda said, 'then I need help here. I need a Domestic, someone to assist me. The Islander nurse tries, but what if I'm asleep and Arianna decides to become fire again?'

The Shaman sighed and pulled away from the window. 'You will have to trust in the Powers and Mysteries,' she said. 'They gave you to Arianna. You are up to the task.'

'I did not ask for this duty,' Solanda said.

'You were destined for it the moment you boarded a ship for Blue Isle,' the Shaman said.

'I had no choice in boarding,' Solanda said.

The Shaman stared at her for a moment. 'No,' she said. 'I suppose you did not. But you need to make choices now.'

Solanda shook her head. 'You just told me I had no choice.'

The Shaman leaned against the sill as Solanda had been doing earlier. 'We are not speaking of Arianna now. We're speaking of Rugar. You can no longer do as he says.'

Solanda smoothed the hair on Arianna's forehead. The girl's skin was warm with sleep. 'He doesn't know I'm here. I won't come back when he calls.'

'I know, child, but it is more than that. He will try to steal Arianna to Shadowlands as he did her brother. He cannot succeed.'

'Why can't she go to Shadowlands? She is part Fey.'

The Shaman stared at Solanda for a moment. A flush built in Solanda's cheeks. She had asked a rude question of the Shaman. The Shaman often spoke in riddles. It was the duty of the Fey to abide by those riddles, not to question the riddles, but to live with the future that the Shaman spoke of, to allow the Shaman to lead in the small, yet important things.

Then the Shaman reached up and pulled the tapestry over the window. She went to the other two windows and did the same, leaving the room in darkness. Only the glow of the fireplace provided any light at all.

The Shaman walked toward it and sat beside it, her face in profile. 'I am a young Shaman,' she said, 'far from my peers and learning as best I can. Jewel died because I was not clear to her father about his role in the future of the Fey. I will be as clear to you as I know how. On some of this I do not have clarity. I have only knowledge.'

Solanda stayed beside the crib, unwilling to leave Arianna unguarded in the darkness. Once, in a Shift, Arianna had made no noise at all.

'Arianna is a Shape-Shifter, born to a Visionary. Such a birth is rare, but would be thought part of the Mysteries if not for two other things. Her brother had his first Vision this year, and nearly died with his mother, so their Link was strong. He was saved by the child you rescued.'

'Coulter?' Solanda asked. She remembered the trail of grief she had followed, the trail Coulter had left when he was not much older than Arianna, a trail he hoped would guide his parents to him. His parents had died the same day he was rescued by a kind old woman whose heart Solanda shattered. One of the few completely cruel acts Solanda had ever committed, and the only one she regretted.

'The boy has the ability to Enchant.'

'But he's not Fey.'

'Exactly,' the Shaman said. 'We have traveled halfway across the world before we meet a people like our own.'

'But they can't Shift. They have no Doppelgängers or Warders.'

'They have no need,' the Shaman said. 'They are the most protected people we ever encountered. They only had to defend themselves against each other. They did that through their religion.'

'The poison,' Solanda said.

'And their god, the Roca.'

'He isn't a god,' Solanda said. 'But a man they claim was Beloved of God.'

'Who ascended, but still lived.'

'Like a Power,' Solanda said as the realization sank in.

'Which creates a Mystery we may never solve.'

The baby sighed and rolled over in her sleep. Solanda kept a finger on the baby's shoulder, to make certain nothing changed while she wasn't paying attention.

'But if they're like us,' she said, 'then this child is not unusual.'

The Shaman bowed her head. 'If the races intermingle, we will have even more powerful children.'

'So we should be encouraging that,' Solanda said. 'We are always to follow the magic.'

'As long as we have the approval of the Black Throne,' the Shaman said.

'The Black King is in Nye. We don't need his approval.'

'Then the approval falls to his son.'

Her words hung in the room. A log snapped in the dying fire and sparks scattered like red Wisps.

'Rugar doesn't understand this, does he?' Solanda asked quietly.

'Rugar is a warrior,' the Shaman said. Her hair caught the firelight like cobwebs. She might be a young Shaman, but she was an old woman, with an old body that was carrying the weight of Fey on its shoulders.

'Rugar has always been a warrior,' Solanda said. 'But you no longer trust him.'

'I –' the Shaman's voice broke. She turned her head away from Solanda, toward the fire. 'I never trusted him. Never. I only came along because I could not get out of it. I was the youngest of the Shaman, and the Black King decreed that one had to go on this trip.'

'Do you think he knew that Rugar was Blind?'

'I think he knew that we would be trapped on Blue Isle,' the Shaman said.

Solanda shuddered. No wonder Rugar had opposed Jewel's travel here. No wonder he had let Rugar go so easily. No wonder he had insisted that Solanda come as well. 'Does he know, then, of Arianna?'

'I can only guess,' the Shaman said. 'And my guess is that he could not See past the loss of Rugar. If the Black King had known of the magick here, he would have come himself.'

'But to send his own son away, to almost certain death ...' Solanda shook her head. 'It seems wrong somehow.'

'It's been done before.'

The Shaman spoke softly. It had only been done a handful of times before, each time to prevent the Blood turning on itself. Murder within the Black King's family, his legitimate family, was unspeakable.

'You don't think Rugar's crazy enough to kill for the Black Throne, do you?' Solanda asked.

'What I think doesn't matter,' the Shaman said. 'What the Black King thinks is all that is important.'

Solanda longed to pick up Arianna and hold her tightly. Instead, she wrapped her forefinger around the baby's fist. 'So Rugar truly didn't care when we thought Gift died. And all he wants Arianna for is her power.'

'And what she can give him.' The Shaman folded her hands together and looked away from the fire. The side of her face nearest Solanda was in darkness. The Shaman appeared to be a shadow of herself, surrounded by a halo of light.

'But if he's Blind, she can't give him anything,' Solanda said.

'She's a baby. He can make her what he wants. That's the power of adulthood. If he has that powerful little soul to mold, her brother who is already his toy, and the Islander Enchanter, he will have more power than I do, more power than anyone else on this Isle, and probably more power than his father. Even now, he may have too much power. But that baby would make matters worse.'

'So let me steal Gift from Shadowlands,' Solanda said. 'Nicholas will care for him.'

The Shaman shook her head. 'Jewel should have stolen the child back, but she never Saw what happened. I Saw it, but I did nothing. Another of my mistakes. Gift has lived three years among the Fey. He is Fey now. All my Visions of him show that he cannot leave Shadowlands.'

Solanda was silent. It always felt wrong to be near the lump. It would have been nice to tell Nicholas, to bring the real child here. But if the Shaman said Gift belonged in Shadowlands, then in Shadowlands he would stay.

The Shaman apparently took Solanda's silence for disapproval. 'The boy has already given his Visions to his grandfather,' the Shaman said softly. 'We have no idea what Rugar has learned. All we can hope for is that he never holds Arianna, that she never speaks to him, that she never even sees him.'

The baby stirred, as if the words had disturbed her. They certainly disturbed Solanda. 'Shaman are supposed to support the Black Throne,' Solanda said. 'You should be helping Rugar.'

'Rugar's father cast him from the Black Throne. Rugar lost all of my support when he allowed Jewel to die. My support now goes to the heirs to the Throne.'

'Jewel's brothers are in line,' Solanda said.

'Jewel's brothers don't stand a chance if the Black King learns of Arianna's powers,' the Shaman said. 'Jewel had more potential than anyone born into Rugad's family. Jewel had no powers at all when compared with her own children.'

'She made the right choice, then, when she married Nicholas.'

The Shaman nodded. 'Who knew how her Vision led her, but it led her to the best place possible. If Rugar had let King Alexander live, we would already be in a better world.'

'Jewel could never have tended this child,' Solanda said.

'You never got along with Jewel,' the Shaman said.

Enough. Solanda had heard enough. She had been giving everything to Arianna. 'I have had to Shift twice in order to save this child. Jewel could never have done that. Without you, without the Domestics, and with only Island healers, Arianna would have died in the middle of her birth and you know that.'

'Are you saying Jewel's death was the wish of the Powers?'

Solanda paused. She wasn't certain if she was saying that. She thought for a moment, rubbing her thumb against the soft skin of Arianna's wrist.

'No,' Solanda finally said. 'I'm saying that the Powers decreed that we could have Jewel or Arianna. We were not allowed to make that choice. But Rugar made it for us.'

'Do you think he made the right choice?' The Shaman sounded as if she were testing Solanda.

Solanda bent over and kissed Arianna's head. If Rugar hadn't made that choice, Arianna would not exist. But if Rugar hadn't made that choice, Solanda would still have her freedom.

'How do you value one life over another?' Solanda asked. 'Jewel is dead. We cannot change that. Arianna is alive. We must make sure she remains that way.'

'Exactly,' the Shaman said. 'We must forever keep Rugar from this child.'

Arianna's grip had tightened on Solanda's finger. She wished it

324

weren't so dark. She couldn't tell if the baby was awake or not. But the Shaman had closed down the room so that no one would hear them talk, and to make conversation easier. Confidences were always easy in the dark.

Solanda bowed her head. 'You know that I swore my life to Rugar,' she said.

'I've always thought that a hasty and ill-conceived act,' the Shaman said.

'But you knew?' Solanda asked.

'I suspected. A woman of your talent does not spy easily. Nor does she come on foolish missions without just cause.'

'If he comes for Arianna —'

'I trust you will tell him to leave,' the Shaman said.

Solanda's thumb kept moving on Arianna's soft skin. The one worry she had, the one she had never spoken of, had to come out now. The Shaman would tell her what to do. 'He owns me,' Solanda said.

'Does he?' The Shaman turned in her chair, leaning toward Solanda. Now her entire body was in shadow. 'It seems to me to be a feline concept, this concept of owning. Fey do not own each other.'

'They do when they vow. The Black King owns you.'

'The Black King protects me, along with the other Shaman. It is a different arrangement.'

Solanda nodded. She had been very young when she pledged herself to Rugar. In the beginning it hadn't seemed like much. But now, it was everything. It affected her entire life.

'You can't have loyalties to two people,' the Shaman said. 'Either you are loyal to Arianna or you are loyal to Rugar.'

'Rugar saved my life,' Solanda said.

'And you saved Arianna's. I think the debt is repaid.'

'But I pledged him my loyalty for life,' Solanda said.

'Have you given it to him?' the Shaman asked.

'For decades.'

'Then declare the debt paid. Move on.'

'But will the Powers allow that?'

'The Powers allow nothing and everything,' the Shaman said. 'You tell me you've saved Arianna's life a dozen times since her birth. Rugar saved you once. Does Arianna owe you her life?'

'Arianna is too young to make that decision. I owe her my powers.' Solanda held the baby fist tightly.

'Based on what? She is too young to hold anything over you.'

'We are sisters under the skin,' Solanda said.

'You and Rugar are not.'

'But I wouldn't be here without him,' Solanda said.

'Really?' the Shaman asked. 'Or did he make it seem that way?'

Solanda frowned. She remembered that afternoon – the dogs, the soldiers, the blood everywhere. And Rugar swooping down like a god to save her.

Someone had ordered the soldiers into place.

Someone had brought the dogs.

Rugar?

He would have known how to gain a Shape-Shifter's loyalty. In those days his Vision was strong. He might have even known the plan would work.

'He wasn't that devious then,' Solanda said.

'Rugar was devious from the beginning,' the Shaman said. 'He is part of the Black King's family. None of them work in a straight-forward fashion.'

'Such accusations,' Solanda said. 'This babe is too young to be devious.'

'Is she?' the Shaman asked. 'She has tied you to her more effectively than any other being has ever been able to.'

'Her mind isn't formed yet. How can she manipulate me?'

'Coulter's mind wasn't formed yet either, but he left a trail for his parents to follow that was so clear you were able to pick it up a year later.'

'Are you saying I shouldn't trust Arianna?' Solanda couldn't be-lieve that. How could a person not trust a newborn?

'I'm saying love her. Trust her. And keep her away from her grand-father. From both of her grandfathers – Rugar and Rugad.'

'And if I can't?'

The Shaman stood. She seemed taller than she had when she came into the room. 'Then the destruction that follows will be on your shoulders.'

Forty

Lord Stowe flanked him on one side, Monte on the other. They wouldn't let him into the Tabernacle alone. Nicholas thought it odd; he was King, yet he was taking orders from his own men. They threatened to keep him prisoner in the palace if he didn't listen to them, and by the looks on their faces, he realized they were completely serious.

Rather than risk another schism within his community, he allowed them to come with him.

He was actually glad for the protection.

The gates to the Tabernacle were open. The place looked harmless in the daytime. Hard to believe the substance that killed his wife was made within.

The courtyard was covered with painted tile depicting scenes from the Roca's life, and from Rocaanism's history. Nicholas had never bothered to study them. He had never bothered to spend much time on Rocaanism at all. Matthias always saw Nicholas's disinterest as something aimed against the church, but in his boyhood, Nicholas had seen no point in understanding the church. He had figured it was constant, believed it would never change. He had not thought that something like this would happen.

Nicholas's cape fluttered behind him as he walked. They had left their horses outside the gate – Stowe believed the more surprise they had the better – and they walked the rest of the way. Nicholas's boots clicked on the tile. His sword slapped against his leg, and his favorite dirk was tucked in his right boot. He wore his finest linen shirt and the best breeches he owned.

This was an outfit that Jewel had loved.

He needed her beside him for this, even if it was just in spirit.

As they passed the Auds by the main door, the Auds gasped. 'Highness,' one of the Auds said. 'We need to announce you.'

Nicholas ignored him.

'You'll announce no one,' Monte said.

The inside of the Tabernacle was dark. Candles burned on tables, and the antechamber smelled of wax. Swords hung, point down, from the walls. The ornate chairs beside the tables were meant for decoration, not sitting. Some of the chairs still bore the damage the Fey had done to them years before. The tiles below Nicholas's feet also bore scars of that day, but those scars were seared in from burning Fey flesh.

A Danite blocked the entrance into the rest of the Tabernacle. His hands were pressed together in a praying position in front of his chest. 'Highness,' the Danite said, and bowed. 'We were not expecting you.'

'Where's the Rocaan?' Stowe asked, leaving off the Danite's honorific.

'The Rocaan is seeing no one. Perhaps Elder Porciluna –'

'The Rocaan will see the King,' Nicholas snapped.

The Danite bobbed his head. 'Of course. He's in the worship room. Allow me to lead you.'

The Danite took them through corridors that wound around the servant's chapel, past portraits of the Rocaans, and down an ancient stairway. There was no railing, and the stone walls crumbled as Nicholas placed a hand on them. Torches burned from their pegs, and only the Aud guards at the base of the stairs reassured him that this was not a dungeon.

The air smelled musty, and an old water trail limed the floor. The Auds leaning against the door stood at attention when they saw the Danite.

'The Rocaan asked not to be disturbed,' the first guard said to the Danite.

'Then the Rocaan will not get his wish,' Nicholas said, pushing past Stowe and Monte, past the Danite, to the guards. 'Open the door.'

'He wished –'

'It's the King, fool.' The Danite's whisper echoed in the small space.

The Aud gave the Danite a panicked look. The other Aud pushed on the door handle and shoved the door open. Stowe grabbed Nicholas's arm so that he wouldn't go through first, but Nicholas shook him off.

'Matthias,' Nicholas said as he walked through the door, 'You're a coward.'

Matthias was kneeling in front of a small altar. A ceremonial sword hung from one wall. The slitted windows had a view of the Cardidas. This room must have been where the old Rocaan had first seen the Fey.

Matthias turned at the sound of Nicholas's voice. 'This is a worship room,' Matthias said. 'Not for unbelievers.'

'Then I suggest you leave, *holy* man,' Nicholas said. He glanced at Stowe and Monte, who flanked him again. 'Wait for me outside.'

'Sire, he could be dangerous,' Monte said.

'Then let him be. Wait for me.'

'Yes, sire,' Stowe said. He and Monte backed out. The door closed behind them.

The room was chill and the smell of mildew was strong here. Matthias's blond curls hung limply around his face. He looked as if he had not slept for days.

He braced one hand on the altar and slowly got to his feet. 'You have no place here.'

'I have more place than you,' Nicholas said. He put a hand on the hilt of his sword. 'I could run you through now and the entire Kingdom would think I was justified.'

'Would they?' Matthias asked. 'Too many believe that you should never have united with the Fey. Look at your son.'

'You should see my daughter. She is more powerful than any Fey,' Nicholas said.

Matthias frowned. 'Daughter?'

Nicholas nodded. 'Yes, daughter. The Fey saved the child, even though they couldn't save Jewel. And if you so much as touch her, I will have your head.'

'Idle threats, Nicholas,' Matthias said. He raised himself to his full height, nearly a head taller than Nicholas. Matthias was older – Nicholas's father's age – but still young enough to do harm if he had to.

'I don't make idle threats,' Nicholas said. 'I'm in no position to.'

'The child will need to be Blessed in the Roca,' Matthias said.

'And my wife needed burial, but I would not let any of your kind near her.'

Matthias crossed his arms in front of his chest. He walked to the window, deliberately turning his back, as if taunting Nicholas. If the window were just a bit wider, Nicholas would have reacted the taunt and pushed Matthias through it.

'You're free now, Nicky, to choose the right kind of wife.' Matthias spoke softly.

'Are you telling me you killed her on purpose?' Nicholas asked.

'No,' Matthias said. 'It was God's will that she died. I'm merely saying that now you can go back to the business of governing Blue Isle. Set her children aside, and do the right thing.'

'I was doing the right thing,' Nicholas said. 'Just as I am doing the right thing now. I came to warn you, Matthias.'

'You need me, Nicholas. Threatening me is not constructive.'

'If I thought it best that you die, I'd kill you without warning,' Nicholas said. He reached into his boot and pulled his dirk. The blade glistened in the candlelight. He walked to Matthias and pushed the tip of the blade into his back. 'I could kill you now.'

'Then do it,' Matthias said. 'You'd guarantee that your friends the Fey would take over Blue Isle.'

Nicholas's hand was shaking. So simple. One quick movement and Matthias would be dead.

But Nicholas had more to think of than himself. He had the Isle. He had Arianna. What would happen to her if he killed the Rocaan? Most of the Islanders would not understand his action, and they would turn against him.

They would turn against her.

'I came here,' he said, leaving the tip of the knife in place, 'to prove to you that I am a better Rocaanist than you are.'

'By forgiving me?' Matthias's voice held disdain. 'You can't forgive me when I did you a favor, Nicky.'

Nicholas tightened his grip on his dirk. He clenched his teeth and thought of Arianna. He had to be subtle. He had to take care of things in a different manner than he would if he were not King.

'You did me no favor, Matthias. I loved my wife, and my marriage to her brought peace to Blue Isle. We were going to work together to find my father's killer. You ruined all that.'

Matthias started to speak, but Nicholas grabbed his arm, bracing himself.

'It's my turn,' Nicholas said. He stood so close that he could feel the river breeze through the window. Matthias's curls trembled in the wind. 'I am going to prove to you that I am a good Rocaanist because I know that you killed her, Matthias. I know that you deliberately covered that cloth with holy water. You don't believe in God's will. You don't believe in God. The Fey frighten you, and Jewel frightened you. You got revenge that afternoon, for my father who was one of your few friends, and for the old Rocaan who put you in this position in the first place. You figured you could use Jewel's death to warn the Fey, to remind them that you had the power to kill them.'

Matthias remained completely still. His long angular body was pressed against the window sill, and he stared straight ahead. Nicholas's grip on Matthias's arm was so tight that Nicholas's fingers actually hurt. It took all of Nicholas's strength to keep his right hand steady, to keep the dirk pressed lightly against Matthias's back.

'The Fey have tried to kill you once,' Nicholas said.

'The boy was Islander.'

'The boy was once a Fey prisoner. The Fey have many tricks, Matthias. They have targeted you. They know that you acted without my approval. They will succeed. They killed my father and he was well guarded. You use Auds, and the Elders are opposed to protecting you, saying you defiled a religious ceremony. Which you did.'

330

'It was an accident,' Matthias said.

'I thought it was God's will,' Nicholas said.

'Sometimes they are the same thing.' Matthias's voice quavered.

'I'm sure the faithful would love to hear you say that,' Nicholas said. 'Unlike you, I will wait as the Words Written and Unwritten bid us to do. I will allow you to receive your punishment after you die, when the Roca, the Holy One, and God show you all the pain you have caused in this world. See? I do remember the teachings. And unlike you, I act on them.'

Matthias blinked. Once. It was the first time since Nicholas had put the knife to his back. 'Then why are you here?'

'If not to kill you?' Nicholas pulled back on Matthias's arm just a little. 'You have no faith in anything, do you, Matthias?'

Matthias swallowed, but did not reply.

'I'm here to warn you, Matthias.' Nicholas spoke softly, putting his mouth near Matthias's ear. 'Because of your actions, we may go to war again. We need holy water. We need the Secrets in order to survive. See, unlike you, I believe God gave us holy water and the Secrets so that we could use them to help us become better people, to help us resolve our differences quickly instead of prolonging them through needless acts of violence.'

'Spare me the speeches, Nicky,' Matthias said.

'I am your King, now,' Nicholas said. 'Only my father and Jewel had the right to call me Nicky. You may call me Your Highness or Sire. To use my given name without my permission is a crime against the state.'

'I thought you were going to be a good and kind ruler,' Matthias said.

'I thought so too. But you killed any chance of that days ago,' Nicholas said.

'Just tell me what you want.' Matthias sounded brave but his entire body was trembling. The point of the knife had pierced his clothing and was probably scratching skin.

'I want you to think about this,' Nicholas said. 'The Words Written and Unwritten say that the Rocaan's first thoughts should be of God. His second should be of his people, and his third should be of the heavens themselves.'

'Don't quote the Words to me,' Matthias said.

'Someone needs to.' Nicholas pushed slightly on the knife. Matthias straightened. A small bit of pain, then, nothing more. 'Because you're not thinking of anyone except yourself, Matthias. If you thought of God, you wouldn't use him as an excuse for murder. If you thought of the heavens, you would trust in the Roca's heir in this world. And if you thought of the people whose lives are entrusted to you, you would share the Secrets as the fiftieth Rocaan did, in case you were killed.'

'If I had done that, you would have killed me by now.'

The hilt of the knife bit into Nicholas's palm. One quick twist of the wrist and Matthias would be mortally wounded. They were alone in the worship room.

Jewel would do it in a heartbeat.

But Jewel had been Fey. Vengeance was her way. It was not Nicholas's, at least not directly. If he killed Matthias, he would create more problems than he solved.

'No,' Nicholas said. 'The Fey will kill you for me. The question is will you leave us with no protection when you die or will you ensure our future, take care of your people as you were supposed to?'

'You sound so certain of what I should do,' Matthias said.

'I am certain,' Nicholas replied.

'Has the Holy One spoken to you? Do you hear the still, small voice?' Matthias's tone almost mocked him.

Nicholas held Matthias against his chest, twisting the tip of the knife slightly as if he were about to core an apple. Matthias stiffened with pain.

'Your wife's death was God's will,' Matthias said.

One movement. One simple movement and Matthias would live no longer.

'As is yours,' Nicholas said.

'Then go ahead.' Matthias's trembling had increased. 'Kill me.'

'The Words forbid it.' Nicholas let Matthias go. 'And unlike you, I follow the Words.'

Matthias turned, the movement a bit stiff as he favored his back. His face was pale.

'The Fey will kill you,' Nicholas said. 'The question is when.'

'They can't get me if I stay in the Tabernacle.'

'Don't be so certain,' Nicholas said. 'They've been here before. They also have other ways, as that boy showed you. You will die and I won't protect you.'

'What protection can you offer from those creatures?' Matthias actually sounded hopeful, as if he believed that Nicholas would save him.

As if Nicholas would want to.

'None,' Nicholas said. 'If they succeed in killing you, it will be God's will. But if you die with the Secrets untold, you will destroy the religion you were sworn to protect.'

Matthias's right hand slid to his back, rubbing the spot where

Nicholas had turned the knife. 'And whom would you suggest I tell the Secrets to?' Matthias asked. 'The Elders want me overthrown.'

Nicholas's dirk had blood on it. He continued to hold it, the weight a comfort in his hand. 'A schism in the Tabernacle,' he said, mimicking Matthias's mocking tone. 'How delightful.'

'You wouldn't think it delightful if one of the other Elders ran the Tabernacle.'

'Any of them would be better than you, Matthias.'

'The old Rocaan believed none of them worthy of taking his place.'

'Yes,' Nicholas said. 'He put you into office. Look what wonders that has done for Blue Isle.'

Matthias's gaze flickered down to the knife. A tiny bit of blood dripped off its tip. 'I did the right thing for Blue Isle,' he said.

'No, Matthias.' Nicholas stepped forward, still holding the knife tip out. 'If you had done the right thing, we would not be arguing now. The country would be united and at peace instead of on the brink of war. You did not do the right thing.'

Matthias took one step back. 'We would still be at war. The Fey murdered your father.'

'One Fey, and I even know who it was. I would have been able to get to that Fey with Jewel alive. I doubt I can now.'

'Who?' Matthias asked.

'It no longer matters,' Nicholas said. 'You took our advantage away.'

'Advantage. You sound as if we're playing a game here. We're talking lives.'

Nicholas took another step forward. Matthias was again pressed against the window. This time, Nicholas placed the tip of the knife against Matthias's heart. 'We've been talking lives from the beginning. You have made this worse than it was. You, Matthias, and now we're talking your life. I will not protect you from the Fey. I would give you to them if I could. If you value the lives you were sworn to protect, then you will give up the Secrets.'

'To whom?' Matthias glanced down at the knife. Sweat beaded on his forehead. He was truly afraid, and Nicholas, for the first time in his life, enjoyed someone's fear. 'If I give them to the Elders, they'll kill me.'

'It's what you deserve.'

'But we can't have that in the church.'

'Why not?' Nicholas said. 'We had it just a few days ago.'

'It wasn't the same.'

Nicholas grabbed Matthias's collar, pulling his face close. Matthias had to bend at the waist to prevent the knife from penetrating his chest. He brought up one hand, his right hand, and it was smeared with blood from his back.

'It is the same,' Nicholas said very softly. 'Just because you didn't value Jewel's life doesn't mean that God didn't. Many of us valued her. Your opinion is not the only one.'

'But I'm a leader in the church. The Beloved of God.'

'And horribly misnamed, because I'm willing to wager that God isn't very happy with you right now.'

'You don't know the Mind of God.'

'*And neither do you.*'

They were both breathing hard. The cool river breeze caressed Nicholas's forehead, keeping him calm. A bead of sweat ran down Matthias's cheek and dripped onto his robe.

'I won't give them the Secrets,' Matthias said. 'They'll kill me.'

Nicholas let him go. Matthias staggered, caught the edge of the window with his left hand, and steadied himself.

'Then teach the Secrets to me,' Nicholas said.

'To you?' Matthias stood, wiped the hair off his face with his right hand, leaving a small spot of blood on his temple. 'You haven't the training.'

'No,' Nicholas said. 'But at least I understand what the Roca was trying to do. When he offered himself to the Soldiers of the Enemy, he was trying to prevent war, prevent death, not trying to cause it.'

'I wasn't trying to cause anything,' Matthias said. 'I thought you were next. I thought she would slaughter you and try to steal our Island that way.'

It sounded plausible. For one brief moment. But Nicholas knew better. 'Jewel was too smart for that. She knew that you and the others would depose her as soon as possible. You might have even killed her.'

'I was just thinking of you,' Matthias said.

'You were thinking of yourself, and your hatred, and your revenge.' Nicholas waved the dirk to punctuate his words. 'Do you know how I know? I know because you aren't justifying this with scholarship. You're trying to justify it with emotions, and you don't understand how emotions work.'

'I know how emotions work,' Matthias said. 'If I give you the Secrets, you'll kill me.'

'I can't kill you and step into a proper place within Rocaanism,' Nicholas said. 'As usual, you worry about yourself before others.'

'The Rocaan chose me.'

'He made a mistake.'

'If he made a mistake, then let God strike me down.'

'God will,' Nicholas said, 'in the form of the Fey. And when you die, the Secrets die with you. Selfish to the end, Matthias. You will be the one – all by yourself – who destroys an ancient religion, maybe even a nation. All by yourself.'

'You're not convincing me to trust you with the most sacred parts of Rocaanism, Nicholas,' Matthias said. 'I was your tutor. I know the contempt you hold for this religion.'

'I hold no contempt,' Nicholas said, 'for anything except you.'

Matthias's mouth thinned. His eyes held something dark – hatred? Nicholas didn't want to think about it. It no longer mattered. He shrugged. 'I'm doing right by my people,' he said. 'When you're dead, and the people come to me wondering why we can no longer worship, and no longer protect ourselves against angry Fey, I'll tell them I came to you and you refused to help them.'

'Who is trying an emotional argument now, Nicholas?'

'Emotion?' Nicholas held up the knife. 'Be glad I don't let emotion rule me like it rules you, Matthias. If I did, we would never have talked. You'd be dead already.'

'Threats again. Nicholas, you will never get the Secrets from me. You may as well stop trying.' Matthias crossed his arms in front of his chest. 'If you kill me now, you'll be to blame for the death of Rocaanism.'

'I told you already, Matthias, that I do my duty as King, no matter how much it hurts me,' Nicholas said.

'If you understand your duties as King,' Matthias said, 'then you understand why I cannot give you the Secrets. The Roca separated these jobs for a reason. I am the spiritual side. You are the physical side. It is by the Roca's words that we are separate.'

Nicholas smiled. It was clearly not the reaction that Matthias expected. He tried to back up, but couldn't since he was already braced against the wall.

'Finally,' Nicholas said. 'The scholarly argument. Too little too late, Matthias.'

'I won't give them to you, Nicholas.'

Nicholas tucked his dirk in his boot. The blade was cool, the blood sticky against his foot. 'That's your choice. It won't matter to you much longer anyway. By this time tomorrow, you'll probably be dead.'

'Even a timetable,' Matthias said. 'Are you sure you're not helping these Fey get to me?'

'I offered,' Nicholas said. 'They refused my help.'

Matthias went white. 'You're not serious,' he said.

'I'm quite serious,' Nicholas said. 'You deserve to die for what you've done. Any other murderer would already be part of the Infrin Sea.'

'I thought you said you care about our people,' Matthias said.

'I do,' Nicholas said. 'Rocaanism would still be a religion without you. The difference was this: If the Fey had taken you in exchange for my father's killer, we would no longer need holy water as a weapon. Any Danite can Bless water. We would still have lived in peace.'

'That would never have worked,' Matthias said. 'The people wouldn't have stood for the murder of the Rocaan.'

'I'm sure Porciluna would have helped them accept the change,' Nicholas said.

'You're a cold man,' Matthias said.

'If I am, it's because of what you've done to me,' Nicholas said.

'You're going to let them kill me,' Matthias said.

Nicholas shook his head. 'No,' he said. 'I'm just not going to stop them. I've warned you. I've done all I can do.'

He turned and walked toward the door, half wondering if Matthias would attack him.

'Nicholas?' Matthias said.

Nicholas stopped. He kept his back to Matthias.

'Ask them to stay away from me. They listen to you. If you do that, I'll make sure I share the Secrets.'

Nicholas bowed his head. 'Nice try, Matthias,' he said. 'But the Fey don't listen to me any more. You've seen to that.'

'I demand protection,' Matthias said. 'If not for me, then for the religion.'

'Denied.' Nicholas spoke firmly. 'You can protect the religion yourself by giving away the Secrets. As for you, you cannot demand anything from me.'

'Nicholas, we have to work together here.'

'That's right, Matthias. We should have worked together. Instead, you took the fate of Blue Isle in your own hands.' Nicholas looked over his shoulder. Matthias was still standing against the window, his face white with fear. 'When the Fey come for you, Matthias, realize that I will not help you. In fact, I will be praying that your death will be twice as slow and four times more painful than Jewel's.'

Matthias said nothing.

Nicholas nodded to him. 'I suspect this will be the last time we see each other. I will not miss you.'

'You've become as heathen as they are,' Matthias said.

'No,' Nicholas said. 'If anything, I have finally begun to understand the power of faith.' He looked at the man who murdered his wife. 'You're a lucky man. You still live. I suggest you make the most of your last few hours in this world. If the Words are to be believed, those few hours will be the last moments you ever spend without feeling pain.'

'I haven't caused any Islander pain,' Matthias said.

'Except me.' Nicholas bowed once, mockingly imitating the respectful bow due a Rocaan. 'Good day, Matthias. May the hand of the Holy One take my words to God's ear.'

'God doesn't listen to unbelievers,' Matthias said.

'I know.' Nicholas smiled. 'I have faith in that. You'd do well to remember it yourself.'

Forty-One

Adrian sat on the edge of the cot. One of the candles was guttering, sending flickering light throughout the tiny room. He was shaking. Somewhere, during these long years, he had accepted the fact that he would never leave this gray place. Now, when the opportunity presented itself, he was frightened.

Coulter had left a few moments before to tell Gift about the strange occurrences. Adrian had hinted that Coulter ask Gift to come with them, but didn't say so outright. He didn't know Gift. Gift was a little boy who might not be able to keep things quiet. Gift might run directly to his grandfather, the last place Adrian wanted him to go.

He was putting Luke at risk; he knew that. But he had a plan for that as well. He would go directly to Nicholas and tell him that Rugar held his son in Shadowlands. With the force of Blue Isle behind him, they might be able to make Luke survive.

They might not.

But it was a risk he would have to take. Adrian's life was not the only one at stake any more. Coulter was important too. Knowing the Warders, they might kill him as they search for the secret to his 'powers.'

Adrian stood and scanned his small cabin. He had nothing to take with him. The clothes he wore were Fey made – he would get rid of those as soon as he could. He had collected nothing, owned nothing since he arrived in Shadowlands. All this time, he had done nothing to make his existence permanent. He was a prisoner in a very large cell.

He had promised Coulter an hour. He could give him that.

But only that.

Any more and Adrian might lose his own resolve. He clasped his hands behind his back and paced, causing the candle to gutter farther. If Coulter truly had magical powers, then Nicholas needed to know that as well. The Islanders might have always had the power to completely defeat the Fey, they just might not have known it.

Now, with Coulter's abilities, they would know.

And if Coulter learned magic as Fey children did, then perhaps, Adrian – or Nicholas – could find a disgruntled Fey to teach them.

Anything was possible. He had learned that this afternoon, with Coulter sobbing on his chest.

Anything. Even magic where there had been none before.

A knock on his door made him start. His heart raced before he caught himself. The panic didn't belong. Most Fey just let themselves in. Only two people knocked.

Coulter and Mend.

Adrian pulled the door open, expecting Coulter. Instead Mend stood there, looking small and frightened. She slipped past him.

'Close the door,' she said in Islander. Her mastery of the language was good, but her accent was so strong that most Islanders would never be able to understand her.

He closed the door behind her, fear a palpable thing. Had Rugar discovered his plan already? Was Coulter all right? He couldn't even ask without endangering the boy.

'I only have a moment,' she said. 'Then I have to be in the Domicile.'

She took his hand and led him to the cot. She pulled him down beside her, and for a moment, he thought she was going to make love to him. She had tried, more than once, but he had refused. He was not going to accept this place any more than he already had. If he had allowed himself to fall in love with Mend, he never would have made these plans with Coulter. Adrian would have lost himself entirely.

Not that she wasn't beautiful. She was. All the Fey women had an ethereal charm that he found very appealing, Mend even more so. Her dark hair fell past her knees, and she left it unbound, contrary to custom. Her eyes were as sharply pointed as her ears, and the line of her eyebrows defined the ridges of her forehead. Her nose was slender and delicate, her lips dusky rose. So many nights he had lain awake on this very cot, thinking of her.

Even though he knew that sometimes the Fey used attraction as a trap.

'What's so urgent?' he asked.

'I should not tell you this,' she said. She took his hands in her own. Her hands were slender like the rest of her body, her fingers longer than his. 'But I cannot be silent. You have kept your side of this bargain in good faith.'

He stiffened. Whenever the Fey spoke of his bargain, they usually did so with derision, as if they would never have made such a trade themselves. But Mend had asked him about it many times, and she had never spoken with a lack of respect. She had always seemed interested and compassionate.

'The last night your son was here, he was in the Domicile.' She lowered her voice to a whisper. 'We Spelled him and his clothes so that we could track him.'

'Jewel said you would do that.'

'Then we left him. Others saw him. I know they Charmed him. And I know they gave him to Dream Riders for false memories. But until today I did not know what else they had done.'

'Charmed?' Adrian asked. The translations were so poor in Islander. 'Tell me in Fey.'

She shook her head. 'Those spells are minor. It is this one you need to know of. Burden used your son as an Assassin.'

'What?' Adrian asked. 'Is he all right?'

'I believe so,' Mend said. 'But I don't know.'

'How could he use Luke? Luke was outside Shadowlands.'

'Burden has Charm. Solanda brought him to the awareness of that, and Luke was Charmed. He was also given many orders so that he would be useful to us if anything happened to you. But that was the key, Adrian. As long as you kept your bargain, Luke would remain untouched.'

Adrian felt as if he had just been punched in the stomach. He was glad he was sitting down. 'I had been warned not to bargain with the Fey. I knew that you people never kept your word. I had just thought that this was different.'

'It was different in two ways,' Mend said. She put her hand on Adrian's. He pulled away. 'First, Jewel made the bargain with you and she's dead. Second, it was to our advantage that we maintain that bargain.'

'And it's not any more?'

Mend bowed her head. 'Burden wasn't thinking clearly.'

'Such an excuse for using my son as a weapon.'

Her jaw worked as if she were trying to find the words to express what was on her mind, but couldn't. 'Burden loved Jewel.'

'And I love Luke. I gave my entire future so that Luke would have one. And you people Spelled him and Charmed him and made a mockery of what I did.' Adrian stood up. The cabin seemed even smaller than usual. He was glad now he hadn't gotten involved with Mend. Glad that he had found his own way in this place. Glad the only person he had truly allowed himself to care about was the other Islander.

'It was just a protection,' Mend said. 'We always make protections. It is our way.'

'Just as it's your way to break agreements.' Adrian rubbed his temple. His whole body was shaking with the rage he felt inside. 'What a fool I've been. A stupid, stupid fool.'

Mend watched him from the cot, her hand resting in the spot he had vacated. 'Not all of us are bad,' she said. 'I came to you as soon as I found out.'

'And what do you expect me to do now? Warn my son? I'm sure he knows about your little spells.'

She shook her head. 'We broke the agreement,' she said. 'I think you're free to go.'

He held his breath. Of all the things he had expected her to say, this was not one of them. Had they other powers he didn't know about? Could they read his mind? Did they know he had already decided to leave, taking Coulter?

'I'll help you,' she said. 'I think this is wrong. I will open the Circle Door for you and you'll be free.'

'And Luke will die.'

She shook her head. 'I'm not sure anyone will even notice when you leave. You haven't had duties for a long time.'

Again, his thought. A chill ran down his back even though the cabin had grown too hot. 'You'll know,' he said.

'Adrian, you and I have been friends. Good friends, I thought.'

'A man cannot be friends with his captors,' he said.

'I'm not your captor. I'm willing to set you free.'

'After five years! What did you people do to Luke during those five years?'

'Nothing, Adrian.' She turned her hand over so that the palm was out. A small, but obvious supplication. 'You saw him each year as we agreed. You know that.'

He shook his head. 'I only know what he told me. And you people could have Spelled him to tell me anything.'

'Adrian.' Her voice was soft. 'I took a risk, coming to you.'

'Did you?' he asked. 'Did you really? Or are you merely here to tempt me? I'm in the way, aren't I? I no longer have a use to you people, so you'll kill me and continue to use my son as a weapon.'

'We could use him without killing you,' she said. Her cheeks were flushed. He was clearly making her angry.

'Then why not just slaughter me in my sleep? Why go through such a ruse?'

'Good question.' She stood and pushed past him, grabbing the door. 'Perhaps you should ponder it as you remain in this prison of your own choosing. I gain nothing from helping you. It's better for the Fey if you die. Yet I offered, at great risk to myself. I offered.'

She shoved the door open and left. Adrian winced as the door slammed shut behind her. He had done that wrong. Clearly wrong. But the closeness of her words, her decision to tell him now, unnerved him. No waiting for Coulter any longer. If they were going to leave, they had to leave now.

Adrian paced around the small room. Coulter had gone to see Gift. If Rugar was there, the escape would be ruined.

But that was a risk Adrian would have to take.

He rummaged through his clothes pile until he found the clothes he was captured in. The Domestics had cleaned them at his insistence. They had wanted to throw out the clothes instead. He hoped they hadn't Spelled the clothing, but there was less of a chance that Spells were woven into his Islander clothes than in the Fey clothes he now wore.

He put on the shirt. It hung on him. He had known that he had lost a lot of weight since he came into Shadowlands, but not how much. The sleeves were torn on the wrists and the shoulders – flayed from his bindings and the beatings – but there were no bloodstains.

The pants fit so loosely that he had to double-knot the waist. His boots were long gone. He had only the soft shoes the Fey had given him.

It had been so long since he had seen the sun that he wasn't even certain of the season. He might emerge in winter, and then he would need the shoes. But if it were summer, he could leave the shoes in the Dirt Circle.

He had to get out of here quickly, before anyone noted the clothing.

He pushed open the door and looked both ways. The Sprites were messing with the weather again – they should have given up long ago – and the mist was thick and damp. He stepped into it, actually glad for the cover it gave him. He rounded the large Domicile and headed for the Wisps' cabin.

Gift's cabin.

By Shadowlands standards, the Wisps' cabin was small. By his standards, it was huge. They had an extra room to work with, space enough for three people, when he and Coulter were crowded with two.

He rapped on the door and took a step back when it opened. Niche answered. Her bandaged wings looked fragile and useless, bound to her back, her eyes shadowed and haunted. It probably wasn't easy raising Rugar's grandchild. A thankless, ugly task at best.

'I am supposed to bring Coulter to the Domicile,' he said in Fey.

Gift sidled up beside her and clung to her legs. In action and gesture, he was closer to a young boy than Coulter had ever been.

'He's not here,' Niche said.

Adrian sighed. He hated this part. A lot of Fey wouldn't trust him with children, not even an Islander child. 'He came here a while ago. It's important that he get to the Domicile. They want me to bring him.'

'He hasn't been here,' Niche said. 'If he were, I would let him go with you.'

Adrian looked at Gift. The boy's face was eerie. His features were Fey, but his look belonged to the Royal House of Blue Isle. He was so clearly Nicholas's son that Adrian wasn't certain why he had had to be told in order to see it.

'I never seen him,' Gift said. His eyes were large, frightened.

Coulter had nowhere else to go. Sometimes he hid by the Domicile, but Adrian had walked past his spot. Coulter had been very clear; he wanted to see Gift. After that, they would leave. When Coulter was clear, he did what he said he would.

'Not at all?' Adrian asked.

'Why are you doubting my son?' Niche said.

Nicholas's son. The thought came unbidden, but Niche didn't seem to react to it. Perhaps they couldn't read minds after all.

'I'm not,' Adrian said. 'I just know Coulter. When he says he's coming somewhere, he does it.'

'How come they don't like him?' Gift asked.

Niche looked down at him, a frown on her face. 'Who?'

Gift watched Adrian. 'My grandfather. My grandfather and his friends, they don't like Coulter.'

Adrian went cold. The experiments. Touched and Rugar had no reason to wait. The next time they saw Coulter, they would take him.

'Do you know where Coulter is?' he asked Gift.

The boy shook his head.

Adrian looked at Niche. 'When two people are Linked,' he said, 'can they See each other across that Link?'

'Sometimes.' She said the word slowly as if she were thinking through it.

Adrian crouched in front of Gift. 'Can you See Coulter?'

Gift glanced at his mother, looking even younger than his years. She nodded at him. He closed his eyes. Adrian could almost see the boy stretching across Shadowlands.

'No.' Gift's voice sounded very far away. 'He's wearing a wall.'

A wall. Adrian glanced at Niche, but she didn't seem to understand the reference either. A wall.

I blocked them, Coulter said.

With a wall?

Adrian put his head in his hands. He was already too late.

Forty-Two

The door closed behind Nicholas.

Matthias collapsed against the wall, and slid toward the floor. His feet wouldn't hold him any more.

He had thought he was going to die. He had thought Nicholas was going to kill him.

Matthias's back ached, his heart was pounding, and he could barely breathe. He was bleeding, too. He could feel the blood running down his skin. He touched his back and his fingers came away bloody.

Damn Nicholas. Damn them all.

The door had barely closed when it opened again. Two Auds came in, the Auds he had assigned as guards.

Seeing him like this. So weak and frightened.

'Get out,' he said, his voice still strong.

'But Holy Sir,' one of the Auds said, 'we had to see if you were all right.'

'I'm fine,' he said. 'Get out.'

'Holy Sir –'

'Get out! This is a place of private worship. I am praying. Get out.'

The Auds backed out and closed the door. He leaned his head against the wall and caught the faint odor of blood mixed with the scent of the river. Blood. His blood.

He would have to get someone to look at that wound.

Nicholas. That arrogant boy. Telling Matthias that he was more of a believer than Matthias was.

Neither of them believed.

Perhaps that was the problem.

Matthias took a deep breath. It was difficult. He had been breathing shallowly since Nicholas arrived. The fear had nearly overwhelmed him.

That was the second time in two days he had been afraid for his life.

The second time he had not turned to the Holy One for help.

He shook his head. The fiftieth Rocaan had never been a scholar. He probably hadn't remembered the stories that separated the church,

344

even when Matthias had brought them up. He probably thought un-belief a problem that Matthias could solve.

But he couldn't. If anything his disbelief was getting worse.

There was a knock and before he could answer, the door opened.

The Aud guard stood there with a Danite.

Young Titus, the one who had brought Nicholas down.

Titus, the believer. Matthias had envied him for so many years. Envied the boy's belief.

'See?' the Aud whispered. 'The blood?'

'I told you to get out,' Matthias said to the Aud.

'Forgive me, Holy Sir, but —'

'He asked me to see you,' Titus said. He nodded at the Aud, then pulled the door closed. 'You're bleeding, Holy Sir. He was worried for your health.'

'My health is fine.' It was his strength that wasn't. He couldn't take many more shocks to his system.

'Beg pardon, Holy Sir, but a man is not fine when he leaves a bloody smear along the wall.'

'Young Nicholas thought to teach me a lesson.' Matthias smiled. As if Nicholas could teach him anything. Nicholas had been his pupil and a poor pupil at that.

'And did he, Holy Sir?' Titus remained by the door. His head was unadorned and he wore no shoes, proclaiming himself in the world of Danites as a true believer. His black robe was spotless.

'No.' Matthias had to get up. He had to show Titus he was all right.

Matthias put a hand on the cold stone floor and pushed. His feet slid from under him, and he almost fell. Titus crossed the room quickly and crouched beside Matthias.

'I'm fine,' Matthias said.

'You're bleeding.'

'A little,' Matthias said. 'Nothing serious.'

'You let me see.' Titus had stopped using formal titles. He moved to Matthias's right side and twisted Matthias's robe, touching him more intimately than anyone had touched him in a long time. 'I can't see — oh, here it is.'

Matthias closed his eyes. The area around the wound throbbed. Titus's fingertips made the throbbing worse.

'It's small,' Titus said. 'Just deep enough. What did he do?'

Matthias knew that Titus wouldn't leave him alone until he told. 'He used the tip of his knife to remind me of his anger.'

Titus nodded. 'You're lucky, Holy Sir. He could have killed you.'

'He wouldn't have killed me.'

'Nothing is certain in this world any more,' Titus said. Something in his tone made Matthias open his eyes. Titus still crouched beside him, his fingertips stained with Matthias's blood. The blood was a light red.

'You don't approve of me, do you?' Matthias regretted the question the moment he asked it. But he was so alone and so exhausted. He wanted something, a crumb of anything, even if it was begged-for affection.

'I believe murder holds no place in the high ceremonies of this church.' Titus sat down, grabbed the hem of his robe, and ripped.

'Murder?' Matthias asked. How could everyone think the death of a Fey murder?

'The death of the queen should never have happened.'

'It was God's will,' Matthias said.

'If God had willed it, she and the first child would have died at birth.' The hem of Titus's robe came off all the way along the bottom. Strands hung around his pale hairy legs. He took the ripped portion of the robe and held it out. 'Forgive me, Holy Sir, but I think we need to bind that wound to staunch the bleeding.'

Matthias leaned forward. The stretch pulled the skin along his back, making him wince at the pain. Titus wrapped the hem around him about Matthias's sash and pulled tight. 'My,' Matthias managed. 'It might stop my breathing as well.'

'It will help. I volunteered to work with the wounded during the Invasion. Yours is a small wound.'

Matthias heard the implications behind Titus's words. Trivial. Unimportant. The suffering you proclaim is an act to give you sympathy. Perhaps it was.

'Forgive me, Holy Sir, if I speak out of turn, but you could have died this afternoon. You nearly died last night. I heard parts of your discussion with King Nicholas. He is right. You need to pick a successor. Someone else needs to know the Secrets.'

The Secrets, the Secrets. Didn't anyone care about him? Matthias sat up. The hem was tight across his ribcage.

'I thought you didn't believe in church-sanctioned death,' Matthias said. Deep breaths hurt.

'I am not thinking of holy water,' Titus said. 'That's an entirely different discussion.'

For a Danite, he had no fear. Titus was half Matthias's age, and had one-quarter the experience, yet he felt he could lecture Matthias.

'It's the same discussion,' Matthias said. 'Whoever possesses the Secrets knows how to defeat the Fey.'

Titus leaned back. The blood had dried dark on his fingertips. 'They say, in the Aud dormitories, that your scholarship enabled the fiftieth Rocaan to use the holy water as a weapon.'

Matthias shook his head. 'It was an accident, that discovery.'

'But the decision to use the water after that accident, after that discovery, was made because you argued for it. You used the Words Written and Unwritten to show the Rocaan how to justify the use.'

'Justify,' Matthias said. 'How do you know that the Roca didn't leave us the water for just this reason?'

'You twist logic well, Holy Sir, but logic doesn't always serve the faithful.'

The throbbing had settled into a dull ache. 'Don't paraphrase the Words to me,' Matthias said. 'Sometimes one must use logic to understand the Words.'

'No,' Titus said. 'One must use faith. If it seems wrong to the heart, it is wrong. You have used the holy water as a weapon, as a tool to commit murder. Not just one death, but hundreds, rest at your feet. The King was right to come to you. His own logic was wrong.'

'Nicholas was reacting. He will understand what I did, in time.'

'The King knows that peace is better than war. It's a lesson that you might remember, Holy Sir.'

'And you might remember that you are addressing the Rocaan, your leader.'

'I do not believe you represent the Roca. I do not believe you are Beloved of God. I believe that the fiftieth Rocaan chose you because he believed he would return, and I think that's where he made his mistake. He tried to make you his guarantee, thinking God would never allow a man like you to become fifty-first Rocaan, and God showed him otherwise. "An arrogant man always suffers for his pride."'

Matthias looked at Titus. Titus's cheeks were flushed with a fervor that Matthias had never experienced. 'You're the one who is being arrogant now,' Matthias said. 'You have no knowledge of the fiftieth Rocaan. You were a child when he died.'

'I was fourteen,' Titus said, 'and I had survived my Charge. I went into the Fey's shadow world unprotected and alone.'

'You think that gives you a moral superiority over the rest of us?' Matthias asked. 'It shows only that they had a use for you alive.'

'You see things only as they exist in this world, not as they exist in the spiritual realm,' Titus said.

'I see things as they are,' Matthias said. He put a hand on the wall and eased himself up, holding back a moan as he did so. He would be sore, thanks to Nicholas's moment of temper.

'If you saw things as they are, you would know that the King is right. God cannot allow you to live.'

Matthias straightened and looked down on Titus. 'If there's anything I've learned in my years in the Tabernacle, it's to not second-guess God.'

'Yet you speak with such surety of God's hand in the deaths you've caused.' Titus stood as well.

'You know I could take your robe for this insolence.'

'But you won't,' Titus said.

'No,' Matthias said. 'I won't.' He studied the boy for a moment. Titus was shorter than Matthias, and stockier, but hardy. No one would think him important because he wasn't important. 'I have something else in mind for you.'

Titus wiped his hands on his robe, then shook the dirt from the floor off. Some of the threads hung to the floor. The breeze from the window had grown chill. Matthias was tired. He wanted nothing more than to rest in his apartments. But he didn't have time for that. He couldn't ignore this many warnings. To do so would be foolish.

'I am not certain I will do what you tell me,' Titus said.

'Based on what?' Matthias said. 'I am still Rocaan.'

'But not rightly so.'

'You cannot determine the right or wrong of any situation. You are only a Danite.'

'I still know what feels proper.'

Matthias smiled. 'You follow your heart because you're unwilling to study. But now you will have to study.'

Titus clasped his hands in front of him. 'Why?'

'Because I am going to give you the Secrets.'

Titus took a step backward. He hit the altar, nearly knocking it over, and caught it with his left hand. 'You can't,' he said, finally appearing his age. 'I'm a Danite. You have to teach an Elder.'

'I don't have to teach anyone,' Matthias said.

'But that means I'll be your successor.'

Matthias shook his head. 'I warned you, Titus. You need to study more.'

Titus was gripping the altar with his left hand, the knuckles white.

'The fiftieth Rocaan gave me the secret to holy water long before he made me his successor. It was custom among the early Rocaans to give the Secrets to a trusted Aud.' Matthias smiled. 'Of course, if the Aud did not progress in his studies, he often died when the next Rocaan was chosen.'

'That's not true!' Titus said.

'It's very true,' Matthias said. 'The history of the Tabernacle is full of unexplained deaths, betrayals and counterbetrayals. The early Rocaans were not as secure in their powers as some of the later ones.

348

The practice died out around the Tenth Rocaan. But it was allowed, even encouraged, for the very reasons you're encouraging me.'

'I'll check the history before I agree,' Titus said.

Matthias crossed his arms, ignoring the pull in his back. 'Why, Titus? Are you afraid?'

'I'm not afraid,' Titus said.

'You're not? You don't want the power of life or death over the Fey?'

'I would never use holy water as a weapon,' Titus said.

'Never?' Matthias asked. 'Not even if I die?'

'I don't know what your death has to do with it,' Titus said.

Matthias was beginning to feel stronger. Titus was right. The binding helped. He could no longer feel the blood running down his back. 'If I die without choosing the next Rocaan, the Elders will choose him. What if that Rocaan wants to use holy water to attack the Fey? You have to teach him the Secret, Titus.'

'And if I won't?'

Matthias shrugged. 'The death of the church will be on your shoulders, not mine.'

Titus moved behind the altar, using it as a block between himself and Matthias. 'You're a cruel man, Holy Sir.'

Matthias shook his head. 'A realistic one.'

'Why teach me?'

'I thought you heard my conversation with the King.'

'Only the parts he shouted.'

'He didn't shout, Titus.'

'He raised his voice.'

Matthias remembered Nicholas speaking in whispers. He would have to see if there were echo chambers built around this room. It was old enough, and it had been used as a headquarters once. Such devices might make sense.

'I will teach you because you are a Danite,' Matthias said. 'You cannot, even by a vote of Elders, become Rocaan. You cannot kill me for the privilege of taking my power. And one of the conditions of knowing the Secrets is that you reveal that knowledge to no one.'

'That can't be a condition,' Titus said. 'We know you know them.'

'I am Rocaan,' Matthias said. 'You know I now possess the Secrets, but you don't know when I learned them.'

'We know you learned about holy water the day of the Invasion.'

'Did I?' Matthias asked. 'Or did the Rocaan say that to reassure the others?'

'Are all Rocaans as devious as you?' Titus asked.

'If they want to survive,' Matthias said. 'Only if they want to survive.'

Forty-Three

The boy huddled in the middle of the table, his arms wrapped around his legs. He peered over his knees, watching Touched's every movement. Rotin sat at the head of the table, staring at the boy. She had not had any herbs since the morning, and was clearer than Touched had seen her in a long time.

The other Warders were gone; they had scattered after the meeting. Touched had tried to send for them, but Rotin said she had already done so. He didn't believe her, but he didn't know how to contradict her.

It felt as if she were testing Touched, seeing if his judgment was as good as he claimed. And she was using the boy to do it.

At the moment, the boy, Coulter, seemed very small and powerless. He hadn't moved since Touched grabbed him and dragged him to the Warders' cabin. Touched had been afraid the boy would defend himself in some way, but the boy had done nothing. Still, Touched was prepared. He had all of his guards up, waiting for some blistering bit of light, some elegant piece of magick to come his way.

So far nothing had.

The boy had been sitting on the table for a long time.

'Awfully young,' Rotin said.

'So's Gift,' Touched said. 'They have to have some differences.'

'Untapped magick. Do you know what possibilities that has?'

Touched nodded. He knew. He wondered how it was funneled, how the Islander society used such magick. Aside from the poison, he had no idea.

Rotin stood and put her hands flat on the table. 'You gave him all the mental tests and he passed. There are others.'

'Shouldn't we wait for the other Warders?'

She shook her head in a way that made Touched realize the other Warders weren't going to come. 'Get me a pouch,' she said.

He had been afraid of that. 'Rotin, we need him alive.'

'The Islanders don't need an Enchanter.'

'He's not theirs,' Touched said. 'He's ours. Raised here, remember?'

'I'm not anybody's.' The boy's voice was high and childlike, but his inflection had strength.

'It would be better for all of us if you worked with the Fey,' Touched said.

'Not necessarily,' Rotin said. 'We can certainly test some poison theories with this little one.'

'It's not the magick,' Touched said. 'We were wrong about that. There's something about being Fey that makes us react to the poison. We lost Red Caps because of it.'

'Did we?' Rotin said, her gaze still on the boy. 'Or did they take advantage of the situation and run away?'

'I saw one of the bodies myself,' Touched lied. The boy gave him a sharp look, the only real movement he had made since he huddled on the table. The boy had heard the lie.

But Rotin hadn't. 'You saw one?'

Touched nodded. He wasn't about to lose this boy because Rotin wanted to test poison on him. If things went right, the boy could provide the antidote to the poison. But Touched wasn't about to tell her that yet.

She might be jealous enough to block him. Warders were odd that way, particularly Warders who had been twisting their mind with herbs.

'Then I need a pouch,' she said.

He swallowed. He couldn't refuse her on this. They had a lot of pouches left from the battles years before. The pouches contained blood, skin and muscle from the dead: some from Fey, some from Islanders. The matter was used in spellmaking, in power expansion, and in experimentation. They had used some with the poison, but discovered what they already knew: Fey skin melted and transformed in the poison. Islander skin did not.

Aside from the occasional pouch used in Domestic spell development, none had been used since those poison experiments.

'Wait until I get back before you try anything,' Touched said.

'Of course,' Rotin said.

The boy's lower lip trembled. He was afraid of Rotin.

'I mean it,' Touched said. 'Don't start without me.'

Rotin nodded.

Touched went through the doorway leading into the hall. The Warders' cabin was larger than many of the cabins, with storage rooms in the back, and two sleeping rooms used by any Warders who worked too late. The sleeping rooms were usually empty now, unless Rotin used too many herbs, but when the cabin was first built the rooms were always full. Touched had spent many nights in those rooms himself, dreaming of complex and beautiful spells he could never quite remember when he awoke.

The first storage room was orderly – filled with bowls, pipes and other supplies. It was the second room he went to.

The room had a faintly dry odor to it, as if death waited here. Piles and piles of pouches littered the floor, the counters, the walls. The Red Caps had left a thin path as they stored the pouches. Touched stopped at the edge of the path and stared.

The bloated, faintly-pink pouches were all that remained of hundreds of lives. Inside, stored and preserved, was skin, muscle, and blood from dead Islanders. The third storage room had pouches containing Fey material. Most of the pouches dated from the Battles for Jahn almost six years before.

A Domestic spell he didn't understand kept the material fresh until the pouches were opened. Then the Warders had a day, maybe two before decay set in.

Touched grabbed six pouches. They squished under his fingers. He winced, faintly disgusted. This was the part of his profession that he liked the least. The pouches always felt vaguely alive to him, as if some part of the dead being remained within. It would have helped if he understood Domestic spells, but he did not.

The pouches themselves gave off the dry dusty odor. It coated him. He tucked his six pouches under his arms, and headed back to the front room.

Rotin remained in her chair. The boy hadn't moved either. They were staring at each other. Touched could feel the tension in the air.

She was toying with him.

When he had asked her not to.

Quietly, he set the pouches on the floor, then stood. The boy's eyes were wide. If Touched squinted just a little, he could see light bouncing off the boy's shields. Rotin was having less success than Touched had.

Rotin frowned as she tried again. Her half-second loss of concentration was all Touched needed.

He sent a wall of light and set it up before the boy's. Rotin's spell hit it, and Touched sent it back to her, doubled.

A large bolt of light zoomed toward her. She shot Touched a frightened, angry look before diving from her chair. The light hit the wall, leaving a scorch mark the size of an adult Fey.

The boy still stared at the spot as if that were a way he could maintain his intense focus.

Rotin put a hand on the table and pulled herself up. Her face was flushed with fury.

Touched decided to attack first. 'I told you to leave him alone.'

'Oh,' she said, standing and brushing off her robe, 'I thought you wanted me to wait the actual experiments for you, not my double-checks.'

'There's no need to double-check me,' Touched said. 'I was right.'

'So you were,' Rotin said with just the right amount of surprise. 'Give me the pouches.'

Touched crossed his arms over his chest. 'That spell you sent would have knocked over an adult.'

'Only when you doubled it,' Rotin said. 'Now, let's get to work.'

He still wasn't sure enough of himself. She might have been right. He would keep an eye on her, but follow her for the moment. As he reached for the pouches, he let the wall he had placed in front of the boy go down.

The pouches slid away from his fingers. He stared at them. Then he glanced at Rotin. She grinned at him. Domestic games. It had been years since one of the Warders had taunted him with his lack of simple skills.

But he would show her. He would prove to her that he could do as well or better than she could at everything else.

He picked up the pouches and tossed them at her, one by one. She caught them as if she had expected him to do so, then set them on the table.

The boy hadn't moved.

But his eyes took in everything.

When Touched had tossed her the last pouch, he stood and walked to her side. The entire room smelled dry now. Not even the lingering odor of the herbs or of the woodsmoke could cover it.

Rotin put the pouches on the table, and they jiggled slightly. The boy was shaking. He didn't show it, but it was very clear. He was afraid.

And why wouldn't he be? He was a child. An Islander child, but a child all the same.

Touched had been a child when they first tested him for Warding powers. But that had been only a test. They waited until he hit puberty before actually working with him.

It had been scary then.

It had to be terrifying for someone of the boy's age.

Rotin untied a pouch and the iron scent of blood filled the room. The scent was so strong that Touched could almost see it. The boy buried his nose in his knees. Rotin pulled out a piece of skin. It was long and thick as Touched's finger. The Red Caps had flayed it from the bone – had the Foot Soldiers done it while the victim was still alive, the skin would have been so thin it curled.

'Good choice,' Rotin said. 'We need the thicker skin.'

Light flickered around the boy. He hadn't perfected any of his skills. His terror would burn out his shield. He had it at full strength now. He probably thought they were going to skin him too.

Rotin pushed a pouch at Touched. 'Here,' she said. 'Let's begin.'

He sighed. He hated this part of Warding.

He took the pouch to the side of the table closest to the boy. Rotin went to the other side. She placed the piece of skin on the boy's barrier. It hung in the air, glued to the barrier by the blood, curving an adult arm's length away from the boy. The skin looked as if it were floating, except for the drop of blood that ran along the shield, marking it.

Touched opened his first pouch, wincing at the stench. This one had been taken from a body at least a day dead. Barely viable, and probably useful only for experiments like this one. He reached in, coating his fingertips with slime, and grabbed the first jelled mass he could find.

The skin came out, pale and thick, covered with dark blood.

Heart blood.

No wonder they had harvested this. It had strong magick.

He laid the skin on the shield. On this side also the boy had maintained protection an arm's length away. The dark blood ran down, staining the table, and marking the side of the shield.

A child, even an enchanted child, normally had shields that were attached to the body, not feet away.

Rotin looked at Touched and straightened her eyebrows in surprise. Suddenly she was as interested in this boy as he was.

He hoped that was a good thing.

The shield sparkled as the boy tried to strengthen it. Rotin put pieces of flesh on all sides, then top to bottom, working quickly. Touched did the same. The boy was too young to think his way out of this predicament. If he had dropped the shield and moved, he wouldn't have been trapped, but now, because they had touched the shield on all sides, he couldn't drop it.

Although he could punch a hole in it and crawl out.

Touched moved rapidly, blood running down his hands and into the sleeves of his black robe. His fingers were red, the nails black with blood. The stench had grown worse.

Rotin opened her second pouch.

The boy had buried his head completely, apparently placing all of his concentration on keeping the shield in place. The shield's shape was becoming apparent. It was a half-bubble around him with good curve and strong form.

The bubble seemed to end on the table.

But the boy was smart. Touched remembered that much from their earlier encounter.

He opened his second pouch and crouched, placing the pieces of skin under the table.

Sure enough, the bubble was complete. It put the boy in a protective circle.

Rotin saw what Touched was doing and did the same. They worked quickly and silently, slapping long pieces of skin on the bubble and creating a crazy patchwork in the air. Blood dripped from the bottom of the circle onto the floor. The floor was slightly uneven, and as the puddle formed, a small trickle ran toward the door, as if part of the boy were trying desperately to escape.

Touched finished the bottom first. When he stood, he could barely see the boy through the gaps in the skin. The skin was flat and had adhered so well to the bubble that it was beginning to look as if the boy were trapped inside a circle of flesh.

Rotin had opened her final pouch. She pulled out the strands of skin and pasted them to the gaps in her side of the shield. As Touched worked, he could see the underside of the skin. It looked like a blood-covered river, with tiny tributaries and dry patches. The skin was translucent, so the light in the room filtered through.

The boy watched Touched as he finished placing his pieces of skin on the gaps. The last strand covered an area about as big as Touched's hand. The boy raised his head, his mouth open as if to protest, as Touched covered the last visible spot with skin.

'Excellent,' Rotin said. 'We have him now.'

No protection, no nothing. The skin's blood magick broke the spell. Touched grabbed a towel near the front of the table and started to wipe his arms. Rotin was inspecting their work.

'Very, very good,' she said. A bit of ancient blood smeared the side of her face. Her bald head seemed small compared to the circle of flesh next to her. She looked at Touched and grinned. 'Should we test it?'

'Why else build it?' he asked. The blood wasn't coming off. It had been a long time since he was this covered. He would have to go to the Domestics when he was through and ask for help cleaning his hands and arms.

'Ready?' Rotin asked.

Touched shook his head. 'Give me a moment.' He came over to her side of the table. Her work was sloppier than his, her skin overlapping in places. There were no gaps, however, not even tiny ones.

She rolled up the sleeve on her robe. 'All right,' she said. 'Here goes.'

She shoved an arm through the mass of flesh. It quivered, then adjusted. It looked as if the ball of flesh had eaten to her elbow. Rotin leaned forward.

'He's moving,' she said. Touched couldn't tell if her tone held triumph, irritation, or both.

Make it stop!

The mental blast hit Touched so hard he nearly fell backward. He caught the edge of the table to steady himself.

Rotin didn't seem to notice. She had shoved her arm into the flesh bubble all the way to her shoulder.

Did we hurt you? Touched sent back.

Make it stop!

Terror came with the sending. That was what had sent him backwards. Complete, total terror.

The boy had probably never seen anything like a preliminary shield breech. He probably hadn't even known what his shield looked like outside of his head.

Did we hurt you? Touched sent again.

Keep away! Keep away!

'Better pull out,' Touched said to Rotin.

She glanced at him, frowning.

'The boy is sending. He's terrified.'

'The first breech is always frightening,' Rotin said, but she pulled her arm out. Her skin was covered with long black streaks from the sides of the bubble. The hole in the bubble closed immediately.

'So he's a weak one,' she said.

'No,' Touched said. 'That Sending was strong.'

'He couldn't take my physical touch. Imagine a real one.'

'He's just a boy,' Touched said. 'I don't even know if he's reached six years.'

'Old enough to shield.'

'But too young to know all the tricks.'

'No one taught him,' Rotin said.

'He learns quickly enough.' The bubble below had surprised Touched. The boy was gifted and brilliant.

'Let's see how quickly,' Rotin said. She squinched her face. Touched learned quickly too and this time he recognized the look. She was going to Light-Send again, another attack, like the ones he had leveled at the boy.

A beam of light shot from Rotin's eyes. Touched set up his own block in front of the bubble. When the light bounced back to Rotin, she stopped sending, and the light disappeared.

'You're making things worse,' she said to Touched.

He shook his head. 'That's a boy in there. Little more than a baby. He's talented, but weak. If you kill him, we have nothing.'

'I won't kill him,' Rotin said.

Touched crossed his arms over his chest. 'Your Light-Send is too strong. I won't let it through.'

'You will,' she said. 'Because I head the Warders.'

'No one heads the Warders,' Touched said. 'Not really. And you can do nothing to me.'

'Touched, I can have you removed –'

'When the Black King comes.' Touched smiled for the first time since he brought the boy into the cabin. 'Which may be never.'

Rotin sighed. She obviously realized that threats wouldn't work. 'All right,' she said. 'I'll be gentle.'

'Swear,' Touched said. 'On your powers. Swear.'

She tilted her head toward him. Her expression convinced him that she had no intention of being gentle. 'What would you do to me if I wasn't?'

'This boy is our only chance to understand Islander magic. Our only chance. If you hurt him, I would have to hurt you.'

'Idle threats, Touched. I'm more powerful than you.'

'No,' Touched said. 'You used to be.'

'You can't harm me,' she said.

'Anyone can harm you,' he said. 'All they have to do is catch you after you've taken a few herbs.'

Her face hardened and she turned away. She had clearly heard the truth of that statement. 'I won't hurt him,' she said through gritted teeth.

'Good,' Touched said. He remained behind her, arms crossed, waiting. She sent a very weak light through the bubble's skin barrier.

The boy screamed.

'Is that all right?' Rotin asked with a hint of sarcasm.

'Perfect,' Touched said. 'Just perfect.'

357

Forty-Four

Nicholas dismounted and handed the lathered horse to Ejil. The groom frowned at him – Nicholas had run the horse hard – but said nothing. He murmured words of comfort to the horse and led it into the stables.

Stowe and Monte rode in behind him. Nicholas turned his back on them and walked across the courtyard. The ride hadn't calmed him. If anything it had left him more agitated.

The servants in the courtyard gave him a wide berth. He must have looked as furious as he felt. Matthias had all but said that he had intended to kill Jewel. He had said that Nicholas would be better off without her.

Better off.

The idiot.

No one was better off now.

And Matthias wouldn't listen. He wouldn't give the Secrets away, which would put the entire kingdom in crisis. The Fey would kill Matthias – it was only a matter of time – and when they did, Rocaanism would die with him.

It would all rest on Nicholas's shoulders. The people wouldn't understand why their power and their religion had completely disappeared.

Of course, the Fey hadn't managed to kill this Rocaan so far. They had stopped trying after Nicholas had married Jewel. Who knew what kind of tricks they had now?

Nicholas's cape fluttered behind him as he walked. He felt like Rugar – both powerful and powerless. He hadn't been able to figure out how to use his strengths yet. He had been King for a little over a week, and in that time, he had barely had time to think, let alone learn.

He could use his father's advice at the moment.

Or Jewel's.

He yanked open the kitchen door only to find it stuck. Lord Stowe had his hand on the top of the door.

'Forgive me, Sire,' Stowe said. 'But Monte and I need to talk with you.'

'I'm through talking,' Nicholas said. He needed to get away from the duties for a little while. He needed to spend time with Arianna, to remember why he even tried at all.

'I think not, Sire.' Stowe held the door firmly. 'I know this is irregular, but you need our help.'

Nicholas needed help, but he wasn't sure he wanted to admit it, at least not to one of his lords. 'Let me by, Stowe.'

'Highness –'

'Stowe, the mood I'm in it would be best not to trifle with me.'

'I'm not trifling, Highness.'

And he wasn't. He was looking at Nicholas with the same expression Nicholas's father sometimes used, a bit of compassion mixed with stubbornness.

'All right,' Nicholas said. 'As we walk.'

'Highness, this matter had best be discussed in private.'

'As. We. Walk. Understand?'

'Yes, Highness.' Stowe took his hand off the door. Nicholas pulled the door open and entered the kitchen. It smelled of warm bread and curing meat. The blood near the hearth fire had been cleaned up, but he still saw Jewel there, her body lifeless as it gave life.

Monte flanked him on one side, Stowe on the other, as they had done when they went to see Matthias. The roar of the hearth fire seemed loud. The chefs were pounding meat to tenderize it, and some of the serving women were shouting at each other across the room. A few of the servants saw Nicholas and bowed as he passed. He waved a hand, indicating that they should ignore him.

'Highness,' Stowe said, 'the incident with the Rocaan –'

'Was my choice,' Nicholas said. 'He murdered my wife.'

'Yes, Sire, but –'

'But?' Nicholas was glad he was walking. If he were alone in a room with Stowe, he would grab the man by the throat. 'No but, your lordship. She's dead, and Matthias killed her.'

'We heard the conversation, Highness,' Monte said. He spoke softly, his words barely carrying above the din.

Nicholas took the twisting servants' stairs. He had slid down those in the middle of a battle the day he had first seen Jewel. The stairs were wide enough for two men. Monte, as befit his rank, dropped back.

'Did you?' Nicholas said. The noise of the kitchen was fading away.

'Aye, Sire.' Monte sounded chagrined, as if he could apologize for this entire conversation with his tone. 'We thought we'd better talk with you before this went too far.'

'Did you?' Nicholas kept his voice flat. They were dangerously close to overstepping. He was only allowing this because he felt so alone, because he needed guidance no matter how it came. 'You listened in on a private conversation and feel you have the right to comment on it.'

They had reached the landing. Stowe slowed his steps, but Nicholas didn't. He pivoted and continued up. 'It affects us,' Stowe said.

'Everything I do affects you,' Nicholas said. 'That's the nature of the relationship.'

'Yes, sire, but this one is dangerous.'

Nicholas stopped one step up so that he could look down on both men. Stowe's face was drawn, and Monte's was tight with fear. They were no more comfortable with this moment than Nicholas was.

He wasn't going to make them any more comfortable, either.

'Tell me now,' he said, 'and I'll consider what you have to say.'

Stowe nodded his head once. 'Sire, if the Rocaan dies without revealing the Secrets, we could all die.'

'I doubt that. The Fey won't attack at once.'

'But when they do we have no recourse,' Stowe said. 'We'd lose to them. Rugar would lead us.'

'Rugar won't lead us. I have the children.'

'Babies,' Stowe said, 'and, forgive me, Sire, but one is feeble. We cannot wait for them to grow. We won't last two days without holy water.'

'You're all afraid for your skins,' Nicholas said and started back up the stairs.

'Highness!' Monte's voice was piercing between the stone walls. 'Please.'

'No,' Nicholas said. He continued to climb. No one was on the second floor. The hallway was shrouded in darkness. 'I don't think you men understand. I want them to kill him. I'd have killed him myself if I could have.'

He stopped at the top of the stairs and took a deep breath. He hated coming this way, but he hated going through the Great Hall even more. Jewel's body was gone, but he still saw it there whenever he closed his eyes. The only memories he had of her at the moment were of her death.

Stowe stopped beside him. 'We do understand that, Sire,' he said softly. 'But that's not in the state's best interest. Forgive me for speaking out of turn, Sire, but you need to consider Blue Isle.'

'I am considering Blue Isle,' Nicholas said. 'I didn't kill him this afternoon.'

'Then allow us to protect him.' Monte blurted the sentence from behind Nicholas.

Nicholas turned. 'Protect the man who murdered your Queen?'

'Arrest him then, Sire. But don't let him die,' Stowe said.

'Arrest him? And then what? The people will turn against me as clearly if I arrest him as they would if I murdered him myself.'

'Not if you say you're going to investigate what happens. Not if you force him to appoint an acting Rocaan.'

'It's never been done,' Nicholas said.

'There's never been a need,' Stowe said. 'There is now. The Words don't provide for this, nor does Church history. But it could be the first step in you taking over for the Rocaan. You could even bill it as such.'

'Then Matthias just plays us like a mouse, toys with us, and never gives us the Secrets. If he knows the Secrets are worth his life, he will keep them until he dies of old age. No.' Nicholas walked down the corridor, his boots slapping against the stone.

Monte hurried after him. 'Sire, please, then just let us guard him. You said you thought the Fey would strike in the next few days. let us make certain they don't. Then you can settle this with the Rocaan.'

'You aren't understanding me,' Nicholas said. 'I want him dead.'

Stowe caught up to Nicholas and Monte. He turned to Monte. 'Leave us,' he said.

'But I thought we were to discuss this together.'

'So,' Nicholas said. 'You planned this on the ride back. How charming.'

'Highness,' Stowe said. 'Please. Let me speak to you. Alone.'

Nicholas sighed. He would never get rid of them if he didn't have a real discussion. 'All right. Leave us, Monte.'

Monte nodded, bowed, and hurried back down the stairs toward the kitchen. Nicholas shoved his hands in the pockets of his breeches.

'Make this quick,' he said to Stowe, 'because you're pushing every favor you've got.'

Stowe crossed his arms, apparently unwilling to be intimidated. 'It's time you listen to me, Highness, not as a king, but as a young man. You've lost everything that's important to you this week, and you're not thinking clearly. If you allow the Fey to kill the Rocaan, that will be the last assassination. We will go to war. And with the Rocaan dead, we will have no chance at winning. None at all.'

'The Fey won't attack their own kind,' Nicholas said.

'So your children are safe. Fine, but what about all the other children? What about the people you swore to protect?'

'I swore in a ceremony run by a false Rocaan.'

'You swore before God,' Stowe said.

Nicholas clenched his fists. He didn't want to hear this. 'You would never speak this way to my father.'

'Your father never forgot his obligations.'

'Yes, he did,' Nicholas said. 'He hid in the war room during the Invasion.'

'Because if he died, it didn't matter what happened on Blue Isle. You were too young to rule well. The Fey would have won, right there and then.' Stowe was speaking so forcefully that his entire body shook. He clearly hadn't slept either, and he was one of Nicholas's father's most favored advisors. Beneath all the bluster, beneath the talk, Stowe was terrified. Nicholas had only seen him terrified once before – when the Fey invaded.

'I can't give in to Matthias,' Nicholas said. 'I can't allow him to commit murder with impunity. As long as he is Rocaan, I cannot make any agreements with the Fey. I can't bring my children inside a chapel. I cannot be the leader I need to be.'

Stowe let out a deep breath and brought one hand to his face. He massaged his temples as if he had a bad headache.

'If I arrest him,' Nicholas said, 'he won't give up the Secrets. He'll use them as a weapon against us. But if he's afraid enough of the Fey, he might turn those Secrets to someone else.'

'He's too afraid of his own Elders,' Stowe said. 'And I don't think he cares enough about the Tabernacle.'

Nicholas shook his head. 'That's where you're wrong, milord,' he said. 'Matthias has always loved the Tabernacle. He loves the history and the importance of it. Until he became Rocaan, he was the voice of reason within that building. Making him Rocaan was wrong. He hasn't the – I don't know – the ability for it. He's not political and he doesn't know how to use his power, and he's terrified that someone will discover he doesn't belong.' Nicholas spoke those last words slowly, more to himself than to anyone else. No wonder Matthias guarded everything so closely. It was the only way he had of protecting himself. Perhaps Stowe was right. If Nicholas provided protection, Matthias might give up the Secrets.

The thought made Nicholas's stomach turn.

'If that's true,' Stowe said, 'then fighting him will only entrench him farther. We have to appear to work with him. Then and only then will he feel secure enough to allow the Secrets out.'

Nicholas shook his head. He was actually, physically, queasy. 'I can't work with him. I can't help him. He killed Jewel.'

'Forgive me, Sire, for lecturing you, but these are the difficulties of your position. You must balance everything. And the fate of the Isle is more important now than what the Rocaan did to Jewel. I am sorry to be so blunt.' Stowe was almost bobbing with apology. He clearly knew that he was treading on dangerous ground. But the more he apologized, the more Nicholas listened. 'If we tell Matthias that we are guarding him when, in fact, we will be keeping him under house arrest, then he might relax enough to seek help. He was willing to work with you this afternoon.'

'I'm sure he won't be now,' Nicholas said.

'He actually might,' Stowe said. 'The man is besieged on all sides. He has no support and, if reports are true, he has no faith tö turn to either. You, the Elders, and the Fey are against him. If you embrace him, he will embrace you.'

'I can't tell him that he did the right thing.' Nicholas turned away. His voice was breaking and his eyes stung. 'He didn't.'

'I know that, Sire. But we can send a message along with the guards that you have decided to protect him. Promise the conversation later.' Stowe put his hand on Nicholas's arm. 'Let the lords lie for you. I will. I'll tell him what we must to in order to get him to work with us.'

'And then what?' Nicholas said.

'Once we have the Secrets, we let the Elders voice their opinions to the people. We let them tell the people he was a false Rocaan who seized an opportunity. We let them appoint a new leader, and then you can punish him, Sire, as you see fit.'

Nicholas walked away from Stowe. The hall had a dampness and a chill that came from disuse. These were old family quarters when Nicholas's family had many children, generations ago. Then they became guest quarters. No one had used these quarters since trade broke off with Nye. No guests had come to the palace in years.

'Twists and turns, that's what you're telling me,' Nicholas said. 'I'll never be able to act in a straightforward manner.'

'That's right,' Stowe said. His voice was soft, regretful, as if he knew that Nicholas would be upset about this. 'The days of expressing your every emotion are gone, Highness.'

He was, as best he could without endangering himself, telling Nicholas that he had made a mistake confronting Matthias. Perhaps he had. As a king. As a man, he had not gone far enough.

'I'll never be able to talk with him calmly,' Nicholas said. 'I won't be able to tell him I approve of his methods.'

'With luck, you'll never have to,' Stowe said.

'With luck.' Nicholas spat out the words. 'I haven't had much luck lately, have I?'

'No, Sire.'

Nicholas took a deep breath. Stowe was right. Nicholas had to think about Blue Isle. And about his children.

'I like your idea about house arrest,' Nicholas said. 'Set up a meeting for me with the other Elders. We'll have it here so that Matthias won't know of it. I'll tell them what we plan.'

'No,' Stowe said. 'The fewer who know that the guards are actually prison guards the better. Let's wait until he gives away the Secrets.'

'How will we know?' Nicholas asked. 'He might tell someone and ask them not to say a word.'

'We'll know,' Stowe said. 'He'll have to talk with someone. We'll have guards on him at all times.'

Nicholas shut his eyes. The stinging had ceased. Instead, they felt very, very dry.

As if he would never be able to cry.

'I don't like this path,' he said. 'I don't like it at all.'

'I know, Highness,' Stowe said. 'I take full responsibility.'

'We have no proof that we can stop the Fey.'

'I'll make certain the guards have holy water as well as swords.'

But that wasn't what Nicholas meant. Things had changed with the death of Jewel. Drastically. He felt as if the power had shifted again, and that instead of equality between Fey and Islander, Fey had regained the upper hand. He had nothing concrete for that feeling, just the nagging emotion in his gut.

Perhaps it was the loss of the Rocaan as the moral center. Perhaps it was all the losses combined.

Perhaps it was him. He had placed his own revenge above Blue Isle, a mistake his father would never have made.

A mistake Nicholas would never have made before the last few days. The deaths had destroyed something in him. Something fundamental. Something Stowe was addressing now.

Nicholas clasped his hands behind his back and turned. Stowe hadn't moved from the center of the corridor. The light from the stairwell suffused him, giving him a pale, shadowy look.

'Lord Stowe,' Nicholas said, 'You were my father's most valued advisor. I know that, and that's why I listened to you this afternoon. But do not, ever, take me to task again in front of anyone. Is that clear?'

He could barely see Stowe's face in the dim light. Stowe smiled, as if relieved that Nicholas had said anything at all.

'Yes, Highness,' Stowe said. 'I understand my place.'

'See that you do,' Nicholas said. He nodded, then continued down the corridor.

Alone.

Forty-Five

Burden huddled in the tall grass beneath the great bridge crossing the Cardidas River. He and eight Fey were on the Tabernacle side of the river, not far from the Tabernacle itself. Night had fallen an hour before. The air smelled of mud and the ground had a coolness it hadn't had earlier. Tiny mosquitoes and gnats swirled around him; he continually brushed them off his face and bare arms.

But he didn't move. He didn't want to be seen. He crouched near the edge of the bridge, invisible to passers by but able to see the road and the darkness around it.

He was waiting for Wind to return. Wind, who would scout out the Rocaan's location, and tell Burden. Niche hadn't wanted her mate to come – she was afraid Rugar would find out and if Rugar found out, she was afraid he would take Gift away from them. But Rugar would approve of this mission.

If it succeeded.

And it would succeed. Burden had planned his small troop with care. He had four Infantry with him, all of whom he had worked with in Shima's troop when he had been in the Infantry with Jewel. Then he brought three Foot Soldiers who were careful, meticulous and anxious to be out of Shadowlands. He complemented the group with one Dream Rider, who would give them extra protection, and Wind the Wisp, who could scout locations without being seen.

This was the best troop that Burden could put together given the limitations of Shadowlands, Rugar's leadership, and the deaths since the Fey had arrived on Blue Isle. He had toyed briefly with bringing a few Beast Riders, but they would actually make this small group more conspicuous.

He knew the Tabernacle grounds as well as any Fey. His Settlement had been across the river from it, and he had stared at the spires of the building every day. Some weeks he went past it, almost as a personal dare, to see how close he could get to the most feared place for the Fey without risking his own life. He had a map that Veil had made for him, and he understood the dangers.

Any Fey seen in the Tabernacle would probably die from the poison.

Any Fey. No matter what his reason for being inside. Especially now.

Lights burned on the ground floor of the Tabernacle, but in the private apartments above only a few lights shone. The moon hung over the river, big and golden. It was still early, but apparently the religious Islanders went to sleep early.

Better for him.

A spark floated toward him on the breeze. It flashed like a firefly, but fireflies didn't exist on Blue Isle. They belonged in Galinas, but not here. Blue Isle didn't even have will-o'-wisps, which presented quite a problem for Fey Wisps. They had trouble masking themselves as anything except fire sparks. And a fire spark this close to the river looked suspicious.

Or perhaps that was Burden's own nervousness showing. No one would even see Wind if they didn't know he was nearby.

The spark landed at Burden's feet. The light went out as the Wisp grew to his full size. He huddled, naked, in the tall grass, his wings wrapped around him for warmth. With his change came the smells of sulfur and smoke.

'He is in the room that Veil promised he'd be in,' Wind whispered. His voice had a soft reedy quality. His eyes glowed in the darkness, reflecting the light of the moon. 'His fire is still burning near his bed, but his breathing sounds even. He's asleep, or close to it.'

'Good,' Nightshade said from beside Burden. Nightshade was the Dream Rider. He was twice as old as Burden and bent with the years. His body absorbed light, and he could often pass for a black shape moving across the landscape. Like most Dream Riders, Nightshade could travel in complete silence. His speech was clipped, odd, as if he had learned Fey as a second language which, Burden supposed, he had. 'This is the perfect time, then.'

'We still have to get across that yard,' Amar said. He was Rugar's age and had been in the Infantry since he was a boy. Burden had asked him along hesitantly, wanting experience, but knowing he might not get it. To his surprise, Amar had agreed. On the trip to Jahn, Amar had explained. He had liked Jewel. He thought it horrifying that Rugar was doing nothing about her death.

'We have another problem,' Wind said. 'There's religious guards around the room. One on the balcony, and two in front of the door.'

'They didn't see you, did they?' Burden asked.

Wind shook his head. 'The one on the balcony didn't notice me at all. The Islander boy left a rope tied to the balcony's edge which they haven't removed. I think it would be our easiest way up.'

'The guard will notice us for certain.' Owrie leaned back on her haunches. She was slender and strong, but restless like most Foot Soldiers. She rocked on her toes, and hid her hands under her arm pits. Burden was just as glad for that. Foot Soldiers had an extra set of fingernails in the fingertips, thin, razor-sharp nails that could slice with such accuracy that they could remove a single layer of skin and keep it intact. There was a magic involved there as well, but he was ignorant about it. He only knew that it was dangerous once evoked – as it was now.

Wind shook his head. 'You forget, Owrie. They're not used to us.'

'You have a plan?' Amar asked.

Wind smiled. His face looked almost ethereal in the moonlight reflecting off the river. 'Surprise always works.'

'Not good enough,' Burden said. 'Let's hear it.'

Wind shrugged. 'I'll just transform in front of the guard.'

'Too dangerous,' said Condi. She had been part of Burden's unit in the Infantry, and she was one of the calmest soldiers he had ever seen. 'Startle him like that and you'll be poisoned for certain.'

Burden shivered. A mosquito brushed his arm and he swiped at it. They were all terrified of the poison. Some of the Fey were so frightened that when he asked them to come with him, they refused. Some even refused the Charm.

'Trust me,' Wind said.

'We'll have to,' Burden said. 'I don't want to go through that building if we can help it. We have a lot more chances of running into that poison inside than we do outside.'

'I actually think our greatest difficulty will come crossing that courtyard,' said Llan. He was one of the oldest Foot Soldiers, old enough that Rugar even treated him with the respect due the aging. But he had the same restlessness that Owrie had, and he too hid his hands in his armpits.

'We'll have to be silent,' VeHeter, the remaining Foot Soldier. She had a deep voice, almost masculine. She was the only one of the Foot Soldiers who was perfectly still. But her hands rested, palm up, on her knees and the tips of her fingers glinted in the moonlight.

'Shouldn't be too difficult,' Nightshade said.

'For some,' said Fants. He spoke softly but Burden listened. Fants had been a Leader in Nye, but a scandal that no one discussed forced him back into the Infantry. Most of the time, he said nothing. He had only come with Burden because they had spent so much time commiserating over Rugar's poor leadership. Fants thought anyone could do better – even a Charmer.

'Come on, Fants, we can do it,' said March. She was the only member of this troop that Burden was uncertain about. Her only battles had been on Blue Isle. She had done well, but she was young. She had strength, and little cunning. Amar had asked that she remain, but Burden couldn't find anyone else to round out the troop, and he felt comfortable only in a contingent of ten.

'One should never assume one's ability to succeed in anything,' Fants said.

'If we believed that,' Llan said, 'then we would never get up in the morning. Don't let one bad experience color everything, Fants.'

'Leave him alone,' Amar said.

'Quiet,' Burden said. 'I don't care about your disagreements. We have to do everything right here, or we might not return to Shadowlands.'

'Wouldn't that be a shame?' VeHeter asked.

'For some of us it would be,' Wind said. His wings were wrapped so tightly around his body that he looked as if he were swaddled.

'Yes, I forgot,' VeHeter said. 'Some of us are raising Islander children.'

'This isn't going to work,' Burden said. 'We can't fight.'

'We can fight,' Fants said. 'The energy is here. We just have to turn against an enemy instead of ourselves.' He glanced at Burden as if asking for permission. Burden nodded once. 'The enemy is inside that building. You need to think of two things. The first is that he, in cold blood and with complete duplicity, slaughtered the Black King's daughter when she stood before him in good faith.'

'Her mistake,' VeHeter muttered.

'Shut up,' Condi snapped.

'The second,' Fants said as if he hadn't heard the women's interchange, 'is that if we succeed, we'll light a spark under our people again. We'll be able to leave Shadowlands for good and get off this horrible Island.'

'Dreamer,' Owrie said, but she said it with fondness. They all knew the truth of his words. If they succeeded in killing this man, the one with the secret to the poison, they would return to Shadowlands heroes. The moral victory would be worth any price.

Burden squeezed Fants' arm in thanks. 'We cross to the rope and climb,' Burden said. 'Wind goes ahead of us as a diversion, and Nightshade follows Wind to prepare our victim. Are we ready?'

'As ready as we're going to be,' Llan said.

'Good.' Burden stood, keeping to the shadows. Nightshade disappeared along the dark rim of the bridge. Burden wouldn't be able to watch him. Dream Riders always traveled at their own pace.

Wind shrank until he was the size of a blade of grass. Then he turned into a spark and swirled through the air ahead of them. Fants moved ahead of Burden, leading the troop. He kept them low in the tall grass, pushing it down as he moved, somehow doing so silently. Burden thanked the Mysteries that Fants had agreed to come. Burden wouldn't have been able to move that quietly without him.

The Foot Soldiers slinked off to one side, moving as a unit, almost looking like a creature themselves. The grass continued to the wall, and then there were hedges along the side. But when they reached the wall, Fants slid along the side, moving to the road. It wasn't until Burden followed that he saw the open gate.

So trusting, these Islanders, even in the middle of a war.

Or perhaps they didn't think it was war yet, not with only two casualties. It was the importance of those casualties that escalated this conflict.

A dark shape slithered over the wall. Nightshade was inside.

Fants worked his way around the gate, keeping to the shadows. Burden and the remaining infantry followed. The Foot Soldiers climbed over the spot that Nightshade had used.

Burden could no longer see Wind. The light from four torches burning over the arched doorways made sparks of their own. Wind probably played in those sparks, waiting for his companions. The courtyard seemed unusually light. The tiles depicted scenes of some sort, religious scenes. Burden's heart began to pound hard. He didn't know if he could safely touch those tiles. If the Islanders were smart, they would have poured poison on every surface in this place.

Nightshade slithered along the tiles, heading toward the flowerpots lining the building's wall. He was a giant black shape that remained unchanged. No poison here. He apparently didn't even have any fear of it.

Fants signaled with his hand and the entire troop moved as one unit to the pots near Nightshade. The edge of the rope was tied to a tree. The Islanders had probably forgotten about it in the excitement from that night.

A spark floated past Burden, swirling up and up and up. Nightshade wrapped his body around the rope and parts of it disappeared under his darkness. Burden climbed up next. It had been a long time since he climbed a rope. Fortunately it was sturdy. It curled around his hands. He pulled himself up slowly so that he wouldn't touch any of Nightshade's darkness.

The rest of the troop would follow, two on the rope at all times, in rank order. The Foot Soldiers would climb next, followed by the Infantry. Fants would bring up the rear, partly because he had lost all of his rank, and partly because it would work better to have a competent pair of eyes at the bottom.

When Nightshade reached the edge of the balcony, he got off the rope and slithered along the stone, hiding in the shadows. Wind was floating over the rope, waiting for the others.

Burden pulled level with the stone floor of the balcony. The guard had torches around him. His feet were bare and black with dirt. He couldn't have been more than sixteen. His angular face didn't even have the trace of a beard. The pockets of his light robe bulged, probably with poison, and a vial of it sat on the table beside him. Behind him, the double doors leading into the room were closed, and the room was dark.

Nightshade had reached the edge of the doors. Burden clung to the rope, his arms aching from supporting his weight. He looked down. Owrie was behind him, several feet lower on the rope.

Wind floated past him, a tiny light in the darkness, as if checking the position of the others, then floated up. He was a spark the size of Burden's fingernail – almost big enough to see the little man in the center of the light – and he looked vaguely threatening, more as something that would start a fire than as something that would become alive.

He floated toward the Islander and Burden held his breath. He moved one hand higher so that he could see better. The Islander didn't notice.

Wind floated around the Islander's face. Burden's heart was pounding. If Wind did this wrong, he would die.

Suddenly Wind shot up four sizes until he was the size of the Islander's head. He slammed his small body into the Islander's nose. The boy screamed and clawed at his face.

Nightshade rose to his full height and pulled open the doors.

Burden climbed on the balcony.

The boy grabbed at Wind, but Wind shrank to spark size. The boy's shaking hand found the vial and tried to uncork it. Wind landed in his hair and pulled. The boy got the cork off.

The rope below Burden shook as another Fey climbed on it.

The Islander boy had enough poison to kill them all.

The Islander grabbed at Wind with his other hand. The poison was shaking out of the vial, drops landing on the stone. Burden grabbed his knife as Nightshade slipped inside.

Wind raised his small head, saw Burden, and placed his hands over the Islander's eyes. It was a dangerous move, because the boy was very likely to pour poison on Wind. The boy splashed the poison toward his own face as Burden let his knife fly.

It caught the boy in the chest. He grunted and toppled backwards. Wind floated up with the air, becoming small again, and floated inside the open doors.

The poison spilled all over the stone. Burden grabbed the railing around the balcony and sat on it, raising his feet above the liquid. He hadn't counted on this. Other vials smashed as the boy fell.

The sound was deafening.

Burden waved Owrie to a stop. She rested halfway up the rope, with Llan behind her. The rest of his troop were huddled near the wall, open and vulnerable to anything that appeared on the courtyard below.

Wind landed on Burden's shoulder, sending a warmth down his arm. 'Warn them about the poison,' he whispered.

The boy wasn't dead yet. He raised his head and pulled at the knife, making whimpering sounds as he tried to free it. Burden would have to finish him off, but he couldn't get near. The boy was soaked in poison.

Wind floated down the rope, pausing beside Owrie and then beside Llan on his way.

Burden crawled along the railing toward the boy. It shook beneath his weight. It wasn't made for more than decoration. If an Islander had hit it at full speed, the railing would shatter.

The boy didn't see him. He was muttering something – a prayer? – the words were unfamiliar, but their pattern was ritualistic. His hands were dry as they latched onto the knife.

Suddenly Wind was beside Burden. He was tiny, about the size of a finger. He grinned at Burden then hovered above the boy and shouted. The boy started, his hands falling back. He groped for a vial of the poison as Burden leaned over, grabbed the knife, and twisted it as he yanked it free.

Blood poured out of the boy. He wouldn't last long now.

Wind floated past Burden and toward the door. Burden shoved the knife back into its hilt. He braced himself on the railing, holding himself in place with his hands. He would have to leap past the boy and hope that the stone was dry.

The railing shook as Owrie climbed on it. It creaked under the strain of their combined weights.

'Watch out for the poison,' Burden whispered, but she didn't appear to hear him. She was staring at the Islander. His hands were groping, but otherwise he wasn't moving. The blood coated his robe.

'Let me finish him,' she whispered. She almost licked her lips as she did so.

'No.' Burden spoke louder than he had planned. Were these

Islanders deaf? He had never had a troop make so much noise. 'He's coated in poison.'

'Pity,' she said, her voice matching his. 'Such a waste of marvelous materials.'

Wind opened the doors from the inside. He had transformed to his full height, his wings ghostly shapes in the darkness. If Burden leapt carefully, he wouldn't touch the balcony at all.

'This thing isn't stable,' Owrie said.

'I know.' Burden rose on his toes and launched himself toward the doors. Wind stepped back. The railing clanged behind him as it shook.

'Careful!' Owrie snapped.

Burden landed on the rugs and rolled away from the balcony. His back hit a piece of furniture.

The room wasn't as dark as he had expected. A fire burned in the next room over, sending a bit of orange light into this room. He stood, rubbing his back, and Owrie jumped inside.

She rolled and banged herself too. Llan was crawling along the railing, looking hungrily at the dying Islander.

'Keep your people off that Islander,' Burden whispered to Owrie.

'Don't worry,' she whispered back. 'We don't like dying any more than you do.'

He brushed himself off. Light filtered under the door across the room, and when he squinted, he saw two pairs of bare feet pacing. What were these Islanders thinking, guarding their religious leaders with children?

Still, that made things easier for Burden.

Llan landed in the room, but didn't roll. He picked himself up with grace, and stared out the door at the boy. VeHeter was on the railing. The others were coming up.

Apparently the Islanders outside hadn't heard them at all.

Burden threaded his way around the couch. It all rested on Nightshade now. He didn't see Nightshade or his quarry, so he headed toward the light, keeping in the shadows as best he could.

When he reached the other door, he looked in.

The room was sparsely furnished: two tables and matching bedside chairs, a fireplace in which flames were dying, and a large bed covered with quilts. Vials sat on the tables like sentries, but they hadn't been used.

A man lay on the bed, long and thin, his golden curls spread along the pillows. He was on his back, his hands pinned to his side, his face completely hidden by Nightshade's darkness. The dreams hadn't started yet or the Rocaan would be twitching with them. But Nightshade had barely had a chance to begin.

372

Owrie came up behind Burden and started to go in, but he caught her arm. He had forgotten about the Foot Soldiers' enthusiasm for their work. He pulled her out of the room and closed the door halfway behind him.

'Give Nightshade a moment,' he said.

She frowned and wrenched her arm from his grasp. Then she stuck her hands under her armpits and wandered back to the balcony. VeHeter was inside now, and Condi was on the railing. It looked precarious, but Burden figured it would hold.

By the time all of the troop was inside the room, Nightshade would be ready for them.

Then the Fey would be rid of this menace once and for all.

Forty-Six

Adrian ran across Shadowlands. The mist swirled around him almost as if it could stop him. He had never moved this fast, not in Shadowlands. The cabins seemed closer than they had before, and more than one Fey watched him run.

He had to get to Coulter.

He was probably already too late.

He remembered seeing bits of Ort's broken body after they finished with him. He no longer looked like a person. Most of his skin was gone, his mouth had been grafted shut, and his hands were solid slabs of flesh. Only his eyes remained, opened and filled with terror.

Coulter was too young to die.

Especially like that.

'Wait!' Gift's reedy voice called out to Adrian in the fog, but he wasn't going to wait. For all he knew the Black King's great-grandson had handed his best friend over to the Warders when Coulter told Gift he was going to leave.

No one stood near the Warders' cabin. Smoke rose from the chimney. Adrian bounded up the stairs and hesitated. All the years of training, all the years in Shadowlands had taught him not barge anywhere, to figure he was unwanted instead of needed.

He was unwanted.

They were probably killing Coulter.

He shoved the door open.

And stopped.

Touched and Rotin stood beside each other, their arms covered with blood. The room smelled of fear, iron, and smoke. But those were only details. The thing that caught his attention was the giant circle of skin resting on the table.

'My god,' Adrian said. 'What did you do to him?'

The boy had no face or limbs left. He was just a circle of skin with blood dripping off the sides.

'Get out,' Rotin said.

'Not without Coulter.'

'You have no place here, Islander,' Rotin said. 'Get out.'

374

'No.' He walked toward the table. He didn't know what he would do with the boy once he had him. Mend couldn't fix this. Only the Warders could. 'Coulter?'

He thought he heard a whimper from inside the circle. As he got closer, the stench was nearly overpowering.

Touched put a finger on Adrian's arm and he winced. 'You'd better leave,' Touched said softly.

'Not without Coulter,' Adrian repeated.

'Or you'll do what, Islander?' Rotin asked. 'Melt us all with your poison?'

Adrian whirled. He'd lost five years of his life to these people trying to protect his son, and still they'd ruined Luke. Now they were killing Coulter. He had nothing left. Nothing.

'If I had holy water, I'd pour it on you first, Rotin. You're the most evil, useless creature I'd ever seen. And you, Touched, preying on a child. Coulter did nothing to you. Give him to me. Now.'

'So tough,' Rotin said, her voice almost a caress. She came closer to Adrian. He had to keep his feet planted so that he wouldn't back away. Some of the stench was coming from her. Pouches lay at her feet. Empty pouches.

His stomach turned.

'Give him to me,' he said.

The stench had grown stronger, almost like burning flesh instead of rotting flesh. His stomach rolled, and a wave of nausea swept through him. Someone pounded on the door behind them.

'You have no rights to the boy, little man,' Rotin said. 'He's ours now.'

A curl of smoke rose off the flesh circle. Touched made an odd sound and placed a hand on the circle's side. It jiggled.

'Rotin!'

She turned, saw the rising smoke, and glanced at Touched in confusion. Adrian grabbed the flesh circle, wincing as it squished against his hands. It was hot. He pulled his hands away. They weren't burned, but nearly so.

The smell of crisped flesh grew stronger.

Then a hole broke through the circle and a beam of light slammed into Adrian, knocking him against the wall. The light held Coulter in it, not his physical self, but his mental self. He was terrified, assaulting Adrian with deep emotion, words and babbled phrases inside his mind.

The air had left Adrian's body. 'Stop, stop,' he said, but he didn't know if he was speaking or thinking the words. Coulter didn't stop. The light encircled Adrian like a protection. He couldn't see for the brightness. Outside the pool of light and emotion, he could hear vague voices, and more pounding, but he could make no sense of it.

Finally the breath came back into his body. His chest hurt from the lack of air. It almost felt as if Coulter were clinging to him in that light. Adrian stood, slowly. His vision was coming back, studded with red and green dots as his eyes adjusted to the brightness.

Touched and Rotin had backed away from the light stream. Smoke rose from the flesh circle. It was melting, and as it melted away, it revealed Coulter inside, huddled in a ball.

Adrian had never felt such relief.

Apparently Coulter felt his relief too and some of the emotional assault eased. *Coulter,* Adrian thought, *We have to get out of here. Quickly before they can recover.*

Coulter's grip on Adrian seemed to tighten. The light got brighter. Suddenly Coulter flew through it, his small body ensheathed in it. He landed beside Adrian, both wrapped in light.

We have to go, Coulter thought, the words so powerful they felt like blows. *They know how to break through this.*

Adrian picked up Coulter. The boy wrapped his legs around Adrian's waist. Coulter felt as strong as his emotions had. The light tightened until it was close around them. Rotin was shouting at Touched – something about a pouch. The door had opened and Niche came in, holding Gift's hand.

Coulter was right; they would only have a moment before the Fey would converge on them again.

Adrian ran for the door, bumping the table with his hip. He felt odd, moving with such light around him, but the light didn't seem to protect him from anything except the people. Niche moved away from it. Gift was yelling at Coulter. Coulter sent a beam of light in Gift's direction, but Adrian only saw it. He felt nothing.

'Nooooo!' Gift wailed, his voice echoing around Adrian's head.

Adrian ignored him. He slipped through the door, into the gray mist.

The light that Coulter wrapped around them reflected the mist like a hundred tiny prisms. Adrian ran down the steps and into the mist itself. He knew where the Circle Door was – he used to pass it every day – but he couldn't go through it.

He was breathing hard. He hadn't run in years, and he hadn't carried more than a few bundles of wood in all that time. Coulter was clinging to him so hard that Adrian found it difficult to draw breath. The Fey they ran by shouted at them, but those shouts didn't echo as Gift's had. Apparently Coulter had done something to bring Gift's voice inside the light.

The Meeting Rock loomed like a dark thing out of the mist. The Circle Door was across from it. Adrian looked behind him. The Warders were following. He had left a man-sized hole in the mist, and a trail of fading light through the hole. The mist did not close up after him. It was as if he had burned something through the center of Shadowlands.

Coulter pushed away from him. *We can't have the light and get through the door.*

I think we need this light, Adrian sent back.

Not if we want out. Coulter ran to the precise place where the door was. Adrian followed as the light winked out around them.

Suddenly the grayness had returned to Shadowlands. He hadn't realized how much the light refreshed him, warmed him, made him feel strong. He stopped beside Coulter as the Warders caught up.

'Stop!' Touched yelled. 'Now!'

Coulter didn't even glance at them. He stuck a hand through the mist and the Circle Door opened. Sunlight streamed around the Dirt Circle and the scent of fresh air and pine trees flowed in. Adrian grinned at the familiar sight.

Home.

He was getting out of the grayness and going home.

Touched had almost caught up to them. Rotin was farther behind, her misused body unable to keep up with the rigors of the run.

'Let's go, son,' Adrian said to Coulter. He put a hand on Coulter's back to propel him out of Shadowlands, but Coulter wouldn't move.

Adrian looked at him. The boy's face was white, his eyes huge. His hand still extended through the door, keeping it open, but he wouldn't move.

'Coulter?' Adrian asked.

'You go,' he whispered. 'I'll stay.'

'They'll kill you,' Adrian said.

'I can't,' Coulter whispered.

Touched sent a beam of light their way. Adrian pulled Coulter out of the way. The light went through the door and started a small fire in the Dirt Circle.

'Now,' Adrian said.

'No,' Coulter said.

Then Adrian understood. Coulter had spent his entire life in grayness. He couldn't handle the smells, the colors, the sounds.

But he had no choice.

Adrian wrapped himself around the boy, protecting Coulter's eyes, and jumped through the Circle Door. They landed in the Dirt Circle, near the fire, and Adrian rolled away from it, holding Coulter's head to protect it.

The Circle Door winked closed, but the lights around it started flashing again a moment later. Adrian knew what that meant. Touched was coming through.

But they were on Adrian's turf now.

He didn't have time to enjoy the sunlight or the birds or the fresh air. He picked up Coulter, who was shivering, and plowed through the trees away from the road, heading toward the gurgling river. The river was deep here, but they could follow its edge into Jahn. The Fey were sometimes linear thinkers. They might try the road first, which would give Coulter and Adrian some extra time.

Coulter's terror was as strong as it had been in the Warders' cabin. 'Stay with me,' Adrian whispered as he clung to the boy. 'You'll be safe as long as you're with me.'

Coulter said nothing. He kept his face buried in Adrian's shoulder. The strong, powerful child Adrian had seen in Shadowlands had been replaced by a tiny terrified boy.

Adrian hoped he could keep his promise as he slipped down the embankment toward the river. They only had one chance to survive – and all of it rested on Adrian's wit, and his five-year-old memories of Blue Isle.

Forty-Seven

The gates to the Tabernacle were open. Stowe cursed under his breath. The fools. They should have had guards everywhere, and locks on all the doors. That way, if the Fey wanted in, they would have to work at it.

In fact, if he were planning for a Fey attack, he would have vials of holy water rigged to spill on anyone who passed through. The Islander visitors would be angry but fine, and the Fey ones would die.

Simple as that.

But he had not been planning for such an attack until sundown. That was when Nicholas finally gave him permission to round up the guards.

Monte had given fifteen of his best men. Monte had wanted to come along, but Stowe wouldn't let him. Confident as Nicholas was about his relationship with the Fey, it didn't seem quite right. Stowe lacked that confidence. He felt that the person behind Alexander's murder might kill Nicholas as well.

The chances were slimmer now that Jewel was dead, but they still existed. With Nicholas gone, the children still babies, the entire Isle would be thrown into chaos. If Nicholas didn't want to prepare for such a contingency, Stowe would. After all, he would be the one left to clean up the mess.

The wind was off the river, cool and smelling faintly of damp ground. The full moon provided more light than Stowe had planned on – he wondered if any of the Auds were watching him and the guards. If so, they were doing nothing about the large group just standing outside the wall. Stowe continued to stand for a moment longer as a test, hoping that someone would emerge, anyone who would tell him to go away.

No one did.

They left the gates open and did not monitor who came in and out. He would wager that once he crossed the courtyard, he would find the main doors unlocked and unguarded as well.

Matthias should have ordered protection. After the attack the night before, he should have known what was going to happen. But

Matthias had gotten careless since he became Rocaan, almost as if he felt he weren't worthy of the position, and he was strongly disliked. No Elder would countermand Matthias's orders to protect him, like Stowe would do for Nicholas.

Right now, Nicholas needed protecting. He was doing well, considering.

Considering.

But now was not a time to do marginally well. Now was the most crucial time of Nicholas's kingship. Everything rested on the next few days.

If Matthias died without sharing the Secret of holy water, the kingdom died. Nicholas didn't realize that. Nicholas, in his own way, was expendable. Matthias had ensured that he was not.

Torches burned over all the windows and over the double doors. Faint curlicues of smoke rose toward the moon. The torches burned every night, leaving scorch marks on the whitewash. Stowe used to come here as a boy and peer over the wall, watching the Auds go through their morning rituals. He had always wanted to be part of the Tabernacle, but he could not.

He was the eldest son. It had been his lot to become Lord Stowe. His younger brother had been forced into the religion. Last Stowe heard, his brother was an Aud in the Snow Mountains where the discipline among the Rocaanists was lax. His brother had hated the church as much as Stowe had loved it. If only they had been able to change roles. But rules were rules, as his father used to say, and existed for reasons that were beyond the ken of normal men.

Stowe agreed with that.

The Fey's arrival had violated his sense of rules, of fairness, and continued to do so. He admired Nicholas's ability to flow with the changes, and knew such an ability was necessary, but wished Nicholas also knew when to apply hard and strict rules on everything.

Like now. If Nicholas had given more than a begrudging permission, he would have made it easier for Stowe to bring his guards into the Tabernacle. Stowe faced a long discussion with either an Elder or with Matthias himself. Stowe was half worried that Matthias would throw them out after his little scene with Nicholas that afternoon.

Clearly, though, the Tabernacle needed his help. He would convince Matthias to take the guards no matter what it took.

He strode through the gate and across the courtyard. Halfway to the double doors, a movement on the balcony above caught his eye. He looked up, but saw nothing.

Except a rope, hanging from the balcony railing.

Stowe swore under his breath. He went to the rope. It was tied to a

380

tree. This had to be the rope that Luke had used to get in. Damn the Elders. They knew and had done nothing. They wanted Matthias out as badly as Nicholas did.

And Matthias, the man Stowe had seen that afternoon, had been in no real condition to take precautions for himself.

Stowe tugged on the rope. It was hanging loosely from the balcony. The rope swinging in the slight breeze had been what caught his eye.

He posted two guards beside it, and went to the double doors. As he thought. No Auds standing guard. The light from the torches provided him with a good view of the area. Except for his own guards, he was alone.

With his fist, he pushed down on the handle. It turned easily, but he didn't open the door. Instead, he pounded on the knocker, allowing the sound to echo throughout the Tabernacle. Good to scare these people just a little, and let them know that Matthias wasn't the only one jeopardized by the Fey.

No one answered. The discomfort he felt grew. He glanced at the guards behind him. One was looking up at that balcony. It bothered Stowe as well. The rope should have been gone. As it was, it pointed clearly to the Rocaan's rooms. He hoped that Matthias had been smart enough to change locations.

He doubted that Matthias had.

But Matthias may have spent another night in the worship room. He had done so after Luke left. There was no telling with these religious people.

When no one answered the knock, Stowe rapped again, hard this time so that the sound not only echoed through the Tabernacle, but through the courtyard as well.

Finally the door swung open. An Aud poked his head out. His hair was tousled and his eyes were half open. He had been sound asleep.

He couldn't have been more than twelve.

No protection. No protection at all.

When Stowe returned to the palace, he would check the systems that Nicholas had in place. Sometimes the old ways were taken for granted without taking change into account.

Nicholas might not have implemented new systems with all the deaths. Guards might be awaiting orders from the new king.

The thought made Stowe cold.

The Aud was staring at him as if he hadn't seen a lord before.

'I'd like to see the Holy Sir,' Stowe said.

The boy shook his head. ''Tis sorry I am, sir, but the Rocaan beds down just near twilight.'

'I think he'll see me,' Stowe said.

'I canna bother him, sir. Tis orders I have, and tis strong ones.' The boy was not from Jahn. He would never be in the Tabernacle if he were from a farming family, but his speech marked him as a member of the serving class. He had to be from the mountains or the Cliffs of Blood.

Or the Kenniland Marshes.

Stowe had had enough.

'He'll see me,' Stowe said, and pushed past the child as Nicholas had done earlier that day.

Darkness made the Tabernacle gloomy. Candles burned in lamps around the entry area, but the entire effect was one of deep blackness. Another Aud came toward Stowe from the gloom. He was older than the first, but not by much.

'Is there an Officiate here?' Stowe asked.

The newer Aud shook his head. 'The Officiates are traveling right now,' he said.

'Then who is running the Tabernacle?'

'Elder Porciluna,' said the first Aud. 'He is still awake if you would like to speak with him.'

'No,' Stowe said. 'I will talk with the Rocaan.'

The new Aud crossed his arms and blocked the stairs. 'The Rocaan said none of the king's men could visit him.'

That was the first evidence of smart thinking Stowe had seen since he arrived at the gates. 'I need to see him. You'll wake him.'

'No, your lordship.'

The guards were crowding the door, blocking the light. The young Aud looked frightened. After the scene with Nicholas that afternoon, who could be surprised that they were afraid of the guards?

Stowe clenched his fists. Once this had been a wonderful place to live. Before the Fey everyone had gotten along. The Tabernacle and the palace had worked together. Now they were frightened of each other.

The Fey would conquer the Isle by making the Islanders fight among themselves.

'Very well,' Stowe said. 'Let me see Elder Porciluna.' Perhaps he would have more sense than the Auds. No sense arguing with boys when he could talk to someone with more power.

The young Aud nodded. The newer Aud waved him away. The young Aud disappeared down the corridor.

Stowe wasn't certain whether Porciluna would help him or not. Porciluna's desire to be Rocaan was well known. He would probably want Matthias out of the way – and keeping him unguarded was a good way to do it.

Stowe's own guards were crowding him. He turned. 'Get back,

men,' he said softly. 'Scout the area. Tell me if you see anything suspicious.'

'I don't think that's wise,' the newer Aud said.

'Either they look or I bring them inside,' Stowe said. 'This delay isn't wise. It is, in fact, angering me. The King sent his guards here in an effort to protect the Rocaan.'

'Frankly, Milord, there is no way we can know that. The entire Tabernacle has heard of their fight this afternoon. If I were the King –' The Aud interrupted himself and shook his head.

He didn't need to finish the sentence. Stowe knew what he was going to say. The King had every right to seek revenge against Matthias. Every right. Even the Auds knew that, and they should support their own leader.

The guards had backed away. Some were walking through the courtyard, quietly discussing the tile design. Others were pushing aside bushes. Still others were examining the rope.

Stowe tried not to sigh. He hated waiting more than anything else. The Aud was a small barrier. He could push past the man and hurry up the stairs. But a door opened on a side corridor, and Porciluna came out. He wore a satin sleeping robe. The sword around his neck was the only sign of his office. His cheeks were ruddy with sleep, and his eyes looked as if he had rubbed them awake.

'The Aud says you were sent by the King to guard the Rocaan,' Porciluna said. 'Are we talking about the same king? Alexander hasn't been raised from the dead, has he?'

Porciluna's words stung. No wonder the old Rocaan had passed him over. Porciluna would never be a diplomat.

'No,' Stowe said, making certain that he spoke evenly. 'He is not back from the dead. King Nicholas regrets his burst of anger and has thought about the things the Rocaan told him. The Rocaan is right; Blue Isle needs him. The King will provide him with trained protection.'

'Blue Isle needs the Rocaan's knowledge,' Porciluna said, almost under his breath. Stowe watched him warily. If he had ever heard one of the lords speak that way about Nicholas, he would have reported it to the King immediately. He felt no such loyalty for the Rocaan.

'The Isle needs the Rocaan,' Stowe said. 'I would like to station guards at his doors, and on his balcony, as well as throughout the Tabernacle.'

'Considering the relationship between the palace and the Tabernacle at this moment, the Rocaan would be a fool to allow this.' Porciluna grinned. 'I, of course, think it's a wonderful idea.'

'I'm sure you do,' Stowe said, managing to speak without the sarcasm that he felt. 'Let me talk with the Rocaan. After all, it is his decision.'

Porciluna fingered the small sword around his neck. 'It's most irregular, you know. This sort of thing.'

Stowe suppressed a sigh. Was the man angling for a bribe? That would be even more irregular. 'The King believes that something might happen soon. Maybe even tonight. The Fey take revenge quite seriously.'

'I'm sure they do,' Porciluna said with the same guileless tone Stowe had used a moment before. Stowe hadn't fooled him at all.

'So I would like to see the Rocaan now.'

'Really, milord, I do think I would need to discuss this with him. We have Auds at the door. Tomorrow morning –'

'Your Auds are untrained children. I have soldiers who learned to fight the Fey in the Invasion and the subsequent battles.'

'You have soldiers who are really guards, men who were lucky enough to survive until we provided you with holy water. Milord, we are capable of taking care of ourselves.'

This time, Stowe did sigh. 'I have orders, Respected Sir. My orders are to talk with the Rocaan. At least allow me to perform my duties.'

'I do think this discussion can wait until morning.'

'I don't,' Stowe snapped. Actually, Porciluna probably was right – the discussion could wait – but it was becoming a matter of principle for Stowe.

'Milord.' The voice came from behind him. It was tentative, as if it knew it shouldn't be speaking.

Porciluna had looked over his shoulder. His face had gone pale.

Stowe's heart began to beat faster. He turned.

One of the guards he had posted near the rope stood behind him. The man's face was streaked with blood.

'What happened?' Stowe asked.

The guard held out his hand. Blood was smeared on his fingers. 'Forgive me, milord, but I think we should go upstairs.'

'We don't provide protection in here on a whim,' Porciluna snapped. 'A fake emergency will not get you through the doors.'

'It's not fake, Respected Sir,' the guard said. 'The blood isn't mine.'

'Then where's it from?' Porciluna asked.

'The balcony, Respected Sir.'

'The Rocaan's balcony?' Stowe asked.

'Yes, milord.'

Suddenly Stowe was not going to wait for permission. 'Gather the guards outside and send someone up that rope. Send five in here. Have them go up the stairs to the Rocaan's apartment.'

The guard nodded and hurried out.

'You can't go up there,' Porciluna said.

Stowe shoved him aside. 'I don't care what you say or want. If I discover something wrong up there, I'll put you in the keep forever.'

'You can't –' Porciluna started.

'I can.' Stowe was already halfway up the stairs. He shouted the last. 'Because your actions probably cost a man's life.'

Forty-Eight

Adrian could barely breathe. He had run a long way along the river's edge. His pants were torn and his legs were bleeding. Thorns on nearby bushes had scratched his arms and face. More than once he had been hit in the head by a tree branch. All the way, though, he had managed to maintain his footing, something which astonished him, considering the thick mud and the steepness of the bank.

Coulter clung to him, small body wrapped around Adrian's like a second skin. As the brambles hit them, Coulter clung tighter. The boy lifted his head once, whimpered, and lowered it again. Adrian had not planned on this. He had hoped Coulter could take care of himself. At this speed, the Fey would catch them in no time.

The darkness grew until finally, Adrian had to stop near a large oak tree that hung over the river. 'Coulter,' he whispered, his voice barely audible over the river's current, 'let me set you down.'

The boy shook his head against Adrian's chest.

'Please, Coulter, I have to rest a moment.'

The boy clung tighter. Adrian leaned against the tree for support. His back ached, his shoulders ached, and his arms ached. He wasn't certain how much farther he could go. A full moon was rising, casting light almost as bright as day across the water.

The river was wide here, and the current suggested that it was deep. He couldn't wade across even if he wanted to, nor could he swim. With Coulter this panicked about the common things, he would be even more terrified in the water. Adrian couldn't swim across a calm river with the boy this scared, let alone one that raged like this one did here.

Twigs snapped behind him. The Fey were getting close. They had to be.

'Coulter,' he said, 'I can't keep moving and carry you at the same time. You'll have to walk, son.'

Coulter shook his head.

'This is what the real world is like, Coulter. You were born here. It's all right. If it isn't, son, please, use one of your special powers. But I need to set you down.'

After a moment, Coulter loosened his grip on Adrian. Adrian tried not to sigh with relief. He lowered the boy. Coulter clung to his leg with one hand like a two-year-old would, and stared at the world around him.

Adrian stared too. It had been so long since he had seen anything real. The grayness that filled the Shadowlands made even bright colors seem muted. Here, even in the moonlit nighttime, the greens were vivid, the browns vibrant, the blues astonishing. The smell of the trees and grass almost overpowered him, and the rush of the river was deafening.

'It's all like this?' Coulter asked, his voice trembling.

'All,' Adrian said. There was no way to explain how different and yet similar other areas were.

'I can't,' Coulter whispered. He clung so hard to Adrian's legs that his fingers were digging into the skin.

'You have to.' Adrian looked around the tree. He couldn't see the Fey, but he knew they were there. Somewhere, searching for him and Coulter.

Coulter shook his head and buried his face in Adrian's thigh. Adrian pried the boy away and crouched, holding Coulter so that he could see his face. 'I know you're frightened,' Adrian said. 'But they would have killed you back there. This is our only choice.'

'They never hurt me before,' Coulter said.

'They didn't know what you were before.'

Tears lined the bottom of Coulter's eyes. He rubbed at them with his free hand. 'I don't want to go anywhere,' he said. 'I hate it here.'

Adrian rested his forehead against the boy's, wishing he could absorb some of the child's power and protect them both. But he couldn't.

'Try walking with me,' he said. 'Just a ways.'

Coulter's lower lip trembled. A tear spilled down his cheek. Adrian took Coulter's hand, but before he could stand, Coulter grabbed Adrian's wrist with his other hand. 'Don't leave me,' he said.

Adrian frowned. He didn't know where that comment had come from. 'I would never leave you,' he said.

'But if I can't – if something tries – if they catch us, please don't leave me,' Coulter said.

'I will be beside you the whole way,' Adrian said.

Coulter nodded. Adrian glanced around the tree, but saw nothing. He hoped something in Coulter's heightened senses would notice if the Fey were following.

They took a step forward. Coulter was staring at his feet, placing them gingerly between brambles and fallen twigs. Each time he moved forward, he winced as if he expected something to bite him. He had never seen ground beneath his feet, only grayness.

'Pretend like you're inside,' Adrian said. 'It's like being on a floor.'

'What is all this stuff?' Coulter asked.

'Grass and sticks and plants. Growing things,' Adrian said.

They took only a few steps, before the bank rose to a muddy edge. Adrian glanced over his shoulder again. Their footprints were visible in the mud.

'Can you tell if they're coming?' he asked.

Coulter shook his head. His face was streaked from the tears.

Great. The boy was terrified of everything, the Fey were after them, and Adrian didn't know where they would go. He couldn't take them to Luke because the Fey knew how to turn Luke into someone else. That left the palace as his only choice, but after the murder of King Alexander and the attempt on the Rocaan, he wasn't certain if he'd be welcomed there.

The Fey would come. They would find Coulter. They had to. They couldn't let this boy escape. He held too many secrets, too much information within his small person. Even if they killed him, they would learn whether or not he was similar to the Fey.

Adrian carried a lot of secrets too. They didn't want him to get away either.

They reached the narrow bank. A mud slide had formed into the river. Tree roots were hanging over the water. They couldn't go around the tree because of the tangled undergrowth on the other side. They would have to cross on the roots. Coulter would never stand for that, and Adrian wasn't sure if he could cross and handle Coulter's weight.

No Fey yet. They were safe on that front.

Coulter stopped in front of the uncovered roots, his eyes wide. 'What is it?' he asked. 'A frozen monster?'

'A tree,' Adrian said. 'A plant.' Then he realized that Coulter probably had no idea what plants were. 'Remember when the Domestics tried to grow things in the dirt box? They were trying to grow plants.'

Coulter ignored him. The boy was staring at the water several feet below the roots. 'What happens if I slip?'

'You fall in.'

The voice made Adrian jump. He scanned the bushes. He saw nothing, no one, not a face among the undergrowth.

Coulter wrapped his arms around himself. He was standing too close to the edge of the bank for Adrian's comfort.

Adrian put his hand on the boy's shoulder and pulled him closer. 'That was Fey,' he whispered to Coulter.

'I would hope so,' the voice said, just as loud as it had before. The voice was male. 'That's what you were speaking.'

'Touched?' Coulter asked, his voice shaking, but the strength he had shown earlier returning. 'Rotin?'

'Bah, Warders,' the voice said. The comment was followed by the sound of spitting. 'If you're bringing them, I'm going now. You can get across on your own.'

'No, wait!' Adrian said. Coulter pressed close to him. They wouldn't get much farther tonight, and he still wasn't certain where they were going. If they found a safe place to bed down, they might be all right in the morning. 'We're trying to get away from the Warders.'

'Sure you are,' the voice said. 'And what kind of reward do you get now that you found me?'

'Found you?' Adrian said. 'You're the one who found us. We didn't even know you were here.'

'We can't even see you,' Coulter said.

'Well I can see you,' the voice said, 'and, unless I miss my guess, you're either Doppelgängers or Spies sent to flush me out.'

'We're Islanders,' Adrian said. 'You can check our eyes or touch us. If I remember right that should prove to you that we aren't Fey.'

'You're hiding from the Warders too?' Coulter spoke softly, almost hesitantly.

'Evil, evil creatures those Warders,' the voice said. 'They have no value for life. I'm not even sure if they know what life is.'

'Really?' Adrian said. He wasn't sure if he should keep going. He didn't know if this was a trap. Maybe it was a trap, or a way to force Adrian and Coulter to hurry across the fallen bank, and plunge to their deaths.

'Really,' the voice said. 'They experiment on living people. Try to get those people to die for their spells. They figure anyone without magick isn't a person, so it doesn't matter. I say it does.'

'I have magick,' Coulter said, his voice small. 'But they experimented on me.'

'Sure you have magick, kid. You have as much magick as I do.'

'I do,' Coulter said. Adrian squeezed his shoulder to silence the boy. Something about this meeting wasn't right. If the voice's owner knew about the Warders and spoke Fey, then Adrian would have to assume the speaker was Fey. But the bitterness that came out over the Warders and the lack of magick sounded distinctly unFey.

'That kid has quite a complex,' the voice said, apparently addressing Adrian.

'You would too if you had grown up among the Fey,' Adrian said.

'Oh, trust me. I understand completely.' The voice chuckled and the sound carried across the river.

'Shhh,' Adrian said. 'I don't know how close they are.'

'I do,' the voice said. 'They sent a contingent down the main path and another to Daisy Stream. They haven't figured out yet that you're too smart to travel on the road, but it will only be a matter of time. They'll probably send out Gull Riders for you and you won't even know you've been spotted.'

This conversation was growing stranger, and it was making Adrian very uncomfortable. He pulled Coulter even closer. 'Thank you for your help,' Adrian said. 'But we need to continue. I hope to make Jahn by morning.'

'Not at the pace you're going,' the voice said. 'And the Riders will be out by then. Beast Riders, Gull Riders, some soft furry little Rider, anything that you won't notice. They'll snatch you back up and bring you to the safety of the Shadowlands in no time.'

'You sound very knowledgeable about the Fey,' Adrian said.

'Well, by the Powers, what do you think I am?'

'Nooo!' Coulter cried and pushed himself hard against Adrian's leg. Adrian lost his balance and nearly fell off the bank. He grabbed a tree branch and held on, heart pounding.

'Well,' Adrian said, trying to sound calm, 'if you're going to take us back, you'd better do so now.'

'Take you back?' The bushes rustled. 'Why would I do that?'

'Isn't that what you're supposed to do? Follow your orders and return us to Shadowlands?'

'I haven't followed orders in years.' The bushes rustled some more and a little man emerged from them. He was just a few inches taller than Coulter, and built very square. His skin was dark, though, and his features were Fey. He looked like a Fey inexpertly carved from a tree stump.

'You're a Red Cap,' Adrian said, unable to keep the surprise out of his voice.

'I *was* a Red Cap,' the little man said. He held out his hands and pirouetted. 'If you'll notice, no smell of decay, no dead flesh hanging off the skin, no blood coating the garments. I have been clean since Caseo's death and I plan to stay that way until I die.'

Coulter had brought his head up. He was staring at the Red Cap as if he had never seen one before. Adrian must have been staring the same way. Neither of them had seen a clean Red Cap. Caps were usually tending the dead – those killed in battle – pulling skin and blood off them. When they weren't doing that, they were doing similar duties for the Domestics, taking the place of Butchers (whom Rugar had not brought along) by butchering the animals for meat.

Adrian frowned. He hadn't heard of a missing Red Cap, except, of course, for the ones that died during the Invasion.

And the one who murdered the head Spell Warder.

'You killed Caseo,' Adrian said softly.

The Red Cap shrugged. 'A man has to do a good deed at least once in his life.'

'You killed someone?' Coulter asked, his voice breathless. Red Caps were forbidden to kill people. Such actions were punishable by death.

'He was trying to kill me. Seems only right, don't you think?'

Coulter didn't answer. Adrian didn't want to address the question. 'You've been hiding ever since?'

'It was either that or let them kill me.' The little man glanced toward the sky. The moon was directly overhead. 'They're going to start searching the woods soon. Tell me, boy. Are you folks running from Warders?'

Coulter nodded despite Adrian's grip on his shoulder.

'Good,' the little man said. 'Then come with me.'

'I'm sorry to question you,' Adrian said, 'but where would you take us?'

'To my home,' the little man said. 'We'd better hurry.'

'And why should we trust you?'

'Because I hate Warders, same as you.'

'There's no proof of that.'

The little man crossed his arms and grinned. 'There's no proof that you folks are running from the Fey either, but I figure you wouldn't be here otherwise. Now, why would I be here?'

'Because you're looking for us. Because you expect some sort of accolade for finding us,' Adrian said.

'As if they'd pay any attention to a Red Cap. Bet you never even heard my name. Bet as far as you're concerned my name is That Red Cap Who Killed Caseo.'

Adrian's cheeks grew warm. He was glad that the Red Cap wouldn't be able to see that in the dark.

'I'll bet most of them don't know my name either. I bet my name is long forgotten.'

'What is your name?' Coulter asked softly.

'See? If I were anything but That Red Cap Who Killed Caseo, the boy would know.' The Red Cap crouched in front of Coulter and stuck out his hand, Islander fashion. 'I'm Scavenger. Nice to meet you.'

Coulter gave Adrian an uneasy look.

'Take his hand,' Adrian said, 'and introduce yourself.'

Gingerly, the boy slipped his hand in the Cap's. 'Coulter,' the boy said. 'And Adrian.'

'Well,' the Cap said, 'Now that the social niceties are over, I suggest we get out of the light.'

'Where is your cabin?' Adrian asked.

'Through the woods,' the Cap said. 'Someone else built it for me, but I fixed it up. And I've been wanting company for a while.' He ducked under the bushes. Adrian stared at the hole for a moment, uncertain what to do next. If the Cap were actually working for the Fey, he would take them back to Shadowlands. But the little man sounded convincing.

'Is he Linked?' Adrian whispered to Coulter.

Coulter frowned, then shook his head. 'Not anywhere,' he said with a bit of surprise as if that were unusual.

The little man poked his head out of the hole. 'If you're going to come,' he said no longer sounding quite as friendly, 'come now.'

Adrian shot another glance at the tree. Crossing those roots in the dark, with Coulter so afraid of the air around him, was probably not a good idea. They couldn't backtrack, so they would have to try these woods anyway. Better to have someone lead them through. It was still two against one. If the Cap looked as if he were taking them to Shadowlands, they would run for it.

'Well?' the Cap asked.

'We're coming,' Adrian said. The Cap still sounded close, a bit too close for Adrian's comfort. He wanted the opportunity to warn Coulter not to discuss his own magick. Magick was a touchy subject with the Caps. They had none of their own – the only Fey with no magick and no possibility for it. The Fey said it was in the Cap's size. If they were small, they were magickless. All the Caps Adrian had seen bore this out.

'Do we have to go in there?' Coulter asked.

Adrian nodded. 'I'll be right behind you,' he said. He wanted to promise the boy they'd be safe, but he couldn't.

He had no idea if the Red Cap would hurt them or help them.

But he would find out.

Forty-Nine

Matthias dreamed he was on the Cardidas River, on the barge the Fey and Islanders had built together for Nicholas's wedding. The spray was up, the air chill, and the sun a faint haze through high clouds. The water was choppy. The wind buffeted the barge, hitting the sides of his face like a slap. He wore his long ceremonial robes, and he stood off to the side, watching Jewel in her inappropriate green, her long black hair flowing down her back.

Rugar talked with her, pleaded with her, but it didn't matter. She insisted on marrying the Islander. Fool that she was. Wasting the Fey blood and Fey heritage on such an inferior being.

Matthias squinted. His face felt heavy and a great weight pressed on his chest. The air seemed thicker than usual. Each breath was an effort.

The Shaman stood in the corner, silent, as if she approved of this match. He didn't know how she could. She knew, like the rest of them, that this was a pollution of the Black King's line.

An odd feeling of dread rose in his stomach. He didn't care about the Black King's line. Such a thought felt like blasphemy, even though he wasn't sure he believed in blasphemy. He grabbed for his filigree sword and didn't find it around his neck.

But he was supposed to perform the ceremony. How could he do that without wearing his robe? He patted his pockets. He was wearing breeches.

Jewel came over to him, spoke softly to him. She had her mother's voice, soft and yet powerful. No wonder Rugar had married her. She had died in childbirth too, just like Jewel. Jewel's brothers had had a different mother, one not nearly the equal of Jewel.

Matthias smiled at her, wishing she would linger longer, but she did not. She was his favorite of the Fey. She was –

– evil. He had to remember that. She had ordered Alexander's death.

He tried to roll over, but couldn't. This dream was haunting him. It was clinging to him, forcing him to think about things he didn't want to consider.

Nicholas looked like a pale, sickly creature as he stood at the railing. His hair streamed behind him, pale like the rest of him. How Jewel could mate such a one was beyond Matthias. The Fey mingled blood with their enemies, but usually after the land was conquered, not before, and never in a diplomatic way.

Rugar knew that, and still he was letting this go forward. He spoke briefly to the Shaman and she turned her back on him. Odd, that. The Shaman should always listen to the Leader.

Jewel was smiling. She actually looked as if she wanted to marry this man.

The breeze off the river was cold, yet his face was hot. He almost felt as if he were suffocating. The pressure on his chest had grown. It hurt. He brushed at it, startled again by the missing sword.

Jewel had asked that no one bring Rocaanist trappings on the barge. The Islanders and Fey had built the barge together so that no one would trick the other.

It had worked. No one had tricked the other. They were stuck on the river where if one side started a slaughter, the other side would retaliate. Jewel had thought of that too.

She had been brilliant.

A shame she had to die.

A pox on the man who killed her.

...!

He choked, tried to wake, but couldn't. He had been right in killing her. He tried to rub his eyes, but something was in his way. The weight on his chest was crushing. He heard voices, speaking in Fey. They sounded close. Wood snapped and fell in the fire at the foot of his bed. He wanted to wake up. He had to wake up.

This nightmare was killing him.

Jewel took his hand. 'You ruined any chances for your people,' she said. 'We'll have to kill you all now.'

He wanted to remind her about holy water. No matter what kind of threats her people made, they were still vulnerable to holy water. But he couldn't say that. His mouth felt like someone else's.

'The Islanders deserve to die,' he said, and shuddered.

No.

He pushed against the weight on his chest. The pain grew.

The Islanders deserve to die.

The Islanders

Deserve

Deserve?

No.

The words were Fey. He was thinking in Fey. He couldn't be, though. He didn't know the language.

The weight on his chest ...

He couldn't open his eyes . . .

The dream . . .

The dream . . .

The Fey will kill you. The question is when.

By this time tomorrow you will probably be dead.

I've warned you.

. . . warned . . .

. . . you . . .

Matthias tried to speak but something was blocking his mouth. *Nicholas. Nicholas, make them stop. Nicholas.*

The dream was just a dream. Just a dream. He had awakened himself from bad dreams before. All he had to do was open his eyes.

Open.

The weight on his chest.

Darkness over his eyes.

He reached up, feeling awake, and touched a leg that was not his own. He screamed, but the sound was muffled.

Jewel was frowning at him.

You're dead, he tried to say, but couldn't. She seemed to hear him. She shrugged.

I'll never die as long as my children live.

Your son is not alive, Matthias thought at her. *He has no brain.*

You watch out for my son, she said with a smile. *He will destroy you.*

Matthias had forgotten something. The weight on his chest. Was he dying? It felt as if he were dreaming, not dying.

Dreaming.

He had dreamed of a green glow the night before.

And the glow had nearly killed him.

Wake up! Wake up! he thought, but he couldn't.

He couldn't.

Which meant he was awake.

His mouth was dry. Fingers dug into his mind, little sharp points of contact. A face floated in his brain, a Fey face he had never seen before.

A Fey face.

A leg where his ribs should be.

Weight on his chest.

He slid his hand along the blanket, slowly, slowly, so the movement felt like part of the dream. Jewel was standing beside the other Fey, staring at him.

You can't wake up, she said. *I'll never let you wake up. If I don't wake up, how can I fight your son?* Matthias asked.

She frowned at that, as if something about it puzzled her.

His fingers brushed the bedside table. Almost there.

My son is strong, she said.

Your son has no mind, Matthias said.

My son shares his mind, she said. *My father hid him from me.*

Matthias's fingers touched cool glass. The rounded edges of the vial felt reassuring against his skin.

His heart was pounding hard. He couldn't reach over and uncap the vial. He couldn't pull the cork. He would have to –

(smash it)

He tightened his grip around the vial. He would only get one chance at this.

Your father? he asked Jewel, hoping to distract her, or whatever had created her. *Your father is meddling in everything.*

Then he swung his arm as hard as he could toward his chest. His hand collided with the leg and he cried out as glass smashed in his palm. A thousand shards cut him, and his blood mingled with the holy water.

A scream that was not his own filled the room. The weight flew off his chest and the pressure slipped out of his brain. Jewel disappeared. Suddenly the darkness was no longer complete. He took a real breath. The air smelled of burning flesh.

'Help!' he shouted as loud as he could.

Something thrashed on the bed beside him. The light from the fireplace revealed a Fey form melting from the leg up, the Fey screaming.

Other Fey had rushed into the room. Matthias recognized a face. Burden. The one who led the Settlement. Matthias grabbed more vials of holy water from the bedside table, uncorked them and threw them at the Fey.

The bottles shattered as they hit the floor. The Fey woman nearest him yelled and tried to run out the door. The water must have splashed on her, though, because her legs collapsed beneath her. The man beside her fell as well, and the stench of burning grew in the room. Matthias stood on the bed and kicked off the squirming flesh beside him. His hand hurt and his fingers didn't close well. He had damaged it when he smashed the vial.

He uncorked another vial and threw it, then another, and another. The Fey were running for the doors. Matthias got off the bed and ran after them throwing water at them. Three more fell and began melting into pools of flesh.

Burden reached the door of the suite, pulled it open and dashed into the hall. A Fey slipped and Matthias poured water on her. Some of the water splashed on a nearby Fey and he screamed.

Then a flash of light hit Matthias in the face. He brought up a hand to protect his eyes as a spark flew away from him. The air was red and green for a moment. He flailed water all around him in case they tried to attack again, but there was nothing except the screams of the dying around him.

As his sight came back, he saw another Fey halfway out the door, his legs fusing together. For a moment, Matthias thought that was Burden, but it wasn't. This Fey was too old.

'Help me,' he said in accented Islander.

Matthias stood over him for a moment, then shook his head. 'You came to kill me. I have no reason to help you.'

'You're a holy man,' the Fey said. He had to be in great pain, but he wasn't screaming.

Matthias nodded. 'I am a holy man,' he said, 'and my mission is to rid Blue Isle of the likes of you.'

Fifty

Stowe took the stairs two at a time. A bloodcurdling scream echoed from the upper floor. Then he heard a huge crash and a cry for help. The sound of breaking glass and large falling objects filled the area.

Stowe reached the first landing, looking over his shoulder and shouted, 'We need more men!'

Two guards were halfway up the stairs. One of the men relayed the order down. The Aud ran toward a side room. Another Aud stood at the top of the stairs frozen in terror. He had a bottle of holy water in his hands.

The screaming started again. Several voices raised in unison, long chilling cries that blended and clashed. Stowe reached the top of the stairs. He plucked the vial of holy water out of the Aud's hand, and the boy nearly collapsed with fright.

'Get help, son,' Stowe said. He pulled his sword and advanced, sword in one hand, holy water in the other.

The hall was long and wide, filled with lit lamps. As Stowe ran into the corridor, a door at the end opened and a Fey ran out. He wasn't screaming. He didn't need to. The fear was etched on his features. Another Fey followed him out, then shouted and toppled forward.

The first Fey saw Stowe and tried to turn around.

'Don't move,' Stowe said 'Or I will kill you where you stand.'

The Fey half turned and froze in a position where he could see both Stowe and the door. 'Let me go,' he said. 'There's a madman following me.'

'You're the madman,' Stowe said. 'Don't you know it's death for you to be in this building?'

The Fey in the doorway was begging for help. Matthias's voice was soft in answer.

'He'll kill me,' the Fey said.

He probably would too. Stowe put the holy water vial in his pocket. 'Well, I won't,' he said. 'But I will have to hold you prisoner. Come here.'

The Fey glanced at Stowe's pocket, then came close enough for

398

Stowe to grab him and hold him with one arm around his neck. 'One move,' Stowe whispered, 'and I'll coat you with holy water myself.'

'Fine,' the Fey said.

The Fey in the doorway gasped as the melting rose up his chest to his neck. He turned his head as if to beg Stowe for help when his face flattened out. He thrashed. The air smelled of burning flesh. Stowe turned his head away.

The Fey he was holding watched, his body rigid. More guards came up the stairs and surrounded Stowe. 'Take him,' Stowe said, shoving the Fey at some of the guards. 'Be careful. We're taking him prisoner.'

Matthias came through the door. He stepped over the thrashing body, and stopped when he saw the guards.

He was a mess. His robe was sopping wet, his hair tousled, and his right hand was bleeding. In his left he held an open vial of holy water.

'Thanks for catching him for me, Lord Stowe,' Matthias said. 'Since he led them all, he can be the last to die.'

Something in Matthias's voice sent chills through Stowe. 'He's not going to die,' Stowe said. 'We'll take him to King Nicholas.'

'The good King will set him free.'

'The King will treat him like any other murderer,' Stowe said, letting the words hang in the air.

The Fey said nothing. Even though he was being held, he had wormed his way behind the guards so that no water could touch him. 'If he deals with me the way he has dealt with that murderer,' the Fey said, 'then I will live.'

At that moment, Stowe recognized him as Burden, the one who started the Settlement. Even Fey who had been rational and support-ive of the truce between Fey and Islander had gone crazy over Jewel's death.

'It's not murder when the thing you're killing isn't human,' Matthias said.

'Is that how you justify it?' Burden asked.

'I'm not justifying anything,' Matthias said.

'You have to be,' Burden said, 'because you're just like us.'

Auds, Danites, and Elders were arriving from all over the Taber-nacle. Most crowded behind Matthias. A few put their hands over their noses to block the stench that was coming from the Rocaan's apartment.

Matthias took a step toward Burden, his hand clenched so tightly around the vial of holy water that his knuckles were white. 'You and I are nothing alike.'

'We are exactly alike,' Burden said, keeping the guards between him and Matthias. 'We didn't find out about our magickal abilities until we were adults.'

'Magick?' Matthias laughed. 'I have no magick.'

Stowe didn't like how this conversation was going. 'I think we should get him downstairs.'

The guards put their hands on Burden's arms. The guard in front of him moved. Stowe signaled that the guard should continue to block Burden. Burden peered over his shoulder. 'You have magic,' he said. 'Or else you would never have awoken from that dream.'

'What?' Matthias spoke in a harsh, disbelieving whisper.

Stowe held up a hand so that the guards paused. He wanted to hear the end of this one himself.

'Only magickal beings can break a Dream Rider's spell. Only Fey.'

'I'm clearly not Fey,' Matthias said.

The world was shifting here. Stowe moved near Burden as well. The muscles stood out in Matthias's left arm as he squeezed the vial of holy water. He would break it if he wasn't careful.

'That's right, you're not,' Burden said. 'But you have magick. You broke out.'

Matthias shook his head. His face was paler than it had been before. A slender Danite came up beside him and took his arm with a familiarity Stowe had never seen in the Tabernacle. 'We should go,' the Danite said.

'Leave me alone, Titus,' Matthias said and shook himself free. 'I have no magick. The spell was a thin one.'

'Nightshade is – was – our best,' Burden said. 'No one broke from his spells. Not even Red Caps. No one except Fey with magick of their own.'

Matthias took another step. His eyes appeared glazed. Stowe stepped toward him, keeping his body between them. He knew he should get Burden out of there, but he couldn't. Not yet. He wanted to hear the end of this logic himself.

'You're lying,' Matthias said.

'Really,' Burden said, his voice ringing with sincerity, 'I have no reason to lie. Especially right now.'

'You think that if I believe we're kindred spirits, I will let you go.'

'I heavily doubt that,' Burden said. 'But I think you should know what you are.'

'I am the Rocaan!' Matthias shouted. Spittle flew from his mouth. He looked half crazed.

'And the one who discovered that your "holy water" acts as a poison, right?' Burden asked.

'He did,' Porciluna said from the back. Stowe glanced at him. He didn't trust Porciluna. The man's ambition colored everything.

'As well as escaping one of our Charmed assassins.' Burden shook his head. 'I've been thinking about this. It seems odd that you would survive three separate attacks. I think you should talk to our Shaman.'

'So she can kill me?' Matthias said. 'I am not a fool, Burden.'

'No,' Burden said. 'You have a very powerful magic. Your belief in the military use of that poison is so strong that you have converted all of us to your belief.'

'Are you saying holy water won't work any more if we don't believe in it?' one of the guards asked. Stowe tapped at him for quiet, but it was too late. The question was out.

'It'll work now. He changed its properties. His magic is now part of the mix. The sign of a very powerful magick maker. And you survived an attack by a Charmed assassin.'

'He was just a boy. An Islander boy who didn't want to kill me,' Matthias said in a quivering voice.

'I Charmed him,' Burden said. 'I was behind the attack. Few Fey could have escaped that. And no one breaks a Dream Rider spell without magick. No one.'

'You lie!' Matthias tossed the holy water vial at Burden. Stowe moved a step closer and caught the vial in midair, water spilling all over his hand. He turned. Burden was crouching behind the guards.

Safe.

'Get him out of here,' Stowe said.

The guards didn't have to be told twice. They hurried Burden down the stairs. Titus took Matthias's hand and wrapped it in a bandage. Matthias stared after Burden as if he had struck him in the face.

'I can't believe you were going to kill a man who was unable to defend himself,' Stowe said. 'You have no compassion.'

'No, I don't,' Matthias said, his voice flat and devoid of emotion. 'At least not for demons.'

THE THIEF
The Next Day

Fifty-One

Touched stepped through the Circle Door. Shadowlands felt cold and damp compared to the woods, even though he knew its temperature was warmer than the air outside. His bald head was scratched and brambles were stuck in his robe. He had some kind of rash on his arm that itched like everything. And bug bites all over his open skin.

They had found no trace of the missing boy.

Rotin was still out in the woods, guiding a group of Fey on their search. She hadn't listened when Touched suggested that the boy and the Islander took a path other than the road. She said that the boy had never been outside of Shadowlands. The overstimulation would cause him to balk at anything unfamiliar. Unless the Islander worked miracles, he wouldn't be able to get the boy to walk on anything except flat ground.

She was probably wrong.

Touched had tried to tell her that, and as a reward, he got sent back to Shadowlands. To see Rugar. And to tell him that his new Enchanter was missing.

No one sat on the Meeting Block. Shadowlands looked deserted. It mostly was. Burden had taken a small troop with him to the Tabernacle, and Rotin had taken the rest of the Infantry to find the boy. Touched planned, after he talked to Rugar, to get a Beast Rider or two to look for the boy.

Touched ran through the grayness. The Weather Sprites were not experimenting this morning, and Shadowlands looked odder than usual. The grayness had a flat quality to it, the ground, the walls, and the roof marked by sharp corners and a shine that normally wasn't present. He preferred days when they tried to make sunlight or rain. Both resulted in a foggy mist that gave the place a more natural air.

Smoke was coming out of Rugar's chimney. Touched stopped at the base of the stairs, uncertain about this meeting. Rugar had charged him with the care of the boy. Perhaps that was why Rotin had sent Touched back. So that he took responsibility for his own actions.

Probably not, though. She probably wanted him out of the way so that he wouldn't question her any more.

He went up the steps slowly. Rugar hadn't given him an overt charge, but the implication had been there. Rugar thought Rotin incompetent, and had urged Touched to take action against her. Touched had not.

Now he was following her orders after her actions had allowed the boy to escape.

Although he wasn't certain he would have done any differently. He wouldn't have used the skin to find the bubble, but that was personal preference. He hated using pieces of death. He preferred to use his own mind.

He understood Enchanters.

Rotin did not.

Touched took a deep breath and knocked on the door. A curse echoed from within, then the door opened.

'I told you I don't care what –' Rugar stopped when he saw Touched. 'Sorry,' he said. 'I thought you were someone else.'

'Obviously,' Touched said. He even knew who Rugar thought he was. It was common knowledge that Rugar would not go with Burden on his raid, thinking it a suicide mission. Touched had thought it odd that Burden was willing to risk his life to avenge Jewel, but Jewel's father was not. 'May I come in?'

Rugar stood aside.

Touched went in. The small cabin was too hot. The remains of a meal sat on the table, and the place smelled of stale bedclothes. Rugar had been mourning in his own way. It almost seemed that, when he lost Jewel, he lost his fight.

'How's my Enchanter?' Rugar asked. He didn't wait for Touched's answer. He picked the plates off the table and put them in the bin for the Domestics to take care of later. 'I've been thinking about him. We might be wrong about his lack of Fey blood. He was very young when Solanda found him –'

'We were right,' Touched said. 'Rotin and I did some work with him.'

'Islander?' Rugar squinted as he spoke, as if he could see Touched's answer more clearly.

'Completely. Not a bit of Fey in him.' Touched's heart was pounding. He didn't want to tell Rugar the rest of it.

'Makes some kind of sense, I suppose,' Rugar said. 'It explains why we couldn't defeat them.'

'Yes,' Touched said. Rugar clearly needed the justifications. He was the first member of this Black Family to fail at such a large task. 'It also explains something else.'

Rugar leaned against a stool he had pushed near the table. 'What's that?'

'How he got away.'

Rugar clasped his hands in his lap. To Touched's surprise, Rugar didn't shout, didn't even get off the stool. He put one booted foot on a lower wrung and leaned forward. 'He got away?'

That tone was even more menacing than a shout would have been.

Touched nodded. 'I – that is, Rotin and I – we were experimenting on him –'

'You let Rotin near him?'

'I have no jurisdiction over her, Rugar,' Touched said. His arm itched. He scratched it, drawing blood from the rash. 'She wanted to test him.'

'She had no right.'

'She's head of the Warders.'

'And I told you that wasn't acceptable.'

Touched swallowed. 'I'm the youngest Warder. I have no way of getting rid of her.'

'You are a fool.' Rugar was still speaking softly. He got off the stool and clasped his hands behind his back. 'Well, he couldn't have gotten far. We'll let a Domestic search for him. He's probably hiding in the Domicile anyway.'

'He got out,' Touched said.

'What?' Rugar's voice was even softer.

Touched clasped a hand over his bleeding arm. The itching was worse. 'He got out.'

'You let him out.'

'No,' Touched said. 'He escaped.'

'From the Warders' cabin?'

'Yes, sir.' Touched let his hand drop. It was sticky with blood. The itching hadn't ceased but he could do nothing about it right now.

'How did that happen?'

'He's – ah, he's very powerful,' Touched said.

'He had better be,' Rugar said. He paced around the small room, then kicked at a leg of the table. The table shuddered.

'We're searching for him right now,' Touched said. 'We've got the Infantry out looking for him. Rotin is supervising them.'

'Rotin,' Rugar sneered. 'Rotin couldn't find her feet with explicit written directions.'

Touched agreed with that but loyalty among Warders kept him quiet. Rotin was still the head Warder, whatever her level of competence.

'If she's still searching,' Rugar said, 'what are you doing here?'

'She sent me to tell you he was gone.'

'Afraid to face me herself, was she?' Rugar's smile was grim.

Touched was glad Rugar was not referring to him. 'And you were able to face me. She thinks I won't notice that. Well, the boy won't get far. He hasn't been outside Shadowlands since he was a baby. The colors and smells will overwhelm him. We'll probably find him huddled in a patch of weeds not far from the Circle Door.'

'I don't think so,' Touched said.

Rugar crossed his arms. 'You don't think so.'

Touched shook his head. 'We checked.'

'You and Rotin.'

'And the Infantry. If he had been by himself, maybe. But your Islander servant was with him.'

'Adrian?' Again, Rugar spoke in that low tone. 'You let Adrian escape.'

'I – It seemed like they had it planned. When Adrian arrived, the boy took them both out of the Warders cabin.'

'I'm amazed you captured him in the first place,' Rugar said.

Touched nodded. 'I don't think he's used to his powers yet.'

'Well, he knows enough about them.' Rugar ran a hand through his thick black hair. 'Finally we have answers, and the person who could help us disappears.'

Touched scratched at the rash on his arm. 'I have – I was wondering if we could use a Beast Rider. I was thinking maybe a Gull Rider might notice the two of them better than the Infantry.'

Rugar squinted at him. 'Your idea?'

Touched nodded.

'Of course. It's the first one that makes sense. All right, we'll get you a Gull Rider. But I expect results.'

'You'll get them,' Touched said. 'We have to find that boy.'

'Actually,' Rugar said, 'we don't. We have learned most of what we needed to know from him. The Islanders have their own magick, that much is clear. Types of magick differ from person to person, and its usage apparently differs from culture to culture. This means that we'll have to treat the Islanders like equals instead of like people we can easily conquer.' He dropped his arms and rubbed his hands nervously on his breeches. 'It's something we probably should have done from the beginning.'

Touched agreed with that, but didn't know how to answer Rugar's comment. Rugar might take his agreement as a criticism. And as much as Touched found to criticize about Rugar, Touched was still aware that Rugar was the Black King's son, and the Leader of this band of Fey.

'Actually,' Touched said cautiously, 'I think we need to find him for another reason.'

'What's that?' Rugar said.

'The poison.' Touched licked his lips. He hadn't told anyone what he was about to tell Rugar. 'When Caseo was still alive, I thought of an Enchanter's spell to get rid of the poison. But Caseo rejected it because we didn't have an Enchanter in camp.'

Suddenly Rugar's entire being looked alive. He moved forward until his face was inches from Touched's. 'You have a spell?' he asked. 'A spell that will counteract the poison?'

'I thought I'd lost it,' Touched said. 'But as I was roaming the woods last night, I remembered all of it.'

'And it'll work?' Rugar asked.

'Perfectly,' Touched said.

'It's an antidote?' Rugar asked.

Touched shook his head. 'Actually, it would turn the poison back on them. That's what stalled us. We needed an Enchanter spell from the beginning.'

'An Enchanter spell,' Rugar murmured. Then he clapped Touched on the arm. 'You'll get your Gull Rider, and any other Beast Rider we can find. We have to locate this boy.'

'I know,' Touched said.

'No, you don't know,' Rugar said. 'We have to find him soon. If he realizes he's Islander, he'll never help us. We have to find him while he still thinks of himself as Fey.'

Fifty-Two

Adrian awoke to the sound of birds chirping. He lay on the thick mattress, breathing shallowly, listening to something he had thought he would never hear again.

The sunlight, filtered through the trees, came in the windows and warmed him. Scavenger's cabin, built over many years, was divided into several sections. He called this the Recovery From Shadowlands section. It had windows cut into two walls, windows without glass, so the floor was littered with dirt and leaves. But it also smelled of pine trees, the river, and grass, scents that Adrian adored. A lilac bush was blooming outside the nearest window and the overpowering smell filled the room.

Coulter huddled against him, face buried against his side. The boy grew calmer when they got inside the cabin, as Scavenger predicted he would. Coulter was used to wood walls, floors, and ceilings. It was the brightness he had trouble with.

And the sounds.

And the smells.

The cabin was long and narrow. It wound around the trees, and branches rested on the roof. Adrian had glanced at it the night before, noted the strangeness, but waited for Scavenger to tell him about it.

Scavenger did not.

But it was clear whoever had built the cabin had gained skills as time progressed. The Recovery From Shadowlands room had boards nailed every which way. Some of the boards had knots in them that opened to the outside. But the room farthest in the back, Scavenger's private room which he promised he would only show them once, had even boards and no windows. It was clean to the point of immaculate, and nothing got in.

Nothing at all.

Adrian stretched. He felt a joy he hadn't felt since his son was born. The simple things made him happy. He hadn't known that, wouldn't have known that until someone took the outdoors away from him, with its weather and flowers and mud.

Coulter was another problem.

410

The boy was almost gibbering by the time he got into the cabin. Scavenger had said such a reaction was normal for someone imprisoned in Shadowlands, maybe a bit extreme, but what did Adrian expect? The boy thought the world was gray, not alive with color and beings. It would take time and patience to get him to accept the difference.

The problem was that Adrian had neither. Now that he was outside Shadowlands, he wanted to get as far from it as he could.

He wanted to see Luke.

He wanted to see the rest of his family and the farm and the river in the daylight and Jahn and the bridge and –

And everything. Everything he had missed for so very long.

Scavenger unnerved him a bit too. The Red Cap had given his history, including his own escape from Shadowlands after killing Caseo, but he hadn't said much about what he had been doing since he left. Adrian could guess. An undisguised Fey couldn't be too welcome in any Islander communities. Scavenger had probably spent the intervening years alone.

No wonder he was happy to have them here.

Adrian pulled the blanket over Coulter, then adjusted his own pillow so that Coulter would still have something to shield his eyes. Then Adrian rolled off the mattress. Scavenger could not have made this mattress. He had to have stolen it from one of the Islander communities nearby. It was too soft, the stitches too perfect, the stuffing too even to be made out of twigs and brambles and leaves. Besides, Scavenger had no weaving equipment or sewing tools anywhere in the cabin.

The soft mattress after Adrian's run had left him stiff. He stood and stretched again, thankful that he even had the chance to exercise. Scavenger had not turned them into the Fey, and had promised to protect them, a promise that Adrian would hold him to.

His stomach rumbled. He had to get breakfast for himself and Coulter, and then decide what his next step would be. He opened the door at the far side of the room, and left it open.

Scavenger sat at his table, several pastries on a small plate before him. In the one of the back rooms, he had built himself a clay oven. In order to bake, he had to be awake most of the night.

Adrian was obscurely touched. No one had thought of him as an individual in years. Not even Mend. She had felt sorry for him, felt attracted to him, but she had not treated him as a person with his own feelings, his own beliefs, and his own joys.

'Good morning,' he said as he slid into a chair.

Scavenger grinned at him and pushed the plate of pastries forward.

411

'Thought you might want real food. Can't tell you how long it took me to learn to cook. But I'm glad I did.'

Adrian picked up one of the pastries. It was round and flat and soft. He took a bite. The center was still warm. 'So am I,' he said around the food.

He had never really talked with a Red Cap before. He had always avoided them as the Fey did. But he had done so for a different reason. He had avoided them because he was partially afraid of them. They never bathed, and worked with the dead, and seemed to be a bit dead themselves. The Fey avoided them because they had no magick, and so were not considered real Fey.

But here was a Red Cap who had stood up for himself, had killed because he hadn't wanted to die, and had created a life for himself away from the death and the stink. He had learned trades that most Fey believed beneath them, and had made himself comfortable.

'You live alone here?' Adrian asked.

Scavenger had two pastries on his plate. He fingered one of them. 'Who would live with me?' he asked. 'You're the first Islanders I've seen since I left Jahn, and the Fey – well, you know how they are.'

Adrian did know. He knew very well.

'I hope you realize that you have a unique problem here,' Scavenger said. 'They're searching for you right now. They don't like it when people escape.'

'Did they search for you?' Adrian asked.

Scavenger shrugged. 'A little, probably. But I wasn't important. It would have taken them a long time to discover which Red Cap had killed Caseo, and then they would have sent out the searchers. I already had a place to hide by then, and a plan. You don't seem to have a plan.'

'And they know who we are.'

Scavenger took a bit from a pastry. 'Islanders in Shadowlands are hard to miss.'

Adrian smiled. The man had a wry sense of humor. He liked that.

He finished the pastry. It tasted wonderful, light and flaky and warm. Even the food tasted better outside of Shadowlands, as if the grayness had affected everything.

'Adrian?'

Coulter, crying for him.

'In here,' Adrian said.

'Adrian!' Coulter's voice grew louder, more terrified. He was waking up.

'Better go to him,' Scavenger said. 'He has the Overs real bad.'

Adrian didn't wait for a definition of the word. He had a hunch about what it meant. He pushed away from the roughly hewn table and went through the door.

Coulter was wrapped in a small ball, the pillow shoved against his face, his body as far away from the light as it could be. Adrian sat on the mattress and held a hand over the boy, but didn't touch him.

'Coulter?' he said. 'It's me.'

Coulter didn't move. Adrian put his hand on Coulter's back. Coulter started. Then Adrian gathered him close. 'It's all right,' Adrian said.

Coulter shook his head, the movement small and frightened against Adrian's chest. Adrian put a hand under Coulter's chin and brought his head up. 'Coulter,' he said. 'This is what the world looks like. You lived in a created environment. It was fake, like a building is fake.'

Coulter's eyes were wide. He wasn't saying anything. Adrian stuck a hand into the sunlight. Coulter jerked.

'Light comes from the sky, and sometimes water does too,' Adrian said. 'Then there is darkness like there was last night. That's how we determine days. We don't do it because the Domestics keep us on a schedule. That mimics the schedule of the outside world, of this world.'

'The sounds,' Coulter whispered. 'I've never heard so many sounds.'

The chirping birds, the rushing of the river, the wind in the trees. Even after his years in Shadowlands, Adrian knew what those sounds were. Coulter didn't.

The smells were probably equally terrifying. Shadowlands had a distinct odor, that of woodsmoke and slow-moving air. It didn't even have cooking smells because the Domestics made most of the food using their magic skills. Fey soldiers, apparently, never cooked while on a mission, and Rugar still considered the Fey on the battlefield.

'There are many other sounds as well,' Adrian said. 'I'll help you learn them. Once you know what they are, you won't be as frightened.'

Coulter swallowed, clearly unbelieving, but willing to understand. 'The squeaking?' he asked. 'What's that?'

Adrian had to listen a moment before he even knew what Coulter meant by squeaking. 'Chirping,' he said. 'Birds.'

Coulter blinked at him, still confused. Adrian's heart pounded. This task would take a long time. The boy hadn't seen any creatures except Fey in all his years in Shadowlands.

'You mean like Gull Riders?' he asked finally.

Adrian nodded, trying to keep the pity out of his eyes. 'Gull Riders are Fey who look like a bird called a gull. I'll show you some when I can.'

'It's so bright here,' Coulter said. 'My eyes hurt.'

'And they will for a while.' The voice belonged to Scavenger. He was leaning against the door. He had a plate in one hand, a mug of water in the other. 'From what Adrian said you were a baby when you came to Shadowlands. Your eyes learned about this stuff but you don't remember it. But that means you can get used to it again.'

Like a baby. Adrian said nothing but smiled over Coulter's head at Scavenger. The little man was right. Babies went through this transition. They spent the first weeks of their life adjusting to the new environment.

Scavenger knelt on the mattress and extended the plate to Coulter. Coulter had to reach into the sunlight in order to get the food.

'What's that?' Coulter asked.

'A roll,' Scavenger said. 'I made it myself.'

'You're a Domestic?'

Scavenger shook his head. 'I'm a Red Cap.'

'But Red Caps have no magick.'

'People can make food without magick,' Adrian said softly. 'That's how Islanders have survived for generations.'

'But Islanders have magick.'

Scavenger suppressed a smile. Adrian was silently thankful that Coulter had said Islanders instead of referring to himself.

'Most of them don't,' Adrian said. 'And they take care of themselves just fine. Maybe when you're ready, you can ask Scavenger to teach you how to make rolls.'

'We'll be gone before that,' Coulter said.

Adrian patted him on the back, and pushed him away just a little. 'Why don't you eat?' he said.

Coulter glanced at him, knowing that something had shifted, but not knowing what. Adrian wasn't going to tell him. Not yet.

Scavenger shook the plate a little. The pastry looked warm and tempting on the plate's rough brown surface.

'It won't hurt me?' Coulter asked.

Adrian wasn't certain if he was referring to the pastry or to the sunlight. 'No,' he said, 'it won't.'

Coulter gingerly extended his right hand, slowing the movement when it approached the light. Light had a different meaning for magical creatures. Adrian was just beginning to understand that. The light that Coulter had wrapped him in the day before had been a live thing, a wall between them and the rest of the Fey in that room. Perhaps Coulter expected the same thing from this light.

414

'It's all right,' Adrian said softly.

Coulter nodded, then plunged his hand into the stream of sun-light. He moved with such force he almost knocked the plate out of Scavenger's hand.

'Hey!' Scavenger said. 'It's no barrier! It's sunlight.'

As if Coulter would know the difference. He put his fingers on the plate. 'It's warm,' he said to Adrian.

'That happens sometimes when something's been in the sun,' he said.

Coulter nodded and pulled the plate toward him. Then he moved away from Adrian, set the plate on his lap, and picked up the pastry. He picked at an edge with his fingernail, then pulled off a piece and bit it.

'It's good,' he said with surprise.

Adrian grinned. The boy had to learn that some of these new things were enjoyable.

Coulter ate quickly, then took the water cup from Scavenger and drank. He looked up, again with surprise. 'It's sweet.'

'It's fresh,' Scavenger said. 'Unlike water in Shadowlands.'

Coulter bent over his food again. Scavenger watched him for a moment, then sighed. 'You know,' he said to Adrian, 'you'll have to keep him here for a while.'

'I don't think we should,' Adrian said. 'We're not very far from Shadowlands. I'm not sure how safe we are.'

'Safer than you'd be if you go out again. This boy has the Overs. If you take him into the woods again, then to the city, you'll rob him of his mind.'

Coulter had stopped eating. He set the plate down. 'The Overs?'

Scavenger nodded. 'It happens to people who've spent a long time in Shadowlands. Mostly Fey saw it in prisoners before we came to Blue Isle. It means that you're used to seeing gray everywhere, that colors and scents and temperatures overstimulate you. It can drive some people insane.'

'I don't think you need to tell the boy this,' Adrian said. The last thing he wanted Coulter to know was the dangers of being away from Shadowlands.

'I think he needs to know. Then he won't feel so alone.'

'I don't want to go crazy,' Coulter said in a small voice.

'You won't,' Scavenger said. 'If you get used to things gradually.'

Adrian crossed his arms. 'I think you're just lonely. You want us to stay.'

'You remember the boy's terror last night. It'll only get worse. He's never seen bugs or birds or fish. Everything will frighten him unless we introduce him to it in the right way.'

'How come you're talking like I'm not here, then,' Coulter said.

Scavenger looked at him. 'Sorry,' he said softly. 'I didn't mean that. I just want your – father? –'

Adrian nodded before Coulter could say anything.

'– to do the right thing.' Scavenger picked up the dishes with shaking hands. 'And, yes,' he said without looking at Adrian. 'I am lonely.'

Scavenger managed to say the words without making Adrian pity him. The little man had an amazing amount of dignity for someone brought up with none.

Adrian glanced out the window. The leaves were blowing in the light breeze. The birds had stopped, but the rustling sounds moving vegetation continued. A fly floated in and landed on some crumbs beside Coulter.

He squeaked and moved away, backing into Adrian. 'Souls,' he muttered in Fey.

Scavenger shook his head. 'No,' he said. 'Sometimes the beings in Fey lamps look that way, but no. That is a bug. A fly.' Then he looked up at Adrian. 'See?'

Adrian did see. But his responsibility to Coulter and his responsibility to himself left him torn. He had to take care of Coulter, but he also wanted to find Luke and see if his son was all right.

Coulter must have sensed the thought, because he clasped Adrian's hand hard. 'Let's stay, please? I don't want to go crazy.'

Scavenger was watching him.

'How far is Jahn from here?' Adrian asked.

'A day's hard walk,' Scavenger said.

Coulter's grip tightened. 'Don't leave me,' he said.

'I won't,' Adrian said, although he had been thinking about it, if only for a few days. Both of the boys needed him equally. But he could do less for Luke than he could for Coulter.

'They'll be looking for you,' Scavenger said. 'They'll watch all the ways into Jahn. They'll probably be watching all your friends and family, if you're that important to them.'

'I'm not,' Adrian said.

'But they kept you for years. You know more than they want the enemy to know,' Scavenger said. 'They'll look for you.'

Coulter held on so tight he twisted the bones in Adrian's hand. 'Don't go.'

'I'm not going to,' Adrian said and tried to keep the resignation out of his voice. He wouldn't leave. Not yet anyway. Maybe Coulter with his magic and his quick mind would get used to the strangeness of his new world faster than most. Maybe they'd be able to leave in a few days. 'You really think they'd find me that easily?'

Scavenger nodded.

'Then why haven't they found you?'

'Because I know how to hide from them,' Scavenger said. 'I've done it all my life.'

'Can you teach us?' Adrian asked.

'If you're willing to listen,' Scavenger said.

'We're willing,' Coulter said. His grip on Adrian had loosened. The fly had left the crumbs and landed on Coulter's leg. He didn't brush it away. Adrian saw that as a good sign.

'We'll listen,' Adrian said. 'But if there's trouble, we'll leave.'

'There hasn't been trouble here in years,' Scavenger said. 'I loathe trouble.'

'So do I,' Adrian said, wishing he had never seen the Fey in the first place. 'So do I.'

Fifty-Three

Gift pressed his back against the wall of his cabin. There was no mist in Shadowlands, nothing to hide in. His mother stood beside him, her hand on his shoulder. Even that didn't comfort him.

His grandfather was angry.

He had stood outside the house and asked for Gift to come out. Niche had brought Gift out against his will. He had stopped at the door when he saw his grandfather.

His grandfather had always looked bigger than the other Fey. Not that he was. Gift had seen other Fey who were taller, but his grandfather had presence – a way of looking at the world that made him scarier than anyone Gift had ever known.

He looked very scary now. His cape was draped over his shoulder, his shirt laces were undone, and his boots shone. His hair flowed loose around his face. Gift had never seen him this disheveled, but that wasn't what scared him.

It was his grandfather's eyes.

They flashed with a dark anger that coursed through Gift's dreams. A blackness surrounded his grandfather, a blackness Gift had always seen, but had always attributed to the cloak.

But not today.

'I haven't seen him,' Gift said, knowing his grandfather would ask about Coulter again.

'I know that,' his grandfather said. 'But I want you to find him.'

His mother's hand tightened on his shoulder. Her face was still gray with pain. Her wings weren't healing well and she had to work harder with his father away.

'I don't want Gift to leave Shadowlands,' his mother said.

'I'm not talking about Gift leaving,' his grandfather said. His gaze was still trained on Gift. It was as if his mother didn't even exist, as if only he and his grandfather were having the conversation.

'I don't know where he is,' Gift said again, knowing what his grandfather was asking, but preferring to ignore it.

'You could, though,' his grandfather said.

Gift pushed against the building. The unfinished wood bit into his back. He couldn't move any farther away. 'Mom doesn't want me to leave.'

'You're not that dumb, boy,' his grandfather snapped. 'You know what I want.'

'I can't ask for Visions,' Gift whispered. His grandfather wanted to hurt Coulter. He knew that as clearly as he knew his own name.

'I'm not talking about a Vision. I'm asking you to look along your Link. He Enchants, right? And he Linked the two of you. Look through the Link and tell me what you see.'

His mother's hand tightened on his shoulder. Her fingers weren't very strong. 'Perhaps we should go inside,' she said.

'He can do as well out here,' his grandfather said.

'But you might want privacy,' she said.

They already had privacy. The Fey were hiding in their cabins. No one was outside. No one at all.

His grandfather shook his head. He was too impatient to go inside. He wanted Coulter now. Gift could feel that. He could feel and see it in the blackness surrounding his grandfather.

His grandfather reached for Gift, but Gift slid away.

'Find the boy, Gift,' his grandfather said.

Gift shook his head. Coulter had saved his life. They all knew that. If Coulter thought it best to hide from his grandfather, Gift wasn't going to question it.

'Gift,' his mother said, 'it might not hurt.'

'Look,' his grandfather said. 'The Islander servant stole Coulter from Shadowlands. It's not safe out there for us. He'll die.'

'He's not Fey,' Gift said. 'He told me.'

His grandfather sucked in a breath. He frowned for a moment, then the expression disappeared from his face. He crouched in front of Gift. 'It's still not safe. He's never left this place. He doesn't know the world.'

'He's strong,' Gift said. 'He can take care of himself.'

'Gift,' his mother said. 'Your grandfather is only asking for help to find him.'

With both of them against him, Gift couldn't fight. At least not directly. 'I don't know how to find him,' Gift whispered.

'Sure you do, boy,' his grandfather said. 'You're Linked.'

'He may not, Rugar,' his mother said. 'He did come to his talent very young.'

The frown was back, but so small his mother probably couldn't notice it.

'Maybe the Shaman could help,' Gift said.

His grandfather slid out a hand so quickly that Gift couldn't get away. The touch sparked Gift's Vision, like it did before. Gift saw all the Links: the one between him and his mother, three others leading out of Shadowlands. Those Links were all white. But a fifth Link appeared, black and ugly, and faded. It had clearly been severed.

There was no Link between him and his grandfather. None at all.

That lack gave Gift courage.

'I think,' he said quietly, 'the Shaman should help.'

His grandfather let go of him, apparently unaware that Gift's Sight had changed. The blackness was roiling around him, as if it were ready to explode.

'I won't see the Shaman,' his grandfather said. 'You will find him. Now.'

'I can't,' Gift said.

'Gift,' his mother said. 'Your grandfather has been very good to us.'

Gift didn't agree with that. His grandfather only came by when he wanted something. He squinted at his grandfather. 'You don't have the magic to make me,' he said.

'Oh, but I do,' his grandfather said. He grabbed Gift by the shoulders, and his touch sent waves through Gift's body. They were bound somehow. Not Linked, but connected through their magic. His grandfather's magic was gone, long gone, but enough remnants remained to trigger something within Gift.

For a moment, Gift clung to his grandfather. Then Gift's consciousness slid down one of the white Links leading out of Shadowlands. Gift could feel Coulter's terror along that Link, and he saw bits of light as he traveled, protective light.

'Good,' his grandfather said. His eyes were wide. Gift pulled himself away, stumbling against the wall, but it felt too late. His mind was still traveling along the Link. If his grandfather touched him again, his grandfather would see Coulter's trail as clearly as Gift did.

Gift closed his eyes, touched the wall, and felt very far away from his body. He concentrated as hard as he could, and when the Links merged in the Circle Door, he jumped from Coulter's Link to another.

The Link Gift landed on felt old and familiar. He skidded down it fast, his mind traveling along the pathway as it had done a thousand times before.

But never consciously. He never remembered taking this journey. He only knew he had done it.

If he looked back along the Link, he could see the Circle Door closing, and farther beyond that, he saw his grandfather and mother crouching over his collapsed body. His grandfather was about to touch him as the Door closed.

Gift suddenly found himself in a room made of stone. Everything was bright here and warm. He was leaning against a woman who held him tightly, crooning to him. He felt as big as he did at home, too big to be held, but it felt good nonetheless. There were square holes in the walls, and someone had placed fabric on those holes. A crib stood in the middle of the room, and in it, a baby girl cooed.

His sister.

He remembered her.

He patted the woman's hand and walked to the crib. He was about to peer down when he felt another presence in his body. His grandfather's consciousness pushed him aside. Gift's head swiveled and he toppled over, landing with a thud on the floor.

The woman cried out something in a language he did not understand. A cat came over and sniffed him. His grandfather made the body recoil. The cat had a cool expression on its face as if it saw something it disliked. It made a whoofing noise through its nose, then backed away, hair rising on its neck.

His grandfather cursed. Then he grabbed the part of Gift that had traveled down the Link.

Take me to Coulter.

Gift shrugged. The body responded, shoulders scraping on the floor. *I thought he was here.*

You lie, boy. I'll find him. His grandfather slid along the Link, heading toward the Circle Door, toward the place where Gift had split away. Gift closed his eyes and stretched out on the floor. His grandfather would not find Coulter, not without Gift's help. And for the moment, Gift wasn't leaving.

He knew this place. He had been here before. It had been safe here. He used to come here in dreams. It was his secret place.

Now his grandfather knew about it.

But at least he hadn't led his grandfather to Coulter. At least he hadn't done that.

His friend was safe.

Gift was safe.

For the moment.

Fifty-Four

Matthias's hand throbbed. Titus had cleaned it and wrapped it, but the pain in the palm was excruciating. He wasn't certain if he would be able to use it again.

He was sitting in the big Sanctuary, directly beneath the Roca's sword, the large sword that hung point down from the ceiling. In this room five years ago, he had discovered the blood that made him believe a Fey had infiltrated the Tabernacle. In this room, he had conducted hundreds of Sacraments.

Hundreds.

As a representative of the Roca.

And now he was the Roca's representative in Blue Isle. The Roca's representative to the world. Beloved of God.

They had called him a murderer.

But they had been trying to kill him. The Fey had attacked him in his sleep, not once, but twice.

The Auds were cleaning his rooms now, getting rid of the spilled holy water and the blood. All the blood. Someone had told him there was a body of an Aud on the balcony.

The young boy who had guarded him.

He hadn't even heard the boy die.

And that, apparently, had been before their dream-maker invaded his mind.

He sighed and rested his head against the wooden edge of the pew. The air smelled faintly of holy water and candles. He had lit a few candles after he had come in, then asked not to be disturbed. He couldn't go to the old Rocaan's worship room, not after what Burden had said.

A magical being. Impossible. Burden had to be trying to invade his mind, trying to drive him crazy as a punishment for Jewel's death. Matthias had never been magical, had no idea, really, what Burden meant.

But ever since he had discovered holy water's properties, he had helped make it. His hand had been on the weapon from the beginning.

At first he had thought that beginning was going to be the last moment in his life. He had been terrified, certain he was going to die, and unwilling to. The Fey had trapped him in the servant's chapel. He was the only Islander left alive in that room. And when he had seen the holy water, he thought it would save him. As a distraction maybe, but just enough to get him free.

He had flung it at the Fey, all the while hoping, perhaps even praying, that the vials would save his life.

They had, in a most hideous fashion. But they had.

All his life he had been accused of being demon-spawn. He had been too tall. In the Snow Mountains, they took children that were born too long and thin, and left them in the snow to die. His mother had refused, and the villagers wouldn't talk to him, all the while saying he was cursed.

He had to prove to them he wasn't. He went to Sacrament every night, and when the time came, he got his family to sponsor him into the Tabernacle. He spent years as an Aud, studying, wishing he could move up. He had been such a good scholar he had even studied with King Alexander when they had both been boys.

There were only two wishes Matthias never had granted.

He did not want to be Rocaan.

And he wanted to believe. He had never been able to believe. All his life he served the Roca and believed only that the Roca was a myth, a story, or – at best – an historical figure whose importance was exaggerated over the centuries.

Demon-spawn.

You have no compassion.

At least, not for demons.

He shook the voices out of his head. He was Rocaan. Wasn't that good enough?

Apparently not. And he couldn't forget Burden's face. The Fey kept saying he had no reason to lie. And he was right. He had no reason to lie. None at all.

Except to play with Matthias's mind.

They couldn't kill him. Perhaps that was because he was God's Beloved instead because of magick. The Fey tried to explain everything in terms of magick.

Maybe if he were alone with Burden, Burden would admit that to Matthias. He would admit he lied.

He had to admit that. If he didn't, Matthias would never have any peace.

He couldn't be as bad as those people. He couldn't be. It wouldn't be right. No just God would do that to him.

No just God.

The God he wasn't sure he believed in.

Matthias sighed. His back still ached from Nicholas's knife. They all hated him. Nicholas, Porciluna, the Auds. Everyone, not just the Fey. They all would love him to be something that would interfere with his duties as Rocaan.

Interfere more than his disbelief did.

He shook his head. All his life he had wanted the purity that Titus had shown that afternoon. Titus held the vials of holy water as if they held the spit of the Roca himself. Titus had spoken in awe of each Secret as if he were given a sacred trust.

And apparently he was.

Matthias had been awed by the trust. He had just not seen it as sacred.

He stood and slid into the aisle. The vials of holy water he had taken from his room were in his pocket, weighing down his robe. He wasn't used to walking on bare floor anymore. When he came into this Sanctuary as Rocaan, he walked down a red carpet. Everything was given to him. It was the best position in the kingdom, after the King's itself.

But unlike Porciluna, he hadn't craved the luxuries. He had just accepted them as part of the job. Like the Words. Like the pretense at belief.

Demon-spawn.

Lord Stowe had left a group of guards at the Tabernacle. Matthias had been too tired to argue and uncertain whether he wanted to. It would be foolish to remain vulnerable to the Fey.

Although foolish was how he felt.

He had always felt unworthy of his position. Now people were trying to get him to protect it at the same time as they accused him of misusing it.

Accused him of having magick.

Of being like the Fey.

The idea made him shudder. He glanced up at the sword. He was standing directly beneath its point. The written history of the Tabernacle stated that the Elders had argued about hanging the sword, worried that it would fall on a worshiper. One of the Elders had said that if the worshiper deserved the wrath of God, the sword would fall.

For two hundred years, the sword had remained in place. Matthias half wished it would fall now. It would save everyone the trouble of dealing with him. It would save him the trouble of thinking about his own future.

You have no compassion.

Not for demons.

He sighed and headed up the aisle. His sandals whispered against the polished wood. When he reached the double doors, he stopped. Carved into the wood were hundreds of tiny images of the Roca's life. One was of the people greeting him with joy.

Joy.

No one had ever greeted Matthias with joy. Not even the old Rocaan who had chosen him.

He pushed the door open and stepped into the hallway. The guards silently flanked him as he walked through the corridor. Never again would he be able to go anywhere alone. Nicholas had thought of a good trick, a great way to keep Matthias in line. Protect him. He wouldn't refuse protection.

Except now.

'I have some private worshipping to do,' he said to the guard beside him.

'We will stay outside the room as we did before,' the guard said.

Matthias shook his head. 'I walk.'

'We'll follow,' the guard said. 'As far behind as we can, not to disturb you.'

Matthias shook his head. He didn't need to try too hard. It didn't matter if they followed him or not. The loss of privacy would be the price he paid for protection.

At the moment, his hand throbbing at his side, he was willing to pay that price.

He left the Tabernacle without telling the guards where he was going. The morning air was fresh and clean, blowing in from the west, from the Stone Guardians.

As the Fey had done.

The sun was out. Its light was bright. The birds were chirping overhead and the river gurgled playfully. Except for a few blood spatters on the tiles, there was no evidence of violence here from the night before.

Matthias clasped his hands behind his back and went through the gate. He walked quickly as if he were surveying his domain. People who recognized him bowed to him and backed away as was appropriate, but they did not show joy.

And why would they? He had never given joy in return.

But neither, to his knowledge, had the Roca. The life of the Roca himself was only revealed to them in small incidents, small stories. Perhaps the stories of joy had been left out.

Matthias walked past the reeds beside the river, and saw places where they had been crushed. Perhaps the Fey had hidden there as they planned to attack him. Or perhaps a fisherman had taken a nap beside the water. He was looking for enemies everywhere.

425

The enemy is with us always, within ourselves.

He cringed as that portion of the Words Written and Unwritten rose unbidden in his mind. That was what Burden had said in a different way – that Matthias was just like the thing he hated.

The foot traffic on the bridge was heavy this morning: women crossing with children at their sides and baskets on their backs, men carrying tools and pouches. Auds passed him on horseback, not even noticing him, and King's guards rode in the opposite direction, greeting the guards that followed him.

Except for the occasional greeting, Matthias felt as if he were invisible to all who passed him, as if he didn't matter at all.

He wasn't certain he liked that feeling.

The bridge seemed longer than it used to, and the walk took more effort. He hadn't walked across it since the Fey came. He had ridden, of course, but never walked. He used to enjoy the bridge – its masterful engineering, the wide wooden surface that the bridgeworkers kept clean and in good repair. He had forgotten the view, how the waters of the Cardidas sparkled below him, how the sun felt warm against his head and shoulders. Since the Fey had come, his life had been the Tabernacle, being Rocaan, and defeating them.

Sometimes he felt as if he were the only person who concentrated on defeating them instead of accepting them. No one else seemed to realize that the Fey wouldn't stop with acceptance. They wouldn't stop until the entire Isle was theirs.

Demons. Evil, evil demons.

Just like he was.

If Burden was right, if Matthias's desire had somehow changed the purpose of holy water, then he would be responsible for all the deaths.

Every single Fey death since the Invasion.

He shook his head as if he could dislodge the thought. A woman leading a little girl carefully across the boards frowned at him. He probably seemed crazy. He felt crazy.

He was terrified. Now that the old Rocaan was dead, he had no one to talk with, no one to confide in, no one who believed in him. He didn't even believe in himself.

When he reached the other side of the river, he glanced down the forked road. To his left was the remains of the Settlement. The buildings were already falling down. The Fey who had moved there hadn't known much about carpentry. They hadn't known much about living like Islanders. Perhaps that was why they conquered, because they couldn't do so many mundane things on their own.

The shops weren't yet open. Some children played in the cobblestone street, and a dog sniffed at the side of the road. He missed the

426

cats. At least Nicholas had changed that edict. Matthias had come to believe it extreme. God's creatures were God's creatures.

Except when they were Fey.

He took the road that wound behind the palace. As he got closer to the palace, the guards moved closer to him. He suspected they weren't protecting him, but protecting Nicholas. Even the guards assigned to him didn't trust him any more.

He didn't even glance at the palace. Instead he walked to the keep. It was located at the back of the guards' quarters on the other side of the palace gate. The keep itself was isolated from the rest of the city by a row of trees, planted in a square around the building. Guards stood inside the grove, watching the entrances.

The building was also square and made of whitewashed stone. It had no windows, and the doors were reinforced with iron. Matthias had last been inside as a Danite, when it was his duty to minister to the condemned.

Decades ago.

The two guards before the main entrance blocked it as he approached.

'I would like to see the prisoner,' Matthias said.

The first guard, a stocky man barely twenty, shook his head. 'I'm sorry, Holy Sir. We have orders that no one is allowed to see him.'

They all knew who Matthias was talking about, even though he was certain there were other prisoners inside. He wanted to see Burden. They weren't done with their discussion yet. He had to get Burden's words out of his mind.

'You'll refuse him religious counsel?' Matthias asked.

'Our orders are from the top,' the guard said. 'He's not to be bothered.'

'I will see him,' Matthias said. 'By law, only the King can overrule me. Are your orders from King Nicholas?'

The young guard glanced at his companion. The other guard shrugged. 'The head of the guards told us that no one could enter,' he said.

Monte. He wasn't even a lord, although he was accorded equal status. 'Then I may enter,' Matthias said.

The young guard held out his hand, both blocking and supplicating Matthias. 'Forgive me, Holy Sir, but we have orders that no holy water may be brought inside the premises.'

An anger surged through Matthias. He hadn't realized his own plans. Revenge had become so ingrained in him that he went after it without a thought.

But he could go in without the holy water and still clear his mind. A conversation. That was what he had initially told himself he was after. That was what he would pursue.

He reached into his pockets, pulled out both vials of holy water and handed them to the guard. Then he clasped his hands behind his back. 'May I go in?'

'Forgive me, Holy Sir,' the young guard said again. 'But we have to make sure.'

A shudder ran through Matthias. They were going to search him. For a moment he didn't know what to do – suffer through the indignity or to order them to desist. Finally he decided to suffer. It suited his mood.

He held out his arms and looked at the door while the guard patted his sides. The door was made of thick wood. Iron ran along its strips. Unlike most doors in the Tabernacle, this one had no carvings, nothing to make it unusual.

When the guard finished, Matthias put his arms down. 'Take me to the prisoner,' he said in the most imperial tone he could manage.

The guard's face was flushed. He nodded, clearly embarrassed by the position the job had placed him in. The other guard pulled out a large ring of keys and unlocked the main door. The first guard went inside. Matthias's guards started to follow, but he held up his hand.

'I doubt the Fey will attack me in here, don't you?' he said.

They stopped. Matthias turned his back on them and followed the first guard through the door.

The stench made him recoil. The building hadn't been cleaned in a long time. It smelled of urine and fouled clothing. The odor was so strong he could almost touch it.

Torches hung on the walls, their flame casting a dim light on the narrow hallway. They were an arm's length from each door, casting each door in darkness. The doors all had narrow slits in them – Matthias remembered that from his Danite days – but he could see nothing through them. He recalled this hallway as being noisy, but he heard nothing now, although he suspected the keep had more prisoners than it had ever had. He had not checked on conditions as the old Rocaan occasionally did. A thread of unease worked its way down his back. A man imprisoned in darkness should cry out at any sound, for help if nothing more.

The guard took him through twisty corridors until Matthias lost track of the way. The corridors got narrower as they got older, and the torches were farther apart. Finally, the guard took a torch off its peg, and carried it the rest of the way. Using his own ring of keys, the guard unlocked the heavy oak door and went inside.

This room didn't smell as strong as the hallway. Very few prisoners had been kept here. The guard went inside and lit a row of torches with the one he carried. The light revealed a cage at the back of the room. The cage was made of metal bars. Hay stood in one corner, and water in another. Burden leaned against the stone wall, his arms crossed. A spark from one of the torches floated around his head like a mosquito.

'Ah,' Burden said to Matthias in Islander. 'Your curiosity bested you.'

The words struck home. Matthias did not respond. He didn't know what he could say without sounding defensive. He turned to the guard and took the torch from the man's hand.

'Leave us,' he said.

'But, Holy Sir –'

'Leave us.'

The guard couldn't countermand the Rocaan. Still Matthias felt a moment of compassion for the situation he put the man in. If the Rocaan died, the guard would be executed. If the prisoner died – well, that would depend on Nicholas. And considering how the King had been enchanted by the Fey, the guard would probably die in that case as well.

'I'll have to lock you in,' the guard said.

Matthias nodded. He had done this a hundred times as a Danite. He was prepared.

'I'll be outside,' the guard said.

He left, pulling the door closed behind him. After a moment, the lock clicked, imprisoning Matthias just as it imprisoned Burden.

Another spark had found its way into the cell. Matthias frowned at it. If it fell wrong, it would start the hay on fire. Then the spark hit the wall and winked out.

'Aren't you afraid I'm going to kill you?' Burden asked.

'If you could do that across this distance, I would have died in the hallway,' Matthias said. 'You need others to do your killing for you.'

'Like you need poison.'

Matthias shrugged. 'It works.'

'Only because you created it.'

This was what he had come for. This revelation – or this lie. 'Every Rocaan makes holy water.'

'But until you it had no magic properties.'

'We don't know that. Until you, we had no Fey.'

Burden laughed. The sound was deep and warm, a sound Matthias could like if he gave himself half a chance. He would not give himself half a chance.

'Still,' Burden said, 'you had to come to see.'

'I had to see you here, behind bars, to make sure I was safe,' Matthias said.

Burden grinned. It made him look even more devilish. 'What's the matter? Don't you believe your god will protect you?'

'He has so far,' Matthias said.

Burden shook his head. 'You've protected yourself.'

'Why are you so determined to convince me that I'm part Fey? Is this another way to "defeat" me?'

'No.' Burden crossed his arms. The smile left his face. 'It's more of a way of explaining, to myself, what happened in that room. Twice now. No one should be able to defeat us.'

'You know, you people always say that, but I have seen no proof,' Matthias said. 'We have been able to defeat you rather easily.'

'We murdered your Rocaan, we murdered your King, and you think us defeatable?'

'And we killed the Black King's granddaughter,' Matthias said.

A spark hit him in the face. He brushed at it and moved away from the torches. He had never seen torches spark like this.

'I thought it was an accident,' Burden said.

'It was no more an accident than you showing up in my room.'

'Killing never used to be the way of your people.'

'We had to learn something from the invaders.' Matthias's hands were cold. He wished he hadn't let them search him. He wanted to kill this Fey too. They were evil. All of them. Evil.

Burden pushed off the wall and came toward the bars. 'You want to know how I can tell you have magick?'

'I don't have magick,' Matthias said. 'I am just Beloved of God.'

'You're tall,' Burden said. 'Islanders usually aren't tall. Height seems to go with the magick for reasons we don't understand.'

'The last Rocaan wasn't tall,' Matthias said. And he died.

He died.

'You cannot be easily killed. Three times we trapped you. Three times you escaped.'

'I have great luck,' Matthias said. His mouth was dry.

'But most importantly, it is the way you look. If a person squints, he can see magick energy flickering off another person. It crackles off you. I am amazed no one else ever noticed. I think it was because no one else was looking.'

'I think you're making all of this up,' Matthias said.

Burden gripped the bars with his long slender fingers. 'Should we test it?'

'We can't test anything in here,' Matthias said. 'And I am not getting you out of here.'

'Then why did you come?' Burden asked.

The answer was too complex to admit. He had come to kill Burden. He had come for answers. He had come to see for himself the man who had tried to kill him.

'I came to discover if anyone else is trying to kill me,' Matthias said.

'In the Fey?' Burden asked.

Matthias nodded.

'And why should I tell you that?'

'Because,' Matthias said. 'I could kill you where you stand.'

'Your precious poison,' Burden said. 'Someday we'll learn the antidote, and then you'll know the meaning of Fey wrath.'

'I think we've seen enough Fey wrath to last us a lifetime,' Matthias said.

'We haven't even started yet,' Burden said. 'Just wait.'

'So someone else will try to kill me,' Matthias said.

Burden grinned. 'I think someone named Wind will try. I suspect Rugar might. I think even your own king hates you enough to try.'

'Nicholas had his chance,' Matthias said. 'We are less –'

The spark floating past him suddenly became a hand-sized man. The man held a tiny sword and plunged it at Matthias's eye. He ducked, then slapped at the man. The man shrank back into a spark and disappeared.

'How did you do that?' Matthias asked, approaching Burden.

'I didn't do anything,' Burden said.

'You lie.' Matthias's voice had grown softer. It was a growl.

The spark came close, but Matthias pushed it away with his hand.

'See?' Burden said. 'Fey can do that. Nonmagical beings can't.'

Matthias looked at his hand. It was up, but it wasn't pushing the spark away. An opaque wall had formed in the air, inches from his hand, as if mimicking it.

'Stop that,' Matthias said.

Burden laughed. 'I'm not doing anything.'

'Stop that,' Matthias repeated.

'I can only Charm, not Enchant,' Burden said. 'You're doing that.'

'I'm not doing anything.' Matthias was shaking. The opaque screen was shaking too. The spark waited outside it, like a bug trying to get in a door.

'You have a great magick, holy man,' Burden said. He shook his head. 'Aren't you ashamed of killing the very thing you are? Or is that why you did it?'

'I'm not like you,' Matthias said.

'You're just like me,' Burden said.

'I'm not.' He brought his hand down. The screen went down too

431

and the spark came toward him. Instantly another screen went up before his face. He felt the screen go up before it appeared. He felt it like he would feel his arm lifting a shield.

The thought infuriated him. He wasn't a demon spawn. He was a good man. All his life he had worked to be a good man. He was Rocaan. The Holy Sir.

Beloved of God.

'I'm not like you,' he whispered.

'That's probably true,' Burden said. 'Your power is reckless, out of control. You have no idea why you hate us as intensely as you do. You hate us because we remind you of yourself.'

'I'm Islander,' Matthias said.

Burden nodded. 'We've discovered a couple others like you. It's why you have been able to hold us at bay. That magick of yours.'

'I have no magick!' Matthias shouted. White light shot from his eyes and stabbed into the cage. He felt the light pouring from him, burning out of him, taking his anger with it.

Burden jumped out of the way, but Matthias turned his head. The light moved with his eyes.

'Stop it!' Matthias yelled. 'You're doing this! Stop it.'

Burden sprinted away from the light. He held up his hands and they sizzled. He screamed.

Something slammed Matthias in the side of the head, making his ears ring. He blinked and the light stopped. The room smelled of burning flesh. Something was on his ear, pulling his hair, sticking needles in his skull. He brushed it away. The little man tumbled through the air, but turned into a spark before he hit the ground.

'You did that,' Matthias said to Burden.

Burden's face was gray. His hands were bloody masses of flesh. 'I wouldn't hurt myself like this for a demonstration,' he said. 'Go ahead. Finish me off. With your magick, oh religious one. With your magick.'

The door opened, and the guard hurried inside, sword drawn. 'Are you all right, Holy Sir?'

Matthias shook his head. He was not all right. He turned, grabbed the guard's pouch, and pulled a vial of holy water from it. Then Matthias poured the holy water on his own hand. Then he looked up at Burden. 'You lie.'

Burden shook his head. He was staring at his ruined hands. 'I don't lie about pain.'

'You promised me, Holy Sir,' the guard said. 'Please, give me the water.'

Matthias clutched it in his hand and approached the cage. 'You're trying to drive me crazy. All this time. You want me dead like the old Rocaan. And if you can't kill me, you'll drive me crazy.'

'Holy Sir, please –'

The spark circled his face, but his shield went up again. He wouldn't let anyone near him. He took the vial and held it up. 'Before the Roca,' he said, 'the Islanders believed in revenge.'

'You believe in your god, though,' Burden said, his voice small.

'The Roca is not God,' Matthias said.

'Please, Holy Sir,' the guard said. He was approaching, his sword out, and pointed at Matthias. 'Don't make me defend the Fey.'

'Defend me,' Burden said. 'I'm not proud.'

A shield went up behind Matthias. The sword clanged against it. 'You people believe in revenge,' Matthias said. 'You tried to take my life twice in revenge for Jewel's.'

'You had no right to take hers,' Burden said.

'But I have a right to take yours.' Matthias threw the water at him. Burden screamed and tried to dive out of the way, but the water hit him.

'Holy Sir!' the guard cried.

The spark left the shield and hovered over Burden. Burden was screaming, twisting and turning. Mist rose off his body, carrying the stench of burned flesh. He was cursing Matthias in Fey. Then his face collapsed in on itself. He struggled for a few moments more, then stopped moving.

There was still a bit of holy water left in the vial. Matthias searched for the spark. It zoomed past him and out the door, so fast that it looked like a streak of light.

Matthias leaned against the cage, the stench sickening him. The iron was cold against his forehead. He was trembling. This time he had killed. Purposely. No accident here. For revenge.

As the Fey did.

'Forgive me,' he whispered, hoping the Holy One would take the words to God's ear. 'Please, someone, forgive me.'

Fifty-Five

Solanda sat on the windowsill, her feet braced against one side of the stone frame, her back braced against the other. The wind blew in from the river, carrying with it the smell of sunshine and mud. Flowers were blooming in the garden below. Someday soon, when she was certain that Arianna wouldn't spontaneously change into a thorn or something even more wicked, she would ask the nurse to accompany them into the garden.

She hoped that would be before winter.

Since the Shaman had come, though, Solanda was calmer. She was seeing some of the benefits of Nicholas's care. The food was good. She had just finished a plate of fish cooked over a slow fire. The cook had added delicate herbs which she picked off and placed on the side, and she hadn't eaten her asparagus, but saved it for the lump, who inexplicably loved green food.

He was standing in the other window, as he had since he woke up, holding the tapestry back with one hand and staring over the garden to the river and Tabernacle beyond. The nurse had taken the morning off – Solanda wanted her rested because the nurse had no real idea how difficult the next year would be.

Neither did Solanda. She only knew she had to take it one day at a time. And last night, the nurse had borne the brunt of Arianna's playfulness. Arianna was learning some control after a week of life. She would change only enough to panic the nurse, but not enough – and not long enough – to give the nurse time to wake Solanda. By the time Solanda did wake, the nurse was shaking and crying, frightening Arianna who started crying too.

The child had learned, in the last day, to change a single finger without shifting anything else. Solanda supervised the non dangerous Shifts, but did nothing. Better to let Arianna Shift under observation than to order her not to Shift at all.

The door to the room opened, and the nurse came in.

'I think I told you to rest,' Solanda said.

The nurse nodded. 'I canna sleep away from me babies.' She looked at the lump. 'Has it been all day he's been looking out there?'

'I'm afraid so,' Solanda said. She put her plate on the floor so that she could get the fish oil off it later, when she was in her cat form, and got off the ledge. Arianna was still sleeping, exhausted from her play the night before.

'Come on.' The nurse took the lump's arm. He turned and allowed her to lead him near the fire. Then he hugged her, the movements slow and gentle. Solanda found it amazing that the nurse tolerated such handling. But she actually seemed to like it. 'Tis sleep ye need, boy. Ye was up with me all night. Tain't good for ye.'

Solanda wondered if anything was good for that lump, but instead of commenting on that, she said, 'I think I'll take a catnap. Wake me if you need me.'

The nurse smiled at her and went to the lump's favorite corner. He followed her. She leaned against the wall, and he sat on her lap, resting his head on her shoulder. After watching them for weeks now, Solanda marveled at the lump. By rights, he should have died before he reached Arianna's age. But unless someone knew that he wasn't real, he seemed like a child continually moving underwater, never hearing properly, never speaking properly, never moving properly. She wondered how Arianna would deal with him.

Not that it mattered at the moment. Arianna was asleep in her favorite position, her small fist pressed against her cheek. Her eyelashes twitched as if she were dreaming. What did she dream about? Shifting? The loss of her mother? Already her life was full of activity and loss.

The fish scent under Solanda's nose was driving her cat side crazy. She took a deep breath and Shifted, feeling her body shrink into its familiar second form. She ended up on her haunches beside the crib, her front paws on the legs. She brought her paws down and immediately cleaned her face, getting oil and flavor from her whiskers. The meal had been good – excellent in fact – if she could just get the cooks to forego the green.

She walked over to the plate and pushed the asparagus aside with her nose. It reeked worse in this form, and almost turned her strong stomach. She ignored it, and licked the remains of her meal off the plate, beginning on the lower left rim and working her way into the center.

The nurse started cooing, as she often did to soothe the lump. Islanders frowned on song, as Solanda had learned on Arianna's second night of life. They had learned somewhere that music was evil, and they had outlawed it. *Only birds do that*, the nurse had told her.

Birds, heh. Fey did it too.

Birds. That was one irritation of the window overlooking the garden. All the birds that landed on the trees below. Meals, waiting for her hunting skills. But she didn't dare launch herself from the window, so the delicious creatures sang in blissful ignorance, waiting for the day when Solanda became free again, the day she made a meal of every bug, bird, and mouse in sight.

At least they had fish here. Good fish too.

Above her Arianna giggled. Solanda cursed under her breath. The child catnapped. Solanda sat on her haunches and cleaned her whiskers a second time. The nurse would warn her if Arianna began to Shift. A cat had a right to finish her meal in peace.

Then a movement caught her eye. The lump stood up. The nurse stopped cooing. The lump walked to the crib and looked down. He did that periodically, and it always unnerved Solanda. It was as if the lump suddenly remembered he had a sister, and wanted to protect her.

He clutched the edge of the basket. Solanda couldn't see Arianna's physical response, but she giggled again. She liked her lump and usually reached toward him when he looked at her.

The nurse looked at Solanda and shrugged. Solanda sighed. She would have to change back. She didn't want the lump to inspire Arianna to do anything stupid.

Then the lump whipped his head around. The sudden movement unbalanced him. His arms pinwheeled, bumping the crib, and he toppled sideways.

He had never moved that fast. Ever.

The nurse hurried across the room, and caught the crib before it fell over. Then she crouched beside the lump, brushing his hair from his face and asking him if he was all right.

Solanda hadn't moved.

He was looking at her. His eyes were alive. They had an intelligence she recognized, a presence she felt she should know.

The fish taste went stale in her mouth. She stood and crouched, inching up to the lump as she would to a dead body. Then she stopped by the face. The lump had never had this kind of adult intelligence glowing from its eyes. Occasionally she had seen it look smart – she had wondered if Jewel was coming back as a Power or if Gift was looking through him. But she had never seen this.

The lump's mouth was curved in almost a sneer. He seemed to recognize her too. The nurse was still exclaiming over him, trying to get him to show her that he was all right. He wasn't bleeding, but he wasn't moving either.

She sniffed his face, wondering if he smelled different. He had the dry polished scent of stone, and a bit of the egg he ate for breakfast.

His eyes followed her every movement. When she got close to his lips, he blew at her to scare her away.

She huffed, a cat noise of disgust that she couldn't control, and the ruff on the back of her neck rose. She backed away from him, unwilling to take her gaze from his face.

'By the Powers,' the lump said in disgust, and then the presence left his eyes.

'What did he say?' the nurse whispered.

But the intelligence remained. Solanda saw it, wondered at it. The intelligence was boyish, now, not as malevolent. The lump closed his eyes and stretched, like a child would do before sleep.

'What did he say?' the nurse repeated.

She hadn't understood him. The lump had spoken in Fey.

Again.

The hair was still up on the back of Solanda's neck. Her tail had poofed with fear. The lump was alive because someone had visited this nursery through him. Probably Gift. But now he brought someone else with him.

Even though she wanted to clean this memory away, she didn't have time. She had to check on her baby. Solanda Shifted, rising back to her Fey form, feeling her muscles lengthen, her tail disappear, her eyes grow.

'What did he say?' This time, the nurse's tone held fear.

Solanda brushed her hair away from her face with one hand. 'He swore in Fey,' she said.

'In Fey?' the nurse asked. 'Did you teach him that?'

Solanda shook her head. She peered into the crib. Arianna was awake, her eyes wide and frightened. Solanda picked her up and held her warm body against her own naked shoulder.

The baby was all right.

For now.

Fifty-Six

Matthias paced the audience chamber in the Tabernacle. He couldn't sit. He couldn't wait much longer either. Soon Nicholas's people would come after him.

The guards had helped him escape from the keep, thinking he was the one in danger. They had procured him a horse, and let him ride alone across the bridge, following as quickly as they could. When he got to the Tabernacle, he ordered the first Aud he saw to get Titus and Porciluna and to have them meet him in the Audience Chamber.

That had been a few moments ago, but it felt like hours. He had already paced the room twice, ignoring the drawings of the Rocaan, keeping his hands away from the swords.

No matter how much he wanted to lie to himself, he couldn't forget the clank of the sword against his shield, his ability to keep the spark at bay, and the feeling of the light pouring out of him.

Burden had told the truth, and for that Matthias had killed him.

Perhaps this magic was the key to his lack of faith. Perhaps he was a demon spawn as they had said.

The side door opened and Titus came in. His robe hung loosely. He wasn't wearing a sash. His filigree sword looked almost white against the black of his robe.

'You all right?' he asked. He was looking at Matthias's hand. Matthias had already forgotten the injury. The pain seemed part of him. He almost glanced at his hand to see if it had healed itself.

'No, I'm not all right,' Matthias said. He paced away from Titus. Ahead of him was a sword. Past that were carvings of the Roca. Everywhere he turned were signs of this religion.

'What can I do?' Titus asked.

Nothing. Everything. Throw holy water. Attempt to take the spells away from him. Give him faith. 'Wait,' Matthias said. 'Porciluna will join us.'

And he had better do so soon before Matthias lost his nerve.

Before Nicholas and his guards got here.

Before the entire kingdom was turned upside down.

'The guards said you went to the keep,' Titus said.

'What I did doesn't matter,' Matthias said. He kept his back to Titus. Titus, with his eagerness and his intuitive understanding of the Roca, was exactly what Matthias didn't need.

The door creaked open. Matthias turned, half afraid to see Nicholas in the doorway. Instead Porciluna stood there. His robe was pressed, and he wore rings on each finger. His biretta was placed to cover his balding scalp. He looked official and omnipotent.

'They're saying you were attacked at the keep,' he said.

'Close the door,' Matthias said. No secrets here, except the ones God ordered them to keep. God or a Rocaan long forgotten. All those years he had planned to spend in scholarship, lost to the day-to-day running of the Tabernacle. All those years of prayer, lost to a morning of revenge.

Porciluna closed the door and came into the chamber. He looked as if he belonged here, his robes flowing behind him, his size giving him a stature and power that Matthias never had.

Matthias bit his upper lip. He wasn't certain how to proceed. But he had to. He had to move forward somehow.

And he didn't have much time.

'I am stepping down as Rocaan,' he said.

'What?'

'You can't!'

Porciluna and Titus spoke at the same time. Both men had identical expressions of shock on their faces.

'No one has resigned as Rocaan,' Titus said. 'It's a post appointed by God.'

'It's a post given to one man from another,' Matthias said.

'The Elders will have to approve this,' Porciluna said.

'The Elders have no say. Besides, you begged me to step down days ago.' Matthias clasped his hands in front of his robe, wincing at the pain that flared suddenly in his palm. 'You were behind that, Porciluna. Don't play with me now. You wanted this position so badly you would have done anything to get it.'

'Holy Sir, do you know what chaos this will place the church in?' Titus asked.

'The same kind of chaos it has been in all week,' Matthias said. 'My leaving will probably help the Tabernacle. That, of course, depends on how you play this.'

'You said nothing of leaving,' Porciluna said.

'Trust me.' Matthias clasped his hands tighter to keep from shaking. 'You don't want me here.'

'But the Secrets –'

'Titus has the Secrets,' Matthias said.

439

'Titus?' Porciluna's flush grew deeper. He glanced at Titus then at Matthias. 'But he's a Danite.'

Matthias nodded. 'Someone else had to know the Secrets, and it had to be someone who wouldn't try to get rid of me immediately.'

'You can't give the Secrets to a Danite!'

'I already have.' Matthias swallowed. Titus was staring at him, eyes wide. He was little more than a boy, early twenties if he was that old, faithful and strong. He had to be to endure what was coming next.

'So now you give the Secrets to me,' Porciluna said.

Matthias shook his head. 'I don't think you should be Rocaan, Porciluna. I think you lack faith, and I think you are motivated by greed, two elements that have no place in the Rocaan's suite.'

'You lack faith,' Porciluna said.

'And I'm stepping down,' Matthias said.

'If you aren't planning to give me the Secrets, why did you bring me in here?'

Matthias shook his head. Whatever his crimes, they had none of the self-absorption that Porciluna had. 'To let you know, as the ranking Elder, that I'm leaving. To let you know that Titus has the Secrets.'

'And we're to accept this boy as our next Rocaan?' Porciluna said.

Matthias shrugged. 'The Elders must decide. I am leaving the post of Rocaan for reasons I will not discuss with you. The old Rocaan thought I had God's Ear. But I don't. And I don't trust any decision I make about my own successor. The council has to decide now.'

He walked around them. Titus hadn't moved. Porciluna was shaking with anger.

'You won't be here?' Titus asked, his voice rising.

'I'm leaving,' Matthias said.

'But what am I supposed to do?' Titus asked.

'Follow your heart,' Matthias said. 'Of all the people in the Tabernacle, you're the only one who seems to be listening to God.'

'Although you said you can't tell,' Porciluna said.

'Do you see what I mean?' Matthias asked. Now that his decision was made, he felt calmer. But he did have to leave as quickly as he could.

'Where are you going?' Titus asked. 'How do I find you?'

'You won't,' Matthias said.

Porciluna squinted at him. 'What happened in the keep?'

Too much. And fortunately, most of it had died with Burden. Matthias certainly would never speak of it. 'You'll find out soon enough.'

'Are you sure the boy has all the Secrets?' Porciluna asked. His tone had an edge that Matthias didn't like.

440

'All of them,' Matthias said. 'Keep him alive, Porciluna, because I'm not going to tell you the Secrets.'

'Elders should know,' Porciluna said.

Matthias shook his head. 'I may be nothing else, but I am a scholar of Rocaanism. Nothing in the Words or in the Teachings state that Elders must keep the Secrets. Nothing even says that Elders should become Rocaan. That's been tradition.'

'You're destroying the church,' Porciluna said.

Matthias's hand throbbed. Porciluna had no idea how badly Matthias had hurt the church nor how badly he would hurt it if he stayed. He turned to Titus. 'Please explain this to the others,' he said. 'I'm doing this because it's for the best.'

'You don't have to resign, Holy Sir,' Titus said. 'I'm sure we can work this out.'

Matthias shook his head. 'The Tabernacle is better off without me. You all are.' He held up his good hand. 'Blessed Be.'

Then he let himself out of the Audience Chamber. He was shaking. His last act as Rocaan. His last act in the church. Now he would get as far away from it as he could. As far away from people as he could.

He was demon-spawn. No one should get near him. No one would be safe.

The guards had left, as he thought they would. That meant that someone knew what had happened.

He stopped by one of the ornamental chairs and pulled off his filigree sword. He felt naked without it. Then he removed his sash and placed it on the chair. He couldn't remove his robe – he had no other clothes. He would worry about that later, when he got out of Jahn.

Matthias let himself out of the side door. The sun was still shining. The air was still fresh, and the day was still lovely.

He was the only thing that had changed.

Demon-spawn.

He would never go anywhere holy again.

Fifty-Seven

The boy leaned against the building, his eyes rolled into the back of his head. Niche hovered over him, her hands barely touching him. Rugar sat across from him, seething. The Shadowlands swirled around them, gray and barren, more of a prison than a home.

Rugar grabbed the boy's wrist. 'Get back here,' he whispered.

'Don't hurt him,' Niche said. 'Please.'

Rugar ignored her and pulled the boy close. His body was limp. His consciousness was still in Nicholas's palace, in the golem, in the same room as his sister. The boy fell forward, hitting his head against Rugar's knee.

Pain shot through his leg, but he ignored it. He put his hands under the boy's armpits and pulled him upright. 'Get back here,' Rugar said.

'Please,' Niche said. 'He's a baby. Don't –'

'He's not a baby,' Rugar said without looking at her. 'He already knows how to manipulate. I was wrong letting you raise him. You have corrupted him. I wanted to find that Enchanter, and your son led me to the palace.'

'I'm sure he didn't mean –'

'He meant.' Rugar shook the boy. 'Get back here.'

Gift's head lolled back and forth. Niche crouched beside them. 'Please, Rugar, don't hurt him. He can't hear you.'

Rugar pushed her. She flew backwards, the strength of his shove unnecessary for her light bones. She landed on the ground and cried once in pain.

The boy opened his eyes. He had returned. 'Mommy?' he asked.

Rugar was holding the boy's arm tightly. 'She'll be all right,' Rugar said. 'But you might not be. You were following the Enchanter's Link. Then you veered. Why?'

The boy's face was gray. He swallowed, looking suddenly like his father. His small mouth worked.

Rugar shook him. 'Why?'

'He saved my life,' the boy whispered.

'Gift.' Niche sat up. Her injured wings looked flat and she didn't move from the place where she had landed. 'Help Rugar. He needs you.'

'I don't need anyone,' Rugar said.

'But I thought you wanted him to find Coulter,' Niche said. 'Maybe if I ask, he will.'

'No.' Gift's small jaw was set.

Rugar pulled him close. 'What did you say?'

'I said no.' Gift's eyes flashed like Jewel's used to when she was being stubborn.

'No one says no to me.'

'I do,' Gift said. 'I hate you.'

He stated the words as if they were fact. They hit Rugar like a blow. 'I don't care how you feel about me,' Rugar said, pulling him so close that their noses touched. 'I want you to find that Enchanter for me.'

'No,' Gift said.

'He didn't save your life,' Rugar said. 'I'm the one who brought you here.'

'I don't belong here,' Gift said.

'That's not true.' Niche's voice wobbled with pain. She put one hand on the gray bottom to Shadowlands and slowly eased herself up. 'You belong with Wind and me, Gift.'

Gift pulled his head away from Rugar's. 'I belonged with my real parents. You stole me.'

'You're Fey,' Rugar said. 'You belong here.'

'I'm half Fey. Coulter told me.'

Niche gasped. Rugar let go of the boy's left arm and placed his hand behind the boy's head, holding it still. 'You are my grandson. You are to be loyal to me.'

'I hate you,' Gift said. 'You're a mean old man.'

The back of the boy's neck was fragile. One quick turn and he would be gone. Rugar wondered if he knew that.

He nearly squeezed, then shoved the boy away. Gift slammed into the building so loud that the sound echoed through Shadowlands.

Niche stood, blood dripping from her injured wings. 'He's a child. He doesn't know any better.'

Rugar got up and stood beside her. 'He knows what you taught him.'

'I never taught him to defy anyone.'

Rugar clenched his fists. He had done enough damage this day. 'I thought having him raised by a family would be good for him. I thought it would teach him about love and respect. I was wrong.'

Niche raised her chin so that she looked directly at him. 'We did teach him about love and respect. That's why he's protecting Coulter. The boys were best friends.'

Rugar grabbed her wrist and pulled her close. Her bones shattered beneath his fingers. She whimpered. 'You failed to teach him to respect family. He's not Fey. He's not anything.'

A little body slammed into Rugar. Arms circled his waist and a head pushed against his stomach.

'You let her go!' Gift cried. 'Let go!'

He grabbed with all his strength, then kicked Rugar repeatedly. With his free hand, Rugar pried Gift loose. Then Rugar put his hand on Gift's skull and pushed him back. The boy flailed at him. Niche didn't fight at all.

'Madam,' Rugar said to her, ignoring the boy slapping his hand, 'I still have use for your child. See to it that next time he obeys me.'

Then he let go of her. She fell to her knees and cradled her wrist against her chest. Her hand flopped forward, useless.

Rugar turned to Gift and grabbed the boy's flailing hands with one of his one. 'You, child, are flesh of my flesh, blood of my blood. You may hate me, but you will do as I say.'

Gift struggled, but Rugar didn't tighten his grip as he did with Niche. 'I'll never listen to you.'

'Someday, you'll have to,' Rugar said.

'Someday you'll die,' Gift said. 'And I'll laugh.'

'Gift,' Niche said wearily. Her eyes were dark circles on her face.

'You may laugh,' Rugar said. 'But you'll take my place.'

'No,' Gift said.

'You have to,' Rugar said. 'You're my grandson.'

'I don't have to do anything you say.'

'Gift,' Niche said again, warning in her tone.

'I don't! I hate you! I will always hate you!'

Rugar let go of the boy's hands. This would get them nowhere. They had already gone nowhere. 'Then hate me,' Rugar said. 'It will do you no good. You can't fight what you are.'

'I'm not you,' Gift said.

The boy's eyes flashed as he spoke. All traces of his father were momentarily gone from his face. 'Not yet,' Rugar said.

He turned his back on them, and headed to his own cabin, unwilling to fight this any longer. The boy had failed him, and would continue to fail him. As long as Rugar was around, the boy would treat him as the enemy. Niche and Wind had raised him incorrectly. Rugar should have seen that from the Naming Day. Gift was not the name of a warrior, but of a precious coddled child. Precious coddled children ultimately rebelled.

Like Jewel had.

The mist swirled around Rugar's boots. Behind him, he heard Gift exclaiming over his mother. Soon the boy would go for help. No one would rebuke Rugar – no one could – but they would all watch him warily, more warily than they had.

These years in Shadowlands had taken away their fight. He was the only one left who wanted to control Blue Isle. And he would, with or without Gift's help. They had been trapped inside this Shadowlands for five years. No one had even taken the ships out of the First Shadowlands in two years. A few more wouldn't matter.

He would get the Enchanter back, but first he would do something he should have done weeks ago.

He would bring his granddaughter home.

The Shaman had spooked him while he was grieving. He should never have listened to that old woman. She had made it clear that she never liked him, and would do anything to supplant him. She had told him to stay away from his granddaughter because she didn't want him to have the child's power.

But the child belonged in the Black Family. The power was his until he decreed otherwise. He would raise her properly, and make her gifts work for the Fey.

He had seen Solanda at the child's side. Guarding a baby with a cat seemed preposterous at most, silly at best.

Besides, Solanda was sworn to him. She would do what he asked.

She would give him the child.

Fifty-Eight

Titus watched the door close. The Rocaan was gone. Suddenly the Audience Chamber seemed empty.

'Shouldn't we go after him?' Titus asked.

Porciluna was staring at the door, his expression blank. He appeared to be as shocked as Titus was. 'I don't think so,' Porciluna said. 'I think for the first time in years, he made the right decision.'

That's because you want to be Rocaan, Titus thought but didn't say. He couldn't say anything. Yet.

He walked to one of the chairs and sank into it. The cushions were hard as wood. When King Alexander died – which seemed like years ago even though it had only been a few weeks – Titus had believed that the Rocaan cared for nothing but power.

Now he was walking away from it as if it mattered not at all. And Titus, who had only wanted to worship in his own way, was suddenly in the middle of a struggle he only dimly understood.

If he had realized the day before that the Rocaan had been thinking of this when he passed along the Secrets, Titus would never have accepted them. He wasn't an Elder. He didn't have the experience or the training to work the complicated political paths that he would have to walk now. Already he knew that he would have to make decisions he had never considered before.

He would have to give the Secrets to the Elder chosen by the Council.

Or he would have to refuse.

He leaned his head back. The glass in the chandelier glimmered in the light of a single torch. The ceiling panels were carved. He had never noticed that before. All the little details in the Tabernacle. Rocaanism was a series of tiny details, some centuries old.

He wasn't ready for this. He would never be ready for this.

'We need to call the Elders together,' Porciluna said.

'I'm not an Elder,' Titus said and sighed.

Porciluna was silent for a moment. 'Right now we have no time to discover what you are. We have to find leadership for the Tabernacle.'

'I still say we go after the Rocaan,' Titus said. It would be easier. He was arguing the easy path, something he used to ridicule others for. But now he understood it. If they found the Rocaan before he got too far, Titus wouldn't have to make any choices.

Porciluna clapped a hand on his shoulder. Titus found himself looking at the underside of Porciluna's chin. Porciluna's skin was soft and acne-scarred. It smelled faintly of rosewater. He didn't look happy.

'You think he should have chosen you,' Titus said.

Porciluna started. 'An Elder would have been a logical choice to keep the Secrets,' he said. 'That's what the fiftieth Rocaan did.'

'And then kept that Elder in charge even when he shouldn't have been.' Titus shook his head, and pushed out of the chair. Already he felt older than he was. 'When the Rocaan told me that he was choosing me for the Secrets, I argued against it. But he said that it was the best choice. I would never have any expectations of becoming Rocaan, so I wouldn't try to kill him. That was yesterday. It seemed like he wanted to stay in the position then.'

'Something happened in the keep,' Porciluna said.

'He murdered the Fey.'

Both men whirled at the third voice. Elder Reece stood in the door. He didn't seem as nervous as usual, as if the crisis had somehow given him strength. He was standing straighter, and his thinness made him seem powerful for the very first time. Apparently neither Porciluna nor Titus had heard him come in.

'Murdered?' Titus said.

Reece nodded. 'The man's dead, and the guard says he tried to stop the Rocaan. This time there can be no claim of accident.'

'But the Fey tried to kill him,' Porciluna said.

'Still it would make things clear that the Rocaan is out to get the Fey.'

'I see nothing wrong with that,' Porciluna said.

Reece sighed. 'But the King does. The Rocaan left, I would guess, before the King can arrest him for the murder of the Queen. He did us a favor.'

'By leaving?' This conversation was moving too fast for Titus. He was afraid, however, that all conversations would move too fast for him from now on. These men knew so much more than he did.

Porciluna nodded. 'By making us choose a leader now, he prevents a long period of turmoil in the Tabernacle. We have never had a Rocaan arrested. We would have debated procedure until we were old men.'

'But now he's fleeing justice,' Titus said.

'That's probably why he wanted to leave so quickly,' Porciluna said. 'That's another reason we should find him.'

'No,' Reece said. 'He did us a favor. We can do him one.'

'The King's guards will catch him anyway. He has nowhere to go. He won't get far.'

'I don't understand any of this,' Titus said. 'A man commits murder, not once but twice that we know of, and we let him go? It makes no sense. We're supposed to be leaders in this community. We're supposed to know right from wrong.'

Porciluna glanced at Reece. 'The boy has a point. We need to make a decision tonight about the new Rocaan. When we make the announcement, we'll say that we knew of Matthias's flaws for a long time now, and were trying to deal with him.'

'That's not what I meant!' Titus said. 'We need to find him, and to bring him to the King ourselves. And then we need to figure out what to do about his position. No Rocaan has ever resigned, just like no Rocaan has ever been arrested. What's the difference between one and the other?'

'The future of the Tabernacle,' Porciluna said. 'If we let the Rocaan be imprisoned, then we can never be leaders in this community again.'

'But how can we be leaders if we do something like this? Just because people don't know doesn't make it right.'

Porciluna and Reece looked at each other. Titus's cheeks warmed. That look implied that he was young, that he didn't know what he was talking about, that he had no understanding of the world.

And he didn't.

'It's our job to make these kinds of decisions,' Porciluna said.

But Titus wasn't going to let go. 'I thought it was our job to follow God's will.'

Porciluna shrugged. 'It will be God's will if the guards capture Matthias.'

'God would have stopped him if he hadn't wanted him as Rocaan. God would have stopped the killings, too.'

'That's dangerous ground,' Reece said. 'We can't know if God ever condones killing.'

'Not even killing of Fey?' Titus asked. The Rocaan's argument had been that Fey were demons and therefore not worthy of life.

'Any killing at all.'

'But we kill to eat,' Titus said. This was what angered him about the Rocaan, this arguing about words without listening to the heart of a subject.

'Do you condone killing Fey?'

Titus shook his head. 'But I think we should always listen to the man God appointed Rocaan.'

'Another man appointed the Rocaan, not God.'

'Acting with God's still small voice speaking in his ear!' Titus said.

Again the two Elders glanced at each other. Titus felt his flush deepen. 'You're not going to tell me that the still small voice doesn't exist,' he said quietly. 'I know it has. I've heard it.'

Porciluna nodded almost imperceptibly at Reece. It was well known that Reece was the believer of the two.

'Have you heard it on every decision?' Reece asked.

'No, but if you hear it once, then you know it's working in the other cases,' Titus said. He couldn't believe he was having this discussion with Elders. He had had it as a young Aud, with other young Auds, some of whom became Rocaanists only because their family asked them to. But Elders should have worked this out a long, long time ago.

'Exactly,' Reece said.

Titus shook his head, suddenly confused. Exactly what? They were dismissing him as if he were a child. He wasn't a child. 'I think we should get the Rocaan. I think we should face what's coming for us as a unified body. If our leader believes that the Fey are threats to us and to God, then we should listen to him.'

'We don't have a leader,' Porciluna said.

'We did just a few moments ago,' Titus said. 'Send some Auds for him. Bring him back.'

Reece glanced down the hall, and closed the door. Then he came over and took Titus's arm. 'You're frightened, aren't you?' he asked.

Titus shook his arm away. He didn't want this fake compassion. He had decisions to make, a church to save, ideals to hold. Some of those decisions had to be made now, before the Rocaan was gone for good. 'I just think we should be certain of our choices,' he said.

'The Rocaan made his choice,' Porciluna said.

'Based on politics and fear, not on belief!'

'How do you know that?' Reece said. 'How do you know what's in a man's heart?'

They reversed the argument on him, and he had no answer for that. None at all. Titus shook his head. 'I just think we should get him.'

'And save you the embarrassment of sharing the Secrets with one of us?' Porciluna asked.

Titus swallowed. He was frightened. But he suspected the fear was healthy. 'What if the Elders don't decide on a new Rocaan? What then?'

'We'll decide,' Porciluna said.

'No,' Reece said softly. 'We have to address this. It's a valid fear. We're already in trouble if none of us has the Secrets.'

'I have the Secrets,' Titus said.

Reece started, his thin body shaking with the violence of his reaction. 'You –?'

449

'That's why he's here,' Porciluna said. 'Matthias wanted to be sure I knew who kept the Secrets, and that I should leave the boy alone.'

'I thought you had them,' Reece said. He put a hand to his face and rubbed the bridge of his nose with his thumb and forefinger. 'This changes things.'

'It changes nothing,' Porciluna said.

'No,' Reece said. 'It makes sense of the boy's question.' He brought his hand down, his faded blue eyes seeking Titus's. 'If we can't agree on a Rocaan in the Council of Elders, son, then you become Rocaan by default.'

'There's nothing in the traditions for that,' Porciluna said.

Reece nodded. 'But it's true. If we can't decide, then the boy has to make holy water and take care of the rest of the Secrets. That's how it will work.'

Porciluna waved a hand dismissively. 'We'll choose a Rocaan.'

Titus was cold, even though his face was flushed. They would choose a Rocaan, and he would give that man the Secrets. Even a man like Porciluna who also had no faith. Who was willing to lie to the people in order to save his own skin. Who was willing the jeopardize the church with no thought at all.

'And what happens if I refuse to give the Secrets to the new Rocaan?' Titus asked.

Porciluna swiveled until he faced Titus. 'You have to.' Porciluna's voice quivered as if the idea had never occurred to him before.

'Do I?' Titus said. 'Is that in the traditions? I know this isn't provided for in the Words. And it was my understanding that the person who possessed the Secrets is the Rocaan.'

'You aren't ready to be Rocaan,' Reece said gently.

'I know,' Titus said. 'So let's bring the Rocaan back.'

'He resigned,' Porciluna said.

'But there's no provision for that either,' Titus said. He smiled. 'See? It works out just fine. You allow him to break traditions of the church, so you'll have to allow me to do the same.'

'This is blackmail,' Porciluna said.

'No,' Titus said. 'It's sense. You cannot have things the way you want them. They have to go according to our understanding of God's will.'

'We never understand God's will,' Porciluna said.

'The Words, the traditions, and the still small voice are all designed to help us understand, however imperfectly,' Reece said.

'You're on his side?'

Reece shook his head. 'There are no sides here. Only a complicated issue that won't be solved simply.' He turned to Titus. 'We won't look for Matthias.'

Titus started to object, but Reece held up his hand.

'He is the representative of God, and he has chosen to resign. Traditions start this way. Perhaps if I had been here, I would have discovered what he thought his action was based on. Matthias is a scholar. He knows what he is doing.'

'But he was never a believer.'

Reece looked pointedly at Titus's unshod feet. 'He was never an obvious believer. But the Tabernacle was important to him. He served it as best he could.'

'Matthias said he did not believe just a few moments ago,' Porciluna said.

'And he said that was one reason he was stepping down,' Titus said, not sure why the sentence had come from him with such obvious anger. He had known that the Rocaan had trouble with his faith, but he hadn't realized that the other Elders did too. The Auds he had grown up with, the ones who questioned everything about the church and the religion weren't that unusual. They were, in fact, able to rise in the hierarchy of the church.

A blasphemy.

'Matthias was always honest about his lack of belief,' Reece said. 'I often thought that made him more valuable than the rigid believers. Or the liars.'

He glanced at Porciluna as he said that last. Porciluna did not look away.

'If you're not going to go after him, what are you going to do?' Titus asked.

'Follow his instructions,' Reece said. 'We're going to choose a new Rocaan.'

'We can't,' Porciluna said, 'as long as this boy controls the Secrets.'

'Of course we can,' Reece said. 'This is how Matthias planned it.'

Porciluna's small eyes got even smaller. 'No. Matthias planned this to insult us all. He knew that child wouldn't give up his power.'

'I'm not a child,' Titus said.

'You're not an Elder either.'

Porciluna's words hung in the room. Titus shivered. Porciluna was right and wrong at the same time. The Rocaan had given Titus the Secrets for a reason. The reason had to be stronger than one of revenge and a manipulation of political power.

The Old Rocaan thought I had God's Ear.

Maybe Rocaan Matthias had always had God's Ear. Maybe the Old Rocaan had been right. Maybe this change was the best for the Tabernacle. Maybe he had given Titus the Secrets for a religious reason.

451

Believing oneself to be Chosen is the way of folly, his old Danite instructor used to tell them.

But what if one was really Chosen? How could he tell?

Titus nodded. 'I'm not an Elder. That's right. But I do hold the Secrets.'

'We'll relieve you of that burden as soon as we can,' Reece said. 'Let's call a meeting of the Elders.'

'And quickly,' Porciluna said with his gaze on Titus. In their own ways, both men had made it clear that they believed Titus would destroy the Tabernacle.

He glanced at them, with their political concerns and their ties to this world. They seemed to have forgotten God, forgotten the Roca, forgotten the reasons they were here in the first place.

Perhaps the Rocaan had given Titus the Secrets because he believed Titus could save the Tabernacle.

Perhaps the Rocaan was right.

Fifty-Nine

Touched sat on the Warder's table, examining the blasted and burnt pieces of skin that had fallen when Coulter escaped. Some of the flesh hadn't been touched. It had decayed as it should have, leaving a slight odor of rotting flesh in the room. Rotin claimed the odor sickened her, and she left to conduct her own experiments.

Probably with herbs.

The other Warders were still working with the Domestics. Touched was in no hurry to bring them into the cabin. He wanted to examine this material all by himself.

The burnt skin had been over the bubble where the light had seared it. Those bits of flesh were blackened and charred, some falling apart in his fingers as he picked them up. Little flakes of ash covered the table's surface, suggesting that even more strips of flesh had been burned beyond recognition.

The light hadn't felt that hot, but it had to have been to sear through that much flesh. The moment had been startling and almost terrifying. Touched had believed that he had captured Coulter, that the boy was incapable of saving himself. But something about the Islander Adrian had allowed the boy to break free.

Touched didn't believe that Adrian had any magick. If he had, he would have used it against Jewel and the others when he was first captured. This was a man who had loved his son so much that he had sacrificed his own life to save him. He would have used any magick he had at that point.

He wouldn't have used it to save Coulter.

Unless he had learned it in Shadowlands.

But how was magick learned? Touched had never heard of that. Fey either had it or they didn't have it. He suspected Islanders were the same way.

Although Caseo would have argued with him about that. Caseo believed that assumptions were the killers of knowledge, that they blinded people who really wanted to learn.

That had been one of Caseo's assumptions.

And it had probably been right.

Touched sighed. The most interesting bits of skin were the ones that had side holes punched through them. Tiny charred areas that didn't seem to affect the rest of the strip. Either the light had shredded somewhere or something else had hit these pieces.

As he looked at the skin, he stretched out the pieces on the tabletop, hoping to reconstruct them into the wall of the bubble. That was probably fruitless, but if he could do so, he might learn something about the nature of Coulter's powers.

Or perhaps about what triggered his ability to rescue himself.

A knock on the door made him jump. He resisted the urge to gather all the skin strips and hide them. He was a Warder now. In truth, he was the head Warder, although Rotin hadn't acknowledged that yet. No one could do anything to him.

'Come,' he said, making certain his voice sounded calm.

Tazy slid around the door. He was a stocky Fey, but strong. He ran the Foot Soldiers as if they were children. Touched had put Tazy in charge of the search for Coulter.

He pushed the door closed with one foot, took off his beret, and turned it around and around in his hands. His nose wrinkled at the stench in the room, but he said nothing.

A Foot Soldier could say nothing. They had collected most of the strips.

From live victims.

'Well?' Touched asked.

Tazy shook his head.

Touched waited, but Tazy said no more. 'A simple shake of the head will do you no good,' Touched said. 'Tell me.'

Tazy's hat was tattered, the material full of tiny holes. His skin had scrapes and bruises and there were grass stains on his knees.

'We saw no one,' he said.

Touched set the last piece of skin down carefully so that he wouldn't rip it. Then he clenched his fists and rested them on his thighs. 'I trust you looked.'

Tazy brought his head up. 'You sent us.'

'I sent you to find the boy, not to come back without him.'

'Then send a Gull Rider. We saw nothing.'

Touched nodded once. 'Nothing?'

Tazy poked a finger through one of the holes in his cap. Even though he was twice Touched's age, he looked younger like he had never left childhood. Hard to believe those fingers had the power and precision to flay skin a layer at a time.

'They didn't take the path –'

'I know that,' Touched said.

'– and they didn't go to Daisy Stream that we can see.'

'I already sent teams to those places. Have you anyone in Jahn?'

Tazy licked his lips. His finger had burrowed a large hole in the cap. 'No one would go.'

'No one would go?' Touched kept his voice calm. 'Even though ordered by a Warder?'

'Your orders weren't that specific –'

'My orders were precise,' Touched said. 'I told you to keep your people out there until they found that boy.'

Tazy turned his hat inside out, then stuffed it in the pocket of his jerkin. 'My people are still out there. But they're not going to find anything. That boy vanished.'

'No one vanishes,' Touched said. 'Everyone from Doppelgängers to Shape-Shifters leaves a trail. You just have to know how to find it.'

'That's why I think you should send a Rider. They might see him from above.'

'Or perhaps I should tell Rugar to get someone else to lead the Foot Soldiers. Obviously you're not suited to the task any more.'

'I do fine,' Tazy said. 'This boy is unusual. We haven't lost anyone like this before.'

'Did you see anything?' Touched asked.

'Broken branches leading to the river. Then nothing.'

'So what, do you think he drowned?'

'It's possible,' Tazy said.

'Possible? *Possible?* How possible is it that someone who has lived in Shadowlands his entire life would approach a running body of water? How possible is it that a boy who has never been in the woods could outwit two dozen Fey?'

'It happened,' Tazy said.

'Because you let it happen.' Touched was shaking. The fools. 'Do you realize what you did?'

Tazy shook his head. He wasn't a dumb man. He knew better than to cross a Warder.

'You let our best hope for the future disappear. He Enchants, that boy.'

'He's Islander.'

'He's magic,' Touched said. 'And I have an Enchanter spell that will neutralize their poison. But we need an Enchanter. He's the only one we've got.'

'If you had told me that before –'

'Before? Before what? Would you have worked harder? Is that what you're saying? Are you glad that the Islander child is gone? You disobeyed my orders because of your dislike of Islanders?'

'I didn't know he had magick.'

'Neither did I until a few days ago. I still need him.'

Tazy took his hat out of his pocket and twirled it. 'We could keep looking,' he said.

'That you could,' Touched said.

'But I think the trail's cold. We didn't find the broken branches until yesterday. They only went to the river.'

'Did anyone check the other side? Did anyone go farther downstream to see if the boy waded a few feet to throw you off the trail? Did any of you think at all?' Touched was having trouble keeping his voice down. He had sent the Soldiers because he believed they would do better than he and Rotin would. They had done worse.

Much worse.

Tazy shook his head. 'The river's deep in that spot and the current is dangerous.'

'I don't want excuses,' Touched said.

'It's not,' Tazy said. 'If you knew tracking you would know that the boy couldn't have crossed there. Not alone.'

'He was with another Islander,' Touched said. 'Or have you forgotten?'

Tazy shook his head. 'We need a Gull Rider.'

'Rugar approved one,' Touched said. 'He should have joined you this morning.'

'We haven't seen one,' Tazy said. 'If we had, maybe we would have something by now.'

'Probably the Gull Rider decided to stay away from you people. He probably thought he had a better chance on his own.'

'But you haven't heard anything from him either, have you?'

Touched sighed. He hadn't heard a thing. The Enchanter and his protector had disappeared.

'I thought you haven't,' Tazy said. 'We're not incompetent, you know. You should have let us know how important this was.'

'You should have figured this out,' Touched said. 'It would seem obvious that if we were going to use so many people to find someone that it was important.'

Tazy shrugged. 'I just thought it was Rugar going off the deep end again. He hates losing prisoners.'

'It's happened before?'

'In Nye once. He went crazy.'

'He's not very pleased now. But I'm less pleased,' Touched said. 'Organize your teams. I want you to look under every leaf, through every drop of water, in every tree for that boy. Understand?'

Tazy nodded. 'If he can be found, we'll do it.' He clicked his heels together, opened the door, and let himself out.

Touched sighed and closed his eyes for a moment. He still wasn't used to giving orders. Perhaps he had done it wrong, or perhaps Tazy's attitude was bad, like everyone's seemed to be around here.

They would look hard now, but their opportunity was probably gone. Each day that went by hurt them and Touched's spell. The boy was probably suffering from Overs. They had to catch him while the symptoms were really bad and he wanted to return. Because the next stage after Overs was an exhilaration as the senses met the world. Once the boy reached that stage, he would never want to come back.

Touched opened his eyes. His fists were still clenched. No one understood his frustration, or how much anger was beneath it. He had finally found a solution to the poison, and the solution had fled. Enchanters came along once a generation. The next Fey Enchanter might be born on Blue Isle, but it would probably be born on Nye.

Useless to them here.

Even an infant would be useless.

Coulter was the right age.

But Coulter was Islander.

The Fey had to find him before he realized that.

Sixty

Nicholas crouched in front of his son. Sebastian had a small lump on the side of his head. The bruise had expanded oddly so that it almost looked as if his skin had cracked. Nicholas touched the injury gingerly. Sebastian flinched but did not turn away. His eyes were wide, trusting, the same as they had always been.

But Solanda and the nurse claimed that for a few moments, he had been someone else.

The room was stifling. Solanda kept the tapestries open during the day, but the nurse always built a roaring fire. The baby routinely kicked off her blankets. She loved to lie naked in the heat. Solanda said that was a sign that her second form might be a comfort-lover like a cat. Nicholas hoped so. Some of the other forms that Solanda had described sounded very unappealing in a daughter.

'He seems fine,' Nicholas said. He gently ran his hand through Sebastian's hair. The boy's hair was black like his sister's. Hers, however, was fine and soft. His was coarse and rough, almost straw-like. He smiled a little as his father caressed him. Nicholas didn't touch his son very often.

'He didn't a little while ago,' Solanda said.

'Twas frightening,' the nurse said. 'He dinna look like our boy.'

He wasn't 'our' boy, but Nicholas said nothing. He hadn't really acknowledged the child until shortly before Jewel died. He cupped the back of the boy's skull, cradling it. It felt solid and strong, as if it could hold a real brain instead of the damaged one it had.

Then he leaned over and kissed the boy's forehead. Sebastian looked up at him – and slowly smiled.

Those smiles were so rare, so precious. Nicholas smiled in return. Our boy. Our boy was a sweet child, even if he wasn't a very bright one.

Nicholas rose and gripped the edge of the mantel for balance. Solanda hovered near the cradle. She wore a long loose robe and her feet were bare. The nurse said that Solanda sometimes Shifted in front of Sebastian. Nicholas would have to talk with her about that. He found it inappropriate that his son saw his sister's caretaker nude, even if his son was slow and young.

'What do you think happened? Do you think he did something when he hit his head?' Nicholas asked.

Solanda glanced at the baby. 'I think someone else was using his body,' she said.

'Beg pardon?' the nurse asked. She stood also, leaving Sebastian to play in the middle of the floor. 'How can it be that someone twould steal into me boy?'

'He's not your boy,' Solanda said, her words echoing Nicholas's thoughts. 'He's not really anyone's boy.'

'Except mine,' Nicholas said.

'Be careful what you own,' Solanda said. She appeared about to say more when someone knocked on the door.

They all turned. The guards had orders not to interrupt. Either this was important or something had gone wrong.

Nicholas nodded to the nurse. She opened the door. Lord Stowe was behind it. He wore his riding clothes, and they were dust-covered. He looked as if he had ridden a long way.

'May I see you, Highness?' he asked.

A shiver ran down Nicholas's back. He was beginning to dislike seeing Stowe. He had started associating Stowe's presence with bad news. Nicholas excused himself and left the room.

A guard stood beside the door, staring vacantly at a spot somewhere above their heads. Nicholas and Stowe walked a short distance from the guard so that the conversation couldn't be overheard.

'A Danite came to my home a little while ago with some information you need to hear,' Stowe said.

'The Fey killed Matthias this time,' Nicholas said. He was amazed that the hope he felt carried into his voice.

'No,' Stowe said, 'he resigned.'

Whatever Nicholas had expected, it wasn't that. He frowned at Stowe, then walked toward the gallery. Jewel's portrait stood out even from a great distance away.

'Resigned?' Nicholas asked.

Stowe came up beside him. 'Resigned and immediately left the Tabernacle. No one knows where he went.'

'And you came to me immediately?'

Stowe shook his head. 'They said Matthias resigned after he went to the keep. So I went there. He murdered the Fey.'

'The prisoner.'

'Yes.'

'I told you he murdered Jewel.'

'I know, Highness,' Stowe said. 'I'm sorry.'

'I am too,' Nicholas said. He gazed at his wife. The portraitist had captured her features but not her aliveness. The painting had a flat, unlifelike quality. He missed her. He missed her with each moment, with each thought, with each glance at their children. She would know what Sebastian's strange behavior meant, and she would find a way to care for Arianna without leaving her in the hands of strangers.

Our boy. Soon Arianna would be their girl.

Not if he could help it.

'Highness?'

Nicholas nodded and turned toward Stowe. 'Let's send guards for him. He's ours now.'

'It's not that easy, Highness.' Stowe spoke slowly as if he had the words memorized. He had had time to think this through. He must have known what Nicholas's reaction would be.

It wouldn't have been that hard to determine.

'I think it's quite straightforward,' Nicholas said. 'He's no longer Rocaan and he's committed another murder. He needs to be punished like any other citizen.'

'Highness,' Stowe said, 'you can't look vindictive here.'

'Can't?' Nicholas raised his eyebrows. 'To whom? To the Islanders? That would be a problem, wouldn't it? But what about the Fey? They expect revenge. I'll look weak if I don't take it.'

'You don't need to take it,' Stowe said. 'Matthias made that easy for you. He's gone. That's all they need to know.'

Nicholas shook his head. That wasn't all he needed to know. He needed to know that Jewel's murderer would be punished. He needed to know that Matthias would not go on to live a healthy and full life.

'You need to let him go,' Stowe said. 'As King.'

Nicholas would take that under advisement. He clasped his hands behind his back to hide their shaking. 'Who's the new Rocaan?'

'That's the problem,' Stowe said. 'There isn't one.'

Nicholas suppressed a sigh. 'Then they expect me to lead?'

Stowe shook his head. 'The council is meeting now. The Elders will choose a new Rocaan.'

'And holy water?' Nicholas asked. He was of half a mind about it. Part of him worried that no one could make it any more and the other part was relieved. His children wouldn't die the same kind of death his wife did.

'Matthias left the Secrets with a Danite.'

Nicholas half smiled. Matthias, for all his professed lack of ambition, had certainly had a lot of it. 'A Danite.' Nicholas chuckled. 'At least he left the Secrets with someone.'

460

'At least,' Stowe said. 'He listened to you that much.'

'Maybe more,' Nicholas said. 'He knew I wouldn't let him get away with Jewel's murder. This second killing would have been the last straw.'

'Sire, one more thing.'

Nicholas hated that tone. He knew the one more thing would be bad news. 'What?'

'The dead Fey is Burden.'

Jewel's friend. The one who ran the Settlement. The one who had kissed Jewel shortly after she died. Burden. Who had sat beside her and guarded her like a lover the day she proposed her truce with the Islanders.

Had Matthias known something Nicholas hadn't?

'So Burden led the Fey to assassinate Matthias?'

Stowe nodded.

'You hadn't told me that,' Nicholas said.

'There is only so much a page can relay. I didn't see you scrambling to the keep to find out more about the incident.'

'I didn't care if they killed Matthias or not. I figured if they did, it would make my life easier. I didn't want to know their plans, because then my kingly side might have to fight with my husbandly side. I didn't want that.'

'Now you don't have to worry,' Stowe said.

'Yes, I do,' Nicholas said. 'Matthias is trying to kill everyone associated with Jewel. I have her children in that back room. As long as he's alive, I'll worry. I'll worry every moment of every day.'

Sixty-One

Gift sat on the porch of the Domicile, his short legs extended into the mist. The Domestics made him wait outside even though he wanted to be with his mother. He had had to run for a Domestic to bring his mother to the Domicile, and then they had had to levitate her. She couldn't walk on her own.

When he told them that his grandfather had done it, the Domestics stopped asking questions. It was as if his mother's injuries had appeared out of the air. Her skin was gray, and she was babbling something about keeping him safe. But he had kept her safe.

As best he could.

If he had known that his grandfather was going to hurt her so badly, he would have helped more. He might even have given his grandfather a peek at Coulter.

Maybe.

He worried that his grandfather had seen too much of his sister. She was so tiny and beautiful. Sometimes Gift went to visit her just to escape the grayness of Shadowlands. She always laughed when she saw him and waved. Even though she was tiny, she recognized him.

A tiny wisp of light floated toward him, then grew into his father. He looked frightened.

'I couldn't find you anywhere,' he said. 'Where's your mother?'

'Inside,' Gift said.

He didn't need to say any more. Everyone knew that when people went unexpectedly into the Domicile they had gone to be Healed.

His father shrank to his wisp form and slid in under the door. Gift wished he could do that. He would become very, very small and go inside and see what they were doing to his mother.

One of her wings had looked crushed against her back. The other wing had flapped around almost like she couldn't control it. They were both bleeding from the tips. Her hand flopped from her wrist. She had been defending him when it happened. And he didn't have the strength to fight his grandfather.

Yet.

Gift hoped Coulter was safe. If all of this was for nothing, Gift would never be able to forgive himself. Coulter had said they didn't belong, and Coulter had been right. No wonder he wanted to leave Shadowlands. He wanted to be as far from Gift's grandfather as he could be.

Gift wanted to be that far away too. But he wanted to take his parents. He hadn't forgotten his grandfather's anger at the way they had raised Gift. It made him shudder to think that his grandfather might have raised him. His entire life would be different.

It still might be. He wasn't certain what his grandfather would do to him. Nor what would happen to his mother. Gift had never seen her looking so fragile, not even when Coulter accidentally hurt her trying to save Gift. The fact that the Domestics wouldn't let him inside frightened him more than anything.

His father hadn't come right back out. Either they hadn't seen him or something was happening. Gift leaned against a post. His father would tell him when everything was all right. All he had to do was wait until then.

Waiting would take forever.

He wished Coulter were still here. When Coulter had told him through the Link that he was going to leave, Gift had cried out like a baby. Now he wished he had asked questions. He missed Coulter. He was half tempted to see if he could find Coulter through the Link, but he was afraid his grandfather would jump in as he had the last time. That had been wrong. It had felt wrong, and it had led to this.

Suddenly the world spun. Gift grabbed the post for support. It was still there, solid beneath his hands, but he couldn't see it. Bright light shone through cracks in the grayness. The floor was shaking. People were hurrying out of buildings, screaming and crying. Wind was blowing through his hair and it smelled fresh. Chunks of the sky split and fell around him. Big hunks of gray nothing landing on the ground, then falling through it.

His grandfather's cabin collapsed through the holes in the ground and shattered when it landed on the dirt below. The Circle Door was spinning crazily as people jumped through it, rolling away from the Dirt Circle. Big tall spindly things surrounded the Dirt Circle – Burden had once told him those were trees – and they were bright green. Gift had only seen green that bright in his dreams, in the world where his sister lived.

Another cabin collapsed and another and another. The Domicile was shaking. His mother was in there. She wouldn't be able to fly. His father floated past him, telling him to get out. People were pushing each other over to get to the Circle Door. The Domestics were leaving. No one was helping his mother.

Gift ran toward the Domicile, his slight weight punching holes in the ground. His feet caught in the holes, but his speed kept him from falling all the way through. He got to the Domicile –

– and found that he was already leaning against the post, splinters digging into his palm. The post had pushed his mouth open and it was dry. Drool slimed his chin. He sat up and wiped his face with his sleeve.

The grayness surrounded him as it always had. The mist had grown thick around his feet. The Domicile was all right, and no one was screaming. His heart was still pounding too fast, though. He felt as if he had survived a nightmare.

Then he looked around for Dream Riders but saw none. His grandfather was nowhere around either. Gift was alone. He had been alone all along.

He took a deep shuddery breath. Everything was going wrong. It would go worse. He had to tell someone that he had had a Vision. The whole place would be ruined. People would hurt each other trying to escape.

No one would save his mom.

He had to tell someone but he didn't know who to tell. His grandfather would know what to do, but his grandfather had hurt people. Gift couldn't see his mother, and his father hadn't come back yet.

He was alone.

Completely alone.

Sixty-Two

Adrian crouched by the river bed. The pants Scavenger had stolen for him were too tight. They dug in all the wrong places. But Adrian had to wear stolen clothes. His own clothes were too dangerous.

Coulter crouched beside him. The boy's new clothes were too big, but he didn't seem to mind. In the last three days, he had gone from being terrified of new things to revelling in them. Scavenger had said that was normal as well. Once the senses got used to the load, the body celebrated. Coulter would spend hours studying a leaf or a blade of grass. More than once Adrian had had to explain to him that sometimes these plants could poison him, because Coulter loved to taste everything. It was almost as though he were going through a stage of his babyhood all over again.

Scavenger cradled their old clothes close to his chest. The riverbank rose up here and moved a bit inland. This area was sheltered by trees on either side and by tree branches above. The only way the three of them could be seen would be from the river itself.

Scavenger had assured Adrian that no one would look from the river.

This outing terrified Adrian, but it was the first step in their plan to fool the Fey. After they got rid of the clothes, they would head out down the road. Scavenger claimed that the searchers would be looking for two people, not three. They would keep Scavenger properly bundled so no one saw his Fey features.

The Fey, Scavenger had said when proposing this plan, wouldn't think a thing of him. They believed their own kind were taller and slimmer than Islanders, forgetting the Red Caps, as always.

Once they had made their way to the outskirts of Jahn, they would go south to Adrian's farm. Scavenger would scout for Fey and if he saw no evidence of them, all three would go to the farm. If he saw them, he would inform Adrian and they would make a new plan.

The problem was hiding from the Gull Riders. Scavenger believed staying far enough away from the river would help. He also thought that if the three of them wore the hats he had stolen, the Gull Riders would ignore them. Beast Riders were simple thinkers. Even Adrian knew that. They wouldn't think to look for more than two people on the road.

That part of the plan seemed the most dangerous to Adrian. One slip and the Riders would catch them. Adrian had one other idea up his sleeve, one he would never tell Scavenger about. He would get holy water from the first Danite he saw. Then if the Fey did catch him, they would never take him prisoner again.

The river burbled below them. Coulter sat on the edge of the bank, his feet dangling off. Adrian kept a close eye on him, half afraid the boy would jump. Scavenger explained drowning three times to Coulter, but neither man was certain Coulter understood it. This new phase of his recovery from Shadowlands was almost as irritating as the old phase. Before Coulter had endangered them with his fear; now he was endangering them with his curiosity.

'Ready?' Scavenger asked.

Adrian nodded. He glanced at Coulter. Coulter was staring at the clothes. He understood the importance of this. If the Fey found the clothing, they might think the two of them had died. Scavenger said it was a likely occurrence – people newly released from Shadowlands often made mistakes because of the Overs. It had happened before.

'All right,' Scavenger said. 'Here goes.'

He tossed the clothes. They soared through the air, the wind catching the sleeves of Adrian's shirt, the legs of Coulter's pants. The boots dropped first, landing with a splash in the roaring current. The clothes fluttered longer, whipping and turning with the wind.

Suddenly bright light hit them. Adrian glanced at Coulter. Coulter was frowning at the clothes. If he was the source of the light, it wasn't obvious. But Adrian had never seen such a thing before – except in the Warders' cabin. He didn't know if a person not enveloped in the light could see it.

Scavenger looked up, then around, searching for the source. The clothes fell, landing in the water with a large splash. As they surfaced, they appeared to be full. Bodies resembling Adrian and Coulter filled the clothes. Only the shoes were missing.

Adrian's mouth had gone dry. He had warned Coulter not to let Scavenger see the magic, but Coulter must have thought this more important. And, in the scheme of things, he was right. The Fey would see these fake bodies and stop the search.

'You did that!' Scavenger screamed. His loud voice was jarring, his panic almost overwhelming. He had turned to Adrian. 'Who are you? You don't look like a Doppelgänger! I thought you were all dead.'

'I'm not a Doppelgänger,' Adrian said.

'But you're not a Spy either. You look Islander.' Scavenger's face was pale with fear. He had back against a tree. 'Are you a Golem?'

'I am Islander,' Adrian said.

'Then it's you!' Scavenger turned to Coulter. Coulter leaned away, and lost his balance. For one heart-stopping moment, Adrian thought he would fall in the river. Then Coulter grabbed a tree branch and steadied himself.

'What'd I do?' Coulter asked Adrian.

'I always wondered why you spoke Fey. I thought maybe it was in deference to me. But it was because you wanted to capture me, wasn't it?' Scavenger hit his forehead with the heel of his hand. 'I was such a fool. I helped you people. I thought I was being so nice.'

'You were being nice,' Adrian said. 'You did help us and we appreciate it.'

'You're going to take me back, aren't you? And then they're going to kill me. You just wanted all my secrets of how I escaped.'

'We know how you escaped,' Adrian said. 'Now you're helping us.'

'I don't ever want to go back,' Coulter said. He was clinging to the branch as if it were a shield.

Adrian frowned at him. If the boy got too frightened, there was no telling what he'd do. And the two of them needed Scavenger.

'I knew you'd find me,' Scavenger said. 'I knew it. No one ever gets away from the Fey. No one ever gets to do what they want. No one.'

'I'm not Fey,' Adrian said again.

'No, but the boy is. What are you, half Fey? You're Jewel's son, right?'

Adrian started. Scavenger had left Shadowlands before Jewel had her children. Before she died. The thought was logical.

'Well, you're not going to take me. You're not.' Scavenger pulled out a knife. It had a jagged edge to it. He had used it earlier to skin some meat.

'That's right,' Adrian said. 'We're not.'

Coulter screwed up his face. Adrian recognized the look as the same one Coulter had had when he sent the light over the river.

'Wait, Coulter,' Adrian said. 'Let me talk to Scavenger.'

Scavenger whipped around. He was crouching, but he moved quickly. He held the tip of the knife much too close to Coulter.

'You're not taking me,' Scavenger said softly.

'That's right,' Adrian said. 'If we were, we would have done so by now. We would have taken you in your sleep on that first night.'

Scavenger didn't move. He acted as if he hadn't heard Adrian.

'But we didn't,' Adrian said. 'And we didn't take you the next night or the next night. We waited until now to reveal the magic we had. Now, when you're going to help us escape.'

'I'm not helping you any more,' Scavenger said. He sounded like a petulant child.

'All Coulter did was make sure the Fey wouldn't follow us. That's all.'

'I thought you said he was Islander.'

'He is Islander.'

'But he's part Fey.'

'He's not Fey at all.'

'How do you know?' Scavenger said.

'Because,' Adrian said, 'he was born before the Invasion.'

'But he has magick.'

Adrian nodded. 'I think it's because he grew up in Shadowlands.'

'Magick can't be learned,' Scavenger said. 'Believe me, I know. I've tried.'

His words hung in the air for a moment. He would know. And there would be no convincing him if he thought Coulter was truly Islander.

Coulter apparently understood too. He glanced at the knife, then at Adrian, then back to Scavenger. 'I'm Linked,' Coulter said.

'What?' Scavenger said.

'Linked,' Coulter said. 'To a Fey boy. I think I use his powers.'

Scavenger whirled again, this time facing Adrian. 'You didn't tell me he was Linked. Now they'll be able to find us.'

'Gift won't turn us in,' Coulter said, his voice pleading.

'He might if Rugar gets his way.'

Coulter shook his head. 'Gift is my friend.'

'Friends turn on you, son,' Scavenger said, his back to Coulter. He held the knife tightly. Adrian finally understood how the little man had committed such a spectacular murder all those years before.

'Not Gift,' Coulter said. 'Besides, I'd know.'

'Only if you made the Link, boy.'

Adrian was trembling. He could, with a quick kick of his foot, shove Scavenger into the water. But the man had helped them. He didn't want to do that.

'They would have found us by now,' Adrian said. 'If they were going to use the Link. We're not that far away.'

Scavenger lowered the knife. 'I never heard of Links giving anyone magical powers,' he said.

'You never heard of a Link with an Islander before, have you?' Adrian asked.

'No,' Scavenger said.

'We're different from you. Maybe Links affect us in different ways.'

'Why didn't you tell me he had magick?' Scavenger said.

'Because it's not always there,' Adrian said. 'If it were, then we could have gotten farther on our own, right?'

Scavenger shook his head. 'Different magick acts in different ways.'

He seemed more comfortable now that he could act the authority again. He hefted the knife, grinned at it as if he were embarrassed, and pocketed it. Adrian let out a breath. Coulter scrambled up the side of the hill, away from the edge of the river.

'You spooked me,' Scavenger said. 'I thought you were coming for me.'

Adrian shook his head. He was trembling but he didn't want to show it. 'You've helped us. We would never cross you.'

'I hope not,' Scavenger said. 'I don't react well to it.' Adrian grinned, hoping that it looked sincere. 'I'll remember that,' he promised.

Sixty-Three

The palace gates were open. Rugar adjusted his Aud's cowl, then shoved his hand back in the pocket of the pale robe. The robe was too long and wide for him. It had to cover his boots, since Auds went barefoot, and it had to allow room for him to hunch. He was much too tall to be an Islander. But anything else he wore made the hunch obvious. He walked with his back straight, his knees bent, and his cowl pulled so far over his face that he couldn't see to either side. He hoped no one looked inside the cowl. They wouldn't see pale skin, blue eyes and round cheeks.

They'd see a Fey.

And sound some kind of alarm. That was the last thing he wanted.

He had to get inside.

So far no one had even stopped him. He was standing just outside the gates. The guards were chatting beside the door. One of the guards was keeping an eye on the flow in and out of the gates, but not checking the people going through.

No wonder something had happened to Jewel. Rugar had never seen security this lax in his life.

Except, of course, the day he invaded Blue Isle.

This day couldn't be more different than that one. The sun shone brightly overhead, and the cobblestone was dry. The air had a bit of a chill that would burn off as the day got longer. And there was no fear anywhere, at least that he could see. Despite the tensions between the Fey and the Islanders, the Islanders were going about their business as if nothing were wrong.

Perhaps they didn't know. Perhaps only the leaders understood the extent of the problem.

Rugar walked through the gate, his back aching from the odd position. The guards didn't stop him. A horse shied as he got too close to it, and a dairymaid nodded at him as she passed by. He nodded back, hoping she hadn't gotten a good look at his face.

The courtyard was full. The day of the coronation – the day Jewel died – the courtyard had been protected and empty. Only the people attending the coronation had been visible, and the only doors that had

470

been open were the ones in use. Everything else had been barred shut. Somehow Rugar expected the same thing.

He expected them to know he was here.

But no one knew. No one even thought a Fey would sneak into the palace. Even after the debacle with Burden and the holy man, the man who had murdered Jewel.

Burden had failed. Ten of Rugar's best people were dead from a scheme that Rugar knew was doomed from the beginning. But Burden hadn't checked it with him. By the time Rugar learned of the scheme, Burden had already left.

Wind was the only one who survived.

Rugar would have been happier if someone else had. But Wisps were lucky. They usually survived battles. All they had to do was change size and fly away.

Rugar had no such options. He actually had to disguise himself, one of the reasons a Visionary never went into battle.

He carried a knife in the pocket of his robe. It destroyed the line, but with his hand inside, he could cup the sheath and use his arm to hide the weapon. He knew his luck would have to be excellent in order for him to make it all the way to the nursery without being caught.

The way out was easy. The tip of the blade to the baby's throat, shouted threats, and lots of speed. He would be away in no time.

No. The difficult moments were these.

He decided to go the way he knew. He rounded the stable. One of the grooms watched him pass, a frown on his face. The groom had a familiar look to him, but Rugar didn't spend much time glancing at him. Too dangerous. Much too dangerous.

The groom did nothing, though. Rugar went beyond him. The path round to the far side of the palace. So far only some of the doors he had seen had guards on them. Others didn't. The kitchen door was wide open, with heat pouring out, and no one guarding the entrance at all. Rugar had avoided it, however, because he thought an Aud might be suspicious, even there.

He had his story ready. He had a message from the Rocaan for the King. Rugar remembered from all those years before that Auds brought messages from the Rocaan. A young Aud had brought him a message five years before, telling him to meet with the Old Rocaan. That was the meeting in which the Old Rocaan died.

No guards stood in front of the doors leading to the coronation hall. The hall was tucked way back in the courtyard, so far from the main gate as to be considered impenetrable. The head of the guards probably thought this place needed no protection either.

The head of the guards was wrong.

471

Rugar tried the doors. They were unlocked. He pulled on the handles and let himself in. The air in the palace was warmer than it had been outside and it smelled stale. The corridor was full of dust. No one had been here since Jewel died.

He walked through the narrow hallway. The first time he had come through here, he had marveled at the marble floors, the ornate trim, the obvious expense someone had gone to build this place that was used only once a generation. He had been right to come to Blue Isle in that regard: The rumors of wealth had been true.

It had been all the other things he had been wrong about.

His Vision was really gone. He had admitted that completely to himself with Jewel's death. He should have been able to see that, as well as his granddaughter's birth. He should have foreseen the initial defeats and the traps that this Isle held.

But he had seen none of it.

And Gift was refusing to help him.

It galled Rugar that a three-year-old boy could outsmart him. But the boy had more power than Rugar. When Gift made that mental turn away from Coulter and headed toward the palace, Rugar had been powerless to follow the abandoned Links, even though he had tried. He had had to follow Gift along Gift's paths. Gift could thwart him and his wishes in this way every time.

But if Rugar raised the girl right, she would be able to do nothing to thwart him. She would help him in every way she could. And judging by her instant Shifts at birth, she would be one of the most powerful of the Fey.

When he reached the double doors leading into the Coronation Hall, he stopped. The doors had been bolted shut, and a chain lock had been wound around the handles. Nicholas wanted no one in there ever again.

No one to see where Jewel died.

The Fey had accused Rugar of not mourning her. But they hadn't known what he was thinking or how he felt. She had Seen that moment many times; Gift had Seen it too. But Jewel's Vision had made it sound as if she would live, and Rugar had just listened to the surface of it. Sometimes words were wrong. It was feelings that were important. Jewel had always felt dizzy and injured after those Visions. Once she had passed out in his arms. He should have understood that sign.

He blamed himself that he didn't.

But he knew that such signs were sometimes easy to miss. The one he should have paid attention to was Gift. The boy's Vision had been powerful; Rugar should have realized that the boy Saw a Turning

472

Event, not a Moment. But Rugar had thought it a Moment. The death of Niche would mean nothing to anyone except her close family. The death of Jewel affected lives on several continents.

He had been wrong from the moment he decided to come to Blue Isle, and staying here only compounded the mistakes. He should never have allowed Jewel to marry, or live away from Shadowlands. He should have forbidden her to participate in that ceremony, and he should have raised her son himself.

He would make no more mistakes.

He would raise the girl, no matter what the Shaman said.

The Shaman was another matter entirely. He had heard that she was talking to the King, that she was giving Islanders advice. His father had forced her to come alone as a kind of guardian, not usual behavior in an invasion force, and Rugar should have opposed the move. She was incompetent, young for her profession, and too power-hungry.

She didn't want Jewel's children in Shadowlands because they were too powerful for a Shaman to deal with.

He touched the door. The wood felt warm against his fingertips. He and Jewel had fought the last time they saw each other. She had berated him for not seeing his grandson – as if she knew – and then she had left him for good.

And he had watched as she died, just as she had predicted he would.

He sighed. He hadn't expected this depth of feeling. Soldiers didn't feel. Soldiers acted.

The corridor was long and seemed to extend forever. Jewel and Nicholas had come from Rugar's right. She had looked toward a flight of stairs when she had yelled at him for not seeing the golem she thought was her child.

After she died, he had seen through that golem's eyes.

The golem lived where his granddaughter lived.

He adjusted his cowl and hurried down the hall where he last spoke to his daughter, the knife clutched in his right hand.

473

Sixty-Four

Charissa carried two buckets of soapy water. Rags hung out of her uniform, and she had her hair pulled back with one. Clean the corridors. As if she had no home, no family. She made one comment about the King. One comment and she wouldn't get any sleep at all tonight.

Clean the corridors.

All of them.

She cursed the Master of the House under her breath. He had been after her ever since the night before the Coronation, when the King had taken her to the kitchen for a meal. The Master of the House had changed her assignments, taken her off the royal wing, and made her work in the guest areas.

That was bad enough. She rarely saw the King any more, and when she did, he looked haggard. She knew how he felt, losing the King his father. It had left her feeling dislocated and a bit frightened, as it had with the rest of the Isle. But then his wife's death – no matter how much Charissa wanted her out of the way – made things even worse.

And the rumors about the baby girl, well, they gave Charissa shudders.

She would have told the Master of the House that if he had asked, but no. He had ordered her to clean the corridors on the basis of one comment.

One.

And she would scrub until her hands bled.

I think the King is the best-looking man in the Kingdom, she had said. Other maids had said the same thing, and in the Master of the House's hearing. She had reminded him of that. But none of them had airs about being Queen, he had countered.

As if she thought she could be Queen.

Really thought it, instead of just dreaming it.

The King hadn't even looked at her at all lately. What with his father's death, running everything, and that horrible child, he didn't have time to sleep, let alone –

She flushed even though she was walking down the hallway alone. Every time she thought of him and *that* she made herself all flustered.

She set down the bucket, stood and stretched. Her back cracked. She had spent the morning cleaning the fireplaces in the guest suites. The Housekeeper demanded that they keep the spring schedule. Fireplaces all week since many weren't in use. The rest of the fireplaces would be cleaned in a month when the weather got too warm. But no one had used the guest suites in so long that some of the fireplaces Charissa had cleaned looked as if they hadn't been used all winter.

The work had been particularly difficult since the coronation. Once news of the baby got out, half the staff quit. They didn't want to be in the same building as the demon child. Charissa had double the work during the same amount of time. The Master of the House was bringing in new people, but they were slow and their work was not yet up to standard.

She picked up the buckets, and some of the water sloshed on her shoes. The wet seeped through the cloth, leaving little footprints in the corridor. She sighed. It was a good thing she hadn't started yet. She would have been quite angry if she had.

She was starting in the Coronation Hall simply because she liked that wing of the palace. She used any excuse she could find to go there. It reminded her of the night she spent talking to the King. Her second favorite place was the kitchen, and her third the Great Hall. She always thought of him in those places.

She wondered if he thought of her.

No one had been in the wing since the devil child was born, and it showed. Lots of dust, even though the place had been sparkling before. She would start in front of the locked Hall doors and then work her way back toward the kitchen, maybe grab a snack and go onto the Great Hall. By then, maybe the Master of the House would take pity on her and let her get some sleep.

He had done that before.

She rounded the corner to the long corridor that led to the Coronation Hall.

And stopped.

An Aud stood before the double doors as if he were confused. He seemed tall for an Aud, and his robe was unusually long. A chill ran down her back. She had heard strange stories about the Rocaanists these days. The King believed that the Rocaan had murdered his wife, and some of the others believed it too. Some of the cooks thought maybe the Rocaan was going to kill the King and take his place.

Would the Rocaan use an Aud to do it?

That didn't make sense. This afternoon, she had heard that the Rocaan had been forced to leave Jahn. She had also heard that he killed a Fey in the keep, so she didn't know which story to believe.

Now an Aud standing in front of the Coronation Hall.

An Aud that was too tall. Like the Rocaan.

She swallowed and slowly backed up. Was he trying to sneak in as someone else? Get an audience with the King? Kill him? Whatever was happening, she would have to tell someone. It wasn't normal for an Aud to be in the palace, at least not without a few other Auds, a Danite, or maybe an Officiate.

Then the Aud reached up, his hand in shadow, and adjusted his cowl, tugging it down even farther over his face.

Fear shot through her, rich and fine. She glanced behind her. Footprints. Her own, going into the corridor and out. He would know he was spotted. He would know he had seen her.

She had only one choice.

She hurried back to the spot where she had first seen him. Then she got down on her hands and knees and started scrubbing. It wasn't a logical place to clean, but it got rid of the double and triple sets of footprints. She made sure the buckets were close to him, so that she had to look in his direction each time she wetted a rag.

He hadn't seen her yet. He was looking down the other corridor as if he weren't certain where to go.

She scrubbed so hard that her arm ached. She was leaving little streaks in the floor, streaks she would have to clean later. This was one of the marble floors and she was cleaning it wrong. She hoped he wouldn't know that either.

Now he was coming toward her. His footsteps sounded firm and purposeful on the marble. That disturbed her. Auds always moved quietly.

As he approached, she moved her buckets out of his path. 'Forgive me, Devoted Sir,' she said, thankful that her voice didn't quiver. 'I didn't see you.'

He nodded as he passed, his face in shadow. He didn't seem to pay much attention to her. Instead he glanced around as if watching for someone.

Or something.

When he reached the fork in the corridor, he ignored the way to the kitchen. He hurried toward the stairs.

The stairs led to the royal wing.

She tossed her rag into the bucket of water. The splash hit her in the face. She had to go to the King, no matter what the Master of the House would say. She had to. He needed to know.

The Aud wore boots, and the hand she had seen on the cowl hadn't been in shadow.

It had been dark.

And long.

And slim.

Like the hand of a Fey.

Sixty-Five

Sebastian screamed.

Solanda whirled. The nurse was already crouched beside him, holding his shoulders. His hands were over his mouth, his eyes were wide, and he was shaking his head back and forth.

He made the sound again. It wasn't quite a scream. Not really. More like a continuous scraping of rocks together. He backed into the corner and stared at the door as if he were afraid it was going to hit him.

Solanda hurried toward him. He didn't look at her. His eyes were empty, as they usually were. That strange person wasn't lurking in them, nor was that startling burst of intelligence she sometimes saw.

This was the lump, the golem, the creature made of stone, screaming.

The thought sent a ripple of terror from her stomach to her heart.

Arianna started crying, deep hiccoughing sobs. Solanda couldn't tell if she was crying because of the lump or for another reason. The lump huddled in the corner, trying to make himself as small as he could. He continued to stare at the door as if it terrified him.

Solanda stood. Arianna looked normal. She was waving her fists and sobbing. Solanda picked her up, but it didn't calm her. She was staring at the lump, crying as if she understood why he was screaming.

'Tis bad, tain't it?' the nurse said. She was trying to hold the lump, but he would have none of it. 'Tis gone he is. Tis gone.'

She thought he had gone crazy. Solanda shook her head. Arianna had gripped the shoulders of her robe so tight that her tiny fists were ripping the fabric.

The hair on the back of Solanda's neck was rising. If she were in her cat form, she would hiss and run away.

'Something's going to happen,' she said. Something the lump knew about. Something he could sense. He was a creation of magic, real and not real. If any of them could sense magic about to happen, it would be him.

But why would it terrify him?

His wail continued, a grating screech that hurt to hear.

'Can we stop him?' the nurse asked.

'No,' Solanda said. Arianna's tiny body shook, but she didn't Shift. This much emotion and she was staying in her most secure form. She felt it too, whatever it was. If they both felt it, why couldn't Solanda? What was wrong?

'He canna keep cryin like this. Tain't good.'

None of this was good. Solanda held Arianna close. Maybe the nurse should take the children somewhere safe. Maybe it was something in the room.

But if it was something magical, the nurse could do nothing. Only Solanda could help.

The problem was she didn't know if the attack was from without or within.

Sebastian was staring at the door. If he were frightened of something in the room, he would be reacting differently.

'Get help,' Solanda said.

'Beg pardon?' the nurse asked.

'Get help.'

'Tis the boy who needs help, mum, and only ye n me ta do it.'

'No,' Solanda said. 'Get guards and the King and as many people as you can bring here. No holy water though. Holy water might kill the child – the children.'

'What's wrong, mum?'

'I don't know,' Solanda said, 'but I think we're going to find out.'

'I canna leave him, mum,' the nurse said. 'He tain't never been like this. I canna go.'

'I'll be with him,' Solanda said. If the nurse didn't leave soon, it would be the two of them against whatever was scaring the lump.

'Beg pardon, mum, but ye dinna know how to –'

'It's magic,' Solanda said through her teeth. 'Whatever has him frightened is magic, and magic he recognizes. Maybe the magic that hurt him a few days ago. You can't help with that. You'll get in the way. But the guards might help. The King might help. Someone might help. But you have to hurry. If you don't hurry, we could all die.'

'Die, mum?'

'My people are ruthless,' Solanda said. 'And these are Jewel's children.'

Then she realized who had looked at her through Sebastian's eyes. Rugar. Rugar knew where she was.

He was coming for Arianna.

And he expected Solanda to help him as she had pledged to do.

'Go, now,' Solanda said.

The nurse looked helplessly at the lump. Then she kissed his cheek, although that didn't stop his crying. She touched his hair, then went to the door. When she had her hand on the handle, she said, 'I'll fight with ye, mum.'

'No,' Solanda said. 'This is something I have to face alone.'

The nurse nodded. She opened the door. 'Blessed Be, mum. I'll bring help soon as I can.'

Solanda only hoped it would be soon enough.

Sixty-Six

'No! Tis wrong. Ye gotta let me see him! Please! In the name of the Roca!'

Nicholas looked up from the papers strewn on his desk. He could barely hear the words, but he recognized the voice. A woman's voice. If it weren't for the dialect, he would have thought it Jewel's.

He was alone in the library. A fire burned in the grate although the afternoon was warm, and a stack of books sat on the side of his desk. He had been researching Rocaanism, trying to see if he had any precedent for taking over the Tabernacle himself. He had stationed guards outside the library door, but hadn't allowed any inside.

'Please, sir. Let me in. Tis important what I tell him.'

Nicholas pushed his chair back and stood. He could hear the guard's voice, low and calm, apparently unconcerned by the woman's anguish.

He pulled the door open. Two guards blocked it. Charissa stood outside, her hair disheveled, and her dress covered with water.

'Ah, Sire,' she said. 'I need ta talk ta ye.'

Once he had promised her that she could talk with him at any time. He had been young then, and he had thought she was beautiful. She had been the first servant to tell him of the abuses of power that went on in the servants' quarters and, instead of seeing them as tragic but normal, he had promised her that he would help. He hadn't regretted that until Jewel's death. He no longer wanted the distractions.

'Come on in,' he said.

'Thank ye,' she said, grimacing at the guards as they got out of her way. She lifted her skirts to reveal thick solid ankles and stepped across the threshold as if it were sacred.

Nicholas closed the door behind her. But she didn't sidle up to him as he expected.

'Twas a Fey,' she said. 'I seen him near the Coronation Hall. Twas dressed as an Aud he was.'

'An Aud?' Nicholas was confused. He had expected her to make a pass at him – she had done so before – and then to complain about one of her bosses, not to tell him of an Aud.

'Boots on his feet he had and twas long and skinny. At first, I thought maybe twas the Rocaan, ye know? But then I seen his hand. Twas long and thin like him, but twas black. I thought maybe twas a shadow, but after I seen the boots I knew twasn't. He wasn't standing in no light.'

She was speaking so fast he was having trouble following her words. 'When was this?' he asked.

'A few moments ago. Twoulda been here sooner but them guards –'

'They were only doing their jobs.'

'Aye, and meanwhile he's gone.'

'He left?'

'No. That's the thing and why I come direct to you. He's not gone. He just went by me.'

'What were you doing in the Coronation Hall?' He had sealed it off. He never wanted anyone to enter it again.

'Twasn't,' she said. 'Twas in the corridor.' Then she wrinkled her nose, and he saw the beauty he had remembered. It was so different from Jewel's. Jewel had been all angles and sharpness. This woman was round and voluptuous and soft. Too soft for his tastes.

'Near the Coronation Hall?'

'Aye, Sire,' she said.

'And now where is he?'

'I dunno,' she said. 'Soon as he left, I come to you.'

They weren't communicating. He found that so frustrating. 'Where did he go? The courtyard?'

'Up the stairs,' she said. The urgency that had brought her was in her voice again.

'The stairs?' His heart was pounding very fast. 'The stairs near the Coronation Hall?'

'Aye, Sire. I thought mayhap he come for you. Thought twas the Rocaan with a knife, but twas a Fey. And I canna for the life a me unnerstand that.'

But he could. He could see it as plain as anything. The Shaman holding his squirming daughter in the air.

I want the child, Rugar had said.

Then what had the Shaman said? Something about stealing Arianna?

He had sent a Fey for Arianna.

Nicholas made a small cry.

His daughter. They were going to take his daughter from him too. They would take her mind, like they had taken Sebastian's.

He yanked open the door. 'Get a contingent of guards and bring them to the nursery,' he said as he passed the guards.

'Weapons, Sire?' the guard asked.

A shiver ran through Nicholas. Suddenly he saw Jewel's face, melted and twisted beyond recognition. 'Swords. But no holy water. If I see any holy water, I'll kill the carrier myself.'

Charissa followed him to the door. She was asking something, but he no longer heard it.

A Fey was after his daughter.

He headed for the stairs in a sprint.

No one, absolutely no one, would take Arianna from him. The Shaman said she had to stay in the palace, and she would stay.

Nicholas would do whatever he had to in order to guarantee that.

Sixty-Seven

After the nurse left, Solanda paced the room. The lump continued his odd crying. He hadn't even made that noise when Jewel died. Then he had been sobbing – a dry, almost silent sound – but this was the cross between a wail and a scream.

Arianna was sobbing. Solanda had placed her back in the crib and every time Solanda passed, Arianna raised her tiny hands, begging for comfort.

Solanda had none.

At least, not yet.

She wasn't quite certain what to do. The guards would bring weapons, but if the foe was magical, that might not be enough. She could get into her cat form and hide, but that might not allow her to protect Arianna.

She did take off her robe. Sometimes during a quick Shift, clothing buried her. She couldn't afford to lose her vision for one moment. She was at least that prepared.

There were no weapons here except the fireplace equipment. The tongs, the poker, and the wood itself. Those were stored high enough so that they wouldn't be a danger to the lump. Everything else was soft and comfortable because this was a nursery.

Sebastian let out a loud scraping cry.

Arianna shrieked.

Solanda turned as the door opened.

An Aud stood in the doorway, his hands in his pocket, his cowl draped over his face.

Solanda grabbed a blanket and threw it over Arianna. It wouldn't be much protection against holy water, but it might be enough.

The Aud brought his hand out, threw back his cowl and grinned.

Rugar.

Solanda's entire body became very cold.

Sebastian stopped screaming. He rolled himself up as tightly as he could, his head buried in his knees. He looked like the rock he had been formed out of. He blended into the wall. If Solanda hadn't known he was there, she would never have seen him.

Rugar came into the nursery and closed the door. 'I need the child.'

Solanda swallowed. Arianna was silent too. Solanda wanted to lift the blanket, to see if Arianna had Shifted, but she didn't dare.

'The Shaman said the baby is supposed to stay here.'

'The Shaman is wrong.'

Solanda shook her head. 'She's happy here. Let her be.'

'We need her, Solanda. The Fey can't survive without her. She's the only viable heir to the Black Throne.'

'What about Gift?'

Rugar made a dismissive gesture with his hand. 'Gift is a traitor.'

'Gift is a child. Children can't be traitors.'

'Children that brilliant can,' Rugar said. The pale robe made his skin look dark, almost black, and his eyes glint evilly.

'How do you know then that Arianna won't turn out the same way?' Solanda stayed beside the crib.

'Because I'll raise her,' Rugar said.

'Where?' If she stalled long enough, the guards would arrive. Rugar had no magickal defensive powers. A knife, a sword, a blow to the head would stop him as quickly and easily as the poison would.

'In the Shadowlands.'

Solanda shook her head. 'The Shaman said she must not go to Shadowlands.'

'The Shaman.' Rugar's voice had a sneer in it. 'When did you start listening to the Shaman?'

Solanda licked her lips. 'When it became clear that she was the only one remaining with Vision.'

'You're fickle, Solanda.' He inched closer.

'It's my nature,' she said. She had a tight grip on the edge of the crib.

He glanced at her hand. 'Right now you look like a lioness guarding her young.'

'Apt,' Solanda said. 'Arianna is my sister under the skin. I care for her.'

'You can care for her in Shadowlands.'

Solanda shook her head. 'She stays.'

Rugar walked toward the crib. 'You can't disobey me,' he said. 'You owe me.'

'I have paid my debt to you,' Solanda said.

Rugar smiled. It wasn't a friendly smile. 'You haven't paid until I say you have.'

Solanda was shaking. She had given him her word so long ago that it felt normal to listen to him. But Arianna had no one. Nicholas couldn't help her. The Shaman didn't want her in Shadowlands. Rugar only wanted to use her. Solanda knew that.

She took a deep breath. 'The Shaman says I never owed you. The Shaman says you set the entire attack up. She says you had those people, those dogs try to kill me so that you could save me.'

He blinked, then frowned. 'That's silly,' he said, but his tone was off. He had planned it. He had used her all these years.

Made her feel a debt to him that she had never ever owed.

All these years of running, of spying, of using her talents for petty theft instead of being a Shifter, one of the greatest of the Fey.

'You're not taking Arianna,' she said.

'Yes,' he said. 'I am.' He moved twice as fast as she expected, shoving her out of the way with such force she lost her grip on the crib. She tumbled toward the fireplace, grabbing at anything to stop her fall.

The lump looked up, his empty eyes filled with terror.

Rugar picked up the baby along with the blanket. For a moment, Arianna looked like herself. Then she Shifted, a full-strength Shift that happened rapidly. One moment she was a Fey baby, the next a tiny white kitten.

Rugar dropped the kitten. It mewled all the way down and landed with a thud. A kitten only a week old was blind. She had given herself movement, but not the vision.

He crouched and grabbed for the kitten, but Solanda flew at him and knocked him out of the way. He grabbed her upper arms, pinching the flesh, and pulled her down with him as he fell. He landed on his back, grunting as the wind was knocked out of him.

Solanda wrenched her arms free. The pain was excruciating. She looked for the kitten, but instead saw the lump crawling across the floor. He scooped the kitten in his right hand and, cradling it gently, returned to his corner and his former position. Solanda almost cheered, but Rugar grabbed her and tried to throw her aside.

She kneed him in the groin and he cried out with pain. Then she rolled away from him, and grabbed the poker, holding it like a club. He rose to a sitting position, one hand up as if to block her.

'You can't hurt me,' he said.

'You stay away from Arianna.'

'Solanda, you know this is best for the Fey.'

'I know that you taking her is wrong. The Shaman told me that. I listen to the Shaman. She has Vision. You don't.'

'You don't know that.'

'No,' Solanda said. Her arms ached from holding the poker in the ready position. 'No, I don't know that for sure. But it seems obvious. You're pathetic, Rugar. You want a power you'll never have.'

'Give me that child.'

'You're not in a position to bargain,' Solanda said.

486

'Neither are you,' Rugar said and with his booted foot, kicked her legs out from beneath her. She landed with a thud that jolted all the way up her spine.

He lunged for the center of the room, only to pause in confusion. He didn't know where Arianna had gone. Then he saw the lump rolled up into a ball in the corner.

'Where is she?' he said to the lump.

Solanda got to her feet. Her entire back ached. She could barely move. She grabbed the poker. 'Leave him alone, Rugar.'

Where was her help? She had sent the nurse for help. How long did it take people to run up those stairs?

The lump whimpered. Rugar moved closer to him. He grabbed a block of wood. If he hit the lump – Sebastian – in the wrong way, the boy would shatter, and maybe kill Arianna in the process.

'Leave him alone, Rugar.'

'You tell me where the baby is, golem,' he said, ignoring Solanda.

Sebastian whimpered again.

Rugar reached toward him –

– and Solanda swung the poker at the back of Rugar's head. The sharp end hit his skull with a smacking thud and he fell sideways toward the wall. He hit the wall and didn't move.

Sebastian scrambled out of his way, Arianna still cupped in his hand. She was mewling, her tiny blind face searching for the source of the sounds.

Solanda had lost her grip on the poker. It was sticking out of the side of Rugar's head. His neck was turned at an odd angle, the cowl of his robe turning black with blood.

She crouched beside him. His eyes were open.

He was dead.

She let out a small sigh, then shivered. The punishment for killing a member of the Black Family was severe. She glanced at Sebastian. The intelligence she feared was not in his eyes. He was holding Arianna close to his face and petting her with his index finger. She was still crying and moving around.

'Solanda!'

Nicholas's voice made her turn. She stood, naked and blood-spattered, trembling in the room's sudden chill.

He had flung open the door and strode into the room. The guards were following him, as was the nurse and a chambermaid. He held up a hand. 'Everyone out.'

'But, Sire, we don't know what's happened,' one of the guards said. He meant whether or not Solanda was dangerous.

But Nicholas was far enough into the room to see whose body it was. 'I'll take my chances,' he said. He closed the door. 'Where's Arianna?'

'Sebastian has her,' Solanda said. 'She Shifted.'

Nicholas crouched beside Sebastian and put his hand beneath the one holding Arianna. She mewled at him piteously.

'I think she's stuck in the form,' Solanda said.

'Is that unusual?'

Solanda shook her head. 'Not when a young Shifter is frightened.'

'We'll have to Shift her back.'

'In a moment,' Solanda said. She wanted to calm herself first. She needed to know what Nicholas would do to her. With her ash-stained hand, she pointed at the body.

'Rugar?' Nicholas asked.

She nodded.

'Dressed as an Aud. That doesn't look good, does it?'

'He wanted to take Arianna to Shadowlands.'

Nicholas moved Rugar's chin. Rugar's head lolled. 'He's dead.'

'I know,' Solanda said. She could barely get the words out. Fear tightened her throat.

'What's the penalty for killing the Black King's son?'

'What would the penalty be for killing you?' Solanda asked.

Nicholas sighed. 'Then I guess his death is my fault.'

It took Solanda a moment to follow his logic. He meant to take credit for the death. 'You can't,' she said. 'You're related by marriage. The Powers would be offended.'

'Wouldn't your powers know that I didn't do it?'

She didn't know the answer to that. She stared at Rugar's body. When he had his Vision, did he know he would die like this? Or had his Vision disappeared so long ago that he never saw his own death?

'I did it,' Solanda said. 'I'll take the punishment.'

Nicholas shook his head. 'My daughter needs you. We need you. You can't turn yourself in.' He stood and pulled the poker from Rugar's head. Bits of blood and brain spattered Nicholas's robe. 'We'll say that it was an accident. Nothing will happen then. No one will question. I doubt anyone will miss him.'

Solanda doubted that too. But she wasn't certain. The Black King's son was still important, no matter what he had done.

Nicholas stuck the tip of the poker into the fire and let the blood and hair burn off. The stench was slight, but enough to make Solanda wrinkle her nose. Then Nicholas placed the poker where it belonged.

'Better put on a robe,' he said. 'I'll let the others in.'

She had forgotten she was naked. She shook her head. 'First,' she said, 'let me help Arianna.'

She took the kitten from Sebastian's hands. Glossy tears covered his cheeks. He still looked terrified. Even though she knew he wasn't a real being, she couldn't help feeling pity. He had saved her life, and quite possibly saved Arianna's as well. Solanda brushed off a tear with her thumb.

'You're a hero, Sebastian,' she said quietly. And when he looked as if he didn't understand, she added, 'You're a real good boy.'

Then he smiled at her, slow and sure and sweet. Solanda smiled back.

The kitten's tiny sharp claws dug into her palm. She put Arianna back into the cradle, then held her and Shifted her own hands into paws. Then, carefully, she Shifted back. Arianna the Fey baby looked up at her, lower lip trembling. For a moment, Solanda thought Arianna was going to cry. Then she giggled, the happy baby sound that had become her trademark.

'So much death around her,' Nicholas said as he came up behind Solanda, 'and still she finds joy.'

His body was warm near hers. She let go of Arianna, and picked up her robe, slipping it on and reveling in the warmth. 'She doesn't understand that death is an ending yet,' Solanda said. 'She sees it as change, and to her, change is fun.'

Nicholas let out a laugh, more of surprise than anything else. 'Would that it be for all of us.' He put a hand on Solanda's back. She turned in surprise.

'I owe you,' he said.

'Me?'

He nodded. 'I didn't think you would care for my daughter, risking your life like this. I thought you would be with her for a while, and then go.'

'It would have been easier,' Solanda said. 'But it wouldn't have been right.'

'I owe you not just my protection,' he said, 'but my daughter's life.'

Solanda put a finger on his lips. 'Don't promise her life to anyone. It is her own. It will be better that way.'

Nicholas nodded, then took her hand away from his mouth. 'I'm sorry I ever doubted you,' he said.

'That's all right,' Solanda said. 'I doubted myself.'

Sixty-Eight

The road was flat and wide, an immobile version of the river. Adrian, Coulter, and Scavenger had emerged from the woods not far from Scavenger's home. They wore the clothes and the hats that Scavenger had stolen. If the Riders saw them from the air, the Riders wouldn't think twice. If Fey found them on the road, Scavenger would claim he was bringing them back to Shadowlands. His assumption was that none of the Fey knew him by name; that they would assume he was a Red Cap from Shadowlands.

The second part of the plan did not give Adrian confidence. After the incident near the river, he couldn't tell if Scavenger was over-confident or if the Fey really wouldn't recognize him. Adrian's own knowledge of the Fey in this area was scant.

They walked in silence. The other two were as frightened as he was. Scavenger's place was still too close to Shadowlands to give them any comfort. Adrian was shocked when he reached the road. It had felt as if he and Coulter had gone a long way that first day, but they hadn't gone far at all.

He was also surprised that Scavenger had chosen to live so close to Shadowlands. Almost in its shadow, as it were.

But where else would he go? And where else would he be safe? That would be something Adrian would have to deal with when he got Scavenger closer to Jahn.

Of course they would stay out of the city. Adrian had finally decided that going directly to the King would be difficult, and hard on Coulter. Besides, he would have a better chance of getting news about Luke at the farm. His family would know what happened. If they didn't, then Adrian could go into Jahn alone.

Getting his family used to the small Fey, on the other hand, would be an even more difficult trick, but it would probably be easier than traveling through Jahn with him.

Scavenger scuffled his feet as he walked, his boots raising small clouds of dust. Coulter would stop every time he saw something which caught his fancy. That would slow them down again, but Adrian was happier to see Coulter's interest than his fear.

490

Suddenly a large boom echoed through the woods, followed by the sound of exploding glass. Adrian, Coulter and Scavenger turned at the same time. Behind them, light shone up and outward through cracks in the sky, like sunlight did through huge gray clouds. As they watched the cracks grew bigger. Thumps and thuds reverberated as chunks of the sky fell.

'Shadowlands,' Scavenger said.

'It's breaking,' Coulter said.

The light expanded and with it, Adrian thought he could hear screaming. They were far enough away that none of the pieces fell near them. It was some kind of trick that even made them feel close.

'We've got to go back,' Coulter said. 'Gift's in there.'

Scavenger put a hand on his arm. 'We can't do anything. It's dangerous to even get close.'

A black cloud formed overhead and suddenly the three of them were being pelted with tiny gray pieces, as hard and sharp as ice. Adrian pulled his hat over his face. The pieces hitting his skin hurt. They tinkled as they fell on the ground.

'Let's get out of here,' Adrian yelled.

They ran off the road under some trees. The branches prevented the worst of the gray matter from hitting them. Through the holes in the leaves, Adrian could see the light emanating from Shadowlands grow brighter.

'We gotta get Gift,' Coulter said.

'We can't,' Scavenger said. 'I'm sorry, son. We can't.'

The gray pellets fell like hard rain. They looked eerie in the growing light.

'What's happening?' Adrian asked.

'It's shattering,' Scavenger said.

'Clearly,' Adrian said. 'But why?'

Scavenger shook his head. 'Usually Visionaries just dismantle Shadowlands. They don't explode it.' He frowned. 'Except...'

His voice trailed off as if the thought were too horrible to contemplate.

'Except?' Adrian asked.

'Except when they die.'

'Someone built Shadowlands?' Adrian asked.

'Rugar did,' Scavenger said. 'He built two of them.'

'What happens to the people inside?' Coulter asked. Tears were running down his face. He was clutching a branch to his chest as if it were a life raft.

Scavenger shook his head. 'I don't know,' he said. 'I just don't know.'

491

Sixty-Nine

The Elders sent him away from the Audience Chamber. They wanted to have a private conference.

Titus left the Tabernacle altogether and found his favorite spot beside the Cardidas. He used to come here in the days after he had seen the old Rocaan die. The water comforted him. It always made him think of the Words Written and Unwritten embodied in the Midnight Sacrament:

Without water, a man dies. A man's body makes water. His blood is water. A child is born in a rush of water. Water keeps us clean. It keeps us healthy. It keeps us alive. It is when we are in water that we are closest to God.

Those words had comforted him after the old Rocaan died. They had seemed right especially when it was holy water that killed Fey. But now water brought him no comfort. He watched the river rush away from him, and it felt like the moments of his life.

He had seen one Rocaan die and another denounce his faith in God.

Now the Elders were deciding whom the newest Rocaan would be. And either he would have to approve that choice or oppose it by not giving the new candidate the Secrets, thereby becoming Rocaan himself.

Even the vote might not be legal. The Council of Elders should have ten men. This one only had eight.

He felt as if he were hiding. There were more people on the river than usual. A group of men were fishing across the water, and some boys were playing along the banks. Some women were washing clothes at the bend west of him.

He was sitting among the weeds and mud near the edge of the bank. He was wearing an old robe, one he often used to sit beside the river. His feet were in the water; it was cool against his toes – a perfect counterpoint to the warm sun. Summer was just around the corner. He welcomed it and its calming heat. This spring had been too difficult for him.

The Rocaan's leaving had been even more difficult.

Titus was terrified of what the Elders would do. He was afraid they would elect Porciluna, and if they did, he would refuse to hand over the Secrets. The man wasn't right to be Rocaan. Titus knew it deep. Titus wasn't the right choice either, but at least he believed. At least he cared.

Something snapped above him. He started and looked into the sky. A gray square had appeared where there had been none before. He had expected thunderclouds, not a long box that extended as far as the eye could see.

Another snap and then a crack. Light extended through holes in the box.

He scrambled up the bank. This was something Fey. Something horrible. The men and boys across the river were yelling and pointing. Cracks spiderwebbed up the box's sides until the gray matter splintered and fell away. Then the bottom came out and boats dropped from the sky.

Not boats.

Ships.

A wall of water smashed into Titus, knocking him flat. Suddenly he had water in his mouth, his nose, his eyes. He clawed for the surface, and found it as suddenly as it had disappeared. The water receded, only to form another wave. He scrambled even farther up the bank and noticed the women scrambling as well, sliding in the mud and water.

Some of the men were in the churning river screaming for help. Bits of wood surrounded them. The ships were sinking and gray matter fell like rain from the skies.

He ran all the way to the road, coughing and sputtering, his entire body covered with mud. Other people were reaching into the water when the next wave hit and it swept them in. He started screaming himself – for help. They needed tons of help – but he wouldn't get near the water again. Those precious moments under the river were too long.

Toward the west as far as he could see, ships were sinking. Fey ships. Parts of the gray box remained in the sky, but it looked like pieces of a child's puzzle, jagged and incomplete.

The waves were smaller now, small enough that he could get close the edge and see if he could help. More people were arriving all the time. Dozens of Auds and Danites from the Tabernacle were already at the water's edge. He climbed back down the bank, his sodden robe hampering his progress.

When he reached the bottom, he extended a hand to a woman trapped in the mud. She grabbed and he pulled. After a moment she broke free.

'Respected Sir,' she said. 'What have we done?'

He looked at the ruined ships. The Fey would never get off Blue Isle now.

'I don't know,' he said. 'Maybe our prayers finally reached God's Ear.'

Seventy

Gift sat on the steps outside the Domicile. Ever since his mother had been injured, he felt as if he had spent his entire life here. He had gone inside with his father each day, but only for a few moments. His presence seemed to disturb his mother. Whenever she saw him, she started to cry, and the Domestics would make him leave. Her hand was bandaged, and she had to lay on her stomach so that her shattered wings would heal.

They weren't sure if she would ever fly again.

His father was inside now. Gift no longer minded. His grandfather had left the Shadowlands a few days ago, and Gift felt a little safer. Every few hours, though, Gift would walk to the Circle Door and then past his grandfather's cabin. He wanted to know when his grandfather returned.

Gift would protect himself and his family.

He didn't know how, but he would.

Suddenly the world spun. He recognized the feeling. This was his Vision. But in the Vision, he saw the Circle Door and his grandfather's house, and no one helped his mother.

He had to stay here.

Large thunderous cracks resounded through Shadowlands. Fey came out of their houses and looked up. A Domestic came onto the porch.

'By the Powers,' she said. She put her hands on Gift's back and pushed him forward. 'Get out. Get out while you still can.'

She turned and shouted the same message inside, then ran past him down the stairs. The ground was shaking. Bits of the sky were falling, revealing a startling blueness above. Fey were screaming.

Screaming.

The Warders' cabin collapsed as the Warders ran outside. The porch that Gift was standing on was coming apart. Domestics poured out the door, running toward the Circle Door.

Gift already knew what was happening there. Fey were trampling each other trying to escape. As the Domestics ran, their feet punched holes in the ground. Mend fell through one of the holes, screaming.

Another Fey started screaming near the side of the Domicile. Pieces of the sky were landing on people. They couldn't move or they would fall through the ground to the green below.

His father scooped Gift in his arms and tried to lift him. But Gift wasn't a baby any more. He was too heavy.

'We have to get out, Gift,' his father said. 'Shadowlands is coming apart.'

Gift shook his head. 'Mom ...'

'She told me to get you out of here.'

The creaks and groans, cracks and screams, thuds and cries were overwhelming. Bits of the sky were flying around him, hitting people and cutting their faces.

'No one will help her,' Gift said. 'She'll die.'

'I can't lift her,' his father said. 'She's too heavy.'

'Make her grow small.'

'She can't. She's hurt too bad. Let's go, Gift, before we all die.'

Gift pulled free. He tried to go in the door, but more Domestics were coming out – Weavers and Menders and Builders. There was no way he could go in.

The buildings were collapsing. The Domicile was one of the few that remained upright, but it wouldn't last long. His father had grown small and was hovering around Gift's head, shouting in a tiny voice. Gift ignored him. They wouldn't get out that way. Already Fey were dying near the Circle Door. Fey were dying under falling pieces of sky. Fey were dying as they fell through the ground.

Shadowlands had to stay together.

Gift reached out with his mind and grabbed the corners of his world. He held them up with all the strength he could find. His father was still shouting, people were still screaming, but the smacking thuds had stopped.

He closed his eyes and imagined Shadowlands as it was. He rebuilt the holes in the walls, replaced pieces in the sky, and patched the chasms in the ground. In his mind, he walked around and tested each part of the Shadowlands, making it stronger than it had ever been.

The screaming stopped.

He opened his eyes.

There was carnage all around him. People lying under slabs of gray matter, or large boards. Bodies flattened. Wounded moaning. But the ground had stopped trembling. The blue holes were gone from the sky, and a mist was rising.

The buildings were ruined.

Except for the Domicile.

The Fey in the doorway had stopped running. Gift pushed his way

496

past them. His mother was on her bed, propped up on one arm. She cried out when she saw him. He ran to her and put both of his arms around her. She held him so tight he thought he would never breathe.

'I thought we were going to die,' she said.

'We would have.' A voice came from above. Gift looked up. The Shaman was nodding at him. 'He repaired his grandfather's work.'

'Gift?' his mother's voice trembled. 'Gift rebuilt the Shadowlands?'

'I had to,' Gift said. They were acting as if he had done something wrong. 'No one wanted to save you. It would have fallen on you.'

His mother pulled out of the embrace. 'Oh, honey,' she said. She cupped his face with her good hand. She looked sad. 'Oh, baby, you don't know what you did.'

'I saved you,' he said.

'No,' the Shaman said. 'You saved us all.'

THE CHANGELING
[One Week Later]

Seventy-One

The farm looked tended. Adrian stood to the side of the road and stared at it. The fields had been turned and the dirt, rich and brown, had long furrows in it. The fence was in good repair and his favorite grove of trees remained, although they were taller than they had been since he left.

'Are we here?' Coulter asked.

Adrian nodded. He couldn't bring himself to go any farther. The air smelled of manure and seedlings. If he followed the road, and rounded to the back of the farm, he would get the scents of last season's hay, chickens, and the pigs that his brother always insisted they keep.

Home.

It hadn't changed at all.

He swallowed the lump in his throat. It was mid-day. Everyone would be inside for a short rest before working the remainder of the afternoon.

'Well, then,' Scavenger said. 'I guess this is it.'

He hiked his pack over his shoulder and turned around.

'No!' Adrian said. 'Wait!'

Scavenger stopped. They hadn't discussed what would happen now. Adrian just assumed Scavenger would stay with them. Adrian couldn't imagine wanting to return to the woods. Not now, not after the explosion of Shadowlands.

When they had realized what was happening to Shadowlands, the three of them took off at a run. The Fey were pouring out of their hiding place, and would soon overtake them. For two nights, the three traveled off the road, because of all the injured and frightened Fey. Then, as quickly as it all happened, it ended.

Scavenger spoke to one of the Fey who was turning back. She said she had heard that Shadowlands was repaired. Scavenger couldn't believe she would return after it had shattered from under her, but she had smiled at him, and told him that she felt safer in Shadowlands than she did around the Islander poison.

Scavenger was still looking at Adrian expectantly.

'I thought you were going to come with us,' Adrian said.

501

Scavenger smiled, but it was a sad smile. 'Around Islanders? You think they'd want me?' His tone said he didn't.

'I think they will if I tell them what you did,' Adrian said. 'You can't go back. There's nothing in the woods for you.'

'Except my house.'

'I want you to stay,' Coulter said.

Scavenger looked at the boy. Adrian watched them. The two were more alike than they thought. Scavenger didn't fit in the Fey because he lacked magick, and Coulter didn't fit with the Islanders because he had it.

'All right,' Scavenger said. 'I'll stay. Until it becomes clear that I can't any more.'

Adrian nodded. He understood that. He also knew that he could make his family accept Scavenger if he had to.

He took a deep breath and then started across the road. Scavenger and Coulter kept a few paces behind. A tapestry moved on the south window, and then it moved again. A door slammed, and suddenly Luke was running across the road.

He was yelling his father's name.

Adrian couldn't wait any longer. His son was alive and coming for him. He ran to Luke and they embraced, his son squeezing him, lifting him off the ground, and whirling him around.

When Luke finally set him down, Adrian stood back and looked for the years he had missed. Luke was taller and broader, resembling Adrian at the same age. A sadness had built around his eyes and a fear around the corner of his lips. Adrian brushed those with his thumb, wishing he could wipe them away.

'They said you tried to murder the Rocaan, that the Fey put some kind of spell on you. I was afraid maybe the King would kill you.'

Luke shook his head. 'The King was good to me. He understood.'

'The Fey Charmed you,' Adrian said. 'When I found that out, I felt I could leave. They weren't keeping their agreement.'

'They never did,' Luke said softly. 'If you put holy water on me, you could see the green of the spell. But it's gone now.'

'Gone?' Adrian frowned. 'After you attacked the Rocaan?'

'No,' Luke said. 'Last week. It just disappeared.'

'The Shadowlands,' Scavenger said. 'Whoever Spelled him must have died.'

Luke gasped and took a step backwards. Adrian caught his son's wrist. 'It's all right,' he said.

'I thought you left them,' Luke said.

'I did,' Adrian said. 'Scavenger helped us.'

'Us?'

Adrian swept his free hand back. Coulter was waiting on the far side of the road, looking lost. 'Coulter and I, we left together. Scavenger found us. He kept us away from the search teams. He escaped Shadowlands a long time ago.'

Luke still pulled against Adrian's arm. 'We really don't want any Fey here.'

'You'll have him here,' Adrian said. 'As long as you have me.'

Luke stared at his father, then looked at Scavenger, then back at his father as if actually considering it. Finally, he shook his forefinger at Scavenger. 'If you touch any of us, or spell any of us, I'll see to you personally.'

Scavenger laughed. Adrian would have smiled himself if he hadn't realized that Luke was so serious.

'He can't spell anyone,' Adrian said. 'He's a Red Cap. They have no magic.'

Luke didn't appear convinced, but he nodded. 'You get to fight this with Granddad,' he said.

'I will,' Adrian said. He slipped his arm around his son's waist. They started forward when Adrian realized that Coulter wasn't coming. 'Hold on a moment,' he said to Luke.

Adrian ran back across the road. Coulter was chewing on a blade of grass, staring back in the direction they came. When Adrian touched his shoulder, Coulter started. His eyes widened for a moment and slowly filled with his personality.

'What were you doing?' Adrian asked.

Coulter swallowed. 'Checking my Links. Seeing if I can still Send.'

Adrian understood the importance of the connection. Coulter had used his Link after Shadowlands stopped shaking to determine if Gift was all right. He was.

'You coming?' Adrian asked.

Coulter shrugged. 'Looks like you don't need me no more.'

'Because of Luke?' Adrian asked.

Coulter nodded. Once.

'Coulter,' Adrian said, 'he's my son, but he's lived without me for five years. You and I, we've relied on each other that long. I'm not going to trade my relationship with you for my relationship with him.'

Coulter kicked at the dirt beside the road. His pants were so dirty that they looked as if they were made from mud.

'I want you to stay with me. I wouldn't have brought you this far otherwise.'

'But you love him better.'

Adrian glanced at Luke. Luke was a man now, no longer the uncertain boy who had been in Shadowlands. Coulter, for all his bravado, was still a child. A brilliant, talented child, but a child nonetheless.

'I love him,' Adrian said. 'But I love you too. It would break my heart if you left now.'

'Gift needs me,' Coulter said.

'They'll kill you in Shadowlands.'

Coulter bit his lower lip.

'The Link remains, doesn't it?' Adrian asked.

Coulter nodded. 'I can reach him,' Coulter said.

'Then that should be enough. If Gift needs you, he'll reach you. You can stay here until that happens.'

Coulter still hadn't said anything. Adrian slipped his arm around the boy's shoulder and pulled him close. 'Don't leave,' Adrian whispered. 'I'd miss you. I haven't been here for a long, long time. I'm as much a stranger as you are.'

Coulter looked up at him, surprise on his face. 'You're scared?' Coulter asked.

'Terrified,' Adrian said.

Coulter grinned. Then he glanced across the road. Luke and Scavenger were talking. Actually, Scavenger was talking, his hands waving as he explained something, probably his own history and why he was trustworthy. Luke was listening intently. Adrian smiled. He had to give his son credit. No matter what he had gone through, Luke was still willing to give a Fey a chance.

'Come on,' Adrian said. He took Coulter's hand. 'Let's go home.'

Together they crossed the road and walked down the incline toward the farm. With each step, Adrian felt his old self returning. He couldn't wait to put his hands in the soil, to plant the new crop, to feel the sun on his back.

He had a boy to raise. He had to get reacquainted with his son. And he had to force his family to get used to a Fey. But he could do it. In the air, and the sunshine, away from the shadows, he could do anything he wanted.

Seventy-Two

Gift put his hands over his ears. He hunched down and closed his eyes. He didn't want to hear any more. He wished they would all go away.

Ever since he fixed the Shadowlands, all the grownups had come to him with questions, just like they used to go to his grandfather. Gift had left the Domicile and had gone back to his cabin. It wasn't badly damaged by the near-collapse. Only a few boards had fallen off the walls. His father had stuffed the holes with rags.

A fire burned in the grate next to Gift and it provided the only warmth in the room. His mother was stretched out on pillows beside him, and his father was manning the doors. The Healers had let his mother come home because they needed the space for all the Fey injured in the Collapse. Almost fifty Fey were hurt, and another fifteen died in that short span of time.

The Shaman said that she was sure it meant that Gift's grandfather had died. He had never returned from his trip, and now the Fey were acting like Gift was in charge.

The only one who wasn't was his father. Gift had asked that everyone leave him alone. His father had let in that Spell Warder, Touched.

Touched wore a bandage over the side of his face, half covering his eye. Apparently some wood sliced his cheek open, and bits of the sky had bruised his arms. Unlike some Fey, though, he didn't let that stop him. He was going back to work.

Unfortunately, his work meant bothering Gift.

'Gift,' he said, crouching down and prying Gift's hands away from his ears. 'I know you and Coulter are friends. I want you to tell him to come back.'

'It makes sense, Gift,' his father said. 'Coulter will know how to stop those Islanders.'

Gift didn't understand all this stop and prevent and keep them away stuff. The only Islanders he had ever seen in Shadowlands were Coulter and Adrian. He had seen some on his Link journey, and one of the ones he had seen was his real father.

'Coulter doesn't want to come back,' Gift said. That much he

505

understood. That much he knew. Coulter liked the Outside. He said it was pretty. He asked Gift to visit sometime. What Coulter didn't know was that Gift had been visiting the Outside his whole life – without leaving Shadowlands.

'We need him,' Touched said.

Gift pulled his hand free and clapped it over his ear. 'No.'

He could still hear through his hands. But the symbolism worked. His father said softly to Touched, 'I think you'll have to try again later.'

Touched stood. 'That's what you said the last time. Can't you make him understand –?'

'He's still a child.' His mother spoke softly, tiredly, as if each word were an effort. 'It seems clear to him. And frankly, I think it is. What you and Rotin did to that boy in the Warders' cabin would frighten anyone away for good. Even if you bring him back he won't help.'

Gift frowned. Help? Help with what? That was the thing they never explained. They said that Coulter could stop some poison, but Gift had never seen that poison. Then they said that poison had killed his real mother – and that had been tricky – but Gift had a better answer than bringing Coulter back. Never get near a black robe. Never leave Shadowlands. Then no one needed to stop the poison. The poison wouldn't get to them.

Gift's father said it wasn't that easy, but Gift wondered. They weren't explaining everything to him, and until he understood, he would listen to Coulter. Coulter had saved his life.

Touched put a hand on his head. Gift moved away.

'Gift,' Touched said very loud, 'please let me talk to you.'

'No!' Gift said. He was done with this. He had saved them, like the Shaman said, and now they wanted more. When they found more holes in Shadowlands, he fixed them. When they asked for a new way to open the Circle Door, he found it. He was tired. He hadn't had a nap in days, and he wanted to talk to his mom. She still seemed really sick and he was worried about her, even though everybody said she was getting better.

'Gift,' his father said. 'Please.'

'No!' Gift said. 'Go away.' Gift stood up. The only way he would get what he wanted was to be bad. He hated it when no one listened to him. Even when he was important no one listened. But they would listen now.

He took his hands off his ears, looked up at Touched, and screamed, 'Get out!'

'Gift . . .' His mother sounded disappointed in him.

Gift didn't care. 'Get out! Get out! Get out!'

Touched took his hand off Gift's head. 'I wish you'd listen –'

'No!' Gift yelled. 'Get out!'

Touched shot a glance at Gift's father, who shrugged. Then Touched opened the door and left. Gift's father closed the door and leaned on it.

'That was wrong, Gift.'

Gift shook his head. 'You guys are wrong. You tell me to listen. I did listen. I said no. He didn't listen.'

'But if Coulter comes back,' his father said, 'then he'll help us.'

'No, he won't,' Gift said. 'He likes those people. He says it's pretty out there.'

His mother propped herself on one elbow. Some color had returned to her face, but there were still deep shadows under her eyes. 'You've talked to him?'

Gift nodded. 'He wanted to know if I was all right. And then he wanted to know if he could still talk to me when I was far away.' Gift made it sound simple, but it wasn't. Coulter had let him look through Coulter's eyes at the new place, the small square building amid all the dark brown. The sky was blue and the air smelled sharp, unlike anything Gift had ever experienced before. Adrian and a yellow-haired man were hugging and laughing and they looked really happy. A Fey was standing with them, and he seemed safe. Gift couldn't understand why everyone here made things seem so difficult.

'If you can communicate with him,' his father said, 'I don't understand why you don't ask him to come back. We need him here.'

'I asked,' Gift said. 'I asked once. And he said he would never come back because they tried to kill him here.'

'The Warders treated him harshly,' his mother said. 'I don't think harassing Gift will bring Coulter back.'

'We need that boy,' his father said.

'We had him for a long time. No one knew what he was.'

'But we know now.'

'And we waited too long.' His mother sighed and adjusted her position slightly so that she rested on the arm that wasn't hurt. Her wings were still damaged and if they wiggled, the pain was evident on her face. 'We chased him away. We can't pretend we didn't. And we can't pretend he'll help us now.'

'But he has no place to go,' his father said.

'Yes, he does,' Gift said. 'He's got a safe place.'

'Where?' his father asked.

'Don't make him answer,' his mother said. 'Gift doesn't belong in this. He's done the right thing. He's said that Coulter wants to remain Outside. I say let him.'

'You didn't see the entire team die,' his father said. 'We need an antidote.'

She nodded. 'We do. But we won't get it if we have to rely on that boy. We treated him too badly. We will need to wait for another Enchanter.'

'You sound so calm.'

'I am,' she said. 'Rugar is gone. Dead, probably. We will be able to take care of our destiny now. Gift will become our Leader one day, and if he does, maybe Coulter will come back and help him. Remember that they're Linked. We just have to have patience.'

'I told him not to come back,' Gift said.

'What?' his father asked.

'I told him not to,' Gift said. He wasn't sure if he was helping his mother's argument or hurting it. 'He asked if I needed help when Shadowlands collapsed. I said no.'

'See?' his mother said. 'That kind of Link is for life.'

Gift frowned. He hadn't realized that Links were forever. Something bothered him about that.

'I hope you're right,' his father said. He sighed. 'I'll explain to Touched that he should wait a while. He won't like that.'

'He shouldn't be pressuring a boy,' his mother said.

'The boy holds Shadowlands,' his father said. 'He's our leader now.'

'Not yet.' His mother smiled at Gift. 'He'll have some time to grow up. The Shaman will help him. She's already promised.'

'I hope so,' his father said. 'This situation is too strange to place on the shoulders of a three-year-old.'

He let himself out of the cabin. Gift watched him go. His mother smiled. 'Let him be, Gift,' she said. 'He was hoping that he could help you Lead. But Wisps have no place in government. Already he is making mistakes. He thinks that he needs to find a solution because he was the only survivor of that attack on their holy man. He doesn't understand that without Rugar, we probably won't be making those attacks.'

'I'd rather listen to you than the Shaman,' Gift said.

His mother eased back onto the pillows. She tired so easily these days. 'I'm a Wisp too, Gift. I can see a little clearer than your father, but not much. The Shaman is the only one who can help you.'

And Coulter, Gift thought, but he said nothing.

'I need some sleep, son,' his mother said. She adjusted her pillow with her good hand, and closed her eyes.

He went over to the fire and stared at it. Seeing Coulter had bothered him. Before when he and Coulter talked through the Links it had been like a conversation in his head. But this time, Coulter's personality had stepped aside to let Gift into Coulter's body. Then Gift was standing on that road, looking out of Coulter's eyes, moving

Coulter's hands, feeling what Coulter felt. Gift had done that before, not with Coulter, but each time he went to the palace.

But there he didn't know whose eyes he used.

He hadn't realized until this morning that he had been using another body at all.

Once he stepped into Coulter's place, he hadn't felt Coulter any more. Only when he stepped out of the eyes – he didn't know how else to think about it, even though he knew he wasn't physically moving – only then did he feel Coulter's presence again. For a moment, they seemed to be in the same place, able to converse without words.

Gift had been pushing someone aside in the body in the palace.

And that was wrong.

He would hate it if someone did that to him.

It bothered him. He hadn't known he was Linked to his real mother, and he had a thin Link to his real father. But his strong Links outside of Shadowlands were Coulter and this person in the palace. The person he had never thought of.

Then a memory rose:

In his bed, another baby lay. His eyes were open, but empty. The nurse brushed her hand on his cheek.

'You're cold, lambkins,' she said.

The little woman huddled in the curtain around the crib. She moved her fingers and the baby cooed. The nurse smiled.

He was staring at the baby that had replaced him. It looked like him, but it was not him. It had been a stone a moment before.

A stone.

He had seen that nurse since, and the room, and now another baby slept in his bed. A girl-baby. His sister.

He was seeing through the Changeling's eyes. Through the eyes of a stone that someone had left in his place.

That his parents, the Wisps, had left in his place.

He didn't want to leave Shadowlands, but maybe, just maybe, he could go Outside whenever he wanted to. That would allow him to see Coulter without anyone knowing. Maybe the stone existed for him to use.

He sat cross-legged on the rug, close to the fire. His father wouldn't be back soon, and his mother's even breathing told him that she was asleep.

He had time to follow the Link.

With his eyes closed, he found the Link and sped along it as he had done countless times. Only this time, when he reached the familiar body, he stopped before stepping into the eyes.

Hello? he called. *Hello?*

He wanted to make certain he wasn't pushing anyone out of the way.

Hello? he called again.

Then he had an answer. It was faint, and it wasn't in any language he recognized. Just a feeling. He followed the feeling until it led him to a tiny place deep within the body.

There a half-formed boy huddled. He had only the outlines of a body. His face was there but his features were indistinct. He was like a drawing of a child instead of a real child. Or Gift would have thought so if he had not noticed another detail. The half-formed boy was shivering.

Who are you? Gift asked.

The answer came to him, not in the child's voice, but in the voice of several people, some women and a man. Sebastian, they all said.

Sebastian.

It felt familiar.

(You will not give him a common name! He is a Prince in the Black King's line. He needs to be named as such!)

His mother's voice. His real mother. Fading now, but it had been mixed with all the other voices in the boy's head.

The boy looked up. He apparently had heard the same snatch of memory.

Gift sent him the memory of the exchange. *Are you the stone?*

In response, the boy sent him the image of a half-woman, half-cat. She was talking to another woman and gesturing at him, calling him *the lump.*

Gift understood bits of Changeling magic. He knew that Golems should not have a life of their own. *Who are you?* he sent again.

The half-formed boy pointed at Gift.

Gift shook his head. *I'm Gift.*

The half-formed boy shot him a series of quick images. The images were clear. First there was light. Then there was Gift riding on the light, and then there was a tiny shadow in the corner, learning from the light. Gift understood although he couldn't explain how. Each time he had visited the stone body, he had left a bit of himself behind. The half-formed boy had taken those pieces and created as much of a self as he could.

You're me, but not me, Gift sent. *You have other people around you.*

The half-formed boy smiled. He sent more images, these wrapped not in light, but in warmth. First he sent one of their mother, the woman Gift watched die. The image was full of a horrible, lonely sadness.

He followed that image with one of their sister, the baby girl

Arianna. Then one of his nurse who held him and talked to him and loved him. And then he sent one of the yellow-haired man Gift knew to be his own father. The images held more emotion than the others.

They held love.

Gift reached out and touched the half-formed boy's hand. Suddenly the boy had language. *You make me leave?* the boy asked. *Make me go?*

He had been afraid of that all along, afraid that Gift would take over his body permanently. If Gift did that, the boy would no longer exist.

No, Gift sent. *You belong here.*

The half formed boy grinned. He could smile and his smile was beautiful. *You let me stay?* Then he answered his own question. *You let me stay.*

Gift nodded. *I don't let you. It's your place. Will you let me visit? I'm sorry I never asked before. I didn't know you were here.*

You can visit, the half-formed boy said. *You give me gifts. You me. I you.*

In a way, Gift supposed, that was true. The half-formed boy, Sebastian, was living the life Gift had been born to. Gift was living his own life now. He didn't want to live here any more.

Besides, he didn't want to hurt Sebastian.

We're not the same person, Gift sent. *Not any more.*

Sebastian frowned. That apparently didn't fit with what he knew.

We're brothers, Gift sent. *The same, but different.*

The same, but different, Sebastian said. He looked at their joined hands. *You come here any time.*

Gift smiled at that. He was glad he would still have his welcome. He liked it here. It was safe.

Thank you, he said. Then he looked around. Sebastian was hidden deep within the body.

You know, Gift sent, *you don't have to stay here all the time. Come with me.*

He took Sebastian by the hand and led him to the body's eyes. Together they looked out at a marvelous world, a world of bright colors and lovely melodies and fresh air. Sebastian giggled.

I can stay here?

All the time if you want, Gift sent.

Sebastian sighed and his relief floated to Gift. Sebastian had been afraid to stay there, afraid that Gift would see him and make him leave.

I like you, Sebastian sent.

Good, Gift sent. *Because I like you too.*

Seventy-Three

The lilacs were blooming. The sweet sharp scent of the flowers reminded Nicholas of his childhood, afternoons spent in the garden, exploring the deep dark shadows made by the hulking trees. His daughter was exploring the garden this afternoon, although in a way he couldn't quite appreciate. She was in her kitten form, and Solanda, in her cat form, was showing Arianna how to hunt, using bugs as prey.

Nicholas still couldn't get used to his daughter's separate selves. He wondered if he ever would.

He sat on a bench, watching the orange tabby lead the tiny white kitten through the underbrush. Sebastian sat near the wall, running his hand through the grass. The nurse was dozing on a different bench, her head cradled on her arms. A slight breeze disturbed the lilac petals and ruffled her hair. Ever since Rugar's death, the nurse had been extremely protective of Sebastian. Even Solanda had watched over him. She had started using his name, and treating him with a bit more respect.

Nicholas understood the nurse's exhaustion. The events of the last two weeks were catching up with him. The Shaman had come and taken Rugar's body away. She had said nothing when she took it; she hadn't even asked what happened.

Solanda said that meant the Shaman knew, but Nicholas had a different theory. He thought that she might not have wanted to know.

That was how he felt about events in the Tabernacle. The Elders were still meeting and arguing. Nicholas had volunteered to take the Rocaan's position and combine it with his Kingship, and they had rejected that outright. Elder Reece had privately predicted to Nicholas that the fights would continue indefinitely and one day the Elders would all realize what they had done. Already young Titus was making the kinds of decisions a Rocaan made, because he had the Secrets.

He was making holy water when it was needed, and scheduling the Sacraments. Soon he would be doing the rest of the Rocaan's duties.

Of that, Nicholas had no doubt.

His daughter the kitten leaped a foot in the air, chasing a fly. Then she disappeared under a bush. Solanda appeared to sleep at the base of a tree, but when Arianna disappeared, Solanda stood, sighed, and followed.

Solanda had done well for him. He still didn't know how to express his gratitude to her. She had saved the lives of his children. She had guaranteed the survival of his kingship, and she had kept Jewel's legacy alive.

Nicholas sighed. He would never stop missing Jewel or her counsel. She would have known what to do with the ruined ships that fell into the harbor when Rugar died. Some Fey had been in those ships and had died at impact. One Islander had drowned, and several others had been injured, but the event was more frightening than dangerous. Nicholas eventually had the guard pick up the remains of the ships. Monte had said he wanted to study them, and Nicholas would let him.

Maybe they could learn even more about the Fey.

But Nicholas felt a lot more secure now that Rugar was dead. The Shaman had promised Nicholas that his children would grow up in peace. He relied on that promise. She had been right before. He could believe her now.

A giggle drew his attention. He looked around the garden for Arianna, but he didn't see her. She loved being a kitten these days much more than she liked being a baby. As a kitten she had mobility. As a baby, she was subject to the whim of others. But she wasn't the one laughing.

Sebastian was.

Nicholas looked at his son. The boy never entertained himself. But this time he was. He was watching the lilac petals drift in the slight breeze. As they sprinkled around him, he laughed.

For the first time in his life, Nicholas's son looked radiantly happy.

Nicholas didn't want to break the moment. He watched Sebastian and smiled with him, wishing he could share the experience with Jewel. She would have been pleased with her children.

At least he had them.

But they didn't replace Jewel.

He would have to get used to being without her. When she died, he had thought being without her was impossible. But now, watching his children, he knew that he could.

Although he would still miss her each moment of each day.

Sebastian reached up toward a petal, saw Nicholas and waved. Nicholas waved back. His son would never be perfect, but he was still a beautiful boy.

Jewel had given him marvelous, unique children. The least he could do was love them.

He got off his bench and walked over to his son. Sebastian giggled a greeting. Nicholas sat beside him, feeling close to the boy for the first time. The wind came up, and together they played, with the petals falling around them like a soft, pink rain.